More praise for

THE GLASS OF TIME

"[*The Glass of Time*] is a gripping narrative full of ingenious twists and turns. . . . The developing relationship between the resourceful heroine and Lady Tansor, whose affection she has to win in order to destroy her, is complex and absorbing. The reader is pulled in different directions by the competing claims of the two protagonists in this clash between emotion and the demands of justice."
—Charles Palliser, author of *The Unburied* and *The Quincunx*

"Cox's gripping second gothic thriller (after *The Meaning of Night*) follows the fortunes of 19-year-old orphan Esperanza Gorst, whose guardian charges her to go undercover as a lady's maid."
—*Publishers Weekly*, starred review

"Multiple mysteries at its heart, and like so many Dickensian and other novels, [*The Glass of Time*] combines realistic details about setting, dialect, and so on with fantastic plot elements, particularly in the form of coincidences and hidden friends, mentors, guides, and protectors. . . . A page turner, a really good read—and one which might send readers back to Mary Elizabeth Braddon, Wilkie Collins, and Dickens (and possibly also to A. S. Byatt and Sarah Waters as well)." —Victorian Web (www.victorianweb.org)

"Michael Cox returns with another epic Victorian-era thriller. . . . [A] gripping tale of psychological unraveling." —*Kirkus Reviews*

"What takes place during this perfectly plotted novel is a complicated web of seduction, intrigue, deceit, betrayal and murder that is impossible to resist." —Bookreporter.com

"An essential read for fans of [*The Meaning of Night*]. But this atmospheric and engrossing work also can stand alone as a treat for anyone who enjoys Victorian thrillers." —*Library Journal*

"In a powerful literary seduction, Michael Cox offers a vivid portrayal of the intermingled insanity and conflict within the lives of people bound by a deeply shared past in his second novel *The Glass of Time*. . . . A stunning new narrative voice in the world of historical fiction."

—*Metro Spirit*

Praise for *The Meaning of Night*

"As beguiling as it is intelligent, full of great country houses, epic loves, fierce anger and vicious habits." —*New York Times Book Review*

"Engrossing and enjoyable." —*Newsday*

"Superb. . . . An engrossing and complicated tale of deception, heartlessness and wild justice, one that touches on every aspect of Victorian society." —Michael Dirda, *Washington Post Book World*

"Resonant with echoes of Wilkie Collins and Charles Dickens, Cox's richly imagined thriller . . . abounds with startling surprises that are made credible by its scrupulously researched background and details of everyday Victorian life. Its exemplary blend of intrigue, history and romance mark a stand-out literary debut."

—*Publishers Weekly*, starred review

"An entertaining love letter to the bizarre and dangerous hypocrisies of Victorian England." —*Independent on Sunday*

"The atmosphere crackles, but beneath all is a sly sense of humor. The plotting is second to none—a finely tuned yet extravagantly complex piece of clockwork." —*Evening Standard*

The Glass of Time

ALSO BY MICHAEL COX

FICTION
The Meaning of Night

BIOGRAPHY
M. R. James: An Informal Portrait

ANTHOLOGIES
The Oxford Book of English Ghost Stories (with R.A. Gilbert)
The Oxford Book of Victorian Ghost Stories (with R. A. Gilbert)
The Oxford Book of Victorian Detective Stories
The Oxford Book of Spy Stories

EDITOR
M. R. James: 'Casting the Runes' and Other Ghost Stories
(Oxford World's Classics)

COMPILER
The Oxford Chronology of English Literature

MICHAEL COX

THE GLASS OF TIME

The Secret Life

of

Miss Esperanza Gorst

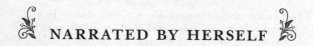 NARRATED BY HERSELF

W. W. Norton & Company

NEW YORK / LONDON

For information about permission to reproduce selections from
this book, write to Permissions, W. W. Norton & Company, Inc.,
500 Fifth Avenue, New York, NY 10110

For information about special discounts for bulk purchases,
please contact W. W. Norton Special Sales at
specialsales@wwnorton.com or 800-233-4830

Manufacturing by RR Donnelley, Bloomsburg
Book design by Brooke Koven
Production manager: Anna Oler

Library of Congress Cataloging-in-Publication Data

Cox, Michael, 1948–
The glass of time : the secret life of Miss Esperanza Gorst /
narrated by Herself
Michael Cox. — 1st ed.
p. cm.
ISBN 978-0-393-06773-6
1. Great Britain—History—Victoria, 1837–1901—Fiction.
2. Identity (Psychology)—Fiction. 3. Lady's maids—Fiction.
4. Secrets—Fiction. 5. Psychological fiction. I. Title.
PR6103.O976G55 2008
823'.92—dc22   2008023909

ISBN 978-0-393-33716-7 pbk.

W. W. Norton & Company, Inc.
500 Fifth Avenue, New York, N.Y. 10110
www.wwnorton.com

W. W. Norton & Company Ltd.
Castle House, 75/76 Wells Street, London W1T 3QT

2 3 4 5 6 7 8 9 0

For Dizzy — again

Dedicated also to the Memory of
Pat Riccioni
Melissa Allen
Chris Davenport

For Truth is like a lone bird singing,
On the edge of day and night —
The unseen herald, ever bringing
Certainty of Light.

P. VERNEY DUPORT
FROM *Merlin and Nimue*
PRIVATELY PRINTED (1876), CANTO III

CONTENTS

ACT THREE / *The Past Awakens*

ACT FOUR / *Duty and Desire*

ACT FIVE / *Time's Revenge*

NOTE ON THE TEXT

The manuscript of 'The Glass of Time' is held in the Houghton Library at Harvard. Although, like the supposedly confessional text published by the present editor in 2006 as *The Meaning of Night*, it purports to be a record of actual events connected with the ancient, and now defunct, Duport family, of Evenwood in Northamptonshire, it is firmly novelistic in character and should be read first and foremost as a work of fiction, or at least as highly fictionalized autobiography.

Consisting of 647 unlined folios of foolscap, tied with a faded black silk ribbon, the manuscript was first catalogued in 1936 as part of the private library of J. Gardner Friedmann of New York, who purchased it on a trip to London in May 1924. After Friedmann's death in 1948, it found its way to Harvard, along with the rest of his extensive collection of nineteenth-century fiction.

As with its related literary predecessor, *The Meaning of Night*, I have supplied explanatory footnotes, where I have felt them to be necessary or helpful to the modern reader, and have silently amended a number of mechanical errors and inconsistencies.

J.J. ANTROBUS
Professor of Post-Authentic Victorian Fiction
University of Cambridge

ACT ONE

A HOUSE OF SECRETS

We twayne are one too many (quoth I) for men saie,
Three maie keepe a counsell, if two be awaie.

JOHN HEYWOOD, *Dialogue of Proverbs* (1546)

PROLOGUE

My Lady and Her Sons

Observed by Miss Gorst, 8th November 1876

I

The View from the Gallery

I WISH YOU, first of all, to imagine that you are standing beside me, peeping over the rail of an arched and curtained gallery, set – like the stage of some aerial theatre – high above a long and imposing room.

From our vantage point, if we push our noses out just a very little way through the narrow gap in the curtains, we may see down to where the assembled company of fine ladies and gentlemen are sitting at table. The thick velvet curtains smell of time and dust, but do not mind them. We shall not be here long.

The room below us, decorated in crimson and gold, is richly furnished and, although grandly proportioned, deliciously warm, even on this chill November evening, from the heat thrown out from blazing piles of pine logs in the two great stone fire-places.

On every wall there are mirrors in gilded frames that give back endless reflections as you pass them. Above us, spanning the whole space, soars a panelled ceiling, curved like a barrel, on which – although you must take my word for it, being now lost to sight in shadow – are painted scenes depicting the marriage of Heracles and Hebe. (I had this information from Mr Pocock, the butler, and, as is my habit, wishing always to improve myself and extend my knowledge, wrote it down as soon as I could in one of the note-books I keep constantly about me.)

The fourteen persons at dinner tonight have come together to pay tribute to Lord Edward Duport, a Government man who lost a finger on this day in November 1605, during the attack on Holbeche House, to where several of the Gunpowder Plot conspirators had fled.

Just below us, on our left, is lumpish Miss Fanny Bristow, stupid but harmless; next to her sits Mr Maurice FitzMaurice, the proud new owner of the Red House at Ashby St John, who thinks he is such a fine fellow, though all the world knows better. (By the look on his face, he appears to have taken it very ill that he has been obliged to sit out his dinner in Miss Bristow's simpering company. It serves him right, I say, for thinking so well of himself.)

Directly opposite is Sir Lionel Voysey, of Thorpe Laxton Hall, with his absurd wife, ugly and coarse; on her right you may see the smirking face of Dr Pordage, who always touches me slyly on the hand with a damp finger when I see him to the door, as if this betokened some secret understanding between us, which it most assuredly does *not*.

The Rector, Mr Thripp, and his captious wife, are sitting next to the doctor, in strained silence as usual. I believe Mrs Thripp harbours some deep and perpetual resentment against her husband, though what it is I cannot say. The remaining guests we can pass over, being of no consequence to my story.

We now come to the three members of this evening's party in which I – and you – have a particular interest: the permanent residents of this great house.

First, of course, my Lady – the former Miss Emily Carteret, now the 26th Baroness Tansor.

Look at her. She sits at the head of the board, as a queen ought, in black and shimmering silver silk. Who can deny that she is beautiful still, or that her fifty-two years have been uncommonly kind to her? In the candlelight below us, fluttering shadows play delightfully across her pale skin (she never allows the gas to be lit: candle-light is so much more flattering).

She captivates and charms the men gathered in her Crimson-and-Gold Dining-Room. See how they ogle her when they think no one else is looking! Mr FitzMaurice, Dr Pordage, even red-faced Sir Lionel Voysey (always comically maladroit in her presence): they all fall under her spell like silly boys, and see her only as she wishes to be seen.

Naturally, her famously tragical past – a father murdered, and the great love of her life slain a month before their marriage – only increases her allure. Men, I think, are such fools, at least men such as these. If she has suffered, well, there is suffering enough in the world, and we shall each have our share before we are released.

Yet she has been richly compensated for her suffering, which is by no means the least of her attractions, especially to her bachelor admirers. Beautiful, romantically scarred by tragedy, the possessor of an immense fortune and an ancient title – and now a widow! Charlie Skinner, one of the junior footmen, who is sweet on me, told me that Mr FitzMaurice could hardly credit his good fortune on meeting his fair neighbour for the first time, and that he returned to the Red House in a perfect jitter of excitement. It was soon reported at his club that he had been heard hinting, to anyone who would listen, that his bachelor days were numbered.

Alas for poor deluded Mr Maurice FitzMaurice! He is scarcely alone in his ambitions. She is far too great a prize, perhaps still one of the greatest prizes in England. His rivals are many and distinguished, his own hand as weak as can be; and yet he persists in entertaining the rosiest of hopes, without ever enjoying the least encouragement from the object of his desire.

The truth is that she will never marry again, and certainly not a prize fool like Mr Maurice FitzMaurice. Marriage would bring her no material advantage. Nor will she succumb to Love again, for her heart is shut fast against all further assault from that quarter. No man can ever displace the memory of her first and last love, whose terrible death has been the great affliction of her life, greater even than the murder of her father. Her late husband, Colonel Zaluski, could not do it – that at least is the common opinion. I never met the gentleman; but Sukie Prout (my great friend below stairs) says that the two of them rubbed along well enough, and that the colonel had a smiling, accommodating way about him that made you instantly like him. I must suppose, therefore, that his wife liked him too, and that this was enough for her.

The fruits of this unremarkable union are now sitting on either side of their mother: Mr Perseus Duport, the heir to her title and fortune, on her right hand, his younger brother, Mr Randolph Duport, on her left. But *they* are not at all unremarkable.

Mr Perseus – who has just raised a toast to gallant Lord Edward Duport – will shortly attain his majority, and is very like his mother in appearance: tall, deliberate in movement, watchful in attitude, and with the same fathomless eyes. His hair – as dark as those eyes – is worn long, so that it falls about his shoulders in a consciously romantic way, as befits the poet he aspires to be. He is very proud of his hair, a trait that he also gets from his mother. A most handsome young gentleman, undoubtedly, made more so by a carefully tended black beard, which gives him a dangerously heroic look, exactly like the portrait of the Turkish Corsair that hangs at the foot of the vestibule stairs, and for which, on first seeing it, I thought he must have sat, had it not been painted over twenty years since.

His younger brother, Mr Randolph Duport, is nearly twenty, and is no less striking than his brother, although very differently composed. He is shorter and stockier, stronger in limb, with warm brown eyes (Sukie says they are the spit of his late father's), a rosy, outdoors colouring, and unruly brown hair. There is not the least resemblance to his mother; nor is there any discernible trace of her temperament in him, which makes people like him far more than Mr Perseus. Unlike his brother, he has none of Lady Tansor's haughtiness and pride. He is, by contrast, a singularly unaffected and spontaneous soul, appearing to take things as they come, and (so goes the general opinion) hardly ever thinking of consequences, for which I am told he has often felt the sting of his mother's displeasure. Yet, possessing the uncommon ability to acknowledge his faults, which Mr Perseus appears to lack, he is said never to complain, but promises to apply himself more soberly in the future to the art of properly considering matters.

Perhaps it is being the younger son that makes him so philosophical. Mr Perseus, on whom all his mother's expectations rest, is ever mindful of his future responsibilities, when he becomes the head of this great family. He takes his privileged position as his mother's future successor very seriously, to the extent that, following the death of his father, Colonel Zaluski, a year since, he insisted on giving up his studies at the University in order to assist Lady Tansor, who had formerly relied on her husband for such things, in overseeing the running of the estate, and to advise her – as he could – on the many other Duport interests.

Mr Randolph does not appear to resent the accident of his brother's seniority, or the material benefits that this will bring when at last Mr Perseus comes into his inheritance. He claims that he would be rather alarmed than otherwise if, by some misfortune befalling his elder brother, he were to succeed in his place.

These three persons have become the principal and constant objects of my attention in this house, to which I have been sent for reasons that – at the time of which I am writing – have not been fully revealed to me. Thus I continue to wait, and watch, as I have been instructed to do.

I AM USUALLY required to be in constant readiness to attend my Lady, day or night; but on this particular evening I had been excused from all duties. After I had dressed my Lady for dinner, the hours that lay ahead had been mine to do with as I wished – a precious respite, during which the bell in my room would (I hoped) remain silent, even through the cold night watches.

My Lady does not sleep well, and I am regularly called down to her when she wakes from her often troubled slumbers, to read to her, or to brush her long dark hair (a service to which she is especially partial) until she is ready to return to her bed. If sleep does not then take her, she soon reaches for the bell-rope to summon me down again.

Sometimes the bell rings only once in my room, two floors above hers; at others, I might stumble, half asleep, out of my warm bed and descend the stairs to her panelled bed-chamber five or six times, returning to my own room vexed and fatigued. But on this particular occasion, my Lady had assured me that I would not be called until the morning.

After performing my evening duties, I had therefore closed my door with the most luxurious sense of relief. At first I curled up on my bed to read a new novel by Miss Braddon (novels are my passion), but found I could not settle; so, throwing the book aside, I tip-toed down to the gallery that overlooks the Crimson-and-Gold Dining-Room, to watch my mistress, her two sons by her side, entertain her guests.

Later, alone in my little room under the eaves, I began writing down in my Book of Secrets what I had seen and thought that day. It was the duty I must daily perform, as instructed by my guardian, Madame de l'Orme, through whose agency I had been sent to Evenwood, to serve the woman whose fourteen guests were now dispersing into the cold November darkness.

II
The Interview

'WHEN YOU ADDRESS me – if, of course, you are successful in your application – I shall wish you to call me "my Lady", never "your Ladyship".'

These had been my mistress's first words to me, after I was shown into her private apartments to be interviewed for the position of lady's-maid.

'Others may use a different form of address,' she had continued, 'but you may not. I hope you understand that, and remember it. Although few of them have deserved the distinction, it is a strict rule of mine that my maid should be looked upon differently by the other servants.'

When I had entered the room, she had been sitting at a little escritoire set before a window that looked out across the Park, lazily holding out her long-fingered hand to receive the character with which I had been furnished. Opening the letter, and still hardly acknowledging my presence, she began to read.

On a sudden, she looked up over her spectacles with a hard, sour expression, and spoke the words I have quoted above, as if I had already wilfully transgressed her instruction, although indeed I had been standing mutely, hands folded demurely in front of me, my face a picture of innocent compliance.

There was a copy of the *Morning Post* on the escritoire. An advertisement had been neatly ringed in red ink.

'Everyone who has come here today for the position has placed an advertisement,' she said, seeing that I had noticed the open newspaper. 'My last maid, Miss Plumptre, may have come from a very respectable agency, but she did not suit at all. I shall never use agencies again. I was forced to dismiss her after a most unpleasant and distressing incident, which I do not wish to speak of. As a consequence I now prefer people who place advertisements. It shows initiative, and reveals character. For a position such as this, I like to decide these things for myself, so it is fortunate for you that your advertisement caught my eye.'

She bestowed on me a frigid smile before returning to the letter.

'Your last employer, Miss Gainsborough, writes that you gave excellent service,' she said. 'And how did you like Miss Gainsborough?'

'Very well, my Lady.'

It was all a well-prepared fiction. 'Miss Helen Gainsborough' never existed, being a creation of Madame de l'Orme's. Everything had been most carefully arranged beforehand, and Madame had assured me that, if Lady Tansor chose to write to this chimeric lady, in order to confirm the opinion of me contained in the letter she was now reading, then a reply would be forthcoming that would amply satisfy her Ladyship on every particular. Even if she called on 'Miss

Gainsborough' in person, or sent some agent, the eventuality had been anticipated, and the necessary means to meet it put in place.

Lady Tansor slowly removed her spectacles, laid them down, and fixed her unmediated gaze upon me.

I had the confidence of youth in my ability to play the part assigned to me by Madame; but Lady Tansor's scrutiny was nonetheless unnerving. She seemed to be sifting through all my secret thoughts, in search of the truth concerning my true identity; and it required considerable effort on my part to maintain my composure.

'It is such a dark afternoon,' she said, her eyes still fixed on me. 'Stand closer, child – here, nearer the window, where I can see you better.'

I did as she asked, for some moments remaining motionless and uncomfortable under her examination.

'You have a most striking look about you,' she said at last. 'Most striking. I imagine people do not easily forget you.'

I thanked her, and said that she was very kind.

'Kind?' she replied, giving me another sharp look. 'No, no; not kind. You will have to earn my kindness.' Then, more absently: 'I do not flatter. It is the simple truth. Yours is a face that would always be remembered.'

She looked down again at the letter.

'I am informed here that you are an orphan, and that you never knew your parents.'

'That is so, my Lady.'

'And you were residing with an old friend of your mother's in London, before taking up the position with Miss Gainsborough?'

'Yes, my Lady.'

'And before that, I read that you lived in Paris, under the care of a guardian, a widowed lady.'

'That is correct, my Lady.'

She once more resumed her reading of the letter.

'Do you consider yourself to be a competent needle-woman?' was her next question; to which I answered that I had generally been considered so.

'I do not often leave Evenwood these days,' she went on, 'but when it becomes necessary for me to go up to Town, I shall require a most careful packer.'

'I am sure I shall not disappoint, my Lady,' I said. 'Miss Gainsborough was a great traveller. I believe she is even now in Russia, although I never travelled nearly so far with her.'

'Russia! How fascinating!'

She thought for a moment, then asked whether I had any followers.

'No, my Lady,' I answered – truthfully.

'No attachment of any kind?'

'None, my Lady.'

'And no living family either, I believe?'

'That is correct, my Lady. The person nearest to a parent is my guardian, Madame Bertaud. My mother's oldest friend, Mrs Poynter, with whom I lived in London before being employed by Miss Gainsborough, I regarded as a kind of aunt; but she has recently passed away.'

After a moment or two's further perusal of the letter, Lady Tansor looked up and once again fixed her great dark eyes on me.

'You are somewhat young, and this is merely your second position,' she said.

My heart began to sink, for it was imperative that I secure the situation.

'I have seen two or three very experienced and competent people today,' she continued, 'who come with excellent references, and who would be well able to fill the position satisfactorily.'

She thought for a moment, and looked intently at the letter again, as if searching for some hidden meaning in it. Then, to my relief, her look began to soften.

'But Miss Gainsborough gives you a very good character, although I do not have the honour of an acquaintance with the lady. In the normal course of matters, I would accept such a recommendation only from someone I knew personally; but I might make an exception, in your case. I suppose,' she added meditatively, almost as if she were speaking aloud to herself, 'that I could write to Miss Gainsborough, or perhaps . . .'

She paused, leaving the sentence unfinished, then suddenly shot one her most severe looks at me.

'Having been brought up in France, I must suppose you to be proficient in the language?'

'Yes, my Lady. I believe you might consider me to be fluent.'

'And do you follow events?'

I replied that I did my best to inform myself concerning the world.

'Then tell me what you think about the Turkish War – in French.'

Now I knew little enough of the matter, no more than the bare, vaguely comprehended fact that hostilities had broken out. As to the causes, or the possible consequences, I was at a complete loss. I made a reply, nonetheless, in French, to the effect that I considered it to be a dangerous situation, and that war, in general, was always a thing to be deplored, and avoided if possible.

She gave me a humourless smile, but said nothing. Then she asked:

'What do you read?'

Here I was on solid ground, for I had ever been a great devourer of books, and Madame had fed my appetite constantly as a child. My tutor, Mr Thornhaugh, who lived at the top of Madame's house, and of whom I shall speak more fully in due course, had also guided my reading. I had a little Latin, too, and some Greek, although I found that I quickly forgot much of what I had so painfully acquired of both languages, and thus had scant aptitude for the serious study of either of the great classical literatures.

My passion was for modern works of the imagination, in French and English; poetry and, above all, novels absorbed me.

'I am very fond of Stendhal,' I said in answer to Lady Tansor's question, with the spontaneous eagerness that I always exhibit when speaking of my favourite books; 'and of Voltaire.'

'Voltaire!' Lady Tansor broke in, with an amused laugh. 'How advanced! What else?'

'And then I adore Monsieur Balzac, and George Sand; oh, and Mr Dickens, and Mr Collins, and Miss Braddon . . .'

Again she interrupted me, raising her hand to prevent me from continuing.

'Your tastes seem a little irregular and ill-disciplined, child,' she said; 'but perhaps that is excusable in one so young, and taste can easily be corrected.'

Then she asked: 'And what of poetry? Do you read poetry?'

'Oh, yes, my Lady. In French, I am very fond of Lamartine, de Vigny, and Leconte de Lisle. Byron, Keats, Shelley, and Mr Tennyson are my favourites in English.'

'And do you know the work of Mr Phoebus Daunt?'

The question was posed with detectable emphasis, as if she had a peculiar reason for asking, which of course I knew that she had. Mr Daunt had been the man she was to have married, before he had been cruelly murdered by an old school-friend, who had harboured a long-standing resentment against him. It was a question that I had anticipated being asked; for Madame had made a point of telling me the story of Lady Tansor's dead fiancé, and of how she had continued to worship his memory with undimmed reverence and passion. Madame had also given me several volumes of Mr Daunt's poems, which I had dutifully read, with little pleasure.

'Yes, my Lady,' I answered, looking straight into her unblinking eyes.

'And what is your opinion of his work?'

I had my answer pat.

'I consider him to have been a poet of singular and remarkable originality, a worthy successor in every way to the epic poets of former times.'

I spoke the words with all the warm conviction that I could muster, and waited anxiously to see whether she had detected any trace of dissimulation in my voice or manner; but she said nothing, only sighed, laying aside the letter of recommendation with a languid gesture of her hand.

'I do not care to see anyone else about the position,' she said after a short period of reflection. 'You have an honest face, as well as a striking one, and I judge you to be a quick learner. My last maid was incurably stupid, as well as being – well, it does not matter now what she was. You, I see, are not stupid at all – indeed, you appear to have been educated to an uncommon degree for someone applying for the situation of lady's-maid. No doubt you have your reasons for doing so, but they do not concern me at present. I have therefore decided: the position is yours. Does that surprise you?'

I said that it was not my place to question her decision, for good or ill, at which she cast me another sharp look, and I once again lowered my eyes submissively, although exulting that my design had been achieved, just as Madame had foreseen. She had promised me that coming to Evenwood would be the making of me, and that I should not entertain the slightest doubt of my power to charm Lady Tansor on sight, as the first and necessary step. So it had proved.

There was a moment's silence as I stood, head bowed, waiting for my new mistress to speak.

'Very well,' she said at last. 'That is settled. Remuneration as set out in my secretary's recent letter, and everything provided, until we see how you go on. Naturally, I expect my servants to observe certain standards of behaviour, and I shall not hesitate to punish insubordination or misconduct; but you will find me a liberal mistress, on the whole, with my own way of regulating the household. Some, I know, would regard me as being shockingly lax, by allowing my servants – those, at least, who have proved themselves deserving of my trust – too much freedom of action; but I do not mind that. It is how I like to do things. If properly managed, it makes for contentment, above and below stairs.

'And now: what shall I call you, I wonder? I see that your Christian name is not given in Miss Gainsborough's letter.'

'It is Esperanza, my Lady.'

'Esperanza! How charming! Although I am not sure that will do either. It is rather . . . Continental. Have you another?'

'Alice, my Lady.'

'Alice!'

She placed a hand, fingers splayed theatrically, against her breast, as if this item of intelligence had momentarily deprived her of breath.

'Nothing could be better. Alice! I like it exceedingly. So fresh! So English! I shall call you Alice.'

She turned away to ring a little silver bell that stood on a table beside her. With surprising promptness, a liveried footman, tall and gaunt, appeared at the door.

'Barrington, this is Miss Gorst. She is to be my new maid. Tell Mr Pocock to send the others away, and then wait outside to show Miss Gorst to her room.'

The footman, giving me a rather queer look – inquisitive and knowing at the same time – bowed and left the room.

'I shall not need you this evening, Alice,' said Lady Tansor when Barrington had gone. 'One of the maids can help to dress me. Barrington will show you where you are to sleep. You will come to me at eight in the morning. Sharp.'

At this, she picked up a book lying open on the adjacent table, and began to read. I caught sight of the title and author blocked in gold on the spine:

ROSA MUNDI
P. RAINSFORD DAUNT

As I was turning to leave, she looked up and spoke once more.

'I hope, Alice, that you and I will suit, and that we might become friends – as far as our conditions allow, of course. Do you think that we shall?'

'Yes, my Lady,' I replied, taken aback by her frankness. 'I am sure of it.'

'Then we are of one mind. Good-night, Alice.'

'Good-night, my Lady.'

Outside, in the now candlelit Picture Gallery, I found Barrington waiting to show me upstairs to my room, a service that he performed in complete silence.

I HAD BROUGHT little with me to Evenwood from my former life in France, except a small valise containing some few clothes, half a dozen books, a handful of precious childhood trinkets, and of course my Book of Secrets.

'We must not trust our cause simply to memory,' Madame had warned me before my departure. 'Memory is often a false friend. Words, my dear, if they be clearly and truly and immediately set down, are our best ally, our best defence, and our best weapon. Guard them well.'

When I first came to Evenwood, the pages in my Book stood blank; but this, as I soon discovered, was a house of secrets, and the pages quickly began to fill.

On the evening of Monday, 4th September, in the year 1876, I slept for the first time in my cramped but cosy room under the eaves of the great house of Evenwood, although not before I had written down in my Book an account, in the shorthand that my tutor had taught me, of my interview with Lady Tansor.

In the darkness, I lay listening to the soft patter of rain against the glass of the two dormer windows. Somewhere, a door banged, and there were voices echoing down a corridor. Then silence.

I was on the threshold of a great adventure, alone in this place, knowing not a soul, ignorant as yet of why I had been sent here. All I knew was that Madame had told me – so often, so urgently – that I *must* be here. Yet as I composed myself for sleep on that first night, assailed by doubts that I could fulfil Madame's expectations of me, I also experienced a tingle of eager anticipation at the prospect of finally understanding what then remained beyond my comprehension.

Tomorrow, then. It would begin tomorrow. At eight o'clock. Sharp.

1

In My Lady's Chamber

I
The Great Task

I WAS AWOKEN by the sound of a clock, somewhere outside, striking the hour of six. If the same obliging instrument had chimed out the hours throughout the night, as I supposed it must have done, it had only now intruded upon the deep sleep into which I had quickly sunk.

Eager to greet the first day of my new life, I jumped down from my warm bed, skipped across the bare boards to one of the little dormer windows, and pulled back the curtain.

Looking down, I could just make out a balustraded terrace stretching the length of the wing in which Lady Tansor's apartments, and my own room two floors above, were situated. Steps led from the terrace to a broad area of gravelled walk-ways and formal flower-beds. Beyond, the densely timbered Park lay partially submerged under a bar of dissolving mist, thicker in the distance about the margins of a large lake, and along the winding course of the Evenbrook, a looping tributary of the River Nene that eventually rejoins the main stream some three or four miles to the east of the Park.

The previous night's rain had gone, and the pale, blue-grey sky was already growing brighter. I took this harbinger of a sunny morning as an omen that, after my success in obtaining the position of maid to Lady Tansor, all would be well for me in this place.

Tuesday, 5th September 1876: my first morning at Evenwood – and such a beautiful one! I had arrived in England a little time before, full of apprehension, but determined – being stubborn once my mind has been made up – not to disappoint Madame in what she expected of me. Although anxious to know why my guardian had contrived to send me here, my true identity disguised, I had resigned myself with difficulty to waiting until she was ready to reveal her purpose to me at last.

TWO MONTHS EARLIER, Madame had come to my room as I was about to retire for the night.

'I have something to tell you, dear child,' she said, taking my hand, her face white and drawn.

'What is it?' I asked, feeling a sudden lurch of anxiety. 'Has something happened? Are you ill?'

'No,' she said, 'I am not ill, but something has happened, something that will change your life for ever. What I have to say will be a shock to you, but it must be said, and said now.'

'Then say it quickly, dear Guardian,' was my reply, 'for you are frightening me dreadfully.'

'There's my brave, dear child,' she said, kissing me. 'Very well. You are to go to England – not quite yet, but soon, when certain matters have been arranged – to begin a new life.'

I was completely unprepared for this extraordinary announcement. Leave the Maison de l'Orme, the only home I had ever known, to go alone to England, where I had never been in my life, so suddenly, without warning, and with no reason given? It was absurd, impossible.

'But why?' I asked, my heart thumping with apprehension and bewilderment. 'And for how long?'

'As to the last,' replied Madame, with the strangest smile, 'if you are successful in accomplishing the task I shall be asking you to undertake, then you may never return here – indeed, I hope, with all my heart, that it may be so.'

As I listened in astonishment, she went on to tell me that, for some weeks past, regular advertisements had been placed in London newspapers setting out my qualifications for a place as lady's-maid.

'Lady's-maid!' I exclaimed, in disbelief. 'A servant!' Had my guardian gone mad?

'Hear me out, dear child,' said Madame, kissing me once more.

It appeared that the intention of the advertisements had been to recommend me for a particular vacancy that Madame knew existed, and to which a reply had now been received. The consequence was that I must go to a great country house in England called Evenwood, there to be interviewed by its owner, the widowed Lady Tansor.

'You must charm this lady,' urged Madame. 'This will present no difficulty, for you charm everyone – as your dear departed father did. She will immediately discern that you are no common servant, but have been brought up as a lady, and this will be your great advantage. But you will have one other. There will be something about you that she will not be able to resist, although she might try. I cannot say more; but this you must believe, and take strength from it.'

'But why must I do these things?' I asked, dumbfounded by her words. 'You still have not told me.'

Again that strange smile, which I believe was meant to set my mind at rest, but only served to alarm me even more.

'Dear child,' she said, 'don't be angry with me, for I can see that you are, and I understand how you must feel. There is a purpose – a great purpose – to be served by your becoming maid to Lady Tansor, but it must be kept from you for the time being. Knowing too much too soon will make it all the harder for you to play your part, and compromise those qualities of innocence and inexperience in your character that you will need to draw on. If you secure this position, as I'm sure you will, you must daily convince your mistress that you are indeed what you present yourself to be. She must have no suspicions of you. Until you have gained her complete trust, therefore, the less you know, the better; for your ignorance will make your behaviour more natural and unstudied. When you have established yourself in her favour, it will be time for you to know everything – and you shall. On that you have my solemn word.

'So will you trust me, child, as you have always trusted me, and believe that what I do, I do to serve your interests alone, to which, since the day you were born, I have always been, and shall always be, devoted?'

What could I say to such an appeal? It was only too true. Her loving care for me had been daily proved. Surely I must trust her now, although blindly? Not to do so would be to repudiate all she had done for me, all she meant to me. I had no mother; I had no father; no brother or sister. I had only Madame, whose lilting voice used to sing me to sleep, or hush me gently when I awoke from the fearful nightmares to which I have always been susceptible. I was certain that she would never deceive me, nor deliberately put me in the way of harm. If the task that she now wished me to undertake was bound to my closest interests, as she continued to insist, what cause did I have to doubt her?

I knew in my heart that, in the end, the duty I owed to Madame would make it impossible for me to reject her assurances that my going to England was absolutely necessary. Nevertheless, I eventually accepted them only with the greatest reluctance, feeling that my guardian had given me no other choice, by exploiting my love for her to overcome my most natural and reasonable objections.

'Dear child,' said Madame, after I had composed myself a little, her elfin face now alive with relief. 'We know only too well that this is a great deal to ask of you, and at so young an age; but we also know that you have it in your power—'

'"We"?' I broke in.

For the first time she hesitated in her reply, as if she had let slip something that she had not wished me to know.

'Why, myself and Mr Thornhaugh, of course,' she said, after a moment's thought. 'Who else should I mean?'

I asked what my tutor had to do with the matter.

'Dear child,' came her smiling reply, accompanied by a soft touch of her hand, 'you know how much I have come to rely on Mr Thornhaugh's advice, having no husband to turn to. I need that advice more than ever now.'

I appreciated why Madame had made my tutor a party in what she kept calling the 'Great Task', for he was in every way a most exceptional individual, in whom I also trusted absolutely; but why had she not told me of this from the start?

'I have taken Mr Thornhaugh into my confidence,' she admitted. 'He must know all, if he is to assist me. I would not have kept this from you had Mr Thornhaugh himself not insisted on it. It is to his credit that he was sensible of the delicacy of the situation. He felt that it would be hurtful to you if I told you that your tutor knew what you cannot yet know. He was right, of course. Will you forgive me?'

We sat in silence, our arms around each other, rocking gently to and fro, until at last Madame said that we would resume our conversation in the morning.

From that day onwards, she set about preparing me for what lay ahead. Her own maid tutored me daily in the various duties that I would be called upon to perform, and I was given a copy of Mrs Isabella Beeton's excellent manual of household management, in which the many onerous responsibilities of a lady's-maid were set out. This I studied assiduously night after night, and later made sure to take the book with me to Evenwood.

It was frequently impossible for me to stop myself from asking Madame yet again about the purpose of the Great Task, and why it required me to quit France.

'It is your destiny, dear child,' she would say, in a most solemn and conclusive manner, which instantly discouraged further enquiry, 'as well as your duty.' This was all the answer she would ever give me; and so, feeling the impossibility of defying Destiny, I at last submitted to the inevitable.

A week or so later, on a hazy August morning, Madame came to me as I was sitting reading in the salon. I saw immediately that she had something of the greatest importance to tell me.

'Are you ready, dear child, to begin the Great Task?' she asked, flushed with excitement.

She stretched both her hands out towards me. I took them, and we stood facing each other, our fingers locked tightly together.

'I am ready,' I replied, although I was sick with renewed apprehension, and still silently resentful at the position of unquestioning obedience to Madame's will in which I had been placed.

'Do not think that you will be alone,' she said, gently stroking my hair. 'I shall be here, whenever you need me – and Mr Thornhaugh too, of course – and you will always have a friend near by in England.'

'A friend?'

'Yes, and a good and trustworthy one, who will make sure that no harm comes to you, and who will watch over you in my place. But you will not know this person, unless – God forbid – circumstances make it imperative that you should do so.'

So the time for leaving the house in the Avenue d'Uhrich grew ever nearer. In the last days, Madame had impressed upon me again and again the need, if I secured the position, to gain Lady Tansor's complete trust, whilst warning me that this might not be won quickly, or easily. She then told me that there had been only one intimate friend of her own sex in Lady Tansor's life, but that, as far as she knew, this friendship had been ended many years ago.

'You must not remain a mere servant for long,' she went on, 'but must become a substitute for that lost friend. The success of the Great Task depends on it.'

For the last time, I ventured to ask what the purpose of the Great Task was, knowing even as I did so what Madame's response would be. For now (it was always, provokingly, 'for now'), I must continue to put my faith in her, although she promised to send me three 'Letters of Instruction', the last of which would finally reveal the goal of the Great Task, and how it was to be achieved.

FROM THAT MOMENT, I have come to feel that my life is not my own, and that it has never been truly mine. Yet until then, on the contrary, it seems to me that I passed a most contented and enviable childhood and girlhood, secure in my own protected world; often alone, but never lonely; and fully alive within myself, where I revelled constantly in bright imaginings – except when the nightmares came, and I would cry out in terror. But even these, while dreaded, did not disturb me so much when the next day broke fair, and I would wake to see the dear face of Madame, whom, if the terror had been severe, I would always find sleeping in the chair beside my bed, her hand closed protectively over mine.

Of my mother, I could recall nothing. Of my father, I sometimes fancied that I had a vague remembrance, as of a place once visited long ago, but of which one retains only the faintest sense, indistinct yet always bringing with it the same indelible impression. Curiously, this fragment of memory never tormented me. It was too insubstantial, and came too infrequently. Only on birthdays did I sometimes feel forlorn at my orphan state; but then I would scold myself for my ingratitude towards Madame, and look upon myself as a very selfish creature indeed. Orphans that I had read of in books were often poor suffering things, cruelly treated by wicked guardians or stepmothers. It was never so with me. Madame was kind and caring; the house in the Avenue d'Uhrich, although its high walls shut out the distant world, was large and comfortable. I wanted for nothing, lacked no bodily comforts or stimulation of the mind; I was loved, knew that I was loved, and loved in return. How, then, should I have been sad or unhappy?

WHEN I WAS quite young, Madame would often take me to the little Cemetery of St-Vincent, to show me where my mother and father were buried, side by side, under two flat granite slabs, in the deep shadow of the boundary wall. My hand held tightly in hers, I would stare down at the slabs, fascinated by the stark brevity of their inscriptions:

MARGUERITE ALICE GORST
1836–1858

EDWIN GORST
DIED 1862

My mother's inscription would always make me sad: such a beautiful name, and – as I one day realized, when I had learned my numbers – so young to have been taken into Death's arms.

For my father's, I felt a strange and fanciful curiosity; for the presence of a single date made it appear to my child's mind that he had somehow never been born, yet had contrived to die. This, of course, I simply could not comprehend, until Madame told me it meant that the year of his birth was unknown or uncertain.

Often, standing with Madame silently regarding the graves, and having no portraits or photographs of them to feed on, I would try to picture what my parents might have looked like – whether they had been short or tall, dark or fair – and wonder, as far as my limited experience of life and the world was able to inform my juvenile speculations, what circumstances had brought them to this, their final resting-place; but I never could.

Throughout my childhood, Madame had often told me that my mother had been beautiful (as all mothers must of course be in the imaginations of orphaned children who never knew them), and that my father had been handsome and clever (as all fathers of such children must also be), for she had known my father before his marriage, and, later, when he and my mother had lived with her for a time in the Maison de l'Orme.

This much, together with the bare circumstances of their first coming to Paris, their taking up residence with her in the Avenue d'Uhrich, my birth there, and their subsequent deaths – my mother's soon after I had been born, my father's a few years afterwards – was all Madame would tell me about my departed parents; and for the duration of my childhood this was all I needed to know. As I grew older, however, I became greatly curious to learn more about them; but Madame would always – in her gentle but immovable way – evade my questions. 'One day, dear child, one day,' she would say, kissing away all further importuning.

Thus I had grown up in Madame's tender care, knowing little more about myself than that my name was Esperanza Alice Gorst, born on 1st September in the year 1857, the only child of Edwin and Marguerite Gorst, both of whom lay in the Cemetery of St-Vincent.

II
The Heir

A KNOCK AT the door roused me from my reverie. Running back to my bed, I quickly pulled on my robe and went to answer it. It was the head footman, Barrington, tray in hand.

'Breakfast, miss,' he said, gloomily.

After placing the tray on the table, he gave a little cough, as if he wished to say something more.

'Yes, Barrington?'

'Mrs Battersby sends to know, miss, if you'll be taking your meals in the steward's room from now on.'

'Is that the custom here for my Lady's maid?'

'It is, miss.'

'And Mrs Battersby is my Lady's housekeeper?'

'She is, miss.'

'Very well, then. Please send Mrs Battersby my very best compliments, and tell her that I shall be pleased to take my meals in the steward's room.'

He executed a meagre bow, and departed.

JONAH BARRINGTON
Footman. Tall and wiry, straight-backed, military bearing, hollow-cheeked, doleful of aspect, full head of stiff grey hair. Large ears with peeping tufts of white, like caterpillars. Fifty years of age? Small pursed mouth giving the impression that he exists in a state of surprised disapproval of the world in which he unaccountably finds himself, although I have a sense that he is a kindly soul at heart. An unobtrusive but watchful air about him.

This was the description of Barrington that I made in my Book of Secrets, after its subject had left, and I had drunk up my tea and eaten my bread-and-butter. Then I washed, dressed myself in the plain black gown, starched white pinafore, and cap that Madame had provided, and went out, for the first time on my own, into the great house of Evenwood.

THE NARROW WOODEN stairs that led down from my room took me, first, to a white-washed corridor, then, becoming wider and grander, to the Picture Gallery, lit by a row of arched windows, in which stood the door to my Lady's private apartments.

It was now nearly seven o'clock, giving me time enough before I must attend Lady Tansor to do a little exploring. So, after examining the pictures in the gallery, I continued my descent until I emerged at last into the great echoing vestibule, with its domed lantern high above, through which the morning sun was now streaming.

Beneath the lantern, in a semi-circular alcove, and surrounded by six candles set in tall wooden holders, hung a painting. It showed a short, stiff-necked, proud-looking gentleman and his wife, the latter cradling a baby lovingly in her arms.

The lady possessed a most exceptional beauty and grace, with an abundance of dark hair gathered up under a cap of black lace, a narrow band of velvet around her long white throat.

I cannot say why it was, but her image instantly exercised a peculiar and lasting power over me. My heart seemed to beat a little faster as I looked upon her. In after days, I would often come and stand intently looking at the picture, as if such an act of dedicated concentration might bring her back to life; for – unaccountable and fantastical though it seemed – I wished with all my heart and soul to know her, speak to her, to hear her voice, and to see her move amongst living creatures once again.

I discovered soon enough that she was Laura Duport, first wife of the late Lord Tansor, my Lady's predecessor, and that the pretty babe had been his Lordship's only son, Henry Hereward Duport, on whom all his dearest hopes for the continuation of his line had briefly rested. The little boy, however, had been cruelly taken from him at the age of seven, after a fatal fall from his pony. Lord Tansor's heart had been broken – yes, and his poor wife's, too; for Sukie Prout later told me that she went quite mad at the last. She was found wandering about the Park, in a cruel frost, dressed only in her shift, bleeding and hurt. They carried her back to the house, but she died soon afterwards, and was buried in the Mausoleum that stands on the edge of the Park.

I turned away from the portrait and looked about me.

To my left was a pair of tall gilded doors surmounted by a shield carved in stone, bearing (as I later discovered) the Tansor arms. One of the doors being partly open, I peeped in, and then went through into a richly appointed room of a predominantly yellow colour, with a great chandelier, suspended by a massive gold chain, that appeared to my mind like some strange crystal galleon floating in mid-air.

I passed through this apartment into another, in which the colour red predominated this time, and then into a third and a fourth, each one sumptuously decorated and furnished. Paintings in ornate frames, many of huge dimensions, rich tapestries, and towering looking-glasses crowded the walls; and wherever the eye rested were accumulations of precious objects of every size, shape, and kind.

The fourth of these rooms, which I came to know as the Green Drawing-Room, opened into the magnificent State Saloon. Its walls and lofty ceiling were entirely covered with brightly painted scenes of ancient Athens and Rome, in which columns and buildings had been so cunningly rendered by the artist that, on first seeing them, I almost believed that they must actually be real, and made of stone.

I sat down for a moment in a gilded chair with a high back, like a throne, the better to drink in the atmosphere of unbounded and unrestrained luxury that the room gave out.

As a child, I had thought that Madame's house in the Avenue d'Uhrich was as large and grand as any house could be; but it was nothing – less than nothing – to Evenwood.

To wake up every morning, knowing that these great rooms, and the treasures they contained, were yours to occupy and savour! What a thing that would be! I amused myself for a moment by trying to fancy what it would be like to experience the daily and absolute possession of such a place. It seemed extraordinary to me that one family, distinguished only by their common blood, could lay perpetual claim to inhabit this faery splendour – more super-abundantly opulent, more ravishing to the senses, it seemed to me, than any sultan's palace that I had read of in the stories told by Scheherazade.

In preparation for my coming to Evenwood, Madame had asked Mr Thornhaugh to tell me something of the ancient Duport family. He had shown me what was written of them in *Burke's Heraldic Dictionary*, from which I learned that the 1st Baron Tansor had borne the name Maldwin, and had been summoned to Parliament by the King in the year 1264. I learned also that the barony was of a peculiar type, known as a Barony by Writ, which allowed inheritance through females as well as males.

The late Lord Tansor had died in 1863. Having no direct heirs, either male or female, his title and property had passed to my mistress, his nearest collateral relative, who had then taken his name. Everything I could see and touch was now hers, to do with as she pleased; one day all this would belong to her eldest son, Mr Perseus Duport. Then he would marry, and a child would be born who would also walk through these very rooms, knowing them as their own.

Thus the great river of successive privilege would continue to flow, carrying the Duports on its calm and glittering waters through this life to the next, from generation unto generation.

BEYOND THE STATE Saloon, a narrow corridor brought me to a huge wooden screen, black with age and festooned with life-like carvings of birds and animals, with an arcaded gallery high above. Through the screen, a pair of double doors opened into the Crimson-and-Gold Dining-Room that I have earlier described.

Here I paused, eager to continue my journey of discovery, but feeling that I had gone far enough for the moment, and fearful of being even a second late to dress my Lady.

I quickly retraced my steps, room by room, meeting no one on the way, until I emerged once more into the great echoing vestibule.

My foot was upon the first step of the staircase when I heard a door open behind me.

A tall young gentleman – black-bearded, with long dark hair – stood looking at me intently. He said nothing for several seconds; then he greeted me, although without any hint of a smile.

'Miss Gorst, I think. My mother informed me of your engagement. Good-morning to you.'

These were the first words that ever I heard from the lips of Mr Perseus Duport, my Lady's eldest son and heir.

His voice was deep and strong for such a young man, and resonated through the lofty space of the marble-paved vestibule. I dropped a little curtsey and returned his greeting.

'Where did you come from?' he asked. 'Are you going up to Mother?'

The voice was softer now, but the handsome face remained fixedly expressionless.

Hesitantly, I explained that I had risen early, in order to acquaint myself a little with the house before attending Lady Tansor at eight o'clock.

'Eight o'clock, eh? She'll expect you promptly, you know,' he said, taking out his pocket-watch. 'She places great store on punctuality. The last girl couldn't oblige; but you can, I'm sure. Five minutes to the hour. You'd better hurry.'

'Yes, sir.'

I curtseyed again and turned to go, but he called me back.

'When you're released, Miss Gorst, you must seek me out. I shall be your guide to the great labyrinth.'

He paused, tilting his head quizzically on one side.

'Do you know what the first Labyrinth was?'

'Yes, sir. It was the lair of the Minotaur, constructed by King Minos of Crete.'

'Splendid! Quite right! Well, well, you'd better run along now. You'll find me in the Library, which can be reached by the little flight of stairs outside Mother's apartments. I often spend my mornings there, when I can. I'm a great reader. Are you a great reader, Miss Gorst?'

'Yes, sir. I believe I am.'

'Splendid again! Well, off you go, or you'll start off badly with Mother, and that would never do, you know.'

He gave me a barely perceptible smile, but his magnetic eyes had a kindly intent about them, which made me feel greatly honoured, and not a little surprised, that the Duport heir had condescended to pay such attention to his mother's new maid. I confess, too, that – to my further confusion – my heart was beating a little faster, as if I had just undertaken some physical exertion, and I could feel my colour beginning to rise under his steady gaze. I was sure – at least, I could in no way allow myself to hope otherwise – that he was only being agreeable to me out of well-bred courtesy, and for no other reason; but I could not account for the way this simple demonstration of good manners had affected me. I would have gladly continued the conversation; but time was pressing and so, bobbing once more, I ran off up the wide curving staircase, arriving at last before my Lady's door on the first stroke of eight o'clock.

Sharp.

III
Lady's-Maid

LADY TANSOR WAS seated at her dressing-table, her back towards me, swathed in a fantastically embroidered Chinese robe of blood-red and emerald-green silk.

'You will brush my hair first, Alice, before you arrange it,' she said, reaching back towards me, a silver hair-brush in her hand.

I began to pass the brush slowly through the thick black tresses, gently pulling out the night's tangles, until all was smooth and to her liking. Then I was instructed on how she wished her hair to be arranged, and in what manner it should be pinned up into the style of knot that she preferred, for she was averse to the use of false hair (her own being so finely textured and abundant), and refused to countenance a chignon.

When I had finished, she took me over to a massive oak ward-robe, where I was shown her many day-gowns; then she opened an adjacent press of similar size containing dozens of dazzling evening-gowns. A third cabinet, with sliding drawers, was packed with Japa-nese silk shawls from the Great Shawl Emporium, and with other expensive accoutrements.

Moving from these, she began to open other drawers and cup-boards for my inspection. Scores of hats and bonnets; trays of pins, buttons, and brooches; shoes and belts of every description; buck-les and bows, fans and reticules; dressing-cases containing crystal scent-bottles; and box after box full to bursting with exquisite jewel-lery – all were laid before my astonished gaze.

'You may dress me now, Alice,' she said at last, pointing to the wardrobe containing her day-gowns. 'The dark-violet velvet, I think.'

At last, my Lady stood before her cheval-glass and pronounced herself satisfied.

'Excellent, Alice,' she said. 'You have nimble fingers, and my hair looks very well, very well indeed. And this brooch matches far better than the other one, as you said it would. You have an eye for these things, I see. Yes, excellent.'

She repeated the compliment, gazing at her reflection in the looking-glass in a quiet, absent way, almost as if she were alone, fin-gering the brooch distractedly as she did so.

'Oh!' she suddenly exclaimed. 'I have forgotten the locket! How could I have done!'

Her voice had taken on a tone of acute distress. She turned towards me, white-faced with sudden anxiety, and pointed franti-cally towards a small wooden box on the dressing-table, which I quickly understood she meant me to open.

Inside was the most beautiful tear-shaped silver locket, attached to a black velvet band, very like the one worn by the late Lord Tan-sor's first wife in the portrait that had so entranced me.

'Here – bring it here!' she snapped. 'But do not touch the locket!'

Snatching the box from my hand, she took out the locket, and went over to the window, where she stood for a moment, breathing hard. Then she began to thread the velvet band around her throat, yet could not secure the clasp.

'Do you wish me to assist you, my Lady?' I asked.

'No! You must not help me. This is the one duty I must perform myself. Never help me, do you understand?'

She was now facing me once more, a fierce emotion in her blazing eyes. But in a moment she had turned away again, to make a second attempt at securing the clasp. At last she succeeded, whereupon she reached forward to open the window, letting a welcome draught of cool air into the stuffy chamber.

She remained by the window, a slight breeze ruffling her hair, her eyes directed towards the distant line of the western woods, now becoming clear to view as the curtain of early-morning mist gradually lifted.

At length, her spirits apparently calmed, she sat down in the window-seat and took up a small leather-bound book.

'You may go now, Alice,' she said quietly. 'I shall not need you until dinner-time. But tomorrow I shall have some work for you to do, and you will bathe me. Please to be here at eight.'

So I left her, with little dabs of watery sunshine illuminating her face and hair, as she placed her spectacles on her nose, opened the book, and began to read.

2

In Which a Friend is Made

I

Introducing Sukie Prout

E VER SINCE I was a little girl, something in my nature has
made me try constantly to improve myself. Words, especially, have always been a passion of mine. From an early
age, encouraged by Mr Thornhaugh, I developed the habit of writing down new ones that I had learned from my reading, and would
then say them over to myself before I went to bed, until I was sure
of their sound and meaning.

Sometimes they would be words that I had heard spoken by others; or I would simply open the copy of Mr Walker's *Pronouncing
Dictionary*, which my tutor had given to me, to see what greeted my
serendipitous (one of my favourite words) eye.

Mr Thornhaugh had once told me that if we are insensible to
the higher powers of language, then we are but crawling things
upon the earth, mutely struggling towards the day of our extinction; but with the proper acquisition and use of language, in all its
plenitude, we can contend with angels. (I immediately wrote these
words down: the piece of paper serves me still as a bookmark.)

I am also an avid collector of facts – another predilection encouraged by Mr Thornhaugh. It is a kind of curse, I confess, to be so
disposed, but an agreeable one at the same time, or at least I think
it to be so.

When I looked at something, I longed to know the one incontrovertible fact about it that made it what it was. I had then to find two or three ancillary facts (I used to call them my 'Little Maids in a Row', attending on the great Queen Fact), that would give greater substance to the first. Then I felt that I had gained some knowledge worth having, and was happy.

Mr Thornhaugh regularly urged me to combine these individual facts, and to rise above the particular to a broader understanding of the whole. I tried hard to do so, but found it impossible. The particular would always draw me to it, leading me on to another fascinating particularity, and then to another. I would be so contented, plucking my knowledge bloom by bloom, and storing each one away separately, that all thought of any higher synoptical or synthetic (two more excellent words) ambition would be put quite out of mind.

Despite this failing, which even Mr Thornhaugh could not correct, the acquirement of factual knowledge was ever delightful to me throughout my childhood, and the habit has remained with me. When I was young, it was another kind of game for me to play, and I did not think it at all strange that a little girl could derive as much pleasure from it as from playing with dolls, or skipping with a rope about the garden.

It might be inferred from these brief remarks that I spent a lonely and sequestered childhood in the Maison de l'Orme, with only my books for company; but I was not without playmates, although they were always carefully selected by Madame.

My especial friend was a girl of about my own age, Amélie Verron, whose father, a government official, was our nearest neighbour in the Avenue d'Uhrich. Monsieur Verron was a widower, and I think Madame felt obliged to demonstrate neighbourly concern with respect to his only child. Every weekday morning, Amélie and I would be taken for walks together in the Bois by my nurse, whilst on Sunday afternoons she and her father would take tea with us.

Amélie was a quiet, nervous child, of a delicate constitution, always content for me to take the lead in our games. When she died, at the age of fourteen, she left a void in my young life that no one else was able to fill. One of our favourite games was to set out a little school-room in the salon or, on fine days, under the chestnut-tree in the garden. Amélie, wearing an expression of the most serious concentration, would sit on a little stool, surrounded by her fellow pupils – a mute company of assorted rag-dolls and stuffed animals – and write slowly and solemnly on a slate, like the obedient little disciple that she was, as I marched up and down in front of her – swathed in a trailing black table-cloth, to mimic a scholar's gown – loudly dictating the names of the Merovingian kings (very much, I am sure, in the manner of Mr Thornhaugh), or some item of knowledge recently gleaned, either from my tutor or from my own reading. I blush now to think how insufferable I must have been; but dear Amélie never complained.

From this school-room game I soon discovered that I had a great liking – and, I think I may claim, a distinct talent – for public declamation, and began to conceive the notion (much to Mr Thornhaugh's amusement) that I might grow up to be an actress. To indulge this predilection, a little stage, complete with a gaily painted pasteboard proscenium arch and red plush curtains, was erected for me in one of the upstairs rooms. Here – before an appreciative audience of Madame, Mr Thornhaugh, and Amélie – I would recite long passages from *Paradise Lost* (a particular favourite of Mr Thornhaugh's), which I had learned by heart, or act out whole scenes from Molière or Shakespeare, taking each part, and giving each one an individual voice. I could not imagine then how these childhood performances, and my ability to hide my true self behind an assumed character, would eventually stand me in good stead for playing the part of maid to Lady Tansor.

I do not wish to give the impression that I was a precocious child, for I am sure that I was not. I was, however, given every opportunity, as well as the means, particularly by Mr Thornhaugh, to use the abilities that God had given me to the full, and I took them.

I was often disobedient and naughty – sometimes so naughty that it exhausted even Madame's patience. Then I would be exiled to a bare attic room, containing only a bed, a chair, and a three-legged table with a jug of water on it, where I had to spend the term of my sentence without books, pen or paper, or any other diversion, until I was released.

I always regretted my transgressions – indeed, would often hate myself for them. The truth was that I could not bear to see Madame or Mr Thornhaugh angered by my bad behaviour. Consequently, when discovered in my misdeeds, I would display a certain inventiveness (I will not say deviousness) in my excuses – not so that I might escape the punishment I knew I deserved, but to avoid causing Madame or Mr Thornhaugh to think ill of me. Afterwards I would resolve and swear never to be bad again. This, of course, despite my best intentions, would always prove impossible; but, gradually, discovering in myself a strong sense of duty, as well as an active conscience, I began to mend my ways somewhat, although even in later years Madame and I would sometimes fall out after some instance of waywardness on my part. Whilst I could no longer be sent up to my former place of correction, guilt for my ungrateful trespasses became an effective substitute.

Now I had heard the governing voice of Duty once more. Madame had set me this task – this Great Task – to perform. Whatever it was, whatever she asked of me, I was determined not to fail her.

BACK IN MY room, after dressing my Lady, I was thinking of Amélie as I took out my note-book to write down the second (the first being the date and artist of the Corsair portrait in the vestibule) of what was soon to become a store-house of facts concerning the great house of Evenwood and its contents:

> Lady T's sitting-room. Small oval portrait. Young Cavalier boy in blue silk breeches. Beautiful long hair. Inscribed by *Sir Godfrey Kneller*.
> *Mem.* Kneller a German.

My Lady having no need of me until dinner, I sat for a while wondering what I might do with myself for the remainder of the day. I must make myself known to the housekeeper, Mrs Battersby, and I had undertaken to write to Madame as soon as I could after my arrival. I also wished to resume my exploration of the house. With that final thought, I remembered that Mr Perseus Duport had offered to act as my guide. His even noticing me, let alone his engaging me in conversation, had taken me by surprise. Had he truly meant what he had said? Perhaps he had been teasing the new lady's-maid, to see whether she would be foolish enough to believe him. Yet although his face had retained a severe and inscrutable expression, his voice had sounded sincere. Very well, then; I would go and seek him out in the Library, and be seen as a fool if I must.

As I closed my door, I heard the sound of someone coming up the stairs. In a moment, a small, panting figure, carrying a mop and a large bucket of slopping water, appeared on the landing below.

It was a freckle-faced girl of perhaps twenty-two or twenty-three, wearing a long striped apron and a strange species of domed cap, a little like a baker's, pulled tightly down over her forehead, from which a few corkscrew curls of light chestnut hair had succeeded in escaping.

When she saw me she stopped, put down her mop and bucket, curtseyed, and smiled broadly.

'Good-morning, miss,' she said.

She moved aside as I made my way down to where she was standing.

'And who are you?' I asked with a smile, for she seemed a most winning little creature.

'Sukie Prout, miss. Upper house-maid.'

'Well, Sukie Prout, upper house-maid, I'm very pleased to meet you. I'm Miss Gorst, Lady Tansor's new maid. But you may call me Alice.'

'Oh no, miss,' Sukie said, visibly alarmed. 'I couldn't do that. Mrs Battersby would never allow it. She'd think it too familiar for one of the servants to address her Ladyhip's maid so, and would scold me if she heard me. I must call you "miss", miss, if you don't mind.'

I wanted to laugh, but she had such a serious look on her funny little face that I quickly checked myself. Not wishing to risk the wrath of Mrs Battersby (of whom I was already forming a distinctly unflattering impression), I therefore suggested that Sukie might address me as 'Miss Alice' out of the housekeeper's hearing.

'Are you afraid of Mrs Battersby, Sukie?' I asked, seeing that she remained apprehensive.

'Afraid? No, not exactly, miss. But she has a way about her that makes you careful to do what she asks. And her words can hurt sometimes, if she's cross, though she never shouts at you, like old Mrs Horrocks did. It seems worse somehow that she don't shout, if you know what I mean, miss. I can't quite explain it, and p'raps I feel it more than others, though everyone – even Mr Pocock – is ruled by her, below stairs, I mean. I've heard Mr Pocock say it's all a matter of character, though I'm not quite sure what he means.'

'I still wish you to call me "Miss Alice", in private,' I said, 'whether the Great Battersby likes it or not. Will you do that?'

Sukie agreed, if somewhat reluctantly.

'That's settled, then,' I replied. 'I'm delighted to have made your acquaintance, Sukie Prout, upper house-maid, and hope very much that we'll be good friends hereafter.'

'Friends! Her Ladyship's maid wants to be friends with queer Sukie Prout!'

She gave a delighted little squeal and put her hand to her mouth.

'Is that what they call you, Sukie?' I asked.

'Oh, I pay it no heed,' she said, with quiet defiance, 'for I know I am indeed a poor queer thing. If I was bigger and cleverer, I dare say they'd call me something else, and so what's the use in complaining?'

'You're not at all queer to me, Sukie,' I said. 'Indeed, you already seem to be the nicest and most sensible person I've met here.'

A little blush began to colour her chubby cheeks.

'Can you tell me one thing I'm curious about, Sukie?' I asked, as she was picking up her bucket. 'Why was Miss Plumptre dismissed?'

Setting the bucket down again, Sukie looked up and down the staircase, and lowered her voice to a whisper.

'Well, miss, that was a great scandal. They said she'd taken a valuable brooch that her Ladyship had left on her dressing-table one day when she'd gone up to London. She denied it, of course, but Barrington swore he'd seen her leaving her Ladyship's apartments at just the time the brooch disappeared, and when they searched her room, there it was. The curious thing was that she went on denying she'd took it, which no one could understand, seeing that the thing had been found in her room, and this vexed her Ladyship something terrible. And so she was sent on her way, without references. Mind you, she'd never been able to please her Ladyship. But it were a good thing in the end, for now you're here, miss, to take her place.'

The sound of a door shutting on the floor below suddenly caused Sukie to look down in consternation.

'I must go, miss – Miss Alice, I mean – before Mrs Battersby catches me.'

Whereupon my new friend curtseyed, wished me good morning, and picked up her mop and bucket, before continuing on her way.

II
The Servants' Hall

I MADE MY way to the head of the circular stone stairs that Mr Perseus Duport had said led down from the Picture Gallery to the Library.

On reaching the stairs, I hesitated.

I was eager to see for myself the famous Duport Library, which my tutor had told me was celebrated throughout Europe; but was it proper to accept Mr Perseus's flattering invitation? What would Lady Tansor say? Perhaps I could just take a peep, to see whether Mr Perseus was there, and then decide what to do. So down the stairs I tripped.

At the bottom, I found myself in a narrow hallway, with a curious ceiling decorated all over with intricate patterns of sea-shells. To my right was a glazed door opening on to the terrace that I could see from my room; at the other end of the hallway was a smaller, white-painted door, which I now proceeded to open, as unobtrusively as I could.

The sight that greeted me made me gasp.

Before me stretched an immense rectangular room of dazzling white and gold. Facing me, giving a view of the terrace and the gardens beyond, eight soaring windows, with semi-circular architraves, rose up to meet the exquisitely plastered ceiling, flooding the great room with early-morning light. Between each window, and running the whole length of the opposite wall also, were tall wire-fronted book-cases, whilst on either side of the central aisle stretched two lines of free-standing cases, and a number of glass-topped display cabinets. I had never seen so many books gathered together in one place, and marvelled at the prodigious outlay of time, industry, and expense that assembling such a collection must have required.

At the far end of the room, sitting at a bureau reading, his back towards me, was the distinctive figure of Mr Perseus Duport.

What should I do? Wishing very much to take up his invitation, but convinced now that I should withdraw, and make an exploration on my own of some other part of the house, I began slowly to close the door. As I did so, I was aware of someone coming into the hallway from the terrace.

The newcomer, I was certain, was Mr Randolph Duport.

The contrast between the brothers was marked. Mr Randolph was a good head shorter than Mr Perseus, with broader shoulders, supported on a thick-set, well-made frame, giving the impression of a robust and active constitution. I would have guessed him to be an outdoors man from his tanned complexion and confident bearing, even had he not been wearing a long, well-worn riding-coat and a pair of muddied and equally well-used boots.

His face, dominated by a wavy mop of thick auburn hair and a pair of soft brown eyes, was to me instantly suggestive of an even and open temper. I will not deny that, all in all, he was a singularly personable young gentleman, with a most taking way about him, to which I was neither insensible not – I further admit – indifferent.

In my previous life, in the Avenue d'Uhrich, I could fancy Mr Randolph Duport making an impression on me that might have been productive of a good many sighs and tears. As it was, in my new existence, allowing myself to imagine feeling an amourous attaction towards my Lady's engaging younger son was, of course, quite out of the question. Nevertheless, I was young and susceptible enough to consider it a pleasant situation, to be living under the same roof as two such elgible young gentlemen as Mr Randolph and Mr Perseus Duport.

On seeing me, Mr Randolph's face lit up in a beaming smile.

'Hullo there!' he exclaimed, closing the terrace door and coming towards me. 'Who's this? Ah, I have it! It's Mother's new maid, ain't it? How d'ye do? Delighted to make your acquaintance, Miss Girst – Garst – Gorst. That's it at last! Miss Gorst!'

He was laughing now – a full, honest, spontaneous laugh, which made me laugh too.

'But, look here,' he said, lowering his voice to a more confidential level, and assuming a suddenly serious expression, 'we shouldn't be laughing, you know. I've come to tell my brother. Slake's dead.'

Seeing my puzzled look, he explained that the Librarian, Professor Lucian Slake, had suffered a seizure that morning and had died.

'Bolt from the blue,' he said, shaking his head. 'Completely unexpected. Fit as a fiddle, old Slake, if you'd have asked me. Saw him only yesterday, looking as chipper as you like. But there it is. Death comes when it will.'

Having delivered himself of this sobering reflection, he wished me good morning, and went into the Library.

Leaving the brothers to their conversation, and feeling secretly gratified that neither of them appeared to find my Lady's new maid wholly beneath their notice, I decided that I would continue my explorations in the open air.

FROM THE TERRACE door, I passed under an arched gateway, then down a shallow flight of steps leading to an area of smooth, sunlit lawn, dotted about with croquet hoops. On the far side of the lawn, opened back against a crumbling fragment of ancient castellated wall, a door – iron-studded and time-blackened – seemed to beckon me.

In a few moments, I found myself in Paradise.

I was standing in an ancient quadrangle, such as one finds in a cathedral, or in one of the colleges at Oxford or Cambridge that Mr Thornhaugh had shown me pictures of. On three sides were dark, fan-vaulted cloisters; the fourth side, in which was set a large painted window, again of ancient date, formed the eastern end of the Chapel. In the centre of the court, a fountain played, sending out delicate, tinkling echoes.

On the petal-strewn flagstones of the central area were a great number of urns and troughs, some fashioned of lead, others of weathered stone, from which tumbled a profusion of late-summer geraniums, ferns, and trailing periwinkles. In between were several low, fluted columns, some bearing sculptured busts of blank-eyed Roman emperors (I immediately recognized Lucius Septimius Severus, whose name used to delight me as a child). Others, wreathed round with glistening green ivy, stood empty and broken.

Threading my way to the far side of the court, I sat down on a little iron bench, and leaned my head against the warm stone of the Chapel wall.

The sound of splashing water mingled deliciously with the gentle cooing of a pair of white doves that had just that moment fluttered down to land on a fantastical dovecote made to represent the great house itself. As I was drinking in the scene, I began to think of Madame, and of what she might be doing at this hour; and then of Mr Thornhaugh, pupil-less now. How he would relish Evenwood, and especially this little portion of Paradise!

It had been Mr Thornhaugh who had first read the legends of King Arthur to me, and shown me such scenes as this, painted in the most brilliant colours, in a Book of Hours from the Middle Ages that he possessed. Now here I sat, in my very body, in just such a place, like Camelot made real – substantial and vividly present to my senses, yet seeming somehow dreamlike, and beyond Time.

A dazzlingly painted, sun-faced clock over the entrance to the quadrangle was now chiming half past twelve, reminding me that it had been a long time since Barrington had brought me my break-fast tray. So up I jumped to go in search of the steward's room, where I hoped some luncheon would be provided.

I HAD NOT gone far in my search when I discovered Sukie emptying her bucket down a drain.

She greeted me with a cheery smile and a shy little half-wave, before looking about nervously, as if to assure herself that no one had observed her committing such a disgracefully presumptuous act.

I asked whether she could show me the way to the steward's room.

'Certainly, miss,' she said, setting down her bucket. Then, glanc-ing over her shoulder once more, and lowering her voice to a gig-gling whisper, she added: 'Miss Alice, I should say!'

She led me over to a door on the far side of the yard, and then down a series of well-worn steps until we came at last to a passage leading into the servants' hall – cavernous, and lit by a row of round windows set high up in the wall opposite the huge fire-place and range that dominated the hall, and before which some half a dozen or so of the below-stairs population were seated round a large table taking their mid-day meal.

'It's the door over there, Miss Alice,' whispered Sukie, pointing to an opaquely glazed screen at the far end.

I felt the curious gaze of the other servants on me as I made my way down the hall. One or two smiled a greeting, and one old gentleman with a grizzled beard rose as I passed to make me a stately bow.

At the open door of the steward's room, I halted.

Three persons were sitting round a table, engaged in earnest discussion.

'Nine o'clock this morning,' one of them – a short, middle-aged man, with a few strands of thin ginger hair pomaded carefully across his otherwise bald head – was saying. This proved to be the butler, Mr Pocock.

'Fifth stroke,' he went on. 'There's something to put on your gravestone!'

'You don't say, Mr Pocock. Fifth stroke. Well, well.'

This satirical remark issued from a rather fleshy young man, sardonic of countenance, and dressed in livery.

'No doubt about it,' replied Mr Pocock, nodding his head definitively. 'Dr Pordage was called, and his repeater, as you well know, Henry Creswick, is never wrong.'

The third man, somewhat elderly, with a weathered face and bushy grey side-whiskers, now delivered the opinion that this was all very well, but exhorted Mr Pocock to remember the rooks. The explanation of this cryptic remark soon followed.

'The rooks know, Mr Pocock. They allus know. I saw 'em plain as day – five or six of the devils, as 'e were walkin' up the Rise yesterday mornin'. They was a-swirlin' and a-swoopin' all about 'im like Death's black servants. I said to Sam Waters, 'e'll be dead by tomorrow night, and sure enough 'e was.'

Then I understood that they were speaking of the sudden death that morning of the Librarian, Professor Slake.

'You mark my words,' the elderly man went on, 'they allus know. Never knowed 'em to be wrong. It were the same with my Lady's father, that day in '53. I saw 'im ride off to Stamford, with the grandsires of those same black devils that followed the Professor a-wheelin' at his back. I said then, 'ed better look out – you won't remember that, Robert Pocock. It were before your time. But I said it, and so it was.'

After refreshing himself from a large pewter tankard, the elderly man – Mr Maggs, the head gardener, as I subsequently learned – was on the point of making some further observations on the subject when a young woman entered the room carrying a bottle of wine and an empty glass on a tray.

III
The Housekeeper

SHE STOOD FOR a moment in the doorway, regarding me with a most curious smile, almost as if she knew me, although I had never seen her before. The others, observing that her attention had been caught by something, all turned their heads towards me.

'I beg your pardon for disturbing you,' I said, feeling quite uncomfortable at the four pairs of curious eyes studying me; but I was an actress now, as I had dreamed of being as a child, with an actress's power to convince my audience that I was someone I was not. On, then, with the character of docile Miss Gorst, newly appointed lady's-maid.

Mr Pocock rose to his feet with a welcoming smile.

'Miss Gorst, I believe,' he said. 'Come in, come in – if I may speak on your behalf, Mrs Battersby?'

He looked enquiringly towards the young woman with the tray, who nodded at him, laid the tray down on a sideboard, and walked over to the head of the table. Making no attempt to greet me, or to introduce herself formally, she stood looking at me for a moment or two before taking her seat.

So this was the fearsome Mrs Battersby. From the little I had gleaned of her from Sukie, I had pictured some tyrannical old retainer, ill-tempered and parochial, a bigoted harridan immovably set in her ways; but the person I now saw was as far from my imaginings as it was possible to be.

She was no more than thirty or so years old, as I guessed, and, whilst not tall, her figure was slim and elegant. Light-brown hair, gathered under a pretty lace cap, framed a small, well-proportioned face, which, despite a slight chubbiness about the chin and neck, many would have considered to be quietly beautiful. I was particularly struck by her hands, with their long, tapering fingers, the nails showing every sign of regular care – not at all the rough country hands of the Mrs Battersby I had pictured.

Equally surprising was her manner. I had expected vulgar truculence and provincial narrowness. Instead, she had a cultivated guardedness about her – the self-confident look of an educated person possessed of an active and critical intelligence. This impression was made both unsettling and tantalizing by the singular cast of her mouth, which tilted upwards on one side, and downwards on the other, seemingly set in a permanent half-smile – at once cynical and inviting. It was as if she wore a divided mask – one half sweetly amiable, the other sour-faced and disapproving, both together producing a mystifying and confused effect in the observer as to the true state of her feelings. As I was to discover, there was nothing outright and unequivocal about Mrs Jane Battersby: everything was held in and considered, or insinuated in the most gradual and ambiguous manner.

'I am glad to meet you, Miss Gorst,' she said at last, smiling, or not smiling, I could not quite tell, 'and happy that you have decided to join us here for your meals, as your predecessor was pleased to do. Will you take a little beef?'

Her voice was low and soft, with an unmistakable refinement of tone, the words delivered slowly and deliberately. She nodded to the young man, Henry Creswick, who, introducing himself as Mr Perseus Duport's valet, drew out a chair for me, then handed me a plate, a glass, and cutlery, before helping me to some beef and potatoes.

The others sat silently observing me as I ate my meal and drank down my barley-water – Lady Tansor, as I was to learn, allowed wine or beer to be drunk by her servants only at supper-time, and then in strictly regulated quantities.

It seemed as if no one felt able to engage me in conversation until liberated by the example of Mrs Battersby, who remained resolutely silent. It was only when my plate was empty that she spoke, to ask how I liked Evenwood.

I replied that it was the most wonderful place I had ever seen.

'Wonderful certainly,' she said, her disconcerting smile having the effect of mitigating what was clearly her real sentiment, 'for those who have nothing to do but live here and look at it; but a world of work, of course, for everyone else.'

Then she turned to Mr Pocock.

'The roof has leaked again in the old nursery, and plaster has come down all over the linoleum. I had to send Sukie Prout up there this morning. I informed Lady Tansor a month since that Badger must be sent up to make the repairs, but nothing has been done, and Badger won't go unless her Ladyship directs him to herself.'

'Mr Baverstock says that the place is becoming sadly neglected,' said Mr Pocock, shaking his head. 'There's money enough, but she's let things go, and Mr Baverstock says that she won't listen when she's told what's required. It wouldn't have happened in old Lord Tansor's time, and the late colonel, God bless him, would have taken things in hand, no doubt about that. I'd thought that Mr Perseus might see it, but he's too busy with his verses.'

'Ah,' said Mr Maggs, 'but then she don't 'old sway like the old Lord. There was a man o' power, if you like. Finger in every pie in the land. They'd all come to Evenwood in them days – even the Prime Minister – just to see what his Lordship thought o' things. The Queen 'erself came once, with German Albert. But the great folk from London don't come no more.'

He too shook his head ruefully.

'No, she don't 'old sway like the old Lord, nor never will.'

'Enough, Timothy Maggs.'

Admonished and abashed, Mr Maggs sought refuge from Mrs Battersby's softly commanding eye by leaning back in his chair and puffing three times on his long clay pipe.

'And where were you before, Miss Gorst?'

It was Henry Creswick who now spoke.

'I had a position as maid to Miss Helen Gainsborough.'

'Miss Gainsborough?'

The question came from Mrs Battersby.

'Of High Beeches?'

'No,' I replied, confidently drawing on the story that Madame had devised concerning my imaginary former employer. 'Of Stanhope Terrace in London.'

The housekeeper thought for a moment.

'Do you know, Miss Gorst,' she said, her smile now broadening,

'I don't believe I know anyone of that name in Stanhope Terrace. I was briefly in a position close by, and thought I knew everyone in that area. Isn't that curious?'

'Miss Gainsborough was a recent resident,' I replied airily, taking a diversionary sip of barley-water, 'and also travels a great deal. I don't care for travelling, and so looked for a new place.'

'Ah,' said Mrs Battersby. 'That would explain it.'

I turned to Mr Pocock.

'Excuse my asking,' I said, 'but when I came in, you were speaking of Professor Slake, I think.'

'Well,' replied the butler, with a kindly smile, 'you're a sharp one, for sure, miss. You know the news almost before we do.'

As I explained how I had been told of the Professor's death by Mr Randolph Duport, Mrs Battersby's face took on a most suspicious look.

Had I somehow spoken out of turn? It seemed that she considered it improper for the newly arrived maid to raise the subject of the Professor's death.

'You were told the news by Mr Randolph Duport?' she enquired.

Her question was politely, and of course smilingly, put; yet it once again made me feel that I was being accused of some transgression. I had no fears that she had any deeper suspicions of me, despite her questions concerning Miss Gainsborough, being confident that I had played my part well, in my first public performance at Evenwood. So I smiled demurely back at her as I recounted my chance meeting with Mr Randolph outside the Library, on his way to tell his brother about the death of Professor Slake.

'Ah,' said Mr Maggs, wryly. 'Mr Chalk an' Mr Cheese!'

Henry Creswick let out an appreciative guffaw at this display of wit, for which he and Mr Maggs both received a stern look from Mr Pocock.

'Now, now, Timothy Maggs,' said the butler. 'That's enough from you.'

'Well, it's no more than the truth, Robert Pocock,' countered Mr Maggs, 'as anyone with eyes in their 'ead can see. Chalk an' cheese they've allus bin since they were babbies, an' chalk an' cheese they'll allus be.'

'And what was your opinion of Mr Randolph Duport?' asked Mrs Battersby, who had continued to fix me with an enquiring eye during the foregoing exchange. 'Did you find him agreeable?'

'Oh yes! A most agreeable gentleman,' I replied, with unthinking eagerness.

'And so he is,' agreed Mr Pocock. 'Ask anyone, and they'll tell you which of the two brothers they prefer. It'll be Mr Randolph over Mr Perseus every time.'

'I suspect Miss Gorst is no different,' observed Mrs Battersby, her enigmatic smile making it again impossible to tell whether or not her remark was intended to censure me, for presuming to express a liking for my employer's younger son, although I could not help taking it as such.

Just then, further conversation was interrupted by the ringing of a bell.

Mr Pocock called out to someone in the adjacent hall, who shouted back: 'Yellow Drawing-Room. Mr Perseus, I'd say. T'other one's gone off.'

'Is Barrington there?'

'No,' came the reply. 'Only Peplow.'

'Then send Peplow,' said Mr Pocock.

The butler was about to sit back in his chair and take a draught of barley-water when Mrs Battersby rose to her feet, at which he also stood up, the glass of untasted barley-water in hand, followed by Henry Creswick and Mr Maggs.

'Well, Miss Gorst,' said the housekeeper, her smile now full and direct, 'I'm very glad to have made your acquaintance, and hope you'll soon feel part of our little family. You will, of course, tell Pocock, or myself, if there's anything you require. Do you attend Lady Tansor?'

'She will not need me until dinner-time.'

'Then you must make the most of a fine day,' came the smiling reply.

Without another word, she turned and went out of the doorway through which she had come.

I, too, made to leave, but then thought of something to ask Mr Maggs.

'I could not help overhearing earlier,' I said, 'that you were speaking of Lady Tansor's father. Did he also die of a seizure?'

'Old Carteret! Seizure!' exclaimed Mr Maggs. 'No, not 'im. Murdered, miss, in cold blood, for 'is money, just as 'e was ridin' into the Park.'

'No, you're wrong there, Maggs,' Mr Pocock broke in. 'Not for his money. As I've told you before, I've heard something about this, and believe it to be the case that he was carrying very little money on him, only a bag of documents.'

'But them what attacked 'im *thought* 'e 'ad money,' objected sceptical Mr Maggs. 'That's the thing, though the rooks didn't care, one way or t'other. It's all the same to them 'ow such poor mortal men as Paul Carteret go to their graves. They jus' know they're a-goin', and that's all there is about it.'

The conversation continued in this vein for some time, with Mr Maggs speaking in unshakeable support of the prophetic capacities of rooks, and Mr Pocock seeking to bring a more rational tone to the proceedings.

I was about to take my leave once more when Mr Pocock offered to show me a flight of back stairs, which he said would take me straight up to my room.

'Of course her Ladyship's maid is free to take the main staircase,' he said. 'But the back stairs are quicker.'

We left through the doorway taken by Mrs Battersby and passed into a narrow, white-washed corridor lined with prints and old maps of the county, coming out at last at the foot of a wooden staircase.

'Here we are, miss,' said Mr Pocock. 'You can't go wrong from here. Just count the floors. You'll come out near your room.'

As I watched him return to the servants' hall, another thought jumped into my head.

'Oh, Mr Pocock!'

He stopped and looked back.

'Can you tell me something? There's a painting, in my Lady's sitting-room, of a little Cavalier boy. Who is he?'

'Ah,' he said, walking back towards me. 'The 19th Baron Tansor as a child. Anthony Charles Duport, painted by Sir Godfrey Kneller. Born 1682 – I remember that particularly because it was exactly a century before my father.'

'Thank you, Mr Pocock.'

'Don't mention it, miss. Always happy to oblige.'

'In that case,' I returned, 'was there ever – or is there still – a Mr Battersby?'

'No, no,' replied the butler, shaking his head. 'Battersby is her own name. It's always been the custom here to call housekeepers Mrs This or Mrs That, whether they're married or not. Ah, I see you're thinking that the name don't suit her, with her good looks and all, and being so young. Well, miss, you're not the first to think so.'

'That's true enough,' I agreed. 'The name certainly *doesn't* suit her. But if there isn't a Mr Battersby, then it's rather surprising that there isn't a Mr Somebody Else by now. I imagine that she wouldn't want for admirers.'

'That I couldn't say, miss,' said Mr Pocock, a little stiffly. 'Keeps herself to herself does Mrs B.'

Then he drew a little closer to me.

'All we know', he said, in a more confiding tone, 'is that she came here from a good family in Suffolk, and before that from a position in London. But she don't have no ties, as far as anyone here knows.'

'No family, then?'

'None to speak of, miss. Father and mother dead, apparently. No brothers or sisters. Only a maiden aunt in London, occasionally visited.'

Just then, the distant sound of a bell from the servants' hall caused Mr Pocock to break off the conversation, leaving me – intrigued by what he had just told me – to clatter up the wooden stairs, emerging at last, three floors up, on the landing near my room.

•   •   •

I LAY ON my bed for half an hour, looking out at the pale-blue sky, and musing on the events of the morning.

After a while, I got up to write a short letter to Madame, assuring her that all was well, and promising to write at greater length in due course. Then I went downstairs again, to place the letter in the appointed place for collection, having addressed the envelope to a lady in London, of whom I shall speak hereafter, to avoid the possibility of awkward questions from my fellow servants.

At a little before three o'clock, I went outside to continue my explorations before it was necessary to attend my Lady.

The September sun still bathed the forest of spires and towers, chimneys and turrets, that gives the great house of Evenwood its bristling distinctiveness in a soft aureate light, and threw muted shadows across the clipped lawns and gravel walks. On the south side of the house I discovered a large rectangular fish-pond, closed in by high walls, profusely colonized by bright-yellow stonecrop. Here I lingered, looking down into the still, dark waters at the fish, many of great size, that swam lazily about, until it was time for me to return to the house.

As the Chapel clock struck the hour of five, and having washed my face, brushed my hair, and smoothed down my dress, I knocked at the door of my Lady's apartments.

3

The First Day Ends

I

Questions and Answers

M Y LADY was reclining in the window-seat, book in hand, exactly as I had left her.

'Come and sit with me, Alice,' she said, laying down the book with a weary sigh. 'I shall not go down to dinner tonight after all.'

'Very well, my Lady,' I said, taking my place beside her.

'Now, tell me what you've been doing. You must think it a strange kind of service to be allowed to do as you like all the day. But you must not become used to it. I shall work you hard from now on.'

She was smiling – a poor melancholy smile, to be sure; but I saw in her eyes that her words were kindly meant.

I recounted my morning exploration through the East Wing, although omitting my encounters with Mr Perseus and Mr Randolph Duport, and my new acquaintance with Sukie Prout.

'You might explore Evenwood for ever,' she said, 'and still discover new things to admire. Someone once described it to me as a house without end, perpetually disclosing new aspects of itself. There are parts of it that even I have never visited; and others, I'm sure, that will remain forever unknown to me. Perhaps, Alice, you may make some discoveries on my behalf, and come and tell me what you've found, for I perceive that you have an enquiring nature.'

Then she asked whether I thought that I would be happy in her service.

'Oh yes, my Lady. Even more than before, now that I've become a little familiar with my new surroundings, and acquainted with some of the people here – especially with you, my Lady.'

She took the compliment with another sad little smile before asking me how I had found Mrs Battersby.

I replied that she seemed a very capable sort of person.

'Capable!' she exclaimed, giving an appreciative clap. 'That exactly describes her! Jane Battersby is certainly capable. A remarkable young woman in many ways, rather mysterious, with a certain worldly wisdom far beyond her station. And whom else have you met today?'

'Mr Pocock, of course; and Henry Creswick, and also Mr Maggs.'

'No one else?'

Her eyes were now fixed on me in that discomfiting way she had. Deciding that a little truth was required, I told her how I had met Sukie Prout on the landing below my room.

'Sukie Prout?'

She thought for a moment.

'Ah, one of the downstairs-maids.'

'The upper house-maid, my Lady.'

'Quite. And no one else?'

I realized then that she knew of my accidental meetings with her sons. For a moment I was unsure how to answer, but she anticipated me.

'My son Perseus tells me that he has already made your acquaintance. His brother, too, I believe.'

I now had no choice but to admit the fact with as much indifference as I could, although I could not see where I had been at fault.

'Was it such a little thing to forget?' she asked.

'I beg your pardon, my Lady?'

'To make the acquaintance of the heir to the Tansor Barony, and his younger brother?'

I thought that she was about to reprimand me, but then I saw that a faint smile was playing round her lips.

'Don't be alarmed, my dear,' she said, leaning towards me and patting my hand. 'I don't blame you in any way for feeling that you could not tell me. You are alive to these little delicacies, I see. But tell me, which one of my sons did you like best? Perseus or Randolph?'

I confess that I found the question rather shocking. What mother could ask such a thing concerning her two sons, both of whom appeared to me to be eminently worthy, each in his own way, of admiration?

'Tell me, do!' she prompted, with unseemly relish, seeing my hesitation. 'I long to know!'

'I really cannot say, my Lady. I have so little knowledge of either of your sons, and, really, we spoke only a few words.'

'But Perseus is the more handsome, is he not?'

'He is handsome, certainly,' I readily conceded. 'But then Mr Randolph Duport is handsome also.'

'But very differently composed, would you not agree? There is less refinement in poor Randolph's features, alas, which in some moods can look a little coarse. He has more of his late father in him, and of his father's family, I dare say, than Perseus. I am also sad to admit that Randolph lacks his brother's higher talents. It pains me to speak so, but it is only the truth.

'Perseus, you know, has been blessed with great literary gifts,' she went on. 'He has written a most impressive drama in verse, which we hope to see published very shortly. The subject is Merlin and Nimue, which I consider to be a most original one for a poetic drama.'

'Has not Mr Tennyson written of them in the *Idylls*?' I enquired, knowing very well that he had. 'Although I believe Nimue is there called Vivien.'

She threw me a sharply reproachful look for presuming to question her son's originality of conception.

'Mr Tennyson's treatment of the characters is wholly different from my son's,' she said coldly, 'and is, in my view, inferior in every way. He does not make them live as people, as Perseus does by means of the dramatic form. It is his great gift.'

I asked if Mr Perseus Duport intended to make poetry his profession.

'A gentleman in the position of my eldest son has no need to follow a profession, as you put it, of any kind. But it is impossible to put shackles on natural genius. Like good breeding, it will out. I have no doubt that, when the work is published, it will be universally recognized as possessing uncommon merit. I shall show you the manuscript another time, so that you may judge for yourself. You told me, I think, that you were a great reader of poetry.'

'Yes, my Lady.'

'And how did a lady's-maid acquire such a taste?'

'My guardian read poetry to me from an early age,' I replied, ignoring the implied insult. 'Even when I was unable to understand the meaning of the words, their sound would soothe me, and send me dreaming. And then I was constantly encouraged to read widely, in both English and French, by my tutor, Mr Basil Thornhaugh.'

'You had a tutor! I've never had a maid before who enjoyed such an advantage. And what manner of man was Mr Basil Thornhaugh?'

'One of the cleverest there could be,' I replied, 'possessing, in addition, great discernment and taste.'

'A most remarkable tutor, by your account. In my experience, such men are always dull failures; but your Mr Thornhaugh appears to have been singular in every way. Yet he was content, it seems, with tutoring a little girl. Why was that, do you suppose? Had he no other profession to follow, or any higher ambitions?'

I could not give a satisfactory answer, knowing almost nothing of my old tutor's former life. All I could say was that Mr Thornhaugh had private interests to pursue, in addition to his pedagogic duties, and that he had long been engaged on a great work of scholarship.

'Ah!' cried Lady Tansor. 'A private scholar! I know the type. Forever dreaming of writing the *magnum opus* that will make their name live on for generations. I understand now. Few of these men realize their ambition. It simply consumes them, for there is never an end to it.'

She turned her head away for a moment and laid it against one of the leaded window-panes. Then she raised her finger to the glass and began absently tracing some pattern, or perhaps a sequence of letters, as she spoke.

After dinner, she asked me to read to her from another work by Phoebus Daunt, *The Heir: A Romance of the Modern.**

'Do you know it?' she asked, handing the volume to me.

I told her that I had not yet had the pleasure of reading it.

'Then this will please both of us,' she said. 'Shall we begin?'

I opened the book, and started to read.

Mr Daunt's poetical gifts appeared to have found their natural expression in the epic form. I imagined that *Paradise Lost*, which I had known and admired since first being introduced to it by Mr Thornhaugh as a child, had been ever before him as the great model for his own essays in what might be called the poetry of magnitude. In Milton's case, the description would signify the higher character of the subject-matter, as well as the sublime capabilities of the poet; in Mr Daunt's, a narrower definition of 'magnitude' is required; for he appears to have believed that the more lines he wrote, the more impressive the effect would be. Consequently, an hour or more passed and I had barely reached halfway through the second of twelve books.

'Does it tire you, Alice?' asked Lady Tansor, hearing me stumble over a particularly inept couplet (the bard had rejected the sterner

---

*Published by Edward Moxon in 1854, the year of Daunt's death. Like Elizabeth Barrett Browning's later verse-novel, *Aurora Leigh* (published 1856), it has a contemporary setting, but its form (as Miss Gorst rightly observes), and its language, are consciously based on the Miltonic epic model. It concerns the heir to a great estate, Sebastian Montclare, who is cheated out of his inheritance by an unscrupulous cousin, Everard Burgoyne. The absurdity of the plot is matched only by the ineptitude of much of the verse, yet the work was popular and well received; even now, some passages retain a certain swaggering grandeur and verve that display a distinct, though wasted, talent.

clarity of blank verse in favour of rhyming couplets, at some frequent cost to sense).

'No, my Lady. I am very happy to continue for as long as you
wish.'

'No, no,' she insisted, 'you are tired. I can see it. I have kept you
long enough. There! What a considerate mistress I am! You must
not think, however, that I treat all my maids with such partiality, for
I never have before.'

She was looking at me expectantly; but when I made no reply,
she moved away from the window and stood staring into the fire.

'No,' she said, quietly, 'I have not always been so partial. But you,
Alice,' looking now over her shoulder at me, 'have qualities that set
you apart. I saw them immediately.'

She paused, as if a thought had suddenly occurred to her.

'Do you know, it now strikes me that your situation is not a little
like Mrs Battersby's.'

She saw the puzzled look on my face, and gave a little laugh.

'I mean that, like you, she now occupies a station in life that
is somewhat beneath the one in which she appears to have been
brought up, although you, of course, seem to have enjoyed superior
advantages to Mrs Battersby – a tutor, you now tell me! You speak
French. You read novels and poetry. And I dare say that you can
play and sing, draw and paint, and generally comport yourself like a
lady. Indeed, I should say that you *are* a lady, by birth and education.
Yet – a little like your clever Mr Thornhaugh, who sounds in every
respect to be a gentleman – you have taken up a situation that is
beneath both your abilities and your natural condition. Is that not
a curious symmetry?'

'You must remember, my Lady,' I countered, nervous of her
questioning expression, 'that I had no choice in the matter. When
Mrs Poynter died – the old friend of my mother's, with whom I was
then living in London – I had no means of supporting myself. I had
only a small life-interest from my father, which was barely sufficient
for my needs. As I did not wish to return to France, I went to an
agency and was put forward for the position with Miss Gainsborough, which I was fortunate to secure.'

'Fortunate indeed,' she said. 'For someone without previous experience of domestic service, one might have expected you to be put up for a petty place or two, perhaps with a clergyman, or some person in a small way of trade. But then I am not in the least surprised that you impressed Miss Gainsborough, who sounds a very sensible sort of person. I have no doubt that she was of the same mind as I myself. She must have seen, as I did, that you were exceptional, which is a rare quality in a servant.'

She had hardly finished speaking when there was a knock at the door, and a footman came in carrying a letter on a small silver tray.

'This has come for you, your Ladyship.'

He bowed, and turned to leave.

'Wait!' Lady Tansor cried out. 'This must have been delivered by hand. Where is the person who brought it?'

'I cannot say, your Ladyship,' replied the footman. 'It was slipped under the front door. No one saw who brought it.'

I was able to make out that the letter contained only half a dozen or so lines of writing; but their effect on my mistress was dramatic. As she read, the colour began to drain from her face. When she had finished, she crushed the letter into a ball, and placed it in the pocket of her gown.

'I think I shall take a short walk on the terrace before retiring,' she said, trying to act as if nothing had happened. 'There are some slops to be emptied in the bedroom, and please to light the fire. It has grown a little chilly. Then lay out my night-things, and remain in the bed-chamber until I return. Do not leave the bed-chamber. Do you understand?'

'Of course, my Lady,' I replied, happy to comply with her orders, although puzzled by them nonetheless.

Still pale and ill at ease, despite her efforts to appear unconcerned, she crossed to the door, but then stopped.

'Remember what I said, Alice,' she said, without turning to face me. 'Do not leave the bed-chamber until I return.'

She opened the door and swept out into the Picture Gallery, leaving me alone in the suddenly darkened room.

II
The Coming of Mr Thornhaugh

AFTER MY LADY had returned from her walk on the terrace, and I had performed the various duties she required, I was allowed to retire.

My mistress had dismissed me rather brusquely, seeming both cross and anxious, and as disinclined to talk as she had earlier been eager to engage in conversation.

As I was leaving, I had asked whether she was feeling well.

'Of course I am well,' she snapped back. 'Do not fuss so, Alice. I cannot abide fussing.'

'I don't mean to fuss, my Lady,' I replied, contritely. 'But you look so very pale. May I fetch you something before you retire?'

Her face relaxed a little, and she slumped down in a chair beside the bed.

'No, nothing,' she said. Then, with an attempt at a smile: 'But thank you, Alice. Few of my other maids have been so concerned for me.'

'Then they did not deserve to occupy the position of maid to you, my Lady,' said I, in a moment of inspiration. 'I consider it to be a most important part of my duty to give constant thought to your Ladyship's well-being.'

'That,' she said, 'is a most original sentiment for a maid to hold; but then of course you are no ordinary maid. Good-night, Alice. The usual time in the morning, please.'

As I turned to go, I saw that there were tears in her eyes.

STILL PUZZLED BY Lady Tansor's strange behaviour, I devoted half an hour to writing up the evening's events in my Book of Secrets. Then I lay down on my bed, and let my thoughts wander where they would.

It was not long before I began to think once more of Madame, and then of my old tutor, in whom my Lady had taken such an interest.

Dear Mr Thornhaugh! How I missed him! Like Madame, he had been a constantly reassuring presence in my life, almost for as long as I could remember. The first clear memory I have of him is of watching his tall, stooped figure walking up and down in the garden of the Maison de l'Orme one hot summer's afternoon, for twenty minutes or more, in close conversation with Madame. With the exception of Jean, Madame's serving-man, I had become accustomed to living solely amongst females. The sight of this strange man, with his long, lined, dark-hued face and prematurely greying hair hanging down about his shoulders, alarmed me at first, until Madame brought him to me later, to introduce him as my tutor. As soon as I saw his wonderful eyes, my fears instantly evaporated, and I knew that I had a new friend in my life.

'How do you do, miss?' he said.

'*Réponds en anglais, ma chère*,' said Madame, smiling.

As English was already as familiar to me as French, Madame being herself a fluent English speaker, I told Mr Thornhaugh, in his native tongue, that I was honoured and charmed to make his acquaintance, holding out my hand with prodigious earnestness as I did so, and then, for good measure, giving him a most lady-like curtsey.

He laughed at that, and called me 'Little Queen', after which he asked me a number of questions to judge how well I knew my lessons. Although they all required some concentrated thought, I acquitted myself well, to my great pride and delight.

'You have done well, Madame,' I heard him say to my guardian. 'I can see that she will go to her lessons like a true-born scholar.'

I hope I do not present myself as an unbearable prodigy. My cleverness, if that is what it was, consisted merely in the possession of a naturally capacious memory, and a desire to fill it with factual knowledge. Beyond this mechanical capability to take in and then regurgitate what I had learned, however, I believe I was rather slow and stupid – I never could master long division or fractions, had a perfect horror of multiplication, and found geometry and algebra incomprehensible, whilst all the various branches of Science were for ever to remain closed books to me, even when Mr Thornhaugh tried later to open them.

My examination having been concluded to everyone's satisfaction, Madame suggested that we should go back out into the garden, where we sat together, the three of us, beneath the shade of the chestnut-tree, drinking tea and eating lemon-cake.

Mr Thornhaugh talked incessantly, although I cannot now bring to mind anything of what he said. Only the impression of an unstoppable flood of glorious words and original opinions has stayed clear in my memory. To one who was already burning to acquire knowledge, he seemed little less than some magician of legend who had been granted the power to know all that had ever been known by man, and all that would be known hereafter.

Thus Mr Basil Thornhaugh took up his place in the house of Madame de l'Orme in the Avenue d'Uhrich. He was given four spacious rooms on the top floor, one of which, next to his book-filled study, was my school-room. Access to this floor was by way of a separate staircase, which led down into the rear garden, and allowed Mr Thornhaugh to come and go as he pleased. I rarely saw him in any other part of the house except his own, or in the garden; and he took his meals alone. If I woke during the night, I would often hear him pacing about his study, which was directly above my bedroom, and drew comfort from knowing that he was always there, just a few feet away, above my bed.

I wondered what he would do now that his pupil had flown the nest. He had remained a resident of Madame's establishment after my childhood, engaged with his own reading and researches, although continuing to instruct me informally in those subjects that I found most to my liking, and when it was agreeable to both of us that he should do so. Yet although I had by then come to think of him as a friend, far more than as my teacher, he could never be encouraged to speak about himself or his family, and would always – sometimes a little intemperately – brush away my questioning. Consequently, I knew nothing about him, or where he had come from. No doubt because of this settled disinclination, he appeared – more than anyone I have ever known, before or since – to wish to live entirely in the present moment, almost by an effort of will; and if I enquired – as young ladies are, of course, obliged by nature to do – about some aspect of his past, before he came to Madame's house, he would always say that his former life was no longer of any concern to him, and should therefore be of no concern to anyone else.

Only once did he give me an answer, when I asked him where he had been born. He told me that he had taken his first breath under French skies, which pleased me greatly, but he would tell me nothing further.

III
Mrs Ridpath

IN DUE COURSE, all the arrangements for my departure to England had been put in hand, and I finally left Paris in the second week of August 1876.

Madame and Mr Thornhaugh accompanied me to Boulogne, where we stayed in the Hôtel des Bains for the night. The next day, we drove to the station in the Faubourg de Capécure, from where I was to take the tidal-express to Folkestone. There, on the crowded and noisy platform, I said my tearful good-byes to Madame.

'Be strong, my dearest child,' she said, as she kissed me. 'I know how hard this is for you, but all will be well, if you only trust in me, and patiently allow me to guide your actions. As you come to know more about why you are embarking upon this great enterprise, you must also learn to follow your own instincts, and act accordingly. For be assured, there is that within you that will lead you to the fulfilment of your destiny.'

And so we parted. I waved from the window until she disappeared from view, and then sank back in my seat, overcome with every emotion that parting from a loved one – perhaps for ever – can engender in a human breast.

My only comfort was that it had been agreed that Mr Thornhaugh would accompany me to London, to see me settled into my temporary lodging, where I was to stay before journeying to Evenwood. Without him beside me on the journey, I do not know how I could have borne the terrible sense of separation from everything I held most dear. Little by little, however, as the shores of England grew ever closer, I began to feel better, as my old tutor brought me back – with such gentle and considerate persuasion – to my former state of determination.

Arrived in Folkestone, we put up at the West Cliff Hotel, taking the train to London the next morning. At last we arrived in Devonshire Street, where I was to remain, under the care of an old friend of Mr Thornhaugh's, until the time came for me to attend my interview with Lady Tansor.

My temporary guardian was a slight, sandy-haired lady, of some fifty years, with a kind face and bright, darting eyes, who immediately put me at my ease. She ushered us in with many solicitous enquiries about our journey, sat us down in the drawing-room, and rang for refreshments.

'Esperanza, this is Mrs Elizabeth Ridpath,' Mr Thornhaugh had said as we entered. 'She's an old and trusted friend of mine and will take the greatest care of you while you are here.' Then, more seriously, he added: 'She knows everything, Little Queen.'

Mrs Ridpath leaned forward and took my hand.

'I know that being here must be very strange and unsettling for you, my dear; and so you must tell me if there is anything I can do to make you comfortable and happy, for the little time you are with me. Mr Thornhaugh and Madame de l'Orme have taken me into their confidence, and I want you to know that I shall never betray the trust that they have placed in me. You may depend on me to the last, just as you depend on them.'

She kissed me on the cheek, and said that, after tea, she would show me to my room, and then I might have a rest if I wished, or we could all walk out together for a little into the nearby Regent's Park.

'Oh, let us go out!' I cried, feeling suddenly full of hope and confidence. 'I'm not in the least bit tired!'

And so, after we had drunk our tea, we all three set off, and soon found ourselves in the Park.

Mr Thornhaugh wished me to see the Zoological Gardens, where we passed a pleasant hour or so. Then we strolled back through the Botanic Gardens, and past the grounds of the Toxophilite Society, before returning to Devonshire Street. Throughout the whole of this little excursion, Mr Thornhaugh had entertained us, in his usual effervescent manner, with his knowledge of the Park, and of London in general. I wanted him to remain in England longer than he had proposed – indeed, I importuned him as hard as I could to do so; but he had a return ticket for the tidal-express that left Charing Cross the next morning, and was adamant that he must not leave Madame alone in Paris any longer than they had arranged, for she would be anxious on my account, and eager to know how I was.

Having been absent for many years from the city where he had once lived, Mr Thornhaugh had arranged to see several old friends at a hotel in the Strand, where he also intended to stay the night.

'Good-bye, Little Queen,' he said, as we stood on the steps of the house in Devonshire Street. 'I do not need to tell you that you will be constantly in our thoughts, and that we have made every effort to shield you from any kind of peril.'

He then asked me a most unexpected question.

'Did Madame ever tell you why you were named "Esperanza"?'

I had to admit that I had never considered the question before.

'She once told me that it was because you were your late father's dearest hope,' said Mr Thornhaugh, 'in whom he placed all his trust. Do not ask me to explain her words: you will comprehend them by and by. And now I must leave. I have no other parting speech to make. Madame has said all that is needful. I will say only this: be brave, Little Queen, for this is a great thing that you do, as you will one day understand.'

So saying he shook my hand warmly; but then, instead of releasing it, took it in both of his and held it.

Then he broke away, smiled, and was soon lost to view.

THE TIME CAME at last for me to leave Devonshire Street, just a few days after celebrating my nineteenth birthday with kind Mrs

Ridpath. The journey north to Northamptonshire was uneventful; and, as I have already described, I duly secured the position as Lady Tansor's maid.

Now my first day at Evenwood had come to an end. The succeeding days and months were to be very different; but this one most memorable day marked a boundary between the life I had known with Madame, and my new one serving Lady Tansor. It also constituted the first stage of the yet unrevealed Great Task that Madame had set me.

I had at least achieved my first goal. The seeds of my future had been sown; but what harvest would eventually be reaped?

For now, I had a day of vivid memories and tumbled impressions to store away: a great room of crimson and gold; sombre ancestral faces looking down at me as I passed; the smell of countless long-unopened books, asleep in their coffins of leather; Sukie Prout's wayward curls and freckled face; a secret, silent court, with a fountain playing in its midst, and white doves fluttering down from a clear blue sky; my Lady's dark tresses pulled through the bristles of a silver hair-brush, and her fingers tracing out letters on a window-pane; a beautiful long-haired Cavalier boy in blue silk breeches with rosettes on his shoes; still, dark water, with fish moving silently beneath; and, lingering in my mind's eye as sleep began to creep gently over me, the faces – each so striking, each so strangely contrasting – of my Lady's two sons.

4

Nightmares and Memories

I
A Dream of Anthony Duport

T HAT NIGHT, I awoke from sleep in terror, wrenched into
trembling consciousness by a new nightmare.

I dreamed that I was being pursued through a white
void, impenetrable on every side. It was neither mist, nor snow, nor
the clinging miasmic fog of London, but something denser and
stranger. I felt the most intense, stinging cold about my bare feet
and face as I ran, not knowing to where, or why, I ran, nor who my
pursuer might be, only that I must escape at all costs. My terror
increased with every step as I began to hear the sound of someone
breathing hard at my back, and gaining on me second by second.

At last I could run no more, and cried out for help. Yet even as
my cries were absorbed into the surrounding void, all fell suddenly
silent.

The breathing had stopped; the pursuing footfalls could no longer be heard. Had I escaped?

I stood a while, looking about me, straining to see or hear
whether anyone was there, until, out of the thick white blankness,
stepped a little boy, with hair to his shoulders, wearing blue silk
breeches, and rosettes on his shoes.

He smiles at me – such a beguiling, innocent smile.

'I do not know my name,' he says, with tears in his eyes. And then, so imploringly that it nearly breaks my heart, he asks: 'Please, can you tell me who I am?'

I yearn to reach out and comfort him, and tell him that I did indeed know his name; that he was Anthony Charles Duport, born in 1682, a hundred years before Mr Pocock's father, and that he would one day grow up to become the 19th Baron Tansor. But as I move towards him, to enfold him in my arms, his beautiful, entreating face begins to distort, and then dissolve slowly into corruption – hair, and flesh, feature by feature – until it degenerates at last into a hideous grinning skull, still set atop its former elegantly clad little body.

I HAD WOKEN from my dream with the sound of a bell ringing in my ears.

As the nightmare began to recede, I realized that it was the bell that hung in the corner of my room, just above the fire-place, with which my Lady had said that she would summon me if I was required during the night.

Putting on my robe, and all of a tremble still from the nightmare, I lit a candle, and ran down the stairs to my Lady's apartments.

She was sitting up in bed – a monstrous black thing with heavy, blood-red velvet hangings, densely carved with grotesque figures of fauns and satyrs, and other mythological creatures – her head thrown back against the piled-up pillows.

I had put the candle down on a table by the door, leaving the rest of the room illuminated only by the flickering remains of the fire that I had earlier lit. The glow, however, was enough to show me Lady Tansor's shadowed face, pale as death, and her disordered hair, spread out across the pillows like a billowing cloak.

She was looking at me intently, yet her mind seemed to be in some other, more terrible, place, as if she were being held fast in a mesmeric trance. I rushed to her, fearing greatly that she had been taken ill.

'My Lady!' I cried out. 'What is the matter? Can you speak?'

She turned her stricken face towards me, and I saw tiny beads of perspiration standing out on her forehead. I saw, too, the encroaching marks of irresistible time.

She stared at me mutely; then, gradually, colour began to return to her cheeks, and she opened her mouth to speak.

'Alice, dear,' she said, in a hoarse whisper. 'I heard a scream. Was it you?'

'A bad dream, my Lady,' I replied. 'Nothing more.'

'A bad dream!'

She gave the most dreadful, mirthless laugh.

'How bad was your dream, Alice? As bad as mine? I do not think so.'

'May I fetch you something, my Lady?' I enquired. 'Some water, perhaps? Or shall I send Barrington for the doctor? I fear you may have taken a chill from your walk on the terrace this evening.'

'What did you say?'

She was now sitting upright, staring at me with a most fearful expression of alarm.

'Did you stay in the bed-chamber, as I instructed?'

'Yes, my Lady, of course. I only thought that the night air might have—'

She raised her hand to signal that I should say no more, then sank back against the pillow.

'I am quite well now,' she sighed. 'I require only the sweet oblivion of a dreamless sleep. Is it possible, do you suppose, to sleep without the intrusion of dreams? I think that it must be, and that it is a most enviable condition. Do you often have nightmares, Alice?'

I told her that I had been afflicted with periodic night-terrors since childhood, although they were now less frequent disturbers of my sleep than formerly.

'Then we are fellow sufferers,' she said. 'But you are more fortunate than I am; for I find that mine increase alarmingly with every year that passes. Oh, it is a fearful thing, Alice, to have your precious sleep constantly taken from you, night after night, and never given back!'

She had reached forward to grip my hand as she spoke, and I saw the dread returning momentarily to her great dark eyes.

'Perhaps you might read to me again,' she said, quietly, 'just for a very little while.'

She pointed to a small volume, with marbled boards and a gilded spine, lying on the table beside her bed.

'Page one hundred and twenty,' she said. 'The first poem.'

I picked up the book and opened it, briefly glancing at the title-page as I did so. Of course it was yet another work from the pen of Mr Phoebus Daunt: the miscellany of poems, lyrics, and translations entitled *Rosa Mundi*,* which she had been reading on the day of my interview.

I turned to the poem she had requested me to find. Placing the open book on my lap, and lighting the bedside candle, I began to read.

The poem was only six stanzas long. When I had finished, Lady Tansor asked me to read it again. All the while she remained motionless, her head laid back against the pillows, staring out beyond the thick red hangings of the bed towards the window, which framed a pale, lunated moon hanging above the distant woods.

'Again, Alice,' she said, without stirring.

And so I read the poem for a third time, and then a fourth, by when I had it perfectly by heart.

'Enough,' she sighed. 'You may leave me. I shall sleep now, I think. I shall ring for you, should I need you. If not, then you must be here early tomorrow. I have a great deal to do. Seven o'clock, if you please.'

She closed her eyes, and I put out the candle. Softly shutting the door behind me, I returned, exhausted, to my room.

Rosa Mundi; and Other Poems (London: Edward Moxon, 1854), the first of the two works by Daunt (the other being *The Heir*: see note to p. 71) to be published in the year of his death. The concluding two stanzas of the poem in question, entitled 'From the Persian', were copied out by Daunt's murderer, Edward Glyver; the piece of paper on which they had been written was later found thrust into the victim's hand. A final irony is that the author had previously sent his murderer – a former schoolfellow – a complimentary copy of the book.

II
Penance and Punishment

AT A LITTLE before four o'clock, I settled down in my bed again and drew the coverlet over my head. Within minutes I was sound asleep, and remained so, untroubled by dreams, until I was roused by someone knocking at my door.

When I opened it, there stood Mrs Battersby.

'Miss Gorst,' she said, with apparent relief. 'Here you are. You'll excuse me, I hope, but you're wanted by Lady Tansor. I believe you're late in attending her this morning. I happened to have been called up to her Ladyship on some small household matter, and so offered to come and find you.'

I turned to look at the clock. It was almost half an hour past my time.

'I shall go immediately,' I said. 'Thank you, Mrs Battersby.'

'It's no trouble, Miss Gorst,' she replied. 'You'll know, I'm sure, that her Ladyship puts great store on punctuality.'

The remark seemed intended as a friendly reminder, but I could not help feeling, once again, that I was being gently put in my place, even though the housekeeper had no authority over me.

'Oh, Miss Gorst,' she said, as she was turning to go. 'I thought perhaps you might care to take tea with me, if your duties permit of course. Come down to the servants' hall and ask anyone to show you to the housekeeper's room. Shall we say four o'clock?'

WHEN I ENTERED my Lady's sitting-room, I found her, dressed in her red-and-green silk robe, seated at her escritoire writing a letter.

'You will make and light the dressing-room fire, Alice,' she said without looking up, 'lay out and air my linen, and then draw my bath.'

'Yes, my Lady. I'm sorry—'

'Say nothing,' she broke in, continuing to write.

These duties concluded, I returned to the sitting-room.

'I shall bathe now,' she said, sealing the envelope of the letter she had been writing and laying it down. Without even once looking at me, she rustled past in her trailing gown and went into the dressing-room, where I had prepared her bath.

No words were spoken during my Lady's ablutions. It was not until she had finished bathing, and I was lacing up her stays, that she finally looked me in the eye.

'You have disappointed me, Alice,' she said, holding me fast with her unyielding gaze. 'Did I not distinctly say that I would need you at seven o'clock?'

'Yes, my Lady.'

'And what is your excuse?'

I told her straight out that I had none.

'Good. To have prevaricated would have done you no service. You took the honest course, as I hoped you would. But it must not happen again, Alice, no matter what the circumstances are, or there will be consequences. When I name a time, I expect it to be kept. I hope that is clear?'

'Perfectly clear, my Lady.'

'I am displeased with you, of course,' she continued, walking over to the dressing-glass, 'for I expected better from you, and I distinctly told you that certain standards must be observed. I shall not punish you this time, however, but you must do a little penance.'

Moving away from the glass, she seated herself at her dressing-table and began fingering through a box of jewellery.

'Penance, my Lady?' I asked.

'Oh, it is nothing,' came the consciously careless reply. 'A walk, on this fine September morning, that's all. To Easton, to take a letter. That will not be too arduous, I suppose?'

'Not at all, my Lady.'

'You may go after my toilet is completed – I think I shall wear the blue taffeta today.'

I dressed her hair in the way she liked, and helped her into the day-gown she had indicated, which, following Mrs Beeton's instructions, I brushed and gently smoothed with a silk handkerchief as my mistress stood observing herself in the glass. When she was satisfied, she went back to her dressing-table and opened the box containing the tear-shaped locket on its black velvet band, which she then placed round her neck.

'You are curious, are you not, Alice,' she asked, 'about this locket of mine, and why it is so precious to me?'

'A little, my Lady,' I confessed.

'Well, I shall tell you about it, but not at present, for you have your penance to perform, and I have more letters to write. The one I wish you to take is on the escritoire. You are to go to the Duport Arms, in the Market Square, and leave it at the desk for collection – for collection, mind. Do not, under any circumstance, give it to the recipient yourself. Then you must come back directly. Of course there is no need to mention this little penance of yours to anyone – for your own sake.'

Then, to my surprise, she announced, almost as an afterthought, that she must take the express-train to London, on an urgent matter of business.

'It is so tedious,' she sighed, 'and I do so hate London these days. But it cannnot be helped. I shall return this evening. While I am gone, after you have delivered the letter, there are a few small tasks I wish you to carry out.'

Here are the 'few small tasks', additional to my 'penance', to which I had to look forward to on my return from Easton.

The gown she had worn the previous day had sustained a small tear in the hem that required mending; her chaussure had been left in the most disgraceful state by Miss Plumptre, and every pair of shoes required a thorough clean; her hats were in the same deplorable condition ('I adore hats,' she said, turning to me with a smile, 'and have a great many'), and each one would need brushing, the decorations renovated where necessary ('Although I cannot now remember where the flower-pliers are. Ask Mrs Battersby'), and putting away afresh.

'The bed-chamber, of course,' she went on, 'will need a good sweeping, which I really should insist that you do now; but you may do it when you return from Easton. There! I think that's all. Now, run along and make the bed, whilst I put on a little scent and finish my letters. Be as quick as you can, so that you can get off to Easton. And remember – for collection, and come straight back. No need to wait for a reply.'

III
The Old Woman

MY WAY TO Easton took me over the Evenbrook, and through the South Gates into the village of Evenwood. As I approached the gate-house – fashioned like a little Scottish castle, gaunt and black, with the rusty spikes of a pretend portcullis poking down into the dark archway – a pretty little house could be glimpsed through a thick plantation of trees to my right. This, I thought, must be my Lady's former home, the Dower House, where Madame had told me my mistress had lived with her widowed father, Mr Paul Carteret, until his untimely death.

I stopped for a moment to take in the scene.

The house reminded me of nothing so much as the doll's-house that Mr Thornhaugh had caused to be made for my eighth birth-day. It was a gift of such size and magnificence that it had aston-ished even Madame; but he said that every little girl should have a doll's-house, even clever ones who loved their books almost more than their dolls, and had smilingly shrugged off Madame's protes-tations that it must have cost a great deal of money, which he might not have been able to afford.

It entranced me from the moment Mr Thornhaugh removed the canvas cover in which it had been wrapped, and told me that I could open my eyes – which I had closed as tightly as I could at his request, to heighten the anticipation.

How I had longed to become small enough, by some temporary act of sorcery (for I had always been accounted tall for my age), to push open the tiny front door and go exploring through all the rooms! I particularly wished to be able to look out of its windows, with their curtains of sprigged muslin, at the Brobdingnagian world outside, and then scamper up the beautiful curving staircase, to skip and dance through the upper rooms, and curl up at last in one of the miniature beds.

The Dower House had the same delicious perfection of form as my doll's-house; and I found myself experiencing something of the same childhood desire to peep inside it. But, mindful of Lady Tansor's strict instructions, I proceeded instead through the archway of the gloomy gate-house, and out into the road.

As I entered the village, the church clock began to strike half past nine. At the corner of the lane that led down to the church and its adjoining Rectory, I noticed a familiar figure come out of one of the cottages and begin scurrying, like a little mouse, down the lane.

'Sukie!' I cried out.

She stopped, turned, and began running back towards me.

'Miss Alice! What are you doing here?'

I explained that I was on my way to Easton, to take a letter from Lady Tansor to a person staying at the Duport Arms.

'Who can that be, I wonder?' she said. 'And why would they be staying in Easton, and not in the great house?'

'Is that where you live?' I asked, looking towards the cottage from which she had just emerged.

'Yes,' she replied. 'The doctor has been to see Mother, and Mrs Battersby allowed me half an hour to come down while he was here.'

I said I hoped her mother's condition was not serious.

'No – thank you – not serious, as far as we know. She'll be seventy-two soon, which is a grand age, I think, though of course it brings its troubles.'

At the mention of Mrs Battersby, I was about to ask Sukie whether she could tell me a little more concerning the housekeeper, in whom I had begun to take a decided interest; but I knew that I must get to Easton as soon as I could, before beginning the various tasks my mistress had set me. Sukie, too, was anxious to return to the great house, in order not to risk Mrs Battersby's displeasure. So we parted, and I watched Sukie's little figure run back down the lane, her curls flopping and bouncing as she went.

ONCE OUT OF the village, and having passed through the hamlets of Upper Thornbrook and Duck End, I took the road that climbed the gentle wooded escarpment on which the town of Easton stands, the trees on either side forming a most pleasant canopy of branches, through which the early-autumn sunlight was now streaming.

The Market Square was already crowded when I reached the town, for it was market day, and there was a great press of people outside the Duport Arms, and in the public rooms.

As there was no one at the desk, I rang the bell several times until a sour-faced old man, bent of back, and with a greasy black patch over one eye, appeared from behind a curtain.

'I wish to leave this for collection.'

He took the letter and examined the inscription by holding it up close to his remaining eye.

'"B.K.",' he muttered to himself, and then said the initials over again, more slowly this time, rolling his eye upwards to the ceiling, as if the information he was seeking might be written there. Then he began to nod his head.

'Do you know the gentleman?' I asked.

'Genlemun? Bless you, no. No genlemun.'

'Not a gentleman? A tradesman, perhaps?'

'Hah! Not 'er.'

'Ah, I see. It's a lady.'

I turned to go, but he called me back. Lowering his voice, and leaning his whiskery face towards me, so close that I could smell his beery breath, he said:

'No lady neither. Initials of old 'ooman. Over there.'

He nodded towards the tap-room door, through the glass of which, in a settle by the fire-place, I could see a woman of about sixty years in the act of draining a glass.

'Gin-an'-water,' the man informed me, with a rasping chuckle.

'Third or fourth.' Still chuckling, he laid the letter face up on the desk, next to the bell, and disappeared back behind the curtain.

I should have immediately left the Duport Arms to return to Evenwood, as Lady Tansor had instructed; but then, remembering that Madame had encouraged me to use my initiative in the pursuit of my great task, I decided to remain a few moments longer, in order to make some observations concerning the mysterious old woman.

These were my impressions of her person, jotted down in my note-book, and later transferred *verbatim* to my Book of Secrets:

OLD WOMAN ('B.K.') AT DUPORT ARMS

Age: sixty, or thereabouts. Grey hair, and a pinched, mean face, much lined about the eyes, and red about the nose. Short. Bent back. Dirty finger-nails. Wearing a dress that might have been in fashion twenty years since, but now faded, and darned in several places. Scuffed and dusty boots, the heel of the left worn almost to nothing. Hole in right stocking just above the ankle.

I stood, watching the woman call for another glass of gin-and-water, and wondering what had brought her here, to receive a letter, delivered by hand, from Lady Tansor. What could my Lady have to do with such a person?

Having drained her glass to the very bottom, the old woman was now wiping her mouth with the dirty sleeve of her dress. There was an intimidating look of seasoned cunning about her. Even in her present half-inebriated condition, her eyes were alert, darting here and there, as if on the watch for some danger. Gripping the table for support, she now pulled herself to her feet, and began to walk unsteadily towards the tap-room door.

I moved away as she approached; but my further progress was prevented by a group of farmers, who were just then coming in from the Square. Being obliged to step back to let them pass, I soon felt the old woman's presence close behind me.

When the last of the farmers had gone by, I began to make my way as quickly as I could towards the front door; but then the one-eyed hall-porter appeared from behind his curtain once more and called to the woman.

'Ma'am! Ma'am! Letter for you.'

Half walking, half stumbling, the old woman went over to the desk and took the letter from the porter.

'Who brought it?' she snapped.

'Young lady over there,' replied the one-eyed man, directing her to where I was standing.

'And who might you be, miss?' she asked, putting on a quickly assumed, but wholly unconvincing, smile as she drew near. 'I don't believe as I've had the pleasure of your acquaintance, my dear.'

I had no wish to tell this unpleasant person my name, and so said simply that I was Lady Tansor's maid. Then, quickly excusing myself, I began to head for the front door again.

'No, no, stay a while, my dear,' she said, placing a grubby claw-like hand on mine. I felt her fingers tighten, and instantly began to pull away; but there was uncommon strength in that grip, which held me back.

For a brief moment I was afraid, and angry at myself for not returning to Evenwood when I should have done.

'Lady Tansor's maid, you say?' the old woman was saying. 'And a pretty maid you are, my dear. Won't you come and talk for a while to a poor old woman with no friends in the world?'

Before I could reply, and with my hand still held fast, my attention was suddenly caught by the silhouette of a well-built man appearing in the doorway.

'Hullo, who's here?' said the man on seeing me. 'Why, it's Miss Gorst, ain't it?'

5

A Walk with Mr Randolph

I

I Hear Confession

THE VOICE greeting me is that of Mr Randolph Duport.

As soon as the old woman sees him enter and walk briskly towards me, her bony hand immediately releases its grip and she scuttles back into the tap-room, where she sits glowering as Mr Randolph comes up to me, beaming broadly.

'And what brings you here, Miss Gorst, on market day?' he asks. 'Have you come to buy a cow?'

I did him the courtesy of giving a little laugh at the joke, although his arrival presented a dilemma.

I could not tell him why I had been sent to the Duport Arms, for Lady Tansor had wished my errand to remain confidential; yet neither could I bring myself to tell him an outright lie. I resorted instead to a near-truth: that I had been allowed a morning's liberty by his mother, and that I had gone into the Duport Arms for some refreshment before returning to Evenwood. I disliked the need for even this venial falsehood; but more such subterfuges – and worse – doubtless lay ahead of me in the prosecution of the Great Task, and I must learn to accustom myself to them.

'And have you taken your refreshment?' he asked. 'You have? Capital! Now, what about your companion?'

'Companion?'

'The old lady you were with when I came in. An acquaintance met by chance, perhaps?'

'Oh, no,' I hastily reply. 'No acquaintance. She mistook me for someone. I've never seen her before in my life.'

'Well, then,' he says, with every sign of satisfaction, 'if there's nothing more to keep you here, may I accompany you back to Evenwood? No, no! No trouble at all. Indeed, I insist. Just the morning for a walk. Do say yes.'

I gladly agreed, whereupon he went off to arrange for his horse to be taken back to Evenwood, whilst I remained in the hall for his return.

As I waited, I glanced behind me into the tap-room. The mysterious 'B.K.' had vanished.

Mr Randolph soon came back, offered me his arm, and out we stepped into the bustling, sunlit Square, thronged with all manner of country-folk, pens of bellowing livestock, and stalls selling various goods.

My companion chattered away, in a most merry and easy fashion, as if we were already old friends, pointing out as we went along the various public buildings – the Town Hall, the Corn Exchange, the Assembly Rooms, the imposing Church of St John the Evangelist – and the houses of some of the town's principal residents, including the stately red-brick dwelling of Dr Pordage, Lady Tansor's country physician.

'So, Miss Gorst,' says Mr Randolph, as we leave the town and begin to descend the long, tree-canopied hill leading to the hamlet of Duck End, 'tell me how you are finding Evenwood.'

I tell him that, from my early impressions, it seems a place in which I thought it must be very difficult to be unhappy.

'I wouldn't wish to disagree,' he says, doubtfully; 'but unhappiness must come to us all, you know – even to those who live in a place like Evenwood.'

I venture to observe that that such a beautiful and ordered place might make unhappiness, when it came, easier to bear, just as ugly and unpleasant places have the opposite effect.

'I'd never thought of it like that,' he replies, brightly. 'How clever you are, Miss Gorst—'

He seems about to say something more, but then checks himself.

'Did you mean to add "for a lady's-maid"?' I ask; but seeing him colour slightly, and not wishing to embarrass him, I immediately confess that my question has been meant to tease, and that I have taken no offence – indeed that I am wholly conscious of my position at Evenwood.

'And yet you're quite unlike Miss Plumptre, and the other maids Mother has had,' he says, adding, in a quieter tone, 'quite unlike.'

I affect not to understand him, wishing very much to know the view he has formed of me.

'What I meant was,' he explains, 'that it seems to me that you weren't born to be a lady's-maid – that you had a very different life once. That's why Mother preferred you to the others. You weren't at all like them – not ordinary in the least. She saw it straight away, as I did.'

'I'm not at all sure I know what I was born to be,' I reply, warming now to my adopted character. 'I only know that circumstances have made it necessary for me to make my own way in the world, with only the few small advantages my upbringing has given me – as I think has also been the case with Mrs Battersby.'

'Mrs B?'

He appears momentarily non-plussed by my mentioning the housekeeper, until I explain that Lady Tansor had observed how similar our situations appeared to be, both of us apparently coming into domestic service from higher stations in life.

'Ah, yes,' he says, with a kind of relief, as if he expected a different answer from me, adding that any comparison with Mrs Battersby would be very much in my favour. Of course I demur, but he seems determined to press home his compliment.

'Come, come, Miss Gorst!' he cries, in mock remonstrance. 'No false modesty! Mrs B's father was – or, at least, so I've heard – a clergyman of limited means. Financial misfortune deprived him, and his children, of the little he had. Died a bankrupt – as I understand. You, on the other hand—'

I regard him expectantly.

'Well, there's a difference of degree between you and Mrs B – that's what I think. Naturally, I wouldn't presume to press you, having just made your acquaintance, to see whether my guess is right. All I know, from Mother, is that you're an orphan. Brought up by some relative, I suppose?'

'By a guardian, named by my father before he died.'

'And did you grow up in the country?'

'No, in Paris.'

I am suddenly conscious of having let my guard down. I must be more circumspect, even though I have said nothing that is not known to his mother. To prevent any further, perhaps more awkward questions, however, I change the subject, by asking whether he has read his brother's poem on Merlin and Nimue.

He throws his head back and laughs.

'Read Perseus's poem! No, no. Not my line of country at all, I'm afraid. Give me a fishing-rod and a good hunter any day. No, Miss Gorst, I haven't read it, and don't suppose I ever will. My loss, I know. I'm sure it's a great thing, but there it is. I'm generally accounted the dunce of the family, you see, especially by Mother. It's a case of brawn and brains, and Perseus was given all the brains.

'It all comes from Mother,' he is now saying. 'She encouraged Perseus early. He was always scribbling, always had his head in some book of verse, and she used to read to him constantly – mostly from Mr Tennyson or Mr Phoebus Daunt, the man she was once to marry who was killed by some maniac he'd known at school. Terrible business. Mother never recovered from it. You've heard of Mr Daunt, I suppose?'

I tell him that I am familiar with his name, and that I am now becoming acquainted with his work, through reading it to his mother.

'Well,' he says, smiling drily, 'I don't envy you that. Mother, of course, won't hear a word said against the ever-lamented bard. It's the great taboo. I suppose that's why she's always spurred Perseus on to emulate him, and make him a kind of substitute. As for Mr Daunt, he still haunts Mother's life – he's there, day in and day out, constantly in her thoughts, and always will be. And next week is the 11th.'

'The 11th?'

He lowered his voice.

'The 11th of every month is observed by Mother as a kind of memorial to Mr Daunt, who died on the 11th of December in the year 1854. On the day itself, she'll go to the Mausoleum, where the poor fellow lies.'

'It must have gone hard for your father,' I remark, 'living with the perpetually present ghost of his wife's former love.'

'No,' he says, looking into the distance in a sad, abstracted way. 'Father always accepted it. He knew that nothing would change her. Poor Father! He could never live up to the memory of Mr Daunt – just as I'll never live up to Perseus. Mother was very fond of Father, in her way; but she lives too much in the past – in the time before she met him. She doesn't see the harm in it, but there *is* harm in dwelling overmuch on what can't be changed, don't you think?'

'There can be, certainly,' I agree, thinking now of the parents I had never known. 'But then don't we also owe a duty to the past, and to the memory of those we've lost, to keep them fresh in our hearts?'

'Oh, yes,' he says. 'Absolutely. Especially in a family like mine. You can't escape the past if you're a Duport.'

I could not help feeling flattered by these confidences, freely given to a virtual stranger, and a servant to boot. It was foolish of me, I am sure, but I took them as a compliment, showing that he liked me, and perhaps somewhat more than he appeared to like everyone.

As for my own feelings, I once again fancied, as I had done on first meeting him, that, under different circumstances, I might have found it hard to prevent myself from falling a little in love with Mr Randolph Duport. Yet here, in this place and time, as I embarked with uncertain steps on the first stage of the Great Task, I found that my heart was able to withstand what should have been – and might yet be – irresistible.

'Your father was a military man, I think?' I said, after we had walked some way in silence.

'Prussian army. Rose to the rank of colonel. Polish by birth, though.'

'Polish? How interesting.'

'Is it? Haven't given it much thought, I'm afraid. Never been to Poland, and Father never spoke much about it. He always said he preferred England, and that meeting Mother and coming here had been the making of him. We've had little to do with that side of the family. Mother never encouraged it.'

'And were you born in Poland?'

'No, here – at Evenwood. Perseus was born in Bohemia, where Mother and Father met. Wasn't there a king of the place in Shakespeare?'

'Yes,' I laughed. 'In *The Winter's Tale*. King Polixenes.'

'That's the chappie. Well, my brother's a sort of king-in-waiting, I suppose. But I don't mind that. Fact is, Miss Gorst, I'm rather grateful to Nature, for putting all the responsibilities on Perseus. I'm afraid I wouldn't have made a good heir, and am heartily glad it's him and not me who must one day bear the crown. I find, you see, that I'm pretty happy as I am, and have no wish to be anything other.'

He appeared to entertain no trace of resentment or envy of his brother's superior position in the family, both as the heir and as his mother's favourite, as some younger sons might have done. I then pointed out that his brother's seniority was a mere accident of birth.

'But could I have carried it off – being the heir to all this, I mean – if I'd been born first? That's the question. No, I'll always stand in my brother's shadow. If I minded, it would be different, but I don't. It sets me free to—'

He hesitated for a moment, then gave a good-humoured shrug.

'Well, free to continue looking about me, for some suitable opportunity. I'm by no means idle by nature, and must do *something* with my life.'

'And do you know what you might wish to do? Have you settled on any particular course?'

He regarded me for a moment with an uncharacteristically evasive expression.

'No, not exactly,' he replied at length. 'I had a mind once to become an engineer, but Mother wouldn't hear of it. Of course if I'd gone up to the Varsity, like Perseus, I might have a clearer notion of what I'm fitted for; but Mother felt it wouldn't suit me, and sent me to a private academy instead. So I continue to look about me – in the hope, as I say, of something eventually presenting itself.'

After a little more probing, he told me that Mr Perseus had received every advantage in his education, whereas his own appeared to have been sadly, almost wilfully, neglected.

The heir had been sent to Eton – where the Duports had a long connexion – and had then proceeded to the school's sister foundation at Cambridge, King's College. Mr Randolph, meanwhile, had been placed in the hands of a succession of private tutors of doubtful competence, before being packed off to reside with a clerical gentleman in Suffolk – a former Fellow of Brasenose College in Oxford – to complete his studies. Here, with half a dozen other similarly constituted young gentlemen, he had remained for nearly two years.

'Of course it wasn't the same as going up to the Varsity, but I've never been happier than I was at Dr Savage's,' he said wistfully, looking away as he spoke, 'and made some good friends there – one in particular. But then I was taken away and had to come back home, and here I've stayed – looking about me.'

WE HAD NOW passed through Upper Thornbrook, a small group of thatched cottages ranged on either side of the main road from Easton, and were coming into Evenwood village. On our left was a broad area of common land stretching down to the river. Here we stopped, at the top of a lane that divided the Common from the church-yard and adjacent Rectory, the former home of Phoebus Daunt when his father was Rector, and now occupied by Mr and Mrs Thripp.

'We can go this way,' said Mr Randolph, pointing towards the Rectory. 'It's quicker than going up to the gates.'

So down the lane we went, and into the Park. From here, a narrow track wound up gently rising ground to join the main carriage-drive. At the junction, we were presented with a magnificent view of the great house laid out below us, its eight cupola-topped towers set darkly against a sky of the most delicate powder-blue.

'Are you going back to attend Mother?' he asked, as we began our descent towards the river.

'No,' I replied. 'Lady Tansor has gone to London.'

'To London, you say? That's strange. She said nothing to me, but then I'm usually the last one to be told about these things. Some matter of business, I suppose, although she usually sends Perseus these days.'

Presently, we halt on the elegant stone bridge that spans the Evenbrook. Mr Randolph is pointing out a spot, a little way upstream, where he likes to take his rod and nets of a morning – fishing being one of his passions – when he suddenly breaks off and turns to me.

'Miss Gorst,' he says, removing his hat, and running his fingers nervously through his hair. 'I don't want you to think badly of me, so there's something I must say – a confession.'

I express surprise that he can possibly have anything to confess to me on so brief an acquaintance.

'That's just it,' comes the reply. 'I don't want to begin our acquaintance on the wrong foot.'

Permission to proceed is duly given, and I wait – with a good deal of curiosity – for him to speak.

Having become rather red in the face, he now takes off his long riding-coat and lays it on the parapet next to his hat.

'The thing is, Miss Gorst,' he begins, 'our meeting this morning – it wasn't quite by chance, you know. I was riding through the village when I saw you take the road up to Easton. So I waited for a while, then rode up through one of the back ways to the town, just in time to see you go in to the Duport Arms. I stabled the horse, and waited in the Square for you to come out. When you didn't, I decided to go in and look for you. There! That's my confession. Will you forgive me?'

'For what?' I ask, amused by his sweetly grave expression, which has somehow brought to mind the earnest face of little Amélie Verron, bending herself to some pretended school-room task that I had set her.

'I thought you might feel it was, well, rather forward of me, having so recently met you,' he admits, 'and I wouldn't want that.'

I assure him that I did not consider it to have been in the least forward, or in any way improper, although adding that Mrs Battersby might not agree.

'Oh?' he says, turning away to pick up his hat and coat from the parapet. 'Why do you say that?'

I reply that she appears to have a rather severe view of the proprieties that ought to exist between domestic servants and those placed in authority over them.

To this observation he merely nods, whilst once again seeming strangely relieved by my words.

As we draw near to the house, he begins to point out the fine iron-work of the gates and of the tall railings on either side, leaning close in to me in order to direct my eyes to the particular features he wishes me to note. We then continue across the wide gravelled Court, past the splashing, Triton-encrusted fountain in its oval of perfect green turf, to the front-door steps.

He is about to take his leave when I interrupt him with a question that has been fluttering around my head since we left the bridge: why had he followed me to Easton?

'Oh, merely a whim,' he says, with a breezy smile. 'Having nothing else to do at that moment, I simply wondered what would take you to Easton at this time of day, when you ought to be attending Mother. Pure curiosity – that's all. It's just that I didn't want you to think I'd done anything – well, underhand – in going after you like that, and then pretending that I'd met you by accident. Well, here we are. Safe home. Good-morning, Miss Gorst. This has been most pleasant.'

He seems suddenly eager to go, tips his hat, and walks quickly off towards the stables.

It is then that I become aware of someone standing in the doorway at the base of one of the towers. It is Mrs Battersby. She watches Mr Randolph leave the Court and then, turning for a moment towards me, although making no acknowledgement of my presence, goes back inside the house, closing the door behind her.

II
A Tea-time Conversation

THAT AFTERNOON WAS spent carrying out the various tasks my Lady had set me while she was away for the day in London – and, Lord, how hot, and piqued, and angry I became!

Shoes, shoes, shoes! Of every type and condition – so many, that I could hardly count them all; and every one to be taken out and brushed, or blacked, or sponged with milk, and then wrapped up and put back again.

Then her hats and bonnets and other head-gear – also seem-ingly without number. Out they all came from their boxes, to be dusted with a feather plume, or the velvet brushed up, and those with crushed or tumbled decorations made good again – although without the flower-pliers, for I did not wish to go down and ask Mrs Battersby for them, as my Lady had suggested.

After the last hat-box had been packed away, it was out with the needle and thread, to mend the tear in yesterday's day-gown, before I set about cleaning and polishing the bed-chamber, emptying the slops, and finally filling the water-jugs with fresh water.

At last, as the bright afternoon began to fade, I slumped down on the sofa in my Lady's sitting-room, exhausted, dirty, and decid-edly out of humour.

I MUST HAVE dozed off, for I woke up with a start, realizing that it was nearly half past four, and that Mrs. Battersby had asked me to take tea with her at four. *Lord, late again!* I thought to myself, hurry-ing down to the servants' hall as fast as I could.

I had awoken from a vivid dream of my recent walk back to Even-wood from Easton, after delivering my Lady's letter to the horrid 'B.K.'; but, in my dream, my saviour had not been Mr Randolph, but his brother. Why my sleeping mind should have substituted Mr Perseus for Mr Randolph, I could not comprehend, but I had no time to puzzle it out as I hastened to keep my engagement with Mrs Battersby.

The housekeeper's room, situated at the opposite end of the hall to the steward's room, and reached by a short flight of narrow wind-ing stairs, was small but cheery, with two mullioned windows over-looking the yard where I had found Sukie emptying her bucket. A comfortable sofa, a button-backed arm-chair, and a low table stood before a gently flaming fire. A venerable oak dresser, laden with crockery; a small gate-legged table and two chairs between the win-dows; a book-case containing a folio bible and a number of other books; two coloured prints of mountain scenery on the wall next to the dresser; and, somewhat incongruously, a child's rocking-horse completed the furnishings.

Mrs Battersby was sitting in the arm-chair before the fire read-ing a book when one of the footmen showed me in.

I apologized for my lateness, admitting that I had fallen asleep after carrying out the tasks Lady Tansor had set me.

'Please think nothing of it, Miss Gorst,' said Mrs Battersby ami-ably, laying down her book (Mr Borrow's *Wild Wales*, as I immedi-ately noted). 'The work of a lady's-maid – like that of a housekeeper – can frequently be arduous, and of course you've also walked to Easton and back today.'

Her voice, I am now aware, has a faintly lilting, musical qual-ity about it – perhaps the residue of some accent with which I am not familiar. But oh, that unsmiling smile! So equivocal, so sug-gestive, so vexingly indecipherable! I know that she saw me return-ing to the house with Mr Randolph; she also knows where I had been, although not, I am sure, why I had gone there. I am certain, too, that she disapproves of Mr Randolph's accompanying me on my return to the house, as she would have disapproved of Sukie addressing me by my Christian name; yet she is all welcoming affa-

bility as she hands me a brimming tea-cup from the tray, brought
in by one of the kitchen-maids, and her face conveys no outward
sign of criticism. It is only when we have finished our tea, during
which our conversation has been confined to trite generalities, that
I begin to detect an undertow of stricture.

'Well, Miss Gorst,' she says, after the kitchen-maid has taken
the tea-tray away, 'I hope you enjoyed your walk with Mr Randolph
Duport. It was a very fine morning for walking, I think, although I
saw little of it myself, being kept indoors by my duties.'

There! The merest pin-prick of challenge and censure, delivered
so artfully; but I feel it, as she means me to do.

'I enjoyed it very much,' I reply, putting on an air of the most
guileless insouciance. 'Mr Duport was excellent company, and the
morning – as you say – was a fine one.'

'You are right,' she says, picking up her tea-cup. 'Mr Randolph
Duport *is* very good company. So easy, so frank – and so unlike his
brother. Mr Perseus is generally accounted proud and unapproach-
able, which could never be said of his brother.'

A pause. A sip of tea. A smile.

'You'd gone to Easton on your own account, I suppose?'

'Yes. As she was obliged to go up to Town, my Lady was good
enough to allow me a morning's liberty.'

'I congratulate you, Miss Gorst. Here you are, scarcely arrived at
Evenwood, and Lady Tansor is already granting you a morning's liberty! I would say such a thing is without precedent here. Certainly
your predecessor never enjoyed such favours.'

'Miss Plumptre?'

'Indeed. Miss Dorothy Plumptre. Of course she lacked the advantage of a winning disposition, which went very much against her.'

'But I've heard that she did not give good service to my Lady,' say
I, disingenuously. 'I have also heard that there was some unpleasantness, which unfortunately led to her dismissal. I hope that I am
not speaking out of turn?'

'Not at all. Anything said between the two of us here, in this
room, is of a private nature, and you are correct in what you say.
There was indeed a most regrettable incident, regarding the alleged

theft of one of her Ladyship's brooches. I may say, personally, that I would never have believed Miss Plumptre capable of such a thing, and she would never admit to taking the brooch, even though it was eventually found in her room. But that's all in the past. Here *you* are, Miss Gorst, her successor, and you – I'm sure – have a very different future ahead of you.'

I smile back at her, as if I am touched by the apparent compliment, but hold my tongue.

'Mr Pocock was right,' she adds. 'A "sharp one", I think he called you? At any rate, you are already very well informed about events here – quite the little intelligencer! First Professor Slake, and now Miss Plumptre – not to mention the way you seem to have so quickly secured the good opinion of both Lady Tansor and Mr Randolph Duport. Mr Perseus Duport will doubtless be next – or perhaps he's already one of your conquests? What a triumph that would be! The heir himself!'

A quiet laugh now complements the ever-present half-smile, and with it a lingering look of teasing cordiality. We are already friends, that siren look would have me believe, and friends can say such things frankly to each other, without fear of offence being given or taken. But I do not believe it. She does not like me, and has no wish to be my friend, although I cannot think what I have done to deserve her antagonism. Was it simply my unwitting presumption in allowing Mr Randolph Duport to escort me – a mere lady's-maid – back to Evenwood? Perhaps jealousy of Lady Tansor's evident partiality towards me is the cause; or it might be that what she considers to be an equality in our conditions poses a threat to her superior position in the household.

I had described her as 'capable' to Lady Tansor, and capable she clearly was, accomplished in ways that set her apart from her fellow domestics. I had no doubt that this gave her a peculiar standing in the Kingdom of Service – almost one of deputy or proxy to Lady Tansor herself – that she was anxious to maintain. Whatever the reason for her dislike of me, I was curious to find it out. For the moment, I knew only that I had unexpectedly made an enemy.

Just then, the kitchen-maid who had brought us our tea knocked at the door to announce that rats had got into the Dry Store and that the housekeeper's presence was immediately required.

'Well, duty calls,' said Mrs Battersby, with a resigned sigh, when the maid had gone. 'It is always calling. This should have been my allotted hour of leisure, but there it is. I'm afraid we must end this most interesting conversation, and Mr Borrow must wait until I retire, which I fear will not be much before midnight. It is always so.'

Another sigh.

'One simply does not have the luxury of – *liberty* – to do the things one really wants to do. There's always some demand or other on one's time – and now it's rats!'

She gets up, still speaking, to take Mr Borrow over to the bookcase.

'But never mind that. This has been most delightful, Miss Gorst. At Evenwood, as you will know, you are answerable only to her Ladyship, and to no one else – as I am. But if there is any help, or advice, I can give you, in these early days, as you become accustomed to the ways of the house, I shall be very glad to do so. Others here, I know, regard me as a little strict in my ways. Perhaps I am. But I am not so with those over whom I have no authority, and so I shall never be strict with you, Miss Gorst.'

She has now opened the door for me to leave. Our eyes meet.

'You'll come again, I hope?' she asks as I step out into the passage.

'Certainly I'll come again, Mrs Battersby, and with the greatest of pleasure,' say I, with my most accommodating smile. 'Duties permitting.'

III
An Act of Charity

MY LADY DID not return from London until nearly seven o'clock, when I was immediately summoned to dress her for dinner. Like me, she appeared tired and fraught after her day's exertions.

'Did you carry out your little penance?' were her first coldly spoken words.

'Yes, my Lady.'

'And you came straight back from Easton, as I instructed?'

She saw me hesitate, and her mouth tightened.

'Have you something to tell me?'

Mindful that I must secure her trust at all costs, I had no choice but to admit my encounter with 'B.K.' On hearing that I had not only seen the letter's recipient, but had also spoken to her, Lady Tansor became visibly agitated, and immediately walked over to the window, where she stood, her back towards me, fingering the black velvet band encircling her neck.

'So you spoke to her?' she asked, still looking out of the window.

'Briefly, my Lady – but only to tell her that I was obliged to return here immediately.'

'Nothing else?'

'No, my Lady.'

'And did she say anything to you?'

'No, my Lady. Nothing of any consequence.'

At this she gave a sigh, and appeared to relax her stance.

'Did you form any opinion of her?' she then asked.

Not wishing to put myself in the way of any awkwardness, I merely observed that she had seemed somewhat in want, venturing the suggestion – the only conclusion, indeed, that I had managed to form of the woman's identity – that she might have been a former servant who had fallen on hard times.

'Yes!' Lady Tansor exclaimed, her mood suddenly lifting. 'You've guessed it! What a wonder you are, Alice. I see that I shall have to be more careful in the future, or you'll discover all my little secrets! She is indeed what you say: an old servant, a former nurse-maid, in fact, who looked after my sister and me for a time. Dear Mrs Kennedy!'

'Her name is Kennedy, then?' I ask.

'It is,' my Lady replies. Then, pausing slightly, she adds: 'Mrs Bertha Kennedy – we always called her "B.K." when we were young.'

'And does she have a husband?'

'She is a widow, alas, and has fallen on very hard times. Of course I was obliged to offer a little help, of a pecuniary kind, when she applied to me – which she did very reluctantly, and on the strict understanding that the arrangement would remain confidential. The letter you took contained a little money, just to see her through this present time of trial. That's why I wished you to return here immediately, you see – to spare her from any embarrassment. Poor thing! To see her in such straits after all these years. It was a great shock.'

'So you've seen her yourself then, my Lady?'

For a moment she seems taken aback, but quickly recovers herself.

'Did I say "see"? I meant of course when I read the letter she recently wrote describing her present troubles.'

She sank slowly down into the window-seat, with a quiet smile on her face that I believe was meant to convey sentimental reminiscence of her former nurse-maid, but which to me, as I stood picturing to myself the grubby and unpleasant individual who had held my hand in her dirty-fingered grip, appeared more like an expression of relief, puzzling though it was to me why I should think so.

After dressing my Lady for dinner, I returned at last to my room, wrote a long account of the day in my Book, and read a little from Mr Wilkie Collins, until it was time to go down and take my own supper.

SEATED IN A line at the table in the steward's room taking their evening meal were Mr Pocock; Mr Maggs; Henry Creswick; and Mr Randolph's valet, John Brimley, a chubby, self-fancying young buck, with heavily oiled hair, and a mocking look about him, as if he were the only individual in the whole of creation who had uncovered the secrets of how the world really worked.

Mrs Battersby was sitting silently in her usual place at the head of the table. By her side was another person, to whom, with John Brimley, I was now introduced: Mr Arthur Applegate, the steward himself.

'You were saying that the interment is to take place next Wednesday, Mr Pocock,' remarked Mr Applegate, a broad-faced, clean-shaven man, with close-cropped grey hair, and a hoarse, breathless way of speaking.

'That's the day,' the butler replied, taking a draught of barley-water. 'The 13th, at eleven. Mr Candy's gravely ill, as I understand, and may not live out the week, so our Mr Thripp is to officiate. Ah, if only Dr Daunt was still here! There was a man for these occasions. No one better.'

'You were here when Dr Daunt was Rector, then, Mr Pocock?' I asked.

'For a time,' he replied. 'I came here in '57, as under-butler to old Mr Cranshaw. The Rector gave up the living the following year, but he's very well remembered hereabouts, Miss Gorst, as a man of great learning and amiability.'

'You're right there,' agreed Mr Maggs, who had now moved away to smoke his pipe in a chair by the fire. 'And what a change we've 'ad with the new man!'

'Hardly new, Maggs,' objected Mr Pocock, 'though you're right that Mr Thripp's a very different individual from his predecessor. No, he took a good funeral, did Dr Daunt, that's certain. I was there when he buried old Bob Munday – pretty much the old Rector's last burial, if I remember aright – and a finer address I never heard. But, ah, it must have been hard, even for a man well used to these things, to bury his only son – and just a year after seeing his old friend, my Lady's father, put in the church-yard. It finished him, that's for sure.'

'That's true enough,' concurred Mr Applegate, shaking his head.

'Lady T will go, I suppose?' asked Henry Creswick. 'To see the old prof buried?'

'Course she'll go,' broke in the all-knowing John Brimley, giving his fellow-valet a supercilious grin.

'And what do you know about it, John Brimley?' came the reply from the other valet.

'More than you, at any rate.'

'Yes, she'll go,' intervened Mr Pocock, giving both the young men a warning look, and taking another quaff of barley-water. When he had laid down his glass, I asked him how long the late Professor Slake had been the Library's custodian.

He thought for a moment before calling through the open screen door to a smartly turned-out man, dressed in an old-fashioned tail-coat with a velvet collar, standing by the fire-place in the main hall talking to one of the foot-boys.

'James Jarvis! When did Professor Slake come here?'

'In '55. February,' came the immediate reply.

'You may always depend on James Jarvis,' said Mr Pocock, with evident pleasure at his own perspicacity in asking the question of such a prodigy of memory. 'Thirty years usher here, and never been known to forget a date. Professor Slake, Miss Gorst, was an old friend of Dr Daunt's, and of her Ladyship's father, Mr Paul Carteret – you know, perhaps, Miss Gorst, that Mr Carteret was a cousin of the late Lord Tansor, though he was also his secretary?'

Before I could reply, a bell rang from an array in the far corner of the room.

'Billiards-Room,' said Mr Pocock, rising from the table with a little chuckle. 'That'll be Mr Randolph thrashing his brother again. Mr Perseus always has to drown defeat with a stiff brandy. Riding to hounds and billiards are about the only things Mr Randolph can beat his brother at, bless the dear fellow. But there's no kinder or truer heart in the world, that's for sure.'

'Who wants to know?'

The demand – unrelated to any aspect of the present conversation – was barked out by the aforementioned James Jarvis, who was now standing by the screen doorway.

'What's that, Jarvis?' said Mr Pocock.

'Who wants to know when old Slake first came?'

'Miss Gorst here.'

Mr Jarvis gave me a deep bow, and said he was glad to make my acquaintance.

'Twenty-one years and seven months, almost to the day,' he then announced to the company, with a look that defied anyone to question his powers either of recall or computation. 'And for most of that time he made a thorough nuisance of himself.'

'And why was that?' I heard myself asking, for I was curious to know, despite feeling Mrs Battersby's disapproving eye upon me.

'Why,' explained prickly Mr Jarvis, with an exasperated air, 'by telling anyone who'd listen – and a great many who had no mind to – that old Carteret was set upon for dockiments, not money. Dockiments, indeed! You can't buy beer with dockiments.'

'Now, now, James Jarvis.'

The reprimand – quietly but firmly delivered – came from Mrs Battersby.

'You've been told before, I think, about speaking out of turn,' she went on, 'and I'm sure that Mr Applegate won't want such talk in his room.'

Mr Applegate, whose authority in his own room seemed negligible, uttered a flustered 'Quite so, Mrs Battersby,' and scratched his head.

'Since when, Jane Battersby, has telling the honest truth been speaking out of turn?' queried Mr Jarvis, throwing his shoulders back, and meeting her gaze – for which act of open defiance I could not help shouting an inward 'Hurrah!'

'You'll oblige me on this, James Jarvis,' replied Mrs Battersby, her perpetual smile now at its lowest ebb, 'before you say something you might regret. Her Ladyship would not care to know that her usher has been gossiping so freely on matters relating to her late father that do not concern him.'

This calmly voiced but sharp rebuke, and its implied threat, might have discomfited a less resilient soul; but the usher appeared well used to such confrontations with the housekeeper, and brushed off her words with an unconcerned shrug, adding that what he had said was no more than the truth, whatever some people might think.

'Dockiments!' he muttered disbelievingly under his breath, as he stumped bad-temperedly back into the hall. 'Who'd want dockiments?'

· · ·

IN THE SUCCEEDING days, my life began to settle into the pattern it was to follow until – well, I shall not complete that sentence; for there is more to tell concerning those early weeks at Evenwood. I felt continually apprehensive, and often fearful, of what lay ahead, being still ignorant of what I would be asked to do by Madame, but I also experienced a strange relish at the prospect of impending adventure.

I would rise early and, if the morning was fine, go down the winding stairs leading to the terrace below my room where Lady Tansor usually took her morning and evening exercise, and then walk about the gardens and surrounding grounds until it was time to take my breakfast in the steward's room. Then I would go up to dress my mistress, and while she went down to take her own breakfast, usually in the company of Mr Perseus and Mr Randolph, I would air and make her bed, and set about making all spick and span for her return, which was usually around eleven o'clock, after she had read her correspondence and conducted various matters of business with her secretary, Mr Baverstock, and the estate manager, Mr Lancing, often with Mr Perseus in attendance.

I had been given a list of tasks (my Lady was a great one for lists), which I was required regularly to undertake. On alternate days, beginning on Mondays, I was to strew dried tea-leaves over the carpets in her rooms, and then sweep them all off again. On Mondays also, all the looking-glasses, of which there were several, as well as various other items of glass-ware, were to be cleaned. On Wednesdays, the books were to be taken down from the shelves and dusted; and on Fridays, the wainscotting and panel-work were to be polished.

Every other Saturday I had to lay out all my Lady's dresses, one by one, whether summer- or winter-wear, and regardless of whether they had been worn or not, and carefully examine them, brushing every one, removing any stains or other dirtying, and making any necessary repairs, before returning them to their respective ward-robes and presses. This proved to be an arduous task indeed, as well as a generally pointless one – several hours of brushing over wool and tweed, rubbing silk gowns with merino, shaking out and ironing tumbled muslin – which made me dread the prospect, for it left me with no time for myself, and I would always return to my room after supper with no other thought than to fall, exhausted, on my bed. Often I would wake several hours later, in the silent darkness, still fully clothed.

One or two afternoons a week, my Lady paid her calls, obliging me to accompany her to various houses in the vicinity, where I would pass the hours in some dark room below stairs, often tucked away in a corner on my own. I was happy enough, however, for I always took a book with me, and soon became blissfully engrossed in some tale of mystery or adventure. Some of the servants in these places considered me proud, I dare say; but I paid no heed to that. It was a relief to be free, even for a short time, from the need to play my usually accommodating character and simply please myself.

In the evenings, of course, I would dress my Lady for dinner, and then prepare her room for retirement. When she returned, she would usually ask me to read from one of Mr Phoebus Daunt's interminable epics, or sometimes (blessed relief!) a few of his more palatable lyrics; then, while she took her evening walk on the terrace, I would make everything snug for her return, when I would undress her, and see her to her bed.

Oh, the tedious and hand-roughening tasks I was required to carry out! The darning; the washing; the preparation of hair-washes, pomatum, and bandoline; the cleaning of brushes and combs, the sponging of collars with gum-dragon in water! The sole task to which I always looked forward was the replenishing of my Lady's scent-bottles. I convinced myself that it was but a very minor transgression – and no more than my due – occasionally to decant a little of some of my favourites for my own private use.

On the Friday afternoon of my first week, my Lady having gone out without me, I had taken one of her lace collars back up to my room to mend, wishing also to write in my Book, which I had been too tired to do the previous evening.

After an hour or so, thinking that she had not yet returned, I went back down to my Lady's apartments with the intention of returning the collar to its rightful place and entered without knock-

ing, only to find her seated on the sofa, a gentleman of most striking appearance by her side.

'Oh, my Lady!' I cried, alarmed at my indiscretion. 'Forgive me.
I thought—'

'Alice, dear,' she said, turning as she spoke towards her visitor.
'We have a guest. This is Mr Armitage Vyse.'

6

In Which Madame's First
Letter is Opened

I

Introducing Mr Vyse

ON SEEING him, I racked my brains for the word – the exact
word – to describe the singular person of Mr Armitage
Vyse.

My immediate impressions of him, later written down in my
Book, were as follows:

MR. ARMITAGE VYSE
Appearance: aged forty or forty-five? A spare, lean, lanky
man: long-bodied, long-armed, long-legged (exceptionally
so). Gives the impression of unusual energy and strength
held back, but in constant readiness. Sinewy. Straight black
eye-brows. Square-boned, clean-shaven, blue-blushed chin.
Clipped side-whiskers. Luxuriant moustache, the ends straight
and waxed – a little like Napoleon III, tho' not near so long,
but which gives him a rather un-English look. Thick black
hair, a little wavy at the sides, pomaded and brushed back
from the forehead and temples. Remarkably long straight
nose, quite pointed. Eyes small and dark – cold but alert.
Striking in every way – handsome even, tho' not to my taste

at all. Expensively suited. Black-and-white checked waistcoat with black silk lapels. Gold watch on heavy chain. Large signet-ring on right hand. Crisp white linen. Boots polished to perfection.

Character: self-regarding, self-assured, and predatory. A selfish, wholly self-interested man, I think, who sees the world as his private domain, and who gives the appearance of believing that everything, and everyone, in it has been placed there for his advantage or amusement.

Conclusion: clever and superficially charming, but devious and dangerous.

As I stand taking in these impressions, and finding myself – very much against my will – drawn to Mr Vyse's still, calculating eyes, the word I have been seeking to describe him suddenly comes to me.

It is *lupine.* Mr Vyse is a wolf; and everything about him is wolfish.

'How do you do, Alice?' he says, getting slowly to his feet and giving me a most agreeable, and no doubt well-seasoned, smile. Six feet tall, if he is an inch, he helps himself up by means of a silver-topped ebony stick. As he takes a step towards me, I see that he has some impediment in his right leg.

'I am well, sir, thank you,' I reply, dropping a little curtsey. I then ask my Lady whether I might take her mended collar through to the dressing-room. Having replaced the collar in its drawer, I am about to return when I hear Mr Vyse say to Lady Tansor:

'So that is the girl?'

'Yes,' she replies, *sotto voce.* 'But Mrs K said nothing to her.'

'You are sure?'

'Of course.'

I could not remain any longer, my ear to the half-open door, without arousing suspicion; so I rattled the handle, and went back into the sitting-room.

'By the by, Alice,' said Lady Tansor, in a careless tone, 'on Mr Vyse's advice, I wrote to Miss Gainsborough requesting confirmation of the character that she provided. Mr Vyse, being a legal man, is scrupulous in matters of business, and says that it was remiss of me not to have done this immediately on offering you the position. But I was unexpectedly charmed by you, and so did not do what I would normally have done, when engaging a new servant. Of course it is a mere formality.'

'A mere formality,' reiterated the smiling Mr Vyse.

'I have, in fact, just received Miss Gainsborough's reply.'

She picked up a letter from the escritoire. I glanced nervously at the handwriting, but saw immediately that it was neither Madame's nor Mr Thornhaugh's.

'Everything is in order, as I naturally expected that it would be,' said Lady Tansor.

'Absolutely as expected,' repeated Mr Vyse, with another archly reassuring smile.

'Thank you, my Lady,' I replied, relieved that Madame's careful arrangements had proved so effective. 'Will you need me at my usual time this evening?'

'Yes, Alice. You may go now.'

AT THE APPOINTED time, I returned to Lady Tansor's apartments to dress her for dinner.

'What did you make of Mr Vyse, Alice?' she asked, as she stood viewing herself in her dressing-glass.

'I do not know, my Lady,' I replied. 'He seems a very amiable gentleman.'

'Amiable? Why yes, Mr Vyse can be very amiable indeed, when he chooses. What else?'

'I really cannot say, my Lady.'

'Cannot, or will not?' she then asked, apparently made peevish by my reluctance to give a fuller opinion of her visitor. 'Come, come, Alice. I know you must have more to say about Mr Vyse than this, even on so brief an acquaintance. We shall not get along, you know, if you cannot be frank with me when I ask you to be.'

'I assure you, my Lady—'

'Assure me! You dare to assure me!'

The look that I had seen when she had told me that I must always address her as 'my Lady' had now transformed her features, like a sudden black cloud blotting out the sun, and she stood before me visibly enraged, although I could not comprehend how my behaviour could have made her react in this way.

'It is not your place to assure me of anything, but to do as I ask, when I ask. You have an opinion of Mr Vyse. I know it, and you will tell me it.'

I stand for a moment considering how I should reply; but then she places her hands against her temples and turns away, as though in pain. I understand then that her angry words have some other cause.

'Are you quite well, my Lady?' I asked.

'Yes, yes,' she snapped. 'Please do not fuss. I wish you simply to tell me what you think of Mr Vyse, and then go. Did you like him?'

I respectfully protested that it was not my place to express any opinion concerning Mr Vyse, especially whether I liked him or not, knowing nothing whatsoever about him; but she would have none of it. I bridled under her ill-humoured stubbornness; but, pressed again, I concocted a bland summary of my impressions, concluding with the observation that Mr Vyse had seemed to be a man possessing great natural abilities, something that was always apparent in a certain type of man (where this confident pronouncement came from, I cannot think), adding that he consequently appeared to me to be someone to whom one could safely turn for advice and help in a difficult situation, and be certain that both would be forthcoming.

'Forgive me, Alice.'

Without saying another word, my Lady walked quickly across to the bed-chamber, closing the door behind her.

I waited for over ten minutes, to see whether she would come out; but her door stayed shut. At last I went back up to my room, expecting to be rung for at any moment.

Half an hour or more went by. When the bell still did not ring, I went downstairs to the Crimson-and-Gold Dining-Room and peeked through the partly open door.

She was there, at the head of the table. Mr Vyse and Mr Perseus Duport were sitting opposite each other, just below her; Mr Randolph sat next to his brother, down the table, and furthest from his mother.

A transformation had occurred. She now looked vivacious and composed, turning first to her eldest son, and then to Mr Vyse, with some observation or opinion, smiling and laughing, exchanging pleasantries, and appearing in every way untroubled by whatever had caused her recent distress of mind.

Of her younger son, she appeared almost unaware, and neither she nor the other two gentlemen made any attempt to include him in the general conversation. Consequently, Mr Randolph sat consuming his dinner and drinking his wine in isolated silence, leaving the others to their talk.

Mr Perseus Duport had only that afternoon returned to Evenwood, after spending a few days in London, and this was the first time that I had seen him since our chance meeting on my first morning.

Sitting now next to his younger brother, the disparity in person between the two was even more marked than I had remembered. Unlike Mr Randolph, the impress of Lady Tansor on the elder brother was most striking – not only in the many physical resemblances, but also in several little mannerisms that I had begun to notice in my mistress: the way he would tilt his head back slightly and look down his nose when Mr Vyse spoke to him, just as I had seen his mother do when she was being addressed; the slight pursing of the lips as he deliberated on some question; above all, his ability to assume, in an instant, a discomposing, unflinching gaze, which turned his handsome face into a frozen mask.

Which of the two brothers did I like best? Or did I like them equally, each in his own individual way? This was a guessing game that I had sometimes amused myself with since my arrival at Evenwood. At first, I had been sure that I liked the younger more than the elder. Mr Randolph's readily bestowed smile soon made me look forward eagerly to his company; and, as our acquaintance increased, I found him to be just as considerate, unaffected, and as touchingly self-deprecating as he had appeared on first meeting him. He seemed also to have inherited his father's reported capacity to associate easily and naturally with everyone, be they high or low. Yet the more I played this little game with myself – in private moments, or when I observed the brothers together – the more Mr Perseus began to assume a dominance in my thoughts, and often in my dreams as well. Whether I truly liked him more than Mr Randolph, I could not say. I knew, and saw, so little of him, for he was in the habit of shutting himself up in his study for long hours, scratching away, to the exclusion of all else, at his Arthurian drama. Yet, curiously, I seemed to think of him all the more for the absence of his physical person. Every day, as I passed through the vestibule, I developed a habit of stopping for a moment to glance at the portrait of the Turkish Corsair, knowing full well that Mr Perseus would instantly rush into my head, the resemblance between the heir and the painted image being, to my eye, so remarkable. As the weeks passed, I also began to grow a little vexed when some of my fellow servants occasionally denigrated him in my hearing for an imagined demonstration of his overbearing and self-regarding nature, being certain in my own heart – although I had not the least reason for believing so – that he did not deserve their censure.

As I stood now, peering at the brothers taking their dinner with their mother and Mr Vyse, I was suddenly aware of someone standing close behind me.

''Ullo? Wot's your game, then? Spy in the camp!'

The grinning speaker was a well-covered youth of about eighteen, in livery, with apple-red cheeks, unruly hair that refused to accept the discipline of copious amounts of pomade, and wearing a collar that was far too tight for him. He was carrying a tray of ices, but seemed in no particular hurry to dispense the dainties to the awaiting diners.

'And who might you be?' I enquired.

'Skinner, Charlie,' he announced, adding, with a wink, 'but you don't need to tell me who *you* are. I already knows. Sukie Prout told me. You're Miss Gorst, and I'm pleased – *very* pleased – to make your acquaintance.'

I was conscious of his eyes travelling up and down my person, but in such a comically undisguised and transparent way that I could not take offence.

'Well, Charlie Skinner,' I replied, 'I'm glad to know you also. Are you a friend of Sukie's?'

'More than that,' he said. 'We're cousins.'

'And do you know where I can find your cousin at this hour? Will she be at home?'

'Most certainly,' said Charlie. 'And once I've finished here, I can take you there, if you'd like.'

I told him that there was no need, as I already knew where Sukie and her mother lived. At this his face fell with disappointment.

'Wait a bit,' he said, suddenly looking over my shoulder towards a nearby window. 'You can't go now, miss. It's already getting dark, and the rain's come on.'

It was true. The last evening light remaining when I had first come down had now quite gone, and raindrops were running in little rivulets down the glass.

'Very well, Charlie Skinner. When you next see your cousin, please to tell her that Miss Gorst sends her very best compliments and requests a word with her, at her earliest convenience. Will you do that?'

'Yes, miss, that I will,' he replied, throwing his shoulders back, like a soldier on parade, and with such gusto that I feared he would drop his tray.

Just then, Mr Pocock emerged from the service door.

'Now then, Skinner,' he said, severely, 'what's all this? Look lively with those ices, boy, before they melt.'

'Yes, Mr Pocock,' replied Charlie, hurrying into the dining-room, giving me another wink as he passed.

'Oh, miss,' said Mr Pocock, 'there was a letter for you in the bag this afternoon. Manners should have brought it up to you, but I've just seen that it's still on the table, by the front door. Would you like me to fetch it for you?'

Telling him that I would get it myself, I quickly made my way to the vestibule, retrieved the letter, and – with a brief glance at the

Turkish Corsair – hurried upstairs to my room, locking the door behind me.

HAVING LIT MY lamp, I sat down at my table, holding in my trembling hands the first of the three Letters of Instruction that Madame had promised to send me, in which she had undertaken to set out, progressively, information that would make clear the nature of the Great Task, and inform me of what she had called 'other matters', which it was necessary for me to know.

Out of the envelope tumbled several sheets of paper, written over in Madame's distinctive hand, and several more printed pages, folded, and held together at the corner by a silver pin. Putting these to one side, I spread the sheets out beneath the light of the lamp, and began to read.

II
Madame de l'Orme to Miss Esperanza Gorst
LETTER 1

Maison de l'Orme
Avenue d'Uhrich, Paris

DEAREST CHILD,—

When you read this, my first Letter of Instruction, you will have commenced yr new life at Evenwood. I can easily picture to myself how you must be feeling – alone, so far removed from everything that is familiar & dear to you, amongst strangers, in a strange house, and still uninformed of why you have been sent there. So let me now begin, as I promised, to set you on the road to understanding, although it must for now be but a very little step.

You must – you shall – know everything needful, as time goes on; & what I shall reveal to you, very soon, will concern your own history, as well as that of others, with whom yours is indissolubly bound up. But, first, you must understand more concerning your mistress; for, as I have often impressed upon you, it is imperative *that you secure her trust – her absolute trust – and also her affection; for without these, you will not succeed in the task you are there to accomplish.*

Her heart, as I have previously told you, is locked against all common assault; and yet, like many proud and self-contained individuals, she is susceptible to the attractions of a single close companionship, in which she can feel herself to be the superior party, and which allows her to control and regulate those confidences with which she has chosen to favour the other. You must become such a companion.

Yet she is fickle, & ruled by iron self-interest. You may not depend on a continuity of approbation or favour from her: both must be constantly earned. Be the complaisant, acquiescent companion she craves; but know this, dear child: she can never *be your friend, however much she may protest otherwise; for her interests and yours are, & will always be, utterly opposed, as shall be revealed to you in due course.*

In a word, although it may be hard for you to believe now, she is – and will always be – your enemy. *Know this; understand only this; let this be your watchword, your one guiding principle, in everything you do at Evenwood; for by knowing what she truly is, you will always have an advantage over her.*

Never let your guard slip; & never succumb *to her flattery. Be always vigilant; mistrust her at all times, as you would a serpent in the grass.*

Above all, seek to understand her weaknesses. The greatest of these – her cardinal passion – is the blind worship of the man to whom she was engaged to be married, Mr Phoebus Daunt. I say that this is a weakness because it deprives her, like all consuming and abiding passions, of reason; and this must always be of profit to you.

I have told you something of Mr Daunt. By way of supplementation, I am sending the enclosed printed pieces, which I ask you to read, note carefully, & then destroy.

This is all I wished to say at present; but you may depend on a further communication from me soon.

I pray for you every night, my dearest child, & think of you every hour of the day. Be strong — have courage. You cannot conceive the prize that awaits you if we are granted success in what we have undertaken.

Write when you can.

Mr Thornhaugh sends his very best regards.

My love always,

M.

I SAT FOR some time, staring into the darkness beyond my window.

I had hoped that Madame's letter would have fortified my resolve, and spurred me on in the prosecution of my task, but it had not done so. All was still vague, and undefined.

Lady Tansor's interests and mine were apparently irreconcilable, yet I did not know why, or, indeed, what those interests were. I must bring my mistress down, yet I did not know why, or how I was to do it. I was a blind soldier, sent weaponless into battle, fighting for an unknown cause, against an enemy towards whom, in my present state of knowledge, I felt no animosity.

Could I believe the little Madame had chosen to tell me? I supposed I must, for she would never deceive me. This was my only comfort, and to this I knew I must cling.

Tearing a dozen or so pages from my note-book, I began to write – row after row, column after column – until my hand ached:

Lady Tansor is my *Enemy*.

Lady Tansor is my *Enemy*.

Lady Tansor is my *ENEMY*.

7

In Memoriam P.R.D.

I

Extract from The London Monthly Review

1ST DECEMBER 1864

LAYING MADAME's letter aside, I picked up the two printed enclosures. Both consisted of pages clipped from the *London Monthly Review*.

The first was an article taken from the December issue for the year 1864. The occasion was the anniversary of the murder of Phoebus Daunt, ten years earlier.

Madame had marked certain paragraphs for my attention, and had also underlined individual words and phrases. I read the article through twice, to fix its contents in my head; then I transcribed the salient paragraphs into my Book, before throwing the original pages on the fire.

IN MEMORIAM P. RAINSFORD DAUNT
1819–1854

The brutal, and apparently senseless, murder of the celebrated poet, Phoebus Rainsford Daunt, on the 11th December 1854, was a national sensation, and for a brief time eclipsed even the news from the Crimea. Those of us who were living in London at that period will never forget the sickening horror of the event.

Following the tragedy, a torrent of outrage naturally flowed from the pages of the public press, and from the justifiably indignant and anxious mouths of all sections of educated society, as they gathered together at table that cold Christmas.

That the author of such deathless, and universally commended, works as *The Pharaoh's Child* and, his most acclaimed achievement, *The Conquest of Peru*, could be struck down in the house of a peer of the realm – and so consequential a peer as the 25th Baron Tansor – seemed to many of us to threaten the very foundations of modern British civilization. The cry went up in every quarter: 'Something must be done!' If a gentleman could not consider himself to be safe from mortal harm as he smoked a cigar in the garden, after taking his dinner in Park Lane, surrounded by friends and guests from the highest ranks of Society, including the Prime Minister himself, where could refuge from criminal violence be found?

At that dinner, Mr Daunt had been toasted as the heir to Lord Tansor's property and business concerns, his Lordship lacking a son or daughter of his own to succeed him. Lord Tansor had always regarded Mr Daunt with exceptional favour – and rightly so. Through his influence, he had been sent to Eton, as a Colleger on the Foundation. Popular and naturally gregarious, he had prospered there, securing the highest academic prizes the School could offer, and then proceeding to Cambridge, as a Scholar of King's College, the recipient of the unfeigned admiration of his many friends.

He duly took his degree, soon after which he commenced his literary career by publishing his first volume of poems, *Ithaca: A Lyrical Drama*, which appeared under the imprint of Mr Edward Moxon in 1841. The success that greeted *Ithaca* was instantaneous. Encouraged by the reception given to his first attempt at dramatic verse, the poet immediately began to compose a more ambitious work, in the epic style this time, entitled *The Maid of Minsk*. Once again, the critics were unanimous in their praise, and the volume sold in gratifyingly large numbers for Mr Moxon. A succession of notable works followed, each one increasing Mr Daunt's reputation as one of our finest narrative poets.

Turning now to the circumstances and motivations that culminated in the poet's death, they remain both mysterious and unresolved. The identity of his murderer, a certain Edward Glyver, is not in doubt. He and Mr Daunt were at Eton together – indeed, they enjoyed a close friendship for much of their time there; but a falling-out in their last year at the School had given this Glyver cause to hate his erstwhile friend, although whether the injury that he felt he had suffered at Mr Daunt's hands was real or imagined remains an open question.

Those who knew him best consider it impossible that Mr Daunt could ever have been capable, even as a school-boy, of behaviour so despicable, and so wounding, that it could have impelled a person to commit murder against him after an interval of eighteen years; a person, moreover, who, by all accounts, was once genuinely attached to his future victim.

After leaving Eton, which he did rather precipitately in 1836, on the death of his mother, Edward Glyver quit England to study at the University of Heidelberg, after which he travelled for several years on the Continent. He did not return to England until the year 1848, when he secured employment, taking the false name of Edward Glapthorn, in the distinguished firm of City solicitors, Tredgold, Tredgold & Orr, of Paternoster Row, for many years legal advisers to the Duport family, where he worked under the direct supervision of the Senior Partner, the late Mr Christopher Tredgold, although it would appear that he had received no legal training of any kind.

It further appears that, through his position at Tredgolds,

Glyver had discovered Lord Tansor's resolve to leave his property to Mr Daunt, and that this reanimated his antagonism towards the latter, compounded now by bitter envy that his hated former school-friend stood fair to inherit so much, when he himself lived on a modest salary.

Yet still he took no action, but seemed content with watching his victim from the shadows. Then, in the autumn of 1854, some crisis occurred that brought on the final catastrophe. What had been smouldering in the depths of Glyver's deranged being for so long now burst forth, to lethal purpose.

It seems probable that the engagement of Mr Daunt to the former Miss Emily Carteret, now Lady Tansor, was the spark that ignited the final conflagration; for it is known that Glyver – still using the name Glapthorn – had visited Miss Carteret in Northamptonshire, ostensibly as Mr Tredgold's surrogate on legal business connected with her late father's affairs. Miss Carteret testified that Glyver soon began to pay her unwelcome attentions, which she found she could not evade, even when staying with a relative in London. To discourage his visits, which became increasingly distasteful to her, Miss Carteret was obliged to absent herself from her home at Evenwood for long periods; but Glyver continued to harass her until, at last, she was forced to tell him of her impending marriage to Mr Daunt, before insisting – in the strongest terms – that he must not call on her again.

Thus jealousy now augmented injured pride and material envy in the disordered mind of Edward Glyver. What had begun as a school-boy quarrel appears to have become an imperative desire to rid himself, once and for all, of the man whom, in his deluded rage, he saw as having irreparably blighted his own amorous intentions – entirely fantastical and unreciprocated – towards Miss Carteret.

So the end came, as all the world knows, on the 11th December, in the year 1854, at the now infamous dinner given by Lord Tansor at his house in Park Lane to celebrate the engagement of Mr Daunt and Miss Carteret, and to mark the conclusion of the legal arrangements that made Mr Daunt heir to his Lordship's material possessions.

In the guise of a footman, Glyver followed Mr Daunt into the rear garden, and there took his long-contemplated revenge by stabbing him to death. He left behind a most bizarre offering: the stiffening fingers of the corpse's right hand were found to be clutching a copy, made by the murderer himself, of lines taken from Mr Daunt's celebrated lyric 'From the Persian', on the association of night and death.

Despite the best and most prolonged efforts of the police, the murderer has remained at large. Whether he is still alive or dead, in England or abroad, no one can say. If he has been called to his Maker, then it is fervently to be hoped that he now suffers in eternity the punishment for his wickedness that he escaped on earth.

At Lord Tansor's generous insistence, the poet was laid to rest in the Duport Mausoleum at Evenwood, on the 20th December, 1854. Ten years have now passed since the world awoke to the news that Phoebus Rainsford Daunt had been cut down at the height of his powers, and with an even more brilliant future before him.

As the anniversary of that dreadful night approaches, it has seemed fitting to offer this brief, and necessarily incomplete, account to the British public, in order to commemorate Mr Daunt's many literary achievements, and to pay tribute to the man himself – a man of instinctive probity and generosity, whose conviviality, perfect manners, and natural wit, endeared him to a wide circle of friends and acquaintances, amongst whom the present writer is proud to have been numbered.

A.V.

As I PONDERED the concluding initials, it did not take long to be convinced that the memorial's author could have been none other than lupine Mr Armitage Vyse, who had taken his dinner with my Lady in her Crimson-and-Gold dining-room that very evening.

What role this distinctive and, I was sure, dangerous gentleman now played in my Lady's life, I could not imagine. Another mystery, then, to add to the puzzle of 'Mrs Kennedy'.

Laying conjecture aside for the moment, I now turned to the second of the printed enclosures.

II

Extract from The London Monthly Review
1ST JANUARY 1865

LIKE THE FIRST, the second cutting had been taken from the *London Monthly Review*, this time from the correspondence columns. It had been written by a subscriber to the magazine in response to the previous month's memorial article on Phoebus Daunt by 'A.V.' It, too, carried inked markings made by Madame, emphasizing points she particularly wished me to note. Along the top of the first page she had written the following note: 'E.— This is sent, as you will immediately see, as a <u>necessary</u> corrective to the other. Note it well. M.'

As before, having studied the cutting, and written out the relevant excerpts in my Book, I committed the original to the flames.

Heath Hall, Co. Durham

26th December, 1864

SIR,—

The article, 'In Memoriam P. Rainsford Daunt', by 'A.V.', which appeared in the December issue of your magazine, has just been brought to my attention. I hope you will allow me space in your columns to offer a reply.

Your anonymous contributor is to be congratulated for remind-

ing the British public of the terrible events of the 11th of December, 1854. I have no desire to speak ill of the dead, especially of a public figure such as the late Mr Phoebus Daunt, who suffered so dreadful, and so entirely undeserved, a death. However, as someone who may claim some personal knowledge of both the victim and the perpetrator, I feel bound to offer another view of the two principal figures in the tragedy.

Having been in College at Eton from 1832 to 1839, I had ample opportunity to observe the respective characters of Mr Daunt (whom I also knew later at Cambridge) and his friend, Edward Glyver. As a consequence, I think I may say, without fear of contradiction, that the impression given by 'A.V.' of the former's character lays itself open to challenge.

I must reiterate that it is not my intention to besmirch the posthumous reputation of Mr Phoebus Daunt. To the assertion of 'A.V.' that, in the opinion of those who knew him best, Mr Daunt was incapable of a despicable or wounding act, I therefore make no reply; except to recall the words of St Paul: that we all fall short of the glory of God, and to observe that some of us fall further than others. Let me, instead, confine myself to facts.

One might infer, from some of the remarks made by 'A.V.', that Mr Daunt had a wide circle of friends at Eton, of which Mr Glyver was but one. This was not the case. Indeed, the future poet seemed rather disinclined, than otherwise, to put himself in the way of approbation by his fellows. Until he was in the Sixth Form, indeed, I cannot remember him having any other companion than Mr Glyver, to whom he constantly attached himself. This signal fact, however, goes unmentioned by 'A.V.', and was the more remarkable because Mr Glyver enjoyed almost a superfluity of friends, Oppidans as well as fellow Collegers, and had no need to confine himself to the company of Mr Daunt, which he often did to the detriment of his own social interests.

Mr Glyver, by contrast with Mr Daunt, was universally admired and liked, and for good reason. He was, in all respects, a rare soul: personable, a most stimulating companion, and gifted with an exceptional and capacious mind. These qualities, combining with great physical prowess, which he demonstrated frequently on the river, the cricket field (for his innings against Harrow in '36 he became a hero in all our eyes), and in the annual Wall Game, made him one of the most popular boys in the School. Here, then, is another material omission in the account by 'A.V.' – all the more puzzling because of Mr Daunt's own fulsome recollections of his friend in the article 'Memories of Eton', which the poet published in the Saturday Review *in October 1848. A man may change, of course, for better or worse; but one's experience of him at fifteen or sixteen is usually a tolerable indication of his mature character. This I would certainly judge to be true of Edward Glyver.*

I hold no brief to defend Mr Glyver – there can be no defence for striking a man down in cold blood, whatever may be urged in mitigation. I write merely as someone who once knew him, and who does not wholly disdain the memory. Nothing can exonerate him for his heinous deed; and that he escaped punishment under the full rigour of the Law is to be deplored by every right-thinking person. I venture to maintain, however, that this atrocious act was not the consequence of some inherent mental deficiency, of which, to my knowledge, Mr Glyver had never shown the slightest sign, despite what 'A.V.' implies.

I am not qualified to judge whether common envy of Mr Daunt's expectations under the terms of Lord Tansor's will, or blind jealousy with respect to the lady (now ennobled) to whom Mr Daunt was engaged, may have combined with some residue of an earlier alienation to produce sufficient cause for Mr Glyver to commit murder. It is a possible view of the case, certainly, although perhaps an incomplete one for those who can claim greater familiarity with Edward Glyver than 'A.V.'

Shunning further speculation, I will only make this final point. To paint Mr Glyver as being other than he was is to do no service to the memory of his victim, who, through several of the most formative years of his life, regarded that gentleman – for gentleman he was – as the truest of friends.

'Mysterious' and 'unresolved' are the words used by 'A.V.' to describe the circumstances that led to the death of P. Rainsford Daunt. I sincerely and utterly deplore the manner of that death, and share the

hope of 'A.V.' that, if still living, his murderer may yet be brought to justice, or, if dead, that he has come to that judgment to which we all must submit. Nevertheless, the facts in the case are few, the unattested conjectures many — to which 'A.V.' has added several of his own. It is to be further hoped that time may one day reveal the plain truth of what uncorroborated supposition and blinkered prejudice continue to obscure.

I remain, sir,
Yours most sincerely,
J. T. HEATHERINGTON

IT WAS APPARENT that Madame had wished me to judge the article by 'A.V.' in the light of Mr Heatherington's critical reply. Yet, taking both at face value, I could not help wondering which of the opposing views was to be believed. For all my instinctual suspicions of Mr Vyse, his almost certain authorship of the encomium on Phoebus Daunt did not necessarily invalidate his estimation of the poet's character, or that of his murderer. Conversely, I had no means of knowing whether Mr Heatherington's opposite view of both could be relied upon.

The greater question, however, was what the murderer, Edward Glyver, had to do with me, or with the Great Task, and why Madame wished me to form a more favourable opinion of him than the one contained in Mr Vyse's memorial. To this, I had been given no answer.

I was wearied with puzzles, and vexed with Madame for putting still more into my poor befuddled head. So, tired and confused, and having written up my Book, to bed I went; for I was needed early by my Lady.

⚜ END OF ACT ONE ⚜

ACT TWO

SECRET STIRRINGS

Then I saw that there was a way to Hell,
even from the gates of Heaven.

JOHN BUNYAN, *The Pilgrim's Progress* (1678)

8

Professor Slake is Buried

I
The Road to Barnack

THE CARRIAGES in which we were to travel to Barnack, for the funeral of Professor Slake, were called for ten o'clock.

At a minute or so past the hour, I followed my Lady down the steps into the Entrance Court, where Mr Perseus Duport and his brother, together with the other members of the party, were already assembled.

The day had broken cloudy and a little chill; but now there was a faint promise of sunshine, and a delicious woody smell of early autumn percolating through the damp air, which instantly called up memories of misty September mornings walking with Madame in the Bois de Boulogne.

My Lady had spoken little as I had dressed her, and I had made no attempt to engage her in conversation. Her face was pale and drawn as Barrington helped her into the carriage; and when she had taken her seat, she turned her eyes wearily towards the western woods. Although she had not sent for me during the night, I could see that the terrors had been upon her once more.

Another carriage had been provided to convey Mr Lancing, my Lady's land-agent; Mr Baverstock, her secretary; the Rector (*sans* wife), who was to officiate for the Vicar of Barnack, Mr Candy; and myself. I was about to make my way towards it when my mistress called out to me:

'No, Alice. You shall come with us.'

'Yes, do, Miss Gorst. There's plenty of room.'

Thus Mr Randolph Duport, who stood by the carriage, an inviting smile lighting up his face, his hand held out ready to assist me up the step.

It was such a signal mark of favour that I felt myself colouring, and hesitated for a moment; but he continued to hold out his hand, and so I took it lightly in mine, and quickly settled myself into my seat, opposite Lady Tansor. Mr Randolph then got in beside me, followed by his brother, dressed in a long black raglan, who seated himself next to his mother.

As Barrington closed the carriage door, I happened to glance back towards the house to see Mrs Battersby standing alone on the entrance steps observing our departure – observing too, no doubt, with disapproval, Mr Randolph's kindness towards me. Then we were off, heading westwards, through the broad tract of trees that bordered the Park wall, and onwards to the gates on the Odstock Road.

My Lady had continued to look fixedly out of the window, her face emotionless, save only for the tell-tale tightening of the mouth, which I had already come to recognize as a sure sign of some held-down turmoil within. Then, as we were approaching the gates, through the band of trees, she suddenly reached out and, almost angrily, drew down the blind. She did not raise it again until we had left the gates well behind us.

From the village of Odstock, our way took us north, through Ashby St John, and then on to the principal road from Easton to Stamford. Mr Randolph had several times tried, cheerfully but unsuccessfully, to engage his mother and brother in conversation, but both had responded to his attempts with barely a word of reply. Then, as we were leaving Ashby St John, he looked over at me and asked whether I knew anything of the late Professor Slake.

'Only that he was the Library's custodian,' I replied, feeling that, in the prevailing atmosphere of the carriage, I should say as little as possible.

'And a great scholar, by report,' returned Mr Randolph, 'though of course I know nothing about such things. You might not know, Miss Gorst, that he had lately completed the history of our family, begun by my grandfather?'

'You refer, I think, to Mr Paul Carteret?'

At my mentioning her father's name, my Lady gave me the most fearsome look, both indignant and angry; but she said nothing, and soon turned away again to stare impassively out of the carriage window.

'Slake may have been a good scholar, but he was far below grandfather in point of character and disposition.'

This from Mr Perseus, who was regarding his brother with ill-concealed displeasure.

'The generality of humankind,' Mr Perseus went on, in a cold censorious tone, 'pass through life like grazing sheep, untroubled by the mysteries that daily surround them. It is for the good of nations that they do so. Professor Slake, however, was of the diametric persuasion, one of that band of troublesome eccentrics who see mysteries and conundrums in everything, even when – as is nearly always the case – there is nothing remotely mystifying or inexplicable to be found. As a consequence, they make themselves an infernal nuisance to everyone else.'

'Enough, my dear,' said his mother softly, still gazing out of the carriage window. 'We must not speak ill of the dead.'

'But what you describe is a kind of higher curiosity, ain't it?' objected Mr Randolph. 'That must surely be something worthy of admiration.'

'Only if it is confined and directed aright,' retorted his brother. 'For a scholar, mental curiosity is, of course, a pre-requisite; in ordinary life, however, that same inquisitive inclination – in certain individuals – can easily become the lowest form of vulgar curiosity, making the enquirer nothing more than a common meddler in other people's private affairs.'

'Perseus, dear, did you speak to Dr Pordage, as I asked?'

Lady Tansor's question brought an end to Mr Perseus's little diatribe, during which I had tried to appear as detached from the exchange between the brothers as I could. I deliberately dropped my reticule, and then, after picking it up, took out my handkerchief to dab my eye, as if I had some speck in it, hoping by these actions to give an appearance of being too engaged with my own petty affairs to pay attention to what was being said.

'Pordage is going directly to Barnack with Glaister,' said Mr Perseus, 'but will return to Evenwood afterwards with Lancing and the others. There's room enough.'

With a cold glance towards me, which I was convinced expressed the view that there ought *not* to have been a vacant place in the other carriage, despite his mother's explicit invitation to me to accompany her and her sons, he pulled his raglan around him, and closed his eyes.

Mr Randolph, seeing my discomfort, raised his eye-brows in a considerate gesture of sympathy, and then gave me a smile, in which I read both apology for his brother's high-handed speech, and a wish to remind me that he and I enjoyed a degree of amity that already set us apart from the other occupants of the carriage.

On we rolled, along the high road to Stamford, which we reached in good time. At the crossroads by the George Hotel, the carriage turned along a road that led us past the gates of Burghley, the great house of the Cecil family, and on to the village of Barnack.

II

Earth to Earth

SINCE LEAVING STAMFORD, Mr Perseus had remained silent, his head laid back against the padded lining of the carriage, eyes closed. Then, as we came into Barnack, he suddenly opened them and looked straight at me.

'You are a great reader of poetry, I believe, Miss Gorst?' he said. 'Have you read mad Clare, one of our local peasant bards?'

I admitted that I had not.

'He used to frequent this place,' said Mr Perseus. 'Over there – what they call the Hills and Holes, where they took out the ragstone.'

He nodded towards a curious tract of broken-up ground, behind a group of cottages.

'You might mention Mr Kingsley also, dear.'

My Lady was now speaking, with a strained smile, as if she did so with considerable effort.

'Kingsley?' queried Mr Perseus. 'Oh, the Water-Babies man. He lived here as a child, I believe, Miss Gorst, when his father was Rector.'

'Your grandpapa told me that Mr Kingsley Senior came to dinner once at the Dower House,' said my Lady to Mr Perseus. 'I can even remember the year: 1829, in the week before my sister died.'

Her voice had taken on a strange, dreamy tone, and her forehead was damp with perspiration.

'Are you feeling unwell, Mother?' asked Mr Randolph, leaning towards her, and placing a solicitous hand on hers.

'Perfectly well, thank you, Randolph. As I told you at breakfast, I have awoken with a headache these past two days, which is why I asked Perseus to get Dr Pordage to come. But it is nothing. Ah, here we are.'

THE CARRIAGE HAD pulled up outside the ancient Church of St John the Baptist, where a numerous crowd of mourners and village onlookers had already gathered.

We descended, and the crowd dutifully parted – like the Red Sea before Moses – as my Lady and her two handsome sons, followed by the other members of the Evenwood party, with me bringing up the rear, processed in solemn order through the church-yard to take their seats in the places of honour that had been prepared for them.

As a measure of his eccentricity (for which I heartily commended him), Professor Slake had long since prepared strict instructions that his committal should be conducted with the utmost simplicity. Consequently, there was a welcome absence of the usual pomp and paraphernalia – no frightful bearded mutes and hideous feather-men, no black-draped coach, like some omnibus of death. I had witnessed such vulgar horrors in London, when I had stayed with Mrs Ridpath, and the sight had filled me with disgust.

The simple wooden coffin was conveyed into the church on a two-wheeled hand-cart, decked out with late-summer flowers and dark-blue ribbons (the Professor having been an Oxford man), and pulled by the deceased's gardener and his son. Behind the coffin walked the solitary figure of Mr Montagu Wraxall, Professor Slake's nephew and closest surviving relative (as I was later informed by Dr Pordage), holding before him – like an offering – a copy of his uncle's great work on the history of the Gentile nations (this infor-mation also being courtesy of Dr P).*

The service duly began, conducted by Mr Thripp – pompously conscious of the dignity that had been unexpectedly conferred upon him – who mounted the pulpit at the appointed moment to give us a full forty minutes of his prolix thoughts on mortality. As he drew at last to a close, to the visible relief of the congregation, the sound of heavy rain began to echo through the building.

'Just such a day as this when they buried Mr Carteret, your pre-decessor,' I heard Dr Pordage, sitting in the pew behind me, whis-per to Mr Baverstock.

'Just such a day,' agreed my Lady's secretary.

*Lucian Rawson Slake (1805–76), An Analytical and Descriptive History of the Gentile Nations (Smith, Elder, 1868), a comprehensive, but unfor-tunately almost unreadable history of the Assyrians, Babylonians, Medes, Persians, Greeks, and Romans. A rival work, by George Smith (1800–68), had been published by Longman, Brown, Green & Longmans in 1853. This must have been a blow to Slake, who had been working on his mag-num opus since 1833, but he continued with his work nevertheless. One fears it found few readers.

III
Pythagoras Lodge

THE DOWNPOUR – sudden, but short – had almost abated by the time we gathered round the grave-side; but it was still necessary for umbrellas to be hastily procured, and for we ladies to mind our skirts as we picked our way through the deep puddles that had formed along the rutted path.

When the coffin, with all due ceremony, had been lowered into the grave, the sides of which still oozed with muddy rivulets, Mr Wraxall moved forward, his uncle's book in hand. This he proceeded to wrap round with one of the long dark-blue ribbons that had adorned the hand-cart; then, kneeling down, he let the ribbon unfurl, allowing the book to fall gently on to the lid of the coffin.

No one, except me, seemed in the least surprised by this singular piece of ceremonial. Indeed, it appeared to have been anticipated by many of the mourners, for I heard one gentleman remark to another that it had long been talked about in the village that the Professor wished his life's work to be placed with him in the grave (although not in the coffin), so that it might be the first thing to come into the light at the Resurrection, which he confidently expected to take place on the first day of the year 1900.

A cold collation had been prepared for the most distinguished mourners – principal amongst whom, of course, was the Evenwood party – at the Professor's former home, Pythagoras Lodge, which stood a little way out of the village on the Helpston road.

From its name, I had expected some forbidding Gothick pile, and my hopeful imagination had pictured a miniature Otranto set down in the quiet East Anglian countryside. Instead, when the carriage came to a halt, I was a little disappointed to find ourselves before a neat little villa, not fifty years old, covered in dark-green trellis-work, and standing in the midst of a large square of perfectly tended lawn, the space broken only by an ancient cedar.

Mr Wraxall welcomed us in, and then escorted Lady Tansor into the morning-room, where the collation had been laid out on two long tables.

The late Professor Slake's nephew had intrigued me from the moment he had entered the church behind his uncle's coffin. He was – as confirmed by Dr Pordage – about sixty-five years of age, clean-shaven, and entirely bald except for the merest wisps of downy, pale-silver hair clustered about each ear. Yet he had an ageless radiance about him, making him appear to be unsullied and unburdened by the usual human woes and disenchantments. He displayed, in addition, such a vigorous and active intelligence in his smiling grey eyes that he might almost have been mistaken for a young man just embarking on life, full of ambition and boundless optimism.

I followed my Lady and her sons into the morning-room, but then held back as they stopped to be introduced by Mr Wraxall to a group of ladies and gentlemen, before they moved on to take their seats around the fire at the far end of the room. In that moment, Dr Pordage came up and, without my asking, began to tell me something of Mr Montagu Wraxall.

Although now retired from the Bar, in his heyday our host had been accounted one of the most formidable prosecuting barristers in London, with a reputation for rigorous and meticulous preparation of his cases, and for a certain intellectual ruthlessness in argument that few could equal. Many were the celebrated murder trials in which he had triumphed, sometimes against considerable odds. Despite his amiable personal qualities, to be prosecuted by Mr Montagu Wraxall, QC, was, it would seem, a fearsome prospect; and amongst the criminal classes of the capital, it was once held as an almost universal truth that Wraxall would hang you for sure if you came up before him on a capital charge.

'But modest, my dear,' confided the doctor, leaning towards me, and stroking his grey spade-beard by way of emphasis, 'almost incorrigibly so. And, do you know, I believe his modesty to be genuine. What do you think of that?'

I smiled mutely, then asked Dr Pordage whether he would be kind enough to bring me a glass of iced water, as my throat was a little dry.

Off he scampered; but he had hardly gone when Mr Wraxall himself was suddenly by my side and was introducing himself.

Of course I began by offering my condolences on the death of his uncle. I immediately saw that I had been foolish to think he was unsusceptible to universal cares. A shadow seemed to pass across his face.

'You are Miss Gorst, I'm certain,' he said. 'Your reputation precedes you.'

He saw my puzzled look, and smiled.

'I only meant to say that you are seen as being unusual, Miss Gorst, and that always starts country tongues wagging – although you should be flattered to be the subject of so much talk. You are a phenomenon, you know.'

'I'm sure I don't know what you mean, sir,' was my honest reply.

'Consider,' said Mr Wraxall. 'You neither look like a lady's-maid, nor speak like one; and I strongly suspect that you do not think like one either. Other people see the discrepancy, too, and they naturally wonder why such a person has been obliged to enter domestic service. I wonder that myself, you know. Now don't be cross with me.'

'Cross, sir?'

'For being so impertinent as to say what is simply true. I'm afraid that it's one of my principal failings – although of course I've many others.'

'Is it, then a fault to be truthful?'

'The truth is sometimes unpalatable, you know.'

He then said that he hoped he would have the pleasure of continuing our acquaintance at Evenwood.

'You may perhaps know that my late uncle was given use of the Lodge attached to the old North Gates, as a residence on those days his duties required him to be in the Library. There are a great many papers and other effects there to be gone through – I fear my uncle was a little lax, not to say disorganized, in the arrangement of his own affairs, although he was wonderfully efficient in conducting those of his employer. Lady Tansor has kindly allowed me to occupy North Lodge while this work is being carried out; and so our paths may well cross once more. I hope they do.'

So we parted.

I had begun to walk over to join my Lady and her sons when Dr Pordage called out to me.

'Miss Gorst! Your water!'

I had no choice but to turn back and take the glass from his hand, which closed clammily around mine as I did so, forcing me to pull away, spilling much of the water in the process.

'How clumsy of me!' he exclaimed, taking out his handkerchief. 'Do please forgive me, Miss Gorst.'

'It's nothing, sir. Excuse me.'

Handing back to him the almost empty glass, I quickly made my escape.

'And where have you been, Alice?' my Lady asked, in an irked tone. 'You should have been here with us.'

I told her that I had been speaking with Mr Wraxall.

'Speaking with Mr Wraxall! Well, well. Then I suppose I must forgive you.'

'Your dress is rather wet, Miss Gorst,' Mr Randolph broke in. 'Won't you come and sit by the fire to make it dry?'

I thanked him, but said that I preferred to stand.

'Come now, Miss Gorst, you really must dry yourself.'

The admonition came from Mr Perseus, who – to my considerable surprise – was now offering me his own chair.

'See how they compete for your favour, Alice,' said Lady Tansor. 'Was ever a lady's-maid so honoured?'

Whilst the little laugh that followed was meant to disguise the sting of the words, I saw that Mr Randolph had coloured slightly at them, although the face of Mr Perseus remained impassive as he stood, with his hands holding the back of the chair, waiting for me to sit down.

I thanked Mr Perseus for his consideration, which had seemed genuinely given, but politely insisted that I was perfectly comfortable.

'Very well,' he said. 'Then you'll excuse me, I hope. I'm in need of a cigar.'

'Will you not eat first, Perseus dear?' asked his mother. 'You ought, you know.'

'I have no appetite for luncheon,' he replied, somwhat sharply, 'and smoking on an empty stomach is a great stimulant for my work. I have the last canto of my poem to finish, as you know, and a cigar will help me to shape my thoughts.'

After he had gone, Lady Tansor turned to me.

'The demands of genius are very great, you see, Alice. They constantly force postponement of the commonest necessities of life. But where would we be without such rare individuals as my son, who strive only to bequeath beauty and harmony to the world? As the possessor of an uncommon poetic talent, Perseus feels his duty to the present generation, and to posterity, most keenly. We are to go to London soon – have I mentioned this to you? Perseus is to show his poem to a publisher. I am confident that he will like it, and that it will be a great success; but of course it must be finished first. And so he must do what he must, even though I do not quite approve of cigar smoking.'

Then, turning towards her younger son:

'Randolph, dear, I find that I am a little hungry after all. Will you fetch me a small piece of pie?'

9

In Which Madame's
Second Letter is Opened

I
A Vision of Judgment

IT IS now a little past first light, two days after the funeral of Professor Slake.

Mr Perseus has smoked a sufficient number of cigars to enable him to complete his poem on Merlin and Nimuë, and tomorrow we are for London, to visit the prospective publisher, and to spend some days in my Lady's town-house.

The late Lord Tansor's London residence in Park Lane, the scene of the murder of Phoebus Daunt, was sold as soon as my Lady succeeded to the title, in the year 1863. She now has a handsome house in nearby Grosvenor Square, although she spends little time there.

She called me down three times last night. On the first occasion, I was required to brush her hair; on the second, she wished me to read to her from Mr Daunt's *Penelope*;* then, at a little after three o'clock, she was content simply for me to sit opposite her, by the bedroom fire, as she silently contemplated the flickering flames.

'You must have been brought up a Catholic, I suppose?' she suddenly asked.

Penelope: A Tragedy, in Verse (Bell & Daldy, 1853).

I told her the truth: that I had attended church regularly as a child, and that I had learned my catechism and read the Bible regularly, but that my guardian, while devout herself, had chosen not to impose formal reception into the Roman faith on me. This, she always said, would have gone against the wishes of my Protestant father. I had thus been allowed to make my own choice on the matter, once I reached the years of discretion.

'And what was your choice?' my Lady enquired.

'I profess no single, exclusive creed or denomination; but I do have a kind of primitive faith nevertheless.'

'And what is that?'

'I believe,' I replied, seeing an opportunity to test my Lady's conscience, 'that there is an eternal creative Power, which we call God, and that we shall all come to judgment at the last under His all-seeing eye.'

The words were those of Mr Thornhaugh, and reflected his own religious convictions. The effect of them on my Lady was immediate.

'Judgment?'

The log that I had thrown on to the fire had suddenly burst into flame, illuminating her face. It had turned ghastly white, and I saw that she was gripping the arms of her chair, as if some invisible force were trying to wrench her from it.

'Enough of such talk,' she said, after some moments. 'I am tired now, and wish to sleep if I can.'

I helped her back into her monstrous carved bed, and drew the heavy red hangings round her, leaving open only those nearest the fire.

'Will that be all, my Lady?' I asked, when I had poured her out a glass of water.

'Yes, Alice. Good-night.'

She closed her eyes for a moment; and then, with a profound sigh, turned on her side, away from the firelight, her long dark hair starkly black against her white night-gown.

Good-night, my Lady, I thought to myself. *Sweet dreams.*

* * *

WHEN I AWOKE, to the soothing sound of pigeons cooing on the leads above me, I was surprised to find that I felt not the least bit fatigued, despite the disruptions of the night; and so I thought that I would take the dawn air before going to dress my Lady.

Drawing the curtains back, I looked out. The prospect that met my eyes was a dismal one.

A dirty, grey light was struggling into life, and thick, clinging mist, almost like the impenetrable white miasma in my nightmare of little Anthony Duport, obscured the view of the Park beyond the pleasure-grounds – a true early-autumn mist that heralded decay and rottenness. It brought to mind maggoty apples strewn across the damp grass of an untended orchard, and piles of stinking mildewed leaves, fleshy underfoot. Death was in the air. I shuddered, and was about to turn away, having abandoned my plan to walk about the grounds, when something caught my eye.

An indistinct figure – a well-built man – could just be made out, standing on the other side of the ha-ha that terminated the gardens.

I watched him for a minute or more, but he did not move. He was tall, wearing a chimney-pot hat, and was carrying a stick; but these were his only discernible characteristics. What was he doing at this hour, and on such a cheerless morning? Waiting for someone? Surely not, at such an early hour. More likely he was some wandering insomniac, pausing to take in the beauties of the house, which, even on such a drear morning, retained its power to stir the heart.

My warm breath having misted the glass, I began to rub it over with my sleeve. When I looked out once more, the man had gone, swallowed up by the enveloping vapour.

After breakfast, Barrington stopped me at the foot of the back stairs to give me a letter. I saw immediately that it was from Madame; but, having then to dress my Lady, as well as a full morning of other duties before me, it was not until luncheon was over that I was able to find time to return to my room and open it.

It was, as I had hoped, the second Letter of Instruction.

II
Madame de l'Orme to Miss Esperanza Gorst

LETTER 2

Maison de l'Orme
Avenue d'Uhrich, Paris

MY DEAREST CHILD,—

Yr letters are the greatest comfort to me. I keep them by me constantly, & re-read them as often as I can. For I, too, need to take courage; & with yr own example before me — so brave! so strong! — I am better able to ask of you what must be asked. Mr Thornhaugh also sends to say that he has nothing but the highest admiration for the way you are conducting yourself under the exacting circumstances in which you have been placed. I worry constantly about you, dear child, but Mr Thornhaugh has been a great support to me, having an unshakeable confidence in you, from which you too should take comfort and strength.

In yr last, you begged me again to reveal our ultimate ambition. It would be prudent to wait just a little longer before doing so, until yr relations with Lady T are firmly established. But I promise you, dear child, that I shall satisfy you on every particular, as fully and as clearly as I can, in my third letter, before the year is out.

I have said that yr mistress is yr enemy. You shall now know what more she truly is.

She is a deceiver, a liar, a betrayer of hearts; a faithless, false-hearted usurper; a complicit party to the most heinous crime imaginable.

You may reasonably ask, accepting that what I say is true, what bearing it has on the Great Task.

Be assured, dearest child, that injury & injustice have been done to you by this woman, who now calls herself yr mistress. I cannot say more — yet — for fear, as I have said, of jeopardizing yr position, before you have completely secured yr mistress's regard. And so I must submit to patience, as you must.

Mark but this. Lady T's present condition — the state of material and social grace that she has enjoyed for so long — is founded on duplicity, treachery — & worse. Proof — substantive & legally unanswerable — of her transgressions is what, for the moment, is lacking, but which I hope you will eventually help discover. By securing such documents, yr own interests will be served in ways that you cannot possibly imagine.

And now to a more immediate matter: Mr Armitage Vyse.

Yr news concerning this gentleman interests me greatly. As you guessed, he was undoubtedly the author of the highly prejudiced memorial to Mr Phoebus Daunt that I sent you. From enquiries that Mr Thornhaugh has managed to make, we know him to be a barrister, of Old Square, Lincoln's Inn, although he gave up his practice several years ago, & now lives as an independent gentleman. We know also that he was introduced to Mr Phoebus Daunt by a mutual friend — this provided the connexion with yr mistress (Miss Carteret, as she then was). He began to pay regular visits to Evenwood after the death of his friend Daunt, and these appear to have increased following the demise of Colonel Zaluski. We know further that Lady T has been to his chambers in Old Square several times in recent months. Legal business does not seem to be the reason for their continuing intercourse, for Lady T now retains the firm of Orr & Son of Gray's Inn, whose Principal, Mr Donald Orr, was formerly a partner in Tredgold, Tredgold & Orr, the family's previous legal advisers. It might have been expected that Lady T, on succeeding to the Barony, would have continued the family's long association with Tredgolds; but instead she appointed the new firm of Orr & Son, established after a dispute arose between Mr Donald Orr and Mr Christopher Tredgold.

We must naturally ask ourselves what business Mr Armitage Vyse is conducting with Lady T at present, when she has the services of Orr & Son ready to hand Mr Thornhaugh is of the opinion that a little more delving is required, through the agency of friends & former associates in London. For yr part, any further intelligence on Mr V's present relationship with yr mistress shd be sent to me immediately, & of course noted down in yr Book.

And so I must finish. Write soon, my dearest, for we ache to hear yr news, & to know that yr resolve is as firm as ever. Take every possible care, and believe that I shall always be,

Ever yr devoted,

M.

10

Dark House Lane

I
The Locket

I T WAS half past five by the carriage-clock on my mantel-piece: time enough to go down to the steward's room to take a little breakfast before dressing my Lady in preparation for our departure for London.

My head was still full of Madame's second co-called Letter of Instruction, which I had found as exasperating as the first in frustrating my desire for specific and definite guidance on how I should proceed in the Great Task.

I had been asked to expose my Lady to the world for what she truly was. And what was she? According to Madame, a deceiver, a liar, a betrayer of hearts, a faithless usurper – and much worse. Yet I could not see how the proof that would substantiate these accusations could be obtained. What was it? Where might it be found? Even if such proof were uncovered, how would the destruction of my Lady's character and reputation serve my own interests?

Once again, I had no choice but to accept Madame's words, opposing doubt and confusion with unquestioning duty and blind trust. I was resolved. Two Letters of Instruction had been received; the third was still awaited. If it did not make everything finally and unequivocally clear, then I would abandon the whole business and return to the Avenue d'Uhrich to face the consequences. In the meantime, having come thus far, and – I blush a little to admit it – continuing to find the prospect of adventure and intrigue rather thrilling (for which I unhesitatingly blame Mr Wilkie Collins), I would do my utmost to fulfil the one explicit instruction in Madame's second letter: to search for documents, if they existed, that would help prise out my Lady's secrets.

ON COMING INTO the servants' hall, the first person I saw was Sukie, sitting alone and sipping a mug of tea. Two other servants, neither of whom I knew by name, were talking together in the far corner, but took no notice of me as I entered. Glancing towards the steward's room, expecting Mr Pocock or Mr Applegate to be there, I saw that it was empty.

It had been a week since I had told Charlie Skinner that I wished to speak with his cousin, but I had heard nothing from her, nor had I seen her about the house. As I came into the hall, she looked up.

'Oh Miss Alice!' she exclaimed. 'I'm so glad to see you!' At which she burst into tears.

'Sukie, dear, whatever's the matter?'

I hurried to sit down beside her, and put my arm around her shoulders.

'Mother's been very poorly,' she sobbed, 'but was taken especially bad yesterday morning. Dr Pordage came in the afternoon, but says she may not see out the week. I've been that worried, Miss Alice, I can't tell you. And then Charlie said you wanted to speak with me, but Mrs Battersby sent me to help Kate Warboys clear out the attic in the East Wing, which has taken us all week, what with everything else, and it isn't done yet, and then—'

'Hush, dear,' I said, tucking one of her disobedient curls back under her cap, and reaching into my pocket for my handkerchief to dry her tears. 'It's of no consequence. What I wished to ask you can wait.'

At last she began to recover a little of her usual sunny temper.

Then, the great clock that hung over the fire-place striking a quarter to seven, she suddenly jumped up, saying that she must start her work before Mrs Battersby began her morning round of inspection and instruction, which she did on the stroke of seven.

'We are leaving for London today, Sukie,' I said, 'as I'm sure you know; but I shall come and find you when we return – and I hope, with all my heart, that Dr Pordage is wrong, and that your mother will be well and truly recovered by then.'

After Sukie had gone, I barely had time to butter myself a slice of bread, and pour out half a cup of strong tea from the pot that Sukie had brewed for herself, before I too had to run upstairs as fast as I could, in order to be at my Lady's door for seven o'clock.

When I had finished dressing her, and had performed all the other necessary morning duties, she asked me to bring her the box containing the tear-shaped locket from the dressing-table.

'I promised that I would satisfy your curiosity concerning this locket, Alice,' she said, 'and am minded to do so now.'

'Yes, my Lady. As you wish.'

She sat down, placed the box in her lap, and took out the locket on its black velvet band. When she pressed a little catch, the locket's silver face opened, to reveal a strand of thick, dark hair curled tightly inside.

'This,' she whispered, with awful solemnity, 'was taken from the head of Mr Phoebus Daunt, after he had been murdered. Does that shock you?'

'Why should it shock me, my Lady?' I replied. 'I believe you were once engaged to the gentleman. To keep such a memento by you seems a most natural and commendable thing to do.'

'I am glad you think so,' she said, closing the locket; 'but you do not fully understand, Alice. I cut it from his head myself, even as his life-blood still stained the snow on which he lay. I saw what had been done to him, with my own eyes; and the sight has never left me. It continues to rob me of healthful sleep, and yet I have put this locket on every day since, even when I was married to my late husband, Colonel Zaluski, in commemoration of that terrible event. Do you not find that strange, Alice? To yearn to be free of the perpetual recollection of that night, and yet to enforce constant remembrance of it on myself?'

She sat, staring down at the locket, her hands shaking. Then she looked up.

'And so I continue to wear it; and it is such a strict rule of mine that no one else – *no one* – shall ever touch it, or what it contains. You will respect that rule, I know, Alice.'

'Of course, my Lady. But it's a beautiful piece of work, and looks so well on you.'

With a gratified expression, she told me that the locket had been commissioned specially for her by the late Lord Tansor.

'His Lordship became almost like a father to me, after the tragedy. His exceptional consideration towards me – my own father having been so cruelly taken from me – is something I shall never forget; and so I wear the locket also in remembrance of him, to whom I owe so much. And now, Alice, we must rouse ourselves. The carriage will soon be here.'

She rose from her chair with a sudden rush of energy, and went over to her dressing-mirror. Placing the locket round her neck, she then turned to face me.

'There,' she smiled. 'My daily duty is done, and I am ready to face the world.'

II
In Grosvenor Square

THE CONFIDENCES THAT Lady Tansor had shared with me concerning the locket encouraged me greatly, for they demonstrated that I was already succeeding in securing my mistress's trust, despite her capriciousness and abrupt changes of mood.

The carriage that was to take us to catch the express-train from Peterborough was brought round to the front door at eight o'clock.

Mr Perseus Duport was already walking up and down the Entrance Court, pocket-watch in hand, and showing every sign of impatience, when my Lady and I came down the steps.

'Ah, there you are at last, Mother,' he cried, striding over to the carriage. 'Well, let's be off.'

We took our places and soon left Evenwood Park – still submerged beneath a sea of mist – behind us.

During the whole journey from Peterborough, Mr Perseus remained immersed in reading and correcting the manuscript of his poem, which he had taken out of his bag as soon as we had boarded the train. My Lady, by contrast, although she had provided herself with a book, seemed eagerly disposed to engage in conversation, and was soon asking me once again about my upbringing in Paris, where she too had lived for several years.

Madame had coached me most thoroughly in anticipation of such enquiries, and my Lady listened attentively as I recounted the little fiction that I had committed to memory, concerning 'Madame Bertaud', the supposed English-born widow of a Lyons silk merchant, whom Madame imagined had been the childhood companion of my dead mother.

'And have you no recollection of either of your parents?' my Lady asked.

'None, my Lady. They had come to Paris, I believe, just a short time before I was born, although they knew no one there but Madame Bertaud. My mother died when I was too young to remember her; and then, after her death, my father went away – I've never been told why, or where. I only know that he died in 1862, and that he is buried next to my mother, in the Cemetery of St-Vincent.'

It had been Mr Thornhaugh's suggestion to leaven our invention with a little judicious truth, against the chance that enquiries might be made by some agent of Lady Tansor's. In this event, the graves of my mother and father would be found just where I had said they were.

'And did your father follow a profession of any kind?'

Again, I was prepared.

'He was a gentleman of independent means. That is all I know of him.'

'And what of your mother? You say that she and your guardian were old friends.'

'Yes, my Lady. They grew up together. I believe she introduced my mother and father to each other.'

Still the questions came, and still I met every one with a confident and plausible answer. At last, apparently satisfied that she had informed herself sufficiently on my history, my Lady took up her book once more, and began to read; but after only a short time, she looked across at me to ask whether Mr Thornhaugh still resided in my guardian's house.

'Yes, my Lady. My guardian insisted that he should retain his rooms there, so that he might continue his researches.'

'But I suppose he has not been your tutor, as such, for some time?'

I replied that he had become more like an older friend, with whom I could converse freely, and on whose knowledge and advice I could always depend.

'And will he come to visit you at Evenwood, do you think? I should so like to meet him.'

I said I thought that such a prospect was an unlikely one, as Mr Thornhaugh was reclusive by nature.

'But could he not be persuaded, by some inducement, to forgo his eremitical existence, for just a very little while? The Library, now: that would tempt a man of books, would it not? But how thoughtless of me! Perhaps he is an elderly gentleman?'

'No, not elderly, my Lady.'

'Of what age, then?'

'I am not quite certain, my Lady. Perhaps five and fifty.'

'Not elderly at all, then, as you say. About my own age, indeed. So let us see whether the fascinating Mr Thornhaugh can be drawn out of his lair by the idea of exploring our celebrated Library at his leisure. Will you write to him, on my behalf? Your guardian, Madame Bertraud, would be most welcome to join him.'

I shamelessly thanked her for her kind invitation, and said that

I would convey it to 'Madame Bertaud' and Mr Thornhaugh. Of course I had no intention of doing so, and could not understand why my Lady appeared so desirous of making the acquaintance of my tutor and my imaginary guardian.

All this time, although I was sensible of occasional guarded glances in my direction, which I affected not to notice, Mr Perseus had been perusing his manuscript in concentrated silence. Only when we reached the outskirts of the metropolis did he at last put his papers away, remove the stub of pencil with which he had been making corrections from his mouth, and look about him.

'Well,' he said, turning to his mother, 'I believe it will do.'

'Do!' exclaimed my Lady, with all the indignance of a doting mother. 'Of course it will do. You are too modest, Perseus dear. It's a work of the highest merit, and you know it. Mr Freeth will know it, too, as soon as he reads it.'

Then, to me:

'Mr Freeth is the principal director of a new publishing firm, Freeth & Hoare, with great ambitions. He has been recommended to us as a man of the highest acumen and taste, who wishes to establish his firm as a publisher of the very best up-and-coming poets. Perseus, we are confident, will be one of the first such to have his work published by the firm.'

At the London terminus we were met by carriage and taken on to Grosvenor Square. After unpacking and hanging up her gowns, I was given leave by my Lady to inspect the accommodation that I had been allotted – a small but airy room on the third floor, looking southwards over the square. There I unpacked my own little case with a gay heart, feeling glad to be in the heart of a great city once more, although it was not the city I knew and loved.

An hour or so later, I was sent for by my Lady.

'My son and I shall be leaving shortly, Alice, to meet Mr Freeth at his premises in Leadenhall Street. I then have a little business of my own to conduct. I shall not need you to accompany us; and so, if you wish, you may go out – but be back by five o'clock. And, Alice, make sure you are not late again. We dine at seven.'

Liberty! My heart leaped at the prospect. I had seen a little of

London, during my stay with Mrs Ridpath; but to have the freedom to explore the greatest city on earth on my own was intoxicating.

Where should I go? What sights should I see first? To the shops in Regent Street? To St Paul's, perhaps, or to Whitehall, to see where poor King Charles was murdered; or to view the pictures at the National Gallery? Then I thought I might go instead to the British Museum, for there I could fill many pages in my note-book with glorious facts.

As I considered the many tempting possibilities, however, the sterner voice of Duty began to whisper in my ear, telling me to use the time usefully, and not fritter it away on my own pleasure.

Thus I resolved to put my own inclinations aside. No shops, no sights. Instead, trusting to fortune, I would pay a visit to Old Square, Lincoln's Inn.

III
Mr Vyse Goes East

AFTER LUNCHEON, ARMED with a copy of Murray's Guide to London and a pocket-map of the metropolis lent to me by Mr Pocock, I left the house and began to take my way eastwards, down Brook Street, and along into Regent Street. From here I proceeded to Piccadilly and then to Trafalgar Square, until at last I gained the Strand. Here I entered Morley's Hotel, to take a little refreshment and consult my pocket-map, before resuming my journey.

I soon found my way to Chancery Lane, and at last stood before the gate-house of Lincoln's Inn – a noble brick structure, bearing the date 1518 (which fact I duly recorded in my note-book).

Passing through the gates, I entered a charming three-sided court. Here I halted, having no particular plan in mind, and looked about me.

The court being deserted, I decided that I would walk a little further into the Inn. As I was approaching the Chapel, a portly gentleman, carrying a draw-string bag over his shoulder, and with a great quantity of papers tucked under his other arm, came out of a doorway and began to walk towards me. He had a kindly look about him, and so I stopped him as he passed to enquire whether he could direct me to the chambers of Mr Armitage Vyse.

'Mr Vyse, you say?'

He considered for a moment.

'Hmm. Wait a bit – yes. Vyse. Old Court. Number twenty-four. You must have passed it, if you came in through the gate-house. Number twenty-four. That's it. Thurloe's old chambers. Good-day, miss.'

'Number twenty-four!' he shouted after me. 'In the corner.'

Retracing my steps a little way, I immediately saw across the court the doorway to which the gentleman had directed me, with the number twenty-four carved in stone above it. The door itself, and the four storeys above, were set in an angled projection jutting out into the court. As I stood wondering which of the windows were Mr Vyse's, and what to do next, a lady entered the court through the gate-house arch, walked head down but purposefully towards number twenty-four, and ascended the stairs.

Now a lady may hide her face from the world with a veil; but she cannot disguise the day-dress that her maid has helped her into that very morning. *Well, my Lady*, I whispered to myself. *What brings you here?*

There was now nothing to do but to wait, and ponder this strange and unexpected turn of events.

'I then have a little business of my own to conduct,' my Lady had said. That business, it now appeared, was with Mr Armitage Vyse. It might of course be perfectly innocent business; but that black veil suggested otherwise.

Withdrawing a little way, I settled myself on a wooden bench with a view of number twenty-four.

Fifteen minutes passed; and with every minute the sky grew darker with the threat of rain. As the first heavy drops began to fall, my Lady at last came out of the doorway of number twenty-four, alone, and hurriedly left the court through the gate-house. Moments later, there was a clattering on the wooden stairs, and the unmistakable figure of Mr Armitage Vyse, carrying a canvas bag, appeared in the doorway.

A little to my alarm, he began to walk directly towards where I was sitting. As hastily as I could, head bowed, I removed to the door-way of the nearby Chapel. To my relief, he appeared unaware of me as he made his way across the court.

I watched him lope off, his long coat flapping behind him, his stick tapping out each step on the wet flagstones. On a sudden impulse, I decided to follow him.

THE RAIN WAS steadily increasing, but I was determined to go on with my plan.

My quarry had now turned into New Square. As he disappeared from view, I slipped out of my hiding-place and was off after him.

On reaching Fleet Street, I thought that I might lose him in the dense crowds; but his long coat and tall hat, and his exceptional height, made it easy for me to pick him out, and I soon managed to catch up with him.

A little way along Fleet Street, he stopped at a cab-stand and spoke briefly to the driver of the first vehicle. As soon as he had clambered in, the cab set off.

Now I had never taken a hansom-cab in my life, and was alone in a city I barely knew. To follow Mr Vyse further, to an unknown destination, began to seem like the greatest possible folly; yet my incorrigible impetuosity urged me to put aside my misgivings. I had wanted a little adventure, and here was one opening up before me. Persuading myself that Madame would want me to seize the opportunity that had so unexpectedly presented itself, and as I was also in the more trivial way of becoming soaked to the skin by the increasing downpour, I took a deep breath, picked up my wet skirts, and ran as fast as I could to the cab-stand.

Having given my instructions to the next available cab-man, I was soon rattling up Ludgate Hill, my pocket-map open on my lap to follow our route, in the wake of the cab carrying Mr Vyse eastwards. From time to time, I leaned my head out to make sure he was still in view; but in the deepening murk, and the confused embroilment of vehicles – carts, cabs, carriages, coal-waggons, swaying brewer's drays, and laden omnibuses – it was impossible to tell whether we were still on Mr Vyse's trail, or not. In Poultry, I called back to the cab-man.

'Can you see him still?'

'Yes, miss,' he shouted. 'Just a little ahead. Don't you worry. We won't lose 'im.'

After passing the Mansion House, we turned into King William Street and began heading towards London Bridge. The possibility that we might be crossing the river now filled me with alarm, for the district was becoming highly unsavoury. I was about to tell the cab-man to abandon the pursuit, and take me back to Grosvenor Square, when we arrived in Lower Thames Street, the cab began to slow its pace, and we finally came to a halt.

Mr Vyse's hansom had also stopped a little way ahead of us, at the junction with a narrow thoroughfare that appeared to lead towards the river. The overpowering stench of fish was everywhere. I looked back at the cab-man – a large, round-faced fellow, with a remarkably bulbous, purple-veined nose – to ask where we were. He saw the disgusted look on my face and began to chuckle.

'Billingsgate, miss,' he said; then, pointing his whip towards where Mr Vyse's cab had stopped to let him out, 'Dark House Lane.'

IV
The Antigallican

DARK HOUSE LANE was aptly named: dark indeed, and filthy, the wet and greasy pavements and roadway slippery underfoot with mud and scatterings of shiny fish scales, and all manner of other detritus. The whole lane was thronged with costermongers in strange leather- or hair-caps, many carrying trays on their heads piled high with fish, eels, and shell-fish, or quantities of oranges.

Lord, the deafening *mêlée* of colliding carts and horses, the shouts and calls and roars, and the rank, all-pervading reek of fish! I had never experienced such a noisome, disagreeable place in all my life and stood at the top of the lane in some anxiety, trying to pick out my route if I were to continue following Mr Vyse. Evenwood and Grosvenor Square seemed a world away in that moment; whilst my former life with Madame in the Avenue d'Uhrich took on the aspect of a dream.

As I considered whether to go on or not, I heard a footstep behind me.

'If you're thinkin' of goin' down there on your own, missy, you'd pr'aps best throw this round you.'

The cab-man who had brought me from Fleet Street was holding out a stained and torn plaid shawl, which he suggested I should put over my head and dress, to make myself a little less conspicuous. I saw the wisdom of his advice, thanked him, and took the proffered shawl.

'That's all right, missy,' he said. 'You remind me powerfully of my own dear girl, an' I wouldn't 'ave wanted 'er to go a-wanderin' about Dark House Lane, for all an' sundry to gawp at, an' who knows what else. I'll be blowed if I can think what you might be doin' down 'ere. It's one thing for that 'usband of yourn—'

'Excuse me,' I interrupted. 'I have no relationship with that gentleman.'

'You don't say so?' replied the cab-man. 'Well, it's no business o' mine, I'm sure. But if you'll take my advice, you'll wait in the cab till the genlemun returns to 'is.'

'No,' I said, placing the shawl over my head, and recoiling slightly from the impregnated smell of beer and stale tobacco; 'but I thank you for your kindness. If you wouldn't mind waiting for me, I'll come back as soon as I can.'

'Then if *you* don't mind, missy,' came the reply, 'I'll accompany you, a few steps behind. The party you've been a-followin' 'as just gone into the Antigallican, which ain't no place for an unaccompanied young lady. And so: Mr S. Pilgrim – the initial standin' for the wise name o' Solomon – at your service.'

He gave a little bow, to round off his introduction.

'There's no need, Mr Pilgrim,' I said, firmly; but he held up a large gloved hand to stop me from saying more.

'No, no, missy. If my Betsy were 'ere in your place, then I trust as 'ow someone would do for '*er* what I insist on doin' for *you*. Though of course,' he added, with a sorrowful catch in his voice, 'she ain't 'ere, and won't never be 'ere, bein' now with the angels.'

'Is she dead, then, Mr Pilgrim?' I asked.

'Taken from me these six months since, missy' he replied, shaking his head slowly from side to side in a most affecting way.

'A little girl?'

'No, missy. Not little. About your own age. Typhoid.'

I tell him how sorry I am to hear it, but that I am determined to go on alone.

'In that case, missy,' he says, seeing that I will not be persuaded, 'I'll do the next best thing. I'll put some baccy in my pipe and wait 'ere, where I can see down to the end of the lane, till you come out again. But if you're not out in fifteen minutes, then I'm a-comin' to get you.'

Touched by his concern for me, I agree to the arrangement. Pulling the shawl round me and placing my handkerchief to my nose, I set off down Dark House Lane towards the Antigallican.

ON EITHER SIDE of me, as I gingerly pick my way down the lane, are fish-stalls and terrible places of steam and heat, where lobsters and crabs are being cruelly plunged into cauldrons of boiling water. It is almost with relief that I finally reach the low, mean-looking building within sight of the river that Mr Vyse has just entered – the Antigallican public-house.

Pushing open the door, I stand for a few seconds on the threshold, observing the scene within.

Through a thick haze of tobacco-smoke, I finally make out the figure of Mr Vyse sitting alone at a table in the far corner of the room, his back towards me. He has exchanged his tall hat for an old forage-cap, and is wearing a black muffler across his face and a stained and patched coat, which I suppose have been carried here in the canvas bag.

The sawdust-strewn room – heaving, like the street outside, with costermongers and fish-stall holders, their numbers swelled by groups of river-people – is close and airless, being low-beamed and window-less, the only light coming from a few tallow candles on the bar, and from the sickly yellow glow of three dimly burning lamps hanging by rusty chains from the ceiling. Several of the house's patrons turn to look suspiciously at me as I enter, and I begin to regret my foolhardi-ness in not agreeing to Mr Pilgrim's accompanying me.

As I take a few nervous steps into the smoky gloom, uncertain what to do next, a grimy, red-faced woman comes staggering over to me, roughly lifts away my handkerchief, and cries out to the assem-bled company, 'Why, 'ere's a little beauty!' To a raucous reception of shouts and whistles, she embarks upon a brief dance of her own drunken devising and then, having availed herself of a nearby spit-toon, stumbles back to the bar, cackling to herself in the most vile manner.

Still Mr Vyse sits, alone and unheeding, in his dark corner. I am feeling quite sick from the room's choking atmosphere, but I force myself to continue watching him, for he has clearly come here for a purpose, and I am determined to discover it. Minutes pass, and still he sits there, hunched over his table, impatiently drumming his fingers.

The door behind me creaks open. I turn slightly, to find myself staring into the eyes of a cadaverous young man wearing a peaked leather cap, from beneath which several long strands of greasy black hair hang down about his ears and neck.

We remain for a moment, face to face, eye to eye; and then, with a most vicious look, the young man pushes past me and goes over to the table where Mr Vyse is sitting.

I am shaking with fear, for I know that I have looked into the eyes of a conscienceless killer. Do not ask me how I knew then, by instinct, what was later confirmed to me as fact by others. I can only swear that it was so. What I have glimpsed in those black slits roots me to the spot with sheer terror.

The newcomer sits down opposite Mr Vyse. Heads leaning towards each other, they begin to talk.

As there is no possibility of my hearing what is being discussed in that dark, smoke-filled corner, and as I do not wish to risk being recognized by Mr Vyse, I am about to leave when I see the barrister reach into his pocket and pass a number of coins over the table to his companion. At the same moment, the young man looks across at me, our eyes meet again, and my blood freezes.

Without saying a word, his eyes still fixed on me, he begins to rise from his seat. Sensing the danger I am now in, and before Mr Vyse can turn to see where the young man is going, I immediately run to the door, out into the din of Dark House Lane once more, and into the outspread arms of Mr Solomon Pilgrim.

'Whoah there, missy!' he exclaims as he releases me. 'What's afoot?'

I have no time to answer him, for the young man has now come out of the Antigallican and is scowling menacingly at us. Mr Pilgrim instantly grabs my hand and begins to hurry me back up the lane towards the safety of his cab.

'Billy Yapp,' he shouts, grimly, as we push our way through the teeming hubbub. 'Known hereabouts as "Sweeney".'

'"Sweeney"?' I shout back.

'Of the barbering persuasion.'

He draws a finger across his throat, and then I catch the allusion to the legend of Sweeney Todd, the infamous barber of Fleet Street, which I remember being told as a child by Mr Thornhaugh.

'Young Billy would slice his granny up, feed her to the fishes, an' not lose a wink,' Mr Pilgrim elaborates. 'A bad lot, through an' through. What your fine genlemun 'as to do with such as Billy Yapp would be a thing to know.'

Raising his bushy eye-brows, he gives me a look clearly intended to encourage me into favouring him with some little confidence concerning Mr Vyse, and why I have followed him; but I pretend not to take the hint. Like Mr Pilgrim, however, I can conceive of no good reason why a respectable gentleman of means and reputation like Mr Armitage Vyse should have come in disguise to this foul and dangerous place, to pass money over to such a person as Billy Yapp, and to do so immediately after having received my Lady in his Lincoln's Inn chambers. As I wonder if she knew where he was about to go, and whom he was going to meet, I cannot help feeling a little swell of satisfaction; for here, surely, is something my Lady does not wish to be known – a secret to be uncovered, and exposed.

As we approach the top of the lane I look back, but there is no sign of Yapp. We soon gain Lower Thames Street once more, where I hand Mr Pilgrim his shawl and climb, shaking still, into his cab. In another moment, with a sharp crack of his whip, we have left Dark House Lane and the Antigallican behind us and are heading westwards again.

As we pass St Bride's Church, I hear the bells striking out five o'clock. The sound immediately makes my heart thump with a new anxiety.

I have missed my time; and now I am late to dress my Lady.

11

An Announcement in *The Times*

I

An Invitation Rejected

ALIGHTING FROM Mr Pilgrim's cab in Brook Street, I ran the short way back to Grosvenor Square, not wishing anyone to see that I had returned in a hansom-cab.

'You'll be all right now, missy,' said my new friend, as I got down.

'I believe I shall, Mr Pilgrim,' I replied.

'Well, you get along, then,' said he, affecting a kind of fatherly sternness, but failing utterly. 'I've got a livin' to make. But if you ever go a-ramblin' agin, missy, where you really oughtn't, I 'opes as 'ow you'll seek out the transportation services of S. Pilgrim if you can – allus to be found, when not engaged with paying clients, at the stand in Fleet Street, where you was fortunate enough to find 'im today. Place of residence hard by, if required – Shoe Lane, number four. Knock and ask for Sol.'

And with that, he gave a flick of his whip, and drove off.

Reaching the house, I ran down the area steps into the kitchen, where I found Mr Pocock and Barrington in conversation.

'Good-evening, Miss Gorst,' said the butler. 'We were worried where you'd got to. Her Ladyship has been asking for you.'

He gave me a warning wink, to signal my Lady's displeasure that, yet again, I had failed to attend her at the time she had specified. I hastily thanked Mr Pocock for the use of his guide-book and map, and, with Barrington's expressionless eye upon me, hurried up to my room.

My dress being uncomfortably wet, and reeking of tobacco smoke from the Antigallican, I quickly changed into my only other gown, and then ran down – heart beating with anxiety, hot and a little bilious after my adventures in Dark House Lane – to my Lady's boudoir on the second floor.

There was no reply to my knock; and so I knocked again, and then softly entered.

The first room was empty, but the door to the adjoining bed-chamber stood ajar. To this I now proceeded, and knocked once more.

'Who is it?'

Her voice was agitated, and I heard the distinct sound of rustling paper.

'Alice, my Lady.'

'Wait. I shall be out presently.'

As I withdrew, I smiled to see that a black veil had been thrown over the arm of the sofa.

When my Lady came out of the bed-chamber, her usually pale face had a slight redness about the cheeks, and I noticed that she was wearing her spectacles, as if she had been reading.

'Where have you been?' she asked, seating herself with her back towards the street window.

'I'm sorry, my Lady. It was necessary to take shelter for some time from the rain, and then—'

'Enough!' she cried, angrily cutting me short. 'This simply will not do, Alice. It has now gone half past five, and you were told to be here by five o'clock. You know I cannot abide unpunctuality, and this is the third time you have disappointed me. I was lenient with you last time, but you'll receive no wages for today. Now, tell me where you have been.'

I had expected to be quizzed by her, and so on the way back in Mr Pilgrim's cab I had prepared myself by reading up on a number of the capital's most celebrated sights in Mr Pocock's guide-book.

'I went to the Cathedral, my Lady.'

'To St Paul's? That's quite a distance. Did you walk?'

'Yes, my Lady.'

'And did you consider it worth the effort?'

'Oh yes, my Lady. Well worth it.'

'It has been many years since I was last there,' she said, with a musing sigh as she slowly removed her spectacles. 'Did you go up to the Whispering Gallery?'

'Yes, my Lady.'

'Any further?'

'No, my Lady.'

'You can go up higher, you know. Much higher. Right into the clouds, or so it feels.'

She then fell silent, and sat for several seconds looking towards the fire, her spectacles dangling carelessly from her hand.

'Miss Lucasta Bligh and her sister, Miss Serena Bligh, elderly relatives on my mother's side, are dining with us tonight,' she said presently, in a flat, indifferent tone, still looking into the flames, 'and also Mr Roderick Shillito, a former school-friend of Mr Phoebus Daunt's, whom I have not seen for several years. Mr Vyse will also be joining us.'

The mention of Mr Vyse momentarily unnerved me, and I felt my colour begin to rise.

'Is anything the matter, Alice?' asked Lady Tansor. 'You look a little flushed.'

'It's nothing, my Lady. Only the exertion of running back.'

Further awkward questions were cut short by a knock at the door, and in walked Mr Perseus Duport, carrying a newspaper.

'Thank you, dear,' said Lady Tansor, taking the paper from him. He then turned to me, paused for a moment, and cleared his throat.

'Have you had a pleasant afternoon, Miss Gorst?'

My Lady, suddenly enlivened, answered for me.

'Alice has been to St Paul's, and goodness knows where else, and on such a horrid day! I forgot to ask you, Alice dear, what else did you see on your walk through the rain?'

I fancied that I could detect some vague insinuation in her voice, although she was smiling now. I quickly thought back to some of the sights I had picked out of *Murray's Guide*.

'I saw Nelson's Column, my Lady, and of course the National Gallery – although I did not go in – as I passed through Trafalgar Square on my way to the Cathedral. And then, on the way back, I walked down from the Strand to the Temple Gardens.'

'Oh, I adore the Temple,' said Lady Tansor. 'Such a romantic place! You know that the Wars of the Roses are said to have begun in the Gardens? But of course I see from your face that you do. I forget sometimes how clever you are.'

'The Temple is indeed a romantic place, my Lady,' I agreed; 'but then I suppose that the other old Inns of Court are too. I should like very much to see Lincoln's Inn, which I have read is very beautiful.'

To my great satisfaction, she momentarily coloured up, and was obliged to turn away, seemingly to place the newspaper on a nearby table, in order to hide her discomfort; but she quickly composed herself, clapped her hands gaily, and told Mr Perseus that he must leave us so that she might dress for dinner.

'Perhaps, Miss Gorst,' he said at the door, in a manner that suggested he had been considering his words carefully, 'if my mother is willing to grant you a few hours' more liberty while we are in Town, you might allow me to conduct you to see the pictures at the National Gallery, which you did not see today? You really ought to see them, you know. There are some very fine works there. Are you fond of paintings?'

Feeling that my Lady would not approve of her maid's accepting such an invitation from her son, although I would dearly liked to have done so, I declined, with due deference, justifying my refusal by saying that my duties would not allow me any more liberty. Why it distressed me to observe a marked, though fleeting, look of disappointment pass over Mr Perseus's face, I could not say; but it was soon apparent that I had been right not to give in to my own rather warm inclinations.

'Alice is quite right,' said Lady Tansor approvingly, giving her son a sharp look. 'In fact, I wish to return to Evenwood as soon as possible. I am growing to hate London. How anyone can bear to live here for more than a few days is quite beyond me. We have been here only a matter of hours, and already the place is making me feel quite ill. We shall stay tomorrow, of course, to complete the arrangements with Mr Freeth; but I shall return to the country on Thursday. You may stay if you wish, Perseus. Come, Alice.'

With these words, she beckoned me to follow her into the bed-chamber, leaving Mr Perseus standing, cold-faced, by the door.

WHEN HER TOILET was completed to her satisfaction, my Lady gave me my instructions for the evening.

'You may take your supper with Pocock and the others, when dinner is over,' she said. 'Until then, there is some mending to do. I have noticed a tear on the sleeve of the dress I wore last week, when I called on Miss Bristow. You remember the one? Good. I am a little disappointed, however, to have to bring this to your attention. You should really have noticed it yourself when you packed it. But let that pass.'

'Thank you, my Lady,' I said, bowing my head contritely, but feeling very much annoyed by the reprimand.

'You might also black the patent boots I wore today,' she went on. 'They have got rather dirtied in the rain.'

'Will that be all, my Lady?'

'Yes – no, wait. I have noticed that the combs and hair-brushes I keep here are in a very bad state – I never could get Miss Plumptre to understand the importance of cleanliness in such things. Wash them through, would you, Alice?'

Such tasks are part and parcel of the duties of every lady's-maid; but it was plain that, in laying them on me that evening, Lady Tansor had wished to reassert her authority over me, and to remind me of my station. Although it went against Madame's instructions, I had begun to grow a little fond of my mistress; but on occasions like this, when her mood would suddenly change from cordiality to high-handed disdain, the antipathy that Madame had encouraged me to feel towards her would begin to stir within me. Now, in the face of another display of haughtinesss, I felt it stirring again, even though I knew that I must go on playing the role of the acquiescent lady's-maid.

'And please to make the bedroom fire ready before you go to supper,' she was now saying. 'Miss Lucasta and Miss Serena Bligh will not stay late, and so I shall retire early, and leave the gentlemen to their cigars and brandy. Ah, there's the front door. Someone has arrived.'

II
A Discovery

TIRED AND HUNGRY, having nearly completed my penance by blacking my Lady's boots and washing her combs and brushes, I was sitting before the fire in her richly furnished boudoir, mending the tear in her dress, and thinking over the events of the day.

Laying aside my needle and thread, I sat back, kicked off my shoes, and placed my stockinged feet on the fender to warm my toes.

The square outside was silent. Only the ticking of the long-case clock in the corner of the room, and the distant sound of occasional laughter from the guests downstairs, disturbed the stillness. As I luxuriated in the warm silence, my mind returned to Madame's second letter.

My Lady's secrets – like all secrets, or so I have read somewhere – may long to be told; but they must also be searched out. I must turn spy. Cupboards and drawers must be opened; pockets rummaged through; bags and cases and purses turned out, and their contents examined. Why not start immediately, here in her town-house?

For half an hour, keeping my ears open, and with one eye on the door in case my mistress should return unexpectedly, I went about the room, examining each piece of furniture in turn. I then did the same in the bed-chamber, opening everything, searching with the greatest diligence; but I discovered nothing.

Overcome with fatigue and chagrin, I threw myself on my Lady's bed. How did Madame expect me to uncover proof of my Lady's crimes if she did not tell me what those crimes were? How could I find what was required if I did not know what I was seeking?

I remained in this baffled and impotent state for several minutes until my eye was caught by something protruding from beneath the pillow, not six inches from where I lay.

I reached forward and pulled it out.

It was a folded piece of paper, on which were a few lines of writing:

> *I am relieved that you will soon be returning to the country. London is a dangerous place. Only last Sunday (of all days), as I believe I mentioned to you this afternoon, a woman was found, with terrible injuries, in the Thames. Shocking. If you have not yet seen it, you may read an account of the outrage in yesterday's* Times, *page six. What a world it is!*

As I read the note again, it seemed to take on the character of a cipher. There was another meaning here, skulking beneath the surface, which I was unable to discern. Replacing the note under the pillow, I returned to the sitting-room.

The newspaper that Mr Perseus had brought up for his mother still lay on the table by the window. It was of course the previous day's edition of *The Times*, and was open at page six. Towards the bottom of the page, the following notice instantly caught my eye:

HORRIBLE MURDER

As briefly reported in yesterday's edition, on Sunday last, 17th September, the body of a woman was found in the Thames, near Nicholson's Wharf. She had been most fearfully muti-lated about the throat. The woman has now been identified as Mrs Barbarina Kraus, aged sixty-four years, of Chalmers Street, Borough.

On the previous Friday, Mrs Kraus had been seen leaving the Antigallican public-house in the vicinity of Billingsgate, having gone out that morning in order, she told her son, to meet an old friend.

Her son, Conrad Kraus, became alarmed when she did not return that evening, and the next morning requested the landlady of the lodging-house in which they resided, Mrs Jessie Turripper, to alert the police.

The authorities have so far uncovered no clue as to the identity of the friend that the victim said she intended to visit, and robbery is not thought to have been the motive for the fatal assault. The victim had lived for some years in straitened circumstances with her son, and was carrying no money.

From the condition of the body, the opinion of the police surgeon is that it had been thrown into the water not more than a day before its discovery.

The investigation continues, under Inspector Alfred Gully, of the Detective Department.

Two things in the report immediately seized my attention. The first was the mention of the Antigallican, where I had lately witnessed Mr Armitage Vyse in close conference with Billy Yapp, a known killer. The second was that the victim's initials had been 'B.K.'

It seemed altogether too great a coincidence. Mrs Barbarina Kraus, last seen alive leaving the Antigallican public-house, had the same initials as the old woman my Lady had said was Bertha Kennedy, her former nurse-maid. If they proved to belong to the same person, then it followed that my mistress and Mr Vyse had been involved in her murder.

I had no time to consider this dreadful conclusion further, for just then a noise on the landing sent me running back to my chair by the fire. Picking up my work, I had only just assumed an attitude of innocent industry when in walked Mr Perseus Duport.

III
An Instance of Wounded Pride

HE CLOSES THE door quietly behind him and stands, for several moments, regarding me with that unsettling inscrutability that reminds me so much of his mother.

'Ah, Miss Gorst! I've come for that copy of *The Times* I brought up earlier.'

Then, observing the needle and thread in my hand, he remarks: 'My mother is a hard task-master, I fear.'

What a sweet picture I must have made in my sober black, my work in my hands, compliant to the utmost degree! He could not have guessed the true character and ambition of the dutiful Miss Gorst, the lady's-maid, nor the suspicions – of the most atrocious kind – that she now has of his mother.

In the brief silence that ensues, it is borne in on me once again what an uncommonly handsome gentleman he is: tall, slim, straight-backed, his clipped black beard and long hair making him look like some Assyrian potentate transported through time to the mundane nineteenth century.

Undeniably handsome, then; and I suppose, with his literary dis-position to supplement his manly beauty, that I ought to have con-sidered him a match for all the heroes of legend and fiction that I had ever read or dreamed of. Perhaps I did secretly harbour such a thought, although I was careful not to show it, and determined not to swoon before him, as many young ladies of my age might have done. Yet he fascinated me; and, in spite of his undemonstrative, and often high-handed, manner, I flattered myself that he regarded me with an unaccustomed degree of favour.

'Do you remember,' he is now saying, 'when we spoke about the Cretan Labyrinth?'

'Yes, sir,' I reply, puzzled by the question. 'I remember it very well, and also your kind offer to guide me through the labyrinth of Evenwood.'

'You are right. I did!'

He falls silent again, then looks frowningly at me with his piercing black eyes – his mother's eyes.

'But you didn't come to find me, so that I could fulfil my offer.'

'I'm afraid, sir, I felt that it was not my place to trespass on your time.'

'You seem very conscious of your place, Miss Gorst.'

'That is as it must be, sir,' I reply. 'A lady's-maid must always keep in mind that she has only one duty, and that is to do her mistress's bidding. Beyond that, she has no individuality, as long as she remains in her mistress's service.'

'That is a rather severe philosophy, Miss Gorst, and one that I suspect you don't really hold.'

'Oh, I assure you I do, sir, having no other aim than to serve your mother. My own inclinations are of no account.'

'And what were your inclinations with respect to my offer to show you Evenwood?'

He has now seated himself on the sofa and is resting his index finger against the side of his nose, tilting his head to one side in a gesture of anticipation at my reply.

'It would have been very pleasant I'm sure, sir, to have explored the house in your company; but it would not have been proper. I am certain that, on reflection, you must agree.'

'Proper!' he exclaims, with a humourless laugh. 'No, it would not have been at all proper for me to escort the new lady's-maid around my mother's house. But then I did not make the offer to a common domestic servant, did I? I made it to you, Miss Gorst, *in propria persona*. Do you know what that means?'

'Yes, sir.'

'But of course you do. Tell me.'

'It means "in one's own person".'

'Precisely. And by answering that question correctly, just as you did when I asked you about the Labyrinth of the Minotaur, you reveal a little more of your true self. Lady's-maid, indeed!'

'It is what I am, sir.'

'It is what you pretend to be.'

His words momentarily alarm me; then I see that he is only

expressing what his mother, as well as his brother and Mr Wraxall, have thought was the truth: that I am a lady's-maid only through necessity.

'You say nothing, Miss Gorst,' he continues. 'Come now, admit it. You are not showing us your true self, even though it peeps out most tantalizingly from time to time. What we see is not what you truly are.'

'It matters not a rush, sir,' I return, determined not to let my character's mask slip. 'The life I lived formerly has gone for ever, and I am perfectly content in my new one. And now, if you will excuse me, sir, I have work to do before my Lady returns.'

It is several moments before he speaks again. When he does, it is on a completely different subject.

'You have not asked me about my poem,' he says. 'Wouldn't you like to know how we fared with Mr Freeth? And do not say that it is not your place to ask. That will only vex me, for I know you're curious.'

'I believe my Lady said that you will be seeing Mr Freeth again tomorrow, to conclude the arrangements. I assume, therefore, that your meeting today must have had a satisfactory outcome.'

'Satisfactory is the word. Mr Freeth believes that *Merlin and Nimue* will be a great success, and that it will instantly make my reputation. What do you think of that?'

'Is Mr Freeth a competent judge?'

I see in his eyes disbelief at what he plainly considers to be the effrontery of my question, although I intend neither presumption nor offence.

'Competent? Freeth? Of course he's competent. What a question!'

'But I think my Lady said that Freeth & Hoare was a new concern. I suppose, however, that Mr Freeth and Mr Hoare must have had previous experience of the publishing business before establishing their own firm.'

His face darkens.

'Perhaps you consider yourself to be proficient in these matters, Miss Gorst,' he says, getting up from the sofa and moving across to pick up the copy of *The Times* from the table, 'being – as my mother informs me – such a great connoisseur of poetry.'

'Oh no, sir,' I reply, feeling sorry – indeed, rather distraught – that I appear to have angered him. 'I read only for my own pleasure, and I know that my taste is both conventional and unformed. In any case, I am sure that the opinion of a mere lady's-maid is of no interest to anyone.'

My words are sincerely intended to placate him. I am distressed, however, that he seems to have taken offence at them, and at my apparent denigration of his poem.

'Well, then, Miss Gorst' he says, tetchily, folding up the newspaper, 'I shall detain you no longer.'

When he reaches the door, he turns.

'Oh, I have just remembered. I have several engagements tomorrow, and so would have been unable to show you the pictures at the National Gallery after all. I am sorry to have kept you from your darning.'

12

Mrs Prout Remembers

I
Mr Thornhaugh Considers Possibilities

ON THE morning that we were due to return to Evenwood, my Lady went out early in the carriage, informing me that before we left Town she must pay a brief visit to an old friend who was unwell. This, I was sure, was not the true reason, but as I had to pack up her boxes and tidy her rooms, there was no opportunity to follow her, which I was burning to do.

When she returned, she was visibly out of sorts; and during the journey home remained irritable and uncommunicative by turns, complaining now that the carriage was too hot, or too cold, now that the motion of the train was making her ill, and then relapsing into sulky, fidgety silence, when she would try to read her book, or look listlessly out of the window, but being unable to settle to either.

As we approached Peterborough, however, her face suddenly lightened.

'Nearly home!' she cried, throwing aside her book, and the rug that had covered her lap.

'I shall not go to London again unless it is absolutely necessary,' she then declared. 'Perseus shall go in my stead from now on, if there are matters of business that must be attended to. Or people shall have to come to me.'

'But do you not find London fascinating, my Lady?' I asked.

'Fascinating?'

She took off her spectacles, and looked out of the carriage window.

'Perhaps once, but no longer. It is dirty, and dangerous; and of course it holds memories for me that are far from pleasant. There are beauties and marvels, no doubt, that will always captivate, but I have seen them, and have no wish to see them again. Evenwood is my world now. I shall never tire of Evenwood.'

Then she turned her face towards me once more.

'Oh, Alice, did I tell you? Mr Freeth was captivated – simply captivated – by Perseus's poem. He read the first six pages of the manuscript and said that he did not need to read any more in order for him to declare – categorically – that it was a work of indisputable genius, which the house simply had to publish on its inaugural list. A contract was sent round this morning. He has consulted his partner, Mr Hoare, and they propose publishing the work in December, in a *de luxe* edition of two hundred and fifty copies. Alas, its being a new venture, they are unable to underwrite the costs themselves, the market for poetic works of this scale and ambition, according to Mr Freeth, being a somewhat difficult one just at present. But he has every confidence that a great many more copies will be instantly called for, once the reviewers have informed the public of its singular merits. Ah, here we are at last! We shall soon be home now.'

I HAD MUCH to tell Madame regarding my adventure in Dark House Lane, and the note I had found under my Lady's pillow, obliging me to sit up until well past midnight composing a long letter to her. I had expected to receive an immediate reply, and began to feel both annoyed and anxious when none came. A week went by, then ten days. At last, a letter arrived – but it was from Mr Thornhaugh, informing me that Madame's sister had been taken gravely ill, and that she had been obliged to go to Poitiers to be with her. Mr Thornhaugh, it appeared, had also been absent from the Avenue d'Uhrich, although he did not say why.

'Your information concerning Mr Armitage Vyse, & his visit to the public-house in Billingsgate,' he wrote, 'was of the greatest interest to Madame.'

What a marvellous detective you have become, Little Queen! And what courage & resourcefulness you showed in following Mr V. But you must not take unnecessary risks. That must be strictly under-stood. I add the stern admonition of your old tutor to the advice of your new acquaintance, Mr Pilgrim (whom I desire very much to shake warmly by the hand) that you must never again go to such a place as the Antigallican alone.

Returning to Mr V, Madame thinks as you do: that there is some new mystery here, concerning this gentleman & Lady T, which may be helpful to our cause, if it can be solved.

Madame knows nothing — yet — of this Mrs Kraus, having only read, as you have, the report in The Times, *& so cannot be cer-tain of identifying her with 'B.K.' But she agrees with you that the coincidence of the initials appears too great to fall back on any other conclusion.*

This being so, it would seem that a woman has been murdered, in the most violent manner, who is connected in some way with yr mis-tress. Can it be deduced from these few, though eloquent, clues that Lady T and Mr V were directly responsible for instigating the death of the Kraus woman, through the agency of Sweeney Yapp? Madame and I think it can — but why it was necessary for this apparently insignificant person to suffer such a fate is, I confess, beyond both of us for the moment.

Madame tells me to say that she is conscious that you remain anx-ious to receive her third, and final, Letter of Instruction, in which the true cause of yr being sent to Evenwood will be laid before you at last. She wishes me to assure you, once again, that this will be in yr hands, as she promised, by the close of the year.

In the meantime, she urges you to watch Lady T ever more closely. If our inferences are correct, there will almost certainly be conse-quences to the death of the Kraus woman that even she may not be able to escape — with or without the help of Mr A.V.

Madame also notes that you have made little mention of the Broth-
ers Duport in yr letters, which has surprised her. She is interested to
know what communication you have had with them, and what yr
impressions are of each.
    Ever yr affectionate,
    B. THORNHAUGH

II
The Coming of the Heir

ON A DARK and pinching morning, not long after receiving Mr
Thornhaugh's letter, I awoke from a dream of snow.

Since coming to England, I had often dreamed of snow. In my
dreams, I am running from something through soft, stinging flur-
ries, not from the nightmarish horror that pursued me in the shape
of little Anthony Duport, but from something that, in some inexplicable way, is familiar to me. Yet although I am certain that it
appears to mean me no harm, I am nevertheless anxious to flee
from it; and so to an urgent desire to elude my pursuer is added an
equally urgent curiosity to know why I should be seeking so strenu-
ously to escape from something that I am sure will not hurt me.

At last, I know that I have given my pursuer the slip, and I experience a sweet sense of relief, as if some oppressive burden has suddenly been lifted from me. I sink down into the snow and look up
– with a strange joy in my heart, and with white flakes falling gently
on my face and hair – at the grey, laden clouds high above.

I had been awoken from this dream by a soft knocking at my
door. When I opened it, I was greeted by Sukie's freckled face.

'Did I wake you, Miss Alice?'

'Well, perhaps you did,' I replied, 'but it was time I was up and
about. Come in, dear.'

She puts down her pail and mop, and looks nervously about
her.

'Mrs Battersby?' I ask.

She nods.

'I must be quick,' she says. 'Her Ladyship wants all her old gowns moved over to the North Wing. She thinks they'll be spoiled if the roof leaks again. And such a job! I believe every gown she's ever worn since she was a girl are in those cupboards, even quite new ones she's grown tired of – and shoes as well, and I don't know what, and everything to be taken away, and then the place cleaned out. Megan Bates is already up there, but I had to see you to tell you.'

'Tell me what, dear?' I asked.

'Why, that Mother is quite better! Dr Pordage says that it's the most remarkable recovery he's ever seen – and of course he takes all the credit. But then she's a Garland, and Garlands are sturdy folk, as anyone round here will tell you.'

Of course I was delighted to hear Sukie's news, and we continued to speak for some little time until she said that she must get on, as Mrs Battersby was certain to appear shortly, to assure herself that the removal of Lady Tansor's gowns was proceeding satisfactorily.

'But Charlie said you wanted to speak to me, Miss Alice,' she said, picking up her pail and mop.

I told her that I was curious to know a little more of Lady Tansor's marriage to Colonel Zaluski, if she could tell me.

'Oh, I could tell you something about that,' she replied, 'but Mother could tell you much more, and would, I'm sure, be happy to.'

Thus it was arranged that I would call on Sukie and Mrs Prout after church the following Sunday.

SUNDAY DULY CAME. Mr Thripp's sermon (on the text 'He taketh the wise in their own craftiness') lasted nearly an hour – much to my Lady's ill-disguised annoyance, for she had frequently requested her Rector to limit his expositions to a moderate twenty minutes. Afterwards, by the lych-gate, I saw him turn sickly pale as his patroness, with a face like thunder, spoke a few words to him, before she was helped into her carriage by Mr Perseus.

That afternoon, as arranged, Sukie was waiting for me at the bottom of School Lane. Her mother had been ordered by Dr Pord-age to remain in bed; but when we arrived at the cottage, we found her sitting in a rocking-chair by the kitchen range, a large tabby cat on her lap, humming contentedly, and apparently in the most flour-ishing condition. I saw immediately what Sukie had meant concern-ing the resilience of the clan Garland. Far from being debilitated by her recent illness, Mrs Prout – a stocky little woman, with a bright and lively eye – appeared to exhibit a nonchalant defiance of the body's ailments.

'Don't fuss so, Suke,' she said, when gently admonished by her daughter for leaving her bed. 'That fool Pordage knows nothing about it. Bed-rest, indeed, when there's tatties to be peeled!'

Sukie looked across to the dresser, on which stood a bowl of freshly peeled potatoes, and shook her head in exasperation.

'Now then, Suke,' continued Mrs Prout, ignoring the further strictures directed at her by her daughter, 'introduce me to our guest, and I'll allow you to make us some tea, for I'm sure you think it'll kill me if *I* do it.'

'This is Miss Gorst, Mother,' said Sukie, before placing the kettle on the range. 'Her Ladyship's new maid.'

Mrs Prout expressed herself pleased to make my acquaintance, and we were soon chatting away, sipping our tea betimes, in a most pleasant and companionable way.

As soon as I was able, I turned the conversation towards Lady Tansor and her late husband.

'Oh yes, miss,' said Mrs Prout. 'I knew the colonel. I worked as under-housekeeper then, at the great house, where my late husband was a coachman. We all liked the colonel – a most agreeable gentle-man – though of course it was a great surprise to us all when Miss Carteret, as was, came back with him.'

Once she was engaged with her subject, it took little prompting on my part to encourage Mrs Prout to enlarge, at some length, and in considerable detail, on my Lady's marriage to Colonel Zaluski. This – in summary, and in my own words, drawing on the short-hand notes I made at the time – is what I learned.

* * *

IN JANUARY OF the year 1855, hardly more than a month after the murder of Phoebus Daunt by Edward Glyver, Miss Carteret (as we must call her for the moment), still of course in mourning, left England for the Continent, destination unknown. She appeared to do so with the full blessing of her relative, Lord Tansor, with whom, following the death of his nominated heir, she had quickly established a new, and apparently close, relationship.

The suddenness of the change in their relations was remarkable – occasioned and cemented, it was generally assumed, by their mutual grief. On Lord Tansor's side, where there had formerly been an observable frostiness towards his second cousin, there was now constantly expressed concern for her well-being. Mrs Prout well remembered hearing him, on several occasions, entreat Miss Carteret, in a most anxious tone, to move away from an open window for fear of catching a draught, or to sit a little further from the fire to avoid over-heating her blood. 'Moderation, my dear,' she remembered him saying, 'is the thing. Nothing too extreme. That's the way.'

From Mrs Prout's account, it seems that Miss Carteret, on her part, demonstrated a reciprocal, almost daughterly concern for her noble relative, making it her constant duty to keep his Lordship untroubled by domestic annoyances, however trivial.

Then, to general surprise, Miss Carteret had suddenly quit Evenwood to cross the English Channel, and did not return to Evenwood until the spring of 1856 – fifteen months later.

'When she did,' said Mrs Prout, 'she had a fine ring on her finger, the colonel by her side, and a babbie – Mr Perseus – wrapped up in a great shawl.'

On the day of their arrival in Northamptonshire, the little universe of Evenwood had turned out *en masse* to greet them – tenants, house-maids, cook-maids, dairy-maids, gardeners, gamekeepers, footmen, stable-boys, and every other species and sub-species of menial necessary to maintain Lord Tansor's comfort, all drawn up in eagerly curious, Sunday-best ranks in the Entrance Court.

Lord Tansor himself, Mrs Prout recalled, cooed and beamed – like the proud parent that he almost was – as the fruit of the union between his cousin and Colonel Zaluski was paraded along the clapping and cheering lines to receive the salutations of those who were about to serve him.

It was a warm afternoon, but the future heir was kept close wrapped in a voluminous white shawl, leaving only his eyes and button nose visible – to the vocal disappointment of the many females who strained eagerly, as we females are naturally inclined to do on such occasions, to catch a glimpse of the juvenile wonder.

The colonel and his wife were given a handsome suite of rooms, newly decorated and furnished, on the south side of the house, overlooking the fish-pond; and a nurse was engaged to attend the young prince.

'We all longed to see the little one,' Mrs Prout had recalled, 'but Mrs Zaluski had picked up a strange notion, from some foreign doctor who'd attended her, that the babbie must be kept away from people, and as warm as possible, even in summer, until he was at least eight months old. The little thing was that precious to her, and her trust in the doctor's system so great, that nothing could persuade her to take any contrary advice.

'But then one day, a week or two after they came back, I was passing the open door of the nursery when, happening to glance in, I saw the nurse, Mrs Barbraham, carrying Master Perseus in his night-dress through to his mamma. It was the first time I'd been able to see him properly, and my! What a bonny babe he was, to be sure! The bonniest three-month child, indeed, I ever did see, with his mother's great eyes, and a thick cap of black hair. Why she was molly-coddling him so, I couldn't see, but of course no one dared say anything to her.

'Anyway, a day or two later, I was speaking to dear old Professor Slake, and he'd also caught a glimpse of the child. I remember his words to this day: "They've misnamed him, Mrs Prout," he said to me. "He should have been called Nimrod, for it's certain that he'll soon be about the Park, slaying lions and pards by the score, to lay before Lord Tansor's feet." Then he explained to me who Nimrod was, and that a pard was an old name for a leopard, and I saw then what he meant. I've never forgotten his words, for they seemed so true and apt.'

COLONEL AND MRS Zaluski conveyed to the world at large the strongest impression of contentment. Mrs Prout confirmed that the colonel had been an extremely agreeable gentleman, although his health was poor, and he had a constantly careworn look about him. He spoke excellent English, with hardly a trace of his native accent, and treated everyone with a natural courteousness. Altogether, it could not be argued that he did not possess a great many qualities to attract a wife – but a wife such as the former Miss Emily Carteret, and so soon after the death of her beloved fiancé? This was a question much debated below stairs at Evenwood, and beyond.

Yet the colonel's wife seemed happy enough with her choice, even though her husband was so different, in every point, to the man she should have married. Mrs Prout remembered her smiling contentedly at him, and pressing her hand gently on his, as they sat together of an evening, reading and talking, or when Master Perseus was brought down to them by Mrs Barbraham, to be dandled on Mamma and Papa's knees, before he was taken back to his nursery.

Throughout that summer of 1856, Mrs Zaluski – supported in her determination by Lord Tansor – continued to follow the strict medical advice she had received from her foreign doctor to the letter, keeping her adored and pampered son wrapped up in great shawls, and refusing to allow him to be taken up by anyone except Mrs Barbraham, for fear of contracting some infection. Gradually, however, as the autumn approached, the child was brought out more and more; and what a fine fellow he was pronounced to be!

'Oh, Miss Gorst!' said Mrs Prout. 'You've never seen such a handsome little boy as Master Perseus – so tall for his age, and so strong, and lively. Everyone remarked it. And so like his mother, too, with hardly a trace of the colonel in him. This, of course, made Lord Tansor dote on the child even more; for, though his Lordship liked the colonel well enough – as who could not? – he always treated him like a guest in the house, and not at all like one of his family. But Mrs Zaluski had become like a daughter to his Lordship, and this pushed the poor colonel out of things even more.

'As for his Lordship, no man could have been more proud or happy. I won't say it changed him, for he was a stern old stick – always was, always would be. But it smoothed him out a little, is what I'd say, for the death of his own poor son, Master Henry, and then of Mr Daunt, had made him terrible bitter. And now here comes Master Perseus to replace them both!'

In due course, Lord Tansor's satisfaction was increased even more, with the birth of Mr Randolph the following year, although from the very first the child was over-shadowed by his elder brother, on whom was lavished every possible attention by his mother, and by the man who, in all respects except name, came to be considered as his grandfather. Lord Tansor's former aversion to the collateral line of his family, represented by the Carterets, was no more. The Duport succession, it seemed, had been secured by the birth of Perseus Zaluski-Duport, as he was known before his mother shed her husband's name. The great ambition of his life – that perpetually keen, but formerly unsatiated, hunger to pass on what he had received, which had ruled him for so long – had been achieved. His Lordship was content at last.

III
A Remembered Death

AFTER LEAVING MRS Prout and Sukie, I took the road through the village and entered the Park by the South Gates.

I could not help taking another peep at the Dower House, which had so enchanted me on first seeing it; and so I stood for several minutes, just beyond the plantation of trees between the lawn and the carriage-road, to look again at where my Lady had spent her childhood.

I had not been there long when a gate in a wall at the side of the house opened, and through it stepped Mr Montagu Wraxall carrying a valise. On seeing me, he waved, and began walking towards me across the lawn.

'Miss Gorst, how pleasant!' he said, making me a low bow. 'A large number of letters from my late uncle to Mr Paul Carteret – who, as I'm sure you know, once lived here – have recently come to light, and I've just been to collect them, although I hardly lack for papers to read at present. My dear uncle has left quite an ocean of them behind. But what brings you here?'

I told him how the Dower House reminded me of the doll's-house that Mr Thornhaugh had given to me as a child, and how much I would like one day to live in such a place.

'Would you now?' he said, turning back to look at the building, its red brick glowing warmly in the afternoon sun.

'Yes, it's charming, certainly, if now touched by tragedy.'

'Mr Carteret was an old and dear friend of my late uncle's,' he went on. 'A gentler, kinder man never drew breath. And he was killed for nothing. Nothing.'

'Excuse me, Mr Wraxall,' I said, 'but I'd understood that Mr Carteret was robbed after coming home from the bank.'

'No, no,' Mr Wraxall replied, shaking his head, 'I don't say that he was attacked for no reason; but he was not robbed for money, if that's what you mean. He was carrying very little.'

I ventured to put the opinion of Mr Maggs that his assailants may have thought differently.

'They may have done,' said Mr Wraxall doubtfully, 'though I don't believe so. My conviction is that they – if, indeed, there was more than one attacker, which again I doubt – knew exactly what Mr Carteret was carrying with him, and it wasn't money. Shall we walk?'

We set off through the plantation of trees, emerging again on the carriage-road by the South Gates. Soon we were ascending the long incline known as the Rise, the summit of which presented a wonderful prospect of the great house standing in splendour on the other side of the Evenbrook.

Mr Wraxall seemed somewhat preoccupied, saying little as we walked down towards the bridge.

'May I ask, sir,' I said at length, finding the silences a little uncomfortable, 'what you think Mr Carteret was carrying, if it was not money?'

'Well, that's the great unanswered question,' he replied, with a suggestive smile.

'Something of value, surely?'

'Something of value? Yes, most certainly. But I think you are playing the *ingénue*, Miss Gorst. I am sure that you already know something of this matter, and if you wish me to take you into my confidence, then you have only to say.'

He rested his clear grey eyes on me as he spoke, but there was no rebuke in them, only twinkling sincerity.

'I should like that, sir,' I returned.

'And so should I, Miss Gorst, so should I. But perhaps this is neither the time, nor the place for such confidences. I'm obliged to return to London tomorrow evening, and then I must travel to Scotland on family business. Are you always at liberty on a Sunday afternoon? You are? Then perhaps you might like to come to tea at North Lodge when I return. Would you consider that to be at all improper?'

'Not in the least,' I said.

'Neither would I. Then that's settled. I shall send word when I am back in Northamptonshire.'

We parted at the bridge that takes the carriage-road over the Evenbrook: Mr Wraxall to make his way across the Park to North Lodge, where he said he had several more hours' work to do on his uncle's papers, I to my room, and to Mr Wilkie Collins.

That night, looking out from my window as I was about to blow out my candle before retiring, I could just make out a faint gleam of light far across the Park, in the direction of North Lodge. It was now past midnight, but evidently Mr Wraxall was still at work.

As sometimes happened, I rose early the next morning, well before daybreak, wishing to finish reading my novel before commencing the day's duties.

Darkness still lay across the Park, although fragmented in places by a narrow arc of silver-grey light rising slowly over the eastern horizon, and the Home Farm cockerel had yet to rouse himself. I opened the window to let in a draught of that delicious air one experiences at this time, when night has not quite fled, and the fullness of day has still to break.

The light I had seen when I went to bed burned on in North Lodge. There had been no rest that night, it seemed, for Mr Montagu Wraxall.

13

In the House of Death

I
Waylaid

DESPITE THE impression that Mrs Battersby had contrived to convey, that she wished us to become friends, no further invitations to take tea with her had been made. I had in fact seen little of her, except occasionally at meal-times in the steward's room – which I often missed, either preferring to take something in my room, or because I was busy attending my Lady – when she would sit at the head of the table saying little, and never remaining longer than was necessary. This suited me very well, as I had a great many other matters to claim my attention. Nevertheless, I remained eager to satisfy my curiosity concerning the housekeeper, being now convinced that there was some deeper reason for her antipathy towards me, skilfully disguised though it was, than mere instinctive dislike, or some imagined threat to her standing with the other servants.

More than two months had passed before she asked me to her room again. She appeared everything amiable and attentive, expressing with a most convincing imitation of regret that her duties had prevented her from 'enjoying the much anticipated pleasure' of my company.

Half an hour goes by in general chit-chat; then she asks me whether my present situation is as I had imagined it would be, or

whether – being young and well educated, with a deal of life before
me – I had perhaps considered giving up domestic service for some
other kind of occupation 'more suited to my talents', as she smilingly puts it. This strikes me as a very odd thing to ask of someone
who has only lately commenced her employment; but I let it pass,
saying only that I am very happy serving my Lady, and that I cannot
presently foresee any circumstance that might persuade me to seek
another situation, or some other way of earning my living, which I
must continue to do.

'I'm so glad to hear it,' she says, with such warm emphasis that
I almost believe her, 'for I'm sure her Ladyship has no wish to lose
you – and of course everyone below stairs would feel it to be a considerable loss if you were to leave us. You've made a great impression
here, Miss Gorst, a very great impression, as you must, I'm sure, be
aware – modest though you are. But then we never know, do we,
what Fate has in store? Our situations can change in an instant, for
better or worse.'

To this genially expressed platitude I make no answer, having
none to give; and so we sip our tea in silence for several moments,
each of us understanding that what has been said is not what has
been meant.

To my relief, there is a knock at the door and Charlie Skinner's
pink face looks in.

'Beg pardon, Mrs Battersby,' he says, 'Cook wants a word about
the meat for tomorrow. It's Barker again. The order's short.'

'Thank you, Skinner,' says Mrs Battersby. 'Tell Mrs Mason I'll be
down directly.'

Having delivered himself of his message, Charlie withdraws his
great head, with its spiky crown of hair, and closes the door, giving
me a surreptitious wink as he does so.

'You see again how it is, Miss Gorst,' sighs Mrs Battersby resign-
edly. 'Our all too brief hour of precious leisure was interrupted last
time by rats in the Dry Store, as I recall. Now it's the meat for tomorrow's dinner! It's most regrettable, for I'm sure we both deserve
a little relief from our labours. But there! What help is there? It

wouldn't do for the cream of county society to go hungry – and on such a special occasion.'

Her look seems to express something unsaid, a significance beyond these unexceptional words. It is another instance of that curious ambiguity that characterizes everything about her, and which it vexed me very much to be unable to fathom – as it used to do when I failed to grasp some fine point of philosophy or mathematics that Mr Thornhaugh was trying to get into my head.

The occasion referred to by Mrs Battersby was the grand dinner, to be held the following evening, to mark Mr Randolph Duport's twentieth birthday. I had first learned of it the previous week, when my Lady happened to mention one afternoon that she would be engaged for the next hour or two with her secretary and would not need me to attend her.

'The guest-list for Randolph's dinner must be gone through,' she said, with a world-weary sigh, 'and then I must look at the menu card, and approve the wines, and I do not know what else. All this sort of business bores me so; but he is my son – these things are expected, and so I suppose they must be done. Of course, Perseus's majority in December, falling as it does on Christmas Day, is an altogether different matter. *That* will be an occasion for celebration indeed, and one into which I shall throw myself heart and soul. Oh, by the by, Alice,' she added, 'I wish you to attend me at the dinner tomorrow. It will be of great assistance to me, to have you there, and will also be good for you, and stand you in good stead, for you should know that I have plans to bring you out a little. I shall say nothing more about this for the moment, but if you continue to do well, then it is possible that your situation here may change for the better.

'And so, Alice, you are to attend Randolph's dinner – although not, of course, as a guest – that must be clearly understood. I would not normally countenance my maid's joining the company on such an occasion; but I am prepared to make an exception in your case, wishing – as I say – to accustom you to the best society, and being confident that you know how to conduct yourself in the proper manner.'

Mrs Battersby, continuing to speak of the arrangements for the dinner, and of the many distinguished guests, from both Town and country, who had been invited, had now risen from her chair.

'What a shame it is, Miss Gorst,' she was saying, 'that the likes of you and me are excluded from the company tomorrow evening, especially after all the work we shall have been put to, in our respective spheres. Perhaps her Ladyship thinks we would disgrace ourselves.'

Her eyes show resentment, despite the jesting tone, and although she must know the impossibility of a housekeeper – even one with her advantages of upbringing – ever taking her place amongst Lady Tansor's dinner guests. No doubt she also believes that my Lady's maid is in the same position; but I have a surprise for her.

'Oh,' I say, innocently puzzled, 'has my Lady not informed you?'

'Informed me?'

'That I am to attend her during the dinner. I would not have mentioned it, except that I thought you must already know.'

I saw immediately – with a stab of guilty satisfaction – how my words had hit home. The signs were of the subtlest – only a slight contraction of the eye-brows, a little narrowing of the eyes beneath, and the merest blush of confusion; but they were eloquent of her incredulous displeasure that, yet again, I had been accorded such a conspicuous demonstration of favour.

'Well, well,' says she, looking away, and affecting to tidy up the tea-tray, in a hollow show of equanimity, 'this is a rare honour indeed for my Lady's maid! I congratulate you again, Miss Gorst, and wonder where it will all end.'

She made no further remark, although it was plain that her mind was still busily turning over what I had told her. Excusing herself, and wishing me a rather curt 'Good-afternoon, Miss Gorst', she conducted me to the door, and hurried off – with ill-concealed reluctance – to apply herself to the pressing problem of the meat order.

THE PROSPECT OF Mr Randolph's birthday dinner had been a most pleasant one, and became the object of many idle imaginings – not

with respect to Mr Randolph, but, curiously, to his brother. I immediately began wondering how Mr Perseus would like me in the cast-
off gown that his mother had said I might borrow for the evening;
where I would be placed at table, and whether it would be near Mr
Perseus; what I would say to him – I mean to Mr Perseus; and so on,
in ever more fantastically unlikely elaborations.

Yet perhaps it was not so curious that my mind – with delightful
frequency – should run on such things. Let me now confess what I
have held back from my readers – indeed, what I had hardly begun
to admit to myself.

When Madame had enquired, through Mr Thornhaugh, why I
had made no mention of the two brothers in my letters, she had
unwittingly touched a nerve. The truth was that, although I found
his aloofness and displays of prickly pride occasionally distasteful, I
had begun to feel myself increasingly attracted to the elder Duport
brother. Deeper feelings, of course, were impossible, even if I
believed that the regard I thought he had for me could become anything more than simple liking. Yet still I let my fancy roam, seeing
no harm in dreaming of what, when morning came, I knew could
never be. Being somewhat fearful that Madame would strongly disapprove of any such distraction from the Great Task, I had therefore thought it prudent to keep silent on the matter.

I was unable to give a name to the feelings that I had begun to
form for Mr Perseus. They were entirely new to me, my only experience of such things being a brief infatuation with a nephew of
Madame's called Félix. What, I wondered, did it mean that Mr Perseus crept into my thoughts when I least expected it, at all times
of the day, and that I looked for every opportunity to meet him,
if only for a moment – on the vestibule staircase of a morning,
or in the Library, or wherever else I thought he might be? Many
were the ploys that I began to contrive, to bring about these apparently chance encounters, even though I would receive only a scant
'Good-morning, Miss Gorst', or 'How do you do, Miss Gorst' for
my troubles. Yet these hard-won morsels were reward enough, and
I soon began to feed hungrily on them, and found myself craving
for more.

I date a distinct change in my feelings for Mr Perseus to a morning not long after our return from London, following a little adventure, which I shall now relate.

My Lady – having slept badly, and wishing to remain in bed – had sent me to Easton in the fly to collect some trifling items that she had ordered from the milliners, it being a custom with her to patronize local establishments when she could.

It was one of those crisp and invigorating mornings when you smell the approach of autumn in the air, and when the late-summer sun still dazzles and intensifies the colours of Nature, although its warmth has diminished. I decided that I would return to Evenwood on foot, and so, sending back the fly with the various packages and parcels that I had collected, I set off.

I had reached the point where the road divided – one way turning off towards Thorpe Laxton, the other to the hamlet of Duck End and on to Evenwood village – when a rough-looking man suddenly stepped out of the bordering woods and barred my way.

He is short and slightly built, but with a desperate and threatening glint in his eyes. Bare-headed and stubble-chinned, dressed in stained labouring clothes and wearing mud-caked boots, he conveys a strong impression of someone who has passed the night – perhaps several nights – sleeping under the stars.

'Well, well,' he growls, in a most menacing way. 'Wot 'ave we 'ere?'

I cannot turn and run back up the hill behind me, for he would quickly have caught up with me; neither can I easily get past him, the road being narrow, with deep ditches on either side. The only course, I decide, is to confront him directly, which – very much to my surprise – I find myself determined to do, being rather affronted at being accosted in this manner. Assuming as much boldness as I can, although sensible of the danger I am in, I look the fellow in the eye.

'Excuse me,' I say, preparing to land him a sharp kick in the shins if he does not move aside; but even as I go to step round him, he seizes me roughly by the wrist.

'You're a fine-looking gal, an' no mistake,' he says, licking his lips in the most disgusting manner. Then his eye is caught by the sequinned reticule – a gift from Madame – hanging from my other wrist.

'Oh ho!' he exclaims, with a vicious leer. ''Ere's somefink better nor a pretty face.'

Releasing my hand, he is reaching to tear the reticule from its strap when he suddenly lets out an oath, turns, and runs back into the woods.

At the same moment, I hear the sound of hooves on the road behind me. Looking round, I see a figure on horseback coming down the hill. As the rider draws closer, I realize – with amazement and relief – that it is Mr Perseus.

It would, I am sure, meet the breathless expectations of every female reader of fiction, or lover of legend, had Mr Perseus – like some knight-errant – galloped down the hill on his grey mare (the penny-plain surrogate for a white charger), whip (substituting for a sword) in hand, and knocked the ruffian to the ground; but it was a most welcome second-best rescue nonetheless, for which I was inexpressibly grateful.

'Miss Gorst!' he cries, reining in his horse, and dismounting. 'I thought it was you. I saw you earlier, outside Kipping's. I had some business at the auctioneer's, and when I came out the fly had gone. You were on an errand for Mother, I suppose?'

'Ribbons, sir,' I reply.

'Ah, yes, ribbons. Quite so.'

He looks towards the woods, into which my waylayer had lately disappeared.

'Did I see you with someone, just now?'

'No, sir,' I return, seeing little reason to involve him further, and not wishing to appear like some weak and defenceless maiden in his eyes, 'only a local man crossing the road on his way to Odstock.'

He gives me a kindly sceptical look.

'Has anything happened, Miss Gorst?' he enquires. 'You are very pale.'

Gratified by his concern, and having assured him that nothing is wrong, we continue on our way, Mr Perseus leading his grey mare by the reins.

I can recollect little of what was said as we walked, side by side, through Evenwood village and into the Park. Mr Perseus tethered his horse by the gates, to be collected by one of the grooms, and we took our leisurely way past the Dower House, up the Rise, and down to the bridge over the Evenbrook. Our conversation was inconsequential enough, I am sure, certainly on my side, and of no importance in itself. Yet by the time I arrived back at the great house, I felt that a change had come upon my life during the previous half an hour.

Half an hour! Such a short time, and yet the world now seemed remade. It puzzled me very much that I should feel this. My little room under the eaves was just as I had left it, with everything in its accustomed place. The view from my windows – the terrace below, the gardens and parkland beyond, the dark outline of distant woods – was exactly as I remembered. My physical senses told me that nothing had changed since I had set out that morning; but my heart knew better.

For an hour or more, until it was time to attend my Lady, I lay on my bed, thinking of Mr Perseus Duport, and happily wandering through the Land of Fancy, where everything is possible.

THE SUNDAY FOLLOWING my adventure on the road from Easton, as we were coming out of church, Mr Randolph announced that he wished to walk back to the house rather than take the carriage. He then asked whether I would care to accompany him. This seemed a most ill-judged suggestion, and I looked enquiringly at my mistress, certain that she would not countenance such a thing. Mr Perseus, standing within earshot of his brother, certainly appeared to regard it with disfavour, pulling his coat around him and angrily striding off towards the lych-gate and the waiting carriage, his face clearly proclaiming the blackness of his mood.

'I think, sir,' I said to Mr Randolph, 'that my Lady will wish me to go back with her.'

'No, no,' said Lady Tansor, who, to my great surprise, showed no sign at all of disapproval. 'Go with Randolph if you wish. I have some letters to write when I get back, and Mr Thripp is riding over to discuss some parish business, so I shall not need you for an hour or so. Besides, some fresh air will do you good. You have been looking a little out of sorts lately.'

The carriage taking my Lady and Mr Perseus back to the house soon jingled off, leaving Mr Randolph and me to make our way down the lane we had taken on our first walk from Easton, and thence into the Park.

We speak of Mr Thripp's sermon, and whether that verbose gentleman will ever learn the discipline of brevity; and of Mrs Thripp's perpetual antagonism towards her husband; and then of this, and then of that, a digest of which would weary my readers.

All this time, Mr Randolph has been his usual good-humoured self; but as we are approaching the bridge, a change comes over him. The smiling, easy talk ceases, as if he wishes to say something to me that causes him difficulty. He falls silent for some time as we stand looking out over the Evenbrook, shimmering in the weak autumn sunlight, towards the great house. Then, as if he has suddenly taken courage, he asks whether I have left many friends behind in Paris.

'A few,' I return, puzzled by his question.

'And do you miss them?'

'Some of them, certainly; but I had a largely solitary childhood, and so have grown used to my own company. Self-reliance is a necessity for someone in my position, who has to make her own way in the world.'

'But was there no special friend, whose company you miss?'

'No, there was nobody like that, only when I was very young,' I reply, thinking of Amélie, and continuing to be perplexed by his questions.

He considers for a moment.

'So you have no one – no friend, I mean – to confide in?'

I reply that, having little to confide, I do not feel the lack of an intimate confidante. 'And do *you* have a friend to whom you tell your secrets?' I ask.

'I suppose I do,' he replies. 'My best chum at Dr Savage's academy, Rhys Paget – a very fine fellow. Of course I also have a fairly large acquaintance hereabouts; but Paget is more like, well, more like a second brother – not that I could ever confide in Perseus, of course, nor would ever want to.

'Do you know, Miss Gorst,' he then says, after a little more awkwardly silent reflection, 'I think you *should* have a friend to confide in, and who could do the same for you. You – and they – would find it a great comfort, I'm sure, to be able to talk freely about – well, about things that you can't talk about to others. We all have such things in our lives, and it don't do to bottle them up, you know. Not at all. A secret shared is – well, I can't quite recall what it is, if indeed it's anything. What I mean is that it's a very good thing, at any rate.'

'Perhaps you're right, sir,' I say, thinking of my secret feelings for his brother. 'The difficulty would be finding such a person. My social circle is a rather restricted one.'

'Quite so, quite so,' he says, returning my smile. 'But you concede the principle?'

'Yes,' I reply, with a laugh, 'I concede the principle.'

Just then, Mr Thripp comes trotting down the Rise, his terrier skittering about beside him, on his way to keep his appointment with Lady Tansor. A few words are exchanged as he passes over the bridge, and Mr Randolph and I then proceed on our way, talking inconsequentially once more, before parting at the Entrance Court gates.

II
The Day of Days

THE EVENING OF the dinner to mark Mr Randolph Duport's twentieth birthday finally arrived. My Lady had taken great delight in tricking me out in one of her unwanted gowns from last season, telling me that I looked very well indeed, and really quite handsome, adding – in a sly, woman-to-woman way – that she would not be at all surprised if I did not break one or two hearts that evening.

At the dinner, I found myself placed at the lower end of the long table in the Crimson-and-Gold Dining-Room, next to Miss Arabella Pentelow, a whey-faced maiden of about my own age, with a put-upon look and very little to say for herself. As the heiress to a stupendous fortune, Miss Pentelow was one of several young ladies there present – with their quietly combative mammas – whom my Lady had marked out for consideration as possible matches for Mr Randolph, having a strong desire to see him married and 'off her hands' (as she once said in my hearing) as soon as he attained his majority.

On my other side was seated – of all people – the ridiculous Mr Maurice FitzMaurice, who spent the whole of the dinner responding monosyllabically to all my attempts at conversation, in the many intervals of which he threw yearning glances at my Lady, seated in splendour between her two sons.

With two such neighbours, I was thankful that my Lady kept me pretty busy, throughout the dinner and when we ladies withdrew. A stream of requests was issued via Barrington, who appeared silently at my back at regular intervals to whisper them into my ear. Her Ladyship was feeling a draught – off I was despatched to fetch a shawl. Her Ladyship was a little warm – off I went to remove the shawl to an adjacent room and bring her favourite Japanese fan. Her Ladyship was concerned that the Bishop had been placed too close to the fire – off I tripped to ask his Lordship, on her behalf, whether he was quite comfortable (he was). Still they came, these ingeniously conceived commands, all designed – I had no doubt – to remind me that I was present as her maid and general agent, not as her guest.

There were several toasts to the health of Mr Randolph, after which a neighbouring magnate, Lord Tingdene, a plump, fish-faced gentleman, gave a speech – almost rivalling one of Mr Thripp's sermons in its tedious prolixity – in which he sycophantically extolled the unrivalled virtues and achievements of the Duport family since the days of the 1st Baron, while consigning to eternal perdition all those of the present day who strove against the proven perfection of inherited privilege.

Mr Randolph received all the salutations and congratulations with every appearance of satisfaction. His brother, who had led the toasts, wore his usual imperturbable expression, modified by an occasional weary smile, whilst my Lady shone, and smiled, and was graciously hospitable, although perhaps I alone perceived the little signs of strain and fatigue around her eyes.

The evening finally drew to a close. My hopeful dreams had come to nothing. Mr Perseus had appeared distracted, and we barely exchanged a word. Soon after the ladies and gentlemen reassembled in the Chinese Salon, he had been carried off to the Billiards-Room by a company of young gentlemen, noticeably unsteady on their legs, and I did not see him again. I continued to wait on my mistress until the carriages were called at one o'clock; yet even when the last guests had departed, I had still to undress her and see her to bed, although by then I could hardly keep my eyes open.

'You did well tonight, Alice,' she said as I was about to leave. 'Everyone admired you, as I knew they would. Now off you go. I shall need you at the usual time tomorrow, you know, so no excuses.'

It was a little before two o'clock when I closed the door to my Lady's sitting-room and stepped out into the gallery. As I did so, a figure emerged out of the shadows at the head of the stairs.

'Mr Pocock informs me that the dinner was a great success,' says Mrs Battersby.

'I believe so,' I answer.

'I am glad, for Mr Randolph's sake.'

We stand for a moment, eyes locked.

'Well, good-night, Miss Gorst,' she says at length. 'I still have a deal to do before I retire, but your duties are done, I think. And so I wish you pleasant dreams.'

With these words, she turns, and is gone as suddenly as she had appeared.

MR RANDOLPH HAD left Evenwood soon after his birthday, intending to spend several weeks in Wales with his friend, Mr Rhys Paget, who had been unable to attend the dinner because of some family business. To my disappointment, Mr Perseus had also been absent, in London; and so the days went by in weary succession, as I waited for his return to brighten my dull life of service with new dreams.

To compound matters, I had nothing to report to Madame. Mr Armitage Vyse had made no further visits to Evenwood; and, despite determined efforts, I had found no incriminating or suspicious documents of any kind in my Lady's apartments, and nothing to connect her directly with the murder of Mrs Kraus, except my transcription of the note I had found under her pillow in Grosvenor Square. And still I waited for Madame's third letter. I had no choice, it seemed, but to continue mending, and washing, and cleaning, and dressing my Lady in her finery, until that long-awaited day came, when I would know at last the purpose of the Great Task.

December came on, and with it the anniversary of Phoebus Daunt's death, observed annually by my Lady, as Mr Randolph had told me, by a visit to his tomb in the Duport Mausoleum.

On the morning of the 11th, after I had dressed her, my mistress informed me, in a subdued, strained voice, that she would not need me until two o'clock that afternoon, when she wished me to read to her for an hour or so.

'Do you know what today is, Alice?' she asked.

'Yes, my Lady,' I replied, without hesitation.

'Of course you do,' she said, fingering the locket containing her dead lover's hair.

I left her; but I did not return to my room, for I had determined on a bold plan.

THE DUPORT MAUSOLEUM – a strange, domed structure, in the style of an Egyptian temple – stands in dismal isolation on the south-eastern edge of the Park, in the midst of a clearing bordered by tall, densely planted trees, and smaller clumps of yew and elder. The path leading up to the great metal doors, curiously decorated with inverted torches, was muddy, and thickly carpeted with pine needles and slippery, decomposing leaves blown into the clearing from the tree-lined approach road. The doors – guarded on either side by two stern-looking, sword-bearing stone angels, pitted and lichen-covered – I found to be locked fast; and so I withdrew a little way, concealing myself beneath a dripping tree to await the arrival of my Lady.

I passed a most uncomfortable time, reading through my notebook to relieve the tedium, until at last I heard the sound of an approaching vehicle.

A minute later, my Lady had descended from the carriage, a large key in one hand, and had begun walking slowly up the leaf-strewn path; the carriage then departed, leaving us alone in this melancholy spot.

As she entered the Mausoleum, I quit my hiding-place and ran towards the double doors, one of which she had left ajar, allowing sufficient light into the building for me to make out the general character of the interior – a rectangular entrance hall, beyond which three wings led off a large central space containing several imposing tombs.

I watched my Lady walk, with solemn deliberation, to the wing directly opposite the entrance. As she disappeared from sight, I stepped into the gloom.

The main chamber was dimly illuminated by a dirtied-over lantern at the apex of the dome, by the feeble light of which I stole as quietly as I could towards the arched entrance through which Lady Tansor had just passed. There I halted.

In the walls of the vaulted, semi-circular space that I now saw before me could be made out a number of gated wall-tombs. Before one of these, my Lady was now standing, statue-still. Only the sound of a few desiccated leaves being blown about the floor by a sudden draught of air broke the heavy silence.

For the first time since entering the Mausoleum, I began to be sensible of the danger I was in. Discovery would surely bring catastrophe. Even if my presence remained undetected, I must contrive to make my way out before my Lady, to avoid being locked in this ghastly place. Yet my curiosity was now so great that I foolishly ignored my fears, and tip-toed forwards.

My Lady was no more than five or six feet from me, as I stood in the deep shadows of the arch, hardly daring to breathe. Then she sank slowly to her knees before one of the wall-tombs, and pressed her cheek against the padlocked gates.

With an anguished moan, she reached up and, with sudden ferocity, grasped the gates with both hands. For a moment or two she remained thus; then she began to pull at the iron bars with all her might – harder, then harder still, in a desperate, but pitifully futile attempt, as it seemed, to wrench them out by main force, and so join her lover in his eternal bed-chamber.

Shaking her head from side to side, she now began to sob – such a baleful, inconsolable sound as I had never before heard. Was there any comfort, in heaven or on earth, that could ever assuage such pangs? It was a sight indeed to see my proud mistress humbled so, brought low by what even she, the 26th Baroness Tansor, could never remedy. Death had taken Phoebus Daunt from her, and would never give him back.

How we strive to hide what we really are! In spite of all she could do, the shadow of Time was daily creeping over the once-radiant Miss Emily Carteret, as it creeps over us all, leaving behind the indelible marks of its progress. She would have wished no living person to see her in this condition of utter subjection, just as she would wish no one to see her without her morning mask of subtly applied lotions and powder, with which puny weapons she daily sought to defy the years. But *I* had seen what she tried to hide, as I was now witnessing her powerlessness to break free from the enslaving past.

In the fallen world, beyond this house of death and decay, she was a person of the greatest consequence – envied, still desired, unassailable; but not here. Who would know proud Lady Tansor now, raw-eyed and helpless? She was strong in wealth, mighty in inherited rank and authority; but she was weak and defenceless in this perpetual servitude to the memory of Phoebus Daunt.

The sight of this poor lost creature, on her knees, weeping uncontrollably before the tomb of her long-dead love, is pitiable indeed, and moves me greatly; but I can offer her no succour and comfort, soul to human soul, as I would have done for any other person. I turn away, tears in my eyes.

Minutes pass, and still my Lady remains kneeling before the tomb, pulling at the iron gates in a most frantic and pathetic manner. Then, on a sudden, she rises to her feet, turns, and begins walking towards the archway in whose shadows I am hiding.

III
I Contemplate Mortality

I HAVE HESITATED fatally, and now it is impossible for me to leave without being observed. Heart beating wildly, and as noiselessly as I can, I withdraw a few steps into the central chamber and crouch down behind the nearest tomb. I have barely had time to conceal myself when my Lady re-enters the chamber and passes by on the other side of the tomb, the train of her dress dragging through the scatterings of dried leaves with a thin crackling sound. She continues in her slow, ghost-like progress until she reaches the entrance hall.

Panic now grips me. I must leave – but how can I do so without revealing my presence?

As though in a dream, I watch my Lady's tall, rigid figure proceed across the entrance hall and into the misty outer light. She then turns to pull the metal door shut with a reverberating clang. A moment later, I hear the sound of the key turning in the lock.

I run, heart thumping, to the doors and place my eye to the key-hole.

She is standing, her back towards me, at the head of the path, just beyond the pillared portico. Somewhere in the distance, the mist-muffled bells of St Michael and All Angels are faintly tolling out the hour of eleven. Almost on the last stroke I hear the sound of the returning carriage.

Through the key-hole I watch the coachman assist Lady Tansor into the carriage. There is only one course for me to take.

I begin hammering on the door and shouting out for help; but when I stop, there is only silence. I put my eye to the key-hole once more.

The carriage has gone.

I SINK TO the cold floor, my back against the doors, in numb contemplation of my fate. I cannot stop myself from wondering what it will be like to die – as it seems I must – minute by minute, hour by hour, day by day. At first I am sure that I shall be missed, and have no doubt that a party will shortly be sent out to find me; but as the minutes pass, my confident hopes begin to ebb away. Even if a search is made, will anyone think of looking for me here? And if no one comes, until it is too late, what will they find? Nothing but a grinning, shrunken thing, wrapped in a worsted cloak, sucked dry of life by thirsty Death.

In a futile attempt to keep such horrid thoughts at bay, I decide to try to make some notes – as best I can in the dim light – on my surroundings.

I note down, first, the occupants of the various free-standing tombs in the central chamber, coming at last to that of Julius Verney Duport, the 25th Baron, my Lady's cousin, from whom she had inherited her title and property – a man of almost unrivalled wealth and political power, now reduced to bone and withered flesh, as I must soon be if no one comes to my aid.

I then move away into the adjoining chamber, stopping first before the tomb of Phoebus Daunt to transcribe the inscription thereon:

SACRED TO THE MEMORY OF
PHOEBUS RAINSFORD DAUNT
POET AND AUTHOR
BELOVED ONLY SON OF THE REVEREND
ACHILLES B. DAUNT
RECTOR OF EVENWOOD
BORN 1820
CRUELLY CUT DOWN 11TH DECEMBER 1854
IN HIS 35TH YEAR

For Death is the meaning of night;
The eternal shadow
Into which all lives must fall,
All hopes expire.

P.R.D.

By contrast, the neighbouring tomb carried the briefest of inscriptions, but it instantly held my attention:

LAURA ROSE DUPORT
1796–1824

SURSUM CORDA

Here, then, lay the mortal remains of Lord Tansor's beautiful first wife, whose portrait in the vestibule had so entranced me on first seeing it, and which had continued to exert a powerful fascination over me. Standing before it, I would sometimes feel as if I were looking upon myself in some former life; at others, I would be moved to a strange certainty that I had known her – actually known her, in the flesh, although the remembrance had the indistinctness of something seen from a great distance. Of course this was impossible, for she had been laid here thirty years and more before my birth; yet whenever I looked upon her lovely face, I would always experience a powerful sense of affinity that I simply could not explain, and which drew me back to the portrait time and time again. Now she, too, like her husband, was nothing but dust and bone.

It was no use. I could not hold back the morbid thoughts that naturally arise when contemplating such monuments to mortality. Shutting up my note-book, I returned to the entrance hall and slumped to the floor, overcome once more by the horror of my situation. Here I remained, unable to stem my tears, until at last I could weep no more.

How long had it been since my Lady had returned to the great house? An hour? Perhaps more. Soon I would be late attending her; then another hour would pass, and then another. Darkness would begin to fall, and what little light there was in the Mausoleum would be extinguished. Then, for sure, the terrors would come.

I MUST HAVE fallen asleep, although for how long I cannot say; but I am awoken with a start by a sound, just a few inches above my head.

At first, I think that I have been dreaming; but then the sound comes again. It is the key turning in the lock.

Jumping to my feet, I turn to face the door; but it does not open. I hesitate for a moment, thinking perhaps that it might be my Lady returning. I consider rapidly whether I should conceal myself in the far shadows of the entrance hall, and then attempt to make my escape without being observed. But still no one enters.

I reach forward and open the door.

There is no one there. The clearing is deserted, and there is no sign of anyone on the road.

Startled by my sudden appearance, a wood-pigeon, perching on the head of one of the stone angels, flaps noisily away into the murk; but all else is silence. I step outside, and then turn to look back at the doors.

The key has gone, and with it my unknown liberator.

14

A Gift from Mr Thornhaugh

I

I Receive an Apology

DOWN THE muddy track skirting the Park wall I ran, heart beating furiously, afire with blessed relief that I had been released from a most terrible fate, but anxious that it was now long past the hour when my Lady had instructed me to attend her.

I had half expected to catch up with my liberator; but I reached the southern gates, hard by the Dower House, without encountering a living soul, and the carriage-road winding its way up the Rise was deserted.

On reaching the Entrance Court, hot and breathless, I looked up at the Chapel clock. Ten minutes to two o'clock. I would not be late to read to my Lady.

'What did you do this morning, Alice?' she asked when I entered, picking up a copy of Phoebus Daunt's *Epimetheus*,* which had recently become a particular favourite of hers.

'I spent the morning reading, my Lady.'

'And what were you reading?'

'Mr Wilkie Collins's *No Name*, my Lady.'

Epimetheus; with other posthumous poems (2 vols, Edward Moxon, 1854 for 1855).

She looked at me sourly.

'I am not acquainted with the work of Mr Collins,' she said, in her most preposterously pompous manner.

'I rather wonder, Alice,' she went on, 'that you cannot spend your leisure time more profitably. There must be many books that you have not read, of a more improving character than such trivial stuff. I am sure your Mr Thornhaugh would agree with me.'

I was tempted very much to retort that fiction could be just as improving as poetry, and that my tutor was a great admirer of Mr Collins, and of such fiction in general, but prudently refrained.

'Have you written to him, by the by,' she then asked, 'to enquire whether he would care to visit you here?'

Of course I said that I had written, but that he had been absent from Paris for some time, engaged on his researches.

'Ah, yes. His researches,' she said. 'But that is a pity. I find your Mr Thornhaugh quite fascinating already, and rather mysterious in his way, even though I have yet to meet him. Isn't that curious? Well then, shall we begin?'

She handed me the book.

'Wait—'

She was looking down at the hem of my skirt.

'What are those? Cobwebs?'

I followed her eye, alarmed to see that the hem was indeed laced with a skein of grey and dusty cobwebs, picked up from my temporary imprisonment in the Mausoleum.

'I believe they are, my Lady,' I replied.

'But where have they come from?'

I thought as quickly as I could.

'I have developed a habit of exploring the house, my Lady,' I told her, 'before I come to you in the mornings – I hope you will not disapprove. History is another of my passions, and there is so much here to interest me. This morning, early, I went down to look at the Chapel under-croft, which was very dirty and dark, and I had not taken a light. I suppose the dress must have become dirtied there. I apologize, my Lady, that I did not notice it earlier.'

'And is that mud on the hem also, and on your shoes?'

'I'm sorry, my Lady. I have just taken a walk in the rose-garden. I should have noticed.'

'Well, well, it's of no consequence. No doubt you were too absorbed in Mr Wilkie Collins to pay attention to the condition of your dress. Have you enough light there? Good. I should like to hear "The Song of the Captive Israelites", and then the sequence of sonnets that follows.'

She leaned back in her chair, and closed her eyes.

'Page ninety-six,' she said, this woman who, only a short time before, had been on her knees, in agony of spirit, before the tomb of her dead lover. No sign remained of that pathetic lost soul; gone was that face, racked with unalloyed torment, on which her secret history had been so visibly stamped. In its place was her customary mask of haughty, unfathomable composure. But I had seen what I had seen; and so, with a curious sense of triumph, I began to read.

> *O who can contend*
> *With the wrath of angels,*
> *Or resist the righteous anger*
> *Of the just?*

ALTHOUGH THE HARD frosts of recent days had now abated, they were replaced by several more of bitter driving rain, which denied my Lady her usual habit of morning and evening exercise on the Library Terrace. Confined to her rooms, except for meal-times and the hours spent each morning with her secretary, she became crotchety and impatient, often sending me away angrily when I failed to perform some task to her satisfaction. Then, when I was called down again, she would try to make amends for her bad-temperedness – perhaps by opening a new book of Paris fashion-plates and asking me what I thought of this or that gown, or bringing out for my inspection an item of jewellery from Giuliano's, or some other piece of expensive frippery that had been sent up from Town.

On the day before the weather finally began to improve, as we sat before the fire, she asked me to read to her. I had hardly begun when she suddenly told me to stop, complaining that she had a headache. Then she expressed a wish to discuss some topic of current interest, but quickly became bored with the conversation and threw herself, with an irritated sigh, into the window-seat, leaving me to wait, without instruction, for nearly half an hour, while she gazed morose across the rain-lashed Park towards the dimly grey outline of the western woods.

I had picked up my needle and thread, to re-commence some work I had earlier laid aside, while carefully keeping one eye on my Lady as she sat in distracted contemplation. I wondered what she was thinking. What rough gales of guilt and fear were roaring beneath that impassive exterior? I was used to her abrupt changes of mood; but it was only too apparent that her mind was more than usually perturbed.

Towards four o'clock, she suddenly rose to her feet, announcing that she wished to rest.

'Please come and take out my pins, Alice,' she said, walking towards the bed-chamber.

I put down my work and followed her to her dressing-table, where I began to loosen her long black hair.

'Oh, Alice,' she sighed. 'What a world of trouble it is!'

I saw by her look that she did not expect a response, and so I continued with unpinning and brushing out her hair.

'How long have you been here, Alice?' she asked.

'Three months and six days, my Lady.'

'Three months and six days! How like you to be so precise! No doubt you know the hours and minutes also.'

'No, my Lady. But I am particular about these things.'

Our eyes meet in the looking-glass, and for the briefest space I think that she has seen through my disguise; but then she looks away, picks up a silver hand-mirror, and begins to examine her eyebrows with apparent nonchalance.

'Well, you have been a treasure – despite the occasional lapses in punctuality.'

She gives a little smile, which I return demurely.

'Good servants are increasingly hard to find. They are not what they once were, especially the females. I had a maid once, when I lived in the Dower House, Elizabeth Brine by name, who gave very satisfactory service for many years; but she changed for the worse, and I was obliged to let her go. Since then, I've been disappointed with every individual who has been given the position – except with you, my dear. I hope you are happy. I would not like to lose you.'

'Oh no, my Lady,' I assured her gaily. 'I am very happy here, and flattered that you think so well of me. It is a daily pleasure to serve you – and to do so in such a beautiful place as Evenwood. I could wish for no better position, and no other home.'

'That is most kindly said, Alice. If only all one's servants thought as you do, for I'm sure that there can be few places so enchantingly situated as Evenwood, which must be a constant compensation for the labours of service. I hope you will stay a very long time, Alice – perhaps you might even grow old here. My good and faithful servant!'

'I should like that, my Lady, and to be as dear to you as your old nurse, Mrs Kennedy.'

As I spoke, I was reaching forward to lay one of the hair-pins on the dressing-table. At the same moment, my Lady gave a little cry, and dropped the mirror she was holding on the floor, shattering the glass. Pushing back the chair, she turned her face towards me.

Her black eyes were opened to their widest extent, as if transfixed by some sight of the utmost horror; but then, her cheeks colouring, she began to rail at me in the most intemperate manner.

'You stupid, clumsy girl! Look what you've made me do! That mirror was my dear mamma's, and now it's broken because of you. And just when I thought you were different from those other stupid creatures! But you're as stupid as they were, I see. Leave me! Leave me!'

By now she was walking quickly towards the great carved bed with its blood-red hangings, her loosened hair tumbled all about her. Throwing herself on to the coverlet, she pulled one of the pillows towards her, cradling it in her arms like a child.

•   •   •

I HAD BEEN back in my room for no more than ten minutes when the bell over the fire-place started to ring.

As I re-entered my Lady's bed-chamber, she was standing with her arms outstretched towards me, dressed in a black silk robe, with a dark-red scarf of the same material wrapped round her head, like a turban, from which her hair, still loose, flowed down over her shoulders. She was smiling – but such a fixed, unintelligible smile that it put me immediately on my guard.

'Dearest Alice!'

Her voice was low and soft; the smile now broader – inviting, conciliatory, but dangerous, like that of some wily sorceress.

'Come!'

Now she was beckoning to me with her still-outstretched hands, the long fingers slowly indicating her wish for me to take them in mine.

For some moments I stood spellbound, rooted to the spot by the sight she presented; then, feeling my will returning once more, I closed the door behind me and began to walk slowly towards her. This was not Circe or Medusa standing there, but a mortal woman, beset with no common cares, vain and capricious, assaulted constantly by unknown terrors, and desperate to hold back the encroachment of Time. She had wished to display strength, by appearing thus before me; but I saw only impotence and frailty.

Our fingers meet, and lock gently together.

'Dear Alice,' she whispers. 'What must you think of me? Shall we sit?'

She draws me over to the window-seat, still smiling.

'Can you forgive me?'

'Forgive you, my Lady?'

'For my atrocious behaviour. It was not your fault that the mirror was broken. It was inexcusable of me to blame you for it. So will you now accept my apologies?'

Of course I tell her that an apology is neither required nor expected; at which she leans forward and – to my astonishment – kisses me tenderly on the cheek.

'What a marvel you are!' she says. 'So forbearing and tenderhearted! What must you have thought of me? I did not mean those horrid words; but there was a reason, my dear, which you must now hear.'

'If you wish, my Lady.'

She reaches forward and lightly touches my other cheek. The sensation of her long nails on my skin sends a little shiver down my spine, and I cannot help drawing away.

'Oh, Alice!' she cries, removing her hand. 'Are you afraid of me?'

'No, my Lady, I assure you.'

'But you're still upset, I see – and who could blame you? Stupid, indeed! How could I have been so cruel? But, my dear, when you mentioned the name of Mrs Kennedy, it was like a knife to my heart!'

She pauses, as if she expects me to say something. When I remain silent, she rises from the window-seat and walks towards the fireplace.

'I have recently received the most terrible news,' she says softly, head bowed, her back still towards me. 'Poor dear Mrs Kennedy . . . is dead!'

'Dead, my Lady?'

She nods mutely.

'The news, as you may imagine, was the greatest possible shock, and I fear that, when you happened to mention her name, it caused me to act in that most unkind and hurtful manner, for which I hope I am now pardoned.'

I naturally express my own shock at the death of 'dear Mrs Kennedy', for which my Lady thanks me most effusively.

'Did you read of the attack in the newspaper, my Lady?' I ask.

She stiffens slightly, and turns her head away once more.

'No, no. It was Mr Vyse who informed me.'

'There will be a funeral, I suppose, my Lady, which you will wish to attend?'

'Alas,' she sighs, 'the news has taken some time to reach me. My poor old nurse was buried many weeks since.

'And so, Alice dear,' she says, after a period of silent reflection, 'now that we are friends again, there's something I must say to you.'

'Yes, my Lady?'

The indulgent, wistful smile has gone. In its place is a look that throws me into confusion and alarm.

'I no longer wish you to be my maid.'

SUDDENLY, IT SEEMS that the tables have been turned on me. I have been discovered.

'Have you nothing to say?'

Her unflinching eye holds mine for several seconds. Then, as suddenly as it had gone, the smile returns. Taking a step towards me, she kisses me once again on the cheek, and takes my hand in hers.

'Dear Alice! Did you think I meant that you were being dismissed? You silly goose! How could you think so?'

'I don't know, my Lady. You seemed so . . .'

'No, no, I meant no such thing. Of course I have no intention of dismissing you; but I have come to a decision that affects your future here. I have been considering the matter for some time – almost from the day you first came here. And so, Alice, here it is. I no longer wish you to be my maid: I wish you to be my companion. There! What do you say to that?'

Her companion! I could have desired nothing more than an association of greater intimacy with her, one that would afford new opportunities to observe her, and which might admit me into parts of her life that, at present, were closed to me. It was therefore with unfeigned satisfaction that I conveyed my thanks and gratitude to her, for which I received another kiss, and many expressions of pleasure and regard.

'Of course you will have a generous allowance – I cannot have my companion dressed in dreary black; and new accommodation must be found for you – there's a charming set of rooms on the next floor, with a snug little sitting-room, that I have in mind. Naturally, you will occupy a very superior position in the household, although for the time being things must go on as they are, until a new maid can be found . . .'

On she talked, but I hardly heard her. I was already picturing to myself the surprise and delight that Madame would feel at my news, and anticipating the commencement, in earnest, of the Great Task, once I had received my guardian's third letter.

When I was eventually released from my Lady, I ran upstairs to write a note to Madame, and then went down, with a light and triumphant heart, to take my supper – perhaps for the last time – in the servants' hall.

II

On the Threshold

IT IS THE 23rd of December. My Lady is in one of her petulant moods and sends me away curtly after I have dressed her. Having taken a walk in the gardens, I am returning to the Entrance Court when a carriage draws up, from which emerges the lanky figure of Mr Armitage Vyse – the first of the Christmas guests to arrive, and, as far as I am concerned, the least welcome.

I spend the next hour in my room, expecting to be called down to my Lady; but when the bell does not ring, I go downstairs to ask Mr Pocock whether Lady Tansor is still occupied with her morning correspondence.

'No, miss,' he replies. 'Her Ladyship has driven out in the barouche with Mr Vyse. I'm afraid I don't know where they've gone, or when they'll be back.'

Mystified by this secretive excursion, but glad to have more time to myself, I take a book to one of my favourite places of resort – a secluded window-seat high up in one of the towers that overlooked the Entrance Court and gave an enchanting view of the Park and winding river – to await my Lady's return.

• • •

MID-DAY APPROACHED. WHERE had they gone? What was afoot? Then, happening to glance out of the window towards the Even-brook, I noticed a man standing on the bridge, staring towards the house. The distance was too great for me to discern his features; but the set of his tall, broad-shouldered figure called up a distinct memory of the man I had seen standing in the fog and looking up at my room. Now, however, aided by the clear morning light, a new and most distinctive feature of the watcher could just be made out. The right-hand sleeve of his coat hung limply down by his side. I strained my eyes, to make sure I was not mistaken. No; I was now sure of it. He had only one arm.

Just then, cresting the summit of the Rise, a vehicle came into view, which I soon saw was my Lady's barouche.

The man on the bridge immediately turned at the sound of the approaching horses; then stepped to one side to allow the vehicle to pass. As it did so, my Lady looked back at him. The man stood watching the barouche as it turned in through the great iron gates and came to a halt before the front door. He continued to maintain an attitude of the most intense interest, his hand shading his eyes, as Mr Vyse helped my Lady down, and escorted her up the steps. As she reached the door, she turned to look back towards the bridge; but the man had now begun to walk, with long purposeful strides, up the Rise towards the South Gates.

Thinking that my Lady would soon wish me to attend her, I went quickly back to my room to await her summons; but the bell remained silent. Another hour went by, and still no call came. Then there was a knock at the door. It was Barrington.

'This has come for you, Miss,' he said, handing me a brown-paper package.

My first thought was that it must be Madame's third letter arrived at last, and of course my heart leaped with eager anticipation; then I saw that it bore a London postmark, and that it was directed to me in a hand I did not recognize.

When Barrington had gone, I sat at my table and hastily ripped off the paper wrapper.

Inside were a short note; a letter, in Mr Thornhaugh's hand, addressed to 'Miss E.A. Gorst, Private and Personal'; and a small-octavo book bound in dark-blue cloth.

The note was from Mrs Ridpath.

12, Devonshire Street

22nd December 1876

MY DEAR ESPERANZA,—

At Mr Thornhaugh's request, I have obtained, and am now sending, the enclosed volume, which he had difficulty finding in Paris, but which he & Madame wish you most particularly to peruse, after you have read the letter from him that is also enclosed.

The book comes, as I need hardly say, with his very best seasonal compliments, & those of Madame – & of course with mine also.

I am further requested by Madame to say that, to avoid suspicion, she proposes that all letters from Paris should in future be forwarded to you at Evenwood from here, & you should do the same in reverse. A suitable & safe accommodation address in the neighbourhood, to where I can direct letters, would be an additional advantage.

I trust that you go on well at Evenwood, which I have heard is a most lovely place. Lovely or not, you will always remember, I hope, that Devonshire Street is not so very far away, should you ever need a refuge.

I remain, yours very affectionately,

E. RIDPATH

My anticipation now mounting, I tore open the envelope containing Mr Thornhaugh's letter, hoping that it might also contain some communication from Madame. I saw immediately that it did not. This is what I read.

Avenue d'Uhrich
Paris

20th December 1876

LITTLE QUEEN,—

*I am bidden by Madame to inform you that, after much careful &
anxious deliberation, she feels obliged to delay sending you her third
Letter of Instruction, which she had fully intended to do this very
week. Indeed, she has been occupied these past two days with its composition, to the exclusion of all else. The task, however, has proved
more difficult than she anticipated.*

*What it is absolutely necessary for you to know and understand
— particularly with regard to your own history — is so extensive that
Madame does not now feel that it can be conveyed to you in a single
communication. Nor, of course, will it be possible, at present, for her to
speak to you in person, & so satisfy you concerning the many points
on which you will undoubtedly require explanation and elaboration.*

*However, we have recently come across — by quite curious chance
— an unexpected source of information, a copy of which Madame
wished me to send to you via Mrs Ridpath. The circumstances of its
discovery were these.*

*A few weeks ago, an old friend of Madame's, living now in Lon-
don, sent her an advertisement printed in the* Illustrated London
News. *It had been placed by a Mr John Lazarus, requesting Mr
Edwin Gorst, if still living, or any member of his family or acquaintance, if not, to communicate with him at their earliest convenience.*

*You may easily imagine the keen interest that this aroused in
Madame and me. I immediately wrote to Mrs Ridpath, who called
upon this gentleman to inform him that Edwin Gorst was dead, but
that she, Mrs Ridpath, had been authorized by an old and trusted
friend of Mr Gorst's to answer the advertisement. It seems that Mr
Lazarus not only wished to give your father a copy of his recollections,
in which he figures prominently, but also to renew the brief friendship
that they had enjoyed many years previously.*

Madame feels that this gentleman's recollections will apprise you of a great many things concerning both yr father & yr mother, particularly the former, that you would wish to know. I have taken the liberty of marking the two relevant chapters, which will prepare the ground for the letter from Madame that will come, as promised, before the year's end.

By way of supplementing Mr Lazarus's volume, you may also expect to receive, within a few days, transcriptions from a journal kept by yr mother during the period of her life when she met yr father, & which has been in Madame's safe-keeping since his death.

Madame begs that you will forgive her for keeping the journal from you, but she was acting under an obligation to yr father to do so until you reached the age of twenty-one. She now feels that she must break that obligation, for the sake of the Great Task, and because it is wrong that you should be kept in ignorance of what the journal contains any longer.

Madame asked me to make the transcriptions in shorthand for safety's sake. We must be ever aware of prying eyes.

I remain, ever yr devoted friend,

B. THORNHAUGH

My disappointment at not receiving Madame's final Letter of Instruction was naturally great; but the curiosity aroused by Mr Thornhaugh's letter was – for the moment – even greater, engendering the keenest sensation of expectation; for the most insistent and tormenting question of all seemed about to be answered at last.

Who was I?

⚜ END OF ACT TWO ⚜

THE PAST AWAKENS

And diff'ring judgements serve but to declare
That truth lies somewhere, if we knew but where.

WILLIAM COWPER, 'HOPE' (1782)

15

The Resurrection of Edwin Gorst

I

Mr Lazarus

THE BOOK that Mr Thornhaugh had sent contained the privately printed recollections of a London shipping-agent, the aforementioned Mr John Lazarus, of Billiter Street, who had spent several years in the Atlantic wine trade.

This gentleman was unknown to me, the connexion of his profession with what little Madame had told me of my father unclear. Questions and uncertainties began to jostle in my head; but when I turned to the first chapter indicated for my attention by Mr Thornhaugh, I became instantly gripped.

There, on the very first page, was my father's name: *Edwin Gorst*.

To have his name printed there, for all the world to see, sent a thrill through me. I had never seen it set down anywhere, except on that shadowed slab of stone in the Cemetery of St-Vincent. I remembered sometimes as a child having the curious notion that only three living persons – Madame, Mr Thornhaugh, and myself – remembered that my father had even existed. But of course he had been a man living in the world of men, playing his part – large or small – in the dramas of other people's lives; he had made friends and acquaintances – perhaps even enemies; and here was Mr John Lazarus to prove it.

To stand on the threshold, as it then seemed, of possessing the knowledge concerning myself, and of the people who had given me life, which I had secretly yearned to possess for so long, was a most solemn moment, and I felt it to be so to my very soul. I sat for some minutes, hardly daring to begin reading, heart beating, apprehensive of what I was about to discover.

For the past hour or more, a wind had been gusting noisily round the eaves; but now it had fallen quite away, and all was deathly silent, as if the great rambling house, and the wide world beyond, of which I knew so little, was – like me – holding its breath.

It is a most singular sensation to eavesdrop on one's own life. Lacking my own memories of my father, I was now obliged to appropriate those of a complete stranger. Would it not be better to remain in ignorance? Mr Lazarus's recollections – imperfect and fragmentary as they must be – could claim to be only the dimmest of reflections of the living, breathing being who had once walked the earth as Edwin Gorst. Could they even be trusted?

Thus I held back until, at last, after getting up to lock my door against intrusion, and clearing my throat in a business-like manner, as if I were about to begin conning some piece of work set for me by my tutor, I began to read.

Read? No. I was soon devouring the words before me, like some starving animal who has been tossed a few scraps of meagre sustenance. So sit with me now for a while, as I let Mr John Lazarus, of Billiter Street, City, tell you, in his own words, what I had never known until that late December afternoon: the circumstances by which my father – through the agency of Mr Lazarus – reclaimed his life from certain decline and death; how he met my mother, on the island of Madeira, in the year 1856; and the consequences of their union.

II

From J.S. Lazarus, My Atlantic Life: Recollections of
Portugal, the Canary Islands, the Azores, and the Island
of Madeira, during the years 1846 to 1859*

AFTER ATTENDING MY mother's funeral, as related in the previous
chapter of these recollections, I left English shores once more, in
the last week of July 1856, first to undertake some brief business in
Madeira, and then to sail on to the Canaries, having affairs to conduct there with my old friend, Señor J—, in Teguise, on the island
of Lanzarote.

After only three days, however, I was obliged to take ship back
to Madeira; but I did not wish to leave the Canaries without paying
a further visit to the English gentleman, Mr Edwin Gorst, to whom
I had been introduced the previous year, and for whom, as already
recounted, I had been able to do some little service by taking a box
of papers to England, which he desired to be placed in the hands of
his solicitor for safe-keeping.

If it should seem strange to the little circle of family members,
friends, and former colleagues, for whom this book is intended, that
I should devote so many words to this gentleman, it is because my
acquaintance with him, although brief, was one of the most memorable of my life. I have never forgotten this remarkable individual,
and never shall. I therefore make no apology for presenting a full
account of that acquaintance (of which I have never spoken, except
to my dear departed wife), believing that it may be of interest to my
readers in many ways.

Having always been a punctilious diary-keeper, I have every
confidence of the accuracy of my record, although I acknowledge
that it has been necessary, at many points, to compose my own
renderings of conversations, whilst always drawing on my diary for
substantiation.

•   •   •

*Norwich: Jarrold & Sons, printed for private circulation, 1874.

I HAD RETURNED to the Canary Islands on one previous occasion since undertaking the original commission for Mr Gorst, and had made an attempt then to call at his house in the village of Y—, only to find him away from home. I wished, naturally, to assure him that the papers had been safely delivered, as he had requested, and also to inform him that I had been given, in return, a letter from his solicitor, which he had asked me, most particularly, to hand to Mr Gorst in person; but my time was short, and so, being unable to wait more than five minutes, I opened the door of the tiny house in the Calle E— S—, placed the letter, with a short covering note of my own, on a nearby table, and departed.

The next day, however, on board the ship that was to take me back to Madeira, I began to regret that I had not waited a little longer, against Mr Gorst's return to the house, so that he might have received the letter directly from my hands, as his solicitor had been anxious for him to do. I thus determined that, when next I had occasion to return to the Canaries, in three months' time, I would make every effort to call again at the house in the Calle E— S—, in order to make myself comfortable that he had indeed found the letter where I had left it.

Mr Gorst had exerted a powerful fascination over me from our first brief meeting, when I had been introduced to him at a small gathering of English residents. I knew nothing of his history, or of why he had come to such a remote place, apparently to live out his days; but I gleaned enough to be convinced that some great calamity had befallen him, requiring a permanent removal from the country of his birth.

At the time when I took possession of the box of papers he wished to place in my temporary charge, he had been living in Y— for only a few months. In appearance, he was exceptionally tall and well-made, with luxuriant moustachios, and a remarkable pair of limpid brown eyes. Altogether, my new acquaintance cut a most striking and imposing figure. (The local people, I later learned, called him *Il emperador inglés*.) He was, besides, a most stimulating conversationalist, exhibiting an unusually wide knowledge of many abstruse subjects.

Yet though he affected a casual vivacity in his manner, it was clear to me from the first that this was but a carapace or mask, intended to cover over a deeply wounded spirit. From time to time, he would display signs of acute nervousness, which sat oddly with his powerful physical presence. His great hands shook as he poured out a glass of wine, or when he passed one of them, as he did frequently, through his long hair, which, whilst I judged him to be perhaps only thirty-five or thirty-six years of age, was receding fast from his temples.

My initial curiosity concerning Mr Gorst – and, although I could not say why, my compassion for his situation – increased as the afternoon wore on, and was roused, in particular, by something he said as he handed over the box of papers that he wished me to take back to England.

He had been speaking fondly, and with great gusto, of old times in London, a city for which he cherished an apparently unbounded affection.

'It's the very greatest city on earth,' he maintained. 'You cannot imagine how much I miss stepping out of a morning – a bright, sharp, English morning, with the early mist just lifting off the dear old river – and striding down the Strand again, with no particular purpose in view, other than to go where the fancy takes me, and to feel the breath of the great heaving city on my face.'

'You have a romantic notion of the metropolis,' I observed with a smile. 'You speak as though it were a living creature, rather than a thing built by men.'

'But it *is* a living creature!' he exclaimed, with a sudden burst of passion. 'That's the very thing about it that makes it like no other city. It has a heart that beats, and a soul, too. But I dare say you're right.'

He fell silent, passed a trembling hand through his hair once more, and turned away to look out of the window at the little patch of dusty earth that separated the back of the house from a dreary desert of black volcanic ash stretching away into the distance.

'I do have a rather original view of London,' he admitted, 'made more so, perhaps, by absence.'

Then he opened a cupboard and brought out a wooden box, on which was affixed a label bearing the name and address of his solicitor.

'I am placing my life in your hands, Mr Lazarus,' he said, setting the box down on a table. 'You will, I know, guard it well, and see it delivered safely to its destination. What remains here is no life at all, only the merest shred of existence, which I pray will not be long sustained; for I am weary of the world, and long to be out of it.'

He spoke these words in an accent of such unmitigated sorrow and regret that my heart was wrenched to hear him.

'But surely,' I objected, 'you cannot say so. You are a young man still – younger than me, at any rate, and I hardly consider *my* life to be over, far from it. Of course I do not know what has brought you here, nor why you choose to stay in such an inhospitable place, and I would not presume to enquire; but you speak as though you were prevented by some force or other from leaving this place. Why can you not seek out a more congenial haven of retirement, if you are set on sequestering yourself from the world?'

'Because,' he replied, with a strange light in his eyes, 'I *am* a prisoner here, despite the appearance of freedom; and the truth is that I am growing sick and dispirited, as any prisoner must who daily contemplates the removal of those simple but infinitely precious liberties that he once took for granted, but which can never more be enjoyed. Yet I cannot, and do not, complain. I am my own gaoler, you see, and remain incarcerated here by the constant exertion of my own will.'

With these strange and – to me – incomprehensible words, he handed me the box of papers, we shook hands, and I took my leave.

I DID NOT see Mr Gorst again until my business with Señor J— required me to sail once more to the Canaries, as I have already described. I found him much changed. His former weight had dropped from him most alarmingly, leaving him thin and stooping, haggard-eyed, with brittle, thinning hair, a sallow complexion, and other unmistakable indications of declining health.

Sitting together in the dusty back-yard of his house, I told him that the box of papers had been safely delivered to his solicitor. To my relief, he confirmed that he had found the letter from that gentleman that I had left for him.

During the course of the ensuing conversation, Mr Gorst confessed that his little store of money had dwindled away almost to nothing. As a result, he had been obliged to support himself as best he could by offering English lessons, and – as pupils were scarce in this volcanic fastness – by becoming a jack-of-all-trades. He said, smiling weakly, that he had surprised himself by discovering a previously unrealized talent for mending fences and painting windows. By such modest shifts, he claimed to earn enough to pay his rent and keep a little food in his cupboard from day to day; but I could see only too clearly that his condition was increasingly desperate, not to say perilous.

Despite our brief acquaintance, and although I could not guess what force – whether that of a tormented conscience, or some debilitating extremity of grief – maintained him in self-enforced exile from his native land, I found it impossible to leave him in this miserable state. It was only too clear that his days were numbered if he remained in his present neglectful way of life; and so, as I was taking my leave, I made a proposal to him, despite having little hope of its being accepted.

Once again, my business required me to spend an extended period on Madeira, an island whose healthful and equable climate would certainly have an immediately beneficial effect on Mr Gorst. If he could be persuaded to join me for the duration of my stay, I considered it possible that he might contemplate residing there permanently; if not, then I had the means to arrange his return to Lanzarote at no cost to himself.

This, then, was my proposal, which I placed before Mr Gorst as we stood in the doorway of his house, shaking hands.

'Will you give it serious consideration?' I asked. 'I can see for myself that your circumstances are not of the best here, and that your means have become – excuse my mentioning them – somewhat straitened. It would, of course, be improper of me to attempt to argue you out of any fixed resolution that you hold to remain here. All I ask is that you do not dismiss my proposition out of hand. Won't you do that, as a favour from one Englishman to another?'

He smiled, but said nothing; and so I handed him a card on which was printed the address of Señor J— in Teguise, requesting him most earnestly to send word there by the following evening if he wished to take up my offer.

'I have a charming little villa on Madeira, overlooking the harbour at Funchal,' I said, 'where you would be most comfortable, and at complete liberty to come and go, and to do, as you pleased.'

Still he made no reply, but stood regarding the card with a strange intensity of expression. Then he looked up.

'You are very kind, sir,' he said quietly, his hands visibly trembling. 'Kinder than I deserve.'

'Nonsense,' I replied. 'I would regard the arrangement as being entirely in my favour. I'm weary of voyaging about these Atlantic waters on my own; and although I have many old friends on Madeira, I have no English companion there with whom to pass the long evenings. In a word, I would be most grateful for your company – if you are so minded – until it is time for me to leave for England. You'll send word by tomorrow evening, then, if you wish to join me?'

He nodded, and we parted.

I confess that I had not the least expectation that I would ever hear from Mr Gorst again; but at six o'clock the following evening, a note was delivered to Señor J—'s house in Teguise. I have it yet, and transcribe it here:

MY DEAR MR LAZARUS,—

I am writing, as you kindly invited me to do, to take up yr most generous offer of accompanying you to Madeira.

It is but too true that my present way of going on here has had, & is having, a deleterious effect on my health; & tho' I have little appetite for life, I find, on considering the matter in the light of yr proposal, & somewhat to my surprise, that I still entertain the natural human aversion for the alternative.

It is therefore with pleasure & gratitude that I look forward to passing a few weeks in yr company on Madeira — time, I hope, that will fortify me to endure the resumption of my life here with something of my former vigour after you have returned to dear old England; for I must own that I feel as weak as a baby at present, & the indefinite prospect of physical toil — which, although undeniably honest, & my sole remaining means of support, is almost more than I can at present bear.

To Madeira, then (which I now recall — with great satisfaction that my memory for these things is not wholly moribund — was the Purpuraria of the Romans). Although it will be but a short respite, it will be a most welcome one.

I must beg yr forgiveness, however, for presuming to impose a condition on my coming with you. I cannot, & will not, speak of my former life in England, nor of why I chose to immolate myself in exile here. That is a closed book, which will never again be opened. We must therefore content ourselves in our conversations with matters of merely general & objective interest. If this is acceptable to you, then I look forward to yr promised communication concerning the practical arrangements for our journey.

I remain, my dear sir, yours most sincerely,

E. GORST

Although I was naturally most curious to know more about my new travelling companion and house-guest, it was impossible not to agree to his condition. Whatever kept Mr Gorst from returning to his native shores, and to those he had left behind, it was a mystery that I must accept might remain forever unfathomed.

III
Recollections of Mr John Lazarus Continued

THE ARRANGEMENTS FOR our departure from Lanzarote were duly put in hand, and Mr Edwin Gorst and I began our journey northwards to Madeira, on the brigantine Bellstar.

For the first part of the voyage, my new companion seemed distracted and disinclined to talk. He spent long hours by himself, gazing out concentratedly at the horizon, yet in a strange unseeing way, as if he were mesmerized by some other prospect of sea and sky and cloud, distant and unearthly, of which only he was aware.

Then, as our destination drew nearer, he became suddenly loquacious, and began to speak animatedly once more of the glorious vitality of London, and of how he missed the dirty old Thames and the noisy rain-soaked streets. He asked whether I had ever ascended to the Golden Gallery of St Paul's, which I confessed I had never done, although I had lived close by for many years.

'It is a most inspiriting sight,' he said, 'even on a gloomy day, but you must not go alone. Take someone with you to share the pleasure.'

He also spoke fondly of the book-stalls in Leicester Square, where he had once found a copy of Thomas North's celebrated translation of Plutarch, proceeding from this happy memory to another, and then another.

It was impossible not to feel that this passionate attachment to his former metropolitan life must render his separation from it almost insupportable. Yet again, the question naturally arose concerning the unyielding nature of the circumstances that bound him so fast, in chains of his own devising, to a life so opposite in every way to the one he had previously led. However, as I had agreed not to question him concerning his past, I was obliged to let my curiosity – more than curiosity, indeed: rather the keenest interest born out of genuine concern – go unsatisfied.

At last, on a fine August morning, at a little before noon, we tacked into the port at Funchal on a gentle south-westerly, and lay to anchor a little way off from the quay.

High above the town, dark clouds were beginning to roll threateningly across the bare mountain peaks, and long fingers of grey-black mist were seeping down into the densely wooded clefts that radiated from the serrated heights; but in the harbour, the sun was warm on our backs, the waves sparkled and danced, and the white houses reflected a dazzling light. Dazzling, too, were the colours that met our sea-wearied eyes: the vivid hues of oleander, blue hydrangea, and heliotrope, the white blossom of coffee-trees; and, eastwards, beyond the old city walls, up towards the Mount and the Palheiro,* shining swathes of golden broom.

Turning to my companion as we stood together on the fore-deck, I saw that he was smiling to himself. Naturally, I enquired after the source of his amusement.

'Oh, it is nothing,' he replied. 'I was merely reflecting that your name is Lazarus, and yet it is *you* who have raised *me* from the dead by bringing me here, where perhaps I can live again, and be happy, if only for a brief time.'

'Well,' I said, 'I am glad indeed to be the agent of your recuperation; for you are certainly ill, and this, you know, is the very place to make you well again. You'll find the climate entirely beneficial, and I hope to see you back in full working order in no time at all.'

I had spoken with some confidence, for I had seen many remarkable instances, amongst the numerous foreign invalids who had taken up residence on the island, of permanent recovery from serious illness and debilitation. My own dear wife's brother, Mr Archibald Fraser, had spent two years here, having arrived in a most deplorable condition following a diplomatic posting to India, and had returned home completely revivified.

I was recounting the story of my brother-in-law's wonderful restoration to health by the Madeiran climate when we were approached by the visit boat, the Portuguese Bicolour fluttering gaily in the bow, in which were seated the Harbour Master, the Health Officer, and a physician, the duties of the two latter gentlemen being to ascertain whether any vessel coming into the port could be allowed to communicate with the shore, or be placed under quarantine. This party was quickly followed by the Customs House boat; and then,

---

*The Mount is better known now as the hill parish of Monte, famous for the toboggans that have long been provided for the descent to Funchal. The Palheiro de Ferreiro, or Smith's Cottage, was built, and the extensive area around it planted, by João, 1st Count of Carvalhal.

the arrival formalities having been concluded to the satisfaction of all concerned, Mr Gorst and I took our places in the skiff that was to take us off the *Bellstar*.

We landed on the beach, composed here of pebbles mixed with finely granulated black sand, and my companion stood for a moment gazing up at the wooded flanks of the mountains that reared up behind the town – or city, rather, for Funchal boasts an episcopal church, the Sé Cathedral. Then he kneeled down to pick up a handful of sand, which he let trickle through his fingers.

'Thus,' I heard him say in a low voice, 'my life runs away, and is blown to the four winds.'

Whether he intended me to hear his words, I cannot say; but I affected not to, and instead cheerfully clapped him on the back and welcomed him to the island of Madeira.

A *carro de bois**was waiting to take us up through the steep streets and lanes towards the lower slopes of the Serra. Here, surrounded on all sides by close-packed woods of pine and chestnut, was situated the modest *quinta*, or manor-house, the Quinta da Pinheiro, which – as recounted in an earlier chapter – I had purchased in 1849.

On our arrival, I called for tea, and my guest and I sat conversing on the balcony, shaded from the midday heat by the gigantic fronds of an ancient palm, as we waited for our luggage to be brought up from the Customs House.

'Will you be comfortable here, do you think?' I asked.

He did not answer immediately, but continued to gaze out towards the Desertas, the three uninhabited and waterless islands that could be seen rising out of the turquoise and sapphire-blue sea to the south-east of Funchal. Then he turned his long, sun-burned face towards me.

'More comfortable than I deserve,' he said, with a sad smile.

'Come now,' I remonstrated, 'that is harsh. We all deserve a little comfort.'

*A peculiarly Madeiran form of conveyance, being a kind of covered sledge drawn by two oxen.

'I beg to differ,' was all he replied.

Here was an opportunity that I might have taken to begin making some preliminary enquiries into his history, to see where lay the cause of his previous self-incarceration in a place so utterly removed from his former life; but that avenue was shut off, and so I contented myself with remarking, in a general way, that it was often the case that we judge our actions more harshly than they deserve, and that, in any case, no man is beyond redemption.

'If only I could believe that,' he said; and then, before I could respond, he had changed the subject abruptly and asked whether I had any English newspapers in the house.

'It has been a good while since I last saw one,' he continued. 'My only indulgence, from time to time, and when I can, has been to alleviate my exile with a little out-of-date news from home.'

I quickly procured an old copy of the *Illustrated London News*, which I had happened to bring with me from London on my voyage out. He received it with great anticipation, saying that it had always been a favourite periodical of his, settled himself in his chair, and began reading with great attention.

At that moment, a knock at the front door, and the sound of voices in the hall, announced the arrival of our luggage; and so I left Mr Gorst to his reading. When I returned, some ten minutes later, he had gone.

The paper lay tossed aside on the floor. The first two sheets had been ripped out, torn in two, and then evidently trampled on, although whether deliberately or by accident, I could not tell. In amazement, I picked up the torn sheets to see whether they might yield any clue as to why Mr Gorst – or so it seemed – had vented his rage upon them.

On a cursory examination, they appeared to contain nothing of great remark: a leading article on the American Question; an account of a fancy-dress ball at the Royal Academy of Music, and another on the opening of new docks at Hartlepool. Had my guest been enraged by any of these, or by succeeding items on the Civil War in Kansas, or a conspiracy to assassinate the Queen of Spain? I could not think so.

Then I cast my eye over the epitomes of foreign and domestic news printed on the second sheet.

The first, and longest, paragraph concerned the arrival from the Continent of a Mrs Tadeusz Zaluski, the former Miss Emily Carteret, accompanied by her husband, Colonel Zaluski, and their recently born son, at Evenwood, the country seat of the lady's distinguished relative, Lord Tansor. I looked at the remaining, and much shorter, epitomes, but they appeared entirely innocuous. Then I returned to the first item. Was it merely coincidental that it carried the clear impress of Mr Gorst's boot upon it, as if he had tried to stamp out the information it contained?

I went to my study to lock the torn sheets in my desk drawer, although I cannot quite say why I felt it was necessary to retain something whose significance was entirely lost on me. Then I went to look for Mr Gorst.

I finally found him at the far end of the garden, gazing vacantly at the moss-covered base of an old thorn-apple tree. Hearing my approach, he turned a despairing face towards me.

'Mr Gorst – my dear sir! What on earth is the matter?'

'You see,' he said, in a pathetic half-whisper; 'it follows me here. Even here, to this paradise. There is no escape.'

I did not well know what to say in reply to his strange words, which, it was clear, bore reference to whatever he had read in the *Illustrated London News*. He saw my awkwardness, but made no attempt to alleviate it, nor did he offer any explanation for his behaviour, whilst I, for my part, refrained from mentioning the torn sheets from the paper that I had found on the balcony.

'Come now,' I said, as cheerily as I could. 'You are fatigued from the journey. Come back to the house and take some rest. I must go down into the city on business, but shall be back at six o'clock for dinner.'

He nodded his assent, and we walked together in silence down the tree-shaded path and into the cobbled courtyard at the rear of the house, where I left him to make his way up to the room that had been prepared for him.

16

Miss Blantyre Meets Her Fate

I

The Author's Narrative Continued

I LOOKED up from reading Mr Lazarus's recollections as the clock on the mantel-piece began to strike the hour. Four o'clock, and still no summons from my Lady. No matter. I was in no mind to play either maid or companion, and could not think what I would have done, had the bell in the corner of my room begun to ring. How would I maintain my customary role when my heart was on fire?

My father! My dear father! I now saw him so clearly in my mind's eye – and with such a thrill of instantaneous recognition, like meeting an old and dear friend one has not seen for many years. As described by Mr Lazarus, he was how I had come to picture him: a man possessed of no common intellect, and having a largeness and distinctiveness of character that would have made him a presence of note in any company. Such persons are not easily forgotten – they leave a mark on the world. Mr Thornhaugh was one such. My father, I was sure, had been another.

Yet here were also mysteries and secrets, and still more unanswered questions, on which Mr Lazarus was unable to shed any light. My father had lived in London, as it now appeared; but what profession had he followed there? Had he been born in the metropolis, and into what condition of life? Above all, why had he left England, to exile himself on the inhospitable fastness of Lanzarote?

Something greater even than intense curiosity on these points, however, had ignited the conflagration in my heart, and set my mind racing.

The cause had been the incident, described by Mr Lazarus, concerning the number of the *Illustrated London News* that had carried an account of the arrival in England from the Continent of Colonel Tadeusz Zaluski and his wife, the former Miss Emily Carteret – the woman who was now my mistress. It seemed certain that there must have been a connexion between my father and the then Miss Carteret, and of such a character as to cause a temporary fit of rage when he had read of her marriage to the Polish colonel.

This piece of intelligence – which seemed to corroborate what Madame had intimated concerning Lady Tansor's shaping role in my life – made me mad to learn more; but could Mr Lazarus tell me what I now longed to know?

Praying that the summoning bell would remain silent, I resumed my reading.

II
Recollections of Mr John Lazarus Continued

THE FOLLOWING MORNING, I rose early and, leaving Mr Gorst to his slumbers, went down to the harbour, where I had several matters of business that required my attention. These kept me occupied for two or three hours, after which I took a *carro de bois* to the house of an old Madeiran acquaintance, Mr Danvers Pryce.

I had a particular reason for calling on Pryce that was entirely unconnected with the mutual business interests through which we had been introduced when I had first come to the island. As I had hoped, I also found Mrs Pryce at home, for it was to her that I especially wished to speak.

This lady took a close interest in all the doings and begettings of what our grandfathers used to call the 'haut ton'. The *Court Circular* was her constant companion, and I truly believe that she could name every lord and lady in England, as well as all their offspring, their country seats, town-houses, and annual incomes, and knew to the last detail all their comings and goings, either as reported in the public prints, or by the tongue of vulgar gossip. When I mentioned the name of Lord Tansor, therefore, it was with some confidence that my curiosity concerning this noble personage would be amply satisfied.

'Lord Tansor!' she cried, throwing down the piece of work on which she had been engaged. 'Oh my dear John, you must remember!'

'Remember what?' I asked.

'But it was the most shocking thing,' she replied excitedly. 'You surely cannot have forgotten?'

Once again I had to profess my ignorance.

'The murder of his heir, my dear, Mr Phoebus Daunt, the poet. Now you must remember?'

The name of Mr Phoebus Daunt, whose celebrated works had long been greatly admired by my dear wife, was of course instantly familiar to me. I then recollected that I had been in the Azores at the time of his death, in December 1854, and consequently news of this national tragedy had not reached we Atlantic nomads for several weeks. Soon afterwards, I had been obliged to take ship for Lisbon, and so was deprived of further intelligence concerning the event and its consequences.

I now learned from Mrs Pryce that, a little time before his death, Mr Daunt had been named by Lord Tansor as the heir to his extensive property; not only this, but he had also been engaged to marry a relative of his Lordship's, Miss Emily Carteret. Of course I immediately recognized the name as being that of the lady on the page that Mr Gorst had torn from the *Illustrated London News*, and I listened eagerly as Mrs Pryce told me that Miss Carteret had subsequently taken the place of her murdered fiancé as Lord Tansor's successor. There was this difference, however: in addition to her relative's fabulous wealth, and his principal seat of Evenwood, her blood relationship would also qualify her to inherit the ancient Tansor title as the 26th Baroness.

'It hit the old man hard, being childless since the death of his only son,' said Mr Pryce, at which he was instantly admonished by his wife for the use of what she described as 'a disrespectful epithet'.

'Well,' he countered, 'Lord Tansor has two arms and two legs, and walks upright I think, and so may be called a man like any other; and as he is no longer young, then I suppose he may be called old.'

A little more good-humoured banter of this kind ensued; and then Mrs Pryce, warming to her theme, spoke at length of Lord Tansor's distress at the terrible loss of his chosen heir, of whom he had been inordinately fond, and of the lady who had taken his place.

'Miss Carteret – Mrs Zaluski, as I should now call her – is a proud, cold thing, my dear, by all accounts.'

Mrs Pryce leaned confidingly towards me.

'And yet she is accomplished, and a great beauty; and the death of poor Mr Daunt positively broke her heart. Her own father had also been the victim of a murderous attack. Only think! Her future husband and her father, both killed!'

'But she is now married, it seems,' I observed.

'Indeed,' came the reply, with a decidedly disapproving emphasis. 'To a foreigner with hardly a penny to his name; and all done before poor Mr Daunt was hardly cold in his grave!'

At this, Mr Pryce gave a sceptical 'Harrumph!' by way of objection.

'Hardly cold! Six months! Cold enough, I think.'

'As you say, six months,' his wife retorted. 'Some might consider that to be indecent haste.'

Mr Pryce gave another 'Harrumph!'

'Well, you may express yourself in that vexing way, Mr Pryce,' she continued, with a little toss of her head, 'but it does not alter the case. Propriety was offended. Public opinion was against her.'

'Propriety! Public opinion!' cried Mr Pryce. 'What should Lord Tansor's heir care for either? She can laugh in the face of both. And there's this to consider, Mrs Pryce. She acted, as I've heard it said, with the full approval of Lord Tansor. What do you say to that, eh?'

This challenge appeared to hit home, for when Mrs Pryce replied, it was in a more conciliatory tone.

'It's true, I suppose, that her conduct may have been shaped by a very natural desire to accommodate the wishes of her noble relative. That, I admit, would be a very great consideration.'

'What Mrs Pryce means,' said her husband, turning towards me, 'is that *old* Tansor' – here he gave his good lady a benignly significant look – 'had no more prospect of finding – or, indeed, of fathering – another heir than he had of swimming the English Channel. You may tut-tut, Mrs Pryce, but it's the plain truth. That stick of a wife—'

'Second wife,' interrupted Mrs Pryce.

'As you say,' conceded Mr Pryce, 'that stick of a *second* wife will never produce an heir for him, that's clear; and an heir – as everyone knows – is what he desires above all things. Of course he'd prefer a son of his own, or someone he could call a son; but the former Miss Carteret, who has the good old Duport blood in her, will do very well. And now *she* has a son, and so all's well in Lord Tansor's world.'

What all this had to do with Mr Gorst, I could not guess; and so I asked Mrs Pryce whether anyone by that name was known to her.

'Gorst?' She shook her head with oracular certainty. 'No one of that name has been mentioned in any of the accounts concerning the family that I have read, nor have I heard it spoken of.'

'You are sure?' I asked.

Mr Pryce gave another loud 'Harrumph!' as if it were rank folly to suggest that his wife's intelligence on this subject was in any way defective.

'Quite sure.'

'No former admirer of Miss Carteret's?'

'Naturally, I cannot be certain on that point,' she conceded, 'but I do not think I have ever heard of one. It was reported that the murderer of Mr Phoebus Daunt had conceived an attachment to Miss Carteret, but his name was not Gorst.'

I thanked my old friends for their hospitality and set off back home, my curiosity about Mr Edwin Gorst as strong as ever.

III
Recollections of Mr John Lazarus Concluded

FOR THE REMAINDER of August 1856, and into the following month, Mr Gorst remained a resident of the Quinta da Pinheiro.

His health, as I had hoped, steadily improved through these late summer days. He would take long walks through the nearby pine-woods or, more often, up to the Mount, where he seemed particularly fond of sitting before the doors of the Church of Our Lady and gazing out, across the city far below, to the distant line of the horizon. At other times, returning from Funchal after a day's business, I would find him in the garden, asleep in a hammock slung between two apple-trees, a straw hat over his face, or else sitting on the balcony, feet up on the rail, smoking a cigar, and reading.

I had given him the liberty of my modest library, which afforded him evident pleasure, for he was, as I knew well by now, a great bibliophile, and never more content, it seemed, than when discoursing about colophons, bindings, press-marks, and the like, and with an enthusiasm that was most engaging. There was little enough, to be sure, in my own collection to satisfy such a refined bibliophilic taste; but he seemed content to settle down of an afternoon with an undistinguished edition of Smollett or Fielding, and I remember well how a dilapidated copy of *Gulliver's Travels* sent him into a perfect ecstasy.

'I've not read this since I was a boy!' he exclaimed, and I rejoiced to see his careworn face take on an expression of simple, unalloyed delight at his discovery.

So matters continued until the third week of September.

The time for me to leave Madeira and return to England was drawing near. My companion's health had signally improved; and although it had not been completely restored, he said that he felt strong enough to resume his life on Lanzarote. This, however, I was unwilling for him to do, believing that he would quickly sink back into his former state of debilitation.

'Won't you stay,' I asked, 'until I return, and then decide? It would undo all the good work of the kind Madeiran climate if you were to go back too soon and then fall ill again; and besides, it would also be a great favour to me to know that the house was occupied, and in good hands, while I'm gone.'

'I've little reason to go back to Lanzarote, it's true,' he replied, 'except for what's left of my former resolve to live out my days there. And of course it will be hard to leave this Eden. Yet I think I must do so.'

In all the weeks that we had passed in each other's company, he had revealed nothing of his past and, true to my word, I had made no attempt to broach the subject. But something had changed: some weakening of his will to remain in self-subjugation on Lanzarote had taken place. I had seen it plainly, as the September days advanced, and heard it again now in the half-hearted words he had just spoken. Life and hope were returning to Edwin Gorst.

To be short, after several protracted conversations, he agreed at last to remain at the Quinta da Pinheiro until my return, and to decide then whether he would go back to the Canaries, remain on Madeira, or take some other course.

A WEEK BEFORE my departure, a note came from my old friend George Murchison, at the English Consulate. It contained an invitation for my house-guest and me to attend a reception the next evening at his *quinta*, in honour of some new visitors to the island.

When we arrived, a numerous party had already assembled in the principal salon. Murchison, a jocular and rumbustious soul, shook our hands vigorously by way of welcome, and immediately ushered us away to meet the guests of honour.

'Mr Blantyre, may I present my old friend, Mr John Lazarus. John, this is Mr James Blantyre, director of Blantyre & Calder.'

Now here was a name I knew well, for the firm of which Mr

Blantyre was a principal was a leading importer of Madeiran wine, although one with which I had never yet done business. With him was his elder brother, Mr Alexander Blantyre, the other director of the firm. The rest of the party consisted of the son of the widowed Mr James Blantyre, Fergus by name; Mrs Alexander Blantyre and her daughters, Miss Marguerite and Miss Susanna; and Mrs Blantyre Senior, the mother of Mr Alexander and Mr James – a frail, snowy-haired old lady, for the benefit of whose health the trip to Madeira had chiefly been undertaken.

We were introduced to each of the family members in turn, ending with Mr Alexander Blantyre's eldest daughter, Miss Marguerite Blantyre. To everyone else, Gorst had merely bowed slightly and uttered a stiff 'Good-evening'; but to Miss Blantyre, he delivered a most gallant little speech of welcome, assuring her that Madeira was a perfect paradise, and expressing the hope that she would pass a very pleasant winter on the island, as well as the further hope that her grand-mother would find the climate as beneficial as he himself had done.

'You have been here for some time, then, Mr Gorst?' I heard her asking him.

'A few weeks only,' he replied, 'although the effects on my health have been considerable, even in so short a period. And I hope for further improvement to come, for Mr Lazarus has kindly allowed me to remain in his house until he returns.'

A little more conversation ensued concerning my imminent departure, and then Mr James Blantyre intervened to introduce us to a friend of his son's, a Mr Roderick Shillito, who was staying with the family at their rented *quinta* for the duration of their winter residence.

I must confess that this gentleman, who was much of an age with Gorst, as I guessed, did not produce an immediately favourable impression on me – still less on Gorst, who quickly excused himself after being introduced, and made his way over to the other side of the room, where he attached himself to a group that included my friend Dr Richard Prince, one of Funchal's most distinguished

English physicians. During the introductions, Mr Shillito had expressed himself honoured to meet me, but to Gorst he had offered none of the usual civilities, merely nodding, with a perceptible narrowing of his eyes, and a slight furrowing of the brow, as if he were trying hard to bring something to mind.

After Gorst had gone, I stood for a moment regarding Miss Marguerite Blantyre. She was a most comely girl of about twenty, quite short of stature and slightly built, with light-brown hair, a dimpled chin, and a sweet, open look about her. I later learned from her mother, who seemed eager to confide in me, stranger though I was, that there had long been an understanding that she would become engaged to her cousin Fergus as soon as she came of age.

'It is so pleasant,' said Mrs Blantyre, 'to see two young people so deeply attached to each other, don't you think, Mr Lazarus?'

Of course I assented to the proposition, as a matter of courtesy, although I did so in the abstract, as it were, having detected little sign of obvious affection between the cousins. As for her cousin Fergus, a rather puffy-faced youth with a short neck and a narrow forehead, he seemed altogether an unlikely object of any young lady's passion, let alone such a patently sensible, and undeniably pretty, young lady as Miss Blantyre.

His father, Mr James Blantyre, on the other hand, impressed me as a most purposeful individual – clean-shaven, well fed, firm of jaw, and altogether different from his elder brother, a gaunt, long-chinned, narrow-mouthed man, with thick grey side-whiskers, who stood for much of the evening a little apart from the rest of the family party, and only occasionally contributed to the conversation.

It struck me as curious that, although he was the senior of the two brothers, Mr Alexander Blantyre appeared to defer in a most marked way to Mr James, who had immediately assumed a position of authority at the centre of the group. It was Mr James who steered the talk towards topics of mutual interest; who ensured that Mrs Blantyre Senior was comfortable and lacked for nothing; who complimented his nieces on the perfection of their posies; and it was to Mr James that the others looked for guidance when it was suggested by Murchison that the party might wish to take a turn along the terrace, to see the Chinese lanterns that had been strung through the many stately trees that were a principal feature of the garden.

All this time, Gorst had continued to converse with Dr Prince on the far side of the salon; but when he observed the Blantyres, along with Mr Shillito, making their way to the terrace, he returned to where I was standing with our host.

'And how do you find our new residents, Mr Gorst?' asked Murchison.

My companion said nothing, which obliged me to answer for him.

'They seem a most agreeable and interesting family,' I said, 'and of course the reputation of Blantyre & Calder is second to none.'

'You're right there,' Murchison replied, 'and I'll tell you what else. Mr Fergus Blantyre will have to look to his laurels this winter. There's many a young man on Madeira who'd be glad to usurp his place with his pretty cousin – eh, Gorst?'

To my surprise, the reply came immediately.

'Miss Blantyre is most charming, and would certainly be an adornment to any society.'

As he spoke the words, we both saw him cast his eyes towards the terrace, where the young lady was standing with her mother admiring the Chinese lanterns.

'Ah!' said Murchison, with a knowing twinkle. 'That's how the land lies, does it? I spoke more truly than I thought. What d'ye think of that, Lazarus?'

I did not well know what to think. I could not blame Gorst – a single man, after all – for admiring Miss Blantyre; it was simply that I had not anticipated such a display of partiality from a man I knew to be so fiercely disinclined to reveal himself to others. I thought back to when I had first met him – a broken-spirited exile, sundered from common human contact and sympathy by an uncommon act of will, waiting only for death to set him free from the burden of which he would never speak – and I felt both glad and thankful that I had been the humble means of setting him on the road to recovery.

So the evening passed, at the end of which I began to go about the room, to say my farewells to the many acquaintances and business associates that Murchison had invited to welcome the Brothers Blantyre and their family to Madeira. Mr Shillito had remained outside on the terrace for most of the evening, walking up and down in company with Mr Fergus Blantyre, cigars in mouths, deep in conversation. I was glad of their absence from the main gathering in the salon, since it removed the chance of any unpleasantness with Gorst, in whom Mr Shillito, or so it appeared, had unaccountably aroused a deep antipathy. It sometimes happens, certainly, that we experience a spontaneous antagonism towards a stranger; and yet I could not help feeling that something more was at work here, although its cause – as with so much else connected with my new friend – remained mysterious.

My social duties done, Gorst and I prepared to leave. Murchison was standing in the front hall, wishing his guests good-night as they left. Just as he was shaking hands with Gorst, the Blantyre party appeared, preceded by Mr Shillito.

'Ah, there you are, Gorst,' the latter said in a cool, hard tone. 'I wanted to ask you – are you sure we haven't met before? It has been puzzling me all evening where I might have seen you before, for I'm sure I have, you know.'

In that moment was made dramatically manifest the change that had been accomplished in the hours that my house-guest had spent walking in the pine-woods, and the weeks of relaxation and recuperation at the Quinta da Pinheiro.

At Mr Shillito's words, Gorst seemed instantaneously infused with an almost menacing vigour. Standing there, fists clenched, shoulders thrust back, feet planted firmly and a little apart on the stone flags, as if in readiness to spring forwards, he returned Mr Shillito's insolent gaze in the most determined and challenging manner.

I confess I hardly recognized him during the few brief seconds that the incident lasted, so transformed was he from the usually pensive and world-weary individual whom I had come to know since we had arrived in Madeira. His attitude, although he had drawn himself up to his full commanding height, reminded me of nothing so much as a terrier that has caught the scent of vermin, and is about to pounce.

Mr Shillito also observed the startling change in him, and something more, too, that was lost on me. He had gone suddenly pale, and took a nervous step backwards, as if Gorst had called up some fearful, but long-suppressed, memory. Then Murchison was amongst the party, laughing and shaking hands with the gentlemen, bowing to the ladies, and gallantly enquiring of Mrs Blantyre Senior whether he would allow him to escort her to her palanquin.* As the business of departure was going on, Gorst turned and walked out into the darkness.

When I caught up with him, he was standing in the lane that ran along the side of Murchison's *quinta*, looking up at the moonlit peaks of the mountains, and smoking a cigar.

'Is anything the matter, Gorst?' I asked.

'Nothing whatsoever. Care for a cigar?'

I declined the offer, and we walked up the steep lane a little way in silence.

'There's an ox-sledge waiting,' I said. 'Shall we go?'

'I think I'll walk back, if you don't mind,' he replied. 'I can get home this way.'

'I'll walk with you—'

'No,' he broke in, somewhat brusquely. 'Pray don't trouble.' Then, in a calmer tone: 'If you don't mind?'

As I was feeling rather tired, I did not mind in the least for myself, wishing only to be assured that he would indeed find his way back to the Quinta da Pinheiro, a distance of a mile or so; but he seemed confident of his way, and so we parted.

It was a clear, still night. I watched his tall figure make its way up the narrow lane, past high walls overhung with palm-fronds, honeysuckle, and the laden branches of various fruit-trees. At a bend in the lane, he stopped and turned. Above the door of a little turreted house a lantern burned, casting a pale yellow light over the cobbles.

*A covered litter, normally carried by four bearers.

He stood for a moment beneath the lantern, took a puff on his cigar, and waved. Then he was gone.

AND SO THE day came when I was to leave Madeira and return to England. My cases and trunks had been taken down to the harbour, and I had given my three servants their final instructions, impressing on them that they were to consider Mr Gorst as their master until I returned.

Gorst was standing in the hall, hat in hand, having just come back from one of his walks in the woods, when I emerged from my study to take the waiting ox-sledge down to the city.

'Good-bye, Gorst,' I said. 'I shall write, to let you know how things are back in dear old England; and you will write too, won't you, telling me how you are getting on, and what you are doing?'

'I shall,' he said, 'most gladly.'

He paused, and then held out his hand – no longer shaking, as it had been when we had been on Lanzarote, but now strong and steady.

'Thank you, Lazarus,' was all he said, but it touched me deeply, for I knew that it came from the heart.

They were the last words I ever heard him speak.

17

In Which Lady Tansor
Opens Her Heart

I

I Am Admonished

I CLOSED Mr John Lazarus's recollections in a most desolate
state of mind. I now knew something of my father; but the
knowledge had brought no solace, only a desperate, impossible
longing to experience his living presence as he had really been, and
not as the subject of distant recall.

Now Mr Lazarus (of whom I had formed a very high opinion)
had also given me a fleeting impression of my mother, and of my
Blantyre relations, of whom I had never before heard.

Marguerite. The image of that moss-covered gravestone in the
Cemetery of St-Vincent came rushing back to me once more as I
remembered how I had tried so hard to form an idea of what the
person who had borne that most musical name had looked like
in life – tall or short, dark or fair – and whether she had been as
sweetly disposed as her name suggested to my childish imagination.
From Mr Lazarus's account, she seemed indeed to have been just
such a person, indistinct and ghostly though she remained in my
mind. Soon, I hoped, the transcriptions from her journal, which
Mr Thornhaugh had promised to send me, would help to bring
her person and character into clearer view. For the moment, I must

be content with what I had – a little fragment of kind Mr Lazarus's memory.

I lay down on my bed, feeling suddenly dispirited, and oppressed by urgent questionings. A person mentioned by Mr Lazarus – Mr Roderick Shillito, of whom I knew only that he had been a former school-fellow of Phoebus Daunt's, but whose name had struck an instant chord of recognition – gave me particular concern. He had been present at the dinner given in my Lady's house in Grosvenor Square during our recent trip to London – 'a former school-friend of Mr Phoebus Daunt's', as she had described him to me then. To learn now that he had been acquainted with both my parents on Madeira twenty years earlier might be another singular coincidence, like the matter of the initials 'B.K.'; yet although coincidence – sometimes of an extraordinary character – is far more common in life than we often suppose, I hesitated to ascribe to it Mr Shillito's present association with Lady Tansor. Could my father's evident distaste for this gentleman have arisen from some previous acquaintance? Might there even have been a connexion between my father and Mr Shillito's school-friend, Phoebus Daunt?

At that moment, breaking in on these thoughts, the bell in the corner of my room finally sounded. My Lady was calling for me.

'MISS GORST!' EXCLAIMED Mr Armitage Vyse. 'Come in, come in!'

He had opened the door to my knock, and was standing, leaning on his stick, smiling expansively. My Lady was sitting by the fire, staring blankly into the flames, and holding a sealed envelope.

'How are you, Miss Gorst?' he asked, with the utmost geniality.

'Quite well, sir, thank you,' said I, dropping a dutiful curtsey.

'Splendid! Splendid! Now then, come and sit by the fire, won't you?'

He ushered me over to the little sofa opposite Lady Tansor, and then sat down uncomfortably close to me, still smiling in that odd, sinisterly affable way of his. My Lady made no movement, but went on looking intently into the fire.

At length, she turned towards me. Her face was drawn, and there were dark rings around her eyes.

'This is for you,' she said, coldly, looking down at the envelope. 'From Mr Wraxall.'

'Mr Montagu Wraxall,' added Mr Vyse, stretching out his long legs and cupping the back of his head in his hands, in a highly comfortable and self-satisfied manner. 'Capital fellow! Quite a legend in our profession, you know. Sharp, very sharp.'

His tone was genial and confiding; but the play of his eyes sent a chill through me, making me feel that I had inadvertently stepped on to dangerous ground. I could only guess that an association with Mr Wraxall was something that both Mr Vyse and my mistress wished to discourage, as being in some way threatening to their purposes.

'We chanced to call at North Lodge this morning,' said my Lady, in a flat, emotionless tone, which nevertheless alarmed me, 'and Mr Wraxall asked whether we would deliver this note to you. He also enquired after you, and said that he was sorry that business had kept him away from Evenwood much longer than expected. I confess that I was not aware that you and he were on such familiar terms.'

'Oh no, my Lady!' I protested, with some alacrity, sensing now a hint of challenge in her voice. 'Nothing in the least like that.'

'Forgive me, Alice. I was under the impression that you made Mr Wraxall's acquaintance for the first time at Professor Slake's funeral.'

'That is so, my Lady.'

'But it seems that you have continued the acquaintance without my knowledge,' she went on.

Why was she quizzing me in this manner? I could see no impropriety in the acquaintance with Mr Wraxall; but it was now abundantly clear that my Lady, like Mr Vyse, viewed it with disapproval. The thought then struck me that the reason might be connected with the murder of Mr Paul Carteret, in which the late Professor had taken such a close interest. I therefore resolved to say nothing concerning my conversation on the subject with Mr Wraxall.

Facing her gaze, I explained that I had met Mr Wraxall, quite by chance, coming out of the Dower House, and that he had expressed the intention, on his return to North Lodge, of inviting me there to take tea.

'Oh ho!' exclaimed Mr Vyse with a cynical chuckle. 'To take tea, eh? There's a thing!'

'In that case,' said Lady Tansor with a chilling look, handing me the envelope, 'you may take your note.'

There was a moment's silence.

'The Dower House, you say?' she then asked, in a manner that suggested she had been turning a troublesome matter over in her mind.

'I beg your pardon, my Lady?'

'You said you encountered Mr Wraxall by chance at the Dower House.'

'Yes, my Lady. He was collecting some letters that Professor Slake had written to—'

I hesitated, realizing immediately that I should not have done so. My Lady's face was now fully alert, and her great black eyes were on me.

'Yes, Alice?'

'Letters written to your late father,' I resumed, as coolly as I could.

'Letters to my father?'

'Yes, my Lady.'

'And did Mr Wraxall inform you further on the contents of the letters?'

'No, my Lady. Mr Wraxall had yet to examine them. I know only that there were a great number.'

She rose, and walked over to the window. Mr Vyse coughed, and smiled in an avuncular fashion.

'Well now, Miss Gorst, you are to be raised to a new station in life, I think,' he said. 'Companion to her Ladyship, eh?'

'Yes, sir.'

I lowered my head demurely, determined to say as little as possible; but Mr Vyse seemed equally intent on filling the silence.

'No more than you deserve, I'm sure; and yet less than you might once have expected – as a lady born, I mean.'

'I was brought up an orphan, sir,' I replied, 'as I think you must know; and although I may have enjoyed the advantages of a good education, I cannot – and do not – lay claim to any special privilege of birth. I am perfectly content with my present station, which is so much more than I could once have hoped for, and am grateful for the favour my Lady continues to show towards me, and which I shall constantly endeavour to deserve.'

A pretty speech, I thought, intended as much for my Lady as for Mr Vyse, who was about to make his reply when my mistress broke in.

'I am not at all sure, Alice,' she said, 'that it was right for you to say you would take tea with Mr Montagu Wraxall. However, I shall not positively forbid you from going, although I hope you will now see that it was imprudent of you – and somewhat presumptuous – to accept his invitation without consulting me first. I have made many allowances, as you must acknowledge, with respect to your situation here, allowances that have never been extended to anyone else in your position; but there are limits to my tolerance.'

'Limits,' said Mr Vyse, nodding sagely.

'I had hoped,' she added, 'that there would be no more secrets between us.'

I marvelled at her hypocrisy. Secrets, indeed! She lived and breathed secrets, and yet she would berate me for keeping mine!

'Perhaps,' ventured Mr Vyse, 'if Miss Gorst were to let your Ladyship read Mr Wraxall's note, it would go some way to assure you that no impropriety had been intended, and would put things back on a proper footing. You wouldn't mind that, would you, Miss Gorst? Indeed, I'm sure you had every intention of showing the note to her Ladyship of your own accord, on receiving it. Say now, am I not right?'

He had me, and he knew it, sitting there with his ear-to-ear smile, the light from the fire flashing off his watch-chain and seals, so assured, so studiously affable, so curiously at ease.

With choice denied me, I walked across to where Lady Tansor was standing, and handed her back the unopened note.

'No more secrets, Alice,' she whispered.

'No, my Lady.'

It took but a few seconds for her to read the note, which she then gave back to me with a black look. Saying not a word, she walked quickly to the adjoining bed-chamber, slamming the door behind her.

I glanced down at the paper, and the few lines written thereon:

DEAR MISS GORST,—

I am returned at long last.

Christmas is nearly upon us, but if you are still minded to accept my invitation, then I should be very glad to welcome you next Sunday, the 31st, at three o'clock, at North Lodge.

I shall have another guest, a young friend of mine, who has come up from London to spend this festive time with his ailing father. His wife will be there, too, so you will not be unchaperoned.

Yours very sincerely,

M.R.J. WRAXALL

'Well, then,' I heard Mr Vyse say, as I finished reading and was placing the note in my pocket, 'all done, and everything set to rights. And tomorrow is Christmas Eve! What could be more pleasant?'

He was now standing, his back to the fire, leaning on his stick, and regarding me with another of his unsettling smiles. He seemed everything benign, charming, and considerate, but I knew otherwise; I knew also the danger that he posed to me, having now the vivid recollection of him, disguised, nose to nose with the villainous Billy Yapp.

I was considering whether I should wait for my Lady to come out of the bed-chamber, or to return upstairs to await a further summons, when there was a single tap at the door, which opened to reveal Mr Perseus, standing motionless in the doorway, his face, as ever, an impassive mask. Then I saw that he was clenching and re-clenching his fist as he looked, first at me, and then at Mr Vyse's dandyish figure. It was such a little thing, but something in this involuntary gesture spoke of his resentment at finding Mr Vyse

standing so brazenly before the fire in his mother's private apartments, as if by right of possession.

'Ah, Vyse,' he said, coldly courteous, 'here you are – and Miss
Gorst, too.'

'Here I am, indeed,' replied Mr Vyse, utterly unabashed, and giving an exaggeratedly cordial bow. 'Won't you come in?'

The affront was clearly intended. As if Mr Perseus Duport
needed an invitation by a house-guest to enter his own mother's
apartments!

Closing the door behind him, Mr Perseus stepped into the room
and looked about him.

'Where is my mother?' he asked.

'Alas, she woke this morning with one of her headaches,'
drawled Mr Vyse. 'At my suggestion, we went out in the barouche,
well wrapped up, of course – I have found a strong dose of clean
country air to be a capital remedy for headaches. I'm happy to say
that my recommendation met with her Ladyship's approval, and
that she returned much refreshed, although a little fatigued. She is
now resting.'

You lie easily, sir, I thought, as he gave me a sly, collusive glance.

'Well, then, I shall not disturb her,' said Mr Perseus. 'I merely
wished to inform her that my brother has returned from Wales, and
that Shillito has also arrived. He's in the Drawing-Room, and is asking for you. I suppose you're at liberty to come down?'

His antipathy towards Mr Vyse was clear, although the latter
remained inviolable in his beaming complacency.

'By all means,' came the reply. Then, turning to me: 'I think you
may be excused, Miss Gorst. Her Ladyship will ring for you if you
are needed.'

I gave him a little bob by way of answer, and made to leave. As I
did so, he addressed Mr Perseus once more.

'I've been congratulating Miss Gorst on her good fortune. Her
days of drudgery will soon be over. My Lady's companion now! Altogether a remarkable instance of the triumph of breeding over circumstance. Blood will out, blood will out!'

Ignoring this glib pronouncement, Mr Perseus moved to open the door for me, making a slight inclination of his head as I passed by. Then, for the merest instant, our eyes met, and in that brief span of time I saw something that, I confess, made my heart suddenly pound. What was it? I could not then say; but I left my Lady's apartments with an inexplicably lighter heart than when I had entered them.

MR LAZARUS'S RECOLLECTIONS still lay on the table. Lighting my candle, and idly opening the volume, my eye happened to fall on the account of the reception held for the Blantyre family, at which my father and mother had first met, and on the description of Mr Roderick Shillito – who, even now, was no doubt taking his ease in the Drawing-Room with Mr Vyse.

What would happen when I was introduced – as I surely must be – to this gentleman? Would the name of Gorst call up memories of the man he had encountered on Madeira twenty years ago? This might expose me to suspicion, even danger. I was at least fore-warned, although this gave me scant comfort.

Just then the bell rang, and so down I went again to my Lady's apartments.

II
In Which I Am Elevated Once More

SHE WAS SITTING by the fire, steadily contemplating the brightly flaring logs. There was no sign of either Mr Vyse or Mr Perseus.

As I entered the room, she turned her face – wan and haggard – towards me.

'Come and sit down, Alice,' she said, gently. 'There's something I wish to say to you.'

I took my place again on the sofa opposite her. To my surprise, she leaned forwards, and took my hands tenderly in hers.

'I had a friend once,' she began, in a quiet, reminiscing way, 'the dearest friend in all the world – the only true friend I ever had. When we were together, we were inseparable, like the closest of sisters.'

She looked away for a moment. I saw that her eyes were moistening, and I was about to speak when she raised her hand.

'No, Alice. Say nothing. The memories are painful to me, even now, and are made more so because my own dearest sister was taken from us when I was young – you must, I'm sure, have been told that the poor sweet thing fell into the Evenbrook, and was drowned. Years later, for a period on which I shall ever look back with the fondest remembrance, this friend filled the empty space in my life left by my dear sister. We shared every confidence, every hope and dream; and, in this state of deepest affection and trust, we passed into womanhood together.

'She would come to stay at Evenwood every summer, and became a great favourite of my father's. But then certain – circumstances – sundered the bond between us, making it impossible that we could continue our former intimacy.'

'And you have never seen her since?'

'Never,' she sighed. 'I have had no word of her these twenty years – neither has anyone ever taken her place. I have a numerous acquaintance, of course, here in the country, and in Town; but there has been no one like her.

'There was a most rare sympathy between us, you see, although we were quite unlike in so many ways. She could be skittish and irresponsible – she seemed to dance heedlessly through life, whereas I had grown up serious in my outlook, and cautious in all my doings. But I suppose we completed each other, and made a whole out of our differences. We were so differently made, too. She was a little doll, with the most wondrous fair hair, and the palest of blue eyes, whilst I, of course, was dark, and as tall as a man. We must have made an odd sight!'

Giving a sad little laugh, she released my hands, and leaned back in her chair, lost in fond memories.

We sat for several minutes without speaking, listening to the crackle of the glowing logs. Then she reached forward to take my hands in hers once more, and looked deeply into my eyes.

'Now, dearest Alice, this is what I wished to say. From the very instant I saw you, I knew that, one day, we would be friends – true friends, as this person and I had once been. You came to me as a mere servant; but, as I have told you, I saw through your disguise. I knew you for what you truly were.'

Oh, those transfixing eyes, black as pansy petals, like the eyes of some Byzantine icon gazing steadfastly into eternity! So beautiful, so captivating, so infinitely mysterious! I felt myself sinking into their shifting, treacherous depths, succumbing helplessly to their power, as so many others had done. Her words had alarmed me at first, until it was clear that they contained no suggestion of menace. On the contrary, they had a tender sincerity that I had never heard her give voice to before – and it was bewitching.

'You will find it strange,' she went on, 'that I should speak so – after all, I have known you for only a short time. It is strange to me, I confess, this inexplicable affinity that I feel exists between us. I have struggled to resist it, being naturally conscious of the disparity of our conditions in the world; and I have tried – so very hard! – to maintain the relations that ought properly to exist between mistress and maid, as I attempted to do earlier, over your acceptance of Mr Wraxall's invitation. But I can resist no longer.

'You may not believe it, but I am beset with troubles, and have no one in whom to confide. I see your disbelieving look, but it is only too true. Of course I have my dear son, Perseus; but there are some things a mother cannot say even to her children – and others, perhaps, that must be kept from them, for their own sakes.

'The consequence is that I feel utterly alone in the world. I confess that I can no longer bear the prospect of living out my days bereft of an attachment to someone of my own sex, an attachment of the kind I once enjoyed with my former friend, and for which I daily yearn.

'And so: will *you* be such a friend to me, Alice, as well as my paid companion, from this day forth? My true, devoted friend?'

'I do not know what to say, my Lady,' I said, affecting a look of gratified confusion, although inwardly exultant. 'This is so – unexpected – so undeserved—'

'Oh, Alice, you dear little goose!' she laughed. 'You must say yes, of course; and then you must stop addressing me as "my Lady" – I mean when we are together like this. My name is Emily Grace Duport; and so – except when we are in company, or in the presence of my sons – from henceforth you must call me Emily.'

'But,' I protested, 'you and your former friend were of an age. I am so young, so ignorant of the world. Surely you need a friend of your own age?'

'Nonsense!' she cried. 'You are young in years, of course, but you have an uncommonly wise head on your shoulders. And why should I not have a younger friend, especially one in whom I truly feel there exists such reciprocity of outlook? You feel it, too, I know – that our lives were meant to become entwined. Say you feel it!'

I could not deny it, for it was no more than the truth – the reason, indeed, why I had been sent to this place. Whereupon, on hearing my whispered admission, she fell to her knees in front of me, threw her arms around my neck, and kissed me.

'There!' she said. 'Sealed with a kiss!'

My amazement, on finding my mistress kneeling before me in an attitude of ardent supplication, and speaking to me in such a demonstrative manner, may be readily imagined. It brought to mind the sight of her, overcome by grief, kneeling before the tomb of Phoebus Daunt; but now her face was bright with hopeful entreaty, and – to my further astonishment – I found myself returning her embrace, and sinking into a curious state of willing submission, from which I roused myself only with the greatest difficulty.

I could not conceive what had wrought such a startling change in her – a transformation so sudden and complete that it seemed, even to my suspicious eye, to be wholly untainted by subterfuge. I own that I was in a perfect daze, knowing that I must not trust her, and yet feeling flattered and touched by this effusive offer of friendship from the one person in the whole wide world whom I could never call my friend.

My Lady sat back in her chair once more with a contented sigh.

'Do you remember,' she asked, 'when you first stood before me, and I asked you whether you thought we would become friends?'

I said that I remembered it very well, but had never dared to hope that such a thing could ever come about – 'although, of course,' I added, 'I wished it very much.'

'It's Fate, you see. I am certain – as I have been certain of few other things in my life – and I am truly, truly glad of it.'

'As I am also,' say I, reaching out and taking her hand. 'Truly.'

We sit for several moments, saying nothing, each preoccupied with our own thoughts.

'Naturally, it will not be easy for you, Alice,' she observes after a while. 'You'll feel awkward and constrained, no doubt, by this sudden change in our relations. But I wish you to be as happy in my company as I know I shall be in yours; and so you must strive to overcome your natural delicacy, which does you the greatest credit, and try to treat me as if I were your equal – I mean of course in our private moments, away from the world's gaze, and never in front of the servants. In public we must be more circumspect. You'll then appear as my paid companion, and we must take care to temper our conduct accordingly.'

'Ah, yes,' I say, compliant as you like, 'the proprieties must be observed, of course. Friends in private, mistress and companion in public.'

'Exactly!' she cries. 'You always understand, dear Alice.'

Oh yes, my Lady, I think. *I understand perfectly.*

We talked on for half an hour or more; or, rather, I was content to let my new friend talk away, which she appeared most eager to do, whilst I smiled and nodded in a gratefully accommodating manner, until the darkness began to gather, and it was time to light the lamps.

'Do you know, Alice,' she said, standing up and reaching out her hands towards the fire, 'I think I should like to spend some time in London again after all. It will be quite different now, having you to keep me company. I'm sure I shall not hate it if you are with me. We'll go to the theatre, and to concerts. Oh yes, to concerts! I have not been to one since – well, for such a long time. You'll like that, won't you, dear?'

Rain was now beating against the windows, driven in by a howling wind.

'And then,' she continued, in a rapt, musing sort of way, not waiting for a reply from me, but walking over to the window-seat to look out across the rain-swept Park, 'we can make expeditions – to the Zoological Gardens, perhaps, or to the Tower. Of course there are also people you should meet, to whom I can introduce you, and so bring you out into the best society, as I told you I wished to do.'

She looked magnificent in her trailing dark-grey gown, which hugged her tall figure, and set off her pale skin to perfection. Who would not admire her, and wish to be her friend?

Seeing her standing there, so mysteriously alluring in the fire's glow, I knew that I could never admit to Madame what I could hardly admit to myself: that I was becoming captivated by this woman, whose still unrevealed iniquities I had come here to expose to the world. What a contradictory and perplexing thing is the human heart, that it can be at once attracted to and repelled by the same object, and drawn, despite itself, to what it seeks to destroy!

Thus it was, just three months after my first coming to the great house of Evenwood, that I ceased my employment as maid to the 26th Baroness Tansor, and became the chosen friend of Emily Grace Duport, *née* Carteret – the woman whom my guardian angel, Madame de l'Orme, had assured me was my sworn enemy.

18

Thirty at Table, and What Followed

I
Dressing for Dinner

M
Y LADY and I continued talking by the fire until it was
time to dress for dinner.

'Will you object to helping me dress, Alice?' she asked.
'I mean as a friend would do, of course, not as my maid? There's a
girl coming for interview next week – a relation of Pocock's. If she
answers, then I shall not trouble to see anyone else. Until then—'

I eagerly assured her that I was very happy to go on assisting her
with her toilet until the new maid came, at which she clapped her
hands, and gave me another kiss.

She had been recalling once again, in the most animated terms,
her former friend, and the happy times they had enjoyed together.

'How sad that such times had to come to an end,' I remarked.
'You mentioned certain circumstances . . .'

'Forgive me, Alice.' She had grown suddenly serious. 'I cannot
speak of these things.'

'Well, then, of course I shan't press you,' I replied, deciding that I
would show a little crossness at her refusal. 'I only made the remark
because I thought you wished to have someone in whom you could
confide. But even friends, I suppose, must have their secrets.'

'This is not a secret, Alice,' she said, gently, but insistently. 'The circumstances to which I alluded involve confidences that I simply cannot on any account break, even for a friend.'

Her voice had hardened, and the old imperious light flashed in her eyes. For a moment I feared that I had been too forward; then she seemed suddenly to recollect herself.

'But these things are all in the past,' she said. 'Let us leave them there. This is a new beginning, for us both, and I hope that we shall feel able to share our secrets with each other, like true friends.'

I marvelled again at her hypocrisy, knowing full well that she would never willingly reveal the secret places of her heart to me.

As I finished helping her dress, she told me that she wished me to join the company for dinner that evening, and that I would henceforth take all my meals with the family.

'I suppose tongues will wag,' she sighed, 'and heads will shake, and people will think that I have run quite mad, to raise my former maid in this way; but that should not concern us in the least, dear Alice. Everyone will soon see that you were not born to service, and then they will applaud my good sense in liberating you from it.'

On she chattered, until I had finished dressing her hair and had handed her the box containing the precious locket, on its black velvet band, in which she kept the strand of hair that she had cut from the head of Phoebus Daunt.

'Oh, yes,' she said, placing the locket round her throat; 'I have asked Barrington to take your things to the Tower Room tomorrow morning, so that you may wake on Christmas Day in your new bed. Now, what shall you wear tonight? You must make a good impression on our guests, you know. And Christmas Day is also dear Perseus's coming of age. What a day it will be!'

Jumping up from her chair, she runs over to one of the great wardrobes, like some excitable young Miss on the eve of her first ball, and begins taking out several gowns, which she first holds up for inspection, and then throws impatiently down in a growing heap on the floor.

'Ah!' she exclaims at last, taking out an elegant dress of silver-grey silk, cut low over the shoulders, the skirt looped round with frills and bows of darker grey silk trimmed with red roses.

'Just the thing! It will do very well, I think. Come, let me see you in it. I shall help you.'

So saying, she eagerly begins to unbutton the drab black dress that was my usual daily apparel, and then holds open the gown for me to step into.

It was most unsettling, to find myself being dressed by my Lady, as if she were the maid and I the mistress; but she appeared insensible to the incongruity of the situation. Indeed, she seemed rather to relish it, and prattled on gaily as she buttoned up the gown, fixed a circlet of pearls and paper flowers in my hair, and then took me over to the cheval-glass.

'There!' she cried, admiringly. 'Quite transformed!'

She stood behind me, hands placed protectively on my bare shoulders, as we both looked at my reflection in the glass.

The gown fitted to perfection, for we were much of a height, and, despite the disparity in our ages, my Lady's figure had remained almost as trim as mine. With our dark hair, and the not dissimilar cast of our features, it struck me forcibly that we might almost have been mistaken for mother and daughter. Perhaps the same thought had struck my Lady, for she suddenly started, and removed her hands from my shoulders.

'Good heavens!' she exclaimed, more to herself than to me. Then, under her breath: 'I was right!'

'Is anything wrong, my Lady?' I asked, mystified by her words.

'Wrong? What could be wrong? It is just that – in this light – you look so like someone I once knew. You have always reminded me of this – person; but tonight – here, now – the resemblance is especially strong. It took me a little by surprise.'

'Another friend?' I asked.

This time she did not answer, but turned away, walked over to the dressing-table, and opened an ivory jewellery box.

'One more thing, to make all complete,' she said, bringing out from the box an exquisite opal-and-diamond necklace, which she made to place around my neck.

'Oh, no!' I protested, pulling away. 'I cannot possibly – really, I cannot.'

'Nonsense!' she said, securing the clasp, and then stepping back to contemplate the effect. 'You were born to wear such things. See how well you carry it.'

It was true. My reflection gave back the very picture of a well-born lady, perfectly at ease with expense and luxury. *Where now*, I thought to myself, *was the lowly maid?*

I happened then to glance down at the ivory jewellery box, which still lay open on the dressing-table. Amongst several rings and bracelets jumbled together on the dark-red plush lining, I noticed a small key tied to a piece of black silk. This immediately aroused my curiosity; for where there is a key, there must also be a lock.

'Come, Alice,' said my Lady, taking my arm. 'We must go down. Our guests are waiting.'

II
Mr Shillito's Bad Memory

THE COMPANY OF Christmas guests has already assembled in the Chinese Salon – thirty persons in all. As my Lady and I enter, every head turns to observe us.

We move slowly about the extravagantly appointed and suddenly hushed room, and my Lady introduces me to each guest in turn as 'Miss Gorst, my new companion'.

I am pleased to find that Mr Wraxall has been invited, and as my Lady turns away to speak to Sir Lionel Voysey, we exchange a few brief words concerning my impending visit to North Lodge.

As I am being presented to my Lady's cousin, Major Hunt-Graham, we are joined by Mr Randolph.

'Good-evening, Miss Gorst. I hope you are well,' are his first words to me. He then compliments me on how charming I look, and asks what I have been doing since he has been away in Wales. All the usual enquiries are made, all the usual bland answers given; but his eyes seem to speak another language. For him, it seems, absence has done its proverbial work. There is no doubt in my mind.

I had sensed how it might be, from his first words to me, from his 'confession' on our walk back from Easton, and from other signs and portents. I am now sure of it. For good or ill, amidst the hub-bub and chatter, and the coming and going of servants, I am sud-denly certain – extraordinary though it seems – that Mr Randolph Duport has fallen in love with me.

I am flattered, but also alarmed, for any gratification that I allow myself to feel is immediately tempered by the certainty that I can never return his feelings for me. I like Mr Randolph almost more than I have liked anyone in my life; indeed, I had felt drawn to his unaffected, open-hearted charm from the very moment of our first meeting outside the Library. I could once have imagined loving him, but no longer. I had not given my heart to him at first sight, as I might so easily have done, and know now that I never will.

The man I married might be handsome, or he might not; he might be young or old; he must return my love to the utmost, be kind and caring, and treat me as his equal in all things (a high ambition, but I believed such men existed). Above all, he must be someone from whom I could learn, as I had learned from Mr Thornhaugh, and in whose mental life I could share. Mr Randolph – as I had come to know him, and from the reports of others – was good-natured and sympathetic, liked by all; but it was also plain to me, from my own observations, that he lacked those qualities of mind that I was determined the man I loved would possess.

Mr Perseus, by contrast, matched my ideal far more closely: a poet, a cultivated man of taste and discernment, with the additional mate-rial attractions of one day inheriting an ancient peerage, and becom-ing as rich as Croesus. He had, besides, that element of mystery about him that is naturally alluring to someone of my romantic disposition. He had intrigued me from the first, although I had barely acknowl-edged the fact to myself. As the weeks had passed, however, my fasci-nation had increased. I had felt that there was so much in him to be discovered. His brother seems always to wear his heart on his sleeve, presenting himself to the world as he appears really to be – open, frank, and uncomplicated. Mr Perseus, by contrast, is secretive, reti-cent, continually on his guard. But I do not see Mr Perseus as others appear to do. He is proud, of course: proud of who he is, proud of his ancient family and its lofty position in the world, proud of his own abilities. Yet although I could wish he were less conscious of his own worth, I do not believe that his habitual reserve, or the attitude of arrogant disdain that he is wont to assume towards others less fortunate, or less accomplished, than himself, reflect an inflexible and constricted nature, devoid of the capacity to feel for others. My heart tells me otherwise: that, unlike his brother, Mr Perseus is more – much more – than he seems to be, or than he allows himself to be.

As these thoughts run helter-skelter through my mind, they are interrupted by the arrival of Mr Perseus himself, bowing stiffly, and wishing me good-evening.

'Well, Miss Gorst,' he remarks, sweeping his eye over my borrowed gown, and bringing it to rest on the necklace his mother had insisted on my wearing, 'you have shed your old skin, I see. You stand before us quite new born.'

'Now, dear, you mustn't tease,' reproves my Lady, gently patting her eldest son's arm.

'Oh, I don't tease, I assure you,' replies Mr Perseus, without taking his eyes from me. 'I never tease, as I have told you before. I am perfectly serious. I see nothing but good in the change. You've blossomed, Miss Gorst, most remarkably, in a matter of hours. What next, I wonder? You'll soon be queen of us all.'

'And as I have said before, sir,' say I, still unsure whether he is speaking in jest or not, 'I have no other ambition than to serve my Lady, and shall do so as her companion, as I did as her maid, to the best of my ability. A fine gown changes nothing. I am still the person I was.'

'You are wrong,' he returns, more quietly now, but emphatically. 'You are changed a great deal, or rather you have reverted to what you really are. Don't you agree, Randolph?'

He gives his brother a look of indisputable challenge, as if he were taunting him to disagree; but before anything more can be said, we are joined by Mr Vyse and a perspiring, portly gentleman, whom I immediately presume to be Mr Roderick Shillito.

Now here is the predicament that I had expected. I must be

introduced to the newcomer. Will my name raise a remembrance in him of my father?

Mr Vyse, leaning on his silver-topped stick and beaming in his customary lupine manner, bows a silent greeting to my Lady, and then holds out his hand towards me.

'Shillito, may I have the honour of introducing Miss Esperanza Gorst, her Ladyship's new companion. Miss Gorst has become a great adornment to Evenwood society, and is set to become an even greater one, I predict.'

He then takes a step back, as if better to observe the effect of his words on his friend, whom I shall now present to my readers by transcribing the description of him that I wrote in my Book of Secrets:

MR RODERICK SHILLITO

Age and Appearance: fifty or so years old. Tall – nearly as tall as Mr Vyse – but corpulent, and lumbering in his movements. Pink skin stretched tight over large moon face. Small, mean mouth; moist, pale-lashed, porcine eyes set close together. Across the top of his head is a broad slab of bald, mottled flesh, flanked by swept-back waves of stiff, dirty-yellow hair, like parched grass. All in all, gives out the impression of an elderly, and viciously inclined, *putto.*

Character: presents a complete picture of the dedicated self-seeker. Fixed expression of sly degeneracy, unmitigated by any redeeming quality of spontaneous generosity, or fellow-feeling. An accomplished sponger, I should say – and much worse, no doubt. A strange associate for Mr Vyse (to whom he habitually defers), having none of the latter's flamboyant sophistication, and certainly his inferior in point of intellect.

Conclusion: a repellent buffoon in many ways, but also, I am sure, a bully and a coward.

After Mr Vyse has spoken my name, Mr Shillito scratches his fat head and purses his fat, wet lips.

'Gorst,' he says slowly. 'There's a name I think I know, though

I'm damned if I can remember where. Were you ever in Dublin, Miss Gorst?'

'No, sir. Never.'

'Were you not? Hmm.'

He gives himself up to further strained rumination; and then the light of dim recollection begins to seep into his pale eyes.

'I have it! I met a man once, in Madeira, by the name of Gorst. That's it! Say now, Miss Gorst, have I hit it? Were you ever in Madeira?'

'Never in my life, sir,' I reply, conscious that my cheeks are growing warm, and that both my Lady and Mr Vyse are now taking a close interest in the turn the conversation has taken.

'It's an odd thing,' Mr Shillito retorts, with a deriding snort, and looking round at the others in the apparent expectation of their support for the line he has taken. 'Gorst is an uncommon name, ain't it? It's certain I've only ever known one other person who went by it. Now here's a second, and yet it seems there's no connexion with this fellow I met in Madeira. Rum.'

Another sceptical snort, as if to prove his case.

I decide that my best course is to remain silent; but then my Lady intervenes.

'When did you make this gentleman's acquaintance, Mr Shillito?' she asks.

'Let me see,' he replies. 'It would have been in '55, or thereabouts – no, '56. I remember now, '56. I'm sure of it.'

'No more, then, than a year or so before you were born, Alice,' observes my Lady. 'Is it possible, do you think, that the gentleman in question was a relation – your father, even? Did you ever hear of him visiting Madeira?'

Naturally, I deny having any such knowledge; then a most welcome and unexpected interjection from Mr Perseus, who has remained sternly regarding Mr Shillito throughout the previous exchanges, prevents any further enquiries. Fixing Mr Shillito with one of his most freezing stares, and with barely disguised contempt, he expresses the opinion that it is rather bad form for a *gentleman* (laying particular emphasis on the word) to subject a lady to unwelcome interrogation.

Mr Shillito shrugs indifferently, but says nothing. Mr Vyse then breaks the rather awkward silence.

'Well said, sir. This is a festive occasion, so let us be festive! Ah, Pocock has opened the doors. Shall we go in?'

Offering his arm to my Lady, he leads her out, bowing and smiling to the company as if he were the undisputed master of the house. Two by two, the other guests begin to follow them into the mirrored Dining-Room, to take their places at the great table.

The effect on my Lady's eldest son of seeing Mr Vyse escort his mother into dinner is most apparent. I distinctly hear him whisper, 'Damn the fellow!' under his breath, before walking angrily out of the room.

I am taken into the Dining-Room by Mr Randolph Duport, leaving Mr Shillito to accompany the Rector's daughter, freckled, bony-handed Miss Jemima Thripp, with patent bad grace.

'Dashed bad of Shillito to quiz you in that impudent manner,' says Mr Randolph as we enter the great crimson-and-gold room. 'I'm surprised, too, that Mother encouraged him.'

'And what do you think of his friend, Mr Vyse?'

'Clever fellow, Vyse,' he replies, rather guardedly. 'Since Father died, Mother has become quite dependent on him – I mean for advice on business matters, and so on. Of course Perseus doesn't approve of him. Thinks he has some sort of power over her.'

This remark makes me prick up my ears.

'Power? What can you mean?'

'Well, some hold or influence over her. Perseus is convinced of it. Of course Vyse was a great pal of Mr Phoebus Daunt – thick as thieves, by all accounts – and Shillito was at school with Daunt, which gives them both a special claim on Mother's favour.'

'But surely my Lady cannot like Mr Shillito?' I said.

He shook his head.

'Assuredly not, but she endures him as a kind of duty to Mr Daunt. Now, where have they put you?'

We had reached the sumptuously laid-out table, and I was suddenly anxious that I might have been seated near, or even next to, Mr Shillito; but Mr Randolph, having gone to speak with Mr

Pocock, soon came back to tell me that my Lady had instructed that I should sit next to her. Mr Shillito, I was relieved to see, had been placed halfway down the table, from where he could not easily trouble me.

Thus I found myself, taking my dinner with all the Christmas guests, in the Crimson-and-Gold Dining-Room at Evenwood, sitting at the head of the table with Lady Tansor and her two sons, under the great barrel roof, dazzled by the array of gold plate and glittering crystal, and surrounded by the endless, shifting reflections in the tall mirrors that lined the walls.

I was looking up at the gallery, from where – not so very long ago – I had looked down on just such a fine company as this, when the dusty curtains parted and the face of Mrs Battersby appeared. For several seconds, her eyes remained fixed on me, but then Mr Randolph made some remark, and when I looked up again, the housekeeper had gone.

HOW RADIANT MY Lady looked that night! Such poise and grace! So assured and serene! The eyes of every gentleman in the room were drawn irresistibly to her whenever she rose, which she did from time to time, like the accomplished hostess that she was, to pass amongst her guests at the far end of the great table – bestowing an enquiring word here, a whispered exchange there, smiling and laughing gaily; and then, having dispensed her regal favour, gliding gracefully back down the length of the room to resume her place.

To me, she continued to show the most flattering attention, as a consequence of which I, too, became the object of keen observation and scrutiny – especially from the ladies. But with every smile she gave me, every soft touch of her hand on mine, every affectionate look, the harder it became for me to believe that she was my enemy, whom I had been sent to destroy. Already I could feel myself falling prey to her subtle charms, which I knew I must resist, or all would be lost.

III
In Which an Expedition is Proposed

AS THE THIRD course was being cleared away, Mr Perseus, who had spoken little since we had taken our places at the table, leaned towards his mother and said something quietly in her ear. Then, making his apologies to his immediate neighbours, he left the room. I watched him go, hoping to catch his eye, and perhaps receive a smile; but he showed no sign of noticing me, and as he disappeared through the double doors, I felt suddenly alone and abandoned.

'Perseus is feeling unwell,' explained Lady Tansor, with a sigh. 'I fear he smokes too much. I am always urging him to give up his cigars, and to eat more regularly, but he will not listen.'

'What's your opinion, Miss Gorst?' Mr Randolph asked. 'Do you think my brother smokes too much?'

'I really couldn't say. I believe it's a habit in which many young gentlemen indulge.'

'Young gentlemen must have their pleasures,' observed Major Hunt-Graham. 'Smoking is not so very bad a thing, you know. I've known worse habits in young gentlemen. And I believe, in the case of my young relative, that it's a mighty aid to poetic composition.'

The major was a most attractive character. Tall and well built, with smooth silver hair, and a complexion darkened by his many years in India, he possessed a calm and masterful eye, which, augmented by a patrician refinement of feature, gave his long face an imperial cast that put me much in mind of a bust of Julius Caesar that Mr Thornhaugh kept in his study in the Avenue d'Uhrich.

'My own son is an inveterate smoker of cigars,' he went on. 'My late wife could never persuade him to give them up; but then it's as natural for mothers to fret about such things as it is for sons to abandon themselves to them.'

'I'm fond of a cigar myself,' put in Mr Vyse, who was seated next to the major. 'In my case, I find it aids digestion, rather than poetic composition, and that I sleep all the better for one smoked just before bedtime; but of course one must smoke only the best. My taste was formed by an old friend – he always smoked Ramón Allones, and so, following his example, I've never smoked anything else. The boxes are also delightful. Both colourful and useful.'

He beamed benevolently.

'You've been in Wales, I think,' said the major to Mr Randolph.

'I have, sir – visiting a friend. I am also exceedingly fond of mountains.'

He gave a hollow, barking laugh and threw back another mouthful of wine, giving me the distinct, and surprising, impression that he was becoming a little intoxicated.

'A friend? From your time at Dr Savage's?' asked the major, a little pointedly, I thought.

'Indeed. Mr Rhys Paget, of Llanberis. A very fine fellow. The finest in the world,' replied Mr Randolph, adding more meditatively, 'Wonderful times.'

At that moment, my Lady suddenly rose from her chair, in a sign that it was time for the ladies to withdraw to the Chinese Salon. She swept forth, silent and stiff-backed, leaving me almost to run after her. As I passed hurriedly under the gallery and into the corridor, Mr Randolph caught up with me.

'I must apologize, Miss Gorst.'

'Apologize?' I exclaimed. 'Whatever for?'

'I'm not quite myself this evening. I wouldn't like you to think – that is, it would pain me if you thought badly of me in any way.'

'I don't understand, sir,' I said. 'Why should I think badly of you?'

He hesitated, as a chattering group of ladies passed by on their way to the salon.

'Because I fear I've had a little too much to drink this evening, and – I flatter myself that you must know this, Miss Gorst – because I esteem you so highly. I hope you think of me in the same way, and that you feel you have a true friend in me, as I hope I have in you.'

Again I thought that I read another, deeper, meaning in his eyes. This is what he had been trying to tell me when we had walked back from church together. He does not wish simply to be my friend. He loves me – I am sure of it – and believes, mistakenly, that his love might be returned.

He stands dumbly running his hands through his hair, but no further words come. Then he seems to gain resolve.

'Have you walked over to the Temple of the Winds, Miss Gorst?' he asks at last. 'It's in a rather parlous condition these days, but you get a very fine view of the house from there.'

I tell him that I have not yet explored that part of the Park, and would very much like to see the Temple.

'Capital!' he exclaims. 'Then perhaps we might take a turn together round the Lake, and then walk up to the Temple – if you'd like that?'

So it is agreed that an expedition will be arranged when the Christmas festivities are over, and when my duties allow.

He seems about to return to the Dining-Room when his expression takes on a new intensity – intimate, yet distant, as if he were looking not at me, but through me, at something only he can see.

A slight noise behind me causes me to turn my head.

Mrs Battersby is standing at the bottom of the stairs leading down from the gallery. The three of us stand, silently regarding each other in the suddenly empty corridor with an air of expectation on our faces, as if we have each of us just that moment taken up our positions to begin some strange and soundless dance.

'Was there something you wanted, Mrs Battersby?' I ask, bravely conscious of my new power of authority over her, and eager to demonstrate it.

'No, Miss Gorst,' she replies, and proceeds on her way, her footsteps echoing on the corridor's black-and-white tiles.

Mr Randolph stands for a moment, watching the housekeeper as she disappears through a door at the end of the corridor; then, with a few more words, he excuses himself and returns to the Dining-Room, leaving me to hurry off to join my Lady in the Chinese Salon.

'Where have you been, dear?' she asks.

'A call of Nature,' I whisper.

The card tables have been brought out, and groups of players are now forming. Whist is proposed. I am not fond of whist, but of course I have no choice but to consent to partner my Lady. To my relief, however, just as we are about to sit down, Mrs Bedmore – the former Miss Susan Lorimer, an old friend of my Lady's – comes up to ask whether she will partner *her*, which enables me to give up my place with an appearance of the most sincere disappointment.

I sit by the fire for ten minutes or so, until I am sure that my Lady is absorbed in her game. Then, at a little before ten o'clock, I slip away.

There is something I must do.

19

A Voice from the Past

I
The Secret Cupboard

THE IVORY jewellery box still lay on my Lady's dressing-table. Taking out the little key on its black silk ribbon, I surveyed the room.

Every piece of furniture was familiar to me – I had looked into each drawer and cupboard, examined every box and chest. Now, key in hand, I set about investigating them all again, but without success. Having little time before I must return downstairs, I quickly hurried about the other rooms, but could find no locked receptacle of any kind.

It was possible, perhaps, that I held the key, small though it was, to my Lady's study on the ground floor, a room to which no one but she and her secretary was allowed access; yet I felt sure that I had overlooked some secret hiding-place here, in her private apartments, or why would she keep the key by her in her jewellery box? As I stood debating with myself whether to postpone further searching until some more convenient time, I chanced to look across at the portrait of the beautiful Cavalier boy, little Anthony Duport.

It was hanging slightly askew, as if it had been knocked from its usual position. Through force of habit, having been so lately responsible for keeping the apartments clean and tidy, I walked over to set it right. As I approached the portrait, I chided myself for my stupidity, for I immediately saw what I had been searching for: the outline of a small cupboard set into the panelling, and normally hidden from view by the painting of Master Duport in his blue breeches. The cupboard was, of course, locked.

Taking down the portrait, I inserted the key into the brass escutcheon. It turned easily; the little square door swung open. With beating heart, I gazed inside.

Letters – five or six thick bundles, each secured with the same black silk ribbon as that to which the key had been attached; and, propped up at the back of the cavity, a photographic portrait, in an elaborate gilded frame, surrounded by a funereal mount of black velvet.

The clock above the fire-place struck the quarter hour. I had been gone too long. I would be missed, and could think of no plausible excuse for my absence. The letters must wait, but I could not resist reaching in to take out the photograph.

It showed a gentleman, perhaps thirty or so years of age, of middling height but broad-shouldered, most elegantly and expensively dressed in a silk-lapelled top-coat, light-grey trousers, and brilliantly polished, square-toed boots. He was sitting, in three-quarter profile, in a high-backed chair, against a painted backdrop of a summer garden. Beside him, on a draped pedestal, was a marble bust – the head of a beautiful young man, a god perhaps.

In its physical composition, the subject's handsome, black-bearded face reminded me a little of Mr Perseus; but the impression of character conveyed by the portrait was altogether different to the proud reserve of my Lady's eldest son. The sitter's unwavering and unsettling gaze at once suggested exceptional intellect and physical fearlessness, but also the capacity of will to apply those qualities actively and ruthlessly. A man, in a word, whom it would be unwise to thwart.

I felt as if I knew him already, and for a brief, joyous moment the impossible notion seized me that it might be my father, whom I was now certain had once known my Lady. Then I noticed three initials, 'P.R.D.', with the date 'August 1853', written on the back of the photograph. The sitter was of course none other than the object of my Lady's incorruptible passion – Phoebus Rainsford Daunt himself.

Phoebus Daunt, as he had been in life, was an altogether more impressive and memorable figure than the unprepossessing image I had formed of him. Somehow I had imagined a papery, weight-less sort of man, preening, ridiculously pompous. Instead, here was every indication of an unquestionable strength of character, body, and mind – palpable and present in both expression and bearing. What a superb and enviable couple they must have made – the beau-tiful Miss Emily Carteret and her handsome poet-lover!

A minute passed, then another; still I was held, helplessly fasci-nated, by the brooding, dangerous face of Phoebus Daunt. A bad poet he may have been; but I thought that I now understood why the late Lord Tansor had wished to make him his heir, and how he had enslaved the former Miss Carteret's heart, to the perpetual exclusion of any other man.

I replaced the photograph and was about to close the cupboard door, but at the last moment I could not resist taking out one of the bundles of letters – all written in the same distinctive hand, which, from various inscriptions in the volumes of his poetry that I had read to my Lady, I immediately recognized as being Daunt's. All had been written to my Lady.

Satisfied now that I had made an important discovery, I replaced the bundle, locked the cupboard, and set pretty Anthony's portrait back on its hook.

It was clear that the letters themselves could not be removed from their hiding-place: the risk was too great of my Lady's going to the secret cupboard, perhaps on one of those nights when the terrors were upon her, to gaze on the face of her dead lover. I would have to contrive to read and transcribe them singly, either *in situ*, when I was sure that I would not be disturbed, or by removing them one at a time to the safety of my own room.

Back in the Chinese Salon, I was relieved to find that my Lady was still engaged in her game of whist with Mrs Bedmore and the others, and that it appeared my absence had gone unremarked.

The remainder of the evening passed without incident, although I had constantly to avoid the scrutinizing eye of Mr Shillito. The bells of the great house were heralding midnight when I at last returned upstairs, to sleep for the last time in my little room under the eaves.

THE MORNING OF Christmas Eve was spent packing up my things. My new accommodation consisted of a charming sitting-room, a bedroom, and an adjoining chamber, empty now, but formerly used as a lumber-room. The sitting-room, which had an exquisite plasterwork ceiling of heraldic design dating from the days of Elizabeth, occupied an angle of the tower that stood at the eastern end of the Library Terrace. Like those in Lady Tansor's apartments on the floor below, its tall casement windows gave a view across the gravelled walks of the pleasure-garden to the distant woods of Molesey. There were fine thick rugs on the floor, an imposing stone fire-place, and a capacious sofa. Altogether, it proclaimed my new standing in the household most satisfactorily.

Christmas Day dawned – a red-letter day, indeed, for it marked the additional celebration of Perseus's majority.

In the morning, we took our allotted places in St Michael and All Angels, where we were obliged to endure one of Mr Thripp's wearisome homilies, but which, under the threatening gaze of Lady Tansor, he wisely restricted to a mere twenty minutes. A grand dinner in the evening, of surpassing magnificence, at which the heir was toasted and lauded to an almost embarrassing degree, concluded the day's festivities.

The succeeding days were filled with the usual seasonal activities. We consumed far greater quantities of plum pudding and champagne than we ought to have done; theatricals were organized, in which Mr Maurice FitzMaurice – attempting, in the most ludicrous manner, to impress Lady Tansor with his thespian genius – took a prominent role; and a grand entertainment was got up in the State Ballroom, for which a company of musicians and singers had been brought up from London. We danced and sang; billiards and cards were played; and gossip was given free rein.

Whilst the gentlemen went out with their guns, we ladies spent the long, snow-threatening afternoons by the fire reading our novels, staring vacantly through frost-laced windows at the frozen Evenbrook, or yawning away the hours until it was time to dress for dinner once more.

On the morning following Boxing Day, to my great relief, Mr Shillito, whom I had contrived to avoid as far as I could, received a letter summoning him to London on some urgent family matter. I watched him as he waddled across the Entrance Court to his carriage, accompanied by Mr Vyse, with whom he exchanged a few whispered words, interspersed with what I can only describe as significant looks and nodding glances back at the house. Then he was gone, sparing me any further unwelcome questioning concerning my surname and its association with the person he had met on Madeira twenty years earlier.

Mr Perseus kept to his room for much of the day. When at last he came down to join the company, he seemed distant and preoccupied, and spoke little. A brief remark on the weather, an occasional guarded smile, a sideways glance as I left the room, were all I received from him; yet I did not feel ignored or rejected. On the contrary, I had the most curious certainty that he was thinking of me, even when he appeared at his most distracted and self-absorbed.

As I was obliged to stay close to my Lady, and being often in the company of her guests, there had been little occasion for private conversation with Mr Randolph. Nevertheless, his looks continued to convince me that I was not misleading myself about his feelings towards me, and I was sure that he was only waiting for a suitable opportunity for us to take our walk together to the Temple of the Winds and declare himself. What I would do then, I did not quite know, and so put it from my mind for the time being.

My Lady continued considerate, amusing, warmly confiding (on small matters), agreeable in every way. She kept me constantly by her side in public, whilst in the privacy of her apartments she displayed a most winning and natural charm. We discovered many topics of mutual interest; sometimes we giggled like school-girls, gossiped disgracefully about the Christmas guests, and pored over fashion plates. I even found that I was beginning to look forward, with guilty delight, to our times together, away from public observation, when we would laugh and talk on the sofa in her private sitting-room, or on the window-seat, and act in every respect like the true friends that she wished us to be. When I came across her alone, however, sitting deathly still by the fire, or wandering forlornly on the terrace, it was clear that she was still burdened by some terrible and deep-rooted distress of mind, against which our times of pleasant companionship provided only a temporary solace.

I went on dressing her, and generally assisting with her toilet, as I had promised that I would do until the new maid was engaged; the more menial tasks that I had previously undertaken, however, were now deputed – at my recommendation – to Sukie.

Following the suggestion conveyed by Mrs Ridpath, it had been arranged that all communications from the Avenue d'Uhrich, and from Mrs Ridpath herself, were now to be sent care of Miss S. Prout at Willow Cottage, whilst my letters to Madame would be taken by Sukie to Easton for posting. The dear little thing had been so touchingly eager to oblige me, for befriending her and her mother, that she did not for a moment question why such precautions were necessary.

The first test of the arrangement had been a letter to Madame, telling her how well our plans were proceeding, and that I was now set fair, through my new friendship with Lady Tansor, to commence the next stage of our enterprise.

One evening, while my Lady was occupied in her study, I was reading by the fire in my room, awaiting her return, when Sukie came in with a small package.

'This has come for you, Miss Alice,' she whispered. 'From the lady in London.'

She handed me the package, and I saw from the direction that it was indeed from Mrs Ridpath.

'Thank you, Sukie dear. How is your mother?'

'She is well, thank you, miss, and sends her very best regards. And Barrington gave me this to give to you,' she added, handing me another, smaller, package.

I glanced down at the printed label:

J.M. PROUDFOOT & SONS
QUALIFIED DRUGGISTS & CHEMISTS
MARKET-SQUARE, EASTON

I knew that the brown-paper package contained an order that I had recently placed with Messrs Proudfoot for a bottle of Battley's Drops* – a narcotic preparation my tutor had often taken to combat insomnia, and for which I had a particular use of my own in mind; and so I placed it unopened in the drawer of my writing-table. Then, when Sukie had gone, I turned my attention to the first package.

There was a brief note from Mrs Ridpath and, pinned to the first page of a sheaf of papers covered in shorthand, a letter from Mr Thornhaugh:

LITTLE QUEEN, —

In haste, I send herewith the promised extracts – in shorthand – from yr mother's journal, which you should transcribe, read, & then destroy, along with these shorthand pages. I shall make no further remark on what you are about to read, except to say how much it gladdens Madame's heart that she is able – at last – to lay yr mother's very words before you.

Yr last to Madame cheered her greatly. That you have succeeded – so completely, & in such a short time – in securing Lady T's affection & regard encourages her to believe that the business can now be concluded with complete success, & perhaps sooner than she had anticipated.

But do not, Little Queen, I implore you, take any unnecessary

---

*Battley's Sedative Solution, a patent brand of laudanum containing opium, sherry, alcohol, calcium hydrate, and distilled water.

risks. *Lady T remains a most dangerous and resourceful enemy, &*
her association with Mr V continues to trouble both of us. I have
managed to make enquiries concerning this gentleman, through the
agency of old London acquaintances, & the results do not encourage
me to think that he is anything other than someone you should avoid
at all costs; & as it is clear that he is in some sort of association with
Lady T, you should regard him as another active foe to yr interests.

With respect to yr postscript, I can assure you that Madame's final
Letter of Instruction has been written & will be in yr hands on or by
the last day of the year, as she promised. You will then know all.

Take the greatest care of yrself.

Yr affectionate old tutor,

    B. THORNHAUGH

Locking my door, I began the task of transcribing the shorthand pages. When I had finished, long after completing my evening's attendance on my Lady, I fell on my bed, exhausted, but in a state of the most intense exhilaration.

Here, then, are the first two extracts from my mother's journal. Judge for yourself what I felt, as Mr Thornhaugh's shorthand was transformed, word by word, into the living voice of Marguerite Alice Blantyre, later Mrs Edwin Gorst, whose body lay next to my father's in the Cemetery of St-Vincent.

II
The Journal of Miss Marguerite Blantyre
EXTRACT 1: MEETING MR GORST

Quinta dos Alecrins*
Funchal

---

*'Villa of the Rosemaries'. Rosemary bushes grow to a large size in Madeira, large enough sometimes to form a hedge.

17th September 1856

This evening we were given a most delightful welcome to Madeira by Mr George Murchison, an official in the English Consulate, at his charming villa situated a little way out of the city.

Papa, being distracted and grumpy, had not wished to go, which greatly displeased Mamma, and was the cause of some hot words between them; but of course he could not absolutely refuse, as the occasion was being given in our honour. It pains me so much to see how Papa has changed, and how he now stands constantly in Uncle James's shadow. He could not have foreseen the failure of our estates in the West Indies; but Uncle James will not forgive him, and I fear he makes Papa daily conscious of his misfortune.

Nonetheless, last evening was a pleasant one. Our host, Mr Murchison, is a great addition to any such gathering, being ceaselessly convivial and desirous of pleasing his guests.

He introduced us to a number of distinguished residents of the island, amongst them Mr John Lazarus, a leading man in the shipping business here, and his companion, Mr Edwin Gorst, a striking individual of about thirty-five or thirty-six, I would say, although he has the look of a man of great experience who has lived twice as many years. He is staying for a time with Mr Lazarus, in the villa the latter purchased some years ago.

Mr Lazarus himself is an unaffected, four-square man, brown as a nutmeg, with kind, pale-blue eyes; a person, in short, whom it is impossible to dislike – at least *I* cannot imagine disliking him. My sister, of course, considered him excessively dull; but then Susanna is still dangerously young, and it is an article of her juvenile faith that a man possessing a steady, sensible, and dependable character is a species of blight upon the earth.

Mr Shillito was there. He has become a kind of demi-god in Fergus's eyes, being furiously dedicated to his own whims and desires, as Fergus, in his own weaker way, is to his. To think that, for Papa's sake, I must become the wife of my shallow, selfish cousin is sometimes more than I can bear; but it is the price – together with the assignation of my former expectations under grandmamma's will – that Uncle James has exacted for sustaining us in the comfortable style to which we have been used, as well as for maintaining Papa's position in the firm; and so for his sake, and for Mamma's, I must put my own feelings for ever out of mind. Both Fergus and I are poor helpless captives who cannot live our own lives as we please, but must be bound to the will of our elders.

On the way home after the reception, we passed Mr Gorst walking up the hill near Mr Murchison's villa. He stopped as our palanquin went by and, on an impulse, I leaned out and wished him good-night. For this I was mercilessly teased by Susanna, who kept enquiring – in that provoking way of hers – what Fergus would say; to which I could only reply that I did not much care what Cousin Fergus said or thought about an act of common courtesy. Susanna gave one of her dismissive snorts, which used to enrage Papa so much, but to which he no longer pays any heed, being perpetually weighed down by his broodings.

Yet perhaps Susanna had perceived something in my action that was not immediately apparent to me; for there is indeed a quality about Mr Gorst that intrigues and fascinates me, and which ought (I could admit this in only the privacy of my journal) to make a fiancé jealous, were that fiancé any other but Fergus Blantyre.

Mr Gorst was certainly most attentive towards me this evening, but in a quiet, natural way that put me immediately at my ease. He is tall, much taller than Fergus; and there is a look in his great dark eyes that speaks of suffering long borne, though with no trace of self-pity or resentment. They are beautiful, captivating eyes, and I find that I cannot stop thinking of them. Is this wrong of me? Perhaps it is; and perhaps my simple 'Good-night' signified something more than common courtesy after all.

Yet I doubt I shall see much more of Mr Edwin Gorst. His host, Mr Lazarus, is leaving for England soon, and will not be returning to Madeira for a month or two. While he is away, Mr Gorst will remain in his host's villa; but, as he knows few people on the island, and as he is – as Mr Lazarus told me – reclusive by both nature and habit, it is most likely that he will remain at the Quinta da Pinheiro and shun society. I hope it may not be so.

And on that sinful thought, I shall lay down my pen for the night.

III
The Journal of Miss Marguerite Blantyre
EXTRACT 2: THE MOUNT

Quinta dos Alecrins
Funchal

19th September 1856

We have just returned from our expedition to the Mount, and I hasten to write down my impressions while they are still fresh in my mind.

It began in bright, unencumbered sunshine; but by the time we reached our destination, we found ourselves walking through a dense descending mist. Soon the rain began to come down heavily, obliging us to shelter in the portico of the Church of Nossa Senhora, after scrambling as quickly as we could up the steep flight of basalt steps leading to the church (thankfully not on our knees, like the Catholic penitents).*

---

*The church, with its spectacular views, was completed in 1818 on the site of a fifteenth-century chapel destroyed in the earthquake of 1748. On the Feast of the Assumption (15 August) penitents still ascend the seventy-four steps on their knees.

We stood for some time, looking out into the grey curtain of rain that now obscured our view of the city far below. Papa sat alone inside the church, whilst Uncle James strode impatiently up and down the portico.

There were half a dozen or so other visitors, sheltering, like us, from the downpour, and gathered in a little group at the far end of the portico. At last, the rain easing a little, two or three of these persons moved forward slightly, to reveal a tall figure seated on a stone bench set against the outer wall of the church. I immediately recognized Mr Gorst, dressed in a cape, with a black straw hat on his head, a long walking-stick in his left hand. I confess that my heart leaped a little to see him, although I immediately checked myself, and turned away to remark to Mamma that we might soon be able to make our way back down to the city. However, I found it impossible not to turn again towards where Mr Gorst was sitting, to see whether he had noticed me. He appeared, however, utterly lost in thought, and seemingly unaware of my presence, or of anyone else's.

In a few more minutes the rain had almost stopped, although the clouds overhead remained dark and threatening. Uncle James, briskly clapping his hands together, sent Susanna into the church to fetch Papa, insisting that we must take our chance while we could to return to Funchal before the rain came on again. As we stepped over the little ponds that now lay across the pavement in front of the portico, I looked back. Mr Gorst had risen from his seat and was preparing to follow us down the steps, although it still did not appear that he had recognized us.

I am almost ashamed now to admit my brazenness, but I deliberately held myself back from the others and, in a moment or two, I heard the tap of Mr Gorst's walking-stick just behind me.

As he drew level, I continued to maintain the silly pretence of not seeing him; but just as he was about to move ahead of me, I put out a hesitant greeting, as if I had not quite recognized him. On hearing my words, he stopped and turned his face towards me.

He greeted me with every appearance of satisfaction, smiling as he spoke – such a warm, engaging smile – and gently tipped his hat. Hearing this exchange, Uncle James and the others had stopped a little way from the foot of the steps to look back. I said something stupidly inconsequential to Mr Gorst that I cannot now even remember, and prepared to go down to join my family. Susanna, I could see, was all of a giggle, whilst Mamma – looking first at me, and then at Susanna – was wearing a rather cross expression.

Uncle James, eyeing the rolling clouds suspiciously, called to me to hurry along, or we would all be soaked – our ox-sledges being stationed a little way down the road (Susanna had wished to make the precipitous return descent to Funchal by toboggan, but this had been sternly forbidden by Uncle James). I made a hurried good-bye to Mr Gorst; but, as I took my first step, he stopped me to ask if we planned any further excursions. I told him that we were to go to Camacha the following day.

He said that Camacha was a delightful spot, and that he often walked over to it. Then he wished me good-day and strode off down the steps at a brisk pace, bowing to Uncle James and the others as he passed, before disappearing into the mist.

I find, to my consternation, that this incident – commonplace and trivial though it was – has stayed in my head all day; and now, as I commit the memory of it to my journal, I see even less moment in it. A chance encounter. An exchange of conventional pleasantries. Nothing more. He cannot find me as interesting as I find him. Why, indeed, should I be interesting to Mr Edwin Gorst? Nothing in his face – in those eyes – betrays such a thing, I am sure, and of course I am glad of it; for I am promised to Cousin Fergus; and there is an end to the matter.

20

In Which Mr Vyse Bares His Teeth

I

Mr Vyse Speaks Frankly

O N T H E morning after receiving Mr Thornhaugh's package, I sought out Charlie Skinner.

'Will you do something for me, Charlie?' I asked.

He jumped up from his chair, threw his shoulders back, and saluted.

'Awaiting orders, miss.'

In five minutes he returned, swinging a bunch of keys, which he handed to me, saluted once again, and went on his way, whistling.

On one of my morning expeditions about the house, I had come upon a narrow stone staircase leading from the lower regions to a bare-boarded passage at the rear of my Lady's apartments. Dark and vaulted, it led out through a narrow curtained arch to the Picture Gallery. Halfway along this passage was a low doorway, on the other side of which a closet, used for the storage of travelling trunks, hat boxes, and the like, gave access to my Lady's sitting-room.

I knew from Sukie that the door from this closet into the passage had been locked for some years past. She could not tell me the whereabouts of the key, but thought that Charlie Skinner – the fount of all knowledge on such matters – might know, as indeed it proved.

After leaving Charlie, I made my way up to the passage and soon found a rusting key on the bunch he had given me that fitted the lock. With some difficulty, I eventually got the door to open on its creaking hinges, and I entered the closet, locking the door behind me.

On either side of the interior door were two small round windows filled with pale-yellow glass. These offered a good view of the room beyond and, by opening the door slightly, I judged that I would be able to hear anything that was said within.

I was about to leave when the door to the sitting-room opened and my Lady came in, followed by Mr Vyse.

At first, they remained out of earshot, both standing by the far window talking quietly, with their backs towards me; but then my Lady, her face exhibiting an extreme state of apprehension, went to her chair by the fire, only a few feet from the closet door, where she was soon joined by Mr Vyse.

So stand with me now, to see and hear what passed between Lady Tansor and Mr Armitage Vyse on that crisp winter morning.

Notice, first, the wild look in my Lady's eyes. I have seen it before, many times, when the night-terrors have banished sleep.

'But why is he still here?' she asks plaintively, as Mr Vyse – unsmiling for once – falls wearily on to the sofa opposite her. 'He knows. He must know.'

'Pray don't concern yourself,' drawls Mr Vyse. 'He doesn't know. It's nothing.'

'Nothing?' she exclaims. 'How can it be nothing?'

'It's sheer chance that he's here at this time. No more, no less.'

'But how can you be so sure?'

'I'm told that his father is seriously ill, and that he's been given permission by his superiors to remain in Northamptonshire for a little longer. You should not make more of this than it is, and must trust my judgment in the matter. You do trust me, don't you, my Lady?'

'Yes, of course,' she replies. 'You've been a great comfort and support to me since the colonel's death; and of course I shall always be obligated to you for your unfailing loyalty to the memory of my dearest Phoebus. I simply wish to be sure that we are in no danger of discovery. Gully has a certain reputation, I believe.'

'Pshaw! Reputation! King Minnow!' answers Mr Vyse, with ebullient disdain. 'A mere boy.'

'But he's with Wraxall, another man of some reputation in these matters. You know how his uncle never believed – well, I need hardly say more. And now we learn that he has letters from Slake to my father. Perhaps they contain things from which it might be possible to deduce— '

Mr Vyse interrupts her impatiently.

'The letters to your father may be something or nothing – the latter, if you want my opinion; for if this correspondence with your father contained anything of weight, why did Slake never bring it to public attention? Rest easy, my Lady. All is well. All *shall* be well.'

'If only I could—'

'Listen to me.'

He leans forward, resting both hands on his stick.

'You must put all your worries aside. I am here to make everything right. Your interests are my paramount concern, and you may rely on me, as I hope I've demonstrated, with respect to our recent little problem, to take action – *any* action – should it become necessary.'

She does not answer him, but looks down at her hands, folded in her lap.

'You live too much in the past, my Lady,' Mr Vyse goes on, reprovingly. 'Regarding Wraxall and his uncle, I've advised you before that you must not dwell on the circumstances of your father's – *ahem* – sad demise. Remember: the truth of the matter is known only to our two selves. Slake was an incorrigible busybody; but he's dead and gone, and, with him, all possibility of discovery. Think: he could never bring forward any proof to support his suspicions. For where is it? Where is the palpable evidence to connect you to the business? There is none. Words on paper can kill in these matters, my Lady, but you have assured me many times, have you not, that there are no words on paper concerning the matter – nothing committed to that deadly medium – that might condemn you.

'As for the old woman, I can only assure you, once again, that you – we – are safe. Gully has nothing. He'll soon forget her, if he hasn't already done so. There will always be corpses enough in the Thames – excuse my frankness – to keep him occupied. Besides, the trail is as cold as the weather, the son is a simpleton, and Yapp knows better than to cross me.'

He pauses, and audibly draws breath.

'The girl, however, is another matter.'

'What do you mean?' my Lady asks, patently astonished by his words. 'Are you referring to Alice?'

At the mention of my name, my stomach begins to churn. Has Mr Vyse found me out?

'I'm aware – how shall I put this? – of a new, and rather surprising, familiarity that has lately grown up between you and Miss Esperanza Gorst,' says Mr Vyse, pronouncing each syllable of my Christian name with slow, malicious relish. 'I agreed, somewhat against my better judgment, that the girl should become your companion; but I would not approve of any closer connexion. That would be distinctly dangerous. Who knows what might be let slip? You understand me?'

'You'll recall, Armitage,' she replies, a little tartly, 'that – on your advice – I obtained a satisfactory reference from Miss Gainsborough as to Alice's character, and that we were ourselves able to confirm the truth of what she told us about her upbringing. I have every confidence that she is who she claims to be, and no reason whatsoever to doubt her.'

'Really, my Lady, what an innocent you are!' cries Mr Vyse, with a cynical chuckle. 'You think these things cannot be arranged?'

'But why? If she has lied about her identity, then who is she, and what purpose could she have in coming here?'

He does not reply, but sits back and taps the end of his stick rapidly against the leg of the sofa, as an irritated cat might twitch its tail.

'That, I confess, is unknown to me,' he says at last, adding ominously, 'as yet.'

'So you frighten me with nothing but unsubstantiated suspicions?'

Her consternation is now visibly transforming into anger.

'No, not entirely unsubstantiated. Shillito is sure that she must be related to the man he met on Madeira. He believes, in fact, that she may be the man's daughter.'

My Lady throws her head back, and laughs derisively.

'Well, that's an accusation, to be sure! Related to a man your friend met twenty years ago! Have you forgotten that she's an orphan, who never knew her parents? Even if Mr Shillito is right, where's the harm?'

'That remains to be seen,' he replies. 'But that harm may come of it must be seriously considered, the risks assessed, and appropriate action taken. It is always best to expect the worst. I speak from experience.'

'But I still fail to understand how—'

'Then allow me to explain. Shillito is certain that he'd known this man Gorst *before* being introduced to him on Madeira. Unfortunately, he is still unable to bring to mind the circumstances of their previous acquaintance, but is sure – and this is the point, my Lady – that he did not then go by the name of Gorst.'

'Really, Armitage, this is preposterous! Mr Shillito could be mistaken; and what does it matter to us if this man once went by another name, any more than that Alice might be his daughter?'

'Well,' says Mr Vyse, in a most chillingly significant manner, 'that rather depends on who the man was.'

My Lady shakes her head vigorously.

'No, no, this won't do. I have a keen instinct for these things. It has never failed me yet. There's no harm in Alice, none at all. She is a most innocent, sweet-natured young woman, who has proved herself both loyal and considerate. There's no guile in her, no deceit.'

'What of Wraxall's invitation? Did she not keep that from you?'

My Lady is momentarily taken aback, but soon recovers herself.

'A venial oversight. She meant nothing by it. You are wrong in this, Armitage, although it's true that I have indeed grown very fond of her, to the extent that I now regard her, in every way, as a friend; yes – don't smile in that maddening way – a friend, although of course there are certain matters that I shall never be free to discuss with her, which I regret, but cannot help. You will please oblige me in this, Armitage, and speak no more on the subject. I hope that's clear?'

She fixes him with her queenly eye – the Lady Tansor of old.

'Perfectly,' says Mr Vyse, with another little tap of his stick. I cannot see his face, but I imagine the word has been accompanied by one of his most ingratiating smiles.

They sit for a moment, saying nothing; but then Mr Vyse leans forward once more, and places a long, well-scrubbed hand on hers.

'May I ask, my Lady, whether you have given further consideration to the matter we discussed during our ride out in the barouche?'

'Please don't press me on that, Armitage. I cannot give you an answer yet – and certainly not the answer you want.'

She withdraws her hand from his, rises from her chair, and walks back over to the window, where she stands looking out across the frost-dusted park. Mr Vyse, his long legs stretched out towards the fire, remains on the sofa, swinging his stick to and fro.

'You will permit me to observe,' he says, most sinisterly, 'that you gave me a degree of encouragement, without which I would not have raised the matter so soon. You will also acknowledge, I am sure, that I have shown exemplary patience.'

He is now standing immediately behind my Lady, blocking her from my view. Tall though she is, he is a head taller, and – drawn up now to his full height – he cuts a most menacing figure; but my Lady remains silent.

'Let me put it another way.'

His icy tone makes me shudder. The wolf is baring his teeth.

'There is a debt to be paid. A considerable debt.'

'I promised nothing.'

She moves away a little, but still does not look at him.

'True. However, the debt remains. You have drawn heavily on me, my Lady, and I must – I will – be reimbursed. Yet see how forbearing I can be! Your wish is granted. I shan't press you further – for the moment. But let us understand each other. You have secured your continuing prosperity and position through me, at no little personal risk. It would pain me greatly if – certain matters, as you so delicately put it – became known, to deprive you of what you presently enjoy. You have so much to lose, my Lady, so much. But come, let us be friends again. No more unpleasantness. The air is cleared, and now I shall leave you to your thoughts.'

He begins to walk towards the door, humming quietly to himself, then turns, and makes her a little bow.

'Until this evening.'

When he has gone, my Lady runs to her bed-chamber, slamming the door behind her.

BACK IN MY own room, I read over my shorthand notes of the conversation between my Lady and Mr Vyse.

From what I had just heard, I was satisfied that they had colluded in the murder of Mrs Kraus, although I still could not guess why such a dreadful act had been necessary. I saw, too, what my Lady must be suffering in her private moments, from the weight of guilt, the constant fear of discovery, and – confirming Mr Perseus's suspicions of Mr Vyse – the prospect of ruin if she did not give in to her accomplice's obvious desire to marry her, in return for services rendered.

Another certainty was also beginning to form in my mind: that the death of my Lady's father twenty years earlier was in some way linked to the murder of Mrs Kraus. 'The truth of the matter is known only to our two selves,' Mr Vyse had assured my Lady. But what was that truth, and what part had she played in it?

The significance of Mr Shillito's belief that he had once known my father under another name also eluded me. Mr Shillito might be mistaken; but what did it mean if he was not? Although I could not say why, this question caused me great uneasiness, and only served to increase my already intense desire to learn more about my father.

AFTER DINNER THAT evening, I retired early, to ponder these matters further, and to write up my Book of Secrets; I also wrote a letter to Madame, informing her of what I had overheard, which I intended to take over to the Prouts the next afternoon.

It was late by the time I laid down my pen, but I was not yet ready for sleep, being eager to finish reading the transliterations I had made from my mother's journal.

Return with me again, then, to a former time, and to sunnier climes, exchanging the English winter of 1876 for the sunny island of Madeira twenty years earlier.

II
Scandal in Madeira

A FEW DAYS after first meeting Edwin Gorst at Mr Murchison's reception, my mother, accompanied by her sister and her uncle, made an excursion to Camacha to visit Mr William Lambton, one of the principal wine growers on Madeira.

They left Funchal early in the morning, arriving at their destination in time for breakfast, after which my mother settled herself with a book in a small wooden garden-house situated in the extensive grounds of Mr Lambton's *quinta*. She had hardly done so when she heard the sound of a stick tapping on the flinty surface of the adjoining lane, indicating the presence of some passer-by. Then there was silence. Whoever was there had stopped, just beyond the gate.

She waited, expecting to hear that the traveller had continued on his way; but no sound came. Impelled, it seems, by some keen instinct, she stole quietly to the gate, opened it, and looked out.

She was greeted by the smiling face of Mr Edwin Gorst. As she later recorded in her journal:

We exchanged greetings, and I enquired why he had made the long climb to Camacha on such a hot morning.

He walked a good deal, he replied, as the exertion calmed his spirits. Then he spoke these thrilling words: 'It was, I must now confess, the chance of seeing you, Miss Blantyre, that impelled me to come up here on such a day.'

Those were his very words; and, as I write them now, I experience again the sensation that I felt on first hearing them from his lips; for I saw that he was no longer smiling; the tone of pleasant banter had quite melted away, replaced by one of deep seriousness and unspoken significance.

That moment was, to me, wonderful, both for its utter, intoxicating unexpectedness and – yes! I confess it – because I knew in my heart that it had been most eagerly desired. Yet I was fearful of it also, truly so, for I felt – as I feel again now – a dangerous fascination stirring within me, like a cord of many-skeined silk, beautiful to behold, but deadly, slowly coiling around my heart. For we were still little more than strangers. Whence, then, the cause of this sudden, heart-shaking tumult, which made me so restless and dissatisfied, yet so eager to live over that delicious moment again and again, driving out all thought of duty to what I am, and to what I must be?

My father enquired whether she had been to the Sé Cathedral yet. She said that she had not. He told her that it possessed many points of interest and that, like all such places, it set a necessary distance between ourselves and the world, a reminder of what we truly are. She asked whether he belonged to the Catholic faith. He said that he observed no established religion, yet did not consider himself to be a heathen by disposition. Then, after a little more conversation, he went on his way.

On her return from Camacha, my mother committed the following words to her journal: 'What am I to make of the day that has just passed? Was it a turning point in my life, or a passing trifle? No! It cannot be – it must not be – what I wish *so much* for it to be. In six months' time I shall be Mrs Fergus Blantyre; my life will be over, and all this will be but a lost dream.'

But her prediction was wrong. After church the following Sunday, she contrived to take herself off alone to the Cathedral, but there was no sign of my father. The next Sunday brought a similar disappointment. 'If he had felt but a part of what *I* felt on that hot morning at Camacha,' she wrote, 'then he would have been in the Cathedral, as I had thought he had intimated he would be. He was not there. He has not called. And I am a poor fool for thinking otherwise.'

Three weeks passed. Then, on a bright and windy Monday morning, for what she had resolved would be the last time, my mother returned to the Sé Cathedral. If he was not there, then she would know that her destiny lay elsewhere.

She stood just inside the doorway, intently scanning the people entering and leaving and the few kneeling figures at prayer; then a group of English visitors standing a little way down the nave caught her eye.

She recognized him immediately, talking to a gentleman from the aforementioned group, his hat and stick in one hand, and pointing with the other upwards at the dark wooden ceiling, with its swirling ivory decorations.

She continued to watch him for several minutes, until he shook hands with the gentleman, bowed to the group, and began to walk slowly down the central aisle of the nave towards her:

I remained rooted to the spot, my heart beating wildly, as he approached ever closer to where I was standing.

The door just behind me had been left slightly ajar, allowing a broad stream of golden light to spread across the stone floor. Into this, Mr Gorst now stepped, eyes downcast, lost in the same intense concentration of thought that I had witnessed that day at the Mount. Then, of a sudden, he looked up and saw me at last.

He made no attempt to greet me, but I was not dismayed; for I instantly read again everything I had seen before in that glorious book of his smile, and in the way he regarded me – as if he had wished to see no one else on God's earth but me.

I do not say this to flatter or deceive myself. I say it because

I knew it to be so, beyond all doubt, as surely as, in that moment, I knew that – come what may, and at whatever cost – I loved Edwin Gorst.

After a few more words had passed between them, my father asked her whether she was at liberty to walk down to the sea for half an hour, as the day now promised so fair. I here quote her later description of that walk in full:

In a kind of daze, I accompanied him into the street. I remember that we were conversing as we walked, although I can now hardly recall what was said – nothing of importance, I am sure.

At length, we reached the remains of the pier that had been projected some years since, but which was broken in a winter storm, so that it now only reaches to the water's edge. It is a favourite place of resort for the more active of the island's invalids, and a few such persons were sitting here and there on some of the huge rocks that had been spared from the storm's destruction.

Mr Gorst and I found a convenient place to sit, a little away from the others, and with a view of the distant Desertas shimmering palely in the intermittent sunshine.

The breeze blowing inland from the sea was cool, but not unpleasant, although Mr Gorst was concerned that I might catch cold, and asked me several times whether I wished to go back. But I would not have gone back for the world, even though I remained fearful of someone seeing us together, and reporting us to Uncle James and Fergus. But while I sat with Mr Gorst by my side, with the sound of the booming waves in my ears, and the winds of the wide Atlantic on my face, what did I care about the possibility of unpleasant consequences? There was time enough to consider them when and if they presented themselves.

We spoke but little – an observation from Mr Gorst, a reciprocal remark from me, and mutual wordless smiles at the pleasantness of our situation; nothing more. And then the sun broke forth, in full majestic glory, from behind a looming bank of cloud; and in that shining moment, Mr Gorst turned his eyes full on me – those deep and dangerous pools, in which I longed to drown!

'I wish you to know, Miss Blantyre,' he said softly, 'that I've admired you from the first second that we were introduced at Mr Murchison's.' It was wrong of him, he continued, to speak so, and he had fought against it for the past weeks and days, but now he found that he could no longer keep silent in my presence.

I cannot, and do not wish to, write more, although my heart and head are full to overflowing; for I am unable now to bring back to remembrance every word and phrase those sweet lips spoke, only the sense of overpowering joy that enveloped me, and which envelops me now, as I sit at my little desk by the open window, looking out at the moon shining down on the Convent of Santa Clara.

So it begins, the road that I must now take, away from the duty I owe to my family.

We sat for an hour or more, each of us striving to outrun the other in confessing the secrets that our hearts had been guarding, and which had brought us – so suddenly, so unexpectedly – to this moment.

I felt – I feel – no shame, no remorse; the transgressions that had once seemed so terrible to contemplate, to be shunned at all costs by decency and honour, I now embraced with the alacrity of a martyr. The word – the sacred word of Love – had not been uttered. What need was there? I knew I loved him, and knew that he loved me. He did not have to tell me. He would never have to tell me, for as long as I continued to see what I saw this afternoon in his eyes.

We walked back past the Church of the Colégio, and stood for a moment looking up at the four niches on the façade containing the images of various Jesuit saints. Mr Gorst asked whether he might accompany me to our *quinta*, but I said that I preferred to return alone.

'Then may I call tomorrow?' he asked.

He saw my hesitation, and did not press his request. We had not spoken of my engagement to Fergus, but now it rose up between us, like a black cloud, blotting out the promise of bright day. It fell to me, to face what must now be faced.

A few more words, and we parted.

The die was cast. More surreptitious meetings followed, and momentous plans were laid. At the beginning of December 1856, the final fateful step was taken. As an addendum to the narrative of my mother's final weeks on Madeira, I here set down – without comment – a letter from my father to Mr John Lazarus, printed in the latter's recollections.

Quinta da Pinheiro
Funchal

21st December 1856

MY DEAR LAZARUS,—

As you read this, you will already have received the news that Miss Blantyre & I have left Madeira. You shd also know – which you may not yet – that we are to be married.

I can only too easily conceive what you must think of me. A man whom you rescued from certain decay and death; to whom you have offered the freedom of yr home & introduced to yr friends, & who consequently owes you an infinite debt of gratitude, has repaid you with the meanest demonstration of contempt.

Believe me, dear sir, when I say that I am sensible – no one could be more so – of deserving every epithet of opprobrium and disgust that you can devise, & – which is almost as bad – I have no excuse to offer you for what I have done, only this – which is, indeed, no excuse at all, but rather a statement of plain fact: you succeeded too well by bringing me to Madeira. In doing so, you not only effected the recuperation of my body; you also revived something more, something that I believed had died for ever.

I am still unable to lay the truth of my situation before you, but I can assure you of this: that I shall always cherish the deepest affection for Miss Blantyre, and will do everything in my power to make her as happy as she deserves; that she comes with me willingly, in true mutual regard, with not the least stain of impropriety on her moral character; and that my intentions towards her have been, are, & will always be of the most honourable character.

Finally, know this, and be glad, dear friend. In giving me back my life, you have been – God, or Fate, willing – the unwitting agent of another restoration – far greater, & infinitely worthier of yr efforts, than you could ever have imagined possible.

Yrs in sorrow, eternal friendship, & gratitude for what you have done for me,

    E. GORST

III
Mr Perseus Takes Umbrage

THE NEXT AFTERNOON, dark and raw, with my feet slipping on ragged patches of thin ice that cracked and crackled beneath them, I set off through the Park to Willow Cottage with the letter I had written to Madame, my head still full of my mother's affecting account of her elopement with my father.

As we sipped our tea by the kitchen range, I asked Mrs Prout whether it was known why Lady Tansor had taken Mr Randolph away from Dr Savage's academy.

'That, miss, was a puzzle, to begin with,' she said, putting down her cup. 'Mr Pocock called it a conundrum, for the young man was never happier than when he was at Dr Savage's. Things were said, of course,' she added, mysteriously.

'Things?'

'Why, what else would folk say when a handsome young gentleman of prospects finds himself at liberty for the first time, away from home and the eye of his mamma, and is then suddenly brought back to that home, and to that eye, with hot words spoken when he arrives?'

'I really couldn't say.'

'Why, there was a lady in the case, my dear – that was the general opinion. But nothing seems to have come of it. He moped and sulked for a time, of course, and took himself off to his friend's house in Wales for several weeks. But all things pass, thank God, which is a great blessing, though we never think it.'

'And who was the lady – if there *was* a lady?' I asked, as Sukie refilled the teapot with hot water.

'We never knew, miss, and now never will, I think. The only certain thing was, that her Ladyship took him away from the school immediately, for though he's the younger son, Mr Randolph is still obliged to marry well – and his mamma was determined to make sure she had a say in it. Ah me, he's a dear boy! I hope he can be happy.'

I TAKE MY way home through the church-yard, stopping for a while to sit in the porch.

I have not been there long before I hear the sound of footsteps approaching down the gravel path. As I look up from my reverie, I see Mr Perseus, book in hand, staring down at me from the top of the porch steps.

'Good-morning to you, Miss Gorst,' he says, with an awkwardly half-hearted smile. 'I observed you coming out of the Prouts' cottage and thought you might be glad of some company on your way back to the house.'

I am thrilled by the proposal; but, once more thinking that accepting it might displease my Lady, I make myself politely refuse it, saying that I would prefer to remain where I was for a little longer. I truly believe that I have made him a suitably courteous reply, although it pains me to turn him down. To my surprise, however, his face darkens.

'Upon my word, Miss Gorst,' he exclaims, in a sudden burst of angry exasperation, 'you make it hard on a fellow, when all he wants is to be agreeable.'

His reaction to my gratefully expressed refusal appears out of all proportion to the offence, and I cannot help feeling hurt by his critical tone.

'I hope, sir,' I reply, my colour rising, 'that I have never shown you anything but the respect and consideration due to your station, and proper to my own position in your household.'

He does not reply, and turns on his heel to go; but then he swings back towards me.

'This is badly done, Miss Gorst,' he says, descending the steps into the porch. 'Very badly done. You'll allow, I hope, that from the moment of our first acquaintance I have tried my best to extend the hand of friendship to you?'

Still unsure how I have offended him, I find it difficult to frame a reply, and so make no attempt at one, which only seems to enrage him the more.

'You still say nothing, I see,' he says, giving me the most affronted look. 'Do you play games with me, Miss Gorst?'

To this wholly unjustified accusation I again think it prudent to make no reply. Instead, I get up from the stone bench on which I have been sitting and make to leave, but he puts out his arm so that I cannot pass up the steps.

'Will you just satisfy my curiosity, Miss Gorst,' he says, 'and tell me what you find so objectionable in my behaviour towards you? There are some, you know, who might say that I demean myself by showing such favour to a former servant, even one who was, it seems, born into a superior station in life.'

I see then that all his blustering is only partly due to my refusing his offer to accompany me back to the house, and that it really has some other cause. What is even more curious, as I look into his eyes, is that my own vexation at his intemperate words has now quite melted away.

'If you will excuse me, sir,' I reply, 'but I think that the less that is said on this matter, the better.'

Rightly concluding that I am determined to end the conversation, he steps aside to allow me to ascend the steps.

I leave him standing in the porch and walk hurriedly towards the lych-gate, which I am about to open when he catches up with me.

'This is for you,' he says, not in the least angry now, and holding out the book he has been carrying. 'I've inscribed it, so you may as well have it. Do with it what you will.'

I take the book from him, and he goes on his way back up School Lane towards the main road.

He has given me a copy of *Merlin and Nimue*, in the *de luxe* edition published by Messrs Freeth & Hoare. On the fly-leaf he has written, in an elegant flowing hand:

To Miss Esperanza Gorst, affectionately, from the Author.

December, MDCCCLXXVI.

21

A Child is Born

I

My Lady Seeks Reassurance

MR PERSEUS did not come down to dinner that evening, which spared me the embarrassment that I had anticipated, although I missed his joining us. Mr Randolph was quiet and pensive and soon left the table. My Lady also seemed out of sorts.

Later, as we were sitting with our work by her sitting-room fire, she looked up from threading her needle.

'By the by, Alice,' she said, 'what news from your fascinating Mr Thornhaugh? Is he still labouring on his *magnum opus*?'

'It keeps him continually absorbed,' I replied, 'as all great and worthy enterprises must.'

'Yes, I suppose so. Did you ever tell me the subject of this great endeavour?'

'It is a history of alchemy, from the earliest times.'

'Alchemy? The turning of base metals into gold?'

'It is more than that, or so I understand. Mr Thornhaugh regards it as a system of mystical philosophy – a philosophy of spiritual transformation.'

'Spiritual transformation,' she said, thoughtfully. 'Well, well. A noble subject, indeed. And when will the work be finished? I think, after all, that it would interest me to see it.'

'I'm not aware that Mr Thornhaugh has a definite date in view.'

'That is always the way with these scholars,' she sighed. 'They can never bring matters to a close, but must go on and on, forever delving and delving, until they drop dead, and then the thing is never done. My father was a thoroughgoing scholar, and an unusually systematic one; but even he took too long to complete the history of our family that he had undertaken – and, indeed, he never did bring his labours to fruition, despite all I could do to help him in the latter stages of gathering and arranging the necessary documents.'

She returned to her work. The fire crackled, and the clock ticked; all was warm and cosy, with only the pitter-pattering sound of rain against the window to disturb the comfortable silence.

'Alice, dear.'

I looked up enquiringly.

'I must ask you a question – and I hope you can answer it honestly, and not take offence. Will you promise to do that, dear – as a friend?'

What could I say? Only that I would try my best to satisfy her.

'Although naturally,' I added, mischievously alluding to her previous refusal to divulge the reason why the great friendship of her life had been severed, 'I could not break any pre-existing confidence.'

'Naturally.'

'Then tell me what you wish to know.'

'Well, it's this. Have you been completely truthful with me, on every point concerning yourself, your upbringing, and so on – everything you've told me on that subject since coming to Evenwood? There has been no deceit, has there, dear? No deliberate pretence or duplicity? Can you assure me of that, on all you hold most sacred?'

I express hurt and surprise at the question, and ask whether she has any cause to doubt what I have told her about myself.

'No, no!' she cries, apparently anxious to reassure me. 'You mustn't misunderstand me. Of course I trust you, and have no reason at all for doubting you.'

'I suppose someone has been speaking against me,' I venture, adopting an aggrieved tone.

'No one has spoken against you, Alice. I only wanted to be sure that I am not giving my trust and affection to someone who will reject them, as – you must excuse me . . .'

She lays down her work, and raises her hand pathetically to her brow.

A little compassion seems in order; and so I gently take her hand and, looking sympathetically into her eyes, ask whether she is alluding to her former friend.

She nods, averting her eyes.

'The wound is still raw, I see.'

'Forgive me, Alice dear. I should not have put you in this position. It was wrong of me to ask such a question, as if you've ever given me any reason to mistrust you. But I must be sure – completely sure – that our friendship will be built on a firm foundation of mutual trust and frankness. I could not bear to be disappointed once again, by the painful dissolution of an attachment on which I'd placed the highest value. We *must* be faithful to each other.'

'No secrets,' I say, with another allusive smile.

'No secrets.'

'Well, then,' I continue, in a brisk but conciliatory manner, 'I shall answer your question. I have kept nothing from you concerning myself. I am the person you believe me to be, and no other: Esperanza Alice Gorst, born a month prematurely in Paris on the 1st of September in the year 1857. Would you have her history again, in a nutshell?

'She was an orphan who knew neither of her parents, and was consequently brought up by an old friend of her mother's, Madame Bertaud. She came to England, to reside with another of her mother's friends, the late Mrs Emma Poynter, in October 1875, and secured her first position in service, as maid to Miss Helen Gainsborough, two months later. She then applied to become maid to you, my Lady, in which she succeeded – against all her expectations, but very much to her satisfaction. And that, brief though it is, is the truth – and nothing but the truth – concerning Esperanza Alice Gorst.'

'Bravo, Alice!' cried my Lady. 'You have shown true spirit under fire, and have come through it bravely – as I knew you would. But you *have* hidden something from me, you know.'

'And what is that?'

'Your true character. You are submissive no longer, Alice – I sense that strongly, although you still pretend that it's your nature to be so. Don't look so startled! I like you all the better for it. It is testimony to what I have always known: that we are kindred spirits. It is only circumstance that disguises the person you really are. And now I have released you from subservience, so you may be yourself at last!'

LISTEN! DO YOU hear it? It is the sound of a stick – tip-tap, tip-tap – echoing through the cold evening air. It is Mr Armitage Vyse, descending the front steps on his way to his carriage, for his Christmas visit to Evenwood is over.

As he is about to step into the carriage, he turns and looks up, his lean, flamboyantly moustachioed face illuminated by the lantern held up by his man, Digges. Our eyes meet.

He smiles – such a smile! Broad and lingering, in which is co-mingled ingratiation and intimidation. It seems to say: 'Look to yourself, Miss Esperanza Gorst, for I have you in my sights.' If he means it to frighten me, he succeeds. I strive to maintain my composure; but, knowing what he is capable of, my heart begins to thud. Then, with a slight bow, and still smiling, he doffs his hat, slowly replaces it, and climbs into the vehicle.

I am standing at one of the Picture Gallery windows, watching the bobbing lamps on his carriage as they fade and then disappear into the darkness. My Lady has a headache, and has retired early. As I left her, she confirmed her decision to spend some days in London, having, she says, overcome her previous aversion to the capital, and repeating her desire to take me about a little in society. So we are to depart for Grosvenor Square on the first day of the New Year, which my Lady never cares to celebrate. I feel apprehensive; but, despite the proximity of Mr Vyse, I shall be glad of the change of scene, and for the opportunity, perhaps, of seeing Mrs Ridpath again.

After I had watched Mr Vyse's carriage leave, and was about to go up to my room, Sukie had come panting up the stairs, holding a package.

'I'm so sorry, Miss Alice, I should have brought it over this morning, but I overslept, and it quite went out of my head. It came yesterday.'

The package contained a further sheaf of shorthand extracts from my mother's journal. Two hours later, with midnight approaching, I had completed my transcription of the new extracts.

I poured some water into a bowl to rinse my inky fingers. Then I wept.

II

To France

DRAWN FROM THE JOURNAL
OF MISS MARGUERITE BLANTYRE

AFTER THEIR SECRET departure from Madeira, drawing on the little money that my mother had at her personal disposal, supplemented by the sale of some of her jewellery, my parents took ship for Mallorca. There they took lodgings in a house near the La Seo Cathedral in the city of Palma, temporarily adopting the name of Edward and Mary Gray, supposedly brother and sister. They remained only a short while on Mallorca, my father being certain that they would be pursued, and soon left the island for Marseilles.

After a hard and circuitous route northwards, they were finally married in Cahors, on the 15th of January 1857. These are my mother's reflections on that memorable event, written from the Des Ambassadeurs Hotel the following day:

For the first time in my life, I take up my pen to write my journal as *Mrs Edwin Gorst* – no longer Marguerite Blantyre, or Mary Gray!

Edwin and I were married yesterday, Thursday the 15th of January, in the Church of the Sacré-Coeur. It took such a very little time to become someone else – the wife of my dearest Edwin, whom I shall always love, until Death takes me. And now I am his – truly and completely his – in every way a wife should be, and I cannot think how I may ever live again without his dear presence.

The inn is not very clean, but the food is excellent, and the city – where Fénélon* was a student – is delightful. This morning, on coming down to breakfast, I was addressed by one of the waiters, for the first time, as Madame Gorst! It sounded so strange and matronly – to be considered a *madame*, and no longer a *mademoiselle*! But then, through the day, as I grew used to it, I found myself wishing to hear myself so addressed by every stranger who passed us in the street, so thrilling were the words to my ear. Madame Gorst! Mrs Gorst!

Edwin, who was withdrawn and silent for the last stage of our journey here from Montauban, is altogether changed – optimistic, affectionately attentive, and wonderfully voluble on the various ancient buildings and antiquities that surround us here.

As we walked around the city this morning, arm in arm through the pale winter sunshine, smiling and laughing at the thousand and one little, but infinitely precious inconsequentialities that all lovers make their own, I felt that I would never be so happy again – nor did I care if it were so.

In those all-sufficient hours, I was more truly alive, I believe, than I have ever been in my life, and could conceive of no possible augmentation of that wondrous completeness, in this life or the next. Whatever came, whatever trials I might undergo, I would always be armoured against despair – against even the terrors of death – by the memory that I had once, for a brief instant of time, walked through Paradise with my dearest Edwin.

*François de Salignac de la Mothe-Fénélon (1651–1715), French Catholic prelate and writer.

III
The Avenue d'Uhrich
DRAWN FROM THE JOURNAL OF MARGUERITE GORST

IN THE LAST week of January 1857, my parents at last arrived in Paris, taking lodgings above the shop of a colourman* in the Quai de Montebello, on the Left Bank of the Seine, overlooking the Île de la Cité. Here they intended to make a temporary home until they could safely remove to England without fear of pursuit and discovery by my mother's uncle or his agents: her cousin and former fiancé, Fergus Blantyre, and his friend, Mr Roderick Shillito.

The owner of the shop above which they lodged, a Monsieur Alphonse Lambert, was a softly spoken and ungrudgingly generous man of about sixty years, with an invalid wife under his care. His good nature allowed my parents a considerable degree of latitude with respect to their rent; for by the time they reached Paris, their little stock of money had dwindled almost to nothing.

One day, my mother offered to assist their landlord in the shop, as a way of meeting their obligations until the rent-money then due could be found. She quickly became thoroughly at home amongst the easels, palettes, canvases, brushes, casts, and all the other articles sold by Monsieur Lambert, who just as quickly appears to have regarded her as an indispensable addition to his business.

As well as charming Monsieur Lambert's customers, my mother also displayed an immediate aptitude in the preparation of colours and, having drawn and painted since girlhood, revealed an artistic ability of no common order in the sketches and pictures of the neighbourhood that she soon started to produce, and which she shyly placed before the professional eyes of Monsieur Lambert for his opinion.

Then, one fine spring morning, to the proprietor's surprise and delight, a gentleman, entering the shop with his daughter, for the purpose of buying her some colours and some brushes, chanced to

*A dealer in artists' colours.

see one of these productions, admired it, and enquired whether it
was for sale. Soon my mother was obliged to abandon her duties in
the shop and was given an attic room by her landlord, where she
happily turned out views of the Cathedral and the *quais* that found
an eager market amongst visitors to those picturesque areas of the
city.

My father, meanwhile, occupied himself with occasional literary
work, and with acting as an agent for his wife's artistic endeavours.
He would spend long hours seeking out new patrons, delivering
her drawings and paintings to them, and selecting new views and
subjects for her to depict.

On his return one day from delivering a view of the Concierge-
rie to a gentleman in the Rue de St-Antoine, my father suddenly
announced that they would be leaving the Quai de Montebello
within a matter of days.

My mother was naturally astounded by the news, until he
explained that, quite by chance, he had encountered an old
acquaintance – a Madame de l'Orme, whom he had known,
through a mutual friend, when living in London some years previously. This lady, of about my father's age, was now a widow, but
had been left well provided for by her late husband. On hearing
of their situation, and living alone in a large house in the Avenue
d'Uhrich, she had made the suggestion that my parents should
take up residence with her, free of rent. They could occupy the
whole of the second floor of the mansion, comprising half a dozen
comfortable and well-appointed rooms, amongst which was a spacious, well-lit corner apartment that could be fitted up as a studio
for my mother.

To this proposal my father had agreed, with apparently very little
persuasion on the part of Madame de l'Orme. My mother, less willing to leave the Quai de Montebello, and the modest but perfectly
comfortable life that they enjoyed with Monsieur Lambert, at last
reluctantly agreed to the plan; and so, in June 1857, they moved
their few belongings, together with my mother's artistic materials,
into Madame de l'Orme's house in the Avenue d'Uhrich.

• • •

THROUGHOUT THEIR TIME in the Quai de Montebello, my parents' marriage had continued to be a generally happy one, even though their financial circumstances were often precarious, despite the regular sales of my mother's work. The plan to live in England had accordingly been abandoned, and, by mutual consent, Paris was now to be their permanent home.

Soon after removing to the Avenue d'Uhrich, however, as is evident from several entries in my mother's journal, certain fractures began to appear in their previously happy union – the reason for which, although never explicitly stated, caused my mother considerable pain and anxiety. Disagreement and dissension seem to have arisen, in part, from my father's insistence that no communication of any kind should pass between his wife and her Blantyre relations, a most unreasonable prohibition (it seems to me, as it did to her), which went hard on my mother; for she loved her parents and sister dearly, and had hoped that the irrevocable fact of her marriage would effect a reconciliation – with her nearest relatives, if not with her uncle.

Although it pains me to say it, I have also inferred a degree of unexplained antipathy between my mother and Madame de l'Orme, and must additionally mention two or three veiled references to certain events in my father's former life in England, the continuing consequences of which appear to have contributed, perhaps in no small way, to my mother's growing unhappiness.

Whatever the causes of their troubles, my father became distant and unpredictable in his behaviour, often shutting himself away for long periods, and leaving the house after dark to wander the streets. I cannot be sure whether this sad state of affairs persisted, or whether it was resolved; for from the middle of July 1857, the journal extracts sent to me by Mr Thornhaugh cease. They do not resume, and then only briefly, until September of that year – on the first day of which month, at about three o'clock in the afternoon, I was born in a room overlooking the high-walled garden of Madame de l'Orme's house in the Avenue d'Uhrich.

IV
The Last Words of Marguerite Gorst

MY DEAR MOTHER's health was fatally weakened by the effort of bringing me into the world. She died on the 9th of January 1858, and was buried in the Cemetery of St-Vincent, under the slab of granite that I later came to know so well.

The final entry in her journal, written just three days before her death, speaks of her joy at my birth, and of the many hopes she had for my future life. She also expresses, most poignantly, her sorrow that her own parents continued in ignorance of her marriage, and now of the existence of a fine and healthy granddaughter. These are the last words that she ever wrote, and with them I shall now conclude:

6th January 1858

My life now is over, although Dr Girard persists in the kindly pretence that it is otherwise. I shall never again see dear Papa and Mamma, or my sweet, exasperating sister, with all her impetuous ways; and they will never now see their beautiful grandchild and niece. This is a most terrible and unnatural deprivation, which pains me beyond words; but Edwin has insisted that it must be so, and my love for him remains such – despite all that has happened between us – that I cannot, and will not, go against his wishes, even in the extremity of impending extinction. For I know that Death's net is all about me, and soon I shall be gathered in.

I left Madeira in the highest hopes of lasting happiness; and, indeed, I *was* happy with Edwin for a time – happier than I had ever been in my life. But all has changed – *he* has changed – since we left dear Monsieur Lambert's, and particularly since the birth of our darling daughter, on whom Edwin completely dotes.

When he is not restive and fidgety, he is distracted and preoccupied, as if his mind cannot escape from the unremitting consideration of some irresistibly compelling subject. He locks himself away, scribbling in his note-book, or writing letters – to whom, I do not know; he walks about the garden deep in thought, for hours on end; he goes out at night, returning just before dawn.

He is silent at meals, even with M—; he neglects his work; and now he complains of headaches, for which only his drops – he claims – can effect relief.

Does he love me? Has he ever truly loved me? He has been the dearest, kindest friend and companion, my rock and support; and even through all the dark days of the last months, he has come back to me, on many occasions, as the Edwin I once knew, whom I shall never cease to love, even when I am in my grave. But love? True, entire, enduring love – matching, point for point, the love that I bear *him*, and have so borne since the very moment of our first meeting? Has he ever felt this for me? I ask myself the question over and over, but no answer comes.

M— has insisted on staying with me until Edwin returns, although I wished to be left alone. She is sitting by the window as I write this, looking down into the garden. From time to time, she turns towards me and smiles. We speak little, having now nothing more to say; but we have reached a kind of understanding, for Edwin's sake, which I believe contents us both.

From my bed I can see the bare branches of the chestnut-tree, and the high grey wall, tipped with iron spikes, that separates us from our neighbour, Monsieur Verron. Soon those branches will begin to bud with new life, and my darling girl, my little Esperanza, my precious hope, will lie beneath its canopy of gauzy green in soft sunlight, kicking her little legs, or dreaming unknowable dreams. Although I wish it could be otherwise, I am resigned to the necessity that she must be brought up here, under M——'s roof; but I have the comfort of knowing that she will want for nothing, and that she will go out into the world as a lady.

The pain has returned, and still no sign of Edwin with Dr Girard. I wish so much that he would come!

22

In Which Madame's
Third Letter is Opened

I
By the Lake

THUS MY mother died, and with her the written record of
my early life in the Avenue d'Uhrich came to an end. I had
learned all I could of my parents from the journal extracts
that Mr Thornhaugh had sent me, and from the recollections of
Mr John Lazarus; but, to my bitter disappointment, much was still
unexplained.

I wished particularly to know about the period after my mother's
death, during which my father had been my only parent, and also
the circumstances of his own death in 1862, when I was five years
old.

All I had been told by Madame was that, a year after the loss
of his wife, my father had quit the Avenue d'Uhrich, leaving me
in her temporary care. Long nurturing an interest in the ancient
civilizations of the Near East, his plan had been to travel in those
regions with the purpose of gathering material for a popular work
on the Babylonian Empire, in which the small publishing concern
for which he had been producing translations had expressed an
interest. He had intended the trip to last not more than six months;
but after only two, his letters to Madame had ceased, and no more

was heard from him for several years. At last, in April 1862, a letter came from an official in the British Embassy in Constantinople informing Madame that he had died in that city of scarlet fever a week or so previously.

The necessary arrangements were made, and in due course his body was brought back to Paris, to be buried next to that of his wife's.

Strangely, although I can recall being told by Madame that Papa would not be coming home ever again, I have no memory of his interment, only of being taken, some days later, to see – for the first time – the two stone slabs beneath which lay the mortal remains of Edwin and Marguerite Gorst.

I felt no grief – of that I am certain – at the deaths of my parents, for it was of course impossible for me to remember even the smallest detail concerning either of them. They were little more than names, chiselled into those two inexpressive granite slabs. Madame had become my only parent; and soon she would be joined by dear, kind Mr Thornhaugh. I would have mourned Madame most grievously had they put her in the cold earth, and laid stone over her; but I did not then mourn Edwin and Marguerite Gorst, for they were strangers to me then, their actuality blotted out by the all-sufficient care of Madame. Not until I was older did the keen agony of loss begin to empty its subtle poison into me; and not until now, in the great house of Evenwood, did I weep for them.

SLEEP OVERTOOK ME swiftly that night, and I did not wake until past my usual hour. But it was Sunday, the last of the present year, and church was not until ten o'clock.

Mr Randolph was sitting alone in the Breakfast-Room, sipping his coffee, when I entered. He looked up expectantly.

'Miss Gorst!' he cried, giving me one of his warmest smiles. 'There you are. I've been waiting for you. If you're minded, perhaps you'd care to make our expedition to the Temple today, after church – if it's not at all inconvenient?'

It is perfectly convenient; and later that morning, having endured

Mr Thripp's valedictory sermon to the departing year, we make our way to the Lake, on the far side of which, dominating a terraced mound, stands the Temple of the Winds.

Although the morning is generally overcast, the piled grey clouds are broken here and there by enlarging chinks of pallid sunlight. Our talk has run on the various activities and incidents that took place during the recent Christmas celebrations. We laugh again at Mr Maurice FitzMaurice's unintentionally comic theatrical performance; agree that Sir Edgar Fawkes has grown even redder of face and fatter of girth; and wonder whether Miss Marchpain's sister ever found her missing gloves (Mr Randolph surmises that they were purloined, as love trophies, by gallant Captain Villiers).

We inspect the Temple, once an elegant addition to the Park's amenities, but now falling rapidly into ruin, and slowly begin to retrace our steps back up the path towards the carriage-road. We have been conversing for some time of nothing in particular when Mr Randolph suddenly falls silent. With evident nervousness, he then asks if I would allow him to address me by my Christian name.

'Of course you may,' I tell him, seeing no harm in it. 'Your mother has always called me Alice; but I have another name, as I think you know, if you'd prefer that.'

'Do you know,' he smiled, 'I believe I would. It's so distinctive and mysterious, and suits you so much better than Alice. Yes. Esperanza it shall be. It means "Hope", I think.'

'It does.'

'Well, then, it exactly expresses how I feel – I mean the hope that I've been holding, these long weeks past, that I might be to you what I wish so much for you to be to me.'

Then, almost before I know it, he is asking whether he can come to me privately, at a time and place that would be convenient to me, in order to speak on a matter of the greatest importance to him.

'I have something very particular I wish to put before you,' he continues, his eyes seeming to shine with a great purpose. 'I have wanted to speak to you – that is, to ask you – ever since we walked back together that day from the Duport Arms. In fact I seemed to know from the first moment we met how it might be between us. Don't you find that strange? *I* do – most strange – that I should be so sure so quickly. But it's true nevertheless. I knew straight away, you see, that you'd be – oh, dash it! I'm such a pudding-head at this sort of thing. My brother would know how to put it so that you'd understand, but I don't. So will you let me come to you, when you're ready to hear me, so that I can ask you – well, what I want so much to ask you?'

Was this hesitant declaration a prelude to making a proposal of marriage? Although I can scarcely believe it, that is what I now conclude from his awkwardly fervent words, and from the impassioned look in his eyes. Since my arrival at Evenwood, I have grown exceedingly fond of Mr Randolph. It touches me greatly that he had appeared to like me from the first, and that he had demonstrated so clearly a wish to befriend me. It seems, however, that I am right to suspect that there is now some deeper prompting at work, and that his recent talk of friendship has been meant to convey another, more significant meaning.

To have captured the heart of Mr Randolph Duport was a most wonderful thing, and it makes me feel almost cross with myself, and not a little ashamed, that I must reject the proposal I am certain that he is intending to make. I will do so with every expression of gratitude for the honour he has paid me, and with no small degree of regret; but I can envisage no bond existing between us other than sincere and steadfast friendship. Precious though that might be, it is not enough. When I marry, I must marry for love, true love – nothing less.

'You express yourself perfectly well,' I tell him, 'and of course I shall be very willing to hear what you wish to say to me. My time, however, is not my own, for I am required to be in constant attendance on your mother.'

'Well, then,' says Mr Randolph, breezily, 'we must endeavour to make time, if we can.'

I am about to prevaricate further, but the words die on my lips.

We have arrived at a green-painted boat-house. On one side of the path, the shimmering surface of the Lake stretches away towards the Temple of the Winds atop its terraced mound; on the other, a

broad area of newly planted saplings drops gently down to the glim-
mering Evenbrook.

'Hey, you there!' Mr Randolph suddenly shouts out. 'What the
devil are you doing?'

I follow his eyes.

There, crouching down behind an area of low bushes just beyond
the boat-house, is a man. He is wearing a leather cap, and his black
hair hangs down in long greasy strands. I know him instantly, for he
has often invaded my dreams since our return from London.

It is Billy Yapp, known to the world – as Mr Solomon Pilgrim had
told me in Dark House Lane – as 'Sweeney'.

I think at first that I must be mistaken. Then, as the man breaks
away from his hiding-place and begins bolting towards the river, I
get a clear view of the raw-boned, villainous face that had terrified
me so in the Antigallican public-house. There is no mistake.

In an instant, Mr Randolph sets off in pursuit; but, although
he is fit and strong, he is no match for Yapp, who quickly gains the
cover of the woods that border the northern bank of the Evenbrook
and disappears from view.

I wait for Mr Randolph's return in the greatest consternation,
having concluded that Yapp must have been sent to Evenwood on
the instructions of Mr Armitage Vyse. But for what purpose? To
spy on me – or to do to me what I am certain he had done to Mrs
Barbarina Kraus?

After five minutes or so, to my immense relief, Mr Randolph
comes back up through the trees, hat in hand, and breathing hard
from his exertions.

'Lost him,' he puffs. 'Damned fellow can run.'

'What do you think he was doing?' I ask.

'Nothing conducive to the common good, I'll lay money on that.
Not a local either, by the look of him. But don't alarm yourself.
We'll go back now and I'll send some of the men round the Park,
though I'll wager he won't linger here.'

As we gain the junction with the carriage-road, a tall figure on
horseback is approaching from the direction of the Western Gates.
As it draws nearer, I see that it is Mr Perseus.

He momentarily reins in his mount when he reaches us, throws me a look of the utmost disfavour, and then – without a word to either of us – spurs off towards the house.

As I ENTER the vestibule, I find Mr Perseus, riding-whip in hand, pacing up and down in front of the portrait of the Turkish Corsair. He appears to have been waiting for me.

'You have been out walking again, I see, Miss Gorst,' he remarks, in a most disapproving tone, tapping his whip irritably on the side of his leg as he speaks.

Knowing that I have committed no impropriety, I merely confirm the fact and politely excuse myself.

'You'll allow me to observe,' he then says, as I am about to make my way up the stairs, 'that you appear to entertain a very marked partiality towards my brother. I am not sure that it is quite appropriate for my mother's companion to behave so, but perhaps her Ladyship considers the matter in a different light. She is, I'm sure, aware of your . . .'

He pauses, as if searching for the right word.

'Attachment,' he resumes, with the air of a man throwing down a verbal gauntlet.

'I beg your pardon, sir,' I answer, piqued by his insinuation, 'but you are mistaken. There is no "attachment", in the sense you appear to intend, between Mr Randolph Duport and myself, and therefore nothing for my Lady to consider.'

'Your walks with my brother have not gone unnoticed, you know.'

I have no mind to engage in a debate on the matter, being still agitated after the encounter with Billy Yapp and wishing very much to return to my room. I therefore excuse myself again; but as I am turning away, he suddenly takes hold of my wrist to stop me. Seeing the shock on my face, he immediately releases his grip, but makes no apology for his action.

'Your position here is changing, Miss Gorst,' are his next words, spoken quietly but intently, 'and it will, I predict, undergo further change. I am glad of it, believe me. Her Ladyship is fond of you, and it is altogether a good thing, in my opinion, that you are now occupying a situation in the household that is far more suited to your natural condition. I feel it is my duty, however, to point out something that I am sure you must already know concerning my brother.'

I try to assure him once again that he is mistaken in thinking that any regard I may have for Mr Randolph is anything more than our respective stations permitted, or that I cherish any improper designs on him, but he cuts me short.

'Hear me out, Miss Gorst. I wish only to spare you from disappointment and distress. My brother has an inescapable duty to this great family, and to those who have made it so. Perhaps you are unaware that it has always been the Duport way to expect that even junior sons should marry well. My brother is no exception. It is therefore incumbent upon him to find a wife who will augment and extend the family's interests, and it is Lady Tansor's fixed resolve that he should do so. You understand me?'

He is now at his insufferable worst – pompous, arrogant, the overbearing Duport heir in all his pride. The look I receive enrages me, for of course I understand him only too well. Although I enjoy an unusually favourable position in the household, that imperious stare is intended to remind me that I must be careful not to over-reach myself. I came to Evenwood as a mere servant. I am poor. I am an orphan, with little knowledge of my parents. What advantage could I bring to the mighty Duports? These things, and more, I read in his arctic eyes.

I cannot, of course, reveal my conviction that his brother loves me, that I believe he intends to make me a proposal of marriage; but, goaded to a response at last, and with due deference, I put the hypothetical case that even were I fortunate enough to enjoy the affectionate regard of Mr Randolph Duport, and were I to return that regard, then some might consider it to be a purely private matter.

'There you are mistaken, Miss Gorst,' he returns. 'As I have just been at some pains to suggest, it most certainly *is* a matter on which other persons will, and should, form an opinion – her Ladyship in particular – and the consequences, you may be sure, will not be to your advantage. If I may say so, you appear rather quickly to have convinced yourself that your new position gives you the privilege of acting as you please. Step back, Miss Gorst, step back, for your own sake. You say nothing.'

We stand for several moments in silence as I consider what I should say to him. At length, I tell him that I have some duty to perform for my Lady, and assure him for a third time that any feelings I might have for his brother are of a wholly unexceptional character.

'I am glad to hear you say so, Miss Gorst. You will forgive me, I hope, for speaking so frankly. My only wish is to avoid any unpleasantness.'

He gives me a stiff bow, and I turn to make my way up the staircase, feeling his eyes upon me with every step I take.

I have nothing to conceal from my Lady regarding my feelings for her younger son, and I continue to feel secure in her favour. Why, then, should I care what Mr Perseus Duport thinks of me?

Yet although I pretend otherwise, I *do* care what Mr Perseus Duport thinks of me, and that he might still believe I am in love with his brother. I can deny it no longer. I care very much indeed.

II
Madame de l'Orme to Miss Esperanza Gorst
LETTER 3

I HAVE SCARCELY closed the door to my room, my mind in turmoil, when Sukie knocks and gives me a letter. I know immediately who it is from, and what it contains.

The day had finally come on which I would learn at last who I really was, and why I had been sent to Evenwood; for here, in my trembling hands, was Madame's long-awaited third Letter of Instruction.

It was to be a day like no other I had ever known, and will – I hope – never know again. Madame's words were like flaming arrows to my soul. The fires they ignited are burning still, and will continue to smoulder until I am laid in earth.

Here, then, is what I read, sitting at my desk in the Tower Room at Evenwood, on that ever-memorable day, as the year 1876 drew to its close.

Avenue d'Uhrich
Paris

DEAREST CHILD,—

The time has come, at last, for me to place the Great Task before you in a clear & unequivocal light, & I shall do so as succinctly as I can.

What I first have to tell you — by way of preparation for what follows — will, I fear, cause you great, & perhaps abiding, pain, as it pains me so very much to write the words; and so you must be brave, my angel, & face the final truth about yr history with that same courage that you have displayed so admirably in the role you are playing at Evenwood.

You have looked upon your father's name many times as a child, on his grave in the Cemetery of St-Vincent. As you well know, the stone bears the name of Edwin Gorst, departed this life in the year 1862.

This, however, was not yr father's real name, but the one he adopted after suffering the most terrible calamity, the consequences of which made it imperative that he flee his native country for ever.

Know, then, that your father was born Edward Charles Duport, the legitimate son of Julius Verney Duport, 25th Baron Tansor, & his first wife, the former Laura Fairmile. No doubt you have seen the portrait of Ld & Lady Tansor, with their second son, Henry Hereward, in the vestibule at Evenwood. They were yr grandparents, & the little boy is yr poor dead uncle.

Yet although yr father had been born the true and undisputed heir to the Tansor Barony, both he & his own father, the late Ld Tansor, were denied knowledge of the fact by his mother. He thus grew up in complete ignorance of his true identity, & of his rightful inheritance. He, not yr mistress, should have succeeded the 25th Baron.

The story is a long and distressing one, & must wait to be told to you in full. But, in brief, yr grandmother – without her husband even knowing of his son's existence – gave yr father to be brought up by another, in order to punish Ld Tansor for bankrupting her own father, which, she absolutely believed, sent her adored parent to an early grave. By this act, she set in train the sequence of events that, over fifty years later, have brought you to Evenwood.

By depriving her husband of all knowledge of his son, Lady Tansor did him the greatest possible hurt – although he remained unaware of his loss; & it is true that she repented of her great sin, & suffered grievously, at the last, from remorse for what she had done; but by then it was too late to mend, & the consequences were to prove more momentous & far-reaching than she could ever have conceived.

As you now know, with no heir from his second marriage to succeed him, Ld Tansor elected to leave all his extensive property to his Rector's son, Phoebus Daunt, on the single condition that he assume the name of Duport, which he was more than willing to do. Nor need I rehearse what you have read in Mr Vyse's memorial to Daunt, concerning his murder by Edward Glyver, his erstwhile school-fellow and friend. And now I beg you to be strong, dear child, for what must be told.

The woman to whom Laura Tansor had given her first-born son, Edward Duport, to be brought up as her own child, was her oldest and dearest companion. Naturally, the boy grew up bearing his foster-mother's married name. That name was Glyver. Do you now understand?

Edward Glyver – the man who killed Phoebus Daunt – was yr father.

Oh my darling child! I can all too readily conceive the shock that these words will produce in you. How can the blow be softened, being the simple, terrible truth? Let me attempt to do so.

Never, never believe, dear girl, that yr father was a common mur-

derer, or that he acted out of either vulgar envy or blind vengeance. True, Daunt was the sole agent of his being sent away from Eton, after he was falsely accused of stealing a most valuable book from the Library there; it is true also that this charge, false though it was, prevented him from following the path he desired above all others — of obtaining a University Fellowship, and leading the life of a scholar. The memory of this wholly malicious injustice remained with yr father for many years, during which he harboured an unquenchable desire for Daunt to suffer the bitterness of dashed ambition, as he had done. But he did not wish him to die for it; he began to contemplate such an extremity only when faced with a betrayal and loss so great that no other course seemed open to him.

By the time the deed was finally done, yr father had been temporarily deprived of reason, stripped of every moral sense, driven to the very brink of despair. His former self-possession, & all those higher qualities of which Mr Heatherington wrote, in his reply to the prejudiced eulogy of Mr Vyse, had been shocked into temporary abeyance. All that remained was his formidable will.

Thus he descended into a brief madness, in which nothing mattered but the destruction of his enemy — not for being the cause of his expulsion from school; nor because he had been named as Ld Tansor's heir, for that, yr father was confident, could have been successfully challenged in Law, by means of evidence he had gathered that proved his real identity.

Phoebus Daunt died because he was the instigator, with the woman yr father loved above all others, of a most wicked conspiracy against him. Through the cruellest of deceptions, Daunt & this woman obtained the documents that yr father had laboured so long to discover, proving him to be Ld Tansor's legitimate heir. They then destroyed them, so depriving yr father for ever of the means to reclaim his birthright.

And the name of this deceiving, conscienceless woman, who encouraged him to believe that his love was returned; who then shattered every precious hope he had of future happiness and prosperity, by telling him to his face that she had never loved anyone but Phoebus Daunt, that she intended to marry him, and that the proofs of yr father's true identity, which he had delivered, in the innocence of devoted love, into her very hands for safe-keeping, had been passed to his enemy for certain destruction?

Who else could this perfidious creature be, but the present Lady Tansor – the former Miss Emily Carteret, the woman whose hair you have dressed, whose gowns you have brushed and mended, whose companion you have become, and who now calls herself your friend.

Now do you see, dear child, why Lady Tansor is yr enemy, as she was yr father's, & why she will always be so? She has stolen your birthright, and your children's, as she conspired to steal his.

Yet honesty compels me to admit that yr father loved her, & that he continued to do so, even after she had betrayed him. This you must also understand: somewhere – in the deep places of her black heart – I believe that she felt some affection for him also, weak and ineffectual though it was compared to her consuming passion for Phoebus Daunt.

For a time, yr father refused to blame Miss Carteret for the catastrophe that she had helped bring upon him, finding that he could not condemn her for what she had done in the name of Love, when he, too, would have done anything, committed any crime, for her sake.

Gradually, however, in his lonely Atlantic exile, living on Lanzarote under the name of Edwin Gorst, sundered from everything that had made life sweet for him, and from the country and the city he loved, he began to see things in a different light, viewing his own misfortune against a greater wrong. For in denying yr father what was his by right of birth and blood (and so compounding the actions of his own mother), Miss Carteret and Phoebus Daunt had also denied his descendants what was rightfully theirs. Yr father now resolved that this crime against future generations must be remedied. But what could be done?

At last Fate – as he believed – placed the means in his hands. He was delivered from his exile, as you are now aware, through the agency of Mr John Lazarus. Recuperated & revivified, he began to conceive a plan – desperate, reckless, and with slender chance of success, but which might, perhaps, bring about a restitution, not of his own position, for that had been irrevocably forfeited by the crime that he had committed, but of the right of his lawfully begotten heirs to succeed, in his place, to the Tansor Barony.

His design was simple, although fraught with uncertainty, & perhaps danger; but the responsibility that he felt towards his ancient bloodline negated all practical objections.

Soon after his arrival in Madeira, as you will recall from Mr Lazarus's recollections, yr father had learned — by sheer chance — that Miss Carteret had married Colonel Zaluski, and that a son had been born to their union. This, combined with the further intelligence that Miss Carteret was now Ld Tansor's legal heir, & that consequently her son would succeed to both the title & property after her death, compelled him to action.

The first pre-requisite was to marry, as soon as a suitable wife, whom he could cherish with genuine affection, could be found. Once again, he believed that Fate intervened when, having been on Madeira for only a short while, he was introduced to yr mother, the former Miss Marguerite Blantyre.

As you now know, yr father & Miss Blantyre eloped, were duly married, &, in the course of time, a child was born. That child — you, my angel — became the instrument by which what had been lost could — if Fate allowed — be regained.

For you, too, were born a Duport, legitimately conceived, as he was. Both you and he were thereby subject to a higher duty: to the long, unbroken line of yr ancestors, & to yr future descendants. He had been prevented, by treachery & malice, from fulfilling this duty; but through you, his adored daughter, this great wrong could be set right at last.

Here, then, I come to what yr father wished to accomplish through you.

Before he left for the East, after yr mother's death, I made a solemn vow to him: to bring you up as my own child, and, in the course of time, to set in motion the scheme he had devised: to place you close to the woman who had dispossessed both him & you.

In order to reclaim what had been lost, and so bring the Tansor succession back to the blood of the direct line, yr father laid this great and, to him, binding obligation upon you, his only and dearest *child: to secure the lasting affection — the love, if possible — of the present Duport heir.*

This, then, is what he calls upon you to do, by all you hold most sacred, from beyond the Portals of Death.

You must marry Perseus Duport.

⚛ END OF ACT THREE ⚛

ACT FOUR

DUTY AND DESIRE

Our sins, like to our shadowes, when our day is in its glorie scarce
appear: towards our evening how great and monstrous they are!

SIR JOHN SUCKLING, *Aglaura* (1638)

23

At North Lodge

I

Resolution Renewed

A<small>FTER READING</small> Madame's letter, I descended into a kind
of hell, from which I thought I would never find release.
The foundations of my former life had crumbled quite
away, leaving me in a state of the deepest despondency and mental
disarray, as if I had suddenly been cast upon some barren and featureless desert shore, with no hope of rescue. I returned over and
over again to my guardian's words until they were seared into my
memory – now pacing wildly about the room, weeping uncontrollably, now lying on my bed in a stupor, gazing blankly at the maze of
interlocking patterns on the plasterwork ceiling above me.

I struggled vainly to comprehend what Madame had told me
– that I was Esperanza Duport, the rightful heir, through my dispossessed father, of the late Lord Tansor; that my birthright had
been stolen from me by the present Lady Tansor and her former
lover; and that the hoped-for end of the Great Task – the restoration of that birthright, for my own sake and for the sake of those
who would come after me – was to be achieved by bringing Lady
Tansor to justice at last and marrying her eldest son.

These things were hard enough for me to absorb and understand; but to learn also that my father had been responsible for the
death of Phoebus Daunt was almost more than I could bear.

Was it really true? My dear imagined father, the infamous murderer, Edward Glyver! At first, although the opposing instinct to defend my parent strove to overcome its urgings, my conscience refused to accept Madame's vindication of his crime. She claimed that he had been briefly driven to the brink of insanity after his betrayal by the woman he loved; but was there any justification – even temporary derangement – for such an atrocious act? I pitied my father, I wept for him; but I could not condone what he had done. Everything that I had wanted him to be seemed negated by his crime, the shadow of which now lay over me, his innocent daughter: my perpetual legacy of sin.

Yet slowly, painfully, filial loyalty began to reassert itself. Whatever he had done, whatever name he had gone by – whether Glyver or Gorst, or some other – he was still the father I longed so much to have known, the extraordinary man of whom I had read in the pages of Mr Lazarus's book, and in my mother's journal, and of whose powerful character I had formed such a vivid impression through the accounts of these first-hand witnesses. He had done a terrible, unforgivable thing; but if he had walked into my room at that moment, would I have turned from him in moral revulsion, or thrown myself into his arms?

At length, after many such agonized reflections, and many accompanying tears, I come to a fragile accommodation with my conscience, and my thoughts begin to turn back to the present.

I now knew what I must do to restore my father's stolen patrimony. A great task, indeed, and surely an impossible one. Mr Perseus would never regard me as a suitable wife in my present condition. He had not thought me good enough for his brother. How, then, would he consider me good enough to become the wife of the next Lord Tansor? We were cousins, as it now appeared; but I had no proof, as yet, of my true identity, and such proof might never be found. To Mr Perseus, I would still be Esperanza Gorst, his mother's former maid.

Yet, impossible though the task seems, it does not dismay me. Indeed, as I reflect on Madame's words, I find myself exhilarated by the challenge that I have been given. There is so much that I dislike – even despise – about Mr Perseus; but there is so much more that attracts me to him. I have sometimes caught glimpses – fleeting, but tantalizing – of another Perseus Duport, which has made me believe that he constantly seeks to suppress his true self. He seems to me like some great frozen ocean – cold and featureless on the surface, but teeming with hidden life beneath. It seems that he cannot allow himself to be seen as anything other than the proud, inviolable Duport heir, who must fulfil everything that is expected of him to the utmost, and who must one day apply himself – in emulation of his mother's formidable relation, the 25th Baron – to maintaining the Duports' long-held reputation as one of the first families in the land. It is a mighty responsibility, and it is clear that he feels it to be so. For the first time, I begin to discern a kind of virtue in his pride and self-centredness, and in his stern dedication to something greater than himself. As for my own feelings, I shall say only that the prospect of marrying Mr Perseus was very far – very far indeed – from being an uncongenial one, if by some miracle it could be accomplished.

At length, I fall on to my bed, and into a deep and immediate sleep. When I awake, an hour later, I am strangely calm in both mind and spirit, and filled with new resolve.

I will do my duty to my father, to Madame, to the ancient family I must now call my own, and to those of my blood who will come after me; and I will do it with a glad heart, for the prize is great indeed. I rise from my bed, exhausted but mentally revived, and make a vow to myself, on the innocent soul of Amélie Verron, the dearest and most loyal friend I have ever known.

There will be no turning back. I shall go forward, although with little hope of success, until I can go no further. For I have heard my father calling from beyond the grave. Murderer though he was, I shall not fail him.

II
The Triumvirate

'WE STAND,' SAID Mr Montagu Wraxall solemnly, 'like the prophet, in a valley of dry bones.* It is our duty to clothe these once-vital rel-

---

*Caroline Daunt, *née* Petrie (1797–1874). The 25th Lord Tansor was her second cousin. She married Achilles Daunt in 1821.

ics in the sinews and flesh of truth, and breathe life into them once more, so that justice may be done at last.'

We were seated together, knees almost touching – Mr Wraxall, myself, and a young man, of singular appearance – in the cramped, paper-strewn parlour of North Lodge, taking our tea.

The young man had been introduced to me as Inspector Alfred T. Gully, of the Detective Department in London – the person referred to by Mr Vyse, in the conversation with Lady Tansor that I had lately overheard and, as I had read in *The Times*, the officer in charge of the investigation into the murder of Mrs Barbarina Kraus. Little wonder, I reflected, that my Lady had been alarmed by his presence.

A fourth person completed the company. This was Mrs Gully, a small, neatly turned-out young woman, of a reserved but open and intelligent demeanour, who sat a little way off by the fire, reading a volume of essays by Mr Matthew Arnold, and occasionally raising her head to look affectionately at her husband.

The latter was, as I have remarked, most singular, in both appearance and character. The description of him that I later composed for my Book of Secrets is as follows:

MR ALFRED T. GULLY

Age: about five-and-twenty. Born in Easton, the son of a local police inspector.

   Appearance: boyish. Apple-cheeked, with a wide, full mouth, and a most curious up-tilted nose, giving the strong impression that his nostrils are being perpetually pulled upon by the hook of some invisible fishing-line. Dressed in a dark-blue frock-coat (sadly frayed at the cuffs) and plaid trousers (noticeably shiny at the knee); his hat, being a little too small for his large head, has left a dull red ring across his brow.

   Impressions: his voice has a somewhat grating quality to it, frequently displaying the unmistakable inflexions of what I now recognize as a Northamptonshire accent; and yet he speaks with the fluency and confidence of an educated and well-read person, although not one whose education has been gained by attending the usual institutions of public school and University.

Conclusion: a wholly memorable individual who, I am willing to believe, fully deserves the reputation he enjoys as a detective of no common ability. Amiable, but also formidable in an unassuming way – somewhat like Mr Wraxall in this respect.

After some introductory pleasantries, we had settled ourselves as best we could on three rather unsteady wheel-backed chairs in front of a little bow window that looked westwards towards the Odstock Road. Mr Wraxall rang a small brass bell, and almost immediately Mrs Wapshott, the woman who attended him as cook and housekeeper, brought in a tray of tea, welcomingly accompanied by a large and freshly baked spice-cake.

'And how are you going on, Miss Gorst?' asked my host, passing me a slice of cake.

'Very well, sir,' I replied. 'I am very happy in my new position.'

'Miss Gorst has undergone a promotion. She is now her Ladyship's companion,' said Mr Wraxall to the detective, who merely inclined his head slightly, in a manner that persuaded me that he was already aware of the fact.

'The duties of a lady's companion are very different, I think, to those of a maid,' Mr Wraxall remarked, after a judicious pause, 'and afford many opportunities for observing the character and habits of her employer. Human nature is an endlessly fascinating object of study – don't you agree, Miss Gorst?'

'Ah, human nature!' cried Mr Gully, before I could reply. 'That boundless field in which you and I, Mr W, constantly toil!'

He took out a large, rather grubby pocket-handkerchief and blew his nose with a loud rasp; then he shook his head, and sighed in the most doleful manner.

'You may not know, Miss Gorst,' resumed Mr Wraxall, 'that my young friend here is already a leading man in the Detective Department in London, although he was born in Easton – his father, in fact, was for many years an inspector in the local force. It was my good fortune to have benefited from my young friend's exceptional talents on my final capital case. We've since become – if I may so put it – brothers-in-arms.'

'Most kind, Mr W, most kind,' said the detective, evidently touched by the great man's compliments.

'Mr Gully is presently engaged on a particularly intriguing case,' Mr Wraxall went on, 'in which I am also taking a keen interest – as an amateur observer, you understand. Perhaps you may have read about it in the newspapers? The especially shocking murder – not, alas, an uncommon occurrence in those dangerous parts of the capital with which Mr Gully and I have become professionally familiar – of a woman by the name of Mrs Barbarina Kraus. The business is interesting in several respects.'

'Interesting, Mr W?' echoed the inspector. 'You may say so. And suggestive.'

'Suggestive, certainly,' Mr Wraxall agreed, and then fell silent. 'Enough of this!' he suddenly exclaimed, stamping his foot, and laying down his tea-cup with a clatter. 'I insult you, Miss Gorst, by beating about the bush in this ridiculous fashion. I apologize, most sincerely. I knew you for a friend and ally as soon as I saw you, and I flatter myself that you saw me in the same light – and you were right to do so. So, allow me to make amends and presume to treat you as such.

'I invited you here, Miss Gorst, because you appeared to express some sympathy with the views I hold concerning the death of my uncle's old friend, Mr Paul Carteret. Was I correct?'

I expressed regret that I knew little enough about the matter, 'although it seems to me,' I went on to admit, 'from what I have heard from others, and from what you yourself have told me, that the official verdict might be – open to question.'

Another doleful sigh from Mr Gully.

Mr Wraxall leaned his shining head towards me and, in a deliberately audible whisper, which he clearly intended Mr Gully to hear, informed me that Inspector Gully Senior had been the local officer in the case, and that he had continued to subscribe to the official

view that the attack on Mr Carteret had been a straightforward matter of robbery with violence.

'Mr Gully here was, of course, only a youngster at the time; but
over the years he has, like me, developed an alternative view of the
case. It has, indeed, become something of a private cause with us,
which we've often discussed together, and also with my late uncle,
who made himself rather troublesome in some people's eyes by
steadfastly refusing to accept the inquest verdict, and dismissing
the idea that Mr Carteret had been the victim of a peripatetic band
of ruffians, who waylaid farmers and the like returning home with
market money in their pockets. I have expended a great deal of
midnight oil going through every scrap of paper left by my uncle,
searching for anything that might throw some glimmer of light on
the tragedy, but with little success. We hope – Mr Gully and I –
eventually to establish, beyond all reasonable doubt, what actually
happened on that fateful day, and – which is the point that most
concerns us now, in this present time – *why* it happened.

'Now here *you* are, Miss Gorst; and so – if, of course, you're willing to join us – may I formally, and with great pleasure, extend a
welcome to what is now, I sincerely hope, a triumvirate of enquirers
after the truth?'

He holds out his hand, which, surprised though I am by the gesture, I willingly take, saying that I shall be very happy to join them,
if they were willing to have me, although I could not see what practical contribution I could make to their endeavours.

'Oh no, Miss Gorst,' insisted Mr Wraxall most warmly. 'You do
yourself an injustice. I'm convinced – absolutely – that you'll prove
to be a most useful member of our little alliance.'

'Most useful,' agreed Mr Gully, through a mouthful of cake.

'Your situation here at Evenwood is a singular one,' Mr Wraxall
then remarked. 'Opportunities may – no, will – arise, discoveries
made, perhaps, as a consequence of that situation; and these may
advance our cause in ways we cannot presently know.

'You must understand, however, that our interest in the death of
Mr Paul Carteret, over twenty years ago now, is far from being one
of merely – how shall I put it, Mr Gully?'

'Academic interest, Mr W?' ventured the detective.

'Exactly,' Mr Wraxall replied, with an acquiescent nod. 'And here is my point, Miss Gorst. Mr Gully and I share a common outlook on certain events, of a most dubious character, connected with the noble lady by whom you are presently employed as companion. That outlook may be broadly defined as being sceptical in character – by which I mean that we are in no way persuaded that her Ladyship is entirely innocent of some involvement – be it large or small – in those events. I further believe that you may share that general outlook, Miss Gorst. Am I correct?'

I considered for a moment what to say, having developed a well-practised habit of caution when answering questions concerning myself; but it was impossible to mistrust those wise grey eyes, and so I thanked Mr Wraxall for his frankness, and for the confidence it placed in me.

'And you are right,' I admitted. 'My position here, since becoming Lady Tansor's maid, has put me close to her, and I have indeed become curious concerning certain aspects of her life, both past and present.'

'Aha!' exclaimed Mr Gully. 'Aspects! Past *and* present! There you have it, Miss Gorst.'

'Good!' cried Mr Wraxall, slapping his knee. 'Now one of those past aspects might be the attack on Mr Paul Carteret, in October 1853, of which we have just been speaking. A present aspect might be the very case to which I have already alluded, on which Mr Gully is at present closely occupied: the brutal murder of a woman whose body was found, not three months' since, in the Thames near Billingsgate Fish-market.

'The question I put to you now, Miss Gorst, is this: are these two apparently unrelated crimes – one past, the other present, both still unresolved – in fact part of one single and still-continuing event? My professional opinion is that they are, and Mr Gully agrees with me. If only we had the proof! For who otherwise would accept that a single chain of circumstances connects the savage murder of Mrs Barbarina Kraus, a woman of low condition with known criminal associates, and the fatal attack, so many years ago, on Mr Paul

Carteret, formerly secretary and librarian to his relative, the late Lord Tansor, and father of the present Baroness? It's too incredible, surely. The very idea is laughable, is it not? And yet it's a fact, Miss Gorst – a singular but incontrovertible fact – that, on considering this extraordinary possibility for the first time, Mr Gully's feet began to itch.'

My face must have clearly expressed my utter perplexity at Mr Wraxall's words, for the detective immediately offered an explanation.

'I don't know how it is, Miss Gorst,' he said, 'but whenever I'm on the right track in a case, my feet begin to itch. Martha will tell you.'

Mrs Gully looked up once more from her studious perusal of Mr Matthew Arnold to give an affirmative nod.

'They're itching now,' said her husband, gazing down at his boots.

'I saw her,' I said, wishing suddenly to advance the discussion on my own terms; 'the old woman, I mean. I spoke to her, too, at the Duport Arms.'

'Aha!' said Mr Gully, taking out his note-book and starting to write.

'You refer to the late Mrs Kraus?' asked Mr Wraxall, with eager interest.

'I believe so.'

'And what do you suppose she was doing in Easton?'

'I think she had come to Evenwood to see Lady Tansor.'

'What makes you think that?' was Mr Gully's question.

I recounted how my Lady had instructed me to take a note to the Duport Arms for the attention of 'B.K.', subsequently described by my Lady as a former servant by the name of Bertha Kennedy who had fallen on hard times, but whom I was now certain had been Mrs Barbarina Kraus.

'A former servant!' exclaimed Mr Wraxall gleefully looking significantly at Mr Gully, and then adding mysteriously: 'Perhaps that was not so very far from the truth. We're on to something here, Gully.'

'Indeed we are, Mr W,' the detective concurred.

They continued to look at each other for a moment or two, nodded in concert, and then Mr Wraxall addressed me – quietly now, and with a new seriousness.

'Here it is, then Miss Gorst,' he began, 'in a nutshell. Mr Gully and I are of the settled opinion that the Duport succession is the single strand that unites the deaths of Paul Carteret and Mrs Barbarina Kraus. Our theory – which, in the absence of solid proof must remain as such – is that Mr Carteret was in possession of information that would have dispossessed Mr Phoebus Daunt of his prospects, as the late Lord Tansor's adopted heir.

'We further believe – although here our grounds are, as yet, even more speculative – that Mrs Kraus was murdered because she knew something that fatally threatened the favourable resolution secured by the first crime.

'In short, our conclusion is that the attack on Mr Carteret, more than twenty years ago, was the first act in a greater drama, which led first to the murder of Mr Carteret, then to that of Mr Phoebus Daunt, and now to that of Mrs Barbarina Kraus. Would you like to add anything, Mr Gully?'

'An admirable summary, Mr W,' the young man replied, closing his note-book, 'as one would expect. "Favourable resolution of the first crime" – excellent phrase! Nothing to add, except perhaps a small point of emphasis, which I shall put to you in the form of a question, Miss Gorst: *cui bono*? Or, to come at it the other way, who stands to lose all if certain matters, long hidden from view, were to come to light?'

'You allude to Lady Tansor?' I asked.

'Even she.'

'Then you'd accuse her of murdering her own father?'

The detective glanced enquiringly at the barrister.

'We have no evidence to make that most serious accusation,' said the latter. 'But we cannot dismiss the possibility – even the probability – that her Ladyship, acting with Mr Phoebus Daunt, set the tragedy in motion, although it may be that she did not anticipate its fatal outcome.'

'And Mrs Kraus?' I asked.

'Blackmail,' Mr Gully broke in confidently. 'Pure and simple. Nothing could be clearer. What other reason could the victim have had for coming to Evenwood, if not to lay a demand before Lady Tansor – a demand for money in return for her silence on a matter of the gravest importance to her Ladyship?

'As to the nature of that matter – well, there's the very nub of the mystery. But now, thanks to you, Miss Gorst, we have a definite connexion between her Ladyship and the murdered woman.'

'The latter's demand was either refused outright, or an impression given that it would be met,' observed Mr Wraxall. 'Either way, another course was covertly taken, which resulted in the most unpleasant consequences for Mrs Kraus. Of course Lady Tansor could not possibly have carried out the deed herself, and so must have had an accomplice.'

'Mr Armitage Vyse.'

'Excellent, Miss Gorst! The very man we suspect.'

Mr Wraxall was beaming at me in delight.

'You see, Gully,' he said, turning to the detective, 'what a great addition Miss Gorst will be to our cause? We'll get at the truth yet, mark my words, now that Miss Gorst is with us.'

The long-case clock in the corner of the room struck five o'clock, at the sound of which Mr Gully took out his pocket-watch to check the synchronicity of the two time-pieces.

'I must leave if I'm to catch my train,' he said, jumping to his feet, and brushing a few stray cake crumbs from his jacket. 'And so, good-bye, Miss Gorst,' he said, shaking my hand vigorously. 'We shall meet again soon, I'm sure. Good-bye, good-bye!'

III
Mr Wraxall Exercises His Instincts

AFTER MR GULLY and his wife had gone – Mrs Gully having bestowed on me only the barest 'Good-afternoon, Miss Gorst, so nice to have met you' – Mr Wraxall and I walked out into the little walled garden at the rear of the Lodge.

'You appear to be fond of Mr Gully,' I remarked.

We had now passed through a gate into a small area of paddock. Beyond an enclosing fence, the carriage-road ran up through a fringe of well-set woods to the Park gates on the Odstock Road.

'A decent man was killed over there,' said Mr Wraxall, gazing out towards the darkening line of trees through which I had passed with my Lady and her two sons on our journey to Barnack for Professor Slake's funeral. 'The passage of time has not, and will not, erase the memory of that outrage.'

Overhead, a suddenly startled clamour of rooks, raucously squawking and flapping, took to the air. I stopped to look up at their raggedy antics, while Mr Wraxall walked a little way ahead, his eyes still anchored on the western horizon; then he turned towards me again.

'Forgive me, Miss Gorst. You were speaking of Mr Gully. Yes, I'm very fond of him. Although you might not guess it to look at him, he has a broad and original mind. Not many young men of his upbringing, and certainly none of his compatriots in the Detective Department, read Plato at breakfast, I think! I shall never now have a son; but if I did, I would be proud to have one like Inspector Alfred Gully of the Detective Department.'

'I wish I could have spoken a little more to Mrs Gully,' I said, as we were walking back to the Lodge. 'She seemed a person one would like to know better.'

'Ah, Martha the Silent,' laughed Mr Wraxall. 'A young woman of the highest intelligence and discretion. She's Gully's unofficial right hand, you know. He depends upon her completely, and she has often provided the last essential piece in his investigations that brings success. Her story provides a notable testimony to the benefits of self-improvement. Her father was a ham and beef dealer from Bermondsey, but young Martha conceived the laudable ambition of becoming a doctor. Of course her family circumstances were against her – well, those do not concern us.

'But what *does* concern us – or should – is Mr Armitage Vyse. You must beware of that gentleman, my dear. He is not an ornament to our profession, and things are whispered of him that give me grave concern. His influence over Lady Tansor has become very marked of late, and this leads me to think that he has some plan afoot, which, if discovered, might put the discoverer in danger.'

The look he gave disconcerted me, for he seemed to be offering me silent encouragement to unburden myself. I had been more than willing to join him and Mr Gully in their attempt to establish the extent of Lady Tansor's involvement in the deaths of her father and Mrs Kraus; for if our suspicions could be proved, then my own private cause would be immeasurably advanced, as well as theirs. But I was not ready – yet – to bring even Mr Wraxall into my full confidence. For the time being, therefore, I kept my counsel.

As we reached the back door of the Lodge, Mr Wraxall stopped, his hand resting on the handle.

'I wish to say something, Miss Gorst, and I shall be direct with you, as a friend ought. You have come here to Evenwood for a purpose. Others may believe that a young lady of your education and abilities was content to become a lady's-maid, but I do not. It's the great disadvantage of my calling: to doubt what I'm told until I can prove otherwise. In this case, although I may theorize on the matter, I do not know – and therefore cannot prove – who you really are, and why you are here. I am only sure that I'm right to think that there's more – a very great deal more – to you, Miss Gorst, than meets the eye.'

I was about to frame some prevaricating reply, but he raised his hand to stop me.

'No, hear me out if you please, my dear. Every instinct I have tells me that you're here for no dishonest purpose; but that you have some hidden object in pretending to be someone you are not is, to my professional eye, beyond all doubt.

'Now do not fear. I flatter myself that I'm exceptional in the acuity of my instincts – they provided me with a very comfortable living for many years – and I'm confident that you're safe from discovery. I also see very well that you are unwilling as yet to confide in me – although I hope that may change. Say nothing, my dear. There's no need. We understand each other perfectly, I think. All *I* will say is, that you may depend on me – absolutely – to offer whatever help I can, to the utmost of my ability, in whatever you are engaged upon, feeling certain, as I do, that it must be a matter of the greatest consequence, and that you will tell me what it is in your own good time. Now, let us go in. It's getting rather chilly, and there's still cake to be eaten.'

I found, however, that I did have something I wished to say.

As we sat together by the fire, our tea-cups refilled, encouraged by what Mr Wraxall had said, I had resolved to tell my new friend and ally what I knew concerning Mr Armitage Vyse, including his meeting with Billy Yapp at the Antigallican, and Yapp's recent appearance at Evenwood.

He listened to me with the most concentrated attention. When I had finished, he got up and walked over to the window, where he stood for some time in silent thought.

'Sweeney Yapp. Well, well. Gully was right.'

By which I understood that the detective had already suspected Yapp – well known to the Detective Department – of Mrs Kraus's murder, a conclusion Mr Wraxall soon confirmed.

'Gully was sure this was Yapp's work,' he said, resuming his seat. 'People talk, if approached in the right way; but he lacked – still lacks – the evidence. Now, at least, we know who put Yapp up to it, and perhaps also on whose behalf this person was acting. Well, my dear, Mr Gully will have to look to his laurels, it seems. You have the makings of a fine detective – and an uncommonly brave one, to have ventured into such a place as the Antigallican, which I urge you never to do again.

'But it appears that Mr Vyse's instincts, like my own, are also in full working order. He has his suspicions of you, and that certainly puts you in the way of danger. You are certainly right to think that Yapp was sent here by Vyse, and that must be of great concern to us. I must telegraph Gully as soon as possible.'

'And tomorrow we leave for London,' I said.

'Do you, though?' replied Mr Wraxall. 'Then I beg you to take the greatest care of yourself while you are there. You will please to seek me out, at any time, should it become needful for you to do so, in King's Bench Walk – number fourteen – and you will try not go out unaccompanied unless it is absolutely necessary. Will you promise me that?'

'I fear I cannot,' I answered, shaking my head regretfully, for I was already planning various expeditions, if my Lady allowed me some liberty.

'In that case I shall ask Gully to provide some protection for you. There's a good man in the Department, Sergeant Swann. Let's see what can be done in that regard.'

So it was agreed. Mr Wraxall would make the necessary arrangements, after he had conferred with Mr Gully.

'You've been most forbearing, sir,' I said, as I rose to leave, 'in not pressing me to reveal more about myself than, as things presently stand, I am able to do – although of course I don't admit that your famous instincts are right on this occasion.'

'Of course,' he said, smiling and resting his wonderful grey eyes on me. 'I never claim infallibility.'

'But I do have a question for you – if you're willing to hear it.'

'Ask away,' he said.

'What made you suspect Lady Tansor of being involved in the murder of Mrs Kraus?'

'Ah,' he said, 'an excellent question, my dear. Excellent. And quite worthy of Mrs Gully, who has a wonderful knack of putting her finger on things. The suggestion – no more – came to us in a brief note, sent to Inspector Gully, from an anonymous informant. We have no idea at present who this might be, and so there things must rest for now. Well, this has been most pleasant, Miss Gorst,' he said, handing me my hat and gloves, 'most pleasant indeed. Goodness me!'

'What's the matter?' I asked, anxiously.

'Why, I've just remembered what day it is.'

'The 31st of December?'

'Exactly,' he replied. 'And so I wish you every good wish for the

coming new year of 1877, in the confident hope that all our endeavours will be crowned with success, and that all the dry bones will
be fleshed with Truth at last. And now, my dear, may I accompany
you back to the house? It's growing dark, and it's perhaps best that
you don't go alone.'

24

Snow and Secrets

I
The Night Visitor

WE PARTED, Mr Wraxall and I, at the Entrance Court gates. On our way back from North Lodge, as the evening drew in, the conversation had continued to run on matters connected with the death of Lady Tansor's father.

'You said, I think, that Mr Carteret was an old friend of Professor Slake's,' I remarked.

'Indeed – scholars both, yet their interests were different. Mr Carteret's were of a historical and literary character, whilst my uncle's principal passion was for philology and the religious practices of the Ancients, although of course he devoted himself for many years to his great history of the Gentile nations.'

I then asked Mr Wraxall whether his work on the Professor's papers was proceeding satisfactorily.

'Satisfactorily is perhaps not *le mot juste*,' he laughed; 'but, yes, I believe that I am making some progress, although there is still much to do.'

'And – if you don't mind? – may I ask whether the letters from your uncle to Mr Carteret that you took from the Dower House were of any particular interest?'

Mr Wraxall, clearly guessing my implication, congratulated me again for asking the right question.

'I've been waiting all afternoon for you to ask about those let-ters,' he said. 'There were a large number, and it took me most of that night to go through them and put them in order. The majority concerned subjects of mutual scholarly interest. There were two, however, that particularly caught my attention. The first had a curi-ous link with the murder of Phoebus Daunt.'

I felt my stomach tighten, and was obliged to look away in confusion.

Mr Wraxall, with a look of concern, enquired whether anything was the matter.

'Nothing, thank you,' I assured him, whilst knowing that my face spoke otherwise. 'Please go on.'

From Madame, I already knew that the poet's father, the Rev-erend Achilles Daunt, had been appointed Rector of Evenwood through the influence of his second wife, Phoebus Daunt's step-mother, who had been a relative of the late Lord Tansor's.* Now I learned from Mr Wraxall that he had also been a classical and bibliographic scholar of some repute, celebrated as the compiler of the *Bibliotheca Duportiana* – a complete catalogue of the books held in the Library at Evenwood, to which Mr Carteret had contributed notes on the collection's manuscripts.

It appeared that, some time before the attack on Mr Carteret, Dr Daunt had been preparing a translation for publication of Iam-blichus – an ancient Greek writer whom Mr Thornhaugh had some-times mentioned in our lessons, but of whose works I was entirely ignorant.

When the Rector's translation was in proof, he had sent it to Professor Slake for his specialist opinion, but had then written again requesting that it should be forwarded to a certain Edward Glapthorn, an employee of the legal firm of Tredgold, Tredgold & Orr, who also had extensive knowledge of Iamblichus. This request was the principal subject of the letter that Mr Wraxall had retrieved from the Dower House.

---

*Caroline Daunt, *née* Petrie (1797–1874). The 25th Lord Tansor was her second cousin. She married Achilles Daunt in 1821.

'And here, Miss Gorst,' said the barrister, 'is the link I mentioned. This Glapthorn was the alias of Edward Glyver – Phoebus Daunt's murderer.'

This fact I was already aware of, from the article by Mr Vyse, which Madame had sent me from the *London Monthly Review*, although I expressed a suitable degree of astonishment on receiving this information.

'What is perhaps even more interesting,' continued Mr Wraxall, 'was my uncle's opinion of this gentleman – for gentleman he was – which he expressed in several later letters to Dr Daunt. Although they never met in person, a brief correspondence passed between them, on the subject of the Iamblichus translation, from which my uncle formed a highly favourable impression of Mr Glapthorn – or Glyver, or whatever his real name was – both as a scholar and as a man, an impression confirmed by Dr Daunt, who had met him on several occasions. To learn, just a year later, that the same person had been responsible for the murder of his friend's son came as the most severe shock to my uncle.'

Whilst there was no hint in Mr Wraxall's account of exoneration for the crime my father had committed, it nevertheless gave me great comfort, by adding independent weight to Mr Heatherington's favourable estimation of his character.

'You mentioned a second letter,' I said, as we were about to go our separate ways.

'Yes,' replied Mr Wraxall. 'I found it – suggestive.'

'In what way?'

'It would appear from my uncle's reply to a letter received from his friend that Mr Carteret employed his daughter's fluency in the French language, and used her generally as an assistant, in the course of compiling his history of the Duport family, which my uncle was asked to edit and complete after Mr Carteret's death.'

Puzzled, I asked why this was suggestive.

'Only in this,' replied Mr Wraxall. 'My uncle refers to the fact that Mr Carteret and his daughter had been engaged on arranging certain papers relating to Lord Tansor's first wife, Lady Laura, who, whilst married to Lord Tansor, spent an extended period abroad, in a strange anticipation of Miss Carteret's sojourn on the Continent following the death of Phoebus Daunt.'

'Abroad?' I asked.

'Residing principally, it appears, in the Breton city of Rennes. A curious episode. Very curious.'

'I'm afraid I still don't understand,' I said.

'Well, my dear,' replied a smiling Mr Wraxall, 'neither do I; but all those old instincts of mine tell me that this information is significant in some way, although there, I fear, the matter must rest for the time being, with those other interesting subjects we discussed with Inspector Gully, until the mists eventually begin to clear, as I hope and believe they may, in the course of time.'

IT HAD LONG been a Duport tradition, following the death of an eldest son on this day during the time of the Black Death, not to celebrate the passing of the old year, a tradition that my Lady was happy to observe. Dinner on this New Year's Eve of 1876 was, in any event, a tedious affair.

There were, of course, no guests present, and I expended little effort in making myself agreeable. My Lady, by contrast, affected a gaily voluble mood, twittering away in a most uncharacteristic manner, triviality succeeding triviality, enumerating all over again the places she intended us to visit during our stay in London, and the people she wished me to meet, at such wearisome length that I thought I would scream.

Mr Randolph was absent – his whereabouts unknown – whilst his brother sat wrapped in an attitude of sullen abstraction, broken occasionally by peppery interjections and black looks.

Following the receipt of Madame's third letter, Mr Perseus was now, of course, the object of the most intense interest to me, although I was careful not to show it. As he sat there, silently eating his dinner, I recalled our recent encounter in the church porch, when he had appeared angered by my repudiation of his attempts to 'extend the hand of friendship', as he had put it. I regretted that I had not been more receptive to his efforts; but it could not now be helped. Indeed, I drew some encouragement from his display of displeasure, and from his suspicions of my feelings for his brother to which he had subsequently given voice, thinking that these outbursts may have been the consequence, not so much of entrenched pride, but of chagrin that his regard for me had been spurned. I thought, too, of the inscribed copy of *Merlin and Nimue* that he had given me, a gesture which seemed, on reflection, to have carried more significance than I had realized at the time. Perhaps the task of conquering the affections of Mr Perseus Duport would not be as difficult as I had first thought, although marriage still appeared an impossibility. At least – or so I had begun to persuade myself – I now had a little hope that he possessed a receptive heart after all, and that I occupied a small place in it.

'And how did you find Mr Wraxall?' my Lady asked, as we sat together afterwards in the Drawing-Room.

'As you might expect,' I replied tartly, without looking up from my study of the carpet.

'Really, Alice,' she objected, in a disappointed tone, 'how grumpy you've been this evening. Whatever can be the matter, when we have so much to look forward to? Don't you wish to go to London?'

'Of course.'

'So I would hope. It will be good for you.'

I say nothing, but snatch up a copy of Mr Tennyson's recent play on Queen Mary,* which is lying on a nearby table, and pretend to read; but almost immediately, the pages begin to swim before my exhausted eyes, the book falls from my hands, and I sink back limply in my chair.

'Alice!' cries Lady Tansor. 'Are you feeling ill?'

At this juncture, hearing the concern in his mamma's voice, Mr Perseus, who has been lounging alone on the far side of the room,

---

Queen Mary: A Drama, first performed at the Lyceum Theatre in April 1876 and published the following month.

an unopened copy of *Tinsley's Magazine* on his lap, leaps to his feet and comes quickly over to us.

'All right, Mother,' I hear him say, 'I'll take charge. Now, Miss Gorst, how are you?'

'A little dizzy, sir,' I tell him, 'but I beg you not to concern yourself. It's nothing, I assure you. A little fatigue, that's all. I didn't sleep well last night.'

'Nevertheless,' he insists,. 'we must get you to your room, and then send for Pordage.'

I protest that this is unnecessary, but he brushes aside my objections with brusque concern, and calls out for one of the footmen stationed outside the door. It is only then that I realize that he has taken my hands – lightly, but deliberately – in his, and is now gently rubbing them. Of course I should have instantly removed them, but I did not; for it gave me a most pleasant sensation of comfort and safety, to feel the warm, white hands of the Duport heir encircling mine.

When I had been put to bed, and after the welcome departure of Dr Pordage (whose clammy hands I had been obliged to endure, in repugnant silence, as he had felt my brow, but who rightly diagnosed the need for a good night's rest), I soon fell deeply asleep.

I WAS AWOKEN suddenly by a movement in the bed. With a start, I sat up.

A curtain had been left partially undrawn, through which thin shafts of pale moonlight fell across the bed. They revealed a recumbent figure beside me.

I call out her name. She opens her eyes, and stares sleepily at me.

'Alice, dear,' my Lady murmurs. 'Did I wake you?'

I get out of bed to light my candle. She sits up, her long hair hanging loose about her shoulders and back. She seems somehow shrunken and diminished. Then I see why.

The night-gown she is wearing is a man's. Its sleeves fall down over her slim hands, so that only the ends of the nails can be seen;

her figure is entirely concealed by its ample folds; and on the left breast, underneath the Duport arms, are embroidered three initials: P.R.D.

The night-gown had been her dead lover's.

I stand, candle in hand, looking at her in disbelief, the shadows cast by the flickering flame playing over her face, as white as the gown she wears.

Where had she kept this intimate relic? Her capacity for concealment amazed me. Then she spoke.

'I was unable to sleep. Dreams – such strangely vivid dreams – of you, dear Alice, and yet not you. So then I had to come up, to assure myself that all was well. But you were asleep – so peacefully asleep! And so I thought I would lie down here next to you, just for a very little while; but then I fell asleep myself. Isn't that wonderful! To have fallen so easily into glorious sleep! This bed is so comfortable, more comfortable than my own.'

She gave a soft, mirthless laugh, and slowly laid her head back on the pillows.

'You must go back to your room,' I told her, soothingly, setting the candle down, and sitting on the side of the bed. 'Come, I'll take you down. Have you forgotten that we're to leave for London tomorrow? You must rest.'

'Rest? Oh, if only I could! But I can never rest. Never.'

I held out my hand to her, but she made no movement.

'Take it,' I said. 'You'll rest tonight. I promise.'

She reaches out, places her hand in mine, and together we make our way down to her apartments – although not before I have slipped a small blue-glass bottle of decanted Battley's Drops, supplied by J.M. Proudfoot & Sons, of Market Square, Easton, into the pocket of my robe.

She takes the drops willingly, accepting my assurance that they will help her sleep and do her no harm.

'There,' I whisper, as I pull the coverlet over her and stroke her hair. 'Sleep now.'

'Dear Alice,' is all she says, as she closes her eyes.

I sit by the dying embers of the bedroom fire for half an hour, until I am certain that she is fast asleep. Then I take up the candle, and tip-toe into the sitting-room.

II
A Weapon Made of Words

THE KEY TURNED easily in the little brass escutcheon, just as it had done when I had first unlocked the secret cupboard behind the portrait of Anthony Duport. As I reached inside, the intimidating, black-bearded face of Phoebus Daunt, frozen by the photographer's art, stared back at me from the shadowed recess.

As quickly as I could, hands shaking, and nervously listening out for any sound from the adjoining bed-chamber, I undid the ribbon securing the first bundle of letters, took it over to the table on which I had placed my candle, and began to read.

The letters were all arranged in chronological order. The first, written in November 1852 from Daunt's London house in Mecklenburgh Square, contained a lengthy account of the Duke of Wellington's funeral. Succeeding letters, similarly, offered nothing of interest or significance, except to substantiate the remarkable mutual affection that had existed between the writer and Miss Carteret, whom he constantly addressed in the tenderest of terms.

The second bundle was equally barren: page after page describing how he was passing the time in Town without her, whom he had seen, where he had dined, what so-and-so had said at the Club, the gratifying reception given to his poems by the critics. Then there would be long passages recounting matters of business undertaken on behalf of Lord Tansor – always discharged to the utmost satisfaction of his patron – and others describing, at equally tiresome length, various trifling incidents that had befallen him in the course of his travels.

Then, in a letter in the fourth bundle, I found the following short postscript, which I immediately scribbled down in shorthand, on a piece of my Lady's writing-paper:

DEAREST,—

*In haste. P— has just been here. He is ready, & appears to under-
stand what he must do – if you still wish him to carry out yr plan.
I continue to have qualms about the business, as I have told you,
knowing what P— is capable of – but I have been at great pains to
make him apprehend that no harm must come to P.S.C. & that we
require only the papers. I hope I have succeeded, but cannot be sure,
& so a degree of risk persists. Send word immediately – a single word
indeed will suffice – Yes, or No. I beg you, be sure to destroy this.*

The letter bore the date 21st October 1853 – four days before
the fatal attack on Mr Paul Stephen Carteret – who, I had no doubt,
was the person referred to in the postscript by his initials – as he
entered the Park through the western woods.

I was exultant. At last I had evidence – unequivocal, written evidence – that incriminated my Lady in a plot to ambush her father,
and involved her in its tragic consequences. She had assured Mr
Vyse that nothing existed to link her with her father's death; but she
had lied. Here they were, then: words on paper, which, as Mr Vyse
had warned her, can have fatal consequences.

The postscript had also revealed that the attack on Mr Carteret
had been carried out by one person, the mysterious 'P—', commissioned, it seemed, by Phoebus Daunt acting on Miss Carteret's
instructions, just as Billy Yapp had been recruited by her agent, Mr
Vyse, to kill Mrs Kraus.

The purpose of the conspiracy was also becoming clearer: to
obtain certain papers that Mr Carteret had been carrying. Then
came a sudden rush of realization.

Mr Carteret must have discovered documents indicating that
a legitimate heir might exist who would deny Phoebus Daunt his
golden expectations. Was it even possible that he had made this
discovery during his work on the history of the Duport family,
on which his daughter had assisted him? If so, then the Duport
succession might indeed link the deaths of Mr Carteret, Phoebus
Daunt, and Mrs Kraus, just as Mr Wraxall and Inspector Gully had
suspected.

III
An Encounter in the Fog

MY LADY TOOK breakfast the next morning alone in her private sitting-room, as she sometimes chose to do; I, too, made a solitary repast, downstairs in the Breakfast-Room, disappointed that Mr Perseus had eaten early and then ridden to Easton on estate business.

At a little after ten o'clock, under a snow-threatening sky, and chilled by a biting east wind even as we hurried the little way down the front steps, we took our seats in the carriage, drew the rugs over our laps, and set off to catch our train to London.

With us was the new dressing-maid, Violet Allardyce – a plump, vacant-looking girl, who stood constantly in awe of both her mistress and me, but who performed her duties efficiently enough, although sometimes not to *my* satisfaction.

Emily – I had by now begun to accustom myself to thinking of her, and calling her in private, by her Christian name, as she had wished me to do – was subdued at first, yet not altogether disinclined to converse. Nothing was said by either of us concerning the events of the previous night; and as we approached the terminus, her mood began to lighten. By the time we were nearing Grosvenor Square, she was once more enthusiastically rehearsing her plans for the succeeding days.

As the carriage came to a halt outside the house, gusting swirls of soft snow were coating the pavements, roofs, and front steps of the Square with deepening sheets of still-unsullied white. Emily, head bowed against the wind, her black fur stole starred with melting snowflakes, went straight inside. I lingered at the foot of the carriage steps, savouring the delicious sensation of cold snow blowing against my face, and listening to the delighted squeals of children coming from the rear of a neighbouring house.

We dined that evening with Lord and Lady Benefield at their house in nearby Park Lane – not far, indeed, from the late Lord Tansor's former town-house, in the garden of which Phoebus Daunt had been struck down by my father. I observed Emily closely as we arrived; but if she experienced any distress at the proximity of the place where her lover had died, on another night of snow, she did not show it.

It is needless to rehearse in detail the ensuing evening. Suffice to say that I was introduced to a dozen or so eminently unremarkable people of rank and wealth; that we ate and drank from the finest china and crystal; and that we talked of this and that, and nothing, until we were taken back to Grosvenor Square at a little after one o'clock in the morning.

The next day, we awoke to find that the snow had abated, leaving the streets awash with filthy, viscous slush and mud, which made our progress through them slow and unpleasant. Nothing, however, could moderate Emily's determination to proceed with her plans; and so, despite the difficulties, we contrived to call on several finely dressed, but blithely indolent, ladies of consequence in the vicinity of Mayfair, who all pronounced themselves charmed to meet me. We then went off to view the Queen's Collection at Buckingham Palace, and inspect the Duke of Bedford's Dutch pictures in Belgrave Square; we attended an afternoon concert given by the Philharmonic Society; we saw a play in the evening; and we took an informal late supper *à deux* at Grillon's Hotel, where Emily appeared to be well known.

Our second full day, which brought more of the same, included a visit to St Paul's, where Emily was eager for us to ascend to the celebrated Whispering Gallery, which I had claimed to have visited on our first stay in London. Before we left, she insisted that we make an experiment of its acoustic peculiarities, and so sent me scurrying over to the other side of the Gallery to press my ear to the wall.

'Did you hear me?' she asks excitedly when I return.

'No,' I reply. 'What did you whisper?'

'Oh, nothing. Just the tiniest little secret that I thought to share with you,' she says, with a disappointed sigh. 'I wonder why you couldn't hear me? Perhaps there are too many people here today. Come, let's go down.'

So down we went, back into the mud-splashed carriage, which took us off through the murk and mire to the Tower, and then, with an icy rain coming on, to Madame Tussaud's wax-works exhibition, where, at Emily's insistence, we paid our extra sixpence to view the Chamber of Horrors. The day concluded with a grand dinner at the imposing town-house of the Duport family's banker, Mr Jasper Dinever, at which were a number of eminent people from the financial and political worlds.

I believe that I acquitted myself well that evening, and that I played my allotted part to perfection. By turns I was demure, unobjectionably coquettish, insouciant or serious, as the occasion demanded. Dressed and gilded in my borrowed finery, I listened attentively and sympathetically, flattered and admired, teased and amused, according to each person's sex and disposition. Rather to my surprise, I began to discover that I, too, was capable of enchantment, by the exercise of which I contrived to charm the men, whilst simultaneously recommending myself to the good opinion of their ladies. In short, I triumphed – to Emily's visible delight.

Oh Lord, how proud she was of her creation! As if she were in the least degree responsible! The truth, of course, was quite other. *I* had remade *her*. She was my creature now, although she did not yet know it.

Day after day, I had seen the slow but inexorable transformation of Emily Tansor from the cold and haughty chatelaine – secure in her beauty and power, before whom I had once stood, seeking employment as her maid – into an indulgent, susceptible, and pregnable woman in her middle years, who had revealed – to me alone – an unguessed capacity for impulsive affection.

To others, she continued to maintain her old character of icy unapproachability; but no longer to me. Where now was that unassailable heart, secure against all assault? It seemed that I had found the key to unlock that famously adamantine gate, just as I had discovered the means to open the secret cupboard containing her lover's letters.

AFTER LEAVING MADAME Tussaud's, we had returned to Grosvenor Square in order to rest for an hour before dinner.

I now had a most spacious and comfortable room on the second floor, overlooking the garden at the back of the house, and superior in every respect to the one I had occupied during our previous visit.

Having divested myself of my coat, hat, and boots, I was stretching out my aching feet before the fire, anticipating an hour of glorious solitude, when there was a knock at my door.

It was beaming Charlie Skinner, who had accompanied us, with Mr Pocock, from Evenwood.

'Letter, miss,' he said, in his usual soldierly manner, handing me an unfranked envelope.

'Thank you, Charlie,' I said, returning his salute. 'And how are you finding London?'

'Uncommon dirty, miss,' he replied, before saluting me once more and marching off.

The envelope was addressed simply to 'Miss Gorst'. Inside was a small square of blue paper, with a few lines written in a looping, backward-sloping hand:

DEAR MISS GORST,—

I take the liberty of informing you that my superior officer, Inspector Alfred Gully, has requested that I should accompany you, at a prudent distance, whenever you choose to leave G— Square alone, to ensure that no harm comes to you. This I am very honoured to do — & so send this note to ask if you wd be so kind as to step outside at yr convenience so that I may know you by sight, & you may know me. I am standing at the corner of Brook St & will remain on station here until you come.

I remain, Miss Gorst, yours very faithfully —
WHIFFEN SWANN (SERGEANT)

Mr Wraxall had been as good as his word; and so, with a weary sigh, I laced up my boots once more, threw on my coat and hat, and slipped downstairs to meet my new protector.

●　　●　　●

ON REACHING THE corner of Brook Street, I looked about for Sergeant Swann, but could see no one who might answer to the idea I had formed of him. A plain-clothes detective officer, as I thought, would have a natural unobtrusiveness about him. I had imagined a lean, darkly costumed, flexibly constituted person – attributes, as I conceived, that would enable him to insinuate himself invisibly into the narrow places of life. But there was no one I could see who met my preconceived notion of Sergeant Whiffen Swann. Indeed, there was no one at all, for it was bitterly cold, with a dense fog coming down, and all sensible people were indoors, their chairs drawn up close to their fires, as I should have been.

I continued to walk up and down for several more minutes, increasingly piqued at having been called out on such a night. I was about to return to the house when, out of the foggy shadows, stepped a short, stocky, bespectacled individual dressed in a bright-yellow checked Inverness, of extravagant conspicuousness, and a light-brown bowler hat.

'Miss Gorst, I think?'

He had the deepest, gruffest voice I had ever heard, like the growl of a large and dyspeptic dog.

'I am,' I replied. 'And you are?'

'Sergeant Whiffen Swann, of the Detective Department, at your service, miss. I hope I find you well?'

'Perfectly well, thank you, Sergeant Swann,' I returned, 'although a little cold and uncomfortable.'

'You're not used to it like I am, miss, that's all.'

'You are right, Sergeant,' I said, emphatically, still feeling cross that he had kept me waiting, 'I am *not* used to it.'

'I had a reason, miss, for not making myself known to you straight away.'

His tight-lipped, censorious look rather alarmed me, and gave an entirely different idea of the sergeant's character and competence. His sparse, pale beard and small eyes had at first suggested a man of rather colourless and inoffensive temperament; now a hard and dogged vigour flared quietly behind the misted glass of his spectacles.

'You were followed, miss, as you left the house. Tall, thin party, clean shaven, around forty years of age, large ears, top of index finger on left hand missing, slight limp. Familiar to you, miss?'

'Most certainly not,' I replied, looking nervously about me.

'Thought not,' said Sergeant Swann with a sniff.

'He followed me, you say?'

'Not a doubt of it.'

'Where is he now?' I asked.

Sergeant Swann beckoned me away from the light of the street-lamp under which I had been standing to join him in an area of shadow.

'He's just over there, miss. He'd like to have a word with you, if you wouldn't mind, at your earliest convenience.'

Astonishment briefly robbed me of speech. Naturally, I said that I had no wish to meet the stranger, under any circumstance, and requested Sergeant Swann to escort me back to the house straight away.

'I shall of course accompany you, miss,' he said, 'as I've been instructed to do by Inspector Gully; but – if you'll forgive a little presumption on my part – perhaps I might suggest that you reconsider, and send me over to propose a suitable time and place to meet this person. You wouldn't be alone, you know. I'd be there with you, every second. Your safety would be assured, have no fear. I'm not a man to be trifled with, when push comes to shove.'

'But why should I agree to meet a complete stranger?' I asked, more confused and anxious than ever.

'Because I believe it might be to your advantage, miss,' replied Sergeant Swann. 'I've had several conversations with Inspector Gully, on various matters connected with your good self; and, besides, I know who the man is.'

'You know him?'

'Most certainly. His name is Conrad Kraus.'

25

A Lingering Scent of Violets

I
Sergeant Swann Takes Notes

A T NINE o'clock the next morning, by arrangement, I found myself in the Castle and Falcon Hotel, St Martin's le Grand, Aldersgate.

Two communications had been delivered to me by Charlie Skinner, just as I was going down to breakfast.

The first was from Mr Wraxall, who had been informed by Inspector Gully of my encounter with Sergeant Swann the previous evening.

'Here's a most unexpected, and undoubtedly important, development,' he wrote, 'and I'm gratified – although not at all surprised – that you've bravely consented to meet Mr K. You will be quite safe in Sergeant S's hands – he is one of Gully's best men. So God speed, my dear. I am agog to hear from you further.'

The second note, from Mrs Ridpath, confirmed that she would be pleased to see me later that morning in Devonshire Street, as I had requested.

Emily had been required to attend her solicitor, Mr Donald Orr, that morning, and we were not due to resume our itinerary of activities until after luncheon. At a little before half past eight, I slipped unseen out of the house.

•   •   •

SERGEANT SWANN WAS waiting on the corner of the Square. He made no attempt to acknowledge me, but remained a few yards at my back as I set off towards the hotel in Aldersgate that he had suggested for my appointment with the son of the murdered Mrs Kraus.

We found him sitting in the corner of the empty tap-room, staring vacantly out of the grimy window. He was tall and spare, with a yellowish, underfed look about him; something in the set of his shoulders, and his large hands, spoke of a once strong and robust constitution now reduced almost to frailty by sustained deprivation and misfortune.

Sergeant Swann had judged – or more likely knew – him to be around forty years of age, but he had a curiously juvenile face, and could easily have passed for a man who had lived only half as long, if he had had the benefit of a good wash, a visit to the barber's, several substantial meals, and clean linen.

The sergeant preceded me into the tap-room to speak a few words to the man; then he signalled for me to join them at the table.

'Will you take some refreshment, Miss Gorst?' he asked.

I thanked him, but said that I would prefer to conclude our business as quickly as possible.

'Very well, miss,' said the sergeant. 'You won't mind if I make notes, I'm sure.'

Whereupon he took out a black leather note-book, which he placed open on the table at an empty page, produced a pencil from the inside pocket of his Inverness, and looked expectantly, first at me, and then at Mr Kraus. After a moment or two's silence, he laid his pencil down impatiently, and fixed a disapproving eye on the latter.

'Now then, Conrad,' he growled, 'we're here at your request, so you'd better tell us why. Miss Gorst hasn't got all day – and neither have I.'

Ignoring the sergeant, Conrad laid a dirty hand on the table, and began to trace a pattern of invisible whorls.

'If you wouldn't mind, Mr Kraus,' I said, gently.

He looked up and gave me such a forlorn and piteous look, like a frightened child who knows he must do something that he is most unwilling to do, for fear of chastisement, that my heart almost broke.

'You're so very like 'er, miss.'

He turned his head away to stare out of the window again. A cold, thin rain was falling, sending little snaky streams of soot and grime trickling down the glass.

'Whom do I look like, Mr Kraus?' I asked, as the sergeant began to write in his note-book.

'The lady. Miss Carteret.'

'Do you mean Lady Tansor, Conrad – may I call you Conrad?'

He looked at me for a moment as if trying to remember something, and then nodded.

'And how did you know Miss Carteret, as Lady Tansor then was? Can you tell me?'

My heart was beating faster as I put the question, sensing that this poor inarticulate creature might possess the means to lay bare the reason for his mother's murder.

'When Muvver and me went wiv 'er on the boat,' he said. 'I liked the boat, but not the coaches. We went a long way on the coaches. They made me sick.'

'And where did the coaches take you, Conrad?' I asked.

'Muvver said it were a place called Carlsbad. Where Grandpa lived.'

Sergeant Swann, continuing to write, gave me a knowing nudge, intended, I believe, to communicate that he regarded this piece of information as opening up a promising new line of enquiry.

I then asked Conrad why they had gone to Carlsbad. He said that he did not know, but that Miss Carteret had given his mother money to look after her.

'And a pretty dress,' he added. 'Muvver liked pretty dresses. You've got a pretty dress on, miss. Muvver would've liked it.'

'What did you do in Carlsbad, Conrad?' was my next question;
but he only shook his head, and returned to his tracing. Then I
thought of another question.

'What about the colonel? Colonel Zaluski. Was he with you in
Carlsbad?'

At this prompting, Conrad looked up and nodded once more.

'The colonel – yes. That's where she found 'im. In Carlsbad.'

'What do you mean, "found him"? Had she been looking for
him?'

'Muvver said she was lookin' for someone – I don't know what
for. And then one night she found the colonel, and after that 'e
stayed wiv us, when we went on more coaches. But then she weren't
Miss Carteret no more.'

'You mean she married him?' I asked.

Another nod.

'But we already know that, Conrad. There must be something
else you want of me. What is it?'

He did not reply, only stared blankly at the table-top.

Sergeant Swann now began to display distinct signs of restive-
ness, shifting in his chair, and stamping his boot on the wooden
floor.

'Come along now, Conrad,' he said, his voice descending to a
threatening rumble, like the sound of distant thunder. 'Spit it all
out. What did you want to say to Miss Gorst?'

'I don't want to say nuffink. I jus' want it back,' retorted Conrad,
with sudden vehemence.

'What do you want back?' asked the sergeant. 'Speak up, man.'

'That will do, Sergeant,' I remonstrated. 'What would you like to
have back, Conrad? I shall help you, if I can.'

'The paper wiv 'er writin' on it.'

'And where do you think the paper has gone? Do you know?'

'The man took it,' he replied. 'The tall man who came on my
birfday to see Muvver, and they talked for a long time – 'e got it
from Muvver, when she went out an' never came back. But it were
mine – it's always been mine, though I couldn't never read the
words. It smelled of 'er. It always smelled of 'er. She told me to

take it to the post office, but I didn't. It smelled too nice. So I put it in my pocket, and never told anyone, not even Muvver. When we came home I 'id it in my room, and took it out every night, to remind me of Mrs Zaluski because she were so beautiful, like a queen in the stories Grandpa told me, though she was cruel to us. They thought I'd wanted to 'arm that girl in Franzenbad, but I didn't – I only wanted to make friends wiv 'er. So Muvver and me 'ad to leave very quickly, in the night, and we didn't 'ave enough money for coaches, so we 'ad to walk until Muvver got some money to take us home at last.'

'And so you kept the paper for a long time, did you?' I asked him. 'Until you were quite old?'

'Yes, miss,' Conrad replied. 'Then Muvver found it. She were cross at first, but then she said I were a good boy to 'ave kept it all that time, for it'd be very useful to us, and that we could use it to pay Mrs Turripper for our lodgings. I didn't understand, for it weren't money, only paper that smelled of Mrs Zaluski. But Muvver said that it were as good as money to us.

'Then the man came, the tall man wiv the stick, and she gave it to 'im, but 'e had 'er put in the river. I knows it, true as true can be. She said 'e were an old friend, but I knows 'e weren't. I 'ate the man wiv the stick. 'Ate him! 'Ate him! 'E took the paper, then 'e took Muvver.'

A tense pause followed, as Conrad traced several more whorls on the table.

'So I wants it back, miss,' he said, suddenly looking up, with a pathetically imploring expression in his sad eyes. 'The paper, wiv 'er smell on it, 'er lovely smell. Muvver said it were violets. That's what I wants. I fink the man wiv the stick must've wanted it so 'e could give it back to Mrs Zaluski. That's what I fink. Are you 'er daughter, miss? You can get it for me if you are, though you don't have 'er name. Why's that? Or you can get me another paper, if it smells the same. It 'as to smell the same. Say you will, miss!'

He sat back and closed his eyes, as if it had cost him great effort to speak so many words.

'Conrad, look at me. Will you do that for me?'

He slowly did as I had asked. I saw then what beautiful eyes he had. They were of the softest, deepest brown, like Mr Randolph's, with long dark lashes, and gave out such a depth of sad longing that tears began to form in my own.

'I'm not her daughter, Conrad,' I said, 'and I don't know where your paper is. But if it can be found, then I'm sure you can have it back.'

'Fank you, miss,' he said. 'But now I don't know who you are. Why is everyfink a puzzle to me?'

Another pause, during which the sergeant finished composing his notes, and replaced the little leather note-book in the pocket of his cape.

'One more question, Conrad,' I said as I was about to go. 'You said that your mother went to meet the man who took your paper on your birthday. When was that? Do you know the date?'

Sergeant Swann hurriedly took out his note-book once more.

'Fifteen days after September starts,' said Conrad, with a most touchingly confident air. 'I allus remember that. Muvver used to tell me when I should start counting, for I can count all the way to fifty, though I don't know my letters.'

'And was this birthday the last one you had?'

He gave me one of his assenting nods.

'And just tell me again, Conrad.' I gave him an encouraging smile. 'Whom did your mother give the paper to?'

'I've told you,' he said, turning his face towards the window as he spoke. 'The tall man wiv the stick. And a big moustache.'

SERGEANT SWANN CLOSED his note-book for a second time.

'I think that's all we can do here,' he said, standing up and patting down his bowler hat on his head. 'If you agree, miss, we'll all get a cab back to Grosvenor Square, and then our friend and I will go on to the Department, for a few private words. I think you said you won't need me any more today?'

'That's correct, sergeant. I shall be attending Lady Tansor for the rest of the day.'

'Very well, then. Come along now, Conrad. The inspector would like to see you. You remember the inspector, don't you?'

Conrad nodded.

We left the hotel, and a cab was soon found to take me back to Grosvenor Square.

The door was opened to my knock by Charlie.

'Good-morning, miss,' he said, standing to attention, and saluting me.

Then I saw him glance outside, at the faces of Sergeant Whiffen Swann and Conrad Kraus looking out of the cab window.

'Not a word, Charlie,' I whispered, as I hurried past him.

'Not a word, miss,' he replied, closing the door.

II

The One-Armed Soldier

HALF AN HOUR later, unobserved, I left Grosvenor Square once more, this time to walk to Mrs Ridpath's house in Devonshire Street.

Of course I should have told the sergeant where I was going; but I had had enough of Sergeant Whiffen Swann for one day, and this was my own private business, which I did not care to have reported back to Inspector Gully, and thence to Mr Wraxall.

On arriving in Devonshire Street, I found that I was fifteen minutes before my time, but, feeling somewhat wearied, I knocked on the black front door all the same.

The maid admitted me, took my coat and umbrella, and conducted me up to the drawing-room.

As she was about to announce my arrival, the girl turned to me.

'She's expecting you, miss,' she whispered, 'but the gentleman's still here.'

'Gentleman?'

'He wouldn't give his name, miss.'

So saying, she tapped softly on the door, and we entered.

Her face a sudden picture of confusion, Mrs Ridpath stared across the room at me from a chaise-longue by the fire. Her visitor was sitting with his back towards me.

Tall and broad-backed, with a magnificent head of thick, golden-hued hair that curled around the nape of his muscular neck, he was in the process of raising a glass of cordial to his lips with his left hand. The empty right-hand sleeve of his tweed Norfolk jacket hung over the arm of the chair.

'Esperanza, my dear!' exclaimed Mrs Ridpath, clearly still flustered by my arrival. 'You're a little early, I think?'

She walked across to kiss me on the cheek and shepherded me over to join her on the chaise-longue. As I sat down, I was able, for the first time, to look her visitor in the face.

And what an impressively handsome face it was, exactly like one's notion of some great Saxon king, or sea-roving Viking warrior: weathered, clean-shaven, with the striking exception of a magnificent moustache, the ends of which drooped down almost to his chin; and having a pair of the most delicately pale blue eyes I had ever seen.

'My dear, may I introduce Captain—'

'Willoughby,' the gentleman broke in, getting up to shake my hand. 'John Willoughby.'

There was no doubt now: he had only one arm; and this instantly brought to mind the man I had seen on the bridge over the Evenbrook, on the day my Lady had driven out in the barouche with Mr Armitage Vyse.

'Yes,' said Mrs Ridpath, appearing strangely disinclined to meet my questioning eye. 'Captain John Willoughby. And this – John – is Miss Esperanza Gorst, of whom you've often heard me speak.'

'Delighted and honoured to meet you, Miss Gorst,' said Captain Willoughby, releasing my hand and taking his seat again.

There followed an embarrassing period of shuffling silence, during which Captain Willoughby tapped the fingers of his remaining hand on the arm of the chair, and Mrs Ridpath smiled fixedly in the most abashed and self-conscious manner.

Eventually, a few words were spoken on the subject of the recent snow, and on various other trifling matters. At last I could stand no more.

'I believe I know you, sir,' I said, giving Captain Willoughby the boldest look I could.

'I don't think that's possible, my dear,' Mrs Ridpath began, but she was prevented from saying any more by Captain Willoughby.

'No, Lizzie,' he said, 'Miss Gorst is right. I believe she *does* know me – at least by sight – and so deserves to know a little more about me.'

'As you wish,' said Mrs Ridpath, folding her hands in her lap with every appearance of unwilling resignation.

'That's the thing, Lizzie. Doesn't do to deny what can't be denied, you know. Well, Miss Gorst, you've seen, but not met, me before – that's true; and so I'll lay it out to you, as plainly as I can, for I'm a plain man, and can't do it any other way.'

He gave a preliminary cough, crossed his legs, and sat back in his chair.

'What you must know about me is this. I am – I beg your pardon, *was* – one of your father's oldest friends. Different in every possible way, of course, him and me – I dare say that no two fellows were ever more so. I was once accounted a pretty good sportsman, and could ride any Leicestershire man ragged, before the Russians blew my arm off; but your esteemed pa could hardly get on a horse without straight away falling off. Still, we were chums from the start, and the best of chums we stayed, even when circumstances kept us apart.'

'And where did you meet my father, Captain Willoughby?' I asked.

'Ah, at school. Eton. He was in College, of course – a King's Scholar. We Oppidans lodged in houses in the town, but I hit it off with him from the start, and soon he was taking breakfast with me in the house, and keeping some of his things in my room – Long Chamber, where they put the Scholars, being a pretty inhospitable place. I was put somewhat in mind of it at Scutari.*

---

* The British military hospital (present-day Üsküdar, ancient Chrysopolis, in Turkey), made famous by its association with Florence Nightingale during the Crimean War.

'Well, your pa was as clever as they come – cleverer. Deuced if I know how he kept it all in his head. "The learned boy", that's what we all called him when he came to the school. There never was anyone like him – an absolute demon at his lessons. His masters could hardly keep up with him, let alone the rest of us. I was the most confounded dunce – always had been; but that didn't matter to Glyver.'

'Glyver? That was the name you knew him by?'

'At school, yes. Edward Glyver.'

'Not Glapthorn?'

'No, not then,' said Captain Willoughby, after a moment's consideration. 'That came later, when he lived here – I mean in London.'

'You must also have known Phoebus Daunt at school, then?' I observed.

Captain Willoughby uncrossed his legs, and took out his pipe.

'Mind if I smoke, Miss Gorst?' he asked.

'Not at all.'

Several more moments passed as he reached into his jacket pocket for a pouch of tobacco, dexterously filled his pipe with his remaining hand, and set a match to the bowl. Then he sat back again in his chair, puffing out a blue-grey cloud of sweet-smelling smoke.

'What were we saying?' he asked.

'Phoebus Daunt,' I replied. 'I remarked that you must also have known him, at school.'

'Slightly.'

It was abundantly apparent that the captain had no intention of saying any more on the subject; and so, instead of pressing him further, I put another question to him.

'Captain Willoughby, are you the friend at Evenwood that Madame de l'Orme told me about?'

To this enquiry he gave an immediate answer.

'You may consider me so.'

'The person with whom I should communicate, by placing two lighted candles in my window, should I ever need assistance?'

'Again, you may consider me to be that person.'

'And how did this arrangement come about?'

He blew out another plume of smoke.

'That's easily told,' he said, 'and I'm ready to do so.'

Another long, slow puff.

'Well then, after you were born, and just before he left Paris to go on his travels in the East – which I believe you now know about – your pa wrote to me. He'd conceived a plan for your future, and asked me to watch over you, should I ever be requested to do so. To this, of course, I instantly agreed.'

'But then he died,' I remarked.

'Indeed,' said Captain Willoughby, from behind a fog of smoky tendrils.

'And then?'

'Madame de l'Orme wrote to me last year, to tell me that the circumstances were now right for your pa's plan to be put in motion at last. That piece of intelligence, of course, immediately put things on a war footing, and I began to make the necessary arrangements.

'All went smoothly, and when you arrived at Evenwood, I'd already taken a cottage in the village. You may know it. Curate's Cottage?'

I knew it – a small, two-storeyed dwelling, not far from the entrance to the church-yard – and now recalled Sukie mentioning that it had a new tenant, a former military gentleman who kept himself very much to himself.

'Every morning, mid-day, afternoon, and evening since then,' continued the captain, 'without fail, come rain or shine, I've set off on patrol through the Park, making sure to stop for a moment or two before the West Front, to look up at a certain window. When I'm confident that no candles are burning there, I go on my way rejoicing. You've seen me standing there once, I think, one foggy morning?'

'And once on the bridge,' I said, 'as Lady Tansor passed by in her barouche, with a gentleman companion.'

'Ah,' said Captain Willoughby. 'You saw me then, did you?'

'It was you!' I cried, having been struck by a sudden realization. 'You let me out of the Mausoleum!'

Captain Willoughby nodded.

'Bull's-eye, my dear. No candles burning, just a soldier's instinct – and a little luck.'

It appeared that he had chanced to see me setting off to the Mausoleum, and had decided he would take a detour on the way back from his mid-day patrol, to assure himself that all was well with me.

Arriving at the Mausoleum soon after my Lady had departed, and hearing my cries coming from within that dreadful place, he was at first dismayed to know what could be done to release me. Then he remembered hearing his neighbour, the loquacious Mr Thripp, mentioning that a key to the Mausoleum was kept in the Rectory. This, after walking the considerable distance to seek out the Rector, he eventually obtained, on the pretext of wishing to satisfy an architectural interest in the interior of the building.

'Dashed good luck, of course, that the old boy was at home,' the captain conceded. 'But I'd have got you out, one way or the other, never fear, even if it meant bringing up the artillery to blow the doors off.'

Of course I had to kiss him, which I did, to his great confusion.

'Now, now,' he said, in a vain attempt at bluster, 'that's enough of that. Only doing m'duty, you know.'

I allowed him several more puffs on his pipe, as a reward, before continuing to quiz him.

'Now Captain Willoughby,' I said at length. 'Tell me this. Are you acting strictly under orders?'

'Orders? What do you mean?'

'I have so many large and urgent questions to ask, concerning my father's history, to which I long to have answers. I've a strong impression, Captain Willoughby, that you know a very great deal more about him than you're able to tell me, and that you'd be willing to reveal what you know, were you not constrained in some way. I simply thought that you might be obeying orders, which, of course, a soldier is obliged to do.'

Throughout this exchange with Captain Willoughby, Mrs Ridpath had remained silent, although still visibly discomfited; but now, before Captain Willoughby could speak again, she stood up to ring the bell to summon the maid.

'How rude you must think me, my dear,' she said. 'Here you are, a quarter of an hour in the house, and I've offered you no refreshment. You'll take something, won't you?'

The girl was soon at the door to receive her orders. After she had gone, Mrs Ridpath sat down again, and gently took my hand.

'You must know, my dear, that Captain Willoughby and I are not free agents. As you have realized, we can act only according to the instructions we've been given by Madame de l'Orme, who is in turn fulfilling her own undertaking to your dear father. You may call these "orders", if you like; but they are orders that we can neither countermand nor ignore. It will not always be so. A day will come . . .'

'A day always comes,' I said, wishing to spare her any more discomfiture, 'and so I shall not make myself disagreeable any longer, dear Mrs Ridpath, but shall wait patiently for that day of final illumination. But will you please just tell me this: how did you come to play a part in my father's plan?'

'That's a long story, my dear,' she said, 'and now is not the time to tell it. But this much, at least, I believe that Madame would not be unwilling for you to know.

'I was one of your predecessors at Evenwood. My name then was Lizzie Brine.'

LIZZIE BRINE.

'I had a maid once,' I remembered Emily telling me, 'Elizabeth Brine by name, who gave very satisfactory service.' Mr Pocock had also mentioned her name, and that of her brother, John Brine, who had been Mr Paul Carteret's man-servant at the Dower House.

Mrs Ridpath saw the flash of remembrance in my expression.

'You've heard of me, I see,' she said.

'I have.'

'I've just a little more to say, my dear, and then I think I'll have said enough, for now.

'Not so very long after the death of Mr Phoebus Daunt, when it became known that Miss Carteret, as she then was, intended to go travelling on the Continent, I naturally expected that I would accompany her. Instead, I was informed by Miss Carteret that she required someone to attend her who could speak French and German, and that she would therefore be seeking to engage a new maid.

'So she left Evenwood, and soon afterwards I was dismissed, along with my brother, by the late Lord Tansor. I don't say we weren't treated well: we were given excellent references, and sufficient money to allow us to leave England, where we'd no future, and begin new lives in America. John bought some land to farm in Connecticut, and I became housekeeper to Mr Nathan Ridpath, a Boston banker.

'Well, you may guess a little of the rest. I married Mr Ridpath, and began to improve myself thereby, having always been an eager learner, and greatly fond of the few books I could get – and of course the first thing I did was to learn French and German, not so much to spite my former mistress, although I won't deny that it gave me some satisfaction to acquire the skills I had been dismissed for lacking, but principally to begin turning myself into something better than an English village girl, for my husband's sake.

'But then Mr Ridpath died, only six months after our marriage. He left me very well provided for, and in this comfortable condition I returned to England. This is the house I purchased, and here I've been ever since.'

I listened to her with rapt attention, for of course any scrap of information concerning Emily's past was of the greatest interest to me; and in Lizzie Brine's story I began to divine dim intimations of some momentous, yet still unformed, truth.

'But how did you first come to know my father?' I asked.

'When I was Miss Carteret's maid, we – I mean my brother, John, and I – came to an arrangement with your father.'

She paused.

'An arrangement?'

'Living in London, your father – Mr Glapthorn, as he was then known to us – required to be kept informed of what passed at Evenwood, particularly concerning Miss Carteret and Mr Phoebus Daunt.'

'I understand,' I said. 'But, after you returned from America, how did you find each other again?'

'I came here in 1857,' said Mrs Ridpath. 'When I'd got myself nice and comfortable, I took a trip to Paris – a place I'd always longed to visit, and of course I now had the means and leisure to do so, as well as an ability to speak the language.

'Quite by chance, I happened one day to see some delightful water-colours for sale in the window of a shop in the Quai de Montebello. There was a man – an Englishman – talking to a lady working in the shop, whom I quickly apprehended must be his wife. Although he was much changed since we'd last seen each other, I recognized him straight away, and he recognized me, although neither of us acknowledged the other.

'Well, I bought one of the water-colours, and then left the shop; but he soon caught up with me, and so our acquaintance was renewed.

'After I returned to London, he and his wife – calling themselves Mr and Mrs Edwin Gorst – moved to the Avenue d'Uhrich, at the invitation of Madame de l'Orme. We continued to correspond, and in due course, like Captain Willoughby, I was asked to participate in your father's great scheme to regain his inheritance through you, his only child. And this I agreed to do, most willingly, to put right the terrible wrong that had been done to him, and to you, by my former mistress.'

Light – more blessed light – was now breaking through the obscuring clouds of ignorance and doubt. I kissed Mrs Ridpath, and thanked her for favouring me with her confidence, limited though it was, as we both knew.

'So, Miss Gorst,' said Captain Willoughby, getting up from his chair, and towering over me, 'you now know a little more than you did when you woke up this morning. We've been introduced at last, and I'm heartily glad of it.'

'As I am, Captain Willoughby,' I replied. 'Truly glad.'

'Of course I'll be on patrol once more when you return to Evenwood,' he continued, 'and I trust that your candles will remain unlit; but London is a different matter. A rather sizeable place, London. Can't be everywhere, you know; so you must be careful in your daily routine, especially when going out alone. You're to send word immediately to Lizzie here, if you feel yourself to be in danger from a certain legal gentleman – you know to whom I refer, I'm sure – and she'll call up the cavalry. You'll do that, won't you?'

When Captain Willoughby had gone, Mrs Ridpath gave me a note from Mr Thornhaugh, which had crossed with the report that she had only just forwarded to Madame:

Madame and I are naturally concerned, Little Queen, that what she was bound by duty to tell you about yr father & yrself will have caused you deep distress. So write, as soon as you can, to assure us both that all is well. For the time has now come to put in train the culminating phase of our Great Task. This, Madame knows only too well, will present the most exceptional test of even yr remarkable resourcefulness & strength of mind. I shall write no more at present, except to assure you, once again, that Madame and I continue to have the greatest confidence that your endeavours will meet with complete success, & that what was lost to yr father will be restored to the full – by you.

Having read Mr Thornhaugh's note, I drank up my tea, and prepared to leave.

'Good-bye, dear Esperanza,' said Mrs Ridpath at the door. 'I'm glad, and much relieved, that we understand each other a little better. It has been hateful to me, having to keep my true identity from you, although what Madame will have to say to me when I tell her, as I must, I don't know. But I can see no harm coming from it; and so good-bye again, dear child. Your father would be so very proud of you.'

A cab had been called, and was waiting for me. As it pulled away and set off for Grosvenor Square, I laid back my head and closed my eyes.

A few more small but consequential steps had been taken on the road to the achievement of my great goal, and my father's final and long-awaited vindication. But what still lay ahead?

26

The Old Man of Billiter Street

I

A First and Last Meeting

I was expected for luncheon at half past one, and it wanted but ten minutes to the time when Charlie opened the door to my urgent knock.

'Has Lady Tansor returned from Mr Orr's?'

'Yes, miss,' he replied, saluting smartly. 'Half an hour since.'

I ran up to my room, to change my gown and re-dress my hair, then hurried back downstairs to the dining-room, just as the luncheon bell was sounding.

'What have you been doing this morning, dear?' Emily asked, as the soup was brought in.

I said that I had been out walking.

'Walking? The weather is not very suited to walking.'

'Oh, I pay no heed to that,' I say, nonchalantly. 'I find London fascinating in all weathers.'

'Well,' she replies, dabbing her mouth with her napkin to remove a trickle of soup, 'that is a most original notion, I must say. Where did you go?'

I am all ready with my answer.

'To the Regent's Park, and then to the Pantheon Bazaar.'*

*Originally a fashionable theatre, with the main entrance on Oxford

'The Pantheon Bazaar! How interesting! I've never been there myself, of course. Isn't it a little – vulgar? You must remember, dear, that you should now only be seen in the most respectable places.'

'Oh, the Pantheon is quite respectable,' I say airily, feeling – although not expressing – resentment at her disdainful tone.

'Of course. I didn't mean to suggest otherwise, dear.'

She lays the napkin down, and takes a sip of cordial.

'But it's not quite the sort of place that I would like my companion – and friend – to be seen at. It might give altogether the wrong impression. There are shops, you know, and then there are bazaars. You should really be seen only in the best of the former. You would not see Miss Miranda Fox-More, or Miss Eleanor de Freitas, in a bazaar. They would never think to do such a thing. Did you purchase anything?'

'No,' I replied. 'I'd thought to buy a little gift, for your kindness and consideration in bringing me to London; but there was so much to choose from! I simply couldn't decide what you might like.'

'Well, that was a kind thought in any case,' she said, with an air of frosty relief. 'Which reminds me, dear; you look very well in my old dresses, but you really must now have some of your own. We shall go to Regent Street before we leave next week, to see what can be done.'

After luncheon, resuming Emily's inviolable programme, off we went in the freshly washed carriage to see the Museum of Practical Geology in Jermyn Street, which appeared to delight her excessively, but which almost prostrated me with boredom. Thence to Westminster Abbey, which was much more to my taste, and where I could have happily remained for several hours; but of course I was soon whisked away to see some other celebrated sight, which Emily duly ticked off on the list she kept in her reticule of all the places she had decided beforehand that I – in my novitiate state as a visitor to the capital – must see.

Street. Its attractions included a picture gallery, a toy bazaar, and, on the ground floor, numerous counters offering a wide range of clothing items and fancy goods.

So the day wore briskly on, until it was soon time for us to attend a grand dinner in St James's, at the house of Sir Marcus Leveret, our former Ambassador to Portugal – and grand it was.

My head began to spin at the multitude of persons of privilege and distinction to whom I was introduced: dukes and earls; ambassadors and Honourable Members; foreign princes and Nabobs; judges and bankers; generals and admirals; wives, daughters, mothers, and widowed dowagers, all superbly dressed and coiffured, and brilliantly bejewelled. In addition there was, of course, a generous sprinkling of handsome young bachelors – all of impeccable eligibility, but none of whom interested me in the slightest.

So Friday came, and another dismal morning of bumping along in the carriage from place to place, tunnelling down thickly muddied streets through swirling veils of soot-stained murk. After luncheon, however, Emily complained of feeling unwell, and her London physician, Dr Manley, was called.

'I'm sorry, Alice,' she said after the doctor had gone, 'but I'm afraid that we shall have to abandon our plans for this afternoon. I know how disappointed you'll be, as I am; but it cannot be helped. Dr Manley insists that I must rest, and so you will have to amuse yourself. You won't mind that, will you, dear? Until I feel a little better.'

I am outwardly distraught, naturally, at the prospect of not being juddered and jounced around filthy, cacophonous streets, to spend half an hour staring at this or that object or place of supposed interest and attraction, and then to spend an evening ingratiating myself with the first ladies and gentlemen of English society.

Here, however, I should perhaps insert a little confession, as yet another demonstration of my sometimes inconveniently resilient conscience. Did I feel it pricking me when indulged, to a prodigious degree, by the 26th Baroness Tansor – one of the most admired women in London? I did. And, despite its protestations, did I continue to derive and anticipate a secret pleasure at the privileged consequences of my friendship with this extraordinary woman? Of course. For what young lady of nineteen, with limited experience of the great social world, would not feel complimented and honoured by such attentions? I was as weakly susceptible as any such young lady to the vanities of the world, and to the lure of appearances, and just as apt, on occasion, to want them very badly indeed.

Yes, I was weak enough to be myself, when it came to petting and pampering, and to allow myself to enjoy the experience, although the pleasure was not unalloyed; for, like a perpetually reprimanding second shadow, the stern spectre of Duty would trail me through the great gilded rooms, sit beside me at the laden tables, and enter secretly into my dreams, wrenching me back from shallowness and selfishness to that necessary state of determination, in which nothing mattered but to carry out my fated commission.

I LEFT EMILY to sleep, and went to my room, to consider how best to make use of my unexpected liberty.

I knew that, whatever I decided to do, I ought to inform Sergeant Swann; but I had somewhat taken against my protector, and considered that I would be in no danger if I confined myself to the main thoroughfares.

I was leafing through *Murray's Guide* when an original – and thrilling – idea burst into my mind.

I would seek out Mr John Lazarus, if he still lived.

Fired by this sudden inspiration, I threw on my coat, ran downstairs, and breathlessly asked Charlie to call up a cab.

'Destination, miss?' he asked.

'Billiter Street, City, if you please, Charlie,' I returned, placing my finger to my lips.

A wink, a salute, and he was gone.

THE HOUSE STOOD near the junction with Leadenhall Street – a narrow, half-timbered, tipsy-looking building, with opaque, thickly dirtied, diamond-paned windows, and a forbiddingly studded front door, above which swung a peeling representation of a full-rigged ship, beneath which was the painted legend, 'J.S. Lazarus, Shipping-Agent'.

I knocked, waited, knocked again, and then again, but no one came. I began to think that Mr Lazarus might be dead after all, or that the house had been permanently shut up. Then, as I was about to leave, the door-handle began slowly to turn.

An elderly man, frail and bent, a young ginger-and-white cat rubbing affectionately against his legs, stood before me.

'Good-afternoon, miss. May I help you?'

As he spoke, his look of respectful enquiry suddenly altered.

'Forgive me, miss,' he said, brushing back a wisp of thin grey hair that had fallen over his forehead. 'Have I had the honour of meeting you before?'

'I don't believe so, sir,' I replied. 'But you are Mr John Lazarus, I think?'

'Yes, I am he.'

He was alive! He was here before me – the man to whom my father had owed his life.

'You must excuse me,' he said, 'if I enquire what business you have with me.'

'I am here because you once knew my father,' I replied. 'I am Esperanza Gorst, the daughter of Edwin Gorst.'

He gave a delighted gasp.

'The daughter of Edwin Gorst!' he exclaimed. 'Can it really be? Come in, come in!'

With many warm expressions of welcome, he showed me into a low-beamed apartment, dusty and dark, the walls of which were covered from floor to ceiling with paintings of ships, maps, sea-charts, faded illustrations of exotic birds and flowers, and sundry topographical views of the various Atlantic islands that Mr Lazarus had visited during the course of his long professional life.

Tea was offered and accepted, and we conversed for an hour or more, during which time Mr Lazarus related many small, although – to me – absorbing details of the time he had spent with my father on Madeira. His memories of those far-off days were undimmed, but added little to what I had read in his recollections. On my side, I told him something of what I knew of my parents' history after leaving Madeira, and of how my father had died in Constantinople in the year 1862, which seemed to affect the old gentleman greatly.

There was one question that I was most anxious to ask.

'Mr Lazarus,' I ventured, 'did you ever know what the box of papers contained that my father asked you to take to England, to place in the safe-keeping of his solicitor?'

'They were of a private nature, my dear,' he replied, 'and so of course I did not enquire; but, from something he once said, I believe the box contained some kind of memoir – perhaps a diary or journal, or a more ambitious narrative of his life.'

My heart gave a leap.

'Do you remember the name of the legal gentleman to whom you gave the box?'

My voice was calm; but I felt weak with nervous anticipation of Mr Lazarus's reply.

'Mr Christopher Tredgold,' he replied, without a moment's hesitation. 'I believe he was your father's former employer. He had retired from the firm, after suffering a seizure. My impression, however, was that he was acting in the capacity of a friend, rather than a legal representative.'

'It must be presumed, then,' I suggested, 'that the papers remained in Mr Tredgold's keeping.'

'That, of course, I am unable to say,' replied Mr Lazarus.

'And you had no further communication with Mr Tredgold, after you delivered the papers to him?'

'None, I'm afraid. Will you take some more tea, my dear?'

I saw that our conversation had exhausted him, and that his enquiry had merely been the fastidiousness of a naturally courteous man. I therefore gratefully declined, and rose to go.

'I see now that you have more than just the look of him about you,' Mr Lazarus said, as I stepped out into the cold, wet street. 'You have something of his spirit, too, I think – the essence of a most remarkable individual, whom I consider it to be one of the great privileges of my life to have known, even for so short a time. I have never met his like since, and am sure I never will again. God be with you, my dear. Come and see me again, if you wish. Visitors are few these days.'

It was my firm intention to return to Billiter Street, not only to try and coax more memories of the man he had known as Edwin Gorst from him, but also because I had begun to feel real affection for this enfeebled old gentleman, who had restored my father to life, hope, and purpose; but he died not long afterwards, as I later discovered, and I never saw him again.

II
Pursued

I LEFT BILLITER Street, deep in thought – so absorbed, indeed, that I failed to notice that I was being followed.

It was in Fenchurch Street that, happening to glance back at the clock on the church of St Dionis, I saw him – a squat, pinch-faced fellow of about forty, with prematurely white hair, and a pair of almost perfectly rectangular, perfectly black eye-brows. I had seen him before. It was Digges, Mr Armitage Vyse's man-servant, who had attended him during his Christmas visit to Evenwood.

I quickened my pace; but still my pursuer came on.

What did he want? Was I in physical danger from this man? Surely not – not here, in these teeming streets?

Just as when the ruffian had accosted me on the road from Easton, I felt a sudden fit of indignant anger at being pursued in this way through the public streets. How dare Digges and his master put me to this fright! Momentarily emboldened, I considered turning and confronting the man – I even began to look about me for a weapon of some sort; but discretion happily won the day.

A cab – I must find a cab.

It had now started to rain once more, darkness was rapidly coming on, the streets were thronged with home-going City men, and there were no cabs to be had. I thought at first that I knew my way, having memorized it from the map in *Murray's Guide*; but as I moved quickly on, through an area of mean, narrow tenements, it soon became apparent that I was lost.

I remember the sound of a hammer on metal, and the sharp

hiss of steam escaping from some nearby manufactory; shouts and oaths outside a public-house; and threatening faces staring at me as I hurried along.

Where was I? Where could I seek safety? There was only the slowly imprisoning gloom, windowless walls and fearful alleys, a cold stinging rain in my face, and a desperate sense of helplessness closing in around me.

Then, at last, I emerged into Fleet Street, and started to run. Digges was still behind me; but I was close now – close to where I prayed I might find safety at last.

Even before I reached the cab-stand I saw that it was empty. Should I seek out Mr Pilgrim's house in Shoe Lane, as he had urged me to do if I found myself in need of his protection once more – as I most certainly did? But where was Shoe Lane?

Then, out of the mist, two cabs emerged and came to a halt at the stand. The driver of the second vehicle began to get down from his seat, whip in hand.

'Please!' I panted. 'Can you help me? There's a man following me.'

The cab-man pushed away his muffler.

'Why, here you are again, missy. What's afoot now?' asked Mr Solomon Pilgrim, as large as life.

Relieved but still afraid, I glanced anxiously back at Digges. 'The man with white hair.'

'You'd best get in,' said Mr Pilgrim, opening the cab door.

I clambered in. Seconds later, Digges came up, stopped, and eyed my rescuer belligerently.

'Taken,' growled the burly cab-man, closing the door, and gripping his whip in a most menacing manner.

Saying nothing, but with another warlike look, Digges slouched off. I leaned out to watch him being slowly engulfed by the stream of jostling pedestrians until it closed around him, and he was finally lost to view.

'In a spot o' bother again, missy?' asked Mr Pilgrim, shaking his great round head. 'Though now it seems it's you wot's bein' followed.'

'I don't know the man,' I said, trying to maintain my composure, despite being a perfect jelly inside, 'or why he was following me; but I'm glad to see you again, Mr Pilgrim, and I thank you once more for your kindness.'

'Always at your service, missy, and always to be found here, as I told you before. Will you walk on – which I don't advise – or can Sol Pilgrim take you anywhere?'

I thought for a moment. Not back to Grosvenor Square, not yet.

'King's Bench Walk, Temple,' I said. 'Number fourteen.'

III
A Conversation in King's Bench Walk

IT WAS BUT a short journey to Mr Wraxall's chambers.

Having tendered my grateful good-byes to Mr Pilgrim, I was soon sitting with Mr Wraxall in his comfortable, fire-lit study, recounting my recent adventure, although I said nothing of why I had left Grosvenor Square alone without first informing Sergeant Swann. Neither did I mention that I would do so again if circumstances required.

'You'll forgive me, I hope, my dear,' said Mr Wraxall, when I had finished, 'if I presume to say that I'm a little disappointed that you put yourself in the way of danger once again; but there, the thing is done, and thank God you are now safe.'

His manner was conciliatory; but his disapproval was evident.

'Of course I cannot – and will not – insist that you warn Sergeant Swann in advance of any future expeditions. I only entreat you – for my own peace of mind, if not your own – to consider that it might be prudent to do so. So now, let us put this little unpleasantness aside and get down to business. I take it that there *is* business to discuss?'

Relieved to come at last to my purpose, I told him that I was curious to know whether anything more had been discovered from Conrad Kraus; but before Mr Wraxall could reply, there was a knock at the door, and in walked Inspector Gully.

'Well, here's the very person who can tell us,' said the barrister, getting up to greet his visitor.

'Miss Gorst,' said Mr Wraxall to the inspector, 'has had a little escapade, haven't you, Miss Gorst?'

This, of course, obliged me to tell Mr Gully how I had been followed by Mr Vyse's man.

'Arthur Digges?' enquired the inspector.

Mr Wraxall wondered whether he was known to the Detective Department.

'Slightly,' replied the inspector. 'A former tar. Been with Vyse for the past three years. Nothing more.'

'But why was he following me?' I asked.

'Futile to speculate,' said Mr Wraxall, 'so let us not do so, although my guess is that, like sending Yapp to Evenwood, it was intended to bring home to you that Mr Vyse has his eye closely fixed on you.'

The conversation then returned to Conrad Kraus.

'I believe I've got a bit more purchase on certain matters connected with Lady Tansor's former dealings with Mrs Kraus,' said Mr Gully. 'Perhaps it would interest you to hear where I think we now stand? Very well then, here it is, as tight as I can manage it.'

He took out his note-book, opened it, and cleared his throat.

'*Item.* Miss Emily Carteret leaves for the Continent – date of departure: on or about 19th January 1855 – full approval of noble cousin – acquaintance of noble cousin recommends German-speaking maid and general attendant, recently widowed – name of German-speaking party: Mrs Barbarina Kraus – accompanied on trip by Mrs K's son, Conrad, nineteen years, strapping lad, but somewhat deficient in mental powers.

'*Item.* Miss EC's destination: Carlsbad, where pa-in-law of Mrs K resides – date of arrival: early February 1855 – reason put out for going: to take the waters – true reason for going: to find a husband – suitable party speedily discovered in the shape of Colonel Tadeusz Zaluski, indigent former Polish army officer.

'*Item.* Miss EC and Colonel Z marry – date of marriage: 23rd March 1855, according to information received from local enquiries – union soon blessed with happiest of tidings (facetious query:

effect of Bohemian waters?) – son born in town of Ossegg – date of birth: Christmas Day, 1855 – son christened Perseus.

'*Item*. The family Zaluski returns to England with three-month heir – received by gratified noble cousin at Evenwood on 7th April 1856 – Mrs Z basks in noble cousin's golden beams – second son, Randolph, born November of that year – Mrs Z's triumph complete – Duport succession secure at last.

'*Item*. Miss EC, having become Mrs Z, now becomes Mrs Z-D (Zaluski-Duport) by Royal Licence – legally instituted as noble cousin's successor – on death of noble cousin (November 1863), husband's name shed – former Miss EC now Emily Grace Duport, 26th Baroness Tansor, mistress of Evenwood.'

'Anything else?' asked Mr Wraxall.

'Spot of bother, in the town of Franzenbad,' replied the inspector, 'involving Conrad and – excuse me, Miss Gorst – a girl from the locality. Crisis precipitated. Police called. Flight of Mrs K and offspring. Mrs Z left maidless. That's the long and the short of it, for Conrad can't, or won't, give us any more.'

'And the paper – Conrad's precious paper, which smelled of violets?' I asked. 'Do we know any more of that?'

Having licked his thumb and forefinger, Inspector Gully turned over the pages of his note-book once more.

'A letter, I think we may safely assume. Contents unknown. Recipient? Also unknown, but we might further assume the noble cousin, Lord Tansor – Conrad, of course, could not read the direction.'

Piecing together what he had managed to get out of Conrad, the inspector gave us the following tentative account of how he had acquired the letter.

Conrad, it seems, is waiting to take a letter to the post office; but, just as Mrs Zaluski is sealing it, she knocks a bottle of perfume over the envelope, and Conrad has to wait for it to dry.

Off he trips to the post office at last; but the letter is never sent, for by now he has become infatuated with the beauteous and unattainable Mrs Zaluski and, in his simple devotion, he keeps the perfumed letter. He is unable to read it; but it is hers, and it has her scent upon it, and that is all he cares about.

Mrs Kraus and her son – abandoned, it seems, by their mistress as a result of the unpleasant incident in Franzenbad – at last, and after many hardships, arrive back in England. Conrad conceals the letter in his room, but takes it out every day, for its lingering scent of violets always reminds him of his faery queen.

So things might have gone on, no doubt, if his mother had not discovered his treasured paper.

'Whatever was in that letter,' said Mr Wraxall, 'other than the faded scent of violets, must have offered Mrs Kraus a powerful weapon to use against her former employer, for whom she clearly harboured considerable animosity. It is, without question, the key to the whole business. It unlocks everything. But it was also Mrs Kraus's death-warrant. Bad as she may have been, she did not deserve her fate. Like the death of Paul Carteret, this was a wicked thing that was done to her, my friends, a wicked thing.'

He shook his head.

'What kind of person was Mrs Kraus?' I asked, remembering the unpleasant old woman in the Duport Arms.

'According to what the inspector here tells me,' replied Mr Wraxall, 'she was ambitious to improve herself, by whatever means she could. Her father, I think you said, Gully, was a German immigrant, a watch-maker by trade. She'd received a little schooling, gaining thereby some superficial accomplishments, and married Manfred Kraus, her father's apprentice; but after he died, she took up with a certain Lemuel Burlap, a petty rogue and sharp, long known to the police.

'She then obtained a position in the household of the Duke of Eastcastle, on the strength of which she was recommended by Lord Tansor to accompany Miss Carteret to the Continent.

'On her eventual return to England, after the Franzenbad incident, Mrs K and her son lodged for a time with Burlap; but after he was transported – what year was that, Gully?'

'In '67,' replied the Inspector, without a thought.

'Ah, yes, '67, to be sure. After Burlap had been taken off, Mrs K was thrown back on her own, none-too-scrupulous resources. Time passes, and life gets ever harder; but then she finds the letter.'

'Ah, the letter,' repeated the inspector. 'Back yet again, Mr W, to the letter.'

'Yes, indeed, Gully,' said the barrister. 'Unfortunately, we must presume that it has now gone for ever. Yet although the words on the paper may be lost to us, I believe that some invisible residue of the truth remains, which we can still strive to infer, or guess at, or deduce. Yes, it is my experience that something always remains – like the faintly lingering perfume that entranced Conrad for so many years. It's for us to sniff it out, and put a name to it. And we shall, we shall. It's all a question of time.'

The two men had fallen silent; but I sensed an unspoken intimation of some mutual, although as yet incompletely formed, apprehension.

'Time,' said Mr Wraxall, after a period of significant silence.

He tented his fingers over his mouth and closed his eyes, as if the better to contemplate the implications of the word.

'Of the essence, Mr W?' suggested the inspector.

Mr Wraxall did not answer, but continued to sit, eyes closed, tapping the tips of his fingers together.

'Penny for them, Mr W?'

The barrister opens his eyes, and looks benignly at the inspector.

'I was merely wondering why Miss Emily Carteret was intent on finding a husband so soon after the death of her beloved fiancé. Curious, don't you think?'

IV
An Unwelcome Prospect

UNTIL THE FINAL day, the rest of our time in London proved largely uneventful. Emily, still confined to the house on the doctor's orders, insisted on my keeping her company; and so, to my frustration, I was obliged to remain in Grosvenor Square, passing the long hours reading to her, or conversing on books or public affairs, or the tedious doings of Lady or Miss So and So.

Sometimes, however, a mood of melancholy and listlessness would overcome her, and then she simply wished me to sit by her, with my still unfinished work, as she lay on the sofa under her rugs, silently looking out of the window at the dreary metropolitan sky.

After luncheon, she would usually drift off to sleep for an hour or so, and I would put down my work to study her face in repose. It sometimes seemed as if death had taken her, so still, pale, and life-less did she seem. Once, I even took up a hand-mirror and stood over her, to assure myself, by seeing her breath mist over the glass, that she still lived.

Despite the signs of encroaching age, which she concealed so skillfully, and of which few but myself were ever aware, the striking beauty of her features – her full sculptured lips, the long slender nose, finely arched eye-brows and delicately mounded cheeks, all framed by her still-lustrous black hair – exerted a continual fascina-tion for me, as I now knew that they had done for my father, whose love for her had proved his undoing.

One afternoon, having always been considered by Madame and Mr Thornhaugh as possessing a talent for drawing, a gift, it seems, that I had inherited from my mother, I took out my note-book in an attempt to make a likeness of her as she slept; but it did so little justice to the original that I ripped out the page and threw it on the fire.

It was impossible not to wonder what dreams came to her behind those closed, long-lashed eye-lids. Her afternoon slumbers seemed tranquil, untroubled by the terrors that came to her by night. Per-haps she saw again the sunlit days – before the world was darkened by her iniquities; before she implicated herself in betrayal and murder – when she was simply Miss Emily Carteret, the universally admired daughter of Mr Paul Carteret, of the Dower House, Even-wood, untouched then by the torments of guilty memory, or the deadly darts of foreboding.

As I now read over the foregoing, and what I have written else-where in these pages, I am struck once more by the capricious and inconsistent nature of my feelings for Lady Tansor. I knew now that she had been a calamity in my father's life, and I had been instructed to hate her for it by Madame, my adored guardian angel. Of course I wanted her brought to account and punished for what she had done. I would sit, watching her sleep, knowing that her treachery had driven my father to commit murder, depriving me, too, of the life that I had been born to lead, and then my resolve would revive and harden; but when she woke, giving me a drowsy smile as she stirred lazily beneath her mound of rugs, in a moment all my righteous anger would dissolve quite away.

It sometimes happened – as on this afternoon – that I even began to question once more my fitness for the Great Task. I was so young, so inexperienced, so untested in the dangerous commission that I had been sent to Evenwood to discharge. I felt sick with consternation at what still lay ahead, and by the weight of responsibility that I had been required to bear by Madame and my dead father.

Such discomposing thoughts were running through my head on our last day in Grosvenor Square. I had been sitting, an unopened book on my lap, as Emily slept, reflecting on recent events. Engrossed as I was with my own thoughts, I did not notice that she had awoken.

'Alice, dear,' she said, sleepily, giving me a languid smile, 'there you are, as always when I wake. Like Patience on a monument. Such a good girl – such a good friend.'

More compliments followed, fondly and – apparently – sincerely expressed. Once again, although I tried to resist it, her sorcerous charm began to work on my resolve. Could she really be guilty of the crimes that both Madame and Mr Wraxall had accused her of? Might she not have been compelled, against both will and conscience, to commit them, first by her unquestioning love for Phoebus Daunt, then later by her desperation to keep them from discovery?

She still possessed a troublesome conscience – that was only too apparent from the constant assault on peaceful sleep by her nightterrors; and this might, perhaps, argue for a more lenient view of her character. So, under her drowsily mesmeric gaze, I reasoned; but then, in an instant, the spell was broken.

'Oh, by the way,' she suddenly said, in the most casually peremptory tone. 'Dr Manley has recommended that I should leave England for the remainder of the winter. He believes a change of climate is essential. I shall make the arrangements as soon as we return to Evenwood. Could you please ring for tea? I have a rather dry throat.'

At which, without another word, she took up her magazine, opened it, and began to read.

I was dumbstruck.

'Leave England? For how long?'

She looked up, and removed her spectacles.

'That, I think, is for me to decide.'

'Do you tell me this as your friend, or as your paid companion?' I asked, as calmly as I could. The question produced an immediate riposte.

'Your forget yourself, Alice,' she snapped, her expression tightening. 'This has nothing to do with our friendship. I intend to take Dr Manley's advice, and there's an end to it.'

I saw that further remonstrance on my part would be useless. She had given no thought to consulting me, but had taken her decision only in accordance with her own wishes – as my mistress once again, not as the true friend she purported to be. This, then, was what the equality of friendship meant to her.

Lord, I had been a gullible fool! Madame had warned me that I could not depend on a continuity of favour from Lady Tansor, even when intimacy between us had been established; for her friendship would always be infected by pride and self-interest, and by the constant desire to retain the superiority of her condition.

'You speak as if you don't wish to accompany me,' she said, fixing me with one of her cold stares. 'Is that how it is?'

'Not at all,' I replied, forcing myself to smile in an earnest and propitiatory manner, and reaching forward to take her hand. 'Nothing would be more agreeable to me; and if it is for the benefit of your health, then of course it's what I would wish above anything in the world.'

Although she said nothing, I saw that she had been a little mollified by my acquiescent words; and so I asked her, now mustering up a show of false eagerness, where we were to go.

'I have not quite decided,' she said, 'but Dr Manley has recommended Madeira.'

27

The Temptation of Mr Perseus

I
Mr Perseus Takes My Part

'MADEIRA!'

At a stroke, all my plans had been thrown into confusion. Leaving England was the very last thing that I had anticipated, as well as the least desired. The Great Task demanded that I must put aside all personal considerations, and find a way to marry Mr Perseus if I could, even though I continued to feel that such a thing was beyond my power to achieve. Delay might prove fatal; and for the reason I shall now relate.

Emily had lately informed me that it was her eldest son's intention shortly to take up residence in one of the many London properties owned by the family, as being more convenient for the furtherance of his literary career. Perseus Duport in London! The heir to the Tansor Barony – and a poet to boot! What an irresistible honey-pot he would be for every unattached young lady of fortune and rank in London to buzz round – just as Mr Maurice FitzMaurice and others buzzed round his mother.

Emily had often spoken of her ambitions for her favourite son, the greatest of which was an early marriage, in order to secure an heir of the next generation; for she was as zealous as her predecessor had been to ensure the continuity of her line. What if I returned from Madeira to find that he had been ensnared by some scheming beauty, or had even – Lord forbid! – fallen in love, leaving my father's dream of restoring his birthright through me forever unrealized? Did I also feel a stab of painful apprehension on my own account that, faint though the hope of marrying him was, his affections might be bestowed on another? I did – I own it; but our proposed destination caused me further alarm. Had Madeira really been Dr Manley's unbiased recommendation, or was there some more ominous motive at work?

Plunged as I was into confusion and uncertainty by this sudden turn of events, suspicions began to take hold in my mind that Emily had discovered my true identity; that she did not really intend to go to Madeira at all, but was playing some subtle game with me, using her knowledge of who I really was, first to taunt, and then to expose me.

Detecting the anxiety caused by these disquieting thoughts in my involuntary exclamation, Emily had once again fixed me with one of her most Delphic stares.

'Why do you sound surprised that I should wish to go to Madeira?' she asked, querulously. 'Dr Manley says that it would be the very best place for my recuperation, and for its agreeable English society. Many of my acquaintance have also told me of the beneficent effects of the climate, and yet you seem strangely unwilling to go there. Why is that?'

'I only meant that I am a rather bad sailor – and the voyage is a long one, I think.'

I hoped that she might regard this excuse sympathetically; instead, she became even more indignant.

'Really, Alice, that's extremely selfish of you. Is not my health more important than a little temporary discomfort? It surprises me very much – very much indeed – that you should say such a thing.'

As she continues to chide me, I perceive the absurdity of my earlier fears, realizing now that she is only being herself – the spoiled child she has always been, and will always be: vain, egotistical, and intolerant of the slightest trace of presumption on the part of those – almost the majority of her fellow creatures – whom she considers to be below her. My confidence now restored that she remains unaware of my secret self, I decide to submit apologetically, know-ing also that she will not be argued out of her decision to go to Madeira in her present aggrieved mood.

The effect is immediate. Her look softens; I ring for tea; and tranquillity is soon restored.

'Now, dear,' she says, as the maid comes in to light the lamps, 'we must begin to make our plans. I shall need new clothes, of course, as will you, and so we shall delay our return to Evenwood tomorrow until the afternoon, in order to make that trip to Regent Street I promised. Goodness, I'm feeling revived already! Dr Manley is right. I have been too long in England. A change of scene, and blessed sunshine, is exactly what I need to restore my spirits.'

She is then seized by the notion of writing to Sir Marcus Leveret, to ask whether he would arrange suitable accommodation in Lis-bon, our first port of call before the onward journey to Madeira.

'Paper, dear – quickly! – and something to write with!'

She gestures, with excited impatience, towards the writing-desk.

'We must make notes as we go along, you know,' she says as I return to the sofa with several sheets of paper and a pencil. 'There are so many things to remember.'

For the rest of the afternoon, she feverishly busies herself with making lists of all the things we shall require for our journey, and with scribbling notes to herself. The next morning, we ride off in the carriage to Regent Street. Emily is pale, and I can see that she has not slept well, although she did not call me to sit with her. Once at our destination, however, she appears to rouse herself, and we spend three hours in various opulent, glass-fronted emporia, where of course Emily is treated with the utmost servility, until she has ticked off all the items on her lists and I have been measured for several new gowns. At last we return to Grosvenor Square to rest until it is time to catch our train.

As we set off, I glance idly out of the carriage window.

A man is standing on the corner of North Audley Street. A man with white hair, and thick black eye-brows.

•   •   •

THE FOLLOWING EVENING, Emily and I dined alone in the Crimson-and-Gold Dining-Room.

Mr Randolph was still absent, in Wales once more with his friend Mr Rhys Paget, whilst Mr Perseus was sequestered upstairs, at work on a new poem. Later, however, he came down to the Drawing-Room, where Emily and I were reading by the fire.

'Perseus, dear,' cooed his mother as he entered, 'there you are. Come and sit with us. We missed you at dinner.'

This being the first time that we had met since our return from Town, and no doubt mindful of his mother's presence, he was obliged to put on a show of civility towards me. Settling himself on the sofa next to his mother, he began to ask, in a mechanical tone, a number of predictable questions. Had I enjoyed my stay in London? Which of the sights had I found most interesting? Was not the Victoria Embankment one of the great marvels of the age? To these, and his other enquiries, I replied courteously, but briefly, being aware of Emily's searching eye upon me.

'And now,' he continued, sounding a little piqued, 'you're to go further afield, I think. To Madeira, I hear.'

Emily closed her book, and laid it aside. Seeing this, Perseus enquired what she had been reading.

'Oh,' she said, with a careless air, 'only Mr Harcourt's hand-book to Madeira.'*

Mr Perseus reached over to pick up the book, and then began to leaf cursorily through it. He was on the point of closing it up again when he paused.

'Where did this come from?' he asked, flicking back through the preliminary pages. 'Not from the Library – it has no book-plate.'

To my amazement, his mother began to blush.

'It belongs to Mr Shillito.'

---

* Edward Vernon Harcourt (1825–91), naturalist and MP for Oxford from 1878 to 1885. His *Sketch of Madeira; containing information for the traveller, or invalid visitor* had been published in 1851.

'Shillito? How did you come by it?'

Although she struggled to conceal it, Emily's discomfiture was only too plain; indeed, I could not recall having seen her placed in such an awkward position before, and was on tenterhooks to know the cause of her embarrassment. Yet even under the inquisitive stare of her son, she quickly regained her composure.

'If you must know,' she said, 'it was obtained for me from Mr Shillito by Mr Vyse, who then kindly arranged for it to be sent over to Grosvenor Square.'

The heir did not appear to find this explanation to his liking.

'Ah, Mr Vyse!' he exclaimed, with an ironic smile. 'I should have known. He seems to have become quite indispensable to you, Mother.'

Emily bridled slightly; but nothing her son said, it seemed, could provoke her.

'Not indispensable, dear,' she said, calmly; 'but Mr Vyse has been a good friend to me, and to our family, since your father died, as you must know, and I continue to value his advice.'

'Did Mr Vyse advise on where you should go to recuperate?'

'No. He merely endorsed Dr Manley's recommendation.'

'I see. But has Mr Vyse been to Madeira himself?'

'I do not believe so; but of course his friend, Mr Shillito, knows the island well, having passed several months there some years ago. Don't you remember, dear? It was the most remarkable thing, but he recalled meeting a man there by the name of Gorst. Such a curious coincidence, was it not?'

'Not so very curious,' Mr Perseus replied. 'There must be many people in the world who share the name, and it is not beyond impossibility that one of these may have visited Madeira at the same time as Shillito. Besides, what does it matter, one way or the other?'

I was grateful to him for taking my part, and he saw it. Yet here was a curious thing. Having given him an appreciative look, which he appeared, by the merest inclination of his head, to acknowledge, I experienced a faint, though fleeting, current of mutual feeling flowing between us. It was gone in an instant, but it thrilled and encouraged me nevertheless.

'It matters, dear,' Emily was now saying to her son, 'because it is possible that this person Mr Shillito met on Madeira might have been related to Alice.'

'I think Miss Gorst said that she was not aware of any family association with the island – am I right, Miss Gorst?'

I looked up from my book, which I had been pretending to read with avid attention, and confirmed that he was correct.

'But that means nothing,' Emily objected. 'Your guardian, Madame Bertaud, might not have known that your father, for instance, had visited the island.'

For a second time, Mr Perseus takes it upon himself to interject on my behalf.

'Really, Mother. Miss Gorst has told us that she knows of no family connexion with Madeira, and that should suffice. Even if the man that Shillito met there was her father, I ask again: what does it matter?'

'I merely feel that it would be interesting for Alice to learn something concerning her father that she did not previously know, especially now that she is to visit Madeira for herself.'

'Perhaps,' he returns, looking towards me, 'that's for Miss Gorst to decide.'

'If you please,' I say, feeling their eyes upon me, 'I would prefer it if we changed the subject. I never knew my father, and I have always found a kind of solace in my ignorance, which I would like to preserve if possible.'

'You see, Mother?' says my new champion. 'Miss Gorst finds the subject disagreeable, so let there be an end to it.'

'Very well, dear,' Emily replies, with an indulgent smile. 'You are in a rather cross mood, I see. I expect you've been working too hard, and smoking too much. But by all means let us speak no more about Madeira. In any case, I am feeling rather tired now. I shall retire early, I think.'

So saying, she picks up Mr Shillito's book, kisses her son, and leaves the room, without saying a word to me.

II
I Put On a New Mask

AFTER EMILY HAS gone, and the Drawing-Room door has been softly closed by the footman on duty, I am left alone with Mr Perseus Duport.

I struggle, without success, to think of something to say; and so, after a short period of strained silence, I make to leave but he immediately leaps to his feet.

'Before you go, Miss Gorst, I have something I wish to say to you. Will you hear me out? It concerns our conversation, after you had been walking by the Lake with my brother.'

He hesitates for a moment, and then clears his throat.

'I should not have spoken as I did,' he resumes, 'and so I hope you will forgive me. I promise to conduct myself in a better fashion henceforth.'

His words, though few, are expressed with a simple, unassuming sincerity that touches my heart, for I see how much it has cost his proud nature to speak in this unaccustomed way.

I tell him that I would never presume to seek forgiveness from my Lady's eldest son for anything he might choose to say to me, to which he gives a little dip of his head to signal his appreciation of my words. I then thank him for his kindness in taking my part on the matter of his mother's proposed trip to Madeira.

'As to that,' he replies, 'thanks are unnecessary. You have your reasons, it seems, for not wishing to go there, and I have mine for preferring that my mother should go elsewhere for her recuperation.'

'But it seems that her mind is made up,' I reply, 'and of course I must go with her, wherever she decides.'

'Well,' he says, 'let us see what can be done. My mother ought to consider your wishes in this matter, for it's very clear that you have become more than a paid companion to her. She has been too much alone since my father's death, and has fallen under – let us just say undesirable influences. But you have been good for her, Miss Gorst, for which you have my gratitude.'

'I can assure you, sir, that I shall always do my best to serve your mother as she deserves.'

He assures me in return that he has no doubt of it. I wish him good-night and start to move away, but he takes a step forward to prevent me.

'With your permission, Miss Gorst, I have just one more thing to say.'

He holds me with his beautiful eyes, so like his mother's, in which I can see the flickering flames from the fire behind me reflected back. I am suddenly aware that my throat is dry, and that my heart is beating a little faster.

'I recall that, during our previous conversation, you favoured me with a confidence concerning your feelings for my brother. You assured me, I think, that your regard for him was of an unexceptional character – I believe those were your words?'

I confirm that his recollection is correct.

'May I ask, then, Miss Gorst, whether you would be willing to inform me concerning the nature of my brother's feelings for *you*?'

'Perhaps, sir,' I reply, a little unsettled now, 'you should put that question to Mr Randolph Duport.'

'My brother and I are not in the habit of sharing confidences.' The tone of his voice is now a little harder, the set of his handsome face a little sterner. 'As will have been apparent to you, Miss Gorst, Randolph and I are so very different, in every way. Even as boys we led our separate lives, and have continued to do so. My position in the family has also put a certain distance between us. My brother has a convivial way about him, which wins people over. He is an excellent shot, rides famously well to hounds, and I freely acknowledge his superiority at billiards. But he lacks both ambition and application, and possesses little of the true Duport character. If some misfortune were to befall me, and he should succeed our mother in my stead, what use will billiards be then? The things that matter most – I refer of course to the family's many interests and, above all, to the duty we owe to those from whom we have inherited everything we both now enjoy – mean little to my brother. To me, however, they are everything.'

He has now reverted to his customary manner and is once again the 27th Lord Tansor in waiting, proud and cold.

'We have become strangers to each other, my brother and I,' he resumes, 'which is why I have ventured to ask *you*, Miss Gorst, whether you believe that his regard for you is of the same unexceptional character as you assure me yours is for him.'

How am I to answer him? I am convinced that Mr Randolph loves me, and that he wishes to make me his wife; yet even though I must reject his proposal when it comes, I draw back from confessing the truth to his brother, feeling certain that no good will come of it for either Mr Randolph or myself. A little jealousy on Mr Perseus's part might perhaps aid my cause, but I cannot take the risk that it might also damage it irreversibly.

I therefore boldly meet his anticipating stare and say that I really cannot speak for Mr Randolph Duport, but that I have no reason to believe that his feelings for me are any different from mine for him. I regret the lie, but the gratified look on Mr Perseus's face immediately vindicates the need to tell it.

'I was in error, then?' he asks, after a brief reflective pause.

'In error?'

'To believe that an understanding, of a personal nature, exists between you and my brother?'

'Has he said this?' I ask, confident that he has not.

'As I told you, Randolph and I are not in the habit of sharing confidences. He has said nothing to me.'

'Mr Randolph has been very kind to me,' I admit. 'But as you yourself remarked, he has a convivial way about him, and I confess that I find his company agreeable, as he appears to find mine. But as to an understanding, as you call it, that is altogether another matter.'

'I am glad to hear it,' is his reply. This is all he says, but I see the relief in his eyes that even he cannot conceal.

He accompanies me to the door, and we walk in silence to the foot of the vestibule staircase, where we stand again in front of the portrait of the Turkish Corsair.

'You mentioned certain undesirable influences on her Ladyship,' I hesitantly remark.

'I think you know the – gentleman – to whom I was referring.'

'May I ask whether you believe that this person has had a hand in your mother's decision to travel to Madeira?'

'That is possible,' he returns, 'although the reason for his doing so is unclear to me at present. It is enough, however, that the likelihood of an involvement exists. I shall speak to my mother tomorrow on the subject. And so, Miss Gorst, I shall wish you good-night.'

He gives me an unsmiling bow, and looks towards the glazed front door.

'I see the rain has stopped. I think I shall take a turn on the terrace. I have a good deal to think about. Good-night again, Miss Gorst.'

III
Mr Randolph Returns

ON MY WAY upstairs, I come across Mrs Battersby leaving Mr Randolph's room. It is the first time that we have met for some weeks – no more invitations to take tea with her having been made.

I wish her good-evening and then ask whether Mr Randolph has returned, being surprised to find her in such a place at ten o'clock in the evening. Surely any duties she might have been required to carry out in preparation for Mr Randolph's return ought to have been completed before now?

'I believe he is expected tomorrow morning, with Mr Rhys Paget,' comes the reply. She then makes a little curtsey, gives me one of her most baffling smiles, as if she has got the better of me in some unaccountable way, and departs.

Once in my room, I sit down at my desk to begin writing a letter to Madame, relating the events of the last few days in London, and informing her of what had passed that evening with Mr Perseus; but I soon put down my pen and take myself off to bed.

I am greatly fatigued, but sleep proves impossible. I toss and turn until the Chapel bell strikes six o'clock. With pounding head,

I rise, dress, and go downstairs to take a dose of cold early-morning air.

I walk aimlessly for some time up and down the Library Terrace, but my head continues to whirl bewilderingly. A gauzy mist hangs over the Evenbrook; but there is a promise of a fine day to come, and a sense that, although it is still only January, winter is already slowly slackening its grip.

After a while, I make my way to the Entrance Court. From here I have a clear view of the carriage-road, down which a man is walking. I soon recognize the reassuring person of Captain Willoughby on his regular morning patrol. As he draws closer, he stops to remove his hat in salute, which I return with a wave before he continues on his way.

Seeing the captain brings a degree of composure to my overwrought brain. I then notice two more figures making their way down the Rise to the bridge.

I stand watching them as they draw closer and eventually enter the Court. One is an ascetic-looking, dark-complexioned young man; the other is Mr Randolph.

'Miss Gorst! What an early bird you are!' he cries.

He then introduces me, in his usual genial way, to his companion, Mr Rhys Paget, describing me as his mother's companion; but nothing in his look or manner conveys the slightest intimation that I mean more to him than this; neither does anything in Mr Paget's demeanour suggest that he is aware of his friend's amorous feelings for me. I had naturally thought that Mr Randolph would have confided in his closest friend; but it seems that he has not yet done so. I deduce from this that he is waiting to confess his true feelings to me first.

'We came back late last night,' Mr Randolph announces, 'and put up at the Duport Arms. But Paget was all for getting up early and walking over to take our breakfast here.'

'And do you stay long at Evenwood, Mr Paget?' I ask.

Instead of answering, he shoots an enquiring glance at his companion.

'Paget and I leave for Town in the morning,' the latter inter-

poses. 'A little excursion. We've had our fill, for the time being, of
wild Nature. It's bricks and mortar and smoke for us – for a while, at
least. Paget has some business to conduct, and I'm to be his guide
to the capital.'

'You see how it is, Miss Gorst,' says Mr Paget, in a charming lilting accent. 'I'm but a poor country mouse. Never been to London
in my life – strange, I know; but there it is.'

'And when do you return to Evenwood?' I ask.

'We've no definite plans,' Mr Randolph replies. 'A few days perhaps – a week if the fancy takes us.'

'Then you are not aware of Lady Tansor's intention to go to
Madeira?'

The news surprises him but, curiously, he seems rather relieved
than otherwise.

We stand for several more minutes, conversing on the subject
of Madeira. Mr Randolph appears increasingly ill at ease, and awkward, whilst his friend, towards whom he glances from time to time
in a suggestive way, stands mutely regarding the gravel at his feet in
an almost shamefaced manner that only adds to my puzzlement.

'Well, come along, Paget,' Mr Randolph says at last. 'That walk
has done the trick. I could eat a horse. Will you join us for breakfast, Miss Gorst?'

I demur, saying that I have a letter to finish writing.

We enter the house together.

'Through there,' says Mr Randolph to his friend, pointing
towards the door that leads to the Breakfast-Room. 'I just want a
word with Miss Gorst.' Then, as Mr Paget departs, he turns to me.

'Well, Esperanza,' he says, 'it seems that circumstances have
overtaken us. I'd hoped to speak to you on, well, you know – on the
matter we spoke of on our walk; but I suppose it will now have to
wait until your return from Madeira. Today is out of the question,
I'm sorry to say. Paget and I have a great deal to do, and we're to stay
the night at the George in Stamford – early train, I'm afraid. But
perhaps it's for the best. I'm sure Mother will be keeping you busy
also. I expect she's already making lists! Madeira, eh? Mr Shillito
says it's a capital place.'

His words trail off, as if he is at a loss to know what to say next. Then he suddenly brightens.

'Now then,' he says, 'it's a plate of chops for me, if Paget hasn't eaten them all!'

With a strained smile, he wishes me good-morning, and marches quickly off to the Breakfast-Room, leaving me baffled by his nervous and embarrassed manner, but relieved that the private conversation he wishes to have with me has been postponed until after our return from Madeira.

THE LATTER PART of the morning was spent with Emily in her apartments. Just before luncheon, there was a knock at the door, and in strode Mr Perseus.

'Miss Gorst,' he said. 'Would you excuse us? I wish to speak to my mother on a private matter.'

I was not called again until tea-time. Emily was by the fire in her sitting-room, an atlas open on her lap.

'Come and sit down, Alice dear,' she said eagerly. 'Our plans have changed. We shall not be going to Madeira after all. Perseus has persuaded me that Italy is the place.'

'Italy?'

'He has suggested that we go to Florence. Perseus is to come with us – he has conceived a wonderful new poem, on the subject of Dante and Beatrice. Won't that be splendid?'

28

To the South

I
An Unexpected Visitor

THUS IT was decided. Florence it was to be.

Mr Perseus immediately took over all the arrangements, and we left Evenwood at the end of January 1877, to spend a night in Grosvenor Square, before catching the early boat-train the next morning. It was a great relief to me that the Madeiran plan had been abandoned; and having Mr Perseus accompanying us would, I hoped, present daily opportunities to try what I could to entice him into marriage, as I had been instructed to do.

Mr Randolph and his friend had preceded us to Grosvenor Square. On the morning of our departure, they both came down to the front steps to see us off. Mr Randolph seemed unusually reserved and nervy – Mr Paget also – as he kissed his mother, and coldly shook hands with Mr Perseus. We exchanged a few awkwardly hurried words of farewell, after which the two friends went back into the house.

As we pulled away, I caught a brief glimpse of the pair, huddled just inside the front door, heads together. Mr Randolph had not even favoured me with a departing wave.

We proceeded to the terminus in silence – a most dismal trio. Mr Perseus was in one of his most frostily silent moods; I was musing on the marked change in Mr Randolph; whilst Emily, as I guessed, had another matter on her mind.

Three days earlier, at about ten o'clock in the morning, just as I was descending the stairs from the Picture Gallery, I had heard the crunch of carriage wheels on the gravel of the Entrance Court. Within a few minutes, I learned from Barrington that we had an unexpected visitor.

'Mr Armitage Vyse, miss. He wishes – most insistently – to see her Ladyship on a pressing matter of business.'

I immediately ran back upstairs to fetch the key to the closet from where I had previously spied upon the two conspirators. Once at my point of vantage, I drew out my note-book and pencil, in order to set down in shorthand what passed between them.

Through one of the little yellow roundels, I could see Emily on the window-seat, her eyes open to their fullest extent, black and impenetrable. Mr Vyse was loping backwards and forwards in front of her, shoulders hunched, a furious look on his wolfish face. His tall, gangling figure, dressed in a bottle-green velvet coat and tight mulberry-coloured trousers strapped over his shining boots, presented a strangely mesmerizing sight. All I could think of as I watched him was the horrible picture of the great, long, red-legged scissor-man in Hoffmann's picture-book,* which Mr Thornhaugh used to read to me as a child.

'Not going!' he snarls exasperatedly. 'Not going! When I told you – I mean, of course, *advised* you – that you must go? How else can we begin to prove who your new friend really is? Depend upon it, she knows that the man Shillito met, who called himself Gorst, was her father, although she denies it. There would undoubtedly have been people still resident on the island who also remembered him – and now you say you won't go! How many times have I told you that your precious companion is not who she claims to be, and that she's here

---

*Der Struwwelpeter ['Shock-headed or Slovenly Peter'] by Heinrich Hoffmann (1809–74), an illustrated book of cautionary tales for children first published in German in 1845, and in an anonymous and hugely popular English version in 1848.

to work against us? Yet you continue to trust her! Now we've lost a golden chance to begin uncovering the truth about Miss Esperanza Gorst. This is badly done, my Lady, *very* badly done.'

To emphasize his displeasure, he slams the tip of his stick hard down on the floor-boards, in a most intimidating manner.

'Perseus did not wish me to go to Madeira,' says Emily, calmly defiant. 'And there's an end to it.'

'Perseus! You prefer to take the advice of your coxcomb son? What does he know of our business, or how it should best be conducted? You might as well have asked his fool of a brother.'

The look of insulted contempt that Emily gives him would have withered the nerve of a lesser man; but Mr Vyse continues to glare menacingly at her.

'I did not seek my son's opinion on the matter,' she says, facing him down with admirable composure. 'Perseus suspected that going to Madeira, although originally urged by Dr Manley, had been, in large part, dictated by you – and you know his opinion of you, Armitage. That suspicion was enough for him; and so he came to me and urged me – in the strongest terms – to go elsewhere. On reflection, I saw that he was right. I never wished to go to Madeira. A disagreeable sea-journey, and then to be cooped up on an island with such a small society – no, it would not have suited. I need space and liberty, as well as warmth. My son's recommendation that we should go to Italy instead, and that he should accompany us, perfectly coincided with my own inclinations. And so it's all settled, and everything is in hand. We are going to Florence.'

Her doggedness enrages Mr Vyse even more. He hovers over her, seeming now like some great predatory insect.

'You fool!' he hisses, casting aside all pretence of deference. 'Why will you not listen to me? *She – is – here – to – harm – you*. Why can you not see it? I have yet to discover why she's here, or who has sent her; but it's absurd to believe that she's not this man Gorst's daughter – the coincidence is too great. Every instinct tells me that, if we can once find out who *he* was, then we may begin to understand *her* secret purpose.'

'I ask again,' says Emily, immovably, 'as I've asked you before:

what makes you so certain that Alice is deceiving us? What has she done to make you suspect her?'

With a sigh, Mr Vyse settles himself beside her on the window-seat.

'Tell me, my Lady,' he says, in a wheedling tone, taking her hand in his, 'are you acquainted with a Mr John Lazarus?'

She says that she has never heard of such a person in her life.

'Mr Lazarus is a former shipping-agent,' Mr Vyse tells her, 'of Billiter Street, City. Now then: what reason, do you suppose, would your treasured companion have to visit this gentleman?'

When Emily says nothing, Mr Vyse releases her hand and begins to examine his perfectly manicured finger-nails in a most significant manner.

'Perhaps I should have mentioned,' he says, in a horrid knowing way, 'that Mr John Lazarus passed most of his professional life in the Atlantic wine trade, and that he had a residence on the island of Madeira.'

Emily's face now registers a faint flush of disquiet, although it is nothing to the shock I experience on hearing Mr Vyse's words. What a fool I had been! Of course he knew of my visit to Billiter Street – his man Digges had followed me there.

'Think for a moment,' urges Mr Vyse. 'How do you suppose that Miss Gorst came to know of this gentleman, or where to find him? Shillito didn't tell her, that's for sure. Someone else put her on to him.'

'Someone else? But who?'

'If we knew that,' he replies, quietly now, 'then we might know all.'

Emily now quits the window-seat and begins to pace up and down, her hands pressed to her temples.

'This is too much!' she exclaims. 'My head is fit to burst with all your insinuations. I must follow my heart, and my heart tells me that Alice has nothing to hide, and that there's a perfectly innocent explanation for these things. You must give me proof, Armitage – solid proof – if I'm to believe otherwise. Do you have it? No – I see you don't. This is all Mr Shillito's fault. What does he have to say on the matter? Does he still believe that he'd formerly known the man he met on Madeira under another name?'

'Alas!' sighs Mr Vyse. 'There now seems little likelihood that Shillito will ever be able to confirm the truth of his belief.'

'I knew it!' cries Emily, triumphantly.

'What do you know, my Lady?'

He rises slowly to his feet. They stand face to face.

'Do you know, for instance,' he resumes, 'that, last evening, in Finsbury Square, Shillito was attacked by two ruffians and left for dead?'

On receiving this cruel *coup de grâce*, Emily gasps.

'Mr Shillito attacked! What are you telling me?'

'I am telling you, my Lady, that my old friend Shillito, having sustained dreadful injuries about the head and face, and being presently deprived of the power of speech and movement, is not expected to live out the week. Any other man would already have succumbed to his injuries, but Shillito's skull was always notoriously thick.'

'But this can have nothing to do with Alice,' Emily insists. 'I am appalled, naturally; but surely this was a case of common assault. Was he robbed?'

Mr Vyse is obliged to admit that his friend's pocket-book and gold watch were indeed taken by his assailants.

'But of course it was cleverly done,' he quickly adds, 'to make it appear like an indiscriminate attack. There was a witness, you see, a man with a coffee-stall, who saw the two blackguards speaking beforehand, in what he describes as a familiar manner, to a tall, well-built, well-muffled gentleman – a gentleman, note. I deduce from this that chance played no part in the business, and that robbery was not the principal motive, only payment for the commission.'

This gives Emily some pause; but then, collecting herself somewhat, she asks again what the attack on Mr Shillito could possibly have to do with me.

'Nothing directly and knowingly, perhaps,' Mr Vyse grudgingly concedes. 'But indirectly and unknowingly? Well, then I should say that Miss Gorst is certainly implicated. For here, as in the matter of Mr John Lazarus, I discern the guiding hand of the Shadow.'

'The Shadow?'

Emily gives a derisive laugh.

'It's my name for the intelligence that I believe is directing events,' Mr Vyse explains. 'The person, if you will have it in plain words, who stands behind Miss Esperanza Gorst, like a second shadow.'

'Now you are being ridiculous,' returns Emily, with another derisive laugh. 'I've heard enough of these wild accusations and empty suppositions. First, we have a man Mr Shillito claims to have met twenty years ago who may, or may not, have been Alice's father. Now we have this mysterious "Shadow". They cannot, of course, be the same person, for we know from the enquiries you made in Paris that the Edwin Gorst who was certainly Alice's father is dead and buried in the St-Vincent Cemetery; and if your "Shadow" is not that Edwin Gorst, then who is he, and why – even supposing that he exists – has he sent Alice here? No, it's all nonsense, Armitage, and I'll hear no more of it.'

Mr Vyse, seeing at last that she will not be moved in her defence of my innocence, makes her a little bow of reluctant capitulation.

'Very well, my Lady,' he says, with a conciliatory smile, although patently stung by her wilfulness. 'We'll say no more on the matter of Miss Gorst, until I can place before you – as I'm confident I shall be able to do – the proof that you require. To demonstrate my generosity of spirit even further, you may go to Florence, if that is your wish. There's a condition, however, on which I must absolutely insist.'

He reaches out his arm and, in a most impertinent manner, takes and holds her chin in his hand.

'I think you know what it is.'

Still she stands, rigidly silent.

'I must have my answer when you return.'

A moment passes.

'You shall have your answer, never fear,' she says, pulling away. She then returns to the window-seat and places her cheek against the glass, as I have seen her do so many times before.

'Then I shall wish you "bon voyage", my Lady,' says Mr Vyse, assuming an air of mock affability; and with that, taking up his hat and stick, he leaves the room, humming quietly to himself.

AFTER MR VYSE had gone, Emily remained gazing meditatively out of the window.

I tip-toed from my hiding-place, locked the door again, and ran up to my room.

I was in a perilous situation: that was very clear. Emily appeared immune at present to Mr Vyse's suspicions of me; but doubts – however small – must have been planted in her mind, and he appeared determined to bring her the evidence of my duplicity that she had demanded. As for the attack on Mr Shillito, on this alone Mr Vyse must have been mistaken; for of course I was certain that it could have no connexion with me, or with the Great Task.

One more incident that occurred that day I must mention, trifling though it appeared at the time.

It was a chill afternoon and, feeling suddenly cold as I sat transcribing my shorthand account of what I had just heard into my Book of Secrets, I thought I would put a match to the fire, only to find that the grate was empty. I rang down for Mrs Battersby, to ask why the fire had not been laid; but it was Barrington who answered the summons.

'Where's Mrs Battersby?' I asked.

'If you please, miss,' replied the footman, in his usual funereal way, 'she's been given leave by her Ladyship to visit a sick relation in London – an aunt, I believe. She left yesterday evening.'

I felt a little piqued that Emily had not mentioned this to me; but as it seemed of such little account, I soon put it from my mind.

After the fire had been made up and lit by one of the housemaids, I passed the rest of the time before dinner writing to Madame assuring her that I would write often during our absence from Evenwood. I also sent off a short note to North Lodge, arranging for any communications from Mr Wraxall to be sent *poste restante* to Florence, adding in a postscript a few words concerning the attack on Mr Shillito. A reply was speedily received.

MY DEAR MISS GORST,—

 It shall be done as you request.

 The Shillito business is a strange and unexpected turn of events &
I can make little sense of it, tho' it interests me exceedingly & must, I
feel, have some connexion with our affairs. But do not concern yrself
about it, or about Mr Vyse. You will be safe in Florence, and when
you return, you will have me and others to watch over you.

 Until then, I remain, yours very sincerely,

 M.R.J. WRAXALL

II

The Palazzo Riccioni

OUR JOURNEY TO Florence was uneventful. Mr Perseus had not
wanted to tarry longer in France than was necessary, having a
decidedly disapproving – and, to me, unaccountably prejudicial –
view of the country and its inhabitants. This caused us immediately
to strike south, at all possible speed, to Lyons and Avignon, and
thence to Cannes, where we stayed in the late Lord Brougham's
beautiful villa,* and so on to Nice.

The way into Italy, along the steeply wooded Ligurian coast, was
delightful, even when the January rains sometimes swept in from
the choppy waters of the Mediterranean; but I never minded this,
for to me it rendered the little fishing ports, and the forests of lemon
trees and pine through which we passed all the more deliciously
romantic and picturesque.

Away from England, Emily's temper had quickly improved.
Her son's spirits, likewise, had visibly lightened as we had made
our way southwards. Although he often remained wrapped in
silent thought for long periods, he became increasingly attentive towards me the nearer we came to our destination; and on

---

* The Villa Eléonore-Louise, in the Avenue du Dr Picaud, built by Henry
Brougham, Baron Brougham and Vaux (1778–1868), in 1834–5.

the morning that we crossed into Italy, his manner had changed markedly.

'Italy!' he exclaimed, throwing down the carriage window and breathing in a draught of the clear warm air. 'The most beautiful, most noble country in the world! So much superior to France, in every way.'

Now to this absurd proposition I could not possibly agree; so I took courage, and told him so. There followed a playful duel of words, in which he extolled the scenic and national virtues of Italy, whilst I of course passionately championed those of the country of my birth. This quickly descended into a tit-for-tat exchange of the most ludicrous claims and counter-claims, which ended in laughs and smiles, and in an appeal to Emily to adjudicate on who had got the better of the other.

'I refuse to take sides,' she said, giving us both a smile of maternal indulgence. 'They are both great nations – although not as great as dear old England. But perhaps my son is teasing you, Alice, knowing that you were brought up in France.'

'You know I never tease,' said Mr Perseus. 'I am always perfectly serious. You may depend on it.'

After passing three pleasant days in Pisa, where we established ourselves most comfortably in the Hotel Gran Bretagna, we at last proceeded on the short final leg of our journey to Florence.

At two o'clock in the afternoon, amidst the sound of bells, and beneath a cloudless cerulean sky, we were set down before the imposing façade of the Palazzo Riccioni, within sight of the Church of S. Maria Novella.

THE PALAZZO HAD been secured by Mr Perseus from his godfather, Lord Inveravon; he had also taken a smaller country house, the Villa Campesi, a stone's throw from the Monastery of Vallombrosa.

The Palazzo was of considerable size, on four floors, with over thirty rooms – far more than our needs required. Emily's new maid, Miss Allardyce, had of course accompanied us, along with one of the Evenwood footmen, James Holt, an eager, strongly built lad of about my own age (chosen by Mr Pocock over Charlie Skinner, much to the latter's disgust), who had come as a general factotum. These two, together with a surly Italian cook, his wife, and daughter, constituted all our little household.

Having taken over a large chamber on the first floor for his study, Mr Perseus immediately set to work on his new poem, and on a collection of sonnets, which he had begun before leaving England. To these literary labours he dedicated many hours each day, and for the first two weeks of our residence I saw little of him, except when he would occasionally join Emily and me for dinner.

Being eager for me to see all the great sights of the city, Emily would rise early to compose a list of the palaces and churches and other places that she wished us to explore that morning. In the afternoons, however, overcome by the morning's exertions, she would retire to her apartment, leaving me to my own devices.

Then, of course, we had our social obligations – wearisome dinners with all the most prominent Italian and English residents of the city, receptions, a masked ball, evenings at the opera or the theatre. When even Emily tired of these diversions, we would remove to the Villa Campesi for a few days, to enjoy the country air, and take slow walks through tree-dense valleys. Sometimes we drove to the hamlet of Tosi, with its stone cross and its splendid views of mountains, rushing torrents, and deep, dark ravines, thickly clad with tumbling banks of dusky pine-woods, and wide tracts of beech and chestnut. Although leafless now, they foretold, in their abundance, the aptness of the glorious Miltonic simile describing the innumerable host of the rebel angels.*

I do not intend to present a day-to-day account of what passed during our time in Florence. Three events, however, I must set before you, which I shall now do, as briefly as I can, by recourse to extracts – fleshed out where necessary – from my Book of Secrets, which of course had accompanied me to Italy.

And so let us begin.

---

*Milton, *Paradise Lost* (i. 302): 'Thick as autumnal leaves that strow the brooks / In Vallombrosa . . .'

29

An Italian Spring

Florence: February–April 1877

I

S. Miniato

14TH FEBRUARY 1877

IN THE EARLY afternoon of St Valentine's Day, Mr Perseus came back from composing descriptions *in situ* of the Ponte Vecchio for his new poem on Dante and Beatrice. Usually, after such excursions, he would closet himself in his study; but today he declared himself tired of work. Would I care to walk with him, after he had taken some late luncheon, to S. Miniato al Monte? Gratified by such an invitation, and by the warm manner in which it had been made, I gladly accepted, for it offered the first opportunity since arriving in Florence to be alone with him.

Here follows the account of the first of the three events that I later wrote in my Book of Secrets.

OUR FIRST WALK
We leave the city by the Porta S. Miniato. A steep cypress-lined slope leads up to the Church of S. Salvatore al Monte: a most beautiful situation, with wonderful views of the city – a prospect much admired by Michelangelo, according to Mr P.

Conversation quietly general until returning home.

Mr P (abruptly changing the subject): *Are you happy in your present situation, Miss Gorst?*

EG (somewhat taken aback): *Perfectly, thank you.*

Mr P: *Do you not have any ambition to be more than you are at present?*

EG (unsure as to where this is leading): *Why should I wish to change what is entirely to my liking?*

Mr P: *Everyone should have ambition to better themselves.*

EG: *Most people in this world might regard such an ambition as a luxury they cannot afford. They are too concerned with present struggles.*

He seems a little put out by my Jacobinical tone. Silence descends. Then he asks whether I would not wish to escape my condition of dependence and servitude – for that, in his opinion, despite all its advantages, is what it is.

I enquire how I should escape it, even if I wished, for I have no other course of life open to me, no fortune but my own meagre talents, no expectations or prospects but those I must make for myself.

Mr P (after considering for a moment): *There are other, and better, states of dependency than the one you are presently required to accept. Have you never thought that you might one day marry?*

Of course my heart leaps at the question, even though it seems to have been put with complete disinterestedness.

I ask (assuming an air of mild indignation) how someone in my position could contemplate the possibility of a marriage that would remove the necessity of making my own way in the world. It is a large enough hint, but he does not take it, only nods his head, and says that he supposes that I am right.

We reach the Porta S. Miniato again to find ourselves caught up in a large crowd of people, who jostle us apart for a time.

Once we are reunited, Mr P asks whether I would ever wish

to return to France, or whether I now consider England to be my home.

I tell him that I shall always think of my former life with the greatest fondness and gratitude, but that I could not now foresee any reason for ever quitting England. This appears to please him, although all he says is 'Splendid!' and then that we must hurry back or we shall be late for tea.

On our return to the Palazzo R, he thanks me for the pleasure of my company. There seems to be nothing in his voice or manner beyond politeness, and yet I am sure I see a strained look in his eyes, as if he feels himself in the grip of some strengthening emotion, to which he is unused, and which he can neither control nor overcome. But perhaps my imagination is running away with me.

He ascends the stairs to his study. At the top, he turns for a moment to look back down at me; and then I am certain that I am not deceiving myself. Something is stirring in the heart of Mr Perseus Duport, as it is in mine.

So BEGAN THE almost daily routine of walking out with Perseus of an afternoon, either through the city, of which he had a great knowledge, having visited it on a number of previous occasions, or when we were at the Villa Campesi.

As the days passed, my pleasure in his company increased, in spite of his continuing to display a stubborn and provoking aloofness, and a disposition that seemed instinctively inclined to consider things from his own lofty and exceptional position. The flame of true affection, if not yet that of love, had been lit – of that I became increasingly persuaded, by sundry little signs in his manner towards me, even though his reticent temper checked any outward display of feeling. Having become an accomplished student of his mother's changeable moods, however, and having learned to interpret all the subtle means she employed to mask the true state of her feelings, I began to apply my skills to the similar habits of concealment that she appeared to have bequeathed to her eldest son.

His pride and self-regard being so easily ruffled, I adopted the same submissive and accommodating manner towards him that I had done towards his mother. Despite his frequent lapses into morose silences, I soon discovered that he possessed an enthusiastic volubility on certain topics: the poetry of Milton and Dante; the theories of Mr Darwin; Boccaccio; the organ music of the elder Bach (a passion, strangely, that he shared with Mr Thornhaugh); above all, anything associated with the ancient line to which he was the present heir, and of which I, too, although he did not yet know it, was also a part. When prompting him to hold forth on one of his favourite subjects – which he would do in a rather schoolmasterly, lecturing fashion – I would play the part of the admiring and appreciative pupil, thirsting at the fountain of his superior knowledge. It is an old trick, I dare say, but an effective one: a man, I soon discovered, likes nothing more than to be thought mentally superior to a woman. His knowledge, both specific and general, was not to be compared to Mr Thornhaugh's; but he was exceptionally well informed on a number of interesting subjects, besides his pet ones, and I was a practised and eager listener. I saw the satisfaction that my assumption of intellectual subordination gave him, and as each day passed, by the use of such surreptitious flattery, we began to grow ever more comfortable in each other's company.

II
A Letter from England

OVER TWO MONTHS had passed since we had left England. For some time, Emily had continued in good spirits, and her health seemed much improved by the beneficent effects of the Florentine climate and by the change of scene – aided, I was sure, by the temporary release from Mr Vyse's unwelcome attentions; and by some diminution of the terrible anxieties that had constantly afflicted her in England.

Then, in the first weeks of April, she began to show signs of a decline. Her face took on a worryingly wasted look; her hair, which I still occasionally brushed, became thin and lifeless; the natural, marmoreal paleness of her skin was now the pallor of infirmity; even her eyes – once so captivating in their uncommon size and luminous beauty – were sunken and watery.

She now rose late in the morning, took the lightest of breakfasts, and then sat listlessly in the salon, often with an unread book in her lap, until luncheon, after which she would return to her room until tea. Our explorations of the city ceased; evening engagements were cancelled; and she now rarely required me to attend her. One morning, however, I was called up to her room.

She was lying on a chaise-longue, a plaid rug laid over her, her eyes closed, when I knocked and entered. She said nothing for some moments; then she opened her eyes and looked at me with a kind of startled inquisitiveness, almost as if I were a trespassing stranger. In her right hand she held a partly crumpled letter.

Here follows what I later wrote in my Book:

CONVERSATION WITH LADY T

I sit down beside her and take up her left hand. She smiles weakly, gives a little cough, and says that she has something to tell me: we must return to England, sooner than expected. To my surprise, she admits that a crisis has occurred in her affairs, but will not say more. I show her, with a brief downwards glance, that I have seen the letter she holds in her other hand, and boldly ask who it is from.

Lady T: *It is from Mr Vyse. You will remember Mr Roderick Shillito, who came to Evenwood with Mr Vyse as a guest at Christmas. I regret to say that Mr Vyse informs me that he is dead.*

I naturally affect shock at this terrible news. Was he taken ill? I ask.

Lady T: *No. He was the victim of a most vicious attack, and was not expected to live more than a week. He survived for nearly two months, although he had lost the power of speech and movement.*

EG: *And is this why we must return to England?*

Lady T: *No. There are other reasons – matters to attend to. I have been away for too long. Time is short.*

She makes no further attempt to explain why she wishes to leave Florence. Our eyes meet; hers are tired and frightened. I see that she wishes to say something to me that gives her pain. With an effort she lets go of my hand and raises herself up to a sitting position.

Lady T: *It is time to be honest with each other, Alice. We owe it to our friendship. I must tell you that Mr Vyse suspects you of deceiving me. He believes that you are not who you say you are, and that you came to Evenwood to do me harm. Will you swear to me again, dearest Alice, that he is wrong?*

I give her the assurance she has requested, at great length, and with all the injured fervour I can muster. I tell her, over and over again, of my undying gratitude for what she has done for me, raising me up, a poor orphan, from lady's-maid, to companion, to what I am now: her ever-loving and most devoted friend. To my surprise, I even manage to produce a few tears, which I make no attempt to brush away. My ardent protestations appear to satisfy her; she lies back, and pulls the rug up to her chest, saying that she feels cold, although it is a fine warm day.

Then she says that she has something else to ask me.

Lady T: *It concerns a visit you made, when we were in London, to a Mr John Lazarus. Will you tell me how you know that gentleman, and why you went to his house?*

EG (affecting innocent surprise): *How – if I may ask – do you know that I visited Mr Lazarus?*

Lady T: *Please don't be cross, dear. Someone saw you – a friend of Mr Vyse's.*

EG: *A friend of Mr Vyse's? I see. How fortuitous! Of course I have no objection whatsoever to telling you the reason for seeking out Mr Lazarus, having nothing to hide from you. I merely wished to assure myself that Mr Shillito was wrong concerning the identity of the man he met on Madeira; and so I wrote to Mr Thornhaugh, to ask whether he would make some enquiries on my behalf. It was he who discovered, through a mutual acquaintance, that Mr Lazarus had spent many years on Madeira, and that he was well known amongst the English residents there. And so I went to see that gentleman, to ask whether he had known anyone by the name of Gorst.*

Lady T: *And what did you discover?*

EG: *That the man Mr Shillito knew could not have been my father, who would have been a much older man at the time, and who, from what I have been told of his physical appearance, did not resemble in the least the man Mr Shillito met.*

At this piece of spontaneous invention, Emily smiles in relief, lays her head on the pillow once more, and closes her eyes.

I sit in silent thought for several minutes, thinking she has fallen asleep. But then she startles me by suddenly opening her eyes in a wild stare.

Tears begin to course down her poor lined face, and she gives a low animal moan of despair. I take her hand and ask what is distressing her, but she only shakes her head. I tell her that she must rest, but she says she cannot, and that she has not slept for three nights past.

EG: *Why did you not call me? Perhaps I could have read to you.*

When she does not reply, I suggest that she might take a small dose of Battley's.

Lady T (eagerly): *Do you have some with you, then?*

I fetch the bottle and administer a dose to her. With a relieved sigh, she falls back on the chaise-longue.

'Rest now, dear,' I tell her. 'I shall make sure you're not disturbed.'

Within five minutes she has fallen fast asleep. I gently remove the letter from her cold hand. To my disappointment, it contains nothing of significance beyond the bare intelligence of Mr Shillito's death. Replacing it, I softly quit the room, leaving her to her opium dreams.

III
On the Ponte Vecchio
27TH APRIL 1877

WE BEGAN MAKING the arrangements for our return to England; but then, on the advice of her Italian doctor, our departure was postponed until Emily had regained sufficient strength for the long journey home. As a consequence of this delay, Mr Perseus took the opportunity to visit the distinguished Dante scholar, Professor Stefano Lombardi, in Rome, to discuss his poem. On the afternoon following his return to Florence, we resumed our walks. It was to be our last.

He spoke enthusiastically of the conversations that he had enjoyed with Professor Lombardi, and of the excellent progress he was making on his poem. We talked also of our imminent departure from Italy, both of us expressing regret that the climate had not effected the improvement in Emily's health that had been hoped for.

We were walking back from the Belvedere, speaking of our mutual concern for Emily, when he asked whether I would accompany him to the Ponte Vecchio before returning to the Palazzo Riccioni.

The Ponte Vecchio, like the Rialto in Venice, is a street of shops, mostly those of goldsmiths, jewellers, and other workers of precious stones and metals. Before one of these establishments, we now stopped.

Through the window, I could see the proprietor, Signor Silvaggio, as proclaimed by the sign above the door, looking expectantly out on noticing the distinctive person of Mr Perseus.

CONVERSATION WITH MR P

Mr P: *Will you excuse me for a moment? I have something to collect from here.*

I walk up and down for several minutes until he comes out of the shop holding a small velvet-covered box.

Mr P: *This is for you.*

I take the box, and open it.

Inside is the most exquisite ring of diamonds and rubies, which flash in the gradually westering sunlight gilding the Arno, and streaming through the arches of the ancient bridge.

EG: *Oh, but it's beautiful! But I don't understand. I cannot possibly accept such a gift.*

Mr P: *It is not a gift, Miss Gorst – Esperanza. It is something far more. Have you not guessed?*

He reaches forward to remove the ring from the box. He then takes my hand, and places the ring on my finger.

I am in a daze, almost faint with disbelief.

Mr P: *I have shocked you, I see. But surely you must know?*

EG (lost in delicious confusion of mind): *What must I know?*

Mr P (smiling now): *That this is a token of what I feel for you, and of what I wish us to be to each other. Will you accept it?*

This astonishing declaration is delivered in a stiff, matter-of-fact manner, as if he were offering me a glass of wine; yet I see so clearly in his eyes both that it is most ardently and wholeheartedly meant, and the earnest hope that the implied proposal will be accepted. Against every expectation, every hope, the flame had indeed taken hold, and cannot now, it seems, be extinguished. I am overcome with sheer, irresistible joy that the seemingly impossible goal that Madame set me appears to have been achieved so easily, and in so short a space of time. I am to marry Perseus Duport, the future Lord Tansor, and through our union my father's bloodline will be restored, and the Great Task accomplished. The gratifying sense of a solemn duty done, however, is as nothing to a far greater joy that now floods my heart. As I feel the ring encircle my finger, I know that I truly love Perseus Duport, that I will never love any other man, and – although he has not yet spoken the words I long to hear him say – that he loves me in return.

He tells me that he cannot now conceive of a future life of

any worth or meaning without me. Everything has changed for him. The world has been remade by my coming to Evenwood, and nothing can ever be the same again. He is no longer the Perseus Duport he was only six months since. I have enslaved him completely, heart, mind, and soul. He has been living in perpetual ferment from the day we first met, all the old certainties quite crumbled away, a prey to daily – hourly – pangs of uncertainty, self-doubt, and bitter jealousy that my affections had been given to his brother. Work has been his only solace, his only refuge from the storm that has engulfed him – what he calls this unremitting assault on his peace of mind. But work is no longer sufficient; nothing, indeed, can ever suffice, except the absolute assurance that our lives will henceforth be indissolubly bound together.

These things, these wonderful, unpredicted things, and many more besides, he now confesses, reciting each admission and demonstration of his regard for me in an almost disconcertingly straightforward manner, as if every one were the plainest and most incontestable fact in the world. But I do not mind the steady self-control his displays, or that he has not fallen to his knees like some heart-smitten lover of romance; for a plain and simple fact has ever been my delight, and I almost wish that I could take out my note-book to write down each one, so that I might have them all by me for constant reference, like Mr Walker's *Pronouncing Dictionary*, for the rest of my days.

Thus I stand on the Ponte Vecchio, for five glorious minutes and more, mutely listening to Mr Perseus Duport's declaration, with the afternoon sun in my eyes, in blissful disbelief.

What has happened is so utterly unanticipated, yet so completely in accordance with the entire inclination of my own heart, even though I have barely acknowledged my true feelings for him to myself, that at first I am unable to speak. I find my tongue at last, however, and begin to show a proper reluctance, as a wooed lady ought – at least as they often do in the novels I have read. I dip my head; I blush; I look away;

I take off the ring to give back to him, although he places it insistently back on my finger. Then, to test his resolve, I put up all the obvious objections – of which there are a great many. What will Lady Tansor say? She will forbid the match, surely? What will the world say? The scandal! The gossip! The disgrace! How can I possibly believe that he wishes to marry his mother's former maid? I have nothing to offer him – no fortune, no expectations, no family connexions. Surely such a marriage is impossible for the Tansor heir?

I then make the observation that his feelings towards me appear to have undergone a most remarkable change.

EG: *It is not so long ago that you appeared to dislike me, when you thought I liked your brother better.*

Mr P (vehemently): *No! Quite the contrary, I assure you. I acted out of affection and concern. From the very first moment I saw you, I was certain where our acquaintance would lead, if desire could be crowned with success. But I do not possess a demonstrative nature, and could not easily say what I truly felt in my heart. It made me disagreeable to you, I'm sure, for which I am truly sorry. But I have determined to change – I have changed, as you must see. I have held back, behind a pretence of indifference, for too long. I'll do so no more. You see how eloquent my feelings for you have made me!*

I remind him that he had once spoken of the Duport duty to marry well. He brushes this aside, saying that he is acutely sensible of every objection that could be made to our union, but that he cares nothing for them; that he would once have thought it inconceivable that he could ever be in the position in which he now finds himself, but that he is of age, and able to take his own decisions on his future.

Mr P: *You are an orphan, and you came to Evenwood as a servant. But you were not bred for service; you are a lady born, as anyone can see. I know it, my mother knows it, and soon all the world will know it. You are poor, it is true, but I have money enough, and you are fit, in every other way, my dearest Esperanza, to be the wife of the next Lord Tansor. No one will be able to deny that I have, indeed, married well.*

There is more – much more – in this vein. He tells me again and again that he is a changed man through me; but he is not. He is the same Perseus Duport who quizzed me concerning the Cretan Labyrinth on my first morning at Evenwood, only now Love has uncovered those aspects of his nature that his upbringing had taught him to conceal. I know he will always be proud, always unbendingly conscious of his superior place in the world. He will never suffer fools gladly, or spontaneously exhibit his innermost thoughts and feelings, and he will never wholly break free from his imprisoning self-regard. Yet these outward expressions of his protective instincts do not repel me, as they have formerly done; for they do not represent the whole man. He possesses a far finer nature than his faults have allowed him to reveal. This I know, from what we have shared during the past months – the walks and conversations, the smiles and laughter, the companionable silences. These have disclosed to me what no one else, I am sure, has ever seen: the secret heart of Perseus Duport.

At last, taking both my hands in his, and with sweetly formal gallantry, he puts the question I had hardly dared to hope ever to hear him ask. My amazement is complete when he takes my hand, kisses it, and then, looking deep into my eyes, slowly speaks the words (as I have since verified) of Dante when he first met the young Beatrice: *Ecce deus fortior me, qui veniens dominabitur mihi.**

We leave the bridge and stand, arm in arm, before the Palazzo Pitti. Swallows wheel and swoop above us. All over the city, bells clang out the hour.

I have given him his answer.

AT PERSEUS'S REQUEST, our engagement was to remain a secret until we returned to England and he could inform his mother in

---

*'Behold a god more powerful than I, who, coming, will rule over me.' Dante, *Vita Nuova* (I, ii).

what he called 'the proper circumstances'. There were also many matters, of a legal nature, to be set in train. Finally, he asked – a little shamefacedly – whether I would permit him to take back the ring, until these matters could be finally settled. Seeing no harm in these arrangements, and having my own reasons for keeping our engagement from public knowledge for the time being, I readily agreed, and wrote immediately to Madame to tell her the great news.

We left the Palazzo Riccioni at the beginning of May. The journey home was slow, requiring many extra stops along the way in order for Emily to rest.

Perseus and I maintained a most proper neutrality at all times, only occasionally exchanging little conspiratorial glances and fondly suggestive smiles, as lovers in our situation might be expected to do. Sometimes, as we waited for the carriage to be brought up, and he was sure that we were not observed, he would gently touch my hand, while saying nothing, and often looking into the distance, as if he were unaware of my presence next to him. As for me, I remained quietly receptive during these little dumb shows, although I would try to signal to him, as best I could, that his meaning was fully reciprocated.

He did not travel back with us from London to Evenwood, but remained in Grosvenor Square for several more days – ostensibly, and, indeed, in fact, to inform Mr Freeth on the progress of his new poem, and to obtain that gentleman's professional opinion on the six or so cantos that he had composed in Italy. His principal purpose, however, was to take advice on the various legal matters connected with our impending marriage.

An hour or so before Emily and I commenced our journey back to Northamptonshire, he came up to my room. He said he hoped that it would not be long before he could request an interview with his mother, adding that we could then begin to plan for a formal public announcement. I, of course, gladly made all the appropriate replies, receiving a gentle kiss on the cheek by way of reward; and so we had parted.

At long last, on a most unseasonable day of violent wind and intermittent lashing rain, our carriage drew up once more before the front doors of the great house of Evenwood, on which I now looked with new eyes. As Emily was being helped out by James Holt, striving valiantly to hold an umbrella over her, a sudden violent gust bore away a posy of pale paper flowers from her hat, whirling it rapidly skywards towards the soaring cupola-topped towers and the scudding black clouds high above.

She gave a little cry, almost of pain, and then stood for a moment, watching the fragile petals disperse into oblivion, as if each one were a pathetic emblem of doomed hope.

'They were my mother's,' she sighed. 'And now I shall never see them again.'

Then, with a sad smile of resignation, she turned to me.

'Come, my dear. Time for tea, I think.'

END OF ACT FOUR

ACT FIVE

TIME'S REVENGE

Thus the whirligig of time brings in his revenges.

WILLIAM SHAKESPEARE, *Twelfth Night* (1601)

30

Mr Barley's Black Box

I

Sukie's Secret

EVENTS NOW began to unfold with giddying swiftness.

A day or so after Emily and I arrived back at Evenwood, Sukie brought me a letter from Madame. As she was withdrawing, the little maid had hesitated at the door, before turning back towards me, her face flushed.

'Please, Miss Alice,' she said, plaintively, 'will you tell me something?'

'Of course I will, if I can,' replied I, suddenly alarmed at her distressed expression, for she was such a naturally cheery soul. 'What on earth is it? Come back, dear, and tell me.'

'I want to know if I've done wrong, keeping this.'

Reaching into her pinafore pocket, she took out a grubby piece of paper, which she then handed to me.

'I found this in a gown her Ladyship told me to put away,' she explained, 'with the ones we moved from the old wardrobe in the South Wing, when the roof leaked. It was a lovely gown, and quite new, but her Ladyship said that the colour didn't suit her, and she never wished to wear it again. So I took it away, but a comb fell out of one of the pockets – a lovely tortoiseshell comb, with a pearl inlay. So of course I thought I must look into the other pockets, to see whether there was anything else that might have been left in them.

'And then I found the piece of paper. Oh, Miss Alice, I read it, though I know I shouldn't have done. It was wrong of me, for I saw straight away that it was written to her Ladyship. But when I started, I couldn't stop. It was so queerly written, though I didn't understand it.

'Then when Alf Gully was here at Christmas-time – I always think of him as Alf Gully, even though he's now a great man in the Detective Department, for we grew up together – well, Alf said to keep a look-out for strangers, and it was then I remembered that Charlie Skinner had told me he'd seen a strange old woman, walking with her Ladyship one evening, up and down the Library Terrace.

'When I heard this, I thought at once that it must have been the person who'd written the letter. I don't know why, but I didn't say anything to Alf Gully. I didn't want to get into trouble for keeping the letter, and so I put it back under my mattress. But it's been worrying me something dreadful, Miss Alice, and so at last, when I couldn't stand it any longer, I told Mother, and she said I must give the letter to you, for you'd know what best to do. So there it is. Did I do wrong? Please tell me.'

'No, Sukie,' I said, taking her hand to reassure her. 'You didn't do wrong. And if you did, it was only a very little wrong, and now you've made amends. So run along now, dear, and don't worry any more. I'll decide what best to do.'

She thanked me, with such sweet and touching gratitude, and off she went, leaving me with the soiled and creased sheet of paper, torn in places, on which was written, in an ugly, unrefined hand, badly spelled, and in a ludicrous, half-educated style, with many words heavily underscored, the following extraordinary communication:

MY LADY,—

 Many long years have past & a great weight of water – as I might say – has also past under a great many bridges since I had the honor of adressing yr Ladyship – as you are now but were not then. But I flatter myself that you will not have forgotten me – nor the good service I gave you.

 The manner of our parting in Franzenbad was very unpleasant.

It cost me dear & – what you may not know – has brought me & my poor dear boy much down in the world with suffering and difficulty.

Perhaps you have put those times out of mind – tho I dont think so – & I assure you that I havent. But here is a chance for you at last to make up for casting me & my boy off so cruely.

Now – besides what is in my head concerning those times, wch tho I cannot prove will allways <u>be</u> in my head – I now have something that <u>will</u> prove the cause of all the business & wch I am <u>very</u> sure you will wish to keep privilly to yrself for the rest of yr days.

To put the matter straight & clear before you I will tell you this much my Lady – it is a <u>letter</u> to a late <u>noble person</u> in wch <u>everything</u> is set out as plain as day – wch was careless of you my Lady but good for me as it has now proved. It was written as you may recall on a <u>certain day</u> that meant much to you – & I suppose yr feelings got the better of you. You spilled perfume on it – do you remember? But it was not posted as you thought but my boy kept it for his own reasons and didnt tell me. But now it is found again & is in <u>my</u> hands.

I wd wish you to have yr letter back – as is only right for it is yr property – & I am an honest woman. But I must live & so I am very willing to give it to you – for a consideration of my suffering these <u>20</u> <u>years</u> past – wch is a <u>very</u> long time my Lady.

I have a fancy to see you again & to take some country air – & so wd ask that you send word as soon as may be care of Mrs J. Turripper . . . [paper torn and creased] then I shall bring the [illegible along torn crease: 'letter to show that'?] it is genu[ine]. But you shant keep it until you or an agent have paid what is due to me – I shall tell you how much when I see you at yr grand house.

<u>Write soon</u> my Lady – for old times sake. <u>No tricks</u>.
   Yrs faithfully –
   B.K. (Mrs)

I laid the letter down. Added to my own testimony of encountering the writer at the Duport Arms, it provided powerful confirmation that Emily had met the late Mrs Barbarina Kraus here at Evenwood, not long before the unfortunate woman's body had been hauled out of the Thames at Nicholson's Wharf.

I could easily picture the scene – the old lady slopping along the terrace in her worn and filthy shoes, a bent and ugly goblin figure beside the tall, noble form of her victim, barely suppressing her malicious glee at having haughty Lady Tansor in her power at last for some wrong that she claimed had been done to her, whilst my Lady strives to maintain her dignity and self-command in the face of her tormentor.

Then I imagined the clutch of freezing fear that Emily must have felt when shown the letter in which, as it would appear, some great secret had been carelessly set down, and which she must now prevent from being published to the world at any cost.

Inspector Gully had been right. It was a case of blackmail, pure and simple. Mrs Kraus had met her untimely end because of a forgotten letter, still carrying the faint scent of long-dead violets, over which her poor infatuated son had dreamed for twenty years and more.

Had the killing of Mrs Kraus been explicitly contemplated by Emily from the first? Could I believe this, even of my father's betrayer? Perhaps her instructions to Mr Vyse had been exceeded – deliberately or otherwise – as they had been when her father had been attacked on the orders of Phoebus Daunt. Then I had a sudden vision of Mr Vyse's cruel eyes as he listened to her. I could even imagine what he might have said in reply: *No half-measures in such cases, my Lady, no half-measures* . . . And then the insinuations and circumlocutions, uttered so soothingly, so reassuringly; the knowing looks, no words necessary, everything perfectly understood. *Do not concern yourself, my Lady. All will be made well, if you only place the matter in my capable hands* . . .

The source of his power over her was now plain. She had been so bewildered by events that she had failed to appreciate the folly of taking such a man into her confidence. In delivering herself from the clutches of Mrs Kraus, she had become caught in the toils of someone more dangerous still.

Placing Mrs Kraus's letter in my pocket, I next turned to the communication from Madame.

She began by congratulating me, most warmly, and at some

considerable length, on my success with regard to Perseus, confessing that she herself had doubted whether this absolutely necessary outcome could be achieved. She had also considered whether it would pose any risk to our enterprise to take Mr Wraxall into our confidence. To my relief, she saw no objection to it, and was therefore happy to allow me to use my discretion as to how much I should reveal to him of my purpose in coming to Evenwood, and when it would be best to do so, although I was prohibited from revealing my true identity to him, or to anyone else. To Lady Tansor alone, and to no other person, could the truth eventually be made known, when the proof of her crimes had been finally gathered in.

With her letter was one from Mr Thornhaugh:

LITTLE QUEEN,—

The end of yr Great Task is now in sight. Keep yr nerve, & all will be very well.

I entirely concur with Madame concerning Wraxall. I know him, by reputation, to be a man of the highest integrity & discretion, possessing besides a most extraordinarily penetrating & subtle intellect. You could have no better ally.

Madame and I are so very proud of you, Little Queen, as we know yr father would have been. It is a great thing you are doing, hard though it is. You have shown yrself – in every possible way – to be truly worthy, both of the Great Task, & of the ancient Duport blood that flows through yr young veins. For everything you have accomplished, and for what yet remains to be done, believe me, you will be most amply rewarded.

> *Yr very affectionate old Tutor,*
> *B. THORNHAUGH*

P.S. Madame and I were most shocked to hear of the unfortunate demise of R. Shillito. But London is a dangerous place, even in these modern times, & it wd have been awkward, to say the least, had R.S. finally brought to mind the true identity of 'Edwin Gorst'. It is, I regret to say, an ill wind . . .

Having established that Mr Wraxall had returned to North Lodge a few days earlier, I now sit down to write him a note, asking whether I might call at his earliest convenience.

It then occurs to me that I should seek out Charlie Skinner, to see what he has to say concerning the rendezvous that he had witnessed between Emily and Mrs Kraus. So off I trip, down the back stairs, and into the white-washed corridor leading to the servants' hall. There, to my surprise, I find Mr Randolph.

As he comes down the corridor towards me, the door to the servants' hall is pulled softly shut by some unseen person within; but I pay little heed to this, for Mr Randolph is asking me how I am, and how I had liked Florence, and what I had seen and done there, and telling me how splendid I look, *et cetera*, *et cetera* – a veritable torrent of rapid questions and remarks, to which I hardly have time to respond before another comes my way. Then, suddenly taking my arm, he ushers me, rather unceremoniously, towards the back stairs again.

It is a fine warm day. At Mr Randolph's suggestion, we step outside. Soon we are sitting together on a stone bench overlooking the deep dark waters of the fish-pond, enclosed within its high grey walls.

'And how did my dear brother conduct himself in Florence?' he asks. 'Was he an amenable companion? I do hope so.'

As I cannot tell him the truth, I say that Mr Perseus was much occupied with his new poem, and that we had seen little of each other as a consequence.

'Ah, the great new work!' he exclaims, with a rather forced laugh. 'What a marvel my brother is.'

Falling silent, he gazes distractedly at a shoal of large silver-and-gold fish and their progeny, which is gliding languidly towards a patch of sunlit water.

'You're aware, I hope, Esperanza,' he says of a sudden, nervously passing his hand through his hair, a habit he has whenever he is struggling with some weighty matter, 'how much I admire you?'

'Admire me?'

'Yes, indeed. I consider it admirable, in every way, that you've come here, an orphan and lacking the comfort and support of friends, and yet you've made yourself so much a part of our family – and indispensable, as I well know, to my mother. I hope you're happy. I suppose you *are* happy, aren't you? I – we – would hate to lose you, you know.'

I reply that I have no intention of leaving Evenwood, as long as I can be of service to his mother.

'I believe it's a rare blessing in this world,' he then observes after a little pause, and in a tone of absent reflection, almost as if he were thinking aloud, 'to know what makes us happy – truly happy – and then to be given the means of securing it.'

'And do you know what makes *you* happy?' I ask.

'Oh, yes!' he returns, with a sudden burst of passion. 'Absolutely. Beyond a shadow of a doubt.'

For a moment, I think that he is about to unburden himself at last regarding his feelings for me; but, as Evenwood's bells begin to chime out eleven o'clock, he jumps to his feet to announce that he has business to conduct in Easton.

'I haven't forgotten our last conversation, you know,' he assures me, as we are saying our good-byes. 'It's been constantly on my mind that I promised to speak to you, on a matter of the greatest importance to me. But there have been reasons that have prevented me from saying what I must, and will, say to you, and so I hope that you can be patient with me, for just a little longer. May I beg that of you?'

Greatly relieved that I have been spared once again – for a time at least – the moment when I must reject his proposal and confess that I am to marry Perseus, I tell him that I shall be happy to hear what he has to say to me whenever he is ready.

He gives me a grateful smile and walks quickly away, through the creaking iron gate in the far wall, and down the gravel path leading to the stables, leaving me alone in the bright May sunshine, wondering how I shall tell him that I can never be his.

II
Return to North Lodge

A REPLY TO my note to Mr Wraxall had been immediately sent back, saying that he would be delighted to see me at North Lodge the following Sunday afternoon.

'Come in, come in, my dear,' he said brightly, as he opened the front door to my knock. 'You're just in time. You'll take some tea, won't you? And some of Mrs Wapshott's famous cake?'

'Gladly,' I replied, stepping inside the dark little hallway. Soon I was sitting once more, tea-cup in hand, in the cramped but cosy sitting-room, with its distant view of the western woods.

'Now then, my dear,' Mr Wraxall began, 'I have to tender my apologies. You must be cross with me, for not writing to you in Florence.'

'No, indeed,' I insisted. 'I knew you would send word of anything you wished me to know.'

'Well,' he replied, 'there were such things – I can admit it now; but I thought it prudent not to commit anything to paper, at this critical juncture in our affairs. But here you are, and now I can tell you everything that has happened in your absence. We've made great progress, my dear, great progress!'

As we conversed, in a general way, I asked whether Inspector Gully's feet had been itching. Mr Wraxall laughed.

'They have! They have! And with good reason. So now, my dear, if you've finished your tea, and had quite enough of Mrs Wapshott's excellent spice-cake, I'll begin.'

This, in summary, is what he told me.

IN THE YEAR 1851, through a mutual friend, Mr Armitage Vyse had been introduced to a rising young poet by the name of Phoebus Rainsford Daunt.

The mutual friend was none other than Mr Roderick Shillito, Daunt's old Eton school-fellow. Vyse and Daunt had hit it off immediately, and had soon become close confederates. The bond between them was cemented when they discovered that they shared both a love of the Turf and an aptitude for what Mr Wraxall described as 'activities of a decidedly criminal character'.

Mr Vyse having been recently called to the Bar, his legal knowledge proved invaluable to Daunt in the prosecution of various financial frauds, of which his new friend was the principal instigator. As a consequence of this collaboration, both gentlemen made a considerable amount of money, although the world suspected nothing of their double lives.

This extraordinary disclosure – which, I confess, I would have hardly credited, had it not come from the unimpeachable mouth of Mr Montagu Wraxall – had been obtained by Inspector Gully from a gentleman by the name of Lewis Pettingale, another former legal man and a junior accomplice of Daunt's, lately returned from an extended residence in Australia, and to whom Mr Wraxall and the inspector had been directed by means of a letter, hand-delivered to King's Bench Walk, and signed 'A Well-Wisher'.

'God bless this well-wishing person,' said Mr Wraxall. 'We continue to wonder who it can be. At any rate, he – or possibly she – has given us a good deal of most useful information concerning both Vyse and Daunt – his, or her, knowledge of the latter, in particular, is certainly close, and extensive. But to return to our friend Vyse.

'Continuing to practise the Law from his chambers in Old Square, he was in due course introduced by Daunt to his patron, the late Lord Tansor, and to Miss Emily Carteret. His Lordship was impressed by the shrewd and ambitious young barrister and, through his legal advisers, Tredgolds, Mr Vyse was soon being instructed to act for Lord Tansor in a number of actions arising from his many business interests. Later, after Daunt's death, he was also involved in the legal work connected with Miss Carteret's assumption of the Duport name, and with her being constituted as his Lordship's successor.

'At the beginning of January 1855 – as we already know – Miss Carteret left England for the Continent, with the full blessing and support of Lord Tansor. Her purpose, unclear at the time, became the subject of much speculation and gossip.'

Here Mr Wraxall paused, his face taking on an expression of the utmost gravity.

'What I shall shortly put before you,' he said, 'is of so serious a character that I must ask you to swear that you will not divulge a single word – not the merest hint or suggestion – to anyone. Can you swear, my dear, on your very life?'

Of course I assured him that I would so swear, and that I would keep whatever information he saw fit to vouchsafe to me completely confidential. I did so at some cost to my conscience; for of course I knew that I must break my word by informing Madame of what I was about to be told.

'Thank you, my dear,' said Mr Wraxall, gratefully patting my hand, before continuing with his story.

WHILE MISS CARTERET was away, in order to reduce, if not elimi-nate altogether, the risk of her correspondence with Lord Tansor being opened and read, it was arranged that all communications between them would be directed, in the first instance, to Mr Vyse in Old Square. He would then place each letter, unopened, in a new envelope, which he would forward to the appropriate recipient.

'Why was it necessary to take such elaborate precautions?' I asked.

'All in good time, my dear,' replied Mr Wraxall, before proceed-ing with his story.

These arrangements having been made, their trusted inter-mediary, Mr Vyse, began laying plans of his own. Employing the practical skills acquired during the course of his criminal career, he expertly removed the seals of the letters that passed through Old Square, adding replicated substitutes after having made copies of each letter. But he was even cleverer than this; for in addition to these handwritten transcriptions, he arranged for the originals to be photographed, thus providing him with unassailable evidence of the accuracy and authenticity of the copies.

Following Phoebus Daunt's death, Mr Vyse immediately began – in a quiet but determined way – to ingratiate himself with his late friend's fiancée, his aim being to secure the good opinion and gratitude of the prospective 26th Baroness Tansor. He now had in his hands a powerful weapon to wield against her, should coercion be required; for – as I was soon to learn – several of the letters from Emily to Lord Tansor revealed the true reason for her leaving England in the midst of mourning the death of Phoebus Daunt, and why secrecy had been so necessary.

Mr Wraxall paused once more.

'And so we come to it at last,' he said. 'But before going any further, perhaps you'd like some more tea?'

'No, thank you,' I replied, agog beyond words for him to continue. 'I'm quite refreshed. Do please go on.'

'Very well. You may be wondering how we have come to know so much about Mr Armitage Vyse and his schemes. All will now be made clear. So, if you are sure you are comfortable, then I think it's time to introduce you to Mr Titus Barley.'

III
What Mr Barley Knew

RISING FROM HIS chair, Mr Wraxall walked across to a door leading through to the back parlour. Opening it, he said a few words to some person within. A moment later, a man appeared in the doorway carrying a black tin box – a very small man, not more than four feet and a few inches tall, of about fifty years of age, but trim of form, and rather handsome in his way, with a large head topped with thick, snow-white hair, and wide, thrust-back shoulders.

He cut a most extraordinary figure, dressed in a tight-fitting, dark-blue tail-coat, with gleaming brass buttons and a stand-up velvet collar, matching old-fashioned knee-breeches, dark stockings, and a pair of buckled pumps, the whole ensemble making him seem like some elfin courtier come fresh from attending the Queen of the Fairies herself.

'May I introduce Miss Esperanza Gorst?' said Mr Wraxall to the little man, who instantly gave me a low, unsmiling bow, but made no reply, nor even offered his hand by way of greeting.

'Mr Barley was formerly clerk to Mr Armitage Vyse,' explained Mr Wraxall, who appeared not in the least surprised by the gentleman's offhand manner. 'He served him for many years—'

'Man and boy,' Mr Barley interjected petulantly, in a resonant baritone voice – more impressive even than Perseus's, and almost comically at odds with his minuscule person.

'As you say, sir,' smiled Mr Wraxall, 'man and boy. And as *I* was about to say, as a result of his long-standing service, Mr Barley has come to know a great deal about the character and affairs – both professional and private – of his employer. Would you like to say anything, Mr Barley?'

'Not I,' he replied, with tremendous emphasis. 'But I'll take some tea – and some of that spice-cake, if you please.'

Laying the black box on the floor beside him, Mr Barley sat down to his refreshment, while Mr Wraxall, still smiling indulgently at his eccentric guest, began to speak again.

'You'll remember, Miss Gorst,' he said, turning towards me, 'at the last council of war of our triumvirate, that you asked how we suspected a certain ennobled person of being implicated in the murder of the unfortunate Mrs Barbarina Kraus. I indicated then that we had received the information from an anonymous informant. Mr Barley has been good enough to allow me to tell you today that he was that informant.'

To this statement, his mouth full of cake, Mr Barley gave an affirming nod.

'Of course, discretion has been Mr Barley's constant watchword over the years,' Mr Wraxall went on; 'but circumstances have now arisen, which have – if I may so put it – encouraged him to lay before the authorities certain documents, and other items, which go to the heart of the investigation into the death of Mrs Kraus. So far, so good, Mr Barley?'

Another nod.

'May I go on? Very well. Mr Barley is a single gentleman. For the whole of his life, he has lived in Somers Town with his mother, an estimable lady, to whom he has devoted his life. It is with great sorrow, however, that I have to tell you, Miss Gorst, that Mrs Barley has recently passed away.'

At these words, Mr Barley placed his plate on the lid of the black box and reached into his pocket to draw out a large handkerchief, with which he proceeded to dab away the tears that Mr Wraxall's statement had summoned up, whilst continuing to say not a word.

'While his mother – widowed at an early age – was alive,' continued Mr Wraxall, 'Mr Barley took exceptional care to shield her from all distress or discomfort, of mind as well as body, as a good son ought. Unfortunately, some few years ago, he found himself, through no fault of his own, I am assured, caught up—'

'Enmeshed,' corrected Mr Barley.

'Enmeshed, I should say, in an incident, of a rather delicate – not to say dangerous – character, which, had it become known publicly, would have brought contumely, and much worse, upon both himself and his family. This dreadful possibility had to be kept from Mrs Barley at all costs.'

Mr Wraxall cocked his head on one side and looked at Mr Barley with inquisitively raised eye-brows, receiving another nod by way of his guest's consent for him to continue.

'I do not intend to elaborate on the nature of the – *ahem* – incident. Suffice to say that it came to the knowledge of Mr Vyse, through one of his many London informers.

'Now Mr Barley, as I have said, is a man of the utmost discretion and probity. I have also suggested that, in the course of his employment, he had become aware of certain irregularities in the conduct of Mr Vyse's affairs. Being a thoroughgoing professional man, and the most loyal of employees, he could not at first bring himself to unmask these to the world; but, as time passed, and the iniquities grew in scope and seriousness, he began to overcome his scruples. Finally, he went to Mr Vyse to say that he could no longer, in conscience, continue in his employment, and that he wished to tender his notice forthwith and go immediately to the proper authorities, to inform them of the various criminal schemes in which he knew Mr Vyse had been involved. Right so far, Mr Barley?'

'Right enough,' replied that gentleman. Then, looking down at his empty plate: 'Is there more cake?'

Mrs Wapshott was duly called up from the back regions of the Lodge, and a second cake was soon produced, from which Mr Barley cut himself a mighty slice.

'Pray continue, sir,' he said to Mr Wraxall, with a sniff of majestic condescension.

MR VYSE'S REACTION to his clerk's announcement was perhaps not unexpected. He sat Mr Barley down and told him, no doubt in his sinisterly smiling way, that he ought perhaps to reconsider his position, for the sake of his dear mother.

Mr Barley then realized that his employer knew of the 'incident' to which Mr Wraxall had just alluded, and that he was fully prepared to bring it to the attention of both Mrs Barley and the world at large – a thing the former's son simply could not countenance – should the clerk carry out his threat.

Following a little further discussion on the subject, Mr Barley was persuaded to withdraw his decision to quit Mr Vyse's employment; and so, with the utmost reluctance, he continued in his duties for several more years, until the passage of time, and the death of his mother, gave him the opportunity to liberate himself from his employer's power over him.

Free now to follow his long-suppressed conscience, Mr Barley accordingly put in motion a plan that he had been harbouring for some time.

He secretly gathered together the copies that Mr Vyse had made of the letters sent by the then Miss Emily Carteret to Lord Tansor during her time on the Continent in the years 1855 and 1856, together with the photographs of the originals. These, with some other items, he put in a black tin box – the same box that he had brought with him to North Lodge, and which he had placed on the floor beside him while he took his tea and cake.

'I'd thought to relate, in *précis*, the contents of those letters,' said Mr Wraxall to me. 'On reflection, however, perhaps the best thing would be for you to read them through for yourself – if you have no objection, Mr Barley? Good.

'Well now, before you do, and to bring things quickly up to the present, after removing the box to a safe place, away from Old Square, Mr Barley then removed himself, both from the employ-ment of Mr Armitage Vyse and from his former home in Somers Town, to an equally safe place: to wit, a small, but comfortable, attic room above my chambers in King's Bench Walk.

'What next? Ah, yes. Master Yapp. He has now been taken, and has spoken out against Mr Vyse. We were sure that Yapp had killed Mrs Kraus – Gully had two costers ready to swear that she'd met Yapp in the Antigallican. No doubt Vyse had sent him to obtain the letter she'd found in Conrad's room and made a show of paying the woman off. The costers had then seen Yapp follow her down Dark House Lane towards the river. We don't need to conjecture what happened next.

'All this, however, was circumstantial. We needed solid proof of Yapp's guilt. And now we have it.

'Gully had put a man on Yapp; but then, it seems, Yapp left Lon-don, and for a time nothing was heard of him. A week or so ago, however, Gully received word that Yapp had been seen again in one of his old London haunts, and so the inspector put the business of keeping him in sight in the capable hands of your friend, Sergeant Swann.

'Last Thursday afternoon, Swann followed Yapp to Deptford, where he attempted to pawn a watch inscribed with the name of Mrs Kraus's father, and which both our witnesses will swear that she took out on the day she met Yapp in the Antigallican. It was her one precious possession, of which the poor unfortunate seems to have been inordinately proud.

'As Yapp left the pawnbroker's shop, Swann immediately appre-hended him – and not a moment too soon. He'd been about to make his way to Liverpool, and from there to take ship to America. It seems that he'd come back to London to settle his few affairs, and to demand money for his passage – as well as for his continuing silence regarding the killing of Mrs Kraus – from Mr Vyse. It takes a brave man to face down Billy Yapp; but Mr Vyse, not taking kindly to Yapp's threats, had turned him down flat, and there had been an unpleasant falling out. The consequence was that Yapp had no hesitation in telling the police all they needed to know concerning his former employer's part in the murder of Mrs K. With Yapp's confession in his pocket, so to speak, Inspector Gully now intends to call on Mr Vyse, to pay his compliments, and to request him to step round to the Detective Department. Well now, my dear, do you have any questions?'

'Just one,' I replied. 'You identified Mr Barley as the anonymous correspondent who supplied you with information concerning Mr Vyse; but was he also the person who signed himself "Well-Wisher"?'

'Excellent!' Mr Wraxall cried. 'The answer is that he was not. We appear to have another, invisible, assistant on the case. Whether we shall receive further information from this person, we cannot say; but we now have in our hands sufficient evidence to bring charges against Billy Yapp, Mr Armitage Vyse – and, of course, Lady Tansor – for the murder of Mrs Barbarina Kraus.'

The starkness of Mr Wraxall's assertion shocked me. I cared nothing for Mr Vyse or for Billy Yapp; but to hear Emily's name in such wicked company distressed me terribly. I berated myself for my weakness in feeling sympathy for her, and hesitated for a moment before revealing what I had been about to tell Mr Wraxall. But at last I did speak, reaching into my pocket as I did so to take out the letter from Mrs Kraus that Sukie had given to me.

'Well, well,' said Mr Wraxall after reading it. 'This, I think, clinches it. The whole business is now crystal clear. Blackmail and murder. Blackmail and murder. Just as we thought.'

'And do you have other evidence against Mr Vyse for his part in the murder, as well as Yapp's confession?'

'Assuredly,' replied Mr Wraxall.

'Assuredly,' repeated Mr Barley, rather crossly; and then, suddenly roused to volubility: 'I have eyes to see, and ears to hear. I heard what I heard, one rainy afternoon, when a certain noble lady kept her appointment in Old Square. Mr V sent me away to Blackett, our law stationer, but I didn't go immediately, as he thought. *I lingered.*'

He looked first at me, then at Mr Wraxall; and then, with a kind of belligerent emphasis, he leaned forward and said:

'*I used my ears.* I wrote it all down, in shorthand. Word for word. Transcribed instantly, signed, and dated. Then straight off round the corner to Blackett's – ink hardly dry – for it to be witnessed. It may, or may not, be admissible; but it all adds weight, you know, and weight's the thing with a jury.'

And with this oracular pronouncement, he cut himself yet another slice of spice-cake.

'And Lady Tansor?' I next asked Mr Wraxall. 'You have the evidence you need to – to—'

'Implicate? Certainly. Convict? I believe so. Shall I run through the main points?

'*Item.* A letter, found in one of Lady Tansor's gowns by Sukie Prout, housemaid, from the victim to Lady Tansor, demanding money for the return of a letter, written by her Ladyship twenty years ago, in which certain matters were set out that were, and remain, inimical to her Ladyship's interests, and requesting an immediate interview, at which the aforesaid demand for money was no doubt to be pressed home.

'*Item.* The testimony of Miss Esperanza Gorst, then maid to Lady Tansor, that, on 6th September last, she was instructed by her Ladyship to take a letter to the Duport Arms in Easton for the attention of "B.K.", who could have been no other person than Barbarina Kraus, come to Northamptonshire by prior arrangement with Lady Tansor – *vide* the previous point.

'*Item.* The signed and witnessed statement of T. Barley, Esq., legal clerk, of Old Square, Lincoln's Inn, to the effect that, on the same day, 6th September last, he overheard, and concurrently committed to paper in shorthand, a conversation between Lady Tansor and his employer, Mr Armitage Vyse, during the course of which it was explicitly agreed that Mrs Barbarina Kraus would be a perpetual threat to her Ladyship's interests if she was allowed to live. The meeting concluded with Lady Tansor's consenting to "any means necessary" (her exact words) to remove what she then called "this appalling shadow that has fallen over my life". Mr Vyse's last words were: "You will leave the matter with me, then?" To which her Ladyship replied: "Yes. Gladly." Mr Barley will further swear that he distinctly heard the name "Yapp" mentioned by Mr Vyse as a person "suitable for the job".

'Mr Barley will also testify that Lady Tansor paid a further visit to Old Square soon after the murder of Mrs Kraus. Although he was unable to inform himself fully on the particulars of her conversation with Mr Vyse, he did hear a sarcastically expressed reference by the latter to "the late-lamented Mrs K", to which her Ladyship replied, "Thank God!"

'*Item.* The testimony of Mrs Jessie Turripper, landlady, of Chalmers Street, Borough, that a gentleman answering Mr Armitage Vyse's description had called to see Mrs Kraus on the morning of 15th September last, and that, happening to pass by the door of her lodger's room ten minutes later, she distinctly heard the words "on behalf of Lady Tansor" uttered by the gentleman.

'These, together with Yapp's confession, constitute the principal evidential pegs on which Inspector Gully will hang his case against Lady Tansor. I believe they are more than sufficient for his purpose.'

'What will happen to her?' I asked, breaking the grim silence that had fallen over the room.

'The jury will decide,' came the barrister's stern reply. He then fell silent again.

'And who will act for the Crown?' I asked.

'Sir Patrick Davenport. A most accomplished prosecutor. No man better. He'll see that justice is done.'

I knew then that there was no hope for her, and I shuddered to think of the terrible price that she would be required to pay for her desperate folly.

'But, my dear,' said Mr Wraxall presently, his grey eyes now twinkling genially, 'you still don't know what it was that Lady Tansor wished so much to conceal – the very reason why Mrs Kraus was killed. Are you not just a little bit curious?'

It was true. My imagination had been so seized by a dreadful vision of the judgment that must now fall on Emily that I had altogether forgotten to ask what had impelled her tragic actions.

'Mr Barley, if you please,' said the barrister, nodding to the elfin clerk, who was sitting in his chair blithely licking cake crumbs from the tips of his fingers.

Setting his plate on the table, Mr Barley bent down to pick up the tin box, and handed it to his host.

'I suggest, my dear,' said Mr Wraxall, 'that the back parlour would be a good place for you to peruse the contents of Mr Barley's box. You won't be disturbed, and you have a fine view of the house from there.'

31

A Fatal Correspondence

I

Letters from Miss Emily Carteret to the Late Lord Tansor

JANUARY–MARCH 1855

I PLACE Mr Barley's black box on a table by the window of the back parlour, and open it.

Inside are two bundles of folded letters, both tied with a piece of frayed and dirty string. With every copied letter is a photograph of the original each one written in Emily's graceful hand; and, in the bottom of the box, lie three separate documents.

The letters in the first bundle contain little of significance – mostly brief *résumés* of journeys undertaken, places seen, persons met along the way, the conditions and amenities of hotels, *et cetera*. Setting these aside, I turn my attention to the second, smaller bundle.

Here, on these dozen or so sheets of paper, must lie the final fate of the woman under whose roof I have lived for the past months; who, despite her mercurial temper, has shown me genuine kindness and consideration, and who had implored me – with such touching earnestness – to be her friend. Yet I had been sent to destroy her, for my dead father's sake.

For some minutes, I sit looking out, across the tree-studded Park, glistening under a patina of thin rain, towards the needle spires and battlemented turrets of the great house. At last, drawing up a chair, I take a deep breath, smooth out the first letter, and begin to read.

Here, then, are the ten letters, written from the Continent, by Miss Emily Carteret to her second cousin, patron, and protector, Lord Tansor, during the years 1855 and 1856. In them lurk the dark and dangerous secret that she has sought so desperately to conceal, and which is now about to be brought forth into the light at last, with consequences for my own life that I could never have imagined.

Words on paper, Mr Vyse had warned her, could be fatal. He was right. If only she had heeded his advice, how different things might have been – for her, and for me.

So sit with me now and read these letters, as I read them, and learn what I learned, on that dull, grey afternoon, with rain pattering against the window, in the back parlour of North Lodge.

LETTER 1

Grillon's Hotel
Albemarle Street
London

18th January 1855
MY LORD,—

Since coming here from Evenwood yesterday, I have not ceased to think of the great kindness & sympathetic understanding yr Ldship has shown me – yes, & to weep, too, for joy! I feared – oh so greatly feared! – that you would condemn me, as a lesser man might have done, when I confessed all to you. But you did not! You saw how necessary it was, under the terrible circumstances of those last days, to put aside petty convention for a far greater cause. This I did – & most willingly, expecting no favour or recompense from you, only stern censure. Yet yr compassion was as wonderful to me as it was yearned for, & I cannot conceive how I can ever repay you. An eternal love – for my dear lost Phoebus, yr Ldship's shining hope – and a duty, no less than sacred in my eyes, to the noble line, amongst which I am proud & honoured to be numbered, now bind me indissolubly to yr Ldship's interests, and to those of our family.

The Kraus woman came to see me this afternoon, with her son. She will do very well, I think, & her thorough knowledge of German will be of great service. The son I am less sure of, I admit, but his doting mamma swears that she will not go without him. He said not a word, & never looks me in the eye; but, although simple, he is a tall, well-muscled fellow, & that is the main thing as far as my protection on the journey is concerned.

The tidal-train leaves at eleven tomorrow. I shall send a note – through the arranged channel – of our safe arrival in France, and with directions for our onward journey.

I am, my Lord – & I pray that you will accept the heartfelt designation I give myself – your most loving daughter in gratitude and trust,—

  E. CARTERET

LETTER 2

Hotel Baltazar
Carlsbad

3rd February 1855
MY LORD,—

We arrived here last evening, & I am now comfortably settled in respectable accommodation, obtained by Herr Kraus, a most obliging man who appears to cherish a great regard for his daughter-in-law.

The latter, I regret to report, has been a mixed blessing. Her ability to speak fluent German has certainly been useful at times (my own facility in the language being somewhat limited); and she performs her duties creditably enough. But she often over-reaches herself in point of manners, seeming to believe that she has a claim to consider herself well bred! This, although she has acquired some superficial accomplishments, she most certainly is not, being in truth ill-educated and often uncouth. As she is small of stature, and darkly complexioned, with a low, simian hairline, I have come to think of her as a kind of monkey in fine clothes (my fine clothes, I should add, although cut down to fit her).

To give you an instance of her presumption, in Baden-Baden I overheard her describe herself to the maid of a Russian lady as my companion! For this most unwarranted piece of audacity I was obliged to reprimand her severely, which brought forth an immediate, and rather threatening, scowl. Such a thing I cannot & will not tolerate in a servant. And so more warm words were said, on my part, to the effect that she must immediately mend her ways or be sent back home. All this time, Master K stood in the shadows, silent as usual. If he has said a dozen words on the whole journey here from Baden, I shall be amazed.

Today, however, Mrs K is all smiles, and the light of bloody rebellion has gone from her eyes. She apologized most contritely for trespassing so far beyond her place, & promised that she would be more mindful of her position in the future, which I was glad to hear.

This evening we are to attend an entertainment, at which we are promised fire-eaters, a ventriloquist, & Tyrolean minstrels! A very different prospect to yours tonight at dear peaceful Evenwood, I dare say!

All, then, goes as well as we could hope. I am here, safe & sound, & shall not leave until our business is successfully concluded.

I am, dear sir, your very affectionate,

E.G.C.

P.S. I put off my mourning in Baden. Although it pained me greatly, I thought it best to do so. However, the locket you were so kind to give me, containing my dear love's hair, I shall always wear close to my heart, even when I am laid in my grave.

LETTER 3

Hotel Baltazar
Carlsbad

10th February 1855
MY LORD,—

He is found. I am sure of it. His name is Tadeusz Zaluski, a former colonel in the Prussian Army, although born the youngest son of a Polish nobleman from Lodz. He arrived here a few days since from Gräfenberg, where he had wished to take the water cure; but the place has deteriorated since the death of Herr Priessnitz,* & so he has come here instead.

He speaks excellent English, is forty years of age, in somewhat poor health, & was cut off some years ago by his father. The reasons for this are unclear to me at present, but the separation is apparently permanent, & this has rendered his financial position increasingly precarious. All this I learned within fifteen minutes of being introduced to him.

Mrs K has further discovered, from servant talk, that he travels constantly, to avoid his creditors. It is therefore likely that he will not remain here long, having no doubt already run up debts. All this encourages me greatly, for it demonstrates an acute need – & that is what we seek. He is, besides, cultivated, handsome enough, and – despite his troubles – good-humoured; and so, all in all, I think that he will do very well, if I can get him.

Mrs K, you will gather, continues amenable. I have increased her remuneration, as you suggested, & this, together with the present of another gown (she is inordinately proud of her appearance, & takes the most ludicrous pains to appear à la mode), has, I think, re-invigorated her loyalty. Of course we are taking a risk with her; but I know that I cannot accomplish this on my own, & yr Ldship's judgment

---

*Vincenz Priessnitz (1799–1851), a farmer's son who founded the health cult of hydrotherapy, the centre of which was at the 'water university' of Gräf-enberg in Austrian Silesia (now Lázně Jeseník in the Czech Republic).

with regard to her trustworthiness must override any doubts that I may have on that score.

Colonel Zaluski will be at the Grand Ball tomorrow evening, to which I have also been invited by a pleasant French diplomat and his wife, with whom I have passed several promenading afternoons lately. I hope to send you further news very soon.

Until then, I remain, my dear sir,—

Ever yours in respect and daughterly love,

> *F. CARTERET*

LETTER 4

> *Hotel Baltazar*
> *Carlsbad*

12th February 1855

MY LORD,—

The Polish Colonel escorted me back to my hotel, after the Grand Ball last night, and I took the immediate opportunity to lay my proposal, in the most general terms, to him. My heart was in my mouth, I freely admit, for I feared that he would be shocked by my extreme forwardness, and by the audacity of the business. But my fears proved as unjustified as my first instinct was correct as to his suitability for the role I wished him to play.

We arranged that he would visit me again here at the hotel this morning. He has just left, after two hours, and I hasten to write this to you, so that you may share with me, as soon as may be, the satisfaction of knowing that we have succeeded in achieving the first, and essential, part of our plan, and so soon after arriving here.

He was thoroughly charming throughout, needed no unnecessary justification for our enterprise, and, being of elevated birth himself, professed genuine — indeed, profound and moving — sympathy for the great cause, to which you and I are dedicated. He was unconcerned about the pecuniary arrangements, which only served to reinforce the excellent impression I had already formed of him, saying that all that sort of thing could be discussed in due course. He returns tomorrow to take a room in the hotel.

And so it is done. The heir will have a father.

I remain, dear sir, ever yr loving,

    E. CARTERET

LETTER 5

Hotel Baltazar
Carlsbad

8th March 1855

MY LORD,—

  In haste.

  Colonel Zaluski and I depart from here early tomorrow morning for Franzenbad. Mrs K has been told of a legal man there who will draw up the necessary documents with regard to Colonel Zaluski's position. He will also advise us on making the further arrangements that will be necessary in due course. Mrs K says that the man no longer practises his profession, having been implicated (though never convicted) in a financial scandal in his home city some years back; but she has assured us that he is well able to help us — for a reasonable consideration, of course. From her account, I gather that he has never been over-scrupulous in his professional dealings, even before the scandal, and that one more lapse will not incommode his conscience in the least.

  Ever yr devoted,

    E.

LETTER 6

Hotel Adler
Franzenbad

18th March 1855
MY LORD,—

A dreadful crisis has occurred.

Yesterday morning, while we were in conference with the lawyer, Herr Drexler, at his house, Mrs K's son was apprehended in the act (it is claimed) of accosting a local girl. He escaped, however, & has now fled to the town of Egra, whither his mother (we think) has gone to find him.

After we had come out of the lawyer's house and had been informed of the incident, we returned to the hotel to await developments. The time for dinner arrived, but there was still no word or sign of Conrad. We learned from Herr Adler, the hotel's proprietor, that the girl had not been seriously harmed, & that nothing unmentionable had been done to her, for which we were very grateful. However, the girl's father is an important man in the town and is determined that Conrad must be found and prosecuted. Fortunately for us, no one has so far recognized Conrad as belonging to our party – he and Mrs K were lodging together in a house some distance from the hotel, & we have rarely been seen with him since we arrived.

Mrs K went all about the town looking for her son, & did not return to the hotel until past eleven o'clock. She begged us to take a lenient view of the matter, insisting that Conrad was a good boy at heart and had meant no harm to the young woman. She also promised that there would be no repetition, for she would make sure that he was never again left alone, & assured us that she knew he would be sorry for what he had done.

I told her I found it impossible to accept her assurances, having been deeply alarmed by the wholly unexpected turn of events, which could put all our careful plans in jeopardy. Just then, a messenger arrived with a note for Mrs K. It had been written on Conrad's behalf, being unable to write himself, and bore the three words

'Mother. Egra. Conrad', by way of advising Mamma of his present place of refuge.

The colonel agreed that we must instantly inform the authorities; but on hearing of our intention, Mrs K, with a face of fury, and letting out a kind of howl, rushed to the door, removed the key, and quit the room, closing the door behind her. In a moment, we heard the sound of the key turning in the lock! It took five minutes or more for someone to come, & then another key had to be found to let us out, allowing Mrs K even more time to make her escape.

This morning we learn that the authorities have begun making a search of the lodging-houses in Egra, but with little expectation that they will find either of the fugitives. And so Colonel Z and I must proceed as best we can without the aid of Mrs K, which has not been wholly unwelcome until now. Luckily, the colonel speaks excellent German, & we have already made the acquaintance of Herr Drexler, who, although a little coarse in his manner, & rather too obviously fond of drink, is, in other respects, a man who knows how things are done here, & is willing to do them for us.

Do not be alarmed, my dear sir, by this news. The situation was grave for a time, certainly, but the danger, we are sure, has passed, & we are determined that nothing shall now prevent us from completing the next stage of our enterprise.

We leave here tomorrow, returning through Carlsbad, and then on to Toeplitz. The ceremony will take place there on Saturday week. Herr Drexler is confident that the money we have disbursed will ensure that everything is done as we wish.

With regard to the other impending event, we think of taking a house in Ossegg until the end of the summer, and then move on to somewhere else, before we go to Prague, where the colonel has a sympathetic uncle.

The prospect of being so long away from dear Evenwood, and from yr Ldship, is a dreary one; but the pill must be swallowed, & I am happy to endure any hardship, undergo any deprivation, for yr sake, & for the cause to which I have pledged myself.

Ever yr loving,
    E. CARTERET

II
Letters from Colonel and Mrs Tadeusz Zaluski
to the Late Lord Tansor
MARCH 1855–MARCH 1856

LETTER 7
Mrs Emily Zaluski to Lord Tansor

Hotel de la Poste
Langestrasse
Toeplitz

24th March 1855
MY LORD,—

All is accomplished. I am married, as of yesterday.

Herr Drexler was as good as his word. The documents had been drawn up exactly as required, the officials made content, the priest (pastor, rather) was waiting in the appointed place ready to attend us at the stated time.

The ring I had brought with me looked very well, & was much admired by the impromptu congregation of village onlookers. After-wards, we gave a little dinner at the hotel by way of celebration, to which we had invited the priest & a Belgian cloth-merchant & his wife, whom we had earlier recruited as witnesses. (I concocted a fine story that I had fled England, & the severe displeasure of a preju-diced father, to marry my dashing colonel — who, luckily, still has something of a dash about him. Mme Cloth-Merchant fairly swooned at the romantic daring of it all.)

So all is well, and we are set fair for the next — and most important — part of our adventure.

Only one thing has happened to check the relief I feel, and it is this.

Before we left Franzenbad, after the disappearance of Conrad and his dreadful mother, we received the following epistle, which I here transcribe in all its literary glory:

MADAM,—

Well you have shown yr true colours in seeking to bring down some one who has done you nothing but good & faithful service since leaving England. The girl came to no harm and Conrad as I told you he would be is truly sorry for what he did – but that is nothing to <u>you</u> I see – for you have always disliked Conrad & have never given me my due either for what I have done on yr behalf.

It wd have mattered not a jot to let Conrad be and say nothing – I wd have made certain no such thing happened again while we were in yr service – but you wished only to be rid of us I see – & wanted any excuse to do so – and so you were ready to denownce my poor boy – who deserves yr pity rather than what you are disposed in yr pride to give him, wch is to say contemt.

Well Madam the police shall not have him – I shall find him before they do I can assure you – and by tomorrow we shall be beyond their reach – aye and <u>yours too</u>.

But do not think Madam that I shall forget – I know yr secrets & have them safe in my head. You think you are rid of me for ever – but you are not. Time is my friend. <u>Look for me.</u>

Until we meet again—

B.K.

A charming communication, I think you will agree. I had never trusted Mrs K, and she has shown herself to be both disloyal and vicious. I am most dreadfully sorry that the estimation of the noble friend who recommended her to you, regarding her character, has proved so utterly erroneous, tho' of course no blame whatsoever can attach to yr Ldship for the woman's disgraceful behaviour towards us.

The threat so clearly implied in Mrs K's letter, however, is of great concern to me. I have been as careful as I can not to reveal too much of our business to her; but she knows enough by now (and perhaps can guess more) to make her threat a serious one. Yr Ldship will know better than I how we might prepare ourselves against her. Perhaps we might seek the confidential advice of Mr A.V., who has already proved himself most helpful to us in the present enterprise.

On another matter, my husband – there! I have written the word, for the first time – has been told of a house in Ossegg that appears most suitable for our purposes. We hope to secure it for six months before removing to Dux, and then to Prague for Christmas. I am, I own, happy to think that I shall have somewhere to call home once again, if only for a short time, & although it can never be home in the true sense, for that will always be Evenwood, that ever-blessed haven from the world.

Our immediate task is to find new servants – Tadeusz has just gone out for this purpose. I shall write again with our new address as soon as I know it.

Until then, I am, ever yr loving, & signing myself for the first time,
  E. ZALUSKI

LETTER 8
Colonel Tadeusz Zaluski to Lord Tansor

[Postmarked Ossegg, 16th September 1855]

MY LORD, —

It is with the most heartfelt satisfaction that I write to your Lordship to inform you that my dear wife gave birth to a fine healthy son, at a little after half past four yesterday morning, just as the sun was beginning to rise. We intend to call him Perseus Verney, and hope that this will meet with your Lordship's approval.

My wife is resting now, as the physician has instructed, and as she deserves, and I have come downstairs, at her earnest request, to write this letter to your Lordship so that it can be sent by the next available coach.

Her son – I should say our son – has been placed in the capable care of Frau Steinmann, who has been with us since we left Toeplitz. She is a widow of some sixty years who speaks very little English, and *so we have been able to converse freely in her presence. We have also found here a wet-nurse, who has no English, and a very able young man, Gerhart by name, who has taken a great liking to us both, but especially to my wife, and has so far proved himself to be both eager to serve us and deserving of our trust. He speaks a little English, having been employed for a time in a hotel in Marienbad, and so we are careful what we say in front of him, and always make a point of discussing confidential matters when we are away from the house and en plein air, for of course, after the business with Mrs Kraus, my wife and I are doubly wary. But servants we must have, and these two — in my considered judgment — are exactly what we require, and better could not be easily found.*

The baptism is to take place on Monday week. Drexler has arranged everything, as before, although I regret to inform your Lordship that my wife has been obliged to draw on the reserves that we are carrying with us to reimburse Drexler for what he terms 'unforeseen outlays' with respect to the ceremony.

The house here stands away from the town, and we have hardly been out since we arrived. We are confident that, beyond Dr Weiss (brought in by Drexler from a town some thirty miles distance — another considerable expense) and a handful of tradesmen, as well of course as Frau Steinmann and Gerhart, not more than half a dozen people know that we are here, or of the birth of our son.

I need hardly add that I am acutely conscious also of my debt of duty towards your Lordship, and you may depend on my carrying it out — as I have been ever used to do, as a military man — to the letter.

My wife hopes to write to you herself, if she is strong enough, tomorrow.

I remain, my Lord, yours to command,

T. ZALUSKI (COLONEL)

P.S. I had no sooner finished writing this letter than my wife called down, insisting that I bring it up to her so that she might correct my

English, and so that you might know that it comes from her as well as from me. Thus I was obliged to write it all out fair once again! T.Z.

LETTER 9
Mrs Tadeusz Zaluski to Lord Tansor

[Postmarked Dux, 25th September 1855]

MY LORD,—

We have arrived in Dux. My son is strong and well! And so am I.

The necessary documents were prepared by Drexler as arranged, and with the requisite date — Tadeusz has them all safe. Our task now is to continue to remain as sequestered from prying eyes as we can, until we are able to return to England.

What a tedious time lies ahead! But Tadeusz is excellent company, and we have a good store of books (including, of course, several volumes of dear Phoebus's poems, which I never tire of reading). The house is beautifully situated, with a distant view of the palace, and I can look forward to plenty of healthful exercise, as well as heart-lifting prospects of mountains and forests.

The little one is a delight — more even-tempered than any baby I have known. And, young though he is, I already see such a likeness to his father! It has made me quite gasp sometimes. Tadeusz has been a rock, and I confess that I have grown quite fond of him, although of course I shall never feel for him a fraction of my devotion to dearest Phoebus, whom I have never ceased to think of through all these weeks and months, and never shall, for as long as I live.

What has been troubling me now is how my marriage, and the birth of P—, will be seen by those less charitable souls in society when we return. I expect opprobrium in some quarters for the precipitate manner in which I appear to have conducted myself so soon after the death of P.R.D. But why should I worry about such people? I have Duport blood in me, and so do not need to pay any heed to small-minded tittle-tattle.

Others, I hope, will say, why should an unexpected attachment be resisted, even when it comes so soon after such a loss as I have suffered? Surely that will not be condemned? People will see that Tadeusz and I are happy, for we truly are; and my friends — my true *friends — will rejoice when I return to England a mother, bringing with me a fine son to present to his noble relative.*

So, you see, I have now argued myself out of my anxieties — for I admit only to you that I have greatly feared more often in these last days, when everything, or nearly everything, has been achieved, than ever before, that we shall eventually be found out.

But now I must take the little one out for his walk — under a brilliant sun that I hope is also shining down on Evenwood, the place where I long so much to be once more.

Ever yr loving,

    E. ZALUSKI

LETTER 10

[Postmarked Carlsbad, 11th March 1856]

MY LORD,—

We arrived here from Prague late last evening.

The time, we think, has now come to give out the news of our return. I believe you have in mind to place announcements in The Times *and the* Illustrated London News, *which should suffice. Tongues will do the rest.*

We leave here on Friday. A few days in Paris are proposed, and then home at last.

How I long to see Evenwood again — and, most of all, to place its beautiful heir in your arms!

Yrs ever & truly,

    E.

32

The Consequences of a Lie

I

The Great Secret Revealed

ALMLY FOLDING the last letter, I sit back in the chair, staring out, through a thickening curtain of rain, at the carriage-road winding down to the grey mass of the great house, planted, like some fantastic palace of legend, in its shallow bowl of misty green.

I re-read each of the ten letters in turn, making notes on each, to establish the following sequence of events:

1. The ten letters corroborate what Inspector Gully has gleaned from Conrad: that in January 1855, despite her grief, Miss Emily Carteret had gone to Bohemia, with Lord Tansor's blessing, with the sole but secret aim of seeking out a husband. Fortune quickly favours her, and, soon after arriving in Carlsbad, she discovers a suitable candidate in the impecunious Colonel Zaluski.

2. Certain arrangements are made, and Miss Carteret quickly marries her Polish colonel, apparently towards the end of March.

3. In September 1855, Mrs Zaluski, as she has now become, gives birth to a son, christened Perseus Verney Zaluski.

4. In April 1856, fifteen months after leaving England, Emily returns in triumph to Evenwood with her husband and son.

On the face of it, these facts seem innocuous enough; but behind them is hidden a far less innocent truth.

Time, Mr Wraxall had said, was of the essence in our attempts to unlock the secret that Lady Tansor has gone to such terrible lengths to conceal. As I sit watching the rain-swayed trees in the barrister's unkempt patch of garden, I finally understand what he had meant.

Words on paper. Deadly words. But numbers, too, can be deadly – numbers in the form of dates.

Miss Emily Carteret arrives in Carlsbad on the 2nd of February 1855. She meets Colonel Zaluski on the 9th of February, just a week later. Arrangements – of an unspecified character, although certainly including some financial consideration – are quickly made with him on the 11th and 12th.

Miss Carteret and Colonel Zaluski are married, in Toeplitz, on the 23rd of March 1855. Their first son, Perseus, is born – inferring the date from the postmark on Letter 8 – on the 15th of September 1855, in Ossegg, to where the couple had moved from Toeplitz six months earlier.

Colonel and Mrs Zaluski, with their son, return to Carlsbad from Prague on the 10th of March 1856. They leave Carlsbad four days later, eventually arriving back at Evenwood on the 7th of April 1856 – confirmed by the announcement in the *Illustrated London News*, described by Mr Lazarus in his recollections.

The truth of it all lay here, in a puzzling chronological discrepancy. Why had Perseus's recent majority been celebrated on Christmas Day, when it was clear from the letters that he had been born in September?

Then I recall the afternoon on which I had taken tea with Sukie and her mother, and of what Mrs Prout had said concerning the strange notion of the then Mrs Zaluski that, on the advice of her foreign doctor, her son must be kept away from people at all times, and closely wrapped up, even in summer. I remember, too, how

Mrs Prout had said that Professor Slake, on catching a glimpse of the young heir, had quipped that the boy had been misnamed: 'He should have been called "Nimrod",' Mrs Prout had reported the Professor as saying. Nimrod: the mighty hunter before the Lord, vigorous and strong in body. How had Mrs Prout herself described the infant? 'The bonniest three-month child, indeed, I ever did see.' I had paid little heed to her words at the time; but now they seemed full of unconscious significance.

Time. Dates.

Now I understand. Now I see it.

Perseus was not three months old when Colonel and Mrs Zaluski returned to Evenwood in April 1856, to place the future heir in the welcoming arms of proud Lord Tansor. He was a little over six months old. A bonnie three-month child he must indeed have seemed; and little wonder that his mother had been obliged to concoct a story to keep him from view, swaddled in enveloping shawls, away from inquisitive eyes, until he could be safely brought out, and his uncommon size and robustness displayed to general scrutiny without exciting suspicion.

The contribution to the plot of the unprincipled German lawyer, Herr Drexler, is now also apparent: he must have been paid to prepare the necessary documents, in which he had inserted the fictitious date of 25th December for the heir's birth. All subsequent public computations of the infant's age had therefore been based on this falsified birth-date. With a grudging smile, I reflect on the audacity of the choice of natal day – when both the Son of God and the Duport heir had come into the world of men.

I can draw only one final, momentous conclusion.

Miss Emily Carteret had been with child when she left England in January 1855 – unmarried, and in mourning for her lately slain fiancé. A husband was required, to act as a father to the baby she was secretly carrying. That husband was Colonel Tadeusz Zaluski. That child was Perseus Duport, the present Duport heir, the author of *Merlin and Nimue*, who had lately proposed to me on the Ponte Vecchio. The man I loved.

But who was his true father?

Who else but the man his mother had called Lord Tansor's 'shining hope'; the love of her life; the co-betrayer, with her, of my father?

Who else, but Phoebus Rainsford Daunt?

MADAME HAD BEEN utterly, dangerously wrong. I should not have been instructed to marry Perseus in order to reclaim what had been taken from my father. Perseus was not the rightful heir, as he and all the world believed, and he never could be, for his illegitimacy would now bar him from the succession. It was Mr Randolph, the scorned younger son, the fruit of the legitimate union between Lord Tansor's cousin, Miss Emily Carteret, and Colonel Tadeusz Zaluski, who was the true heir; and it was Mr Randolph whom I must marry.

How can I describe what I feel when this realization comes sweeping over me, in a sudden torrent of despair? To have my heart's true desire snatched away from me – so cruelly, without warning, destroying every hope that I have come to cherish for my future as Perseus's wife – is the most bitter blow imaginable, and I have to force back the tears so that I can continue with my examination of Mr Barley's black box.

Of the three remaining documents, two are single sheets of paper, on which the clerk had set down brief depositions concerning the visits that Lady Tansor had paid to Mr Vyse in Old Square, together with transcriptions of what he had overheard of their conversations on those occasions.

The third and last item is another letter, an original, in Emily's hand, still in its envelope. With the light fading, I raise the letter close to my face, the better to read it.

Then I start back. What is it?

The faintest residue of an odour, almost imperceptible, yet unmistakable: the still lingering scent of long-lost years.

The smell of violets.

•   •   •

OUT OF MR Barley's black box I have plucked the very letter that
Conrad Kraus had kept hidden for over twenty years, the precious
relic that he had preserved of the beautiful lady whom he had
accompanied to Bohemia in his youth, and whom he had continued to reverence – perhaps even love – in his poor, pathetic way
ever since; the letter with which his vengeful mother had thought
to blackmail the object of her weak-brained son's futile infatuation,
but which had led instead to her destruction.

The writer herself had thought the letter destroyed; but when it
at last fell into his hands, the man she had foolishly trusted to protect her had immediately seen its worth, just as doomed Mrs Kraus
had done.

Would you know, at last, what it contained, this deadly epistle,
written to Lord Tansor from Franzenbad by Miss Emily Carteret,
twelve days before her marriage to Colonel Tadeusz Zaluski?

Here it is, then, as I faithfully transcribed it into my note-book
– that constant companion of mine since the day I first began my
employment as maid to the 26th Baroness Tansor.

II
The Perfumed Letter
MISS EMILY CARTERET TO THE LATE LORD TANSOR
11TH MARCH 1855

Hotel Adler
Franzenbad

MY LORD,—

*I had not intended to write to yr Ldship today, for I have no news
of substance; but I was in such distress of mind, on rising this morning to a cold grey dawn, that I did not know what else might relieve
my pain & despair other than to pick up my pen, on this most terrible anniversary day, & set down my thoughts in a few inadequate*

words, & send them to the only other person in the world who is able to comprehend how I feel.

Three months to the day! Three short months — & yet how long, how infinitely long, have been — & continue to be — each week, each day, each hour, each second, without his dear, adored presence in the world! And still the wound of unutterable grief bleeds, day & night, & indeed I believe that it will never be staunched.

I see him constantly in my dreams, his poor white face lying in the hardly paler snow, his open unseeing eyes staring up at the cold stars, his precious life-blood yet spreading all around; but still — even in death — he was beautiful, was still my adored Phoebus!

And then I see, clasped in his frozen hand, the paper on which his murderer had copied out those exquisite lines, with which the name of Phoebus Rainsford Daunt will be eternally associated.

But what is most horrible to bear — & you will think it strange and inexplicable — is the memory of the last cigar he ever smoked, bearing his favorite Ramón Allones brand name, the end still glowing in the freezing gloom, for it had fortuitously fallen from his lips on to the top of a low wall, where the snow lay less thickly. Such a trifling, insignificant thing, and yet I cannot rid my mind of it.

What cuts me to my very soul is that I knew *it would come to this — *knew *that he would perish at the hands of that obsessed madman Glyver, & that I would be left to grieve until death took me too.*

It was on waking one morning from another of the terrible visions of impending, fatal disaster that were then nightly invading my sleep, and which — I truly believed — nothing could prevent, that I suddenly thought of a course of action, which, if successful, might help those who survived the catastrophe — you & I, my Lord — to bear what must be borne.

Certain that the maniac Glyver would not rest until he had wreaked mortal vengeance on his rival, for the injuries that he imagined he had suffered at his hands, I went to dear Phoebus on the day following our dinner in Town with Ld & Lady Cotterstock — do you remember? He laughed at my fears, of course, said Glyver had not the power to hurt him — indeed, that the power was all in his own hands. But in this, my dear love — thinking too little of his enemy's murder-

ous & ungovernable determination to prove his false claim to be yr Ldship's son and heir — was calamitously mistaken. The truth was far otherwise — as you & I now know, to our eternal sorrow.

Having begged him to take the greatest possible care to protect himself, which he promised to do, I then urged that we must seek to arm ourselves against the worst happening, by devising a way to thwart the impostor, if we could, and deny him his illusion of victory.

He listened to my plan; said nothing at first; then sought to dissuade me from the course I had proposed. His objections were many — both moral (as you would have expected of him), & practical — and most earnestly expressed.

Principal amongst them concerned yr Ldship's position, which of course he was ever most anxious to protect from public opprobrium. I could not then answer for how yr Ldship would view the as yet unforeseeable consequences of what I contemplated, tho' I hoped & believed, with all my heart, that yr support & sympathy might at last be secured.

At length, he saw that I was right. With what courage he conceded that the lunatic might succeed, despite taking every precaution, in doing him mortal harm. But he did not flinch from the dread prospect, nor would he fly from it. He was a man, indeed!

And so, as you now know, from that day forth, until the last fateful evening, we became man & wife in all but name and legal form. Then, with mingled joy and grief, I discovered that I was with child! His child! — the son or daughter of yr Ldship's chosen heir, in whom, even if my fears proved groundless, my darling boy would live, and be for ever remembered.

The worst had happened. The madman had succeeded in the exercise of his brutal will, just as I had foreseen. And yet a kind Fate had quickly granted (beyond, I can now confess, my most sanguine expectations) the means of salvation.

I am conscious that I ought not to be so frank in writing to yr Ldship. You will say — rightly — that I have been dangerously injudicious, having already laid some of these things before yr Ldship, and when I promised circumspection, as far as was possible, in our correspondence. But I find I cannot help myself. I must give vent to *the tumult within me — & it is to yr Ldship that I instinctively turn. Besides, once received through our trusted intermediary, you will, I know, destroy this, as we agreed, & as I feel sure that you have destroyed my other letters.*

It is the day, I think, the accursed 11th day of every month, that raises up this tumult within me. I cannot describe the dread I feel as each one approaches — & then the sense of desolation when waking on the day itself, as I did this very morning. It overcomes me utterly, driving away all other thoughts & sensations. Yet it is also a day of sacred observance, on which I must for ever, each succeeding month, & especially on the one *day, worship the memory of him who will always rule my heart, & who has made it impossible for me to love any other man.*

Mrs Kraus has just arrived to dress me, & so I must conclude, & once more find strength — for his sweet sake, & yours, my dear sir — to bring our enterprise to a successful conclusion.

I shall now send Conrad, who is standing sullenly by the door regarding me as I write, in that peculiar abstracted way of his, to ensure that this goes by the first mail coach.

Until my next, when I trust I shall be more myself, I am, my Lord, yr loving & grateful daughter, by adoption & affection,
E. CARTERET

III
The Portrait

'WELL, MY DEAR,' said Mr Wraxall, as I came back into the sitting-room, carrying Mr Barley's black box. 'Is all clear to you now?'

'Where is Mr Barley?' I asked, seeing the vacated chair.

'He was obliged to return to London this evening,' returned Mr Wraxall. 'Mrs Wapshott's son has just taken him to Easton in the trap. Well? Do you see it now?'

He regarded me expectantly.

'I see it.'

I sat down; he drew his chair close to mine, and we began a conversation that lasted for nearly an hour, until darkness began to fall, and Mrs Wapshott appeared at the door to light the lamps. So we continued to talk, until we could talk no more.

For a while we sat saying nothing, listening to the ominous rolling of distant thunder. Then we heard the sound of the trap returning from Easton.

'When will she be—'

Mr Wraxall held up his hand, to prevent my saying more.

'Enough now, my dear,' he said, quietly. 'All that is in Gully's hands, but I do not think it will be long. Now then, let me call John, to take you back to the house.'

DINNER WAS OVER by the time I returned. In the Drawing-Room, as I entered, I could see that Emily, sitting broodingly alone by the fire, was angry.

'Where have you been?' she asked, testily.

There was no reason to deceive her; indeed, I felt seized by a kind of taunting boldness, knowing what I now knew, as I answered.

'To North Lodge.'

She could not prevent a faint flush of apprehension from colouring her sallow cheeks, but as usual quickly contrived an air of unconcern.

'And how goes the brilliant Mr Montagu Wraxall?' she asked, in an affectedly sarcastic tone. 'Surely his business here must soon be finished? Lancing has found a new tenant for North Lodge, and it is now rather inconvenient to us for Mr Wraxall to be here any longer than is absolutely necessary. We have been more than generous in allowing him to remain there for so long, with the freedom to come and go as he pleases, as if the place were really his.'

'I believe there is still some work to be done on his late uncle's papers,' replied I; 'but he is well, thank you, and sends his compliments.'

'Well,' she said, with a dismissive sniff, 'that is kind of him, I'm sure. But I wonder, dear, what you and he can find to talk about. You'll allow, I think, that there is a certain disparity of age and experience between you, which does not – on the face of it – suggest a natural affinity of either opinions or interests.'

'Oh,' I replied, fixing her with a steady look, 'Mr Wraxall has a wide mental view of the world. You would be surprised, I think, how many common interests we share.'

To this she said nothing, but smoothed down her dress, in an exaggeratedly uncaring manner, before pointedly picking up her coffee-cup and taking a sip.

I sat down opposite her and, mimicking her indifference, took up a copy of *The Times* from the low table that separated us, and began to leaf idly through it.

After several minutes' silence, I asked if Mr Perseus had returned from London.

'Yes,' she replied, absently, staring once again into the fire. 'This afternoon.'

'And what was Mr Freeth's opinion of the new work? Favourable, I'm sure.'

She gave a weary sigh.

'I believe so.'

Her fractiousness had ebbed quite away, replaced now by a strange, unreceptive vacancy.

'Are you feeling well, dear?' I asked, laying down the newspaper.

'What did you say?'

'I asked whether you were feeling well.'

'Oh yes, quite well,' she replied, still staring into the dying flames.

'But perhaps you should retire,' I suggested, looking up at the clock. 'You are still feeling the exertions of the journey home, you know, and must take every possible care not to weaken yourself further. Come, let me take you up.'

To this she wearily consented, and took my outstretched hand. Slowly, arm in arm, we went out into the vestibule.

At the foot of the staircase, we paused for a moment to allow her to catch her breath – something I had observed had become increasingly necessary lately, even after the slightest exertion.

'Such a wonderful likeness,' she remarked, seeing me glancing at the portrait of the Turkish Corsair.

'Likeness?' I asked. 'Of whom?'

She laughed in disbelief.

'Why, of Phoebus, of course, you silly goose! Surely everyone in the house knows that. Who else could it be?'

I felt a prize fool for not realizing this before, especially after finding the photograph of Daunt in the secret cupboard. The portrait had been painted in the summer of 1853, as Emily now informed me, soon after the publication of Daunt's tragedy *Penelope,* when his reputation was at its height. After his death, it had been placed in its present position by Lord Tansor, as a memorial to his chosen heir. No doubt the sitter had assumed this consciously Byronic pose to indicate that he was, in point of genius, the noble poet's successor.

Thoughtlessly, I told her that I had always seen a resemblance to Mr Perseus, and wondered that others had not seen it also.

Her mouth tightened. I had unnerved her; but, as ever, her capacity for self-possession soon asserted itself.

'Yes, I'll allow that there is some superficial likeness,' she said. 'It's the beard, I suppose, and I will readily concede that Perseus has a naturally dashing look about him that agrees very well with the original. But they are not so very like, you know, if one looks closely. Come now, dear, won't you help me up the stairs? You have an old lady for a friend now.'

As she did not wish to call Miss Allardyce, I assisted in undressing her, like the old days of not so very long ago, and then helped her into bed.

'Will you take some drops?' I asked. 'Just a few, to settle you?'

'Yes,' she said, laying her head back on the pillow, and closing her eyes. 'I think I will. I don't wish to—'

But she left the sentence unfinished, and I turned to open the bedside cupboard, where the bottle of tincture was now kept.

After I had administered the drops, she asked me to read to her until sleep came. When it did, I replaced the book – one of her dead lover's, of course – on the shelf, quietly closed the bedroom door, and made my way, heart pounding at the thought of what I must do, to the second floor of the South Wing.

33

In Which Certain Truths
are Faced at Last

I
Love Denied

As I stand outside Perseus's study, I begin to wonder whether I should have sought Madame's instructions on what I should do in the dramatically changed circumstances. My mind, however, is quickly made up. I know what must be done, for the sake of the Great Task, and that I must do it as soon as possible, or my courage will surely fail me.

There are tears to brush away; then, taking a deep breath, I am about to knock on the door when it suddenly opens.

'Esperanza!'

He is standing, book in hand, dressed in a plum-coloured dressing-robe that reaches to the floor. His long hair is crowned with a black velvet smoking-cap, his shirt is unbuttoned at the neck, and a lighted cigar is clamped between his teeth. For an instant, the painted image of Phoebus Daunt as the Turkish Corsair, and the photograph of him, coalesce with the living face of his son, and I find myself staring, openly fascinated, at the tall figure framed in the doorway.

'I was on my way to the Library,' he informs me, with a warm smile of greeting. 'Why weren't you at dinner?'

I tell him that I have been at North Lodge.

'With Wraxall?'

'Yes. I hope you approve of him?'

'Approve of Wraxall? Why, certainly I approve of him. We have had little to do with each other, but I hear only good things of him, and of course his professional reputation precedes him. I am glad that he seems to have taken you under his wing.'

Suddenly overcome by a desire to flee from what I have come here to do, I then apologize for disturbing him, and make some excuse to go; but he reaches out and gently takes my hand.

'No, no,' he urges. 'Come in, by all means. I've been working long enough tonight.'

A log fire is burning in the grate, but Perseus finds gloom conducive to poetic composition; and so the only other sources of light in the vaulted stone chamber are supplied by a single candle on his desk, and by a small lamp on a table by the fire.

Being at first unsure of what I should say, by way of preparation for the task before me, I rather stumblingly express the hope that his business in London has gone satisfactorily.

'Quite satisfactorily,' he returns, showing me to a chair by the fire. 'Mr Orr says that the legal side will be perfectly straightforward.'

'And what of Mr Freeth?' I then enquire, struggling to maintain a cheerful tone. 'Come now, tell me what he thought of *Dante and Beatrice*. I've been longing to know.'

'Oh, hasn't Mother told you? He thought that it represents – so far – a signal advance, in terms of poetic achievement, on my previous effort. His considered professional opinion is that it will do very well.'

I tell him that I am delighted to hear it; I then pause, to compose myself in readiness for my next question.

'And – if I may ask – when will you speak to Lady Tansor concerning our engagement?'

'Is that what you really came to ask me?' he asks. His smile has returned, but now it is teasing, in a rather sweet, reassuring way. He does not wait for me to answer.

'Tomorrow,' he says. 'I shall tell her tomorrow, after luncheon.'

He leans towards me, and takes my hand again.

'Please don't concern yourself,' he says, giving me a most tender look. 'Mother will make no objection. I am certain of it. I have an answer to every objection she can possibly raise. My happiness is everything to her, and no one can make me happier than you. She knows what it is to love.'

He does not qualify this remark; but of course he is alluding to his mother's love for Phoebus Daunt, not to Colonel Zaluski, the man he thinks had been his father.

'And do you love me, then?' I ask.

He gives me an incredulous stare.

'Haven't I told you so?' He sounds almost offended.

'You've told me many things with respect to your feelings for me,' I reply, returning in my mind to that ever-memorable afternoon on the Ponte Vecchio; 'but you have not said that you love me – only that you wish to marry me. The two are not necessarily the same.'

'So you wish me to tell you, in plain language, that I love you? Is that it?' His tone is still playful, although his eyes give back a faintly anxious look.

'Only if you so wish, and if it's true.'

'Surely you know by now that I cannot play the lover,' he says, not scornfully or boastfully, but with a kind of regret. Then, more meditatively: 'It's curious. I can write of love, and write well of it, I think; but I've been cursed with a reticent nature, which I deplore, but fear I cannot alter. So you will get no *billets-doux* from me, no rivers of tears, no fervour of abandonment. Will you mind that, my sweet Esperanza? Mind having a poet for a husband who yet cannot tell you he loves you every hour of the day, unless you ask him?'

He releases my hand and reaches down to pick out a log from the basket to throw on the fire.

'No,' I return. 'I won't mind. It's the sincerity of the feeling that counts, of course. You might tell me that you loved me and not mean it. I don't place much value on the mere words, only on what lies behind them.'

He takes my hand again, and my heart begins to beat harder with dread at what I am coming to.

'And you are right to do so,' he says, softly. 'Words mean nothing, in themselves, and are treacherous – dangerous – for that reason.'

'Even the word "love"?'

'Especially the word "love",' he replies, 'which is as pregnant with danger and deception as the passion it describes.'

'So you consider love to be a dangerous passion, then?'

'Most assuredly. Every poet must.'

'But it can be otherwise. Surely, as a poet, you also know that to be true?'

'Certainly – indeed, such love is the subject of my new poem; but the fact remains that words may lie and dissemble, as well as speak the truth. Love can raise the heart to holiness; love can be tender and ennobling; but love can also corrupt and destroy.'

We both fall silent, as the log he has thrown on the fire begins to flare and crackle. Then he reaches forward to touch my cheek.

'But I will gladly speak the words, my dearest girl, and mean them, too,' he says. 'Here they are, then: I—'

'No!' I cry, leaning over and placing my finger on his lips. 'Please, do not say them. It was wrong of me to ask you to tell me something I already know in my heart to be true, just for the satisfaction of hearing the words. But I don't need you to say them, truly I don't.'

'I know!' he exclaims. 'I'll put it all into a poem. How would that be?'

I tell him that a poem will do very well.

'Then it's settled. I'll take up my pen as soon as you've gone, and will deliver the result to you, in person, tomorrow – perhaps in sonnet form.'

As he finishes speaking, I experience such a sharp pang of anguish and despair at what I am about to do that I have to turn my head away, fixing my eyes on the now flaming log in the grate.

'Has something happened?' he asks, seeing my discomfort.

It has come: the moment when I must thrust a knife deep into the precious heart of Perseus Duport – and into my own.

When I still do not answer, he asks again, more urgently, whether anything is wrong.

'Are you still concerned at how my mother will receive the news of our engagement?' he asks, when I continue silent. 'Be assured that—'

'No!' I break in, resolved now to grasp the nettle, come what may. 'It's not that.'

'Then what is it?'

'I cannot marry you.'

My words seem to hang in the air, like the reverberations of a tolling bell. I wait for him to speak, but no words come. The burning log casts a lurid orange light over the chamber. Outside, the wind begins to howl about the many-towered house; and still he says nothing.

At last he rises from his chair, picks up his cigar, which he has placed on the table beside him, and takes a long draw on it. Then he locks his great dark eyes on mine.

'You have a reason, I suppose?'

His voice is cold now, hard and threatening, all its former softness gone.

'I do not love you, Perseus. I never have, and I never will.'

Each word tears my heart asunder. This is the hardest thing I shall ever do in this life: to tell the man I love above all others that I do not care for him.

He takes another long draw on his cigar.

'You'll forgive me for mentioning it,' he says, after briefly considering his reply, 'but you gave me a rather contrary impression in Florence, on more than one occasion. But it seems now that you were – how can I best put it? What is *le mot juste*? Ah, yes, I have it! *Lying.*'

Feeling the sting of his sarcasm, I make a weak attempt to mitigate what I have just said with more untruths.

'I hope you will recall that I have never told you I loved you. I have come to regard you with affection, and of course I cannot help but be gratified – deeply gratified – by the exceptional honour you have paid me by asking me to—'

'Honour! You may say so! Honour! A proposal of marriage from the heir to one of the most ancient and distinguished families in England! An honour indeed, for an orphan of uncertain lineage.'

His anger is now in full flood; but I know that he speaks in this hurtful way because the pride that has sustained him for so long has been grievously – perhaps even fatally – wounded.

'Well, Miss Gorst,' he continues, abandoning himself to every disagreeable trait in his character, 'you've led me a merry dance, I see. You truly are without ambition, to reject a proposal that would have made you one of the most envied women in the land. I was mistaken, it seems. You *were* born to be a lady's-maid after all, and nothing more.'

What can I say to him? He has every right to feel injured and aggrieved by my apparent rejection of what he has offered me, sincerely and unconditionally. At length, head bowed, unable to look him in the eye, I say that I cannot blame him for speaking so, acknowledging that I have done him a great wrong.

'I shall always esteem you, but I do not love you,' I say again, feeling sick to my soul at the lie, 'and it is best that I acknowledge it now. I cannot unite myself to you – or to anyone – without love, although I may lose what the world will think me mad for rejecting.'

'But could you not have learned to love me, then?'

His face is immobile, but the question is put almost pleadingly; yet now it has come to it, I steel myself to give no quarter.

'I do not think so.'

He says nothing, only drops his still-glowing cigar into a metal bowl, brimful of old butts and cold ash. For some moments he sits, tapping his fingers on the arm of the chair, contemplating his reply, and looking so like his mother.

'You say you cannot marry me,' he says at last, 'because you do not love me. I now find that I cannot love someone who does not love me in return. Who, then, holds the superior position?'

In a somewhat more placatory voice, he quickly adds: 'Well, there is no need to answer. It seems to me that we have each been sadly mistaken in the other.'

I do not – cannot – make any reply, but sit, head bowed, as he gets up from his chair and walks over to his desk. Opening one of the drawers, he takes out a small object, and comes back over to stand before the fire.

In his hand is the velvet-covered box containing the ring that he had bought from Signor Silvaggio's shop on the Ponte Vecchio.

'Does this bring back any memories?' he asks, in the most cutting tone.

'Of course,' I answer. 'Very fond memories indeed.'

He opens the box. The brilliant gems flash and gleam in the firelight.

'Hmm. A pretty thing. One of Signor Silvaggio's best. But as you appear to have no need of it any more, well then—'

He turns, and throws the box, ring and all, on to the fire.

'The ring will not be consumed,' he says, watching the flames begin to work on the velvet box, 'for the fire will never be hot enough. But I shall give instructions for it never to be cleared away. It will stay there, in the ashes, to remind me of this charming episode in my life, and as a warning never to trust a woman again.'

I am appalled and distressed by what he has just done; but still I sit, in wordless desperation, as he resumes his seat, and lights another cigar.

'Of course I see how it is,' he goes on. 'Despite your assurances to the contrary, there's another party in the case. My dear brother has got the better of me for once. But I don't care to discuss the matter any further. You've said enough, and done enough.'

Another long draw on his cigar.

I do not even have the strength to deny, once again, that I love Randolph, knowing that it would serve no purpose to do so.

'I shall say nothing of this to Mother, of course,' he resumes. 'However, I shall absolutely insist to her that you must leave Evenwood as soon as matters can be so arranged.'

I try to appear unconcerned, although I ask him what reason he will give for depriving Lady Tansor of someone on whose companionship she has come to depend.

'Oh, I shall contrive something, never fear,' he replies, confidently. 'And if I can't, well then, I shall simply say that you must go, without giving a reason. Mother, you know, can refuse me nothing. It's a very great advantage, to be the favoured eldest son.'

With some difficulty, I persuade him to allow me to tell his mother in my own time that I have decided to leave Evenwood, to seek some new life in France. To this hastily conceived contrivance, he at last reluctantly agrees.

For several moments we both sit, listening to the wind, and staring into the fire. Nothing is said, for there is nothing more to say. He loves me, as I love him; but I have lost him for ever. The Great Task has prevailed.

II
The Tables are Turned

I SLEPT BADLY that night, rising early with an aching heart, and a head to match. The day that lay before me would be a momentous one; for I had determined that I could not wait for Mr Randolph to propose to me in his own good time, but must go to him as soon as possible and bring matters to a speedy conclusion. The prospect of marrying him was not a wholly distasteful one: many happy marriages, I was sure, were made with a great deal less mutual liking than he and I enjoyed. He loved me, I was certain of it; for my part, I felt fondness enough to give myself to him, if it served my father's great cause. None of this, however, gave me any comfort, for my heart had been broken by the sacrifice that I had been forced to make. As the wife of Randolph Duport – now, although he did not yet know it, the future Lord Tansor – I might pass a life of enviable ease and comfort; but that gave me scant consolation for what I had lost.

As I was taking my breakfast, Barrington came in with a note from Mr Wraxall, asking whether it would be convenient to go over to North Lodge later that morning.

'I am expecting Inspector G,' he wrote. 'He has some news, which it is important for you to hear. And so I hope you will be at liberty to join us, in another convocation of our triumvirate.'

On the advice of Dr Pordage, Emily was confined to her bed for the day and did not require me to attend her; and so, after a hasty cup of coffee, I repaired to the Drawing-Room to write my reply, then called for a footman to take it over to North Lodge.

On my way back upstairs, I encountered Charlie Skinner, carrying a tray of coffee and morning comestibles. This, most fortuitously, he was about to take up to Mr Randolph, who, complaining of a headache, had sent down to say that he would take his breakfast in his room.

'If you give the tray to me, Charlie,' I said, 'I'll take it up to Mr Randolph.'

'Well, miss, if you're sure,' Charlie replied, grinning approvingly at this shameless breach of domestic etiquette.

'Before you go, Charlie,' I said, 'do you remember an old woman visiting Lady Tansor, one evening last September, soon after I came here?'

He began to scratch his head.

'Old woman,' he replied, now pursing his lips in a visible effort of concentration. 'Ah!' he suddenly exclaimed. 'The witch! Small ugly party. Hubble, bubble, toil and trouble!'

He gave a gravelly chuckle at this demonstration of his literary wit.

'You saw her, then?' I asked.

'Oh yes, miss. Saw, and heard a bit, too. Then I told Sukie Prout.'

'You say you heard something?'

'Just a name,' he said. 'Gentleman's name.'

'What name, Charlie?'

'Christmas guest, miss. Mr Vyse.'

'Anything else?'

'Something about a letter she'd got with her, the witch I mean, which she kept waving under her Ladyship's nose. She said it was a valuable – what was the word?'

He pursed his lips once more, and furiously scratched his big round head, with its spiky crown of straw-coloured hair.

'Commodity! That was it. A most valuable commodity.'

'Thank you, Charlie,' I said, taking the tray from him.

'At your service, as always, miss,' he replied, taking a step back, winking, and then honouring me with one of his smartest salutes.

OUTSIDE RANDOLPH'S ROOM, I lay the tray down, and knock gently on the door.

'Who's that?'

Placing my face close to the door, I softly say my name.

'Esperanza! What? Just a moment.'

A little time passes before the door eventually opens, and he stands before me – not, as I had expected, in night-attire and dressing-robe, but fully costumed in jacket, buckskin trousers, and top-boots, apparently ready for the day.

'I do hope I am not disturbing you,' I say. 'May I come in – if you are not feeling unwell?'

'Unwell?'

'Charlie Skinner says that you'd asked to take breakfast in your room, because of a headache – look, I've brought your tray.'

'Headache? Oh yes, of course' he replies, looking unaccountably flustered. 'Quite beastly when I woke up, but much better now, thank you. And you've brought up my tray, have you? You shouldn't have done that, you know. Not your place at all. That should have been Skinner's job.'

'Oh, I don't mind about that,' I return. 'I happened to meet Charlie on the way up, that's all. Shall I bring it in?'

'No, no!' he cries. 'I won't hear of it. Leave it there, won't you? Do you know, I find I'm suddenly not at all hungry. I think I'll take something later.'

For some seconds we remain in the doorway, smiling embarrassingly at each other, until he moves aside to usher me in, a little unwillingly, as it seems to me, but saying brightly, 'Come in, come in!'

I step into a small, sparsely furnished ante-room, the floor of which is littered with fishing tackle and old copies of the *Sporting Times*. Through an open door I catch sight of the equally untidy bed-chamber. Mr Randolph continues to seem distinctly ill at ease, inclined only to engage in the most desultory and inconsequential small talk, whilst I, of course, hope that he will seize the moment and make his proposal so that the business can be concluded as quickly as possible. But having exhausted all the tedious topics of general enquiry, and after throwing a brief look out of the open window, he merely remarks: 'A fine day at last, I see. I think I might walk out for an hour.'

Well, here is a thing! Where is the light of expectation in his eyes? Where the relief that his long-delayed proposal can now be put to me? Where the ardent hope that it will be accepted? Has he not guessed why I have come?

For a moment I wonder whether I have been mistaken in believing that what he had said to me, on the day of our walk to the Temple of the Winds, admitted of only one interpretation. Surely his meaning had been unequivocal? And then I had read so much more in his look than his inadequate words had been capable of conveying. Assuring myself that all was well, and once more ascribing his hesitancy to nervousness and inexperience, I resolve to lend some assistance, if I can, to show him that he should have no fear of his proposal being rejected.

'I thought, perhaps,' I begin, 'that *you* might wish to say something to *me*, as you've told me you wished to do. I can assure you that, whatever it is, I am very willing to hear it. *Very* willing indeed.'

'Confound it!' he suddenly bursts out. 'What a booby I am! All I've been wanting to do, these many weeks past, is to find some suitable moment to say something to you – that is, to put something to you, of a, well, personal nature – and now, when *you* give *me* the opportunity I've been looking for, I fumble and shilly-shally, like the dim-witted clodhopper I am, putting it all off again, and thinking that I'll ask you another time. But I shan't be a coward any longer.'

I give him another warm smile of encouragement, and tell him that I am glad to hear it.

'And so,' I proceed, heartened by his admission, 'you had better ask me your question before you change your mind – and I change mine.'

'Oh, I shan't do that,' replies he. 'You can't imagine how much

I've longed to get everything off my chest and unburden myself to you – and to you alone, dear Esperanza, for there's no one else here who would – well, never mind that. It's been such a torment, keeping my secret closed up inside, unable to speak to anyone about it.'

'Tell me now, then,' I urge again, a little more emphatically, for though his words are warmly expressed, there is something in his look that I find worryingly difficult to interpret. Perhaps a little more encouragement is required; and so I reach out, take both his hands in mine, and begin to draw him towards me, careless of the impropriety I am committing.

Mr Randolph, however, seems strangely dismayed and embarrassed by my action. Quickly disengaging himself, he takes a step back.

'No, no!' he exclaims, colouring up. 'You mustn't, really you mustn't.'

'But what is the matter?' I ask, searching his face for some clue to his unexpected reaction. I then attempt once more to give him the courage to open up his heart. I tell him that, if it will help him say what he wishes to say, I am ready to make a little confession, as he had done on our first walk together from Easton.

A puzzled frown is his response.

'Confession?'

'Yes. It's this: I know – I've guessed – what you have wanted to ask me.'

A look of horror spreads over his face.

'You know?'

'Of course,' I declare with a rather forced laugh.

'But how—?'

'How could I not know?' I reply, attempting another reassuring laugh, but now feeling its hollow inappropriateness. 'You made it perfectly clear, when we walked by the Lake.'

He runs his fingers through his hair, and begins pacing distractedly up and down, as if overcome by some sudden and inexplicable shock.

'What do you think you know?' The question is put almost angrily. 'I cannot – will not – say more until you tell me.'

'Since you make me,' I reply, overcome now with confusion, 'then I suppose I must. I believe you wished to put a certain proposal to me – a proposal, as you yourself described it, of a personal nature, and one which I would have accepted. I expected you to ask me a question, to put it as plainly as I can, that I would have answered with the single word, "Yes". There. Are you satisfied?'

He regards me with a dumbfounded expression for several moments. Then the light of understanding breaks over him.

'Do you mean a proposal of marriage?'

'Of course,' I reply, tiring of his obtuseness. 'What else could I mean?'

'But my dear Miss Gorst – Esperanza – you have mistaken me – badly mistaken me. I didn't mean – I couldn't have meant – that is—'

At that moment there is a noise in the adjoining dressing-room, and the sound of a door opening.

I turn my head to see Mrs Battersby step into the ante-room. Without a word, Mr Randolph immediately goes over to stand beside her.

'Oh, Esperanza!' he says, almost in a whisper, and in a way that makes me wince at the undisguised pity in his voice. 'I cannot – could never – ask you to marry me; neither could I have suggested such a thing on that walk. I am already married, you see.'

He turns, and takes Mrs Battersby's hand tenderly in his.

'To my dearest Jane.'

It is beyond my power to describe what I feel on hearing these words. What am I to do? The Great Task lies in ruins, but that means nothing to me now. When I have lost everything that is most precious to me, what is there left to be gained? I have rejected the love of my dearest Perseus, the one-time heir, only to be cast off by his brother, who will soon take his place. Unless I can prove that I have inherited my father's stolen birthright, Mr Randolph will succeed his mother, and Mrs Battersby – Mrs Battersby, of all people in the world! – will become the next Lady Tansor, a reversal of fortunes as astounding as it had been entirely unforeseen.

How had this come about? Here is what I now learned, concerning the younger Duport son and the housekeeper, on that terrible morning.

I BEGIN WITH ever-smiling Mrs Jane Battersby.

Like me, she was a fiction, an invention, being none other than the sister of Randolph's friend and closest companion, Mr Rhys Paget. At the age of seventeen, Randolph had been sent to Dr Lancelot Savage's academy in Suffolk, where it was intended that he should complete his education under that gentleman's direction, the establishment being regarded by Lady Tansor as a kind of substitute for the University.

On his first day at Dr Savage's he met Rhys Paget, the son of a widowed Welsh clergyman. Invited to spend part of the summer holiday at his new friend's home near Llanberis, he there made the acquaintance of Miss Paget, his friend's older half-sister – beautiful, accomplished, of a marked refinement of intellect and manners, and yet possessing, to an exceptional degree, those more practical acquirements that made her an able substitute for her departed stepmother in the running of household affairs.

Very soon, a strong bond of affection developed between the young man and the clergyman's daughter. Despite the variance in their ages, and the disparity of their conditions, their mutual regard soon began to flower into genuine love.

After the death of Mr Herbert Paget, his children had inherited the house at Llanberis but little else, Mr Paget having lost most of a considerable legacy in the infamous failure of the Overend Gurney bank some years earlier.* As a consequence, his daughter had been obliged to seek employment in order to maintain the family home, to which she and her brother were both deeply attached.

Assuming her late mother's maiden name of Battersby, she had first found a governess's position near Shrewsbury, and then a situa-

---

*The collapse of the discount bank Overend Gurney in May 1866, leaving debts of some £11 million, was the most spectacular of the nineteenth century.

tion as under-housekeeper in London. After gaining suitable experience, she had subsequently become housekeeper in a baronet's establishment just a few miles from Bury St Edmunds, and not so very far from where Dr Savage's school was situated.

When Dr Savage became aware, by means of an anonymous note, of his pupil's liaison with a servant, although the latter was not named, he felt immediately obliged to inform Lady Tansor. As Mr Randolph, whilst also refusing to name the lady, did not seek to deny the truth of the assertion, his mother – unwaveringly determined, as always, to stamp out any possibility of scandal attaching itself to the illustrious Duport name – straight away requested her relative, Major Hunt-Graham, who lived in the vicinity of Dr Savage's school, to fetch her errant son away from Suffolk, and bring him back to Evenwood, where he had to face her full wrath for his dangerous and irresponsible folly.

Thus Mr Randolph's time at Dr Savage's was abruptly terminated; but not his love for Miss Paget, which had grown even deeper with time, and which was returned to the full.

For a while, the lovers suffered the agonies of separation; but then fortune had smiled on them.

The position of housekeeper at Evenwood falling suddenly vacant after the death of the elderly lady who had held the situation for many years, Mr Randolph persuaded his mother to interview a certain Jane Battersby, whom, he claimed, had been highly recommended by a friend of Mr Rhys Paget's. The other candidates for the position had luckily proved unsuitable in various ways; and so, as 'Mrs Battersby' had immediately impressed Lady Tansor by demonstrating a highly superior disposition and no common order of capability, and as she had brought with her several excellent references, she was quickly engaged, and 'Mrs Battersby' soon assumed a dominant place in the domestic hierarchy of Evenwood.

I then learn that it had been during the Christmas festivities just past that the two lovers had first begun to lay plans for their marriage. Becoming increasingly anxious that their secret might be discovered, they determined to take this final, irreversible step before Randolph attained his majority, rather than afterwards, which had been their original intention. The ceremony eventually took place in London, soon after Emily, Perseus, and I left for Italy. This of course accounted for the housekeeper's absence from Evenwood, ostensibly to attend a sick relative, and for the changes I had observed in Mr Randolph's behaviour.

All this enlightened many previously obscure and puzzling matters; but how had I so misread Mr Randolph's intentions towards me?

It was simple enough. He had merely wished to recruit me as a sympathetic partaker in his own great secret, hoping thereby to use the intimacy that I had come to enjoy with his mother as a means of bringing her round to an acceptance of their union. The proposal he had wished to make had not been one of marriage, simply of confidential friendship. When I hear this, and recall his former words, I see, with painful clarity, how I had invested them with a meaning that he had never intended.

'I wished so very much to have you as our friend,' says Mr Randolph, 'our true friend, in whom we could confide, and put our absolute trust. You can't know how terrible it's been, keeping our secret to ourselves – except of course for dear old Paget.'

'If that's the truth,' I reply, with some asperity, 'then why has Mrs – your wife, I should say – demonstrated such a dislike of me from the very first?'

'Perhaps, my love,' says Mr Randolph to her whom I shall continue, for the time being, to call Mrs Battersby, 'you should leave us now.'

She has said nothing during the whole time that Randolph has taken to tell the story I have just related, but continues to stand quietly by his side, occasionally squeezing his hand encouragingly.

'Very well,' she agrees. Then, turning her irritating smile full on me: 'This must be difficult for you, Miss Gorst. I feel for you, believe me. I hope, however, that Randolph and I can rely on your discretion? It would be best – for all of us – if this matter remained confidential, for the time being, and did not come to the knowledge of Lady Tansor. I'm sure you'll agree that we should avoid any unnecessary unpleasantness?'

Oh, that two-edged smile! See how we trust you, it seems to say, to keep our secret safe; but if you do not, then there would be consequences for you, as well as for us. I see, and understand, the threat in that smile: that, if necessary, she will have no hesitation in falsely implicating me in their subterfuge.

Without waiting for a reply from me, the housekeeper, bestowing another condescending smile that makes my blood boil, quits the room.

'I thought it best,' says Mr Randolph, when she has gone, 'to answer your question in my wife's absence. The matter is a somewhat delicate one, you see.'

'Delicate?' say I, scornfully. 'Why, then, choose your words carefully, sir. I would not care to be offended, you know.'

'You are angry,' he replies, 'of course you are. It has been a shock, and I am heartily sorry that, in my stupidity, I made you think something you should never have thought. There, you see? I'm doing it again. You know I don't have my dear brother's powers of poetic expression – I wish to God I did, then all this might never have happened. But it has, and now I—'

'Enough!' I angrily interject. 'I have had rather too many explanations for one day, with the exception of why your wife appeared to hate me when you say that you wished me to be a friend to you both and to share your secret. So tell me quickly.'

'Ah,' he says, 'I fear it was all a matter of simple jealousy on her part.'

'Jealousy?'

'Yes. You see, she got it into her head, from the moment you came, that you cherished – well, designs on me. Don't ask me how these things come about, but they do, and they did; and it was quickly made worse when we were seen walking back from Easton together. Then there was my birthday, and other times when she saw us together. She couldn't rid herself of an unfounded suspicion that you – we – might be, well, you know what I'm trying to say. Of course I was able, as I truly believed, to assure Jane that our relation-ship was entirely innocent, and that you'd shown not the least sign of any improper attachment or intent, nothing more than might be expected to exist between us; but she wouldn't have it, and went on believing that you had – excuse the phrase – set your cap at me.

'But she was right, wasn't she, dear Esperanza? I may continue to call you Esperanza, mayn't I, for I wish so very much for us to remain friends, if you feel able? It seems that you *had* formed a regard for me that was – well, you know. If only I'd realized how you truly felt! But I'm a dolt in these matters, as in so much else. I said the wrong things to you, in the wrong way, and that's the long and the short of it.'

I am about to disabuse him, and tell him that he had been right to think that I entertained no amorous sentiments towards him; but I draw back. I feel exhausted and despairing, and have no desire to explain the true state of things.

He stands regarding me with a plaintive look in his eyes, but I can find no more words to say to him – not a single one. So I wish him good-morning, adding that I am glad his headache is bet-ter. I then turn, and leave the room, to the sound of breeze-borne birdsong, sweet and clear, drifting in through the open casement window.

34

Retribution

I

The Triumvirate Reconvenes

I RETURNED to my room, falling on the bed in a state of utter desperation, incapable of conceiving a single intelligible thought. The Great Task had failed. Perseus was not the legitimate heir after all, whilst Mr Randolph, the true heir, was married to another. The exposure of Emily's part both in the murders of Mrs Kraus and of her father would serve the cause of Justice; but how would it now serve my own purposes, or make restitution for my father's betrayal? Mr Randolph, with the erstwhile 'Mrs Battersby' as his consort, would succeed his mother, and I would be left with nothing. How could I tell Madame that my father's great scheme had crumbled to dust?

I sat down at my desk and tried to compose a letter to send to the Avenue d'Uhrich, but the words would not come. After several attempts, I gave up, throwing myself again on my bed in a fit of pique and rage, and hammering at the pillow until the hot tears ceased at last.

As I lay there, watching the sun-cast shadows dance about the ceiling, the striking of the clocks for the hour of eleven reminded me of my appointment with Mr Wraxall, for which I was now half an hour late.

I arrived at North Lodge barely knowing where I was, so stupe-
fied and bewildered was my mental state.

'My dear girl!' cried Mr Wraxall, on opening the door. 'What on
earth is the matter?'

I heard his words, but nothing more. When I next saw the barrister's domed head and anxious eyes, I was lying on the sofa in his
sitting-room, covered with a blanket, a cloth soaked in cold water
laid across my forehead.

'Thank goodness!' said Mr Wraxall, as I opened my eyes and
looked round the room, which, to my surprise, instead of the usual
wilderness of papers, now had an air of tidiness and order about it.

'You fainted, my dear, but are now back with us. I trust you're
feeling a little better now? Very good. And look – here's Inspector
Gully, just in time as always.'

The young detective, who had been walking in the garden, having arrived early at North Lodge, pulled a stool up to the sofa,
and began to add his concerned enquiries to those of Mr Wraxall.
After they had satisfied themselves that I was sufficiently restored
to proceed with business, the inspector produced his note-book,
and then looked at Mr Wraxall, who gave a little nod to signal
that he might inaugurate the second meeting of our investigating
triumvirate.

'Well now, Miss Gorst,' the inspector began, 'I wish to report, firstly
and principally, on a most notable development. Mr W has already
been informed, but he wished me to tell you of it in person.'

Having given us a tremendously consequential look, he briefly
consulted his note-book, and then cleared his throat.

'Two days ago, a body – a man's body – was taken from the
Regent's Canal. It had suffered injuries about the head before being
thrown into the water. The victim was quickly identified, from certain items still on his person, as being Mr Armitage Vyse, barrister,
of Old Square, Lincoln's Inn, and Regent's Park Terrace.'

'Mr Vyse!'

My horrified exclamation was as spontaneous as this extraordinary piece of intelligence had been unanticipated. Mr Vyse, murdered! The wicked wolf, dead!

'But who can have done this?' I asked, looking with shocked eagerness, first at the inspector, then at Mr Wraxall.

'We thought at first that it must have been Yapp's work,' replied the inspector, 'but my dear wife's opinion, with which I entirely concur, is that it was Conrad Kraus. There, you see!'

He reached down and began to scratch inside his left boot.

'A man answering Conrad's description,' he resumed, after paying the same attention to his right foot, 'had been observed, on several occasions, loitering near Mr Vyse's private residence in Regent's Park Terrace. Furthermore, Conrad hasn't returned to his lodgings for some days now, and it seems probable – almost certain, indeed – that he's skipped London altogether, perhaps for good.

'The victim himself had been on the point of leaving the country – his bags and papers were all in readiness. According to the woman who attended him, he'd taken an early supper, and then gone out for a stroll, to pass half an hour until a cab was called to take him to the station hotel, where he'd intended to stay the night before taking the first tidal-train the next morning. But he never returned to the house. We'd put a watch on him, but on that particular night the constable assigned to the job was late arriving at his post, and so didn't see him leave.'

Conrad, simple-minded Conrad. It did not seem to me to be a far-fetched conclusion. I could easily imagine the poor fellow, lacking all care and companionship, abandoned now for the rest of his days in an unfeeling world, driven at last to desperate action by the gnawing contemplation of what the man with the stick had caused to be done to the mother on whom he had depended for so long; and continuing to grieve (the word seemed not at all inappropriate) for the loss of the letter that had led directly to her death – that infinitely precious, violet-scented letter, which had meant so much to him, but which, like his devoted parent, he would never see again.

I asked whether Lady Tansor had been informed of Mr Vyse's death.

'Not by us,' replied the inspector; 'although the newspapers will carry their main notices today.'

I knew only too well that the news would deal Emily a most severe blow. Despite her aversion to Mr Vyse, and her resistance to his attempts to force her into marriage, he had been a party to her secrets, and I had no doubt that she had come to depend on him as her only protector from the storm that had been slowly, but relentlessly, gathering around her. Now, although he had been driven only by ruthless self-interest, she had no one to defend her; and the storm was about to break in earnest.

'Whilst its manner must of course be deplored,' observed Mr Wraxall, reflectively, 'Justice, although of the roughest sort, has been done.'

He sighed.

'I regret very much that Mr Armitage Vyse has escaped answering for his crimes in a court of law,' he went on. 'I confess that I would once have relished the opportunity of questioning that gentleman under oath. I believe it would have been one of the most interesting cross-examinations of my career.'

'And now,' said Inspector Gully, turning over another page in his note-book, 'a word, briefly, concerning Arthur Digges, who has now been questioned concerning his late employer.

'He was recently dismissed, in a summary manner, from Vyse's employment, without receiving the compensation for his services he thought he considered was due to him. Like Yapp, he has now turned against his former master. We don't suspect him of any direct involvement in the Kraus business; but – as you know, Mr W – he's already begun to give us a deal of corroborating evidence, and should prove a most useful witness.'

As I brought to mind the unsettling memory of Digges's pursuit of me, Mr Wraxall, sitting back in his chair, tented fingers to his lips, was giving me a most curious look. I then realized, of course, that he must know from the inspector's interrogation of Digges that I had gone to Billiter Street, to speak to Mr Lazarus. But did he also know why?

'Third, and lastly,' Mr Gully was now saying, 'in the matter of Lady Tansor—'

'Is she taken, then?' I interrupted.

The inspector shook his head.

'Not yet; but I have officers arriving in Easton this evening. We propose to call on her Ladyship tomorrow morning.'

'Tomorrow?'

'Nine o'clock – sharp,' said Inspector Gully, snapping his note-book shut.

Nine o'clock – sharp. The same emphatic qualification that Emily herself had used in order to impress upon me the need to attend her promptly on my first day at Evenwood. The memories of that day flooded over me – my first explorations of the great house and its treasures; my meetings with Perseus and Mr Randolph; dressing Emily's hair for the first time, and seeing the silver locket contain-ing the hair of the murdered Phoebus Daunt. It seemed so long ago, although it had been but a few short months.

Tomorrow. At nine o'clock, *sharp*. They would come for her.

OUR CONVERSATION CONTINUED until it was time for Inspector Gully to return to Easton.

'Well, my dear,' said Mr Wraxall when he had gone, 'it seems as if one of our triumvirate's aims, at least, has now been achieved. Lady Tansor will answer for her part in the murder of Mrs Kraus in a court of law.'

He sighed, and shook his head.

'It will bring terrible consequences for the family – and espe-cially, of course, for Mr Perseus Duport. He is strong, and proud; but it is because of those very qualities that I greatly fear for the effect on him of having the true circumstances of his birth revealed to the world. It will go hard with him, that's certain. He is not like-able, I admit; but he would have made an admirable possessor of the inheritance that he always believed was his by right of birth. And then the irony of his brother's having been the legitimate heir all along! That will be a most exquisite twist of the knife.'

He gave another sigh. I looked away, feeling tears beginning to form.

'Is anything wrong, my dear?' he asked.

Recovering myself, I thanked him for his concern, but assured him that I was quite well, although it was very far from the truth.

'I could have wished, though,' he resumed, 'that we might have been able to congratulate ourselves on making similar progress with regard to the other matter.'

'The other matter?' I asked.

'Concerning the death of Mr Paul Carteret.'

Reaching into my pocket, I drew out my note-book, taking from it a sheet of paper on which was transcribed the letter from Phoebus Daunt to Emily that I had found in the cupboard behind the portrait of Anthony Duport.

'Perhaps this may help you,' I said, handing him the paper. He took it from me, read it in silence, and then, with my assent, placed it in his pocket-book.

'My dear girl,' he said; and as he spoke, I saw that there were tears in his eyes, although he quickly brushed them away. 'What a marvel you are!' he went on, as he walked over to the window, remaining there, with his back towards me, for several minutes as he looked out towards the line of woods where Mr Paul Carteret had met his death.

'Dry bones! Dry bones!' I heard him say quietly to himself. Then, to me:

'I must talk this over with Gully. It's curious, though. I had always presumed that it must have been Daunt who instigated the attack on poor Carteret; but it now seems that it was all the idea of Lady Tansor. Daunt merely provided the means – I guess the initial 'P—' to refer to Josiah Pluckrose, a known criminal associate of Daunt's, and a most dangerous and unprincipled character. Her own father! What wickedness!'

He shook his head in disbelief.

'And there are more letters, you say, which you have not yet been able to examine? Perhaps – no, it's too much to ask.'

'You wish me to bring you the others?' I asked.

'Do you think you can, without discovery? It may, of course, already be too late – they may have been destroyed.'

'No,' I said. 'They are too precious to her, and I have no doubt that she continues to believe that no one will find them.'

So it was agreed that I would try to remove the letters that evening, and put them into Mr Wraxall's hands at the earliest opportunity.

'If only my dear old uncle were here today!' sighed Mr Wraxall. 'How he would rejoice to know that he'd been right all along. It was the succession, as we thought. All done to maintain Phoebus Daunt and Miss Carteret in clover. But now, my dear, we must get you home.'

Patting my hand, in his comfortably avuncular manner, he then went to the door to call for John Wapshott to bring the trap round to the front gate.

Mr Wraxall saw me into the trap and tucked the rug over my knees.

'Will you be there – tomorrow, at nine o'clock – *sharp*?' I asked, although I instantly regretted my levity, for in truth I felt sick at the thought of what lay ahead.

'No,' he replied. 'I have played no official role in the business; and it would perhaps be a little – inappropriate – for me to be present. I shall remain here at North Lodge, and await a report of the proceedings from Gully. Perhaps you ought to join me?'

I shook my head.

'I cannot. She will expect me to be on hand to attend her.'

'Of course,' said Mr Wraxall. 'Of course. Well, we shall see each other soon, I hope, when Gully has done his work. If you're ready, John.'

As John Wapshott flicked his whip and the trap pulled away, bumping down the curving carriage-road towards the great house, I heard Mr Wraxall call out to me.

'Good-bye, Miss Esperanza Gorst.'

II
A Knock at the Door

I DID NOT go down to dinner that evening. How could I have done? To have sat between my dear lost Perseus and his brother, in the company of their doomed mother, making polite conversation after what had so lately passed between us! It was too appalling to contemplate; and so I pleaded indisposition, which was true enough, and rang down for a bowl of thin soup and some cold potatoes (to which I have always been exceedingly partial) to be sent up to my room.

My supper was brought in by Barrington. He seemed at first, as he noiselessly crossed the room, tray in hand, to be his usual uncommunicative self; but as he approached, I saw that he was looking at me with a curiously intent expression, far different from his customary blankness.

'May I ask whether you are feeling ill, miss?' he asked, in a soft, low voice, as he laid the tray down. 'You look rather pale, if I may say so.'

His concern puzzled me, for he was usually a man of the fewest possible words – indeed, the most habitually uncommunicative man I have ever known. We had hardly exchanged a word since I had come to Evenwood; and he had never before shown any degree of interest in my well-being.

I assured him that I was feeling quite well. He bowed, and made to leave; but at the door he turned and said:

'Will you need anything else tonight, miss? Please to ring immediately if you do.'

I said that I required nothing more; whereupon he made me another bow, and left me sitting disconsolately before the window, absently consuming my frugal dinner.

Fatigued and depressed though I was, there remained a task I must perform, while the opportunity presented itself, before giving myself up to sleep. Taking a small travelling bag from my wardrobe, I went downstairs to Emily's apartments, and straight to the portrait of Anthony Duport.

Everything was as I had first found it. I quickly removed the six bundles of letters and placed them in the bag I had brought, leaving only the unsettling photograph of Phoebus Daunt behind in the dark recess.

Back upstairs, at a little before ten o'clock, as I was writing up my Book of Secrets and steeling myself to make another attempt at writing to Madame, there came another knock at my door and, to my astonishment, Emily entered.

Her unannounced presence, and the strained, distracted expression she wore, instantly roused anxious speculation within me. Had she discovered that the letters had been taken?

'Alice, dear,' she said, with a strangely forced smile, followed by a soft kiss on the cheek. 'How are you? Both Perseus and Randolph were asking after you at dinner. Are you feeling better?'

'A little – thank you.'

As she drew away, I saw her glance down to where my Book of Secrets, which I had not had time to conceal, still lay open on the table; but she made no remark as she turned and walked over to the bed. She sat down and patted the counterpane, to indicate that she wished me to come and sit beside her.

'Is anything the matter?' I asked, my anxiety mounting that she was about to confront me about the missing letters; but I need not have worried.

'I don't know,' came the hesitant reply. 'That is to say, I don't know what it means – or may mean – for me.'

She was now staring down at the floor, her body swaying slowly back and forth.

'Dearest Emily,' I said soothingly, my fears now subsiding. 'You must speak plainly, if I'm to help you.'

'Oh!' she cried, as if she had at that moment awoken from some absorbing reverie. 'Didn't I say? How stupid of me! Mr Donald Orr has telegraphed to say that Mr Vyse is dead.'

She gave a grim little laugh.

'Someone has killed him, and thrown his body into the Regent's Canal. There! What do you think of that?'

'This is terrible news,' said I, affecting the greatest shock and surprise, 'although you were not fond of Mr Vyse, I think.'

'No,' she replied, staring down once more at the floor. 'Not fond in the least; but I did not wish him dead. I never wished that. He was ever a true friend to Phoebus, and defended his memory staunchly against those who tried to besmirch it; and for that I must always be grateful.'

She had now turned her face towards me. The ravages of recent events were only too clear. Her deteriorating health also showed in every feature, making her seem suddenly old beyond her years, and weak beyond recovery, all her former strength quite shrivelled away.

'Oh, Alice,' she said, in a most pitiful whisper. 'I am so afraid. What shall I do?'

'Afraid?' I asked. 'What should you be afraid of?'

She shook her head, and then turned away again, her thoughts seemingly imprisoned in some dark and silent place of terror and despair, the living hell that she had made for herself, and from which there was now no escape.

'Can't you tell me?' I urged, feeling my power over her, but curiously taking little satisfaction in it.

Again she merely shook her head; but then, more brightly, she suddenly looked up and smiled.

'Will you brush my hair, the way you used to do?' she asked. 'Allardyce always pulls so, but you have such a gentle touch. Will you do that for me, dear?'

I went to fetch my brush, and began unpicking the long, black tresses until they fell about her shoulders and back.

Through the half-open window came the distant hooting of an owl, and the soft rush of a night breeze. I began to brush, with long sweeping strokes, as she sat, eyes closed, hands crossed in her lap.

At length, she opened her eyes, and looked me straight in the face. I returned her unflinching gaze, and for an instant it was as if we were locked in an unspoken contest of wills, all pretence suddenly stripped away, each knowing the other's secret self. But the moment passed, as suddenly as it had come; she gave me a feeble smile, reached out, and then ran her fingers through my hair, saying that she was glad I was feeling better, and that she now wished to retire.

'Let me come down with you,' I urged. 'You're not well.'

'Oh, but I'm perfectly well,' she replied, almost merrily. 'But, if you insist . . .'

Back in her apartments, she called for Allardyce to undress her and help her to bed. When the maid had been dismissed, I sat with Emily, holding her hand. We did not speak.

She lay with her eyes closed, although still awake. After a while, she opened them, looked down, and whispered: 'Such beautiful hands! They were the first things I noticed about you.'

She was smiling to herself, and softly stroking my palm with her long finger-nails, exactly the way Madame had used to do, whenever I awoke from one of my nightmares. I wanted to pull away, but found that I could not; and so we sat for some moments, in silent intimacy.

Then, the clocks sounding the half-hour, I gently pulled my hand away from hers and reached out to brush away a strand of hair from her damp forehead.

'*Esperanza*,' she intoned quietly. 'It means "Hope", does it not? Your parents named you well, for you must have been their hope indeed. Do you know, dear, the more I say the name, the more I like it. I wish now that I hadn't insisted on calling you "Alice". But there – it's too late now. It's all too late.'

'I'll leave you now,' I said. 'Shall I bring you your drops?'

'My drops?' she exclaimed, in sudden agitation. 'No, no, not tonight. On no account. No need for drops tonight.'

III
The Study

ALTHOUGH EMILY HAD continued to call me down at night – by means of a bell she had instructed to be installed in my room – in order to soothe her when afflicted by her night-terrors, my own sleep had been untroubled by bad dreams for some time. That night, however, one came to me of a most peculiar and disturbing character. It has troubled my slumbers on many nights since.

I am standing, candle in hand, in a large, empty, windowless chamber, the walls, ceiling, and floor of which are entirely plastered over with smooth, white sand. A faint breeze is blowing, scattering swirling eddies of sand about the floor.

All around the room are a dozen or so closed doors. On the sandy floor before one of them lies a small golden key. I pick up the key, and unlock the door.

A sudden gust of salt-laden wind extinguishes the candle as I pass through into a great sea-cave, low and wide, whose huge gaping mouth gives on to a distant expanse of booming surf, with a vista of sparkling turquoise ocean beyond.

I am now standing on a narrow ledge of black, ridged rock, around which the waves slap and suck. Through the mouth of the cave streams the pearly sunlight of early morning, illuminating a great host of identical stone forms rising up out of the solid rock – line upon line of long-haired sea-maidens, their webbed hands outstretched to the rising sun, heads and shoulders bedecked with wreaths of living seaweed, all gazing out towards the open sea, their clinging blue-black draperies glistening in the pallid light as the waves break back and forth over them, sea-water running down the folds of their garments, so exquisitely rendered, frozen for all eternity.

I turn away and return to the room from which I had entered the cave, closing the door behind me; but as I do so, the sand-covered walls begin to shift and buckle, and in an instant I am engulfed.

In utter terror, I struggle to break free from the suffocating mass; but the collapsing sand fills my eyes, my nose, my mouth, with such irresistible rapidity that soon I can breathe no more, and so give myself up gratefully to Death.

THROWING BACK THE sheets, I sat up, perspiration running down my face, my heart pounding wildly.

Once a little recovered from my dream, I lit my bedside candle. The clock showed twenty minutes past the hour of four.

The window was still open; but the breeze had now dropped, and all was silent as a tomb. On a sudden impulse, I felt the need for fresh air; and so, despite the hour, I dressed, and went down to the Library Terrace, where, with light beginning to break faintly in the eastern sky, I walked up and down until the wildness in my head had abated.

Back in my room, as I sat thinking again what my strange dream might portend, the silence was broken by the sound of a door closing on the floor below.

I well knew the sound of that door – the distinctive creak (despite frequent oiling) of the hinges, the hollow note it made when it was pulled shut. I knew also, by the peculiar acoustic properties of the connecting staircase and passage-way, that these sounds could be heard from my room.

Fired by a sudden instinctive certainty that I must make an investigation, I went out into the passage, descended to the first floor, and was soon standing outside Emily's private apartments. I did not enter them, however, for my attention had been caught by a faint light flickering up through the stairwell from the vestibule below.

Down I went; and then I saw her.

It was an uncanny sight. She was wearing the long white nightgown that had once belonged to Phoebus Daunt, which, trailing out behind her in the near-darkness, seemed like the winding-sheet of some poor wandering wraith, newly risen from the grave.

I was now only a few feet behind her, pressing myself close to the deeply shadowed wall of the staircase in order to avoid detection.

Candle raised, her long hair streaming down her back, slippered feet pattering softly on the stone flags, she passed the portrait of the Turkish Corsair, and quickly turned into a long vaulted corridor, flanked on either side with faded banners, shields, crossed weapons, and other martial accoutrements.

On she went, occasionally stopping to take breath, until stopping at last before the one place in the house in which I had never yet set foot in all my ramblings: the late Lord Tansor's study, and now Emily's own inviolable sanctum, the door to which was kept permanently locked.

From the shadowed embrasure of a narrow window that overlooked the rose-garden, I watched as she took out a key from the pocket of the night-gown and unlocked the study door, which she softly closed behind her.

I strained my ears, but could not make out the sound of the key turning again; and so I advanced on tip-toe to the door, kneeled down, and placed my eye to the empty key-hole.

She was standing with her back towards me, in the act of placing the candle on a heavy mahogany desk, which stood before the window on the far side of the room. As I watched her, she suddenly turned, as though she had heard something, picked up the candle, and began walking quickly back towards the door. I had but a second or two to run back to my former hiding-place before the study door opened, and Emily came out into the corridor, looking anxiously about her. After a moment or two, apparently satisfied that she had not been observed, she went back inside. This time, however, the door did not shut properly; and when I ran back, I found that I was able to push it open slightly, to give a better view of the study's interior.

Tall and narrow, its single window giving out over the Entrance Court, the room, including the ceiling, was panelled in dark wood; glass-fronted bookcases covered the right-hand wall; on the left hung a line of portraits.

Having lit a small oil-lamp that stood on the desk, Emily now went over to one of the portraits, depicting a portly gentleman, dressed in the costume of the last century, his wife and dog by his side. I thought at first that she was about to take the picture down, perhaps to reveal some secret compartment, like the one concealed by the portrait of Anthony Duport. Instead, she began pressing the bottom edge of the painting's ornate gilded frame, in what appeared to be a deliberate sequence of actions. Then, with a soft click, the adjacent portrait, of a severe-looking lady of advanced years, suddenly swung open, to reveal a dark cavity. From this she removed a leather bag and what I soon saw was a key, then closed the secret door. Unlocking one of the desk drawers with the key, she took out two envelopes, which she proceeded to place in the bag.

After sitting meditatively for several moments, breathing heavily, she got up again and opened the door of a narrow cupboard set into the panel-work, from which she brought out a long, hooded cloak and a pair of delicate dove-grey evening pumps decorated with black beading. Throwing the cloak over her shoulders, and exchanging her slippers for the pumps, she strapped the leather bag across her chest, extinguished the lamp, and, candle in hand, began to walk towards the door, obliging me to scurry back to my hiding-place once more.

I heard the key turning in the lock of the study door; moments later, Emily's cloaked and hooded figure flitted past.

Slowly, I counted to five, and set off after her.

35

The Last Sunrise

I
The Evenbrook
29TH MAY 1877

A T THE door to the vestibule, Emily halted, looking round to ensure that no one was about. Pausing briefly again, to glance up at the portrait of my grandparents, Lord Tansor and his beautiful first wife, with my father's brother in her arms, she then quickly crossed the great echoing space, and passed through a low green-painted door tucked away in the far corner.

As soon as she had disappeared from view, I was after her: through the green-painted door, down a short flight of stairs, and along a succession of passages and small dark rooms that eventually opened into a little-frequented hallway on the south side of the house. Facing me, a half-glazed door stood open to the chilly morning air.

I confess that I was bewildered. Where could she be going, at this hour, dressed only in a night-gown, and wearing evening pumps? But there was no time to speculate if I was to keep up with her; so out through the door I went.

To the left, the gravel path that Mr Randolph had taken on the day we had sat together by the fish-pond led under the towering South Front to the stables; to the right, it wound away from the house to hug the pond's high walls, before passing through an ave-

nue of venerable trees to join the main carriage-drive. It was now
obvious that Emily had taken this circuitous route into the Park to
avoid being observed. More mystified than ever, I stepped on to the
path.

The nascent morning light was now slowly gaining strength,
enabling me to make out her dark form hurrying towards the far
angle of the fish-pond wall, from which point the path turned
sharply towards the avenue of trees.

On she went, with me following as closely as I dared, through
the trees, on to the drive, over the bridge, and up the long slope of
the Rise, with quick, deliberate steps, as though she was anxious to
keep some pressing engagement, and never once looking back or
pausing for breath.

To avoid being seen, I had kept to the lines of oaks planted at
close intervals on either side of the drive; but the grass was long, and
wet from the heavy dew and the recent rain, and this had made my
progress slow and uncomfortable. As soon as Emily had crested the
slope, I left the safety of the trees, and ran as fast as my legs could
carry me to the summit of the Rise. Below me, in the gradually
expanding light, I could see the dark outline of the castellated gate-
house and, to the right, above the intervening trees, the chimneys
of the Dower House and the tall spire of St Michael and All Angels
silhouetted against the pale eastern sky. But where was Emily?

I scanned the drive for several seconds; then I saw her, hastening
along a path that skirted the boundary wall of the Dower House
and led down to the Evenbrook.

Picking up my wet skirts again, I soon gained the path, and in
another minute found myself on the edge of a clearing in the thick
stands of silver birch and willows that bordered the river.

Here I was obliged to stop, for Emily was now only a few yards
ahead of me, standing motionless on the river's muddy margin,
breathing hard, hair disordered from her exertions, her pretty kid
pumps all wet and dirtied, ruined beyond the skill of any lady's-
maid to repair.

I was on the point of retreating into the trees, fearing she would
turn and see me; but she appeared so oblivious to my presence, so

utterly absorbed by her own thoughts, that concealment seemed, for the moment, unnecessary.

The minutes passed, and still Emily stood, vacantly contemplating the fast-flowing stream, swollen by the late rains, until a sudden noise caused us both to look up.

A swan, its brilliantly white wings beating loudly in the dawn stillness, was slowly rising into the air from a bed of swaying reeds on the opposite bank.

Roused from her reverie by the sound, Emily now took off the leather bag, which she dropped on to the grass beside her. She then began to walk slowly down the muddy slope, and into the river.

I stood frozen in horror, my heart in my mouth.

Dear God! Surely she was not intending to end her life here, wilfully committing her body to the unforgiving Evenbrook? But as the water closed round her feet, still encased in the delicate grey pumps, I knew that no other conclusion was possible. She had come to this deserted place, at this early hour, for only one terrible purpose.

She must know, then, that the final account for her misdeeds had fallen due, for immediate payment in full. But she was proud Lady Tansor. She would not be dictated to – by Fate, or even by Inspector Gully of the Detective Department. She would determine her own fate. But oh, my Lady! How will you answer for this final, most grave offence, when you stand at last before the great Harvester of Souls?

It was all of a piece with the life she now seemed determined to end. Her will was all; her proud, self-regarding nature was her only moral guide – her beacon, her constant touchstone, by which all her actions had been directed. I did not have to destroy her: she had destroyed herself.

You may think it despicable of me, and, indeed, I now suppose that it was, but as I stood amongst the trees watching her, I could not contain an irresistible surge of exultation at this self-inflicted defeat of the woman Madame had instructed me to regard as my enemy. True, it was not the triumphant conclusion of the Great

Task that my guardian had hoped for; but there was justice in it, of a terrible sort, for the betrayal of my dear father, and for the crimes committed as a consequence.

I had to think of *him*, my poor lost father, and of the suffering he had endured because of her. He must ever be *my* beacon, *my* touchstone. For his sake, I must let her die. Her fate was sealed, in any case, whatever she chose to do; and was it not better, perhaps, that her life should end in this way, in this quiet place of water, leaf, and sighing grass, under a brightening morning sky, than face the grim outcome of a guilty verdict in a capital charge?

Let her will be done, then. I would do nothing to prevent it. Why should I care how Death came to the 26th Baroness Tansor? Even though the blood of the Duports flowed through us both, and although she had showed me kindness and called herself my friend, she meant nothing to me, nothing – not now. Friend? How could she ever have been a true friend to me? How could I ever have been such to her? It had all been a sham, on both sides. We had both been working our secret purposes, even as we had smiled and talked, or giggled at Mr Maurice FitzMaurice, or, on rainy afternoons, heads together like school-girls, had pored over pictures of the latest Parisian fashions.

The days of deceit were over at last, and I need dissemble no more. Now I could return to the Avenue d'Uhrich, to begin a new life, consigning my secret existence beneath the towers and spires of Evenwood to the vault of memory.

SHE IS NOW wading ever deeper into the stream, her long cloak spreading out behind her in a dark, undulating arc, making her seem like some strange species of mermaid, and reminding me most uncannily of the stone sea-maidens of my recent dream.

From the Rectory garden, some distance beyond the trees, a dog begins to bark excitedly, followed by a shout. Mr Thripp is an early riser, and is no doubt preparing to walk out with the ebullient little terrier that is his constant companion. The picture that forms in my mind of the Rector – absurd and irritating though he is – making his way up the tree-bowered lane to the church, his dog scampering hither and thither before him, panting with pure instinctual delight, as terriers do, seems to belong to some other world, far removed from this place of contemplated death. As the sound dies away, my conscience begins to awaken.

Can I really stand coolly by and watch this woman die, and do nothing to save her? I urge myself, once again, that it *must* be done: the duty to which I have pledged myself, heart and soul, demands it. I must be as stern and unbending as a judge passing sentence on a convicted malefactor, thinking only of her offences.

Yet as I watch her, my resolve – to let her do what she has come here, of her own free will, to do – begins to falter; and then a new and shocking thought takes hold.

Will not inaction be a kind of killing, and make me a kind of murderer? I have no blade, no pistol, to use against her; no poison to be secretly administered; I would lay no hands on her, to choke off her life. Yet if I do nothing, I will be a silent accomplice in her death. It is an absurd notion; but it produces a stinging sense of culpability that slowly starts to eat away at my former determination to remain a dumb witness to what is unfolding before me.

My heart should have been hardened by now against all feelings of pity or compassion for my former mistress. Yet common human sympathy is sweeping irresistibly through me, and tears start to run down my face.

Even now I can save her, even now. I am young and strong; she is weak from illness, debilitated by sorrow and guilt. I could run to her, pull her back to the bank, and then urge her to fly, no matter where, from the inevitable consequences that await her once Inspector Gully has called, at nine o'clock sharp, to pay his compliments. There is still time. It is not too late.

I cannot believe that Madame, or even my departed father, had either foreseen or desired that things would end in this dreadful way. They had wished only to punish Emily, by depriving her, and her sons, of their illicit inheritance. Why not save her, then – from herself, and from the full rigour of the law? If she escaped, as my father had escaped, she would still lose everything that she had plotted and schemed to maintain.

I can never forgive her for betraying my father, and for driving him almost to madness; but I know that she acted under the spell of her surpassing love for Phoebus Daunt, who had then paid the price for their mutual guilt with his life. Can I be certain that I would not have done as much for Perseus?

I am sick to the heart of plots and secrets and double-dealing, of pretending to be what I am not. The Great Task is no more. All is lost, and I am almost glad that it is so. I am weary also of obeying instructions, even from dear Madame. I, too, have a will of my own. I must – I shall – exercise it. I shall be myself at last.

With painful slowness, dragging the weight of her water-logged cloak behind her, Emily has now passed through the shallows towards the middle of the stream.

In a moment, all confusion has melted away, like mist before the rising sun. My decision is made.

I will not let her die.

A WIDENING STRAND of the palest, purest light is breaking over the eastern horizon as the bells of St Michael's begin to ring out. I hear the sound, but cannot tell which hour, or half-hour, they are proclaiming. It almost seems as if the flow of time has ceased, replaced by a perpetual present moment, poised between life and death.

The water is now waist-deep around her as Emily wades further and further into the Evenbrook. I move forward and stand on the bank to call out to her; but before I can open my mouth, she turns and looks back at me, her chest heaving with shortness of breath, her body rocked gently from side to side by the current.

I now notice, for the first time, that she is wearing the black velvet band with the locket containing the strands of hair she cut from the head of Phoebus Daunt as he lay dead, by my father's hand, in the snow-covered garden of Lord Tansor's town-house. Seeing me about to speak, she places a finger against her bloodless lips, to show that she wishes me to remain silent. Then she stretches out her other hand, palm towards me, by which gesture I understand her to mean that I must stay where I am; and of course I obey these unspoken commands, for she is my mistress still.

Her revived will is impossible to resist. I see now that I cannot save her, for she will not be saved.

She is magnificent, dishevelled and diminished though she is – a queen indeed, unassailable, unconquerable, her beauty transfigured into something strange and unearthly. I wonder how I could ever have believed that I could overcome her. It is only too plain. She has overcome *me*, despite all my stratagems, all the tricks I had devised, under Madame's instructions, to bring her down.

Yet there is something more, something equally incontestable, in the smile she now gives me – sad and affectionate, but charged with a mysterious knowingness – which unnerves me, as though she has uncovered every secret I have striven to keep from her. Such a thing seems impossible; but the mere thought only serves to strengthen her ascendancy over me.

Thus we stand, silently regarding each other, in wordless complicity, as the new day is met by a swelling chorus of bird-song, and a gentle breeze ruffles the fluffy seed-heads of the tall grasses growing between the path and the water's edge, making the overhanging willows whisper and sigh.

She smiles once more; but now that unsettling knowingness has gone; and again, unbidden, my heart goes out to her.

TIME PASSES, AND nothing is said, or done. Emily remains waist-deep in the water, sometimes looking expectantly upstream, towards the Rectory, as though some significant event is imminent.

Then, in a glorious uprush of new-born light, the morning sun rises at last above the wooded horizon laying a shimmering carpet of dazzling, dancing stars over the surface of Evenbrook. Turning towards the rising sun, Emily takes something from the pocket of her night-gown. At first I cannot make out what it is. Then my poor heart begins to beat with wild alarm.

It is the photograph, in its black-bordered frame, of Phoebus Daunt, which should be where I so recently left it – shut away in its hiding-place behind the portrait of Anthony Duport.

She knows, then, that her lover's letters have been taken; but does she know, or has she guessed, by whom?

With her face now bathed in light, she raises the photograph to her lips and kisses it, before pressing it, with rapturous tenderness, to her breast. Closing her eyes, and still clasping the photograph, she falls slowly forwards.

For a moment she remains floating gently, face down, on the bubbling surface of the water, her loosened hair streaming out behind her. Then the weight of her cloak begins to drag her under, as she finally submits to the cold embrace of the Evenbrook.

I can watch no more, and turn away in tears. When I pluck up the courage to look again, she has gone – carried swiftly downstream by the rapid current.

Thus died Emily Grace Duport, 26th Baroness Tansor.

My enemy.

My friend.

II
The Gamekeeper's Bag

HALF AN HOUR has gone by since my return to the house – unobserved, I am certain – bringing with me the battered leather bag that Emily left on the grass by the Evenbrook.

I had decided not to examine the bag's contents until I had returned to the safety of my room. Once there, shaking from head to foot with the shock of what I have just witnessed, and having locked my door, I place the bag on my table under the window, and unbuckle it.

I take out two sealed envelopes: one directed to Inspector Gully, the other to me. The latter I here transcribe in full.

Evenwood Park
Easton, Northamptonshire

28th May 1877

MY DEAREST ESPERANZA (Alice no longer),—

 When you read this, you will know what I am resolved to do.

 I am informed that Inspector Gully & several officers have come up from London & are presently in Easton. I know only too well why they are here, & so shall now put into effect what I have been preparing for these several weeks past.

 Nothing now can turn me from the course I am resolved upon; but there are certain matters that must be set down before I take this final, irrevocable step. A separate letter, for the eyes of my dear eldest son, has been placed with Mr Donald Orr, with instructions that it should be given to him in the event of my death.

 I knew you from the first, my dear girl, when you stood before me for interview. As soon as you entered the room, I was transported to the day, over twenty years ago, when I first met a certain gentleman, in the hallway of the Dower House. You perhaps do not know how much you resemble that gentleman, but I saw it instantly – not merely in the similarities of feature & bearing, striking although some of them were, but more especially in less tangible, but even more powerful, impressions. When I first saw you, I could see – and feel – him standing before me, though I looked upon the form of a nineteen-year-old girl.

 My instinctual certainty of who you were explained so much – the powerful affinity that I immediately sensed existed between us, & why someone possessing such an abundance of attainments, so beautiful, so well-informed, & so assured, despite the attitude of docility you put on, should seek the menial position of lady's-maid. Did you not think it odd that you secured the position so easily, when there were others who applied for the situation who were far more qualified?

 The story you gave me was plausible, and subsequent enquiries appeared to substantiate it; but it was a story, was it not?

 Thus, although I could not be absolutely certain, I knew you in my heart for who you were — the daughter of Edward Glyver, the man who should now be the 26th Lord Tansor. There — I have written his name, or should I say one of his names? What shall we call him? Edward Duport? Edward Glyver? Edward Glapthorn? Or perhaps Edwin Gorst? Plain Edward might be best, which is how I think of him. So let it be Edward.

As for the name by which you are presently known, both Mr Vyse & Mr Shillito strongly suspected you of hiding your true identity, although neither of them discovered that Esperanza Gorst was really the daughter of my dearest love's murderer.

I have no doubt that Mr Vyse would have found you out in time. He had already established, to his own satisfaction, that the man Mr Shillito met on Madeira had indeed been your late father; and Mr Shillito would doubtless have eventually remembered where he had known Edwin Gorst before — at school, as you may or may not know — and under what name. But is it not strange and ironic that I, of all people, should have resolved to keep your secret safe from Mr Vyse and to protect you from him by countering his suspicions, knowing well what he was capable of?

Why had you come here? That was the question I constantly asked myself. To kill me, or to find some other means of punishing me for what I had done to your father? The only certainty was that your presence at Evenwood was no accident, & that it did not augur well for me.

Then I wondered who had sent you, for (like Mr Vyse) I was sure you had not come of your own volition. It could not, of course, have been your father, for I knew him to be dead. I thought perhaps it might have been some old friend or former associate of his, unknown to me, in whom he had confided. Then, later, I was sure that you must be in league with Mr Wraxall, who has long harboured suspicions against me. Only time would tell; & so I decided to engage you, and wait until you showed your hand.

Then certain events intervened, which placed me in extreme jeopardy, and from which there is now no escape. Whether you have been involved, as part of your purpose, in bringing Inspector Gully & his officers to Evenwood, I cannot say; but it no longer matters to me why *you came here, or at whose behest. Indeed, I am glad that it should be so, & that I go from this world in ignorance of these things, wishing in my last hours to think of you as being not wholly indifferent to me and my welfare.*

As for the late Mr Vyse, his loyalty to the memory of dear Phoebus placed a deep, tho' unwelcome, obligation on me; but he possessed certain letters of mine containing information that I wished, at all costs, to remain confidential. This placed me even more in his power, & using these letters he sought to force me into marriage.

One letter in particular, the source of my present troubles, was supposed to have been destroyed by him; but he betrayed me by retaining it, hoping thereby to make it impossible for me to refuse his advances. But he too appears to have been betrayed, & this letter – with the others – has now fallen into the hands of the police. I foolishly put all my trust in Mr Vyse, and now I am utterly undone.

I suspect that you, and your friend Mr Wraxall, possess some knowledge of these matters. Did you also have a hand in Mr Vyse's death, & that of Mr Shillito? I cannot think so. Yet what does it signify? They are both dead & gone, & I am now past all caring.

I betrayed your father, and deprived him for ever of what was his by right of birth – I confess it once more; & in so doing, I sent my dearest love to his grave. Can you imagine what torments of mind & soul I have had to bear as a consequence?

Time is short, & I wish to say only a few more words to you before I conclude with the real purpose of this letter – the first and last I shall ever write to you.

Believing that I knew who you really were, you will naturally find it hard to comprehend why I sought your friendship. You must believe me, dear Esperanza, that I truly desired it – & for this supreme reason.

I loved your father from that first moment in the hallway of the Dower House – although not as I loved Phoebus. Nothing could ever compare to the attachment that had existed between my dearest Phoebus and me since we were children together.

Yet I say, & swear, that I loved Edward Glyver, & believe that he loved me, although at first – having always my darling's interests at heart – I revolted against the notion that I could entertain even the slightest affection for yr father, whilst any deeper regard seemed beyond absurdity.

Nonetheless he entered into my heart on that fatal afternoon when we first met, & his presence there proved impossible either to resist or to root out. He has remained there, defying every natural instinct, ever since.

In public – especially to the late Lord Tansor – I execrated your father's memory at every opportunity. In private I strove constantly to rip him from the place he had occupied in my heart; but I never could do it. I call it love, therefore, this most undesired and unwelcome feeling, for I have no other word for it, tho' it has rendered the perpetual grief & guilt I suffer more unendurable with each passing day.

Thus, loving the father as I did, is it so very strange that I should also have felt a spontaneous affection for the daughter, & have wished her to be my friend?

Whilst of a different character, that affection has grown in strength & preciousness over recent months to rival what I felt for the dear friend, Miss Buisson, of whom I have often spoken, & whose friendship I had never thought could be replaced. But I was wrong. You have been a friend indeed, & I believe that you have also felt some reciprocal affection for me, in spite of your deceits & deceptions, & this gives me the greatest comfort in these last hours.

I have nearly done. Only one thing remains, & that of the greatest importance.

The papers that proved Edward's claim to be Lord Tansor's legitimate son and heir were not destroyed, as he – and my dearest Phoebus – believed. For several years they remained under lock & key, with other private papers, at my London bankers. When I succeeded my cousin, I brought them back to Evenwood and placed them secretly in my study.

I now restore them to their rightful owner – to you, Edward's daughter. You will find them in my apartments, in a place I believe you have already discovered. I do not have to tell you where to find the key.

Why did I not put beyond all reach what I now bequeath to you, when the continued existence of these papers threatened everything that Phoebus & I had risked so much to achieve, and for which I had already paid a terrible price? I could not explain it then, & I cannot do so now. If you will have a reason, put it down to a simple act of conscience, & to the remorse — bitter & insistent — I felt for what I had done. The papers were still for ever lost to your father, & that was enough for our purpose. It was the only time I ever deceived Phoebus, & I suffered much from the guilt of it; but, the decision once made, I found I could not go back on it. Perhaps I knew in my heart that, one day, reparation must be made, & now that day has come.

By thus giving you the instruments of yr restoration, I hope — with all my heart — to gain some measure of forgiveness for the injuries I have done: to Edward, to you, & to others. If I could receive absolution directly from your lips, it would help to ease my final journey. But that cannot be, for the hour is late, & there is still much to do.

Yet honesty compels me to say this. I suffer every day for the wrongs I have done; but I would willingly blacken my soul with fresh sins if my adored Phoebus required it of me.

This, then, is what I wished to say to you, before you and I part for ever. In the bag — that same bag, belonging to John Earl, gamekeeper here in Lord Tansor's day, which my poor father was carrying on the day he died — you will find a letter to Inspector Gully, in which I fully & freely confess all, & which I would ask you to ensure that he receives when he comes — as I am certain he will.

I have one final wish, & it is this: that you might find it in your heart to take my dear son, Perseus, as your husband, & so bring to an end at last the enmity that existed between your fathers, which has proved so injurious to us all. He has lost everything because of me, and he has played no part in any of the events that have brought me to the end I now contemplate. I know also that he esteems you highly, for he has told me so. I hope, & believe, that you may also regard him with a degree of favour & affection that may, in time, grow into something more. I would also wish that you will be kind to Randolph, if you can. He, too, is innocent of my sins.

And so farewell, my dear Esperanza. I go now to join my darling Phoebus, the ever-shining sun of my poor ruined life, in the place that has been prepared for us both.

Your affectionate friend,

E.G. DUPORT

36

Aftermath

I
In Which I See My Future

'YOU'RE UP early, miss,' says Charlie Skinner, tight-collared and red-faced, whom I meet outside Emily's apartments puffing his way up to Mr Perseus's room with a tray of coffee.

I tell Charlie that, having been unable to sleep, I had got up to take a walk in the rose-garden, and watch the sun rise.

'Her Ladyship's been up with the lark, too,' he then remarks, nodding towards Emily's door. He seems uncharacteristically subdued, and I realize that he has not favoured me with one of his customary salutes.

'Miss Allardyce is all of a twitter,' he confides. 'Says she can't understand it. The bed's been slept in, but there's no sign of her Ladyship – or her night-gown.'

'Night-gown?' I ask, assuming a puzzled air.

'Well,' Charlie whisperingly explains, 'Miss A is of the strong opinion that, in the unlikely event that Lady T dressed herself, she would of course have taken off her night-gown. But it's nowhere to be found.'

Then he looks me up and down, dwelling particularly, first, on my wet dress, and then on my boots, which are still spattered with caked mud and clinging blades of grass.

'Are you all right, miss?' he enquires. 'You look a little flushed. Is there anything I can do?'

I assure the dear fellow – for I have grown quite fond of Sukie Prout's eccentric young cousin – that there is nothing wrong, even though I am all afire with suppressed excitement, mingled with recollected horror at what I have so recently witnessed by the Evenbrook.

When Charlie has gone, and with every part of me bursting with nervous anticipation, I frantically push open the door to Emily's apartments and, after retrieving the key from the jewellery box, run to the portrait of little Anthony Duport.

The photograph of Phoebus Daunt, of course, has gone; but in its place I find a shallow wooden box, stamped with the Duport arms, which I immediately take out and open, my hands shaking.

Several documents meet my eager gaze.

The first is a single sheet of paper, headed 'To Whom It May Concern', and consists of a briefly worded admission of the plot to deny my father his rightful inheritance, signed by Emily, and dated two days earlier.

Underneath this covering statement are two letters, written – in a most beautiful hand on thin, fragile paper – from my grandmother to her son, my father.

Next, an affidavit, also in my grandmother's hand, dated 5th June 1820, witnessed and signed in the presence of a notary from the French city of Rennes, swearing that my father was the legitimately conceived son of Julius Verney Duport, 25th Baron Tansor, of Evenwood, in the County of Northampton. With it is another affidavit, signed by two witnesses, testifying to the baptism of Edward Charles Duport in the Church of St-Sauveur in Rennes, on 19th March 1820.

In the first affidavit, my attention is immediately caught by the following declaration:

I, Laura Rose Duport, do hereby further affirm and swear that the aforesaid child, Edward Charles Duport, was born without the knowledge of his father, the aforesaid Lord Tansor, and placed in

*the permanent care of my dearest friend, Mrs Simona Glyver, wife
of Captain Edward Glyver, late of the 11th Regiment of Light Dra-
goons, of Sandchurch, in the County of Dorset, at the express and
settled wish of myself, Laura Rose Duport, being of sound mind and
body, to be brought up by the said Simona Glyver as her own son.*

Now, at last, the year of my father's birth could be inscribed on
the moss-covered slab of granite in the sunless corner of the Cemetery of St-Vincent. He had been forty-two years of age when he died.
Why this simple fact affected me so, I cannot say; but I sat for several
minutes, hands covering my face, unable to staunch my tears.

Lastly, in the bottom of the box, is a bundle of letters from my
grandmother, written to her dearest friend, Mrs Simona Glyver,
in which, as I quickly apprehend, the whole scheme to keep my
father's birth a secret, and then to place him in the permanent care
of Mrs Glyver, is clearly laid out. With these letters is another covering statement from Emily:

*These were the documents that my father, Mr Paul Carteret, knowing
their importance, and that they would deprive Mr Phoebus Daunt of
his expectations, had placed in the bank in Stamford for safe-keeping.
They tell, in Lady Laura Tansor's own words, of how she planned,
with her friend Simona Glyver, formerly Miss More, to keep from her
husband, my late cousin, all knowledge of his son's birth – the son who
should have succeeded him instead of me. My father had discovered the
letters during the course of his researches into the history of our family,
on which I assisted him, and through which work I too came to know of
them. He was carrying them back to Evenwood, in gamekeeper Earl's
old bag, on the day he was attacked and killed by the man, Josiah
Pluckrose, who had been instructed by Mr Daunt to take them from him
– only take them, nothing more, as God is my witness. But Pluckrose
exceeded his commission, as Mr Daunt feared he might.*

*May God forgive me for what I have done. I never meant for him
to die.*

E.G.D.

With these letters, the affidavits, and the evidence that the police already possessed concerning the birth of Perseus, it appeared to my untrained legal mind that the case for the reclamation of my right to succeed Emily, as the 27th Baroness Tansor, was unanswerable. The Great Task would be accomplished. Evenwood and everything in it would be mine – every treasure-laden room through which I had wandered; the unparalleled Library; every corridor and staircase; every turret and soaring tower; the great green Park, over which the morning sun was now throwing its blessed radiance – everything that lay to sight and touch, mine to possess, and to bequeath to my as yet unborn children.

Yet of more consequence by far than this stupendous material inheritance was the now certain knowledge of who I truly was. My ancestors – my centuries-old family – were all around me. I saw their painted, frozen faces every day, in the portraits that lined the walls of so many of the rooms and corridors: proud ladies and self-satisfied gentlemen in their various antique fineries; pretty children dandled on their mammas' knees; steel-suited soldiers, and sober lawyers; well-fed, bewigged prelates, and cautious-eyed men of affairs – every one of them staring out from their frames as they had when they first sat for their portraits, all once living, breathing, feeling people, whose blood I shared.

This place, then, was my true home, not the house in the Avenue d'Uhrich, although it was to my dearly remembered former home that I was now resolved to return, without prior announcement, and as soon as circumstances allowed, to tell Madame in person of our unexpected triumph.

Placing prominently on her escritoire, where it could easily be found, the letter that Emily had directed for the attention of Inspector Gully, I took the box and its precious contents back to my room, changed my dress and boots, and went downstairs to have my breakfast, in the confident expectation that I would soon do so as the next Lady Tansor.

*　*　*

By a quarter to nine, the house is in turmoil. Questions are flying thick and fast.

Where is Lady Tansor? Has anyone seen her? Who saw her last? Had she told anyone that she would be rising early? Why were none of her outdoor clothes missing? (Miss Allardyce is tearfully adamant on this point.) Most puzzling of all, where is her night-gown? Surely she has not gone out in it?

Perseus, who has been up for most of the night working on his poem, paces up and down, saying nothing, his dark face tense with anxiety. His brother moves amongst the throng of servants gathered in the vestibule, talking in quiet enquiring tones to each one. Of his wife, however, there is no sign, for which I am thankful.

I stand alone amidst the hubbub by the portrait of the Turkish Corsair. Although a glance is occasionally thrown in my direction, neither of the brothers seems minded to speak to me.

At nine o'clock sharp, the front-door bell sounds. The door is opened to Inspector Gully, accompanied by four officers, including stony-faced Sergeant Swann. The inspector asks whether Lady Tansor is at liberty to grant him an interview.

'No, sir,' intones Barrington. 'I regret to say that her Ladyship is not here at present.'

On being pressed, Barrington reluctantly concedes that Lady Tansor has not been seen since Miss Gorst left her, in bed, at half past ten the previous evening.

The inspector is at first puzzled, then displeased, and then decidedly put out. His face shows his certainty that this turn of events does not bode well. Something has happened that even he had not foreseen, and he does not like it. Not one little bit. He then rather firmly requests an interview with Mr Perseus Duport instead, and is shown to the Library, with a rueful air, by Barrington, who then goes to fetch Perseus from the Morning-Room.

The ensuing conversation has a marked effect on Perseus, as I later learn from the inspector. When he leaves the Library, some fifteen minutes later, having been told by Inspector Gully that he wishes to question her Ladyship concerning the murder of a certain Mrs Barbarina Kraus, his face bears the unmistakable look of a man in extreme shock.

He storms up the main staircase, deliberately and conspicuously cutting his brother, whom he passes thereon, and slams the door to his study, having shouted back orders to Barrington, who seems to be everywhere this morning, that he is not to be disturbed on any account, except when news is received of his mother's whereabouts.

I AM STANDING by the front door when Inspector Gully returns from the Library.

'May I have a word, Miss Gorst?' he quietly inquires. 'In private.'

We repair to the Morning-Room, recently vacated by Perseus, and the inspector softly closes the door behind him.

'Well,' he begins, rubbing his hands and giving me a look of grim anticipation, 'here's a thing. Where can she have gone?'

There is a new steeliness about my formerly affable co-member of the triumvirate, and I sense now, in his concentrated look, that his reputation is well founded.

'I'm unable to say,' is my instinctively evasive answer, not wishing him – at present – to know that I had done nothing to prevent Emily from taking her own life, so allowing her to escape the due process of the law. I tell him that I have not seen her since the previous evening.

'Quite so, quite so,' nods the inspector, managing nonetheless to insinuate a strong measure of doubt that I am telling the truth. 'Serious matter, though,' he then observes, 'if she's made her escape – perhaps with the help of others. A lot to answer for.'

'Indeed,' is all I can bring myself to say under his discomfiting eye.

There is a brief silence. The inspector taps his right boot on the floor, and purses his lips to make a soundless whistle.

'Anything else you wish to tell me, miss?' he asks at length.

'What else should I have to tell?'

'Beg pardon, miss. Concerning Lady Tansor and her present whereabouts.'

'As I have already stated,' I return, warming to the lie, and knowing that he will learn the truth of Emily's fate soon enough, 'I last saw her at half past ten last night.'

'Up early this morning yourself, I believe?'

'I am often up early.'

'Of course. Why not? Perfectly understandable. Do it myself.'

Another charged silence.

'But you saw no sign of her Ladyship? Apologies for pressing you.'

'I saw no one.'

The inspector now regards me with barely disguised suspicion. I can see that he knows I am lying, although not what I am keeping from him, and that he also realizes he will get nothing more out of me. I feel guilty for the untruth, but it is for the best under present circumstances.

'Well then, miss,' he says, now rubbing the sole of his left boot on the carpet, no doubt to relieve one of his itches, 'it seems there's nothing more to be said – for the moment. And so I'll bid you good-morning.'

I remain alone in the Morning-Room for several minutes, considering what I should do next, my mind still in a whirl from discovering the keys to my lost inheritance, and intermittently assailed by the sickening recollection of Emily's body succumbing to the racing waters of the Evenbrook. At length, I go up to my room, to await the news that must soon come.

THE CLOCKS OF the great house chime out the hour of ten.

Inspector Gully has waited long enough. He calls up Mr Pocock and requests him – with Mr Perseus Duport's permission – to send out as many men as possible to make a search of the Park. Sergeant Swann is then ordered upstairs to Emily's apartments, accompanied by Miss Allardyce and by an insistent Barrington, who seems unusually exercised by the presence of Inspector Gully and his officers in the house.

A little while later, the sergeant returns with a letter, found by Barrington on her Ladyship's escritoire, and addressed in her hand to Inspector Alfred Gully, who immediately turns away to read it. When he has finished, he places it in his coat pocket, and beckons to Sergeant Swann.

They move away from the various groups of anxiously chattering servants towards the portrait of my grandparents in its candle-encircled alcove. I have just come down from my room and am standing at the head of the stairs, from where I can just make out what is being said by them.

'All done, Sergeant,' says the inspector, tapping his coat pocket. 'Full confession. Chapter and verse – delicate matter of the eldest son's natal secret, Mrs Kraus, even the Carteret business. Mr W and his uncle were right – Mrs Gully, too, God bless her! The succession's been the thing from the start. Everything done at first for the sake of Mr Daunt's rosy prospects, and then Master Perseus's ditto. The rest we know. Poor old Carteret had found out who the true heir was, and had the documents to prove it. That did for him, although I'm willing to believe they meant him no fatal harm. And who do you think he was, Sergeant, the cheated heir?'

Sergeant Swann shrugs his shoulders, as if the answer is of the least possible interest to him.

'I'll tell you, then,' says the inspector, with a wry smile. 'Edward Glyver. Now there's a familiar name, Sergeant, to us both, I think, and to the Department. Edward Charles Glyver. Still wanted for the murder of Mr Phoebus Daunt. It's a tangled web, no question, but we're cutting through it now. It's all here. Signed and dated, in her Ladyship's own hand. All we want now is to find her.'

They leave the alcove, and I continue on my way down the stairs, just as Barrington appears, in his usual tight-lipped way, creeping forth from the little green-painted doorway through which Emily had passed earlier that morning, on her final journey to the Evenbrook.

'Ah, Barrington,' says the inspector to the head footman. 'I'll need another word with Mr Perseus Duport, if you please.'

'Mr Duport has gone out, sir,' Barrington tells him. 'He felt the need to take some air. He will be back shortly.'

'Perhaps you'll let me know when he returns,' suggests the inspector.

The footman gives him the merest bow, and slips quietly away.

IT IS APPROACHING eleven o'clock, just as Mr Wraxall arrives and is asking to see Miss Gorst, when one of Mr Maggs's boys, panting and perspiring, runs frantically up the front steps and bursts dramatically into the vestibule.

'Now then, Harry Bloomfield,' says Mr Maggs sternly. 'What's all this?'

'She's found!' the boy gasps out. 'Down by the bridge. Drowned dead in her night-gown!'

An audible thrill of horrified shock ripples round the vestibule. Several of the women begin to cry, and Mr Pocock forgets himself to the extent of sitting down on a red-plush chair and burying his head in his hands.

Mr Maggs gives a low whistle and shakes his head, then turns away and says under his breath: 'Drowned dead. Just like her sister.'

II
Time's Revenge

THEY BRING HER back wrapped in a hastily procured blanket, with her face covered, and lay her on her still unmade bed. As they are carrying their awful burden through the vestibule, to the horror of the onlookers still assembled there, a bluish-white, beringed hand slips from its temporary shroud into full view, causing one of the house-maids to faint.

Dr Pordage has been summoned to give an initial opinion on

the cause of death, although it is plain enough to everyone how her Ladyship has met her end. Mr Thripp then arrives, ties up his whining terrier by the front door, and wheezes his way upstairs to dispense garrulous Christian comfort in this time of trial.

The sight of Emily's poor body, lying under the sodden and dirtied blanket, in the great carved bed where she had spent so many troubled nights, is most terrible. Pretence is unnecessary, for the tears that begin to fall are real, and I make no attempt to conceal them; yet no one comforts me. It seems that I no longer have any standing in the household, now that the protective bond with my former mistress has been sundered, and I find myself ignored by the little group – Perseus and his brother, Inspector Gully and Sergeant Swann, the doctor and the Rector, and Mr Baverstock, my Lady's former secretary – gathered about the bed. All except Perseus are conversing gravely with each other in hushed voices; he stands slightly apart from the rest, staring fixedly down at his mother's now uncovered face.

How like her he is, even now! Her beautiful hair, which I have so often brushed and dressed in life, is now tangled, and matted with river ooze; one cheek is grimed with a jagged sliver of hardened black mud, like a drying wound; and there is an ugly red-black contusion on her forehead. Yet, curiously, Death has also wiped away the years, and her face, beneath these temporary disfigurements, seems almost youthful again. Her skin is smooth and taut, the once visible ravages of tribulation quite gone. She needs no lotions and powder now to mask over what time and guilt have done to her; for she is beautiful in death – beautiful still.

Her eldest son does not look at me, does not even acknowledge that I am here, but continues to stare down at her, in the grip, it seems, of a kind of paralysis. Every vestige of animation has drained from his face, leaving it as pale and immobile as that of his mother's corpse. Then he reaches out to take one of her cold and stiffening hands from beneath the blanket, bends down, and kisses it with such pathetic tenderness that my tears begin anew.

This simple act moves me more than I can say; and when he has gently withdrawn his hold, I see that there are tears in his eyes also, and how much he suffers from the loss, in the most dreadful manner, of a beloved mother. Yet there is another blow that he is struggling to bear; for – courtesy of Inspector Gully – he alone amongst the other gentlemen there present as yet understands the scale of the tragedy, and the shame and dishonour that is about to fall upon the house of Duport.

I look over to where Mr Randolph is talking to Dr Pordage. He appears to be unaware of his brother's suffering; but then he walks over to him and places a consoling hand on his shoulder, which Perseus brushes angrily away before throwing himself on the sofa, where he sits staring into the black mouth of the empty fire-place.

Still no one is paying me the least attention. Only Miss Allardyce briefly acknowledges my presence, although she is too distressed to say anything more than 'Oh, Miss Gorst!' before she is obliged to remove herself from the fearful scene. As she is leaving the room, Mr Randolph comes over to me.

'Perhaps you should leave too, Esperanza,' he says, gently. 'It would be best, I think.'

He speaks kindly, warmly, caringly, as he has always done; but this is his way with everyone – even the servants. I know now that there has been nothing singular in his former manner towards me, only awkwardness and uncertainty arising from his clumsy attempt to bring me into his confidence concerning his feelings for Jane Paget, which I had so injudiciously misinterpreted. He had always been a man in love with someone else, and I failed utterly to see it.

He takes my hand, and leads me to the door. He opens it for me, and smiles. None of the others turns to watch me go.

MR WRAXALL HAS been waiting for me in the Library, examining some ancient document in a glass display case.

He greets me by taking my hand in his and pressing it softly, but says nothing. He then escorts me into an adjacent, curiously shaped chamber, formerly Professor Slake's work-room, and Mr Paul Carteret's before him.

'This is a bad business, my dear,' he begins. 'I confess I did not foresee it ending in this way, although perhaps I should have done. A woman of invincible pride. Yes, I should have considered the possibility that, when all was lost, she might condemn herself, and so cheat the due legal process.

'But we can – and should – speak of this further when we know more of what has happened – and why. What I really came here to say concerns you, my dear.'

'Me? What can you mean?'

'I think you know what I mean,' he replies, momentarily uncovering a glimpse of the fearsome prosecutor he had formerly been.

'Very well,' he resumes, when I remain silent. 'You'll doubtless recall the occasion, in London, when you were followed by Mr Vyse's man, Arthur Digges. What you did not know was that, greatly concerned for your safety, I had earlier instructed my own man, Jobson, to stay close by you when you left Grosvenor Square.

'Jobson stayed with you as far as Billiter Street, where he observed you enter the house of a Mr John Lazarus, a retired shipping-agent. Unfortunately, when you left, Jobson lost you in the crowd, and I thank God that you eventually found your friend Mr Pilgrim. I'm not so certain now, as I was then, that Digges intended you any actual physical harm, but it was still a dangerous situation.

'The next day, I paid a visit to Mr Lazarus – a most delightful and interesting gentleman, and very eager to talk of his former life, in particular of the time that he spent on Madeira, some twenty years ago now, in the company of a certain Edwin Gorst.'

Seeing me begin to colour, he presses my hand again, and apologizes for any discomfort his words are causing.

'Not at all,' I say, as breezily as I can. 'Please go on.'

'Mr Lazarus, it appears, had conceived a great liking for this gentleman, whose name you share, and whom he had first encountered living in precarious circumstances on the island of Lanzarote. It seems that Mr Gorst had requested him to deliver some papers to a solicitor in England, which he had been very willing to do. Fearing for his new acquaintance's rapidly declining health, he then persuaded Mr Gorst to leave Lanzarote for the more beneficial climate of Madeira, where Mr Lazarus had a residence.

'But of course you know all this,' Mr Wraxall then observed, with another penetrating look. 'So let me tell you something of which I think you will not be aware concerning this gentleman, whom we both now know to have been your father.

'Mr Lazarus spoke of a scandal – an elopement, to be exact, as a consequence of which Mr Gorst and a Miss Marguerite Blantyre, the daughter of a well-known Edinburgh wine merchant, secretly and precipitately quit Madeira, never to return. This much, too, you doubtless know.

'That was the last Mr Lazarus ever saw of Edwin Gorst, and it was a great regret to him that he had only one small memento of his former friend. What do you think it was?'

Once more, I felt the barrister's keenly probing eye on me as I struggled, with little success, to maintain an impression of unconcern.

'But there I go again,' said Mr Wraxall, smiling apologetically once more. 'This is not a cross-examination, my dear, and I'm sorry if it seems like one. Old habits die hard, I fear. So let me tell you, friend to friend, that Mr Lazarus's sole memento of Edwin Gorst was the first edition, printed at Cambridge in 1634, of John Donne's *Six Sermons*. It had fallen down behind Mr Gorst's bed, and was only discovered some time after the aforementioned scandal. Mr Lazarus showed it to me – quite a clean and neat example. There was an inscription: "Edward Charles Glyver. Eton College, May 1834".'

I clearly saw where all this was tending, and that Mr Wraxall had correctly deduced that I was the daughter of the man who had killed Phoebus Daunt. I therefore decided, there and then, to bring him fully into my confidence at last, knowing with instinctive certainty that, like Madame, he had only my very best interests at heart, and that I would need his advice and help in the coming days and weeks.

Thus I laid the truth of who I was, and why I had been sent to Evenwood, before Mr Montagu Wraxall.

• • •

AT A LITTLE before mid-day, we walked back out into the Library, that great confection of a room, drenched now in dazzling sunshine.

'It is always satisfactory to have one's suspicions confirmed,' Mr Wraxall observed, as we stood looking out onto the terrace, where Emily had walked so many times.

I had told him everything, ending with an account of the documents that I now possessed, which I hoped would establish my right to succeed to the Tansor Barony, as the grand-daughter of the late Lord Tansor. I even confessed what I had earlier been reluctant to tell Inspector Gully: that I had been present when Emily had ended her life in the Evenbrook.

'Perhaps it was for the best, after all,' said Mr Wraxall, shaking his head sadly, and sighing.

'Do you really think so?' I asked eagerly, having feared that he might have been angered by my failure to save Emily from destroying herself.

'Not with absolute certainty,' he admitted, 'especially, perhaps, because she will never now answer – in this life, at least – for instigating the attack on her father, my uncle's dear friend. But what is done is done, and now we must face the consequences – you above all, my dear. What will you do?'

I told him that I would leave immediately for Paris, to inform my guardian of Lady Tansor's death, and that we now had the means to reinstate my father's bloodline through me.

'And you have also vindicated my dear uncle's convictions concerning the death of Mr Carteret,' said Mr Wraxall, most feelingly. 'He knew, as I did, that there was more to the attack than simple robbery. It was the succession, as we always suspected. And so God bless you, my dear. You cannot know how much this means to me.'

One thing only I hesitated at first to reveal; but I did so at last, and felt the better for it.

'Randolph Duport married! To Mrs Battersby!'

I had never before seen Mr Wraxall so taken aback, and for several moments he seemed quite unable to say anything more by way of reply.

'Does his brother know?' he asked, collecting himself at last.

'I do not believe so.'

Without admitting that I loved Perseus, I then told Mr Wraxall how I had rejected his proposal of marriage, in the belief that Mr Randolph was now the legitimate heir whom I must seek to marry. Mr Wraxall considered for a moment.

'Poor fellow,' he said after a while. 'Do you know, I feel quite sorry for Mr Perseus Duport. He's blameless in all this, after all, but must now pay a heavy price for what his mother has done. Yet it cannot now be helped. You have the instruments, I'm sure, to establish your claim, and so dispossess Mr Perseus, and his brother – unless, of course, you quit this life childless, which I hope, indeed confidently expect, will not be the case. You will be a great catch, my dear, a very great catch indeed.'

He gave a quiet chuckle.

'What is it?' I asked.

'Forgive my levity at such a time,' he said. 'I was merely thinking that you'll need to beware of Mr Maurice FitzMaurice once you become Lady Tansor.'

I returned his smile. Then he regarded me in the strangest way.

'Ah,' he said, quietly, 'I see how it is. You loved Mr Perseus, but had to give him up for the sake of your cause. My poor dear girl!'

The still painful memory of my loss, and my gratitude to dear Mr Wraxall for his touching concern, brought on my tears once more. I was also suddenly overcome by the thought of what now lay ahead for me; but Mr Wraxall soon began to put my mind at rest.

'You must leave as much as possible to me, my dear,' he said, 'if, that is, you are happy to do so.'

'Most happy,' I replied.

It was therefore agreed that Mr Wraxall would take charge of my grandmother's letters and the affidavits, together with Daunt's letters to Emily that I had taken from the secret cupboard. It was further agreed that, during my absence in France, he would consult expert counsel on the legal procedures that would now have to be set in train to advance my claim.

We were discussing these matters when Barrington appeared, to inform Mr Wraxall that Inspector Gully was asking for him.

'Show the inspector in here, if you please, Barrington,' said Mr Wraxall. 'Will you tell him what you've told me?' he then asked me. 'Better if you do, you know, before he finds out for himself.'

The inspector arrives, and the three of us, serious and subdued, walk out on to the sunny terrace. We stand for a while looking across the gardens, in their fresh summer finery.

'Been a bit of a row,' the inspector says, mysteriously. 'The brothers have been going at it hammer and tongs.'

It appears that, on Perseus's return to the house, the inspector had gone up to his study, with the intention of laying his mother's confession before him, only to find the two brothers in the midst of a fierce argument. As he had been about to knock on the door, he had distinctly heard the name 'Battersby' shouted, in an outraged tone, by Perseus, from which of course I inferred that Mr Randolph had at last confessed his secret to his brother, and said as much to Mr Gully.

'Well, well,' says that gentleman. 'There's a turn-up. This is a day for confessions, and no mistake.'

'And I have one, too, Mr Gully,' I say to him, a little abashed.

He gives me a gently satisfied grin, reaches down into his boot, and scratches his foot.

'Just as I thought, miss,' he says, straightening himself up. 'Just as I thought.'

IT WAS LEFT to the capable Mr Baverstock to supervise the many immediately necessary arrangements that now demanded attention; for, within an hour of their argument, both the Duport brothers had left the house – Perseus, in a black rage, for London, Mr Randolph and his wife for Wales, although he announced his intention to return for the inquest into his mother's death.

The little world of Evenwood was of course shocked and scandalized to its very core by these extraordinary events. Lady Tansor dead, and implicated in the murder not only of a former servant but also of her own father! Mr Perseus Duport not the son of Colonel Zaluski! Mr Randolph Duport secretly married to the housekeeper! Even the most inveterate below-stairs gossips were almost speechless with amazement. Where would it all end? And what did it mean for them, now – as it appeared – that the mighty Duports had been laid low?

Mr Pocock and the steward, Mr Applegate, attempted to steady everyone's nerves.

'It'll fall to Mr Randolph now,' the latter told their fellow servants, not knowing that I was now the legitimate heir, 'which will be no bad thing for us, being, as he is, a good and kindly soul. He'll look after us, never fear.'

I LEFT EVENWOOD the next day, travelling to London with Mr Wraxall. He had wished me to stay with him for a few days before taking my onward journey to France; but I was adamant that I must get to the Avenue d'Uhrich with all speed. He agreed with reluctance, but insisted on making the arrangements, and on advancing me some money for any unforeseen expenses.

I spent the night in a dark and dusty hotel, situated in a dismal street close to the station from where I was to depart the next morning – a change indeed from the splendours of Evenwood. It was also the first time that I had ever been truly alone, and thrown completely on my own resources, in the great, smoky, heaving capital.

I was sitting at my lonely supper, in the public dining-room, my mind still swimming with many conflicting emotions, when I became aware of someone standing over me.

'Is everything tasty and tender, miss?'

The question was voiced – without the slightest trace of either geniality or genuine interest – by a lean, lank-haired waiter, with the face of a disappointed undertaker, who concluded his enquiry with the most doleful sigh I have ever heard.

I told him that everything was perfectly satisfactory.

The waiter bowed and moved, with infinite slowness, to the next table, to ask the same question of a capacious gentleman in the act of raising a prodigious portion of dripping beef to his mouth, receiving only an unintelligible grunt by way of reply. The mournful catechism was then repeated, table by table, until at last, having traversed the room, the gloomy interrogator took up a position by the door, placed his wiping-cloth over his right arm, which he proceeded to hold rigidly across his stomach. He then seemed suddenly to subside into rigid immobility, eyes closed, like some lifesized automaton that had run down and now required winding up again.

I do not know why I mention this trifling and irrelevant incident, except that it has somehow fixed in my mind the memory of that day, and of the dismal atmosphere of that dim and dusty diningroom, with its community of transient strangers, each with their own reasons for being there, and each, no doubt, like me, with their own secrets to hide.

37

Inheritance

I

The Four Secrets

1ST JUNE 1877

AFTER SPENDING the night in the Hôtel des Bains in Boulogne, where I had stayed before my departure for England, I finally arrive back in the Avenue d'Uhrich.

Madame is sitting alone, her back to the door, in the high-ceilinged salon on the first floor of the Maison de l'Orme, looking distractedly out at the chestnut-tree beneath which I had played as a child.

For several moments she remains unaware that I have entered, and that I am now standing just behind her; then she suddenly turns her head slightly and, with a little gasp, puts her hand over her mouth with shock and surprise at seeing me.

'Esperanza! Dear child! What are you doing here?'

As she speaks, I too experience a sudden, and most profound, shock, although I seek to conceal it.

She is dreadfully changed. The girlish face that I remembered so well, and which I had dreamed of so often during my months at Evenwood, is now pinched and careworn; her lustrous pale hair has become coarse and thin; and I see, with dismay, that her once smooth and delicate hands are now almost fleshless, like an old lady's, and that they tremble uncontrollably. My beautiful, ever-young guardian angel! What has happened to you?

I found my tongue at last, greeted her, and bent down to place a kiss on her lined forehead. She took my hand, and I sat down beside her, on the little tapestried sofa on which we used to read together when the weather prevented us from walking in the Bois.

'Why did you not tell me you were coming?' she asked.

There was an urgent, unnerving tremor in her voice, as if my return was in some way unwelcome.

'Because I wished to surprise you and Mr Thornhaugh, of course,' I replied, as cheerily as I could. 'Is he here? Shall I ask Jean to call him down, so that I can tell you both my news together? No – let me go and find him myself. I expect he's at his books as usual—'

'Mr Thornhaugh is not here,' Madame broke in, releasing my hand, and looking away for a moment. 'He has gone.'

'Gone? What can you mean? Where has he gone? Will he be back soon?'

'He will never be back. I do not expect to see him again in this world, except in my memory, and I shall soon be leaving this world myself. Dear child, I am dying.'

THE RECOLLECTION OF what followed these words of Madame's festers perpetually within me, like a wound that will never heal.

As the late afternoon darkened into evening, and rain drummed heavily against the tall windows, the secrets came tumbling out.

Secrets! Would there never be an end to them? Where was honesty and open dealing between those who professed to love each other? So much had been hidden away, so much entombed in dark places. Why did they never tell me? I had placed all my trust in them, and they had deceived me. An arrow pulled from my living flesh could not have produced the exquisite and enduring agony that I suffered as the truth was finally laid before me, by the person I had trusted and esteemed more than anyone in the world.

I shall not – cannot – attempt a *verbatim* account of what Madame now told me. Instead, let me have final recourse, as my story draws to its close, to the epitome of that dreadful day that I committed to my Book of Secrets – that brimming repository of hidden things, which I had so dutifully maintained on Madame's instructions.

MADAME'S CONFESSION
MAISON DE L'ORME, 24TH MAY 1877
These are the Four Secrets I learned from Madame on this day.

1. After the death of my mother, 'Edwin Gorst' – who was really Edward Glyver – left the Maison de l'Orme to embark on his eastern travels. This much was true.

   It was then put out that he had died in Constantinople, and that his body had been brought back to Paris. This was a lie.

   He never died. The coffin mouldering beneath the granite slab in the Cemetery of St-Vincent contained nothing more than stones and dirt. He never died, at the age of forty-two, in the year 1862, as his gravestone proclaimed. He lives still. My father lives still.

   This was the First Secret.

2. A year after the supposed death of 'Edwin Gorst', Mr Basil Thornhaugh came to live at the Maison de l'Orme, to take charge of my education.

   Three weeks earlier, Basil Thornhaugh and the widowed Madame de l'Orme had been married secretly, in a village church near Fontainebleau. They have lived together, surreptitiously, as man and wife, ever since.

   This was the Second Secret.

3. Riddle me this.

   The moustachioed 'Edwin Gorst' was thought dead and buried – yet he lived. Clean-shaven Basil Thornhaugh lived and breathed – yet he never existed.

   The answer is simple enough.

Basil Thornhaugh was – is – my father. Basil Thornhaugh was – is – Edward Glyver, who murdered Phoebus Daunt.

Duport – Glyver – Glapthorn – Gorst – Thornhaugh. Five names. One man. One living man. One living father.

This was the Third Secret.

4. Madame had loved my father, since first meeting him, years earlier, when he was attached to another, her dearest friend in all the world. But this friend, together with the man *she* truly loved, had sought to destroy him, in order to gain for themselves what was rightfully his.

Does more need to be said?

The friend was the former Miss Emily Carteret.

Her lover was Phoebus Daunt.

Madame de l'Orme's maiden name was Marie-Madeleine Buisson.

This was the Fourth Secret.

Here my epitome broke off, although more secrets, of less consequence, were still to be revealed.

At intervals in her confession, Madame had been obliged to pause, in order to cough into a large linen handkerchief that she had by her. She attempted to hide them, but I clearly saw the ominous spots of blood staining the white material, and instantly recognized their fatal significance.

'The doctor says that I shall not live to see the leaves fall,' she said, looking out at the swaying branches of the chestnut-tree, barely visible now in the deepening darkness.

Although she had deceived me, I loved her still, and the doctor's prognosis cut me to the heart.

'Well, you must prove him wrong,' I said gaily, trying to force a smile. 'I shall take you away – to Italy. To Florence. And then you'll come back, recovered and happy, to see the leaves falling until the tree is quite bare, and then you'll see the new ones come in the spring, and for many springs to come.'

She returned a sad, indulgent smile, but did not reply.

I got up from the sofa and stood looking down into the wind-swept garden, remembering the golden days of my childhood, and little Amélie Verron, guileless to the depths of her sweet soul, my truest and most faithful friend, as it now seemed.

Love, and the secrets it spawned, had betrayed us all – Madame, Emily, and me. Madame's love for my father had made her his ever-willing slave, ready to do whatever his will demanded. The consequences of Emily Carteret's love for Phoebus Daunt, despite the affection she professed for my father, had driven her, at the last, to the commission of murder and to self-destruction. As for me, I had loved and trusted Madame, and the man I knew as Basil Thornhaugh, to the utmost degree, only to be given deception and lies in return.

THE ATTAINMENT, AT last, of my rightful inheritance, as I could now report to Madame, stood fair to succeed; but the prospect gave me no joy. Lord, what a poor deluded fool I had been! I recalled, with a kind of shame, the bitter tears I had shed on reading Mr Lazarus's memories of my father, and the anguish I had suffered at never having known him in life. The inscription on that shadowed slab of granite had told me that he was dead. Another betrayal. Another lie. He had been with me, throughout my childhood, without my knowing, watching over me as a father ought, day after day, in the guise of my tutor, but never revealing himself to me.

Madame assured me that he had loved me. Why, then, had he never thrown off his disguise? Why had he let me believe that I was fatherless? Could a loving parent be capable of such refinement of cruelty?

'He had his reasons,' Madame had urged, 'and nothing would move him. He could not escape his fate. It pursues him still, and he will never be free of it, until Death releases him. Nothing else matters to him but the restitution of what was stolen by Emily Carteret and Phoebus Daunt. This imperative – implacable and constant – has infected everything he does, and all else must bend to that relentless necessity. It is his curse, and we must all suffer for it, as he does.

'Following his exile,' she went on, 'he could no longer achieve his ambition himself; and so he has directed all his energies, all his will, to making you, dear child, his surrogate. I say again that he loves you – he has always loved you; but there is a power at work here even greater than love.'

'But where has he gone?' I asked her. 'And why has he left you, when you are ill, and in such distress?'

'He left yesterday,' she replied. 'I do not know where he has gone, only that he says he will never return.'

'But why?' I repeated.

'Because I am no longer of any use to him. Because he believes the Great Task has failed. And because *she* is dead.'

I sat in silent disbelief. How could he have known of Emily's death so soon?

My father's reach, it appeared, was a long one. He had recruited a paid spy in the Detective Department, from whom he had learned the nature of the evidence against Emily, and had thus discovered the truth concerning Perseus's birth, and the conspiracy between Emily and Lord Tansor.

'It was a most grievous blow,' said Madame, 'to learn that the Great Task could not now be accomplished through your marrying Perseus Duport. For several days your father shut himself away, eating little, and seeing no one. He had begun to recover his spirits a little when he received a telegraphic message with the news of Lady Tansor's death, and also that the younger Duport brother was already married.'

'A telegraphic message!' I exclaimed in amazement. 'From whom?'

'Your father is a most resourceful man – it comes from his former time as confidential assistant to the late Mr Christopher Tredgold. He has retained many associations with people, not always of the most elevated character, who are willing, and well able, to help him obtain almost any information he may require. He himself has travelled incognito to London, and on several occasions to Northamptonshire, when it was necessary for him to do so.

'You should also know that he has employed someone at Evenwood, who has been constantly observing events there. It was this person who sent the telegraphic message.'

'That will be Captain Willoughby,' I said, confidently.

'No,' replied Madame. 'Not Captain Willoughby, not exactly, although he, too, as you now know, was assigned by your father to keep a daily watch over you. It was Jonah Barrington, the head foot-man, who served under the captain during the Russian War. It has been through Barrington that we have been regularly assured of your safety and well-being, which you must believe have always been our greatest concern.

'As for Captain Willoughby, his real name is Willoughby Le Grice, and he is your father's oldest and most trusted friend, who stood by him through all his years of exile, and on whom he will always be able to depend.'

Barrington! Bleak-faced, ever-silent Barrington, who had brought me my supper on my first night at Evenwood! Every day since then, it now appeared, he had been my unseen and unrecognized guard, for which I supposed I must be in his debt. His familiar presence had never once raised the slightest suspicion in me that he was anything other than he seemed, and as I had described him in my Book of Secrets. Yet I saw now that it was the very fact of his being so unob-trusive and unremarkable that made him a most efficient spy.

To my further astonishment, it also appeared that it was Bar-rington who, at my father's instigation, had contrived to have my predecessor, Miss Plumptre, dismissed. Having removed the brooch that the maid had been accused of stealing, and hidden it in her room, he had then solemnly sworn that he had seen her leaving Emily's apartments, on a day when her mistress was absent in Lon-don, at the very time that the object was thought to have been taken. A search of her room had then been instigated; the brooch had been discovered; and, despite her continued – and most outraged – protestations of innocence, the hapless Miss Dorothy Plumptre had instantly been sent away, so providing Madame with the opportu-nity she had needed to try to place me in Lady Tansor's employ.

• • •

AFTER A LIGHT supper, Madame and I drew our chairs close to the fire, for the wind and rain had made the evening uncomfortably chill.

I had been willing to postpone further conversation until the morning, but Madame, although exhausted by the effort, insisted on continuing her confession.

She implored me, first, to forgive her for what her love for my father had made her do. I told her that forgiveness might come in time; but not yet, not until every secret, every lie, had been laid bare.

'There are no more of any consequence,' she replied, wearily. 'I have told you everything that we have kept from you. But if I have failed to satisfy you on any point, then ask me what you will. I cannot leave this world until I have regained your complete trust and affection.'

I assured her, with a kiss, that she would always have the latter. As for trust—

She seized my hand with sudden and such surprising vigour that I almost cried out.

'Then tell me now, I beg you, how I may earn that trust. What more do you wish to know, dear child?'

'For now,' I replied, 'two things. Tell me, first, did my father have any hand in the death of Mr Roderick Shillito?'

The directness of my question made her hesitate before replying. I had hoped for a categorical denial; but all she would say was that she had not been party to the many 'private arrangements', as she termed them, that my father had made over the past months.

'He never spoke of them to me, or of what may have passed when he himself went to London. He told me of the attack on Mr Shillito, of course – I also read an account of it in one of the English newspapers; but that is all I know.'

Her eyes, however, spoke what we both thought: that my father had instigated the attack on Mr Shillito to prevent him from delving further into the true identity of the man calling himself Edwin Gorst whom he had met on Madeira.

Clearly wishing to avoid further unpleasant speculation on the matter, Madame then asked me to tell her the second thing I wished to know.

'It concerns the death of Lady Tansor,' I replied. 'Why did the news drive my father away? Did you both not insist to me, in the strongest terms, that she was an implacable enemy to my interests, and that we were bent on her destruction? And did you not also tell me that, although my father had loved her once, his former feelings had turned to hatred for what she had done to him?'

'He never ceased to love her,' she answered, in a most pitiful voice, 'even when he pretended to hate her, and even though it did not alter his great ambition to make her pay for betraying him. But her death was never contemplated by us. We worked only to bring about her public shame and condemnation, and then the restoration of your father's line, through your marriage to Perseus Duport. I would go so far as to say that I think your father even harboured an absurd and impossible hope that, when all was done, and in some unimaginable way, he might effect a reconciliation with her. A mad fantasy, of course, but I now believe it to be the case.

'He did not love me, as I once thought he did, when he and his first wife originally came here, from the Quai de Montebello. He had sought me out, with that diligence and perseverance that have always distinguished him; and I thought, in my poor foolish way, that he had done so because of some long-suppressed attachment towards me, which had begun when Emily and I were friends.

'I could not bear what she had done to him – could not for one more moment tolerate such base and determined cruelty; and all for the sake of *him* – that conceited, conscienceless upstart, Phoebus Daunt, who was not fit to breathe the same air as your father.

'So I persuaded myself that your father had brought his first wife to Paris with the express purpose of finding me again, and of renewing something that had been lost to him. Your mother came to think so, too; but he deceived us both in this, as in everything else. He did not love your mother either – although he professed to do so, and although he was always kind and affectionate towards her, except when he was taken by one of his black moods, and then we both suffered. But neither did he did love me.

'No. It was always her. It will always be her. And now she is dead.'

II
Acceptance

I COULD NOT leave Madame alone, in the state of bodily and mental distress in which I had found her; and so, having no immediate reason to return to England until my affairs demanded, I sat down the next morning to write to Mr Wraxall, saying that I intended to remain in Paris until he should send for me. His reply assured me that he would now devote himself to the advancement of the legal proceedings, which, he was confident, having taken provisional advice from several eminent colleagues, could be brought to a successful conclusion as speedily as the workings of the law allowed.

The succeeding days passed quietly, as Madame and I continued to speak of these formerly hidden things. Something of our former intimacy began to return; but it soon became evident that the doctor had been right.

With alarming rapidity, my guardian entered into a terminal decline. I sat beside her bed, morning and afternoon, and often through the night, reading to her, or watching over her in sleep, as she had done for me as a child. I brushed her hair, bathed her face, plumped her pillows, and stroked her wasted hands when she grew restive, or cried out in her sleep. But with every day that passed, she withdrew into some silent and distant world, beyond the reach of all my loving ministrations.

Only once, a few days before the end, did she briefly emerge from her increasingly comatose state, to ask me to take off the little silver crucifix that she wore about her neck.

'I wish you to have this, dear child,' she whispered, so quietly that I had to place my ear close to her cracked lips and ask her to repeat the words. Then, just before slipping back into sleep, she asked: 'Am I forgiven, dear child?'

'Yes,' I whispered back. 'You are forgiven.'

SHE DIED DURING the third week of June, as swallows wheeled dizzily in a cloudless sky above the Bois de Boulogne.

I had left her side, just for a moment, having passed the long night watching over her, to open the window and let in the heavenly summer air. When I turned back towards the bed, I knew that she had gone.

An era of my life ended that day. I now stood truly alone in the world for the first time, on the brink of a new and strange existence.

Alone? Yes. Although I was no longer the orphan I had always believed myself to be, having now discovered that I had a father who lived, I felt no change in my condition. He was as dead and insubstantial to me now as the mythical Edwin Gorst had once been. What other family did I have, now that Madame, my second mother, had been taken from me?

Marie-Madeleine de l'Orme, *née* Buisson, was buried in the Père Lachaise Cemetery. In her will, she left me the house in the Avenue d'Uhrich, together with a substantial sum of money, the remainder of her considerable fortune, inherited from her first husband, being apportioned amongst various charitable concerns in which she had taken an interest, and the two ever-loyal servants, Jean Dutout, and Marie Simon, who, it now appeared, had always known of her secret marriage to my father. To him, she bequeathed nothing.

She also left me a photograph – a self-portrait of my father, taken by him in the year 1853.

His face, of course, was completely familiar to me, for behind the magnificent beard and moustache, it was Mr Thornhaugh's – long and lean, with a dark complexion; swept-back black hair worn almost to the shoulders, and thinning slightly at the temples; large dark eyes, just as my mother had described in her journal.

I have it still, and take it out sometimes, when I wish to remind myself that I once had a father.

BEFORE LEAVING THE Avenue d'Uhrich, I went to the authorities, and in due course the coffin of 'Edwin Gorst' was raised and disposed of. I then had my mother's coffin removed to a new location, open and sunny, away from the constant shadows under which she had lain for so long. I also commissioned a new, upright, headstone to be made, carrying an inscription in English:

IN PERPETUAL MEMORY
OF
MARGUERITE ALICE BLANTYRE
1836–1859

This memorial was placed here by her loving daughter
July 1877

I REMAINED IN Paris for another month, at the end of which time I returned to England, although not immediately to Evenwood.

I had received a letter from Mrs Ridpath, inviting me to stay with her in Devonshire Street until all the legal matters were settled. This I gratefully, but firmly, declined; for whilst the offer was kindly meant, I regarded Mrs Ridpath as being somehow tainted by her association with my father, whom I had now determined I never wished to see, even if he made an attempt to communicate with me. Mr Wraxall then urged me to reside with him; but this invitation, although a far more congenial one, I also refused.

I settled myself instead at Mivart's Hotel, where I was visited almost daily by Mr Wraxall, but where I had the freedom to do exactly as I pleased, when I pleased. I cannot say that I was happy there, still afflicted as I was by grief for Madame and by aching memories of Perseus, and constantly brooding on what the future might bring. Yet when my mind was not beset by troubling, and often irresolvable, thoughts, I experienced a kind of quiet contentment during those strange, undifferentiated weeks, as I explored the seething streets of the city my father had loved, filling my notebook with observations and descriptions, or sat contemplatively beside the great grey river, to wait upon events.

THE INQUEST INTO Lady Tansor's death had returned its expected verdict of suicide and, following the evidence presented by Inspector Alfred Gully, of the Detective Department, the world now knew why the 26th Baroness Tansor had ended her life in the Evenbrook.

The ensuing scandal was immense. The Prime Minister had been immediately notified of her Ladyship's death, and the reasons that had led to it. Her Majesty was then informed. According to Mr Wraxall (who had it on the very highest authority), she had listened gravely to her First Minister, before expressing relief that, despite having liked Lady Tansor well enough, she had never cultivated her at Court.

The nation's public prints produced an ocean of articles and reports – sober, reflective, speculative, prurient, crowing, castigating, or pitying, according to the temper of the organ, or the disposition of the writer. Questions were asked in Parliament, whilst in society friends and enemies alike could talk of nothing else for months.

No objections being made, Emily Grace Duport, *née* Carteret, was buried in the Mausoleum at Evenwood. I did not attend the brief ceremony of interment, but received an account of it from Mr Wraxall. The mourners were few, confined – at the request of the brothers – to Perseus, Mr Randolph, and a dozen or so others. Mr Thripp officiated, managing, for once, to maintain a dignified brevity of expression on an occasion of such poignant solemnity that it robbed even the Rector himself of words.

I SHALL NOT weary my readers with the details of the legal processes, overseen by Mr Wraxall, that followed Emily's death, and the public revelations concerning Perseus's birth. The law duly took its ponderous course, my claim to be the rightful successor to the late Lord Tansor was ratified, and the day finally came when I returned to Evenwood, lady's-maid and paid companion no longer, but as Esperanza Alice Duport, 27th Baroness Tansor.

Mr Wraxall was standing in the Entrance Court, with all the assembled servants and estate workers, as the carriage came down the Rise, rattled over the bridge, where the waters of the Evenbrook had brought Emily's body to rest, and drew up before the front door.

'Welcome home, your Ladyship,' said Mr Wraxall, with a solemn bow.

'Come now, sir,' I replied, in mock admonishment. 'I wish to hear no more "your Ladyships" from you. You will address me by my Christian name, if you please. This is my first command, and I shall expect it to be strictly observed.'

Thus, arm in arm, laughing as we went, and to the applause of the crowd, we entered the great house of Evenwood to take our tea.

ONE OF MY first acts as mistress of Evenwood was to appoint Mr Montagu Wraxall to the position of librarian and archivist. We have become very close, and spend a great deal of time in each other's company. I no longer feel alone in the world. Mr Wraxall is always there, always ready with sound advice, always affectionately solicitous or, when the occasion demands, properly critical, and fiercely protective of my interests. He is my father now. I could want for no other.

For my dear lost Perseus, the calamity of his mother's death, and the circumstances by which he had been dispossessed, were almost unendurable. He immured himself for some months in his London residence, seeing no one, and communicating with the world only through his solicitor. At length he quit England altogether for Italy, where he apparently intended to remain.

Following his mother's death, Mr Randolph, as he had undertaken to do, had returned from Wales, alone, to attend the inquest. He was the subject of much admiration for doing so, being obliged to sit through the painful rehearsal of his mother's iniquities, whilst

enduring the stares and knowing looks arising from the now public knowledge of his marriage to Jane Paget, his mother's former
housekeeper.

With regard to his own position, he made no attempt to challenge my claim to succeed his mother, as he might have done. He
had once assured me that he entertained no wish to be master of
Evenwood, and I had no reason to doubt him; but I hoped also that
he had abstained from legal contention for another reason, and
that, after all, he cherished some regard for me – however small – of
which his wife would not approve.

I DO NOT need to be told that I am blessed. I know it, and thank
God every day for the enviable position in the world that I now
occupy; but I have little contentment. I suffer much from depression
of spirit, and am afflicted almost nightly by bad dreams and painful
memories; for I am imprisoned still in the life my father made for
me. My father – whom I once believed was dead, but who now lives,
or so I must presume. My father – the murderer of Phoebus Daunt.
My father – who stole my life and made it his own. My father – the
ghost within me, the implacable ruler of my existence.

I sit here most afternoons, in the window-seat on which I once
passed so many hours with Emily, reading her dead lover's poems
to her, idly conversing, or looking out over the terrace and the
pleasure-gardens to the wooded horizon.

Sometimes I will pass the time, my back pressed against the
ancient glass, blissfully absorbed in a new novel; at others, I contemplate yet again, as I think I always will, the events that have brought
me to the state of life I now enjoy.

I stare constantly into the Glass of Time, that magic mirror
in which the shifting shadows of lost days pass back and forth
in dumb show before the eye of memory. As for the present, the
days come and go in pleasantly uneventful – yes, and often dull
– succession.

Yet I do not complain. I have new friends; I have become a great
gardener, and have made many much-needed improvements to the

house. I am learning Italian and Spanish, and have emulated Mr Thripp in procuring a terrier of my own – a lovably roguish creature with an infinite capacity for wickedness, Bowser by name, who steals my shoes and is constantly biting holes in my gowns. He has a formidable feline companion, red-haired and noble of aspect, but of a warlike disposition, who keeps him in check and whom I have called 'Tiger', after the cat whose acquaintance I had briefly made at the house of Mr Lazarus in Billiter Street.

I have also fitted out Emily's old sitting-room with shelves that are already groaning under the weight of the novels and volumes of poetry, in English and French, that are sent to me every month; and a week rarely passes that I do not return to my mother's journal, which I now possess in its entirety. It pains me more than ever that I was denied by Death from forming that infinitely precious bond between mother and child, for which – I now believe – there is no true substitute.

My greatest diversion is this house, this wondrous palace of plenty. I have become utterly entranced by its beauty, in a way that I never was before; and when I am obliged to leave it, even on visits to the Avenue d'Uhrich, I dream of its cupola-crowned towers, and especially of the little arcaded courtyard, with its fountain and dovecote, where I had sat and dreamed – so long ago, it seems; and then I yearn to return. I wander through its rooms and corridors constantly, both by day and by night, marvelling, touching, opening; for it is all mine now.

I shall never tire of this place. Even when I am an old lady, drooling and drivelling, wrapped in shawls, frail and bony, and rheumy of eye, I shall still wander these rooms, still wondering at the boundless, dreamlike splendour of it all. Perhaps my ghost will do the same, willingly turning its back on the heavenly home that faith promises, to haunt instead the earthly paradise of Evenwood through all eternity.

Sometimes, although I should not, and strive against it with all my might, I miss her – my former mistress. She comes into my thoughts at all times, and in all places, and I feel her presence everywhere, especially when I am taking my walks on the Library Terrace, or sitting here in the window-seat opposite the closet from where I had spied on her and Mr Vyse. I do not regret the final, unexpected consummation of the Great Task – Justice called for nothing less; yet I wish to my soul that it had not fallen on me to bring it about.

I also sometimes miss the heady days of adventure and intrigue. I would not have them return, of course, for their legacy has been a bitter one; but I confess that my heart beats a little faster as I live over those times once again, when I was Esperanza Gorst, maid and then companion to the 26th Baroness Tansor.

And so I take my leave of my patient readers. Time, in its unfathomable way, and the unknowable workings of Fate, have done their work. The Great Task has been accomplished; and my Book of Secrets can now be put away, never again – I pray – to be opened by me.

E.A.D.
Evenwood, 1879

38

Envoi

Evenwood, December 1884

I
Hope Vindicated

F IVE YEARS have passed since I wrote the words with which –
as I then truly believed – I concluded the story of my secret
life, that bitter-sweet journey from my childhood home in the
Avenue d'Uhrich to the earthly paradise of Evenwood. I must now
crave my readers' indulgence for taking up my pen once more, to
recount certain subsequent events, which I believe those who have
had the patience to journey with me may wish to know. Whether
they will prove to be the end of my story, or constitute the begin-
nings of a new one, I cannot of course yet say. I undertake only to
lay them before you as briefly as I can.

ON A FINE June morning in the year 1880, I was sitting by the Lake,
looking out towards the Temple of the Winds, and thinking of the
past as usual, when one of the footmen brought me the terrible
news that Randolph had died in a fall whilst climbing the mountain
of Crib Goch with his old friend and brother-in-law, Rhys Paget.

Randolph and I had maintained a detached but friendly relationship, when family affairs had occasionally brought him back to

Evenwood; but I had seen nothing of his widow since the death of my former mistress (it is strange that I should still term her so, but it is a habit I easily fall into).

After her husband's interment, Mrs Randolph Duport and I had talked alone for a short time on the Library Terrace, where I sometimes sat on fine afternoons, in an old wicker chair of the former Lord Tansor's, with Bowser by my side.

It was a strange meeting – both of us now sharing the same surname, both of us having once been servants to the 26th Baroness; but she was no longer the woman whom I had known as Mrs Battersby when I was Esperanza Gorst, lady's-maid. She seemed much aged, and subdued in temper, although her curiously fixed half-smile remained, in confusing contrast to the grief so evident in her sunken, reddened eyes. We spoke of Randolph's many amiable qualities: his kindness, his engaging ways, his enthusiasms, his sweet temper and openness of disposition – on all of which points, and many others, we could easily agree. Of more sensitive matters relating to times past, however, nothing was said.

I had risen to go when she put out her hand to touch my arm, asking as she did so if she could say one more word. She then confessed that Randolph had lost most of the money that had been left to him in his mother's will in various failed business speculations. I had also disposed certain sums for his use when I had succeeded to the title; but these, too, it seems, had gone.

'Like my father, he was such an innocent in these things,' she said with a sigh, 'yet so anxious to prove himself as capable as his brother. But he found himself out of his depth, and placed his trust in those who only schemed to take his money, and give nothing back.'

She was looking down into her lap, twisting a handkerchief in her long white hands. I saw how hard it was for the once proud 'Mrs Battersby' to humble herself in this way, and I pitied her. She had hated me once, as I would have hated her had our circumstances been reversed; but she was now my kinswoman by marriage, and I could not wholly abandon her.

I therefore said that I would be glad to offer her some assistance, and I have kept my word, although I shall not receive her here again; and whatever I have done has been for the sake of Randolph's fatherless son, Ernest – a sweet little boy, in whose future prospects I have determined to take a close interest.

RANDOLPH WAS LAID to rest in the Mausoleum, next to the tomb of his mother. Perseus, of course, had been informed of his brother's death, and had written a brief note informing me that he would be attending the interment, although he would be leaving immediately afterwards to spend a few days at his London residence before returning to Italy.

There had been no direct communication between us since his mother's death. All our correspondence on the many matters arising from my assumption of the Tansor title had been conducted – at his request – through intermediaries, principally Mr Donald Orr.

As soon as I became Lady Tansor, I had settled a not inconsiderable fund of money on Perseus, to allow him to maintain himself in an appropriate style; but for this act of genuinely disinterested consideration, intended to provide some small measure of compensation for what he had lost, he had condescended to send me only a few curt words of acknowledgement in a letter to Mr Orr. Despite this rebuff, and after much heart-searching, I had subsequently sent him a long account of why I had been sent to Evenwood, which included a digest of the principal events that I have presented in these pages.

I waited for the expected reply; but none came. The note confirming that he would be returning to England for his brother's interment was the first communication from him that he had written to me personally, in his own hand. Not wishing to part with something so precious, I placed it in a little velvet bag to keep in my pocket, like a kind of talisman, in the foolish hope that it might signify some change for the better in our relations.

Although I had not seen him for nearly three years, Perseus had remained a vivid presence in my life. Hardly a day began but I did not think of him on first waking, and wonder what he was doing, and whether he sometimes thought of me; and hardly a day ended but I did not lay my head on my pillow in the certainty that I would soon be dreaming of him, and of what we had once been to each other. To know that I would be seeing him in person once again filled me with joyful expectation.

The day of the interment arrived. I awoke in the most extraordinarily confused state, grieving for poor Randolph, for whom I had continued to feel great affection, in spite of what had happened between us, but also excitedly anticipating the return of his brother to Evenwood, even though it was only for a day.

The mourners began to assemble in the Entrance Court for the short carriage ride to the Mausoleum; but there was no sign of Perseus. Eleven o'clock struck – the hour when the ceremony should have begun – and still he did not come. Unable to delay any longer, the party began to move off.

In the Mausoleum, the memories of which still sometimes trouble my dreams, Randolph's coffin was committed to its awaiting loculus, and the iron gates were closed and padlocked. Throughout the short ceremony, conducted by Dr Valentine, successor to Mr Thripp, who had passed away the previous autumn, I had stood nervously in the candlelit gloom, hoping that, even now, at this late hour, Perseus would walk through the open metal doors and take his place by my side. But after Dr Valentine had intoned the final prayer, and the mourners prepared to return to their carriages, I knew that my hopes had been in vain.

BY FOUR O'CLOCK that afternoon, the mourning guests, including Mrs Randolph Duport, had departed. For the past hour, I had been engrossed in a recent novel by Mr Thomas Hardy, which my bookseller had sent me some months before, but which I had only lately begun to read.* Laying the book down, I had happened to glance out of the window.

On the far side of the ha-ha, exactly in the place where I had

---

*Presumably, *Two on a Tower: A Romance*, published in October 1882. Hardy's next novel, *The Mayor of Casterbridge*, was not published until 1886.

first seen Captain Willoughby Le Grice, my then unknown friend, one misty morning in 1876, stood a man, staring up at my window. Despite the distance, I recognized him instantly.

In no time at all, I had run downstairs and across the Library Terrace, halting, heart afire, on the edge of the ha-ha. For what seemed an eternity, we stood looking at each other across the steep-sided grassy ditch under the late-afternoon sun – just such a sun as had dazzled me on the Ponte Vecchio years before.

Nothing was said; yet everything seemed understood.

THE DEPARTURE OF the steamer that should have brought him from Boulogne to Folkestone had been delayed for several hours. Being unable to make up the lost time, he had only arrived in Easton half an hour since. Leaving his bags at the Duport Arms, he had immediately taken a fly to Evenwood. This I learn after I have greeted him formally in the vestibule.

We are standing, face to face, at the foot of the staircase – in precisely the same spot where we had first met. The portrait of his father as a Turkish Corsair has been removed, on my instructions, to one of the attic rooms. He glances at the space on the wall where it had formerly hung, but says nothing.

He is as handsome as ever, but in a different way from the Perseus Duport whom I had last seen, on that most dreadful day, when they had brought his mother back from the Evenbrook. His frame is a little heavier; his long hair, of which he had once been so proud, is now worn short and cut closer to his head; whilst the thick black beard, which made him look so like his father, has gone, replaced by a neat wax-ended moustache.

His demeanour has also undergone a most notable change. Although I had longed to see him again, I had feared, from the tenor of his note to me, to find him still hurt and resentful at what had befallen him, and at my part in it. To my great delight and surprise, however, these fears prove groundless. He seems in no way aggrieved or antagonistic towards me. His manner and voice are calm and conciliatory, his smile warm and unforced. He seems, indeed, to have accepted his changed condition to a quite remark-able and unexpected degree, and to have put behind him for good all the rage and shame that had consumed him following his moth-er's death. Most striking of all, his eyes no longer express a nature bound by the constrictions of introspective pride, but shine with sym-pathetic energy, like those of a man eager to engage with the world at large. They are no longer his mother's eyes. Their size, shape, and mesmeric quality are as I remember; but now they declare the char-acter of the whole man, the true Perseus Duport, in all his contra-dictions. For he is no longer obliged to play the role assigned to him from birth by his mother. Like me, he has thrown away the mask that those closest to him made him wear. He now knows the truth about himself, and who he truly is. All this I clearly see in his face, and hear in his voice; and my heart begins to throb with new hope.

'Good-afternoon, your Ladyship.'

'Will you not call me Esperanza, as you used to do?' I ask.

'Certainly, if your Ladyship will allow it.'

'That I shall gladly do – as long as it accords with your own wishes.'

This little game of shuttlecock and battledore continues good-humouredly, until the ice is well and truly broken. We then col-lect ourselves and become serious again as we speak of Randolph, whose death, I see plainly, has affected Perseus more deeply than I might once have supposed that it would.

We continue talking of his poor departed brother as we walk together to the Library, where we stand before one of the soaring windows looking out towards Molesey Woods.

'I misjudged my brother,' he says. 'He was a good fellow, through and through – I can acknowledge that now; but I despised him because I thought he did not deserve to bear the noble name that he and I shared. Yet he had more right than me to call himself a Duport.'

I object that he is being too hard on himself, but he cuts me short.

'No, no. It is the truth. I know now who I am, and what I am, and the name by which I should properly be called.'

'Perhaps you now despise me instead,' I venture, 'for taking from you what you always believed was yours by right.'

He gives me a most tender look.

'Do not say so. How could I ever despise you? I admit that I blamed you once for what has happened to me, but no longer. I know now that you are as blameless as I am, and that you have taken back only what was always rightfully yours. You are a true Duport; I am not. We have both been the unwitting victims of others. All the fault is theirs, not ours.'

We then speak of his mother, for whom he expresses a most unexpected sympathy. To my inexpressible relief, he also assures me that he holds me in no way responsible for her death, blaming everything on her blind passion for his father, Phoebus Daunt.

'Her will was strong,' he says, as we walk down the central aisle of the Library towards his grandfather's former work-room, now Mr Wraxall's, 'but my father's was stronger, even in death. She could never break free from it. She has answered for her sins; but what she did, she did for him. She was his slave to the end.'

The sun is now beginning to set behind the wooded horizon, filling the great room with its glorious dying rays. I am making some trite observation on the beauty of the prospect when he interrupts me to say that there is a matter that must be settled between us, and settled once and for all.

His grave look momentarily alarms me, until he gives me another reassuringly tender smile, and explains that it concerns the enmity that existed between our fathers.

'I must forgive your father, as you must forgive mine. Only then can we be free of them. I believe I can do this – indeed, I have done so. Can you do the same?'

I tell him that I fear we shall never be free of them: their legacy is too great. 'But I will try to pardon them, if I can, for how can my life ever be my own unless I do? We have both paid a bitter price for their sins.'

'Then let it be so,' he says. 'The past shall claim dominion over us no longer. It is time for us both to face the future as ourselves, not as their puppets.'

The hours pass; darkness falls; and still we go on talking of what has brought us to this point in our lives until there are no more secrets left to tell, and I remark that it is growing late.

'Will you not stay?' I ask, my heart in my mouth. 'For tonight at least?'

HE STAYED FOR a week, then for a second; and so it began. It ended at eleven o'clock on a crisp October morning, in the Church of St Michael and All Angels, Evenwood, when I became the wife of my cousin, Perseus Verney Duport.

Two months earlier, as we were sitting together one evening on the lamp-lit terrace, in the twilight of a hot August evening, talking of old times in the Palazzo Riccioni, he had reached into his pocket to take out a small box. Inside was the ring that he had given to me on the Ponte Vecchio, and which he had thrown on to the fire when he believed that I had spurned him in favour of his brother.

'I could not leave it there,' he now admits, taking the ring from its box. 'It had been yours once, and I wished so very much that it might be yours again. Will you accept it for a second time, as a gift of friendship?'

I tell him that I will accept it, with all my heart, but only on the same terms as before.

He shakes his head.

'No, that cannot be. Marriage is impossible. Everyone will think that I want only to regain what I have lost by becoming your husband. You may even think that yourself, and that I could not bear, having no means of proving otherwise.'

He will not be moved by my objections and assurances, maintaining most stubbornly that we must remain cousins and friends, nothing more. Patiently, persistently, however, I begin to persuade him that the world's opinion is of no account, and that we alone must now determine the future course of our lives. For my part, I needed no proof of his sincerity; and why should he not share what is now mine, if I so wish it? He continues to resist; but at last, the ring is on my finger again, the question he asked me on the Ponte Vecchio is asked once more, and the same answer is given.

Thus it was that the son of Phoebus Daunt proposed for a second time to the daughter of his father's murderer, Edward Glyver, and was accepted by her with a grateful and overflowing heart. To their union, on the 23rd of September 1881, was born a son, Petrus, the precious rock on which all his parents' hopes for the future of the ancient house of Duport now rest.

He is on the floor by my feet as I write, contentedly looking at a picture-book – my own childhood copy, in fact, of *Straw Peter*, with its coloured picture of the Long-legged Scissor Man snipping off the thumbs of the naughty little boy who would not desist from sucking them. He appears to find this as horridly fascinating as I did, and has not taken his eyes off the page for these five minutes past.

Petrus is three years old now, strong and healthy, already a strikingly handsome child, and very like his father. Sometimes he can be a little wild and wilful, and then I fear that he may have inherited certain aspects of his character and temperament from one or both of his grandfathers, and that these may prove troublesome in later life without firm correction. Perseus insists that the wildness will pass, and that he will make a fine heir. I hope he may be right.

MY HUSBAND AND I go on very well, and I am now, I believe, as happy as I shall ever be in this life. He has overcome his former reticence and tells me often that he loves me, and that I am his comfort and joy, as he is assuredly and eternally mine. Indeed, there are not words enough in Mr Walker's *Pronouncing Dictionary*, which I still regularly consult, to describe what I feel for Perseus, and what I am certain I shall continue to feel for him, until the day my heart grows tired of beating. Love can corrupt and destroy, distort and betray – this I know from my own bitter experience; but I now also know that, without love, we are nothing.

We walk and ride, and read together; and I often sit beside him as he plays on the Chapel organ, turning over the pages of the Bach fugues that he performs with such admirable dexterity and feeling. Sometimes, when he is unable to sleep, he will rise and go down to the Chapel to play; and then I will lay listening to the majestic cadences and harmonies rising and falling through the still night air, like God's own music, until he returns.

One of my principal pleasures is to help Perseus with his work – reading to him, making fair copies, verifying points of historical fact. His poems, alas, do not sell well, despite his prodigious and relentless industry, and the money paid out to Mr Freeth for their production and promotion; but he looks to posterity to correct the unkind judgments of his contemporaries. It pains me so much to think that he may be disappointed.

However, he has now discovered a new commercial publishing house – Grendon & Co., Booksellers and Publishers, with premises in the Strand – that is willing to take him on at its own risk. I should rather say that the firm discovered *him*; for he was approached directly by the principal, Dr Edmund Grendon, who has deeply impressed Perseus with his erudition and taste, and with the informed enthusiasm he has expressed for his work. Although the firm is still a fledgling one, we begin to hope that, with Dr Grendon's help, the literary success that Perseus so richly deserves, but which has so far eluded him, may be forthcoming at last.

Dr Grendon has already become greatly valued by Perseus as a friend and adviser, for which I am glad, as he has few other companions. Indeed, this gentleman has begun to exert so marked a fascination on Perseus that I am quite wild to make his acquaintance; but, being somewhat reclusive by nature, as well as being often absent on business, he has so far refused several invitations to visit us at Evenwood, obliging Perseus to make frequent visits to Town, sometimes for a week at a time, to consult with his new friend and mentor.

Thus we go quietly on, seeing little of the great world of society and its glittering emptiness, devoting ourselves instead to the care of our son and heir, and to preparing him for the day when he will become the head of this great family. Yet a shadow still hangs over us. We can never escape the legacy of what has been, especially here, in this house, where the past saturates the very air we breathe. Try as we may, for the sake of our son, we find that we are unable wholly to break free from the fetters that bind us to our former selves. I do not think we ever will.

II
Concerning Sleeping Dogs

THERE REMAINS ONE final incident to relate, and then I have done.

A few weeks ago, Charlie Skinner came to me with a message from Mr Wraxall asking whether I would be at liberty to meet him in the Library that afternoon.

On the table in his work-room lay a handsomely bound folio. It bore the title *Historia* on the spine, and the Duport arms were blocked on the front.

'What is this?' I asked.

'Open it,' said Mr Wraxall, unsmiling for once.

I did so, and began to leaf through it. It was not a printed book, as I had thought, but a bound manuscript, written on lined paper. It did not take me long to see what it was, and what it contained.

'How did you come by it?' I asked, closing the book.

'A letter came yesterday. It was signed "A Well-Wisher" – perhaps you may remember that I have previously received a communication from a person using the same *nom de plume*. Our unknown correspondent revealed where the volume had been concealed for these twenty years and longer. It had been in the Library all the time, under our very noses.'

I asked him whether he still had the letter.

He turned to his work-table, opened a drawer, and took out an envelope. Having looked at the direction, I did not have to see the letter's contents, noting only, with a frisson of alarm, that it had been posted in London.

'It is from him,' I said, handing back the envelope. 'I am very familiar with the handwriting of Mr Basil Thornhaugh.'

'Yes, my dear,' said Mr Wraxall, replacing the letter in the drawer. 'I believe you are right.'

He was alive, then, living somewhere in the world, perhaps in England, under some new name, no doubt, beneath the same declining sun that was now throwing shadows over the terrace. I had presumed as much, but my heart lurched at this unequivocal confirmation.

Mr Wraxall saw my look of apprehension, and placed a reassuring hand on mine.

'Be still, my dear,' he said. 'He will not come. His day is done.'

He stood for a moment or two, his grey eyes bent on me with tender intensity.

'What do you wish me to do with it?' he then asked, picking up the volume, the contents of which had been brought to England so many years ago by Mr John Lazarus. 'I spent the whole of last night reading it. It would tell you a great deal that you might wish to know, but perhaps much that you would not.'

Just then, the sound of the latch on the gate outside the workroom window caused me to look up.

Perseus, holding little Petrus by the hand, was coming through the archway on to the terrace. They stood together, looking out across the wintry Park. Then Perseus bent down, gathered his son into his arms, and kissed him.

'Put it back,' I said, in answer to Mr Wraxall's question. 'I do not wish to know where, and you must never tell me, or my husband. I shall be ruled by him no longer.'

Mr Wraxall nodded in agreement. Then he reached into his pocket.

'This was inside,' he said, passing me a small slip of yellow paper. 'The gentleman who wrote it would be glad, I'm sure, that you have chosen to take his advice.'

I took the paper from him and read the few words written on it, in a small, precise hand:

These papers, delivered to me by Mr John Lazarus, shipping-agent, of Billiter Street, City, and bound together by Mr Riviere, using antique materials, to resemble a folio of the seventeenth century, were covertly placed — on the author's instructions — in the Library of Evenwood Park, by me, Christopher Martin Tredgold, solicitor, on 30th November 1856, to be found by others, or not, as Fate or chance decided.

This much I was specifically instructed to say by the author. On my own account, I write only these wise words, to whosoever should read them:

> *Quieta non movere.**
> *C.M.T.*

'Do you remember your Latin?' asked Mr Wraxall.
'Yes,' I said. 'I remember. I shall always remember.'

⚜ FINIS ⚜

---

*'Let sleeping dogs lie.'

Acknowledgements

This novel was written during a difficult period in my life. I wish specifically to acknowledge the contribution to its completion of the following:

At A.P. Watt: my agent, Natasha Fairweather; Naomi Leon; Judy-Meg Kennedy; Linda Shaughnessy; and Teresa Nicholls.

At John Murray: my editor, Roland Philipps; Rowan Yapp; James Spackman; Nikki Barrow; and Caro Westmore.

At W. W. Norton: my US editor, Jill Bialosky.

At McClelland & Stewart: my Canadian editor, Ellen Seligman and Lara Hinchberger.

I acknowledge once again the expert advice of Clive Cheesman – Rouge Dragon Pursuivant – at the College of Arms; and the copy-editing and proof-reading expertise of Celia Levitt and Nick de Somogyi respectively. Thanks are also due to my assistant Sally Owen for her administrative skills.

To all the consultants, doctors, and medical staff who have kept me going over the past two years, no words of thanks can ever be adequate. They principally include: Professor Christer Lindquist; Dr Christopher Nutting; Mr Michael Powell; Mr David Roberts; Mr Nigel Davies; Mr Naresh Joshi; Dr Diana Brown; Dr Peter Schofield; Dr Adrian Jones; and Professor John Wass.

Finally, family and friends. For their love, support, and patience, I mention particularly my wife, Dizzy, on whom I now depend more than ever; our daughter Emily (with apologies again for naming one of my central characters after her) and her partner Kips Davenport; my stepchildren Miranda and Barnaby; our grandchildren – Eleanor, Harry, and Dizzy Junior – and daughter-in-law, Becky; my parents, Gordon and Eileen Cox; my mother-in-law, Joan Crockett; and Jamie, Ruth, Joanna, and Rachel Crockett.

To all these, and to the many others I have not named who have helped and contributed in their various ways, I am properly and sincerely grateful.

Michael Cox
Denford, March 2008

THE GLASS OF TIME
Michael Cox

DISCUSSION QUESTIONS

1. From the first page of *The Glass of Time*, we are transported to a different time and place. How does Michael Cox evoke the world of nineteenth-century England, and how does this setting affect the unfolding story?

2. How would you characterize the relationship between Esperanza and Lady Tansor as the former ascends from lady's maid to companion? Are they friends or is their relationship more oblique?

3. How does Esperanza's nobility shine through when she occupies a modest position as lady's maid? To what extent is this characteristic a mark of "Duport blood," and how does the novel's broader conflict of succession convey the importance of lineage and social station in Victorian England?

4. Why does Madame choose to only gradually reveal the facts and instructions that will guide Esperanza in her completion of the Great Task? Does this method help or hurt Esperanza's chances of succeeding?

5. Esperanza often pities Lady Tansor, even though she knows that Emily once betrayed her father. Is Emily deserving of our sympathy as well?

6. How do love and obsession shape the actions of both Madame and Lady Tansor?

7. Why is Esperanza attracted to Perseus despite his often temperamental manner? What do they have in common?

8. Why don't Perseus and Randolph get along? How does Randolph's carefree, independent nature set him apart from the rest of his family?

9. Esperanza breaks off her engagement with Perseus when she learns that she must marry Randolph in order to take her rightful place in the Duport family line. What does her decision say about familial duty versus individual will, and how does this theme play out in the rest of the novel?

10. Although Mrs. Battersby displays antagonism toward Esperanza, Lady Tansor alludes to a certain similarity between these two women. In what way might these women be alike?

11. Lady Tansor and Esperanza both take pains to hide their true selves. What are the consequences of this behavior? Do these women ultimately unburden themselves of their masks?

12. Even after Esperanza discovers that her father murdered Phoebus Daunt, she forgives him and proceeds with the Great Task. What did her father do that is, perhaps, unforgivable?

13. Does Esperanza allow herself to be ruled by the past? Does the image of her new family with Perseus and their son offer hope for a new beginning?

14. The Great Task succeeds, although not quite in the way that Edwin Gorst had planned. Why would Edwin set this plan in motion, knowing full well that he would never reap its benefits?

15. *The Glass of Time* is full of characters intent on exposing the truth or uncovering it for themselves. Why, after months of searching through letters and documents in her pursuit of the truth, does Esperanza choose to ignore her father's *Historia*?

Wayne Johnston	*The Custodian of Paradise*
Erica Jong	*Sappho's Leap*
Peg Kingman	*Not Yet Drown'd*
Nicole Krauss	*The History of Love**
Don Lee	*Country of Origin*
Ellen Litman	*The Last Chicken in America*
Vyvyane Loh	*Breaking the Tongue*
Benjamin Markovits	*A Quiet Adjustment*
Emily Mitchell	*The Last Summer of the World*
Honor Moore	*The Bishop's Daughter*
	The White Blackbird
Donna Morrissey	*Sylvanus Now**
Patrick O'Brian	*The Yellow Admiral**
Heidi Pitlor	*The Birthdays*
Jean Rhys	*Wide Sargasso Sea*
Mary Roach	*Bonk*
	*Spook**
	Stiff
Gay Salisbury and	
Laney Salisbury	*The Cruelest Miles*
Susan Fromberg Schaeffer	*The Snow Fox*
Laura Schenone	*The Lost Ravioli Recipes of Hoboken*
Jessica Shattuck	*The Hazards of Good Breeding*
Frances Sherwood	*The Book of Splendor*
Joan Silber	*Ideas of Heaven*
	The Size of the World
Dorothy Allred Solomon	*Daughter of the Saints*
Mark Strand and	
Eavan Boland	*The Making of a Poem**
Ellen Sussman (editor)	*Bad Girls*
Barry Unsworth	*Sacred Hunger*
Brad Watson	*The Heaven of Mercury**
Jenny White	*The Abyssinian Proof*

*Available only on the Norton Web site: www.wwnorton.com/guides